C.S. Boag is a former journalist who has also grown potatoes, driven taxis and bulldozers and worked in a hamburger bar. Apart from his published short stories he has worked as a columnist for *Woman's Day* and the *Bulletin*. He won the Walter Stone Memorial Prize for Literature in 1986. He lives on a small 'green' holding near Bathurst, NSW, with his wife, Judith. He has five children.

www.csboag.com

By the same author

The Hood With No Hands
The Death of a Ladies' Man
Horses for Corpses

C.S. Boag

MISTER RAINBOW

in the Case of Bullets at the Ballet

XOUM PUBLISHING

Sydney

 XOUM

First published in this edition by Xoum in 2017

Xoum Publishing
PO Box Q324, QVB Post Office,
NSW 1230, Australia
www.xoum.com.au

ISBN 978-1-925143-57-7 (print)
ISBN 978-1-925143-58-4 (digital)

Cataloguing-in-publication data is available from the National Library of Australia

Cover design by Xou Creative, www.xoucreative.com.au

Papers used by Xoum Publishing are natural, recyclable products made from wood grown in sustainable forests. The manufacturing processes conform to the environmental regulations of the country of origin.

For my sister Annie

If music be the food of love, you're in the wrong restaurant.

Chapter 1

THE KILLER ON CASTANET CLOSE

It's broad daylight – or daylight for broads, however you want to play it – and me and my one-legged mate Rory are busy at 21 Castanet Close turning over the place trying to find out where my ex-wife has taken our daughter. Aunt Rube is outside on the drive, checking the bins, removing bottles, cans, broken CDs, scraps of paper and fish heads and sorting them into piles marked:

Rubbish

For autopsy and

Clues.

Last time I looked, the Clues pile still had the VACANCY sign up.

Without warning, tinny music pierces the suburban quiet, and instinctively Rory dives for the gun he's built into his crutch, a nice little piece adapted to fire .45 hollows – slugs that don't leave the recipient begging for more. 'That's not Mr Whoopee!' he mutters. Rory might have turned Christian, but he's still a killer.

'Cool it, Roarer.' I go over to the window and peer outside. But he's right: the music isn't Mr Whippy, it's the Dance of the Sugar Plum Fairy from Tchaikovsky's Nutcracker and it's coming from the little music box I gave my daughter Imogene when she still believed in fairies. Somebody's lifted the lid, but it doesn't mean we got to run around shooting ballerinas.

It's not like I wasn't warned. I lost count how many times Salina told me to clean up my act or she'd leave and take the kid with her. Now she's done it. They're not alone. It's written up there in neons, something Imogene said during the Horses for Corpses caper: 'Mummy's met a man she calls Mr Perfect – although she says after you anyone would be perfect ...'

And like Rube always says, perfect is as perfect does. The shack is as empty as the eyes of a killer just before he duffs someone. It's like the place has been given a pre-operative emetic and they not only removed all the dust, but the occupants' deoxyribonucleic acid as well. The kid's bedroom, the hall, Salina's bedroom, the lounge, the kitchen, verandah and Band-Aid-sized backyard are as bare as a pole dancer's belly. Even the light bulbs are clean. All bar the one that should be over the side door but isn't. Which confirms they're not alone. My ex never cleaned anything in her life.

I've already worked my way through the worst-case scenario – that Imogene was abducted – but there's no SOS (aka Signs of a Struggle), so she must have gone quietly. All that's happened, I keep telling myself, is Sal cleared out and took Immo with her. Just like she always said she would.

When the music box finally stops playing, Rube carries on with the sieving of the rubbish. Rube is the gumshoe aunt that took me in and set about teaching me the art of detecting after Dad dumped me. She's my safeguard against doubt. Rory's something else. Rory's a professional killer that found God but right now is a one-legged ball of anger stomping around the kitchen on his crutch-gun; like emotion ever solved anything.

'She took the kid!' He stops stomping and stares at his foot. 'It's ratshit, Rain.'

Rory's no Einstein so I keep the dialogue down around cellar level.

'I said cool it, Roarer. We don't know who this Lover Boy is and there's no big arrows telling us where they went. The only place we're going to find a clue is here – their last known place of habitation. So we got to do the search and we got to do it thorough.'

Roarer looks even more confused than usual. 'What are you on about?'

'I'm saying that while this might seem like an exercise in self-delusion, we –'

'I'm not talking about exercise.' He stomps his gun barrel on the swirly-patterned linoleum. It looks like the family dog just vomited on it.

'Like I said – it's ratshit.'

I need to have my wits about me – as opposed to half-wits like Rory

– but he's a mate and his heart's in the right place, even if his brain isn't. Rory can always be relied upon to do the leg-work. As long as the leg-work only requires the one leg. I look where he's looking and see what he sees. Black pellets.

'They're just rodent droppings, Roarer.'

And the sounds outside are rodent sounds, like the ones in The Nutcracker when the Mouse King sets out to kill the dolls.

Rory does that thing with his forehead that suggests deep thought but is only the thing that Rory does with his forehead.

'Yeah, but they're getting up the barrel of my gat, Rain. And when that happens, my gat's –'

Suddenly I sense – no, I know – that something outside has changed. 'Hang on a sec.'

While Rory's been banging on about ratshit I've been half-listening to the orchestra outside – the wobbleboard of the Dixie bins, the tap-tap-tap of the timpani as Rube examines a tin, the wheelie-bin symphony of Rube going about the business of detecting. Which she's no longer going about.

'It's just that –'

'Roarer, shut up and listen!'

'But I can't hear anything.'

'That's just it, neither can I …'

The silence is broken by another squeak-squeak-squeak sound that might be rats, but isn't, and beyond that, the tap-tap-tap of sharp heels hurrying along the footpath.

I'm out of the kitchen like a shot out of Rory's crutch-gun, hat flying as my whitesides hammer the floorboards, a shoulder of my orange-fleck coat cracking against the door. I rip the .45 Taurus Millennium out of the holster as a shadow disappears through the hedge. Then I turn in the direction of the dry-retching coming from the driveway.

'Rube!'

Chapter 2

THE SOUND OF SILENCE

There's rubbish scattered all over the place, the music box is lying on its side and Aunt Rube's down for the count, the lump-knuckled fingers of one hand clutching the edge of a bin while the rest of her is face-down on the concrete, head twisted to one side, her skin fast acquiring the colour of what she's sprawled on. I hear Rory hoof-and-crutch it up the drive as I drop the gat and kneel beside Rube.

At first I think it must have been Pandora who got her, the nemesis that's been after me as long as I can remember. Pandora's neat and bloody-minded. But even as I think it, I know it's not so. *The knee bone's connected to the thigh bone and the doll dances only when you lift the lid.* Pandora clubbing Rube would be a coincidence. And I don't do coincidence.

Rory crutches back down the drive. 'What do you want me to do, Rain?'

I help Rube sit up while pocketing the music box.

'She's copped a thumping. She's got to be seen to. Get the Caddie, quick.' Rube groans as Rory heads for the wheels. 'Take it easy, okay?'

She shakes her head. 'I'm getting old, Rainbow. I taught you everything I know only to forget the basics myself. I was too intent on the rubbish. And he was quiet as a mouse. I should have been more alert. Hell, Rainbow, I was supposed to be helping you and then I go and do this.'

'You didn't do anything, Rube.' I cradle her head. 'Take it easy.'

'I have to help find the kid.' She knots her forehead, turning in on herself. 'I didn't see his face, just the hand. He was strong.'

'Jeez, Rube, if only I hadn't —'

Rube's voice cuts across mine like a scalpel. 'They were after you, Rainbow. I was just in the way, a pawn in a chess game in which the killer was after the King. He took me in passing. But something disturbed him. When he was laying into me I heard this squeaking sound …' She takes a shallow breath. 'Something spooked him. That's my impression, anyway. I know I taught you not to do impressions but …'

I hear the Caddie screech to a stop and Rube's light as pigeon feathers as I carry her up the drive.

'I telegraphed the hospital,' Rory says, holding the door open. I settle Rube in the back while Rory hands me a rug. I retrieve my coat, shrug it on and tuck the rug under Rube. Then I straighten.

'It didn't happen here, Roarer.'

'What?'

'Don't mention 21 Castanet Close. Don't say what happened or where. Rube fell while taking the bins out, okay?'

'You mean you want me to lie?'

'Only if it's not against your religion, Roarer.'

He hands me back my fedora.

'I'll do what God allows me to do.'

I shut the door on Rube as Roarer climbs behind the wheel. I got to trust him but it's like trusting a dingo in a chookyard. 'Drive like you got no licence,' I say. 'Imagine the car's nicked, you just robbed a bank and the cops are after you.'

Rory clunks the jalopy into gear.

'That's how I always drive, Rain.'

The name's Rainbow. You can spit on my card, bend it, twist it, rub it with your shirt sleeve or blast a hole through it with a .38, it will still read: Jack Black's Investigations. Whatever it says, I'm still Rainbow. The card's so I look respectable.

As I'm walking up the drive, Nosy Nora the next-door neighbour is on her porch, arms folded, head thrust forward into somebody else's business, her little shopping trolley sitting beside her.

'I was just coming back from the shops when I noticed …' she says, eyeing me like a snake watching its prey. 'Is everything all right, Mr —'

Nora's front gate requires something like a cast of the runes to open it. I kick it down and get up her path, fast. 'If the cops pay you a visit, Nora, you never saw nothing, understand?'

It comes out *unnerstand* and it comes out hard.

Nora shrugs. 'I been in the next-door neighbour game long enough to know how it works, Mr Whoever-you-are. But that doesn't make me blind and it doesn't make me stupid.'

'So tell me what you saw.'

'Well, I was just coming back from the shops and letting myself in the gate – which, incidentally, you'll have to get fixed ...' Her eyes narrow to dollar signs. 'Was there something I *should* have seen?'

I lift her dolly cart and spin the wheels. They squeak. I put it down again.

'Did you see anyone leaving the premises dressed in, say, black?'

Pandora's favourite colour.

Nora shakes her head.

'I didn't see anyone. I was having trouble with the gate, so of course I wasn't looking anywhere else.'

'What about *before* you weren't looking?'

'I was shopping. And, oh my goodness, the price of food these days!'

I ignore the hint.

'In the days and weeks before you went shopping, did you see anything or anyone out of the ordinary?'

'What's it worth?'

'What's what worth?'

'My silence in the right quarters and my lack of silence right now.'

I feel the need to dramatise things but I keep it slow and breezy like we're discussing the weather instead of Imogene's fate.

'Lady, most people possess what might be called a survival instinct. Know why animals' noses twitch?' I lean in close so she can smell the threat and also so that my gat in its holster is clearly visible. 'Their noses twitch because they hear the hunter's cry, smell the cordite and see the dogs. They're not thinking about food or where their burrow is or the next tree to hide behind. It's more basic than that. All they want to do is survive.'

Chapter 3

WHAT THE NEIGHBOUR SAW

'What exactly are you saying?' Nora asks.

'You wanted to know what your co-operation's worth so I'm telling you.'

Nora takes a deep breath.

'All right, yes – I saw him.'

'The figure in black?'

'No, I'm talking about before.'

'Salina's lover?'

'I think of him as her regular guest.'

'And when did you see this "regular guest"?'

'When he was coming and going.'

'What was his name?'

'We were never introduced.'

'Describe him then.'

'I can't do that, either.'

I shake my head.

'Nora, for years you been hanging over your balcony, peeping around curtains and staring past your secateurs while pruning the camellias. Number 21 Castanet Close is your private stage and you got a permanent front-row view of the action.' I hunch forward again, let her catch another glimpse of the gat, and let her imagine what it might do to bilbies that don't talk. 'So describe the lover.'

Nora pulls her shopping cart between us. It's full of home-brand groceries. Nora knows the value of staying alive.

'I'm sorry but I can't. He came and went at night. There was no light in the driveway' – because Mr Incognito had removed the bulb – 'or I might have seen him. He was never more than a silhouette.'

'Use your imagination. You say he. Could it have been a she?'

'No.'

'Why not?'

'Because of the voice.'

It's better than nothing.

'Tell me about the voice. Was it low and murmurous or sharp and querulous? When he said hello to Salina in the darkness of the night and goodbye in the anonymity of the pre-dawn, did he do it allegro? Or did he do it nice and slow, like he had all night to say it in?'

Nora shakes her head.

'I can't say. But I can say that the voice had an unusual quality to it.' She does a now-I'll-tell-you-the-truth pause. 'I think he was foreign.'

It's not much but when you're desperate you settle for scraps. 'All right, on television, who did he sound like?'

She doesn't even have to think about it.

'Maurice Chevalier.'

'The joker in Gigi?' Nora nods. 'That's all you got? A silhouette that talks like a dead actor?'

'Yeah.'

'So when did they leave?'

'Just recently. A van took away the furniture. They left the same night.'

'And?'

'There's no and.' She's got her confidence back, the confidence that comes with knowing she's going to live. 'Unless, of course, you want me to start using my imagination.'

A nice old Indian V-twin with swept-back handlebars is parked outside the hospital. I like bikes, know my way around them, but I got to stick to the plan. Rory's waiting in Admission while Rube's in Ward No. 2 on the third floor wearing a back-to-front gown, her face as saffron as Mabel's in *The Simpsons*. In the room with her is a joker dying of consumption, a geezer in the last throes of double pneumonia, and a machine. I park myself next to the machine.

'Nice to see you're not dead, Rube.' She aims for a smile but it comes out a grimace. 'Have the cops paid you a visit yet?'

'I told the doctors I was dancing on the porch and slipped. They didn't believe me but at least they didn't call the cops. It doesn't mean they're not going to.' She nods at the machine. 'Meanwhile, they say that without Mr Dialysis here I'd be dead.'

There's something wrong with what she just said.

'People can live fine on one kidney, Rube.'

'That's what I've been doing since I was twenty.'

'What happened when you were twenty?'

'A bullet happened. The doctors had to remove one of my kidneys.'

After that there's total silence, apart from the croaking of the geezers and the thumping of the machine.

'Will it kill you to talk?'

'To the cops?'

'No, to me.'

Rube was facing north when her attacker punched her. The sun was in front, which meant that she didn't even see his shadow. 'There was a rush of cold air in the vicinity of the eleventh rib, just behind the peritoneum, to the rear of the abdominal cavity.' Rube grimaces again. 'It's like my assailant knew what he was doing.'

'You think he knew you only had one kidney? And you call me paranoid.'

'I'm not saying what I think, Rainbow, nor did I suggest you were paranoid. I'm just saying that's what happened. But he might have known about the kidney. These days, everything's in the public domain – phone calls, emails, hospital records, the works. They know everything there is to know about everyone.'

'So your assailant needn't have been someone you knew?'

'He didn't need to be. But that's beside the point. It wasn't me he was after, it was you.'

Back and forth and round about, like batting a square ball over a high net on a court without lines. I don't ask how she's sure, because she can't be sure. Her mind's been affected by the attack.

'I'm sorry, Rube. I shoulda–'

Rube frowns.

'Shoulda, Buddha! How many times must I tell you, Rainbow, that neither exists – neither what might have been nor a Higher Being. So don't let's have any of that malarkey about what should or shouldn't have been, don't let regret get in the way of –' She stops mid-lesson, cocking her head. 'Cops! I can hear them, smell them, taste their bile.' She nods towards a cabinet. 'The nurse put my stuff in that drawer. Open it.'

I open it.

'Now take out the purse and look inside.'

There's a ticket inside the purse.

'It was in the music box. The kid must have put it there.'

'Why would she do that?' I ask.

'I don't know, Rainbow. All I know is that Imogene must have thought it was important.'

Chapter 4

WHILE THE CAT'S AWAY

Rory's gone. He must have decided his responsibility ended when I turned up. I get myself home to the bashed-up old ferry I call the *Wooden No* (What's she called? nosey parkers ask. *Wooden No,* I reply). I then haul out Imogene's music box, place it on the chart table and prise open the tiny stage. Apart from the inner workings, there's one other item inside: Imogene's mini recorder, the one I gave her. The battery's dead. I take the battery out of my torch, insert it in the recorder, and switch on. There's the stuff Imogene recorded in the *Horses for Corpses* caper and after that a slice of the survival-ration German she's been learning – *Haben Sie ein Stuck Brot, bitte?* Then right at the end, a male voice saying one word. It's hard to make out. *Myrtle? Mater?* I turn my attention to the ticket, the one that Rube found. It's a child's concession to the ballet.

The *Wooden No*'s in much the same condition as Rube – dependent on a pump to keep her afloat. The bailing out takes an hour-fifty. Afterwards, I lie in the aft cabin staring out the porthole as the water works its way back in through the hole in the hull and the pump tries to work it out again. Just like I'm trying to work out the rat droppings at Castanet Close. The house was spotless. So why the droppings?

It's 3 am when I finally give up the struggle, grab the torch – along with bolt cutters, pliers and plastic card – unhitch the rowboat and row myself back to shore. After which I hoof it to 21 Castanet Close.

No-one's replaced the bulb over the side door. Why should they?

Right now, the joint's a resident-free zone, containing no more than rats. I see what Nora saw. And that's all I see because my torch battery is in the mini recorder. But there's enough light to note that the bins are empty and the piles of junk have been cleared away. Which means I got a rat's chance of finding out anything via the rubbish.

I slip the plastic card between lock and flange and the front door swings open. The streetlights illuminate the bullet hole made by the psychopath that shot Imogene's three-legged cat, Tripodi, in The Hood with No Hands caper. The absence of the cat would account for the rats.

I get down the hall, through the living room and into the kitchen. I can't see much. But I know the water heater's a storage variety, 250-litre Rheem, the size and weight of a Rugby League front-row forward and about as moveable. There's fireworks when I cut the wires. After that, working by feel, I use the bolt cutters to cut the pipes. There are two – one top, one bottom, inlet and outlet, wet and wetter. Kneeling in the rat dirt, I fold the ends of the pipes and crimp them with the pliers. After that I do the Rheem dance, heel-and-toeing the water heater out of the corner. Rats like it hot and the hottest place in the house is behind the water heater. It's not only hot, it's also dirty. No-one cleans behind water heaters and Mr Clean was no exception.

My hand brushes against a bunch of hairless ratlets. It's a nest and I know I'm clutching at straws but I pocket a handful of the nest anyway. After that, I get the ratlets back in their corner, the water heater back in front of the ratlets and myself back to the *Wooden No*. And with daylight creeping over the horizon and a Manly ferry making too many waves, I sit at the chart table and dissect the contents of the nest.

Hair, toothless comb, scraps of cloth, a couple of feathers, shoelace, bits of plastic and a few scraps of paper. I check the hair. Salina's is peroxide-orange, Imogene's is a finer, tawny-coloured baby fluff, while Tripodi's – when he existed – was black. I find one foreign follicle. It could be significant but I'm not equipped to do hair.

I'm familiar with the threads worn by Salina and Imogene and the fibres in the nest match.

Using tweezers, I turn my attention to the paper: it's glossy and there are seven ragged pieces of it, some containing lettering. I get them all facing the same way. The piece with the capital letter C on it has a straight edge so I place it on the left. Discard all preconceptions, Rube always told me. Don't force the pieces. Rats are no respecters of words and in the end I'm left with five letters and too much chew. The magnifying glass reveals a bit of letter I've overlooked. It makes what I thought was a

C into a G. But is this one an N or an M? Is the R a B? Could the F be an E? That would give me a word: RENCE or RECEN or CEREN or even – GREEN.

The ferry returns, a green boat churning the green water white and shaking my concentration and the table. I slip the letters into an evidence bag and the evidence bag into my pocket. GREEN isn't much to go on, but at least it gives me a crypto-name for Salina's Lover Boy. Courtesy of the rats, I've got Mr Green. And courtesy of Imogene, I've got a ticket to the ballet.

Chapter 5

THE DANCE OF THE DEAD DOLL

The ticket's to the Big Sailbird, the Nun's Cowl, Three Sheets to the Wind – aka the Sydney Opera House – to see the ballet *Coppélia* tonight. No-one frisks me when I enter which means I go in armed but when a dowager bumps the mitt holding the tumbler, the beer splashes the gat and I got lager on the Luger.

The dame in the box office says my ticket is one of three booked in the dress circle, except the kid's ticket was cancelled. Less popular seats are still available – like the balconies along the sides, the loges – or she could sell me a seat in the front row, and that's the one I take. Aunt Rube brought me up on ballet so I could do pliés and demi-pliés, leaps, rolls, high dives and arabesques – moves that might prove useful to a detective – and I was taught dance by the great Madam Blavatsky, who trained a lot of those performing tonight. I'm still wiping beer off my jacket when I note a little man holding forth to a bunch of barely-pubescent neophytes agog with inattention.

'The under title of tonight's ballet,' the little man says, adjusting his pink cummerbund, 'is *La fille aux yeux d'émail*. That's French for *The Girl with the Enamel Eyes*, a description I find so much more *apposite* than the one provided. Think about it – a girl with enamel eyes …'

The little man would like everyone to believe he picked up the voice in Aspen, Colorado, via Paris, France, and Eton and Oxford. But I can tell it's from Bullamakanka, just to the left of the Black Stump in the Back of Beyond.

'It's all about surrogacy,' he continues, looking around him. 'You know what surrogacy is, don't you, girls? Surrogacy is giving your life for others. In the ballet, the old man thinks he's bringing the doll to life but of course he can't.' The girls nod like they know what he's talking about. 'So you could call the ballet an allegory about man's arrogance …'

The bell goes for the first round and I head for the stalls. The rich get richer and they also get all the lookers. The figure on one dame isn't off the hook; what the brunette by the bar's wearing could be the Emperor's clothes, because there's little more to her clobber than the imagination; while the blonde with the unstockinged legs under a silver skirt fashioned from not much more than a pocket handkerchief is looking my way out of eyes a pulp-fiction writer might refer to as sloe: like the ripe, dark fruit of a wild berry.

'Come, come, Hélène,' says the old joker standing beside her. 'I'll take you somewhere afterwards.'

The ultra-riche – the take in the wonderful give-and-take that makes up Sydney society – are always more than willing to do something to their own benefit.

'I'm sorry but I'd prefer to go home,' the dame replies in an accent contemptuous of the aspirate. 'And by home I mean shame-wah.'

That would be *chez moi*, which is French for her own little truckle bed. And because she's looking at me when she says it, I'm half-thinking it might be me she'd like to go shame-wah with …

The only good thing about a front row seat at the Opera House is the leg room. Apart from that, you see far too much of the orchestra and also feel as exposed as the blonde with the silver skirt and the accent – a potshot for any sniper who might happen to be prowling the auditorium. I've got a view of the band, the legs of the ballerinas and the leg room. A hundred stall rows rake behind me, topped by the circle, and all the seats are full except those in the cantilevered boxes along the walls, which are empty.

You got to hand it to Delibes, the music's a knockout. The band does the prelude while the doll in the window stares wistfully at the revellers below. It's all swirling skirts, pink tights and boleros. It's great to look at but I'm not here for looking. This isn't some video on the laptop in the – all right, dis-comfort of the *Wooden No* – with the pump thumping in the bilge, a double whisky sitting beside me on the chart table and my finger on the pause button. There are no second chances here. There had to be a reason why Imogene hid the ticket. And if something happens, I can't just press rewind to find out what it was.

First insight: It's the band that are the automatons, not the dancers. What the dancers are doing isn't easy, it just looks that way. I know because I learnt ballet with a lot of these dancers.

Second insight: My ex-wife would have told Lover Boy I'm a private detective. Which means he would have known to cover his tracks. Hence the ultra-clean house. But why nothing from Imogene, except for a cancelled ballet ticket and a single word (Myrtle? Mater?) on her mini recorder?

The ballet dancers dance and the band plays and the sway of the music and the swirl of the tutus is as real as the rat droppings at Castanet Close. The old doll maker's given Franz a sleeping draught before dragging him across to the … Him? That's when I realise the production's traditional. And the tradition of The Girl with the Enamel Eyes is that Franz is a ballerina in travesty: the dancer's a dame. The hips are too wide, while the legs … Lisette Priée's too good a dancer for anyone to notice her gender, but now that she's in the arms of the old puppeteer and pretending to be male, I can see it. But then I stop seeing it. Because the puppet has risen from the dead and the music suddenly comes alive. As does Swanilda, pretending to be the puppet that's borrowed Franz's life and is launching into the 'Dance of the Dead Doll' while the old man clasps his hands and – Crack, crack, crack!

Chapter 6

CORPSE DE BALLET

No dancer's that good. Apart from which there's no stage direction saying that the old man's got to collapse, as far as I know. He's supposed to be over the moon because the doll's come to life, not –

Dead.

Final-curtain dead.

He's lying flat on his back and in death the years roll away to reveal a much younger dancer than he was pretending to be. I'm close enough to see his inferior maxillary drop and his fingers twitch and his body sag and the blood begin to drain from his arteries.

I'm right in front of the orchestra so a good part of my attention is on the violinists, bassists and bassoonists while the bad part of my attention is on the dancers. And none – I repeat, none – of the musicians was responsible for the noise suggesting the firing of an unsilenced pistol: no drumstick smacked against a drum edge or whip crackers making noises like fireworks. I know because I'm in the front row, with nothing between me and the band but a safety net.

There's a way onto the stage if you're prepared to play it rough and I play it rough as I grapple-hand my way over the safety net. A big man in a rollneck is leaning over the dead dancer. Battered face. A pug. I flash a card. Any card. They never check.

'I'm from the police. What's the deal?'

'They got him.'

I ask the next question and I ask it fast.

'Who's they?'

The bloke doesn't answer. Instead, he says, 'It was my job to protect him and I stuffed it.'

'Who's they?' I ask again.

But I'm not going to get any sense out of him because he's a bodyguard whose CV's just been shot full of holes. I turn my attention to the corpse. And the corpse tells me the calibre of the bullets was .38 and at least two entered his head via the occipito frontalis region and exited via the coccyx.

Which makes it a loge shot – from somewhere up high in the balconies.

Someone's closing the curtains. The stalls are emptying. In the circle I spot an alluringly bare back framed in silver lamé. I shift my attention to the loges. They're empty. What did I expect? A nice man with his hands up saying, 'Arrest me'? I retire behind the curtains.

'Rainbow!'

She's a pair of shapely legs with a bulge in the crotch that doesn't go with the legs. It's Franz – or at least the doll that played him – a girl from Madam Blavatsky's dance squad who always tended to hang around long after the rest had left. Now rebadged as Lisette Priée, but once upon a lifetime ago, Jane Brown.

'Hi, Jane.' I indicate the body. 'Know anything about the corpse de ballet?'

Wrinkles spring into play about her eyes as she smiles, before she decides that undiluted joy at seeing me might be a bad look under the circumstances and plumps for abject sadness instead.

'Yes. Only, please, Rainbow – not here.'

We're standing on the eastern side of the Opera House with the tile-covered sails overhead. Jane shivers, hugging herself because no-one else is offering to do the job. Jazz floats up from a play boat weaving across the Harbour while the sound of sirens – cops, ambulance and fire – ransack the city. Jane's gnawing at her fist. Maybe she didn't have breakfast.

'I was afraid something like this might happen. Not a murder necessarily but still something bad. Sure, Simon had a bodyguard, but dancers can't take bodyguards onstage with them.'

She reaches down into her crotch and extracts the prosthesis that
made her a male. I keep my eyes on her face.

'Why did this Simon joker need a bodyguard?'

Jane clutches the prosthesis.

'He and the lead dancer hated each other. There was even a punch-
up.'

'Professional jealousy?'

She shakes her head.

'It was way beyond that.'

'So tell me about the hatred.'

'Why so impatient, Rainbow?'

'My kid's gone and I need to find her.'

Jane stares past me like she wishes she'd taken up tap. She's still got
the misty-brown eyes set in an oval face she always had. And they still
avoid mine like they always did.

'So you have a child now,' she murmurs. 'That must mean you're
married – or as good as.'

I don't enlighten her. 'Jane, take away the frills and you'll find men
aren't much more than what you just took out of your crotch. So forget
your dreams, stick to the script and tell me what you know.'

Jane tells me that Simon Peter, the dead dancer, was a stand-in for the
main drag.

'But why the hatred?'

'At first I thought it was an affair gone wrong. Then Simon came onto
me so ... Anyway, after that I thought it might be what you just said – a
case of simple competitiveness. But it was more than that, a lot more. It
was like Simon knew something about Janus that he shouldn't know and
Janus didn't like him knowing so he was out to get him.' She pauses,
fingering her prosthesis. 'It would explain the bodyguard.'

'Tell me about this Janus.'

'His full name is Janus King. He made a lot of money from dancing.
But that's all I know. I'm a dancer not a detective.'

'So where is he now?'

'He was called away. Simon is – was – his understudy. Other than that
I – I know nothing.'

She's no longer a boy, not even a ballerina. Just a girl I used to know
who knows nothing except –

'I'm sorry, Rainbow, I wanted to talk to you. But what I've told you
is the truth – Janus hated Simon and the hatred was due to something
Simon knew.'

'How can you be sure?'

'The body language, of course. If dancers know anything, it's body language ...' Her voice trails off, she lets her arms fall to her sides and somewhere deep inside the Opera House an orchestra starts up. 'And there was the bodyguard ...'

'Where is he now – this Jason Robards or Janus McCoy or the Emperor Haile Selassie or whatever he calls himself?'

'Janus King.' The name's a match so I take it as a confirm. 'Like I said, he was called away.'

'Where to?'

'No-one knows.'

'Hazard a guess.'

'I suppose to Europe. Janus was – foreign.'

'Who called him away?'

She shakes her head.

'I'm sorry, Rainbow, but I'm just a –'

'Yeah, I know, you're a dancer not a detective.' Hoofs approach along the concourse, big hairy hoofs, the kind that usually belong to cops. 'They'll want you for questioning, Jane. You'd better go back.'

Lisette reaches out: an appeal for time to stand still, for a past that turned up out of nowhere only to disappear like the play boat that just crossed the Harbour. But no-one can remake the past – not a doll maker, not a dancer, not anyone.

Chapter 7

THE FRENCH CONNECTION

Rube's still got a tube coming out of her and she's occupying a faded-blue hospital caterpillar chair while a dialysis machine thumps away beside her. Rory's brought her the *Complete Works* (*Complete Works of what,* Roarer wanted to know — *bridgeworks, roadworks, the kind of works you give someone when you ex 'em?*), her favourite pillow and her laptop.

'So who's this dancer you're after? And what's he got to do with the kid's disappearance?' she asks.

I tell her Janus King and that I don't know.

She nods and her tube nods along with her as she gets to work.

'The dancer, the dame and the kid all disappear about the same time,' she murmurs. 'So let's start with the name. According to Titus Livius — that's Livy to you, Rainbow, "Janus" means "gateway". That could be a gateway of opportunity. But Janus was also the god of two-facedness. As for King …'

She studies the screen, the eyes in the lined old face hooded with pain and the little body under the coverlet rigid. The stink in the ward is that of a public inconvenience on the cleaner's day off.

'What did the doc say, Rube?'

Her face is grey. It could be the reflection from the computer screen. Or it could just be grey.

'What doctors always say.'

'Would you mind elaborating on that?'

'Oh, you know, malarkey about a build-up of potassium and an inability to process waste. Expressions to make them feel superior; big words to justify their existence.'

'For Christ's sake, you're talking to me, Rube, not the janitor.'

She pauses and looks up. 'Rainbow, I'm shy a kidney and the one that's left has taken a beating. From now on my best friend's Mr Dialysis here. Do you want to know about Janus King or do you just want fairy stories?'

I tell her yeah, but she's not interested in what I was just saying, only in what she's reading, courtesy of some whacked-together public relations guff occupying the ether.

'Janus King was born Vladimir Gregorovich in the village of Petroville, the Ukraine, in 1986. It turned out he had twinkle toes. He came to the attention of the Russian Commissariat and was placed in the State Dance program, quickly graduating to the Bolshoi. He became premier danseur. But Vladimir still wasn't happy. So he defected.'

'He was quick on his feet then.'

Rube's crook so she lets that one pass.

'On his defection, Gregorovich changed his name to Janus King, joined London's Royal Ballet, and blah blah blah. Formed a relationship with a fellow dancer – female – and had a kid.'

I don't know why but I still ask, 'When was the kid born?'

Rube shrugs.

'It doesn't say. It just says he made a fortune out of ballet – it's possible if you're good enough. He joined France's Academie royale de danse from which he's currently on loan to the Australian Ballet.' She snaps the laptop shut and looks up. 'There's no mention of abandoning Coppélia but this is Wackipedia, not breaking news.'

Around us, the other hook-ups are in a state of somnolence. Some people get all the breaks while others just break. I don't know what category Gregorovich is in. All I know is I've got to find Imogene and the odds are lengthening. It's like Rube reads my mind.

'Ex-spouses take kids, Rainbow – it's what happens. You've got a headstart because you're a detective but you still need to sidestep your emotions. It's the only way you're going to find her. Stay calm and marshal your facts – and make sure they are facts – then do the deduction. Forget Imogene's your daughter and park any feelings you might have regarding Salina. Treat it like any other case.'

'I'll try, Rube. But just like you're my aunt and you're sick, Imogene's my daughter and she's missing.'

Rube reaches out a hand the colour of the stuff in the tubes and when it touches me it's shaking.

'I can look after myself but Imogene can't. I've lived most of my life but the kid's just starting. I'm pretty much dispensable but the kid isn't. So …'

She takes her mitt away as a nurse arrives. They call them sisters now – no-one uses real names any more, it's part of the worldwide identity crisis. Rube waits for the pan-handler to leave before resuming speaking.

'So, stripped of emotion,' she says, 'this is what we're left with:

'Ex-wife disappears with lover

'The kid's with them

'Aunt Rube cops a beating

'A dancer is shot.'

She shifts the computer off her knees. 'Now tell me what you're not telling me.'

The paper forms a rough-cut daisy chain next to the words *PROPERTY OF THE NSW HEALTH DEPARTMENT* on the coverlet over Rube's legs. 'I'm sorry if I didn't mention this before, Rube, but you were crook.' I look at the letters. 'It spells *GREEN* if you use your imagination.'

'And if I don't use my imagination?' She shoves the paper aside with barely a glance. 'What then? Look, there are too many pieces missing. What else have you got?'

I don't like hospitals and Rube's too sick to be reliable.

'The neighbour said that Green – that's what I'm calling him – talked funny.'

'Her exact words being …?'

'She said he sounded like Maurice Chevalier.'

'That fat old bugger in Gigi? The one who sang about little girls?'

'Thank heaven for little girls. Yeah, that's the one.'

Rube nods. She's still not herself but she's more herself than she was before.

'Anything else?'

'Yeah, I found something in the music box – Imogene's mini recorder.' I take it out and press play. The word's still muffled. 'On reflection, it sounds like mert. It could be murder.'

'That would be the voice of our friend the lover, the one that the neighbour believes is French,' Rube says. 'If we go along with that, he's not saying murder, but merde – the all-purpose French swearword. Which means that – in the absence of evidence to the contrary – we can assume he's French.'

'But Janus King's not French, he's Russian.'

'All that means is that Janus King isn't our man.' Rube holds up a hand with the tube coming out of it to silence me. 'I know it's a long shot, Rainbow, but it's the only shot you have. You think rats chewed that paper because you're sure it wasn't a platypus, a kangaroo or a frill-necked lizard. All right, it's the same with Salina. Like most practical people, she's a romantic who would fly off to Paris at the drop of a hat. And that's what this case hinges on – romance.'

Rube senses my doubt.

'Look, I might be sick, but it's not my head that's affected. Nosy Nora the neighbour watches too much television but because of it she can pick an accent with her eyes shut. So if she says that someone's Maurice Chevalier, it means that person is French.'

I shake my head.

'In her last call to me Imogene said she'd had a medical and her photo taken for a passport.'

'That confirms the French option.' Rube sighs as she leans back. 'Does Salina speak French? Does Imogene?'

'No and no.'

Rube waves a tired hand.

'Well, then ...'

It gives me something to do, anyway, at a time when I need something to do. At least I won't be twiddling my aquifers on the *Wooden No*. And it just might – I stress *might* – lead to something.

It's a long shot.

But like Rube says – apart from the bullet that took out the dancer, it's the only shot I got.

Chapter 8

C'EST MOI OR SAY NOTHING AT ALL

Out of the blue I get a call from Ace Mollema. I spent the first five years of my life with Ace on the Funny Farm — aka the hippy commune where our parents raised us in Nimbin, northern NSW. While I became a gumshoe detective, Ace joined the Australian Security Intelligence Organisation, commonly known as ASIO — Australia's equivalent of America's CIA. It's what happens to hippies' kids — they go off the rails. I tell him about Imogene. He offers to help and we arrange a meeting.

Sydney's premier clearing house for all things French is a glass-fronted joint in Sussex Street called the Alliance Française. A dame in Paris chic — high eyebrows, low hemline, acid glance — brushes against me as I push open the glass door. 'Oh, excusez moi,' she murmurs because she wants the world to believe that she's French. 'Merde!'

'Same to you,' I say as I saunter up to the guy at the front desk.

'Bonjour, m'sieur. Comment allez vous? Qu'est ce que c'est —'

'In English, pal.'

'How can I help you?'

'I'm looking for a teacher.'

'Why do you want a teacher?'

'I want to learn French.'

'We teach French here.'

Salina's stolen the kid and, knowing Salina, it's an arrangement she wants to make permanent. That means she's got to hide her tracks. Which also means that if they took French lessons she wasn't going to be obvious about it. 'I want to do it like a consenting adult — in private.'

'D'accord,' says the joker behind the counter, like it's not d'accord at all but more like Bugger off and stop wasting my time. 'In that case, I suggest you consult the Sydney telephone directory. Or – on the off chance you've mastered the technology – the White Pages on the internet.'

I lean over the counter and my coat falls open. When in doubt, show them the gat. It tends to remove doubt.

'And I suggest you supply me with a list of private French teachers.'

He supplies me with a list of private French teachers.

Of the teachers on the list, one no longer exists, five no longer teach, and the seventh is a funny little toe living in Bondi going by the name Jean-Pierre Boulevardier. He's got a French accent. They've all got French accents. Some of them even speak French.

'What do you want?' he says when I pay him a visit.

The door's open just enough to reveal a sloppy bottom lip and a suspicious eye. This is Bondi. It pays to be suspicious in Bondi. There've been a lot of muggings lately.

'I want to talk.'

'In French?'

'No, just talk.'

'I don't talk, I only give French lessons.'

I kick the door down.

'That'll do for starters,' I tell him.

The joint's the kind they dole out to people who would otherwise live in cardboard cartons and the man wringing his hands would come into that category long before he'd come into anything else. He's wearing a decade-before-last T-shirt, a crumpled set of underdaks and a scared face.

'I'll call the cops!' he squeaks.

I shove him back into the room that's just this side of being a box.

'And what are you going to call them? Messieurs? Gendarmes? The Boys in Bleu? Or just plain busy. Because that's what they'll be, pal, and they won't appreciate being bothered by someone with a fake accent, dirty underpants and no observable means of support. So shuddup and siddown.'

He shuds up and sids down, giving me the chance to appreciate what a fake French teacher looks like on his day off. 'What do you want?' he asks.

'Information. Starting with the identity of your students.'

'That's private.'

'That's good because I'm a private detective.'

The stench of boiled cabbage and mould wafts through the doorway behind him and the traffic on Bondi Road is as calm as a tsunami.

'Show me some ID to prove who you are,' he says.

'I've got a better idea. You identify your students, thereby proving you want to stay alive.'

I've discovered most people want to stay alive, even ones with fake French accents, soft hands and jowls like badly-set jelly. He climbs to his podcasts, drags himself to an old desk, digs in a drawer and produces a notebook like he's surprised to discover it's there. Holding the book at arm's length so I don't get the plague, I pick my way through the sex shops, wanking salons and spiderweb sites until I find what I'm after. I stab my thumb at a name.

'Describe them.'

'Describe who?'

'It says here: Smith.'

He describes someone that couldn't be Green, Salina, Imogene, or even Janus King. After which I walk him through the rest of the names. The second from last's a possibility — two adults and a skid.

'Got a mobile number for them? Email? An address?'

'They didn't provide any contact details.'

'So give me a description.'

He gives me a description and it's not them. I chuck the book back at him and tip my fedora.

'I won't trouble you again. Unless you trouble me first.'

'How might I do that?'

'In any number of ways but primarily by going to the cops.'

'I won't go to the cops.'

'If you're ever tempted, just remember the Bondi mugger.'

'Who's the Bondi mugger?'

I pick up the door and lean it against the architrave.

'C'est moi.'

After that there are another fourteen futilities. But I don't give up. And it's good I stay with the program, because on the fifteenth go I strike gold.

Make that silver.

Chapter 9

A DAME CALLED DAMNATION

'Why, hello there.'

She's still blonde, she's still beautiful and she's still looking at me out of the same sloe eyes she had at the ballet – only now they're sloer. Her modesty's no longer in danger from the scrap of lamé, but it's a fair bet the khaki affair she's wearing doesn't possess a back either. She's got an accent that's genuine French and I've tracked her down to an immodest four-up, half-a-dozen down, full-brick-and-tile Edwardian mansion in upmarket Mosman. To cover my contusion I pretend to tick a name off the list I got from the bloke in Sussex Street.

'Would you be Hell and Damnation?'

The dame with the eyes nods.

'It's Hélène, actually.' She throws me a glance I could only describe as winsome – or appealing, or lovely, or knee-trembling. 'And it's Dalmation, not Damnation. Which makes my appellation Hélène Dalmation, rather than what you just said.'

Whatever it sounds like, she'll always be Hell and Damnation to me. I get a grip on her mitt – it's more than I got on myself – and her skin feels like the inside of a dream. I check if she's wearing gloves but her hand's as bare as my emotions.

'I'm Harry Golightly and I'm a dick.' It's not how it was meant to come out so I try again. 'What I mean is that I'm a private detective and we need to talk.'

She opens the door and my heart – or whatever I got thrashing around in my ribcage – goes arrhythmic enough to earn me a bed next to Rube's.

'I think you could do with a drink,' she says, crossing to the expensive-looking liquor cabinet under an even more expensive-looking Picasso. She pours a couple of drinks out of an expensive-looking bottle and I see that I was right. Her dress doesn't possess a back, her beautiful neck rising out of her scapulae like a lily out of a pond by Cezanne. She hands me a glass as big as a bidet and sits in a couch that didn't come from Ikea before fixing me with a look and murmuring, 'Haven't we met somewhere before? You look familiar.'

She's brought the bottle with her, she's sitting far too low in the couch for comfort – mine, not hers – and the wine is late-cut Beaujolais.

'You were at the ballet with your grandfather,' I reply. 'So was I, but without the grandfather.'

When the dame laughs, she reveals a set of teeth almost good enough to go with the eyes.

'You say the cutest things, Mr Private Detective.' She wipes what might be tears of mirth out of the amethyst eyes with one of the hands that aren't wearing gloves. 'Yes, I was at the ballet, but not with my grandfather. His name's Albert Flax, he's an ex-Olympian and rather wealthy.' She notes the direction of my glance as well as that of my thoughts.

'French lessons couldn't pay for all this, could they?'

'I don't know, could they?'

The sloe eyes change shape like an amoeba.

'I remember you now. You're the man who leapt onto the stage after that ballet dancer was shot.'

I'm not so far gone that I don't know an inconsistency when I hear one.

'How do you know he was shot?'

The reply comes back as smooth as the Beaujolais.

'Why, it was all over the media, social and otherwise. I should have thought that a detective would keep up with the news.' She crosses to a magazine rack and the afternoon sun gambols in her hair.

'This is what one paper said.' Her beautiful hands flip the pages. 'Dance of Death. A young man playing an old man became a dead man last night when …' She palms me the blatt. 'You read it, I can't bring myself to.'

While the dame resumes her perch, I wade through the purple prose. It doesn't tell me anything I don't know already, except how the dame knew the cause of death. Her hand brushes mine as I hand back the paper. I want to trust her, and because of the hand-brush I want to trust her even more.

'So what's your interest in all this, Mr Private Detective?'

It's like I'm hypnotised – or maybe it's the wine or what I just read in the blatt – but I tell her. Not everything, just enough to give the impression that I'm open without spilling my guts; enough to endear myself without compromising my integrity; enough to set the stage for any pas de trois that might await Hell, me and Damnation in the future.

'Well then,' she croons softly after my spiel, and the amethyst eyes switch to mauve, 'how can I help?'

'You teach French,' I manage. 'And I thought you might have taught my ex-wife and daughter.'

'Why would they want to learn French?'

'Because I believe that my ex-wife's lover is French. Also because I've got nothing else to go on – apart from the crackpot ideas of a sick aunt and the sad hunch of a bereft father.'

'But why me?'

'Because you're one in a million.'

'There aren't a million French teachers in the world.'

'What I mean is that I've interviewed a lot of French teachers and you're the last on a very long list.' I hold up my glass. It's empty. 'So did they?'

'Did who what?'

'Did my daughter and her mother come to you for French lessons?'

The look she gives me is like the one she gave me at the ballet. During which she takes a deep breath and at the same time seems to come to a decision.

'I'll need a description.'

'No, I'll need a description. As well as a list of your students.'

'I'm sorry but I'm discreet.' She considers me for a moment. 'But I suppose that needn't prevent me describing my students.'

It's a long list – she'd be a good teacher if only her students could concentrate on the lessons – and it's a long while before she gets to Salina.

'She's a woman who speaks her mind but is still quite pretty, in a hard sort of way.'

That's Salina, or a close approximation of her. It's my turn to lean forward but I keep the gat covered.

'Did she give you a name?'

The dame shakes her head.

'Not one worth knowing.'

'Describe the kid.'

'A sweet girl who picked things up quickly. She quite liked ice-cream but was somewhat perturbed as to why she needed to learn French.'

'In what way was she perturbed?'

'I overheard her asking her mother why they were here.'

'And what was her mother's reply?'

'She said it would be a shared interest.'

'That's it? She told the kid they were bonding?'

The dame shrugs. 'Correct. But I sensed the girl didn't believe her. She kept quiet.'

That's Imogene. And the liar had to be Salina. But I already know Sal and the kid. It's this dame that I'd like to know better.

'What about the man that brought them here?'

'He stayed in the car; I never saw him. He just dropped them off then picked them up afterwards.'

If I had a description of Mr Green I'd be closer to finding Imogene but all I've got is a foreign accent and a word. It's a dead end. I thought I might have struck gold but it's only Grade 3 dross. Our hands don't touch as I return the glass and the reason for that might lie in the dame or in me or in both of us. 'Thanks. I won't need to trouble you again.'

'I like you,' the dame says slowly. 'So while I might not be able to describe the man, I *can* describe his car. It was a hire car and it came from those people with the inexplicable and possibly sexist motto: NO BROADS. You know, I've always wondered what that actually means ...'

And I wonder about the dame as she follows up with the dates and times of the visits, and the beautiful smile has just become that much more beautiful as she sees me out.

'Just now you said you wouldn't trouble me again,' she says as her hand finds mine. 'But did you ever think I might like to be troubled?'

'What about the ex-Olympian?'

The beautiful smile changes to an even more beautiful grimace.

'Albert's really more like a ... grandfather figure to me.' The hand lingers in mine. 'So let's not say goodbye but *à bientôt*. Or in English, don't be a stranger.'

Chapter 10

GIVE A MAN ENOUGH ROPE ...

A lot of detecting is just standing and waiting and I stand and wait at the car-hire place until the blonde with the kohl-ringed eyes and the plaintive soul lets herself out via a side door and trots off into the night examining her fingernails. When she's gone, I pull on the rubber-duckies and go in.

The security's the kind that companies install to satisfy the insurance. Apart from the insecurity, a cement apron contains a bunch of cars bearing the words NO BROADS, there's a glass-fronted office and a sign in the window says NO CASH KEPT ON THE PREMISES. I punch out the CCTV, check for trip wires and climb in the window the blonde left open in return for money to fix her fingernails with, plus a little left over for her toes.

Once inside, I flick down the blinds, adjust the ex-army torch to high beam, drag the paper serviette out of my jacket, and settle myself at the big black Dell computer in the corner. It's not easy fingering a keypad with gloves on but after a few mis-taps, I manage to enter the security code the blonde wrote on the serviette which gets me LOGBOOK, followed by whorentedwhat, which gets me the rest.

I hit SORT BY DATE and after that I key in the data provided by Damnation. Traffic hums, neon lights flicker, a dog barks and the desktop eventually coughs up a name. Xylophanio Xalades. That's a name? I key in the dates again, blink in the neon, and switch my attention back to the computer like I might surprise it into telling me the truth and the truth might be different to what it's already told me.

But the name's still Xylophanio Xalades and the joker must have used it for the same reason I wear flash clobber and a hat. Because long after

what a witness sees is overtaken by sports scores, that's all they remember
– the funny name, the fancy clothes and the hat.

I ask the computer for the licence and when I hit print, the machine at
the other end of the counter spits out a head-and-shoulders of Xylophanio
Xalades, who might also be Mr Green – the joker that Salina fell in love
with enough to run away to God-knows-where with my daughter.

It's been decades since we've seen each other, so Ace Mollema's little
more than a memory. But he's also an outline in an unlit room, his voice
roughened through shouting passwords to strangers while arresting
enough terrorists to justify a budget that would support a minor royal.

'How've you been, Rainbow?'

I strain to hear him over the background music – which is on loud
because the safe house might be bugged – and nod before realising Ace is
in the same position as me, and just like he can't hear whispers, he can't
see much, either.

'I'm fine,' I say. 'Did you bring a computer?'

I figure he must have nodded because there's a nod-length pause.
After which he adds in a voice that only just makes the high-jump over
the music, 'Plus a scanner and a printer.'

Seen from the road, the safe house could be an electrical sub-station.
It's designed to look like a house without actually being one – a non-
address in a non-street in a non-suburb that wouldn't even show up on
Smoogle Earth, and the music's Beethoven.

'I hear of you from time to time,' Ace says, the glow from the laptop
illuminating his shirt, but not his face. 'You're under everyone's radar
except ours. Because we know everything. I remember when we used to
play cops and robbers – we thought we knew everything then, too.' Pause.
'And, of course, I'll never forget what you did.'

'All I did was get you out of a hole, Ace.'

The computer screen flickers and beyond the Beethoven I can just
make out the sound of Ace's mastic gloves on the keyboard, followed
by the cheese-grater rasp of his voice. 'I remember like it was yesterday.
You were pretending to be a cop while I was a robber on the run when
I fell down that shaft. Hippies don't think about kids falling down mine
shafts, they're too busy being hippies. But you saved me.' I shrug before

remembering that he probably can't see shrugs.

'We were mates.'

'And of course we still are.' It's a spy's voice but I've got to trust him; there's nowhere else to go. 'How could we not be,' the disembodied voice continues, 'seeing that I owe you?'

I don't do the shrug, just raise my voice enough for him to hear me over the music.

'Yeah. And now I'm the one in a hole.'

'And it's my turn to provide the lifeline. What do you need?'

'A temporary passport.'

There's no hesitation. 'We can do passports.'

'It's got to work but no-one can know it's me,' I continue. 'I'm a non-person. I haven't got an identity, and if I didn't need a passport real bad, I wouldn't be asking for one.'

'Okay, I'll have to guess what you look like,' Ace says, 'based on no more than the remembrance of things past. And after that, find a match among the passports of dead men.'

'Can you do that?'

'Consider it done, Rainbow. And after it's done, consider it forgotten. Now is there anything else – apart from the passport of a dead man who looks like what I think you look like after forty years?'

'He's got to be bald.'

'We can do bald. Anything else?'

I reach across the space between us, find his gloved hand with my ungloved one, and palm him the picture from the hire-car joint.

'If you know everything about everyone, tell me who this is and where he went.'

'No problemo.'

The stereo churns out Song of Joy. I like Song of Joy. It's not just the words. Music says stuff you can't put into words.

Like vain hope in the face of impossible odds, confronted in darkness.

Chapter 11

... AND HE'LL HANG HIMSELF

Like Ace says, the spy boys – CIA, ASIO, Mossad, the KGB and the New Zealand Tomahawk Club – know everything there is to know about everyone and then some. I don't like dealing with them but sometimes there's no choice. If I'm going to find Imogene I've got to use every resource I can lay my hands on.

I saved Ace's life when we were kids. That's got to count for something, even to a spook. So after leaving the safe house, I find a nearby café, order an espresso, park my suspicions and study the paperwork. Ace has come up with three starters, each face an inverted triangle, eyes so far apart they might have come from broken homes, and all of them handsome. Salina is a great judge of character – all they got to be is handsome. I suppose that's where I fell short – I look like the backside of a bookcase.

Mr Green no. 1: Real name, Bruno Foxx. Unlikely name, unlikelier person. An orphan, he was fostered young. Ungrateful little bastard proved incorrigible. Finally rejected by his ultra-kind and ultra-peace-loving foster family. After which, in and out of reform school. After which again, in and out of the slammer; offences ranging from taking things that didn't belong to him to attempted murder. When not in jail, a drifter. Believed dead, but you believe what you want to believe in this game.

Mr Green no. 2: Real name, James Hamersley. Single child. No bright spark but apprenticed to an electrician. Married, founded his own business. Became a local politician in the staid backwater where he and Mrs Hamersley set up house. Pillow of the community. Two children and a mistress. Awarded an order of something, the kind that only money can buy. Hypocritical, but I can't let my feelings influence my judgment.

As I wade through the paperwork, Imogene seems further away than

35

ever. That's the trouble with desperation – you leap from one long shot to the next only to end up in the Glebe Morgue. I take stock: there was Rube's mugging, a ticket to the ballet, a death and a voice on a mini recorder. One of these jokers is Lover Boy. Pigs fly. I take a swig of the swill. Talking of pigs, you wouldn't feed this muck to them.

Mr Green no. 3: Serge Lifar. Where would anyone get a name like that? The dossier doesn't say. What the dossier doesn't say interests me. Lifar appeared out of the blue – or rather black, because that's the colour of the ink hiding his origin and just about everything else about him. He attended blacked-out university where he studied blacked-out – six letters or maybe eight. A succession of girlfriends, nothing permanent, names deleted. I check the picture. He's even prettier than the other two. Became blacked-out to various deleted. Deregistered as a blacked-out. Involved in deleted enterprises. Assisted in (see file blacked-out, not attached). Currently deleted.

There's something wrong here. I climb out of my comfort zone, leave the café and head for the station. All of a sudden there's no time for comfort zones.

The off-white car with the mud-spattered and therefore unreadable numberplates sidles off into the streetscape as I board the train. There's no need to follow trains. Unless they go off the rails they always end up somewhere unsurprising. And there's no-one tailing me when I alight from the carriage at Central. But I'm not looking for tails. I'm too busy trying to work out where Salina took Imogene.

That and the blacked-out background of Lover Boy.

It's raining, Rube's been discharged, she's back home and she's got company – a great throbbing lump of a machine next to the day bed in her inner-city hovel. Coffee's bubbling on the rusty Porta-stove while Rube's hooked up to the machine by the usual tubes and gazing up at me, whey-faced.

'I've renamed the machine Mr Heartbreak.'

I rescue the coffee, fill a cup, pass it to her, and she accepts it with shaking hands.

'So how long's Mr Heartbreak going to be around?' I ask, pretending not to notice the shaking hands.

The coffee spills and the planet teeters on its axis. First Imogene, now Rube. She waves the hand that's not spilling the coffee like she hasn't a care in the world, even if she's only got one kidney and it's fried.

'As long as I want to stay alive, Rainbow.'

'You mean forever?'

Her eyes slew away and when they come back to me, she's still trying to make them look calm.

'Of course not. Just a couple of hours every couple of days. But enough about me.' She points to the papers. 'What have you found out?'

After I've filled her in, Rube's nodding. It might be because some of the pieces are falling into place. Or it might be because she's falling asleep. 'Anything else?' she says, opening her eyes.

I look out at the rain and when I look back I'm frowning. 'I'm worried about you, Rube. Other than that, I'm worried about Imogene, I'm worried about Pandora and I'm worried about Ace – I don't like him knowing who I am.'

Rube smiles.

'I can look after myself – always have, always will. As for the rest, Pandora wasn't the thug who biffed me and the spy people know little or nothing about you – I took care of that long ago. Your birth certificate disappeared and you've got no health records and no identity card. You own no property, nor do you have any kind of licence. The marriage and divorce papers are gone. As far as the world's concerned, you don't exist. One fake passport's not going to change that.' Her bony hand lights on mine like a shadow. 'So tell me what else you have.'

'After Ace produced three possible identities for our Mr Green, I asked him to cross-check Imogene and Salina against outgoing air traffic.'

'Does he know where they went?'

'Their departure cards agree with you – Paris.'

Rube taps the papers.

'And which of these Mr Greens is Lover Boy?'

'Serge Lifar ticks all the boxes. He's pretty so Salina would go for him. He's also a crook, but ASIO's protecting him, so I'm guessing he's helped them in some way. He'd be a convenient passport for Salina. She wanted to take the kid and he was her escape route. She knew I didn't have a passport. What she didn't factor in was that I knew Ace and that Ace could get me one.'

Rube shakes her head.

'Rainbow, I can't help on this case.' She lifts an arm and the tubes with it. 'I'm a prisoner of this stupid machine. Worst of all I'm in a negative space emotionally. So you're on your own.'

She closes her eyes then opens them again.

'What about your profile? Who are you taking with you? A sister? A wife?'

'At this stage it looks like I'll be travelling alone.'

Rube's known me since I was a kid. She looks out the window. The rain's bouncing off the rooftops and forming a fine mist on the tar macadam.

'I understand, Rainbow. It's a case of the less I know the better, isn't it?'

Chapter 12

INNOCENCE AND ERMINE

I'm wearing T-shirt, jeans, purple sneakers, hip gun – a nice little .25 Browning Stubby – and I'm fairly sure I haven't been followed. But you can never be certain of anything in this game. For my money – whatever Aunt Rube says to the contrary – Pandora's still a suspect. I've got a bad feeling but I'm used to bad feelings. The Rolls-Rorters, Lexi-Cons and Mercy-Dies sidle between me and the mansion. I got here before lunch and now it's late afternoon, a classless wind dragging the ordure of the hoi polloi across the Harbour while expensive sunlight glimmers off the broad-acre swimming pools of God's favourites.

You can't help the odd idle thought while surveilling – like death it comes when you least expect it. That doesn't mean I don't keep my eye on the doorway of No. 31 Exemplary Parade while relieving myself in a corner of a garden that might have been modelled on Versailles.

She turns up at six. Even in a black suit and carrying a black handbag, Hell and Damnation's still milky-skinned, blonde and knee-knockingly beautiful. I allow fifteen minutes for me to calm down and Damnation to make herself comfortable before rapping on her front door. When she answers I try my best to keep it casual.

'I was past justing and thought I'd good in to say call by.'

She's taken off her day clothes and donned a bathrobe that reveals too much of her to make anyone but herself comfortable, while the tips of her soft hair caress her shoulders and her eyes have got too much violet in them not to be dangerous.

'Oh, it's you,' she says and smiles. 'I was just about to take a bath.'

'Where were you going to take it to?'

The smile turns into outright merriment.

'Why, that's so clever, Mr —'

'Call me Rain. That's what my other friend calls me.'

'Reine? As in Queen?'

I shake my head. It helps to clear it. Not completely, just enough so I can answer.

'No — Rain as in Spain.'

The dame steps back towards the hallstand and her smile goes all the way down to her toenails.

'I notice,' she says sweetly, 'that you said your other "friend", in the singular. I couldn't help wondering: would that be a male or a female friend, in the singular.'

'Yeah,' I tell her and the bottom of her bathrobe flaps a merry little welcome as she lets me in.

While the bathtub's making the kind of noises bathtubs make when they contain dames, I search the house, starting with the bedrooms. I can't move the furniture or she'd hear me over the bubbles, so I feel behind the wardrobe for the hidden safe, get down on my knees to check under the bed for the biscuit tin containing the C-notes, and scratch through the jewellery box for jewels that are far too expensive for a teacher — even one supported by a wealthy ex-Olympian.

But there's no hidden cash, no secret backs to the drawers and no observable skeletons in any of the cupboards. So I go back downstairs and take a gulp of the whisky so she'll think that's all I've been doing. That, and admiring the pictures of the French castles in the magazines she left me along with the whisky.

After that, I check out the rest of the house, starting with the scullery. Inside the sugar bowl, on top of the cupboards, under the freezer, behind the stove — all the obvious places. Followed by the not-so-obvious places. After which, I search the living room containing the Picasso with too many eyes in it, followed by the study. Always with an ear to the bubbles plip-plopping and the body slip-sliding to make sure the dame's not where

I don't want her to be. At least not until I've finished my search.

But the dame's clean. Or as clean as any dame can be that's just taken a bath and is now standing in the bathroom doorway, wrapping herself in a bathrobe and calling out, 'Where are you?'

She's expecting me to be in front of her when I'm behind her, that I'll be in the living room when I'm in the sunroom, and that if she stands in the hallway covering her front with her bathrobe, she'll avoid exposure. I catch a rear view of a beautiful thigh and I'm wondering what else she's trying to cover up when she turns and catches me wondering.

I quickly drain the rest of the J&B.

'I'm here minding my own business. Plus whatever else happens along that might need minding.'

Her face has turned a deep shade of pink. I can't speak for the rest of her because she's finally herded herself back into the robe.

'I – didn't expect you to be – where you are,' she says.

I shrug. 'Neither did I.' I hold up the glass like a shield. 'But I've completed my tour of the whisky and was looking for more.'

The dame's no longer smiling.

'I'm not in the habit of storing drinks in the hallway. Also –'

But I don't hear the also. The double-report of a gun followed by the sound of glass shattering and the noise of a rapid departure puts paid to that. I hit the carpet, taking the dame down with me. When I get back to my feet and into the living room, the Browning's in my fist and the first thing I notice is the broken window; the second is that the Picasso's got even more eyes than it had before; and the third is that there's no glass on the floor.

'Wh – what ...!' cries the dame, trying to keep her gown closed while at the same time keeping her beautiful eyes wide open.

'Stay down!' I yell.

Damnation stays down and I get myself into the garden. The sun has set on the expensive carriageway and there's nothing left but street trees, muted orange lamps and glass on the grass under the window. No sign of any shooter. I come back and check out the dame. She's tied up the bathrobe. I garage the gat.

'You got any enemies?' I ask her.

'No. Have you?'

I busy myself rechecking the window, followed by the painting. And after that, the frame around the painting and the wall around the frame. There's enough lead to make an anchor for the Queen Mary, yet the pellets form no more than a six-inch spread on the wall.

'Know anyone that could shoot that good?' The dame shakes her head like she doesn't understand the question. 'Okay, go and change into something more uncomfortable while I clean up. We'll both feel better that way.'

While she's gone I check her handbag: keys, powder, lipstick, eyeshadow, wallet. Her driver's licence contains the face of a dame with sloe eyes and the name reads like it's supposed to read. There's a Medicare card, health insurance plastic and a library voucher – all the ID other people possess but I don't. An electricity bill proves she lives here. A couple of hundred bucks prove she's not broke. And a passport proves –

The traffic's dying but I don't want to die along with it. I step to the front door and rip it open. Nothing. I close the door and tippy-toe to the base of the stairs. From above comes the soft sound of bare feet and the noise of drawers opening and closing. The shells on the floor are Winchester 12-gauge SSG. I return to the handbag and examine the passport and by the light of the hall sconces make out the following:

The passport's current

The ID in the passport matches the one on the driver's licence

The dame likes travelling from Sydney to Paris and back again.

The sound of espadrilles fluttering down the stairs gets the passport back in the wallet, and the wallet back in the bag. I turn around and there's Damnation standing before me, all clad in innocence and ermine.

Chapter 13

HELL AND DAMNATION

The sloe eyes take a tour and when they return to mine they're wearing question marks.

'I was looking for a broom,' I mumble, 'to clean up the glass.'

'Really. Well, you're not going to find one there.' The voice is as dry as desiccated coconut. 'I keep my brooms in the broom cupboard.'

The breeze through the broken window tries to ruffle the dame's hair as she seats herself next to the table with the bottle on it, but her hair's too wet to be ruffled. She's changed into a nice dress under the coat and she's well into her third whisky.

'I wonder who the gunman was?' She stares at me wide-eyed. 'And I also wonder why you searched my house.'

'I had to make sure you were safe.'

'Which, of course, can be taken two ways ...'

'Most things can.'

She grimaces into her whisky.

'Must you be such a tough guy?'

'Does anyone have to be anything?'

Damnation puts down her glass and hugs herself. She's got beautiful full lips to go with the eyes but the way the mouth's set could make it that of a teacher upset by the behaviour of a student.

'I trusted you, Mr Rain, yet you ...' She clenches her fist; it's a good thing it's not holding the glass. 'But now I feel – defiled.'

'It was for your own good.'

'How could searching my house be for my own good? I didn't invite you into my life – you invited yourself. Along with some cock-and-bull story about an ex-wife stealing a child.'

'Except it's the truth. You were their teacher, remember?'

'But why come back for seconds? Why didn't you just leave me alone.'

I get to my feet.

'It looks like I better go.'

'Good. But before you do, tell me this: did you come back just to search my house?'

I decide to tell her too much. But maybe I intended doing that all along.

'No. I'm leaving the country and I wanted to see you before I went.'

The eyes soften. 'Where are you going?' She answers her own question. 'You're going to France, aren't you? I don't need to be a private inquiry agent to know that. Well, you've seen me so now you can go. *Bon chance a decouvrir ta fille.*'

I play it dumb.

'I beg your pardon?'

She smiles triumphantly.

'I said, good luck finding your daughter when you don't even speak French.'

She moves closer to me. Rube taught me to let them open the door so I step aside. But instead of opening the door the dame gazes up at me out of her sloe eyes and says, 'Mr Rain ...?'

'Mr Rain what?'

'Why don't you take me with you?'

She's put a nice red-and-white check cloth on the table and there's a bottle of French wine, salt and pepper pots in the shape of overstuffed ducks, a red candle, two plates and a hot baking tray containing a margherita pizza with too many olives in it.

'I could be useful,' she says. 'And you might just find yourself in need of useful.' She leans forward. 'I mean, have you ever even been to France?'

'Not in so many words.'

'And you don't speak French.'

Sometimes ignorance can be bliss – hers if not mine.

'Again, not in so many words.'

She sits back. 'So in so many words you'd be *fou* if you didn't take me.'

I know the question's brutal but it's the brutal questions you got to ask in this world. Life's a series of them, even when the answers turn out to be ones you don't want to hear.

'What's in it for you? Dames don't just fly off to foreign countries with strangers, even when those countries aren't all that foreign to them.'

Damnation silently plays with her fork like she's trying to splay the prongs.

'Maybe you feel homesick,' I continue. 'But that's not enough.' I wave a hand at our surrounds. 'You live in a big house. You got a rich lover. Yet you're prepared to toss it away for a trip to France with a stranger. It's what people do when they're teenagers. And it doesn't add up to a row of peanuts when they're not.'

In the dim light of the candle on the red-and-white tablecloth, her amethyst eyes go opaline.

'I – I –'

She's been shot at, which gives her an idea of what could happen if she hooks up with me. And she's had her house strip-searched, which ditto. I'm a lunk with a gun and about as much class as a corpse in a sewer.

'Just answer the question.'

She wipes her eyes on a corner of the tablecloth and takes a deep breath.

'Maybe if I told you something about myself ...'

Chapter 14

THE PROFILE CHANGER

Hélène Dalmation was born in Toulouse, France – about a decade after my mother produced me in a dam in Nimbin, Australia – the result of a union between a Parisian seamstress and a Basque terrorist.

'A what?'

She tucks an errant lock behind a beautiful ear. Thanks to the breeze, her hair's drying nicely and after she tucks back the curl, the shine in the eyes seems no longer due to the tears. 'Oh, Basque terrorists are nothing like – well, people who fly planes into buildings,' she explains. 'In fact, they personify the ideals most French like to imagine they possess, courtesy of the Revolution – liberty, equality and fraternity. The belief that all people are equal and no-one's any better than anyone else.'

When her father was killed, her mother couldn't cope so baby Hélène was sent to a nunnery. At sixteen, she escaped, marrying the scion of a wealthy Australian family, who was in France doing nothing in preparation for doing nothing for the rest of his life. The happy couple drifted to Australia, and after the divorce Damnation discovered herself in the withered but welcoming arms of Albert Flax.

She spreads her hands and the shadows of her fingers play Ludo on the tablecloth.

'Which brings us to now.'

'Tell me about Flax.'

'What's to tell? He's an ex-Olympian, he's rich and he's very generous.'

'And you love him?'

She shrugs. 'What's not to love?'

'Yet you're prepared to ditch him for a trip to France with someone you just met?'

She considers me over the hands.

'Your ex-wife ditched you for as little.' She picks up the pepper pot and puts it down again, raising her eyes to mine. 'I can go back to France whenever I want. Albert isn't possessive.' She takes another deep breath. 'But being able to isn't the same as wanting to. And the reason I want to go to France is because, well, I – I like you.'

She's young and she's beautiful but I've still got half a brain to think with.

'You're being impulsive. From what you told me, you're in the habit of doing things you later regret. You want to go to France with me just like you came to Australia with Mr Useless and later fetched up with Mr ex-Olympian.'

'It's not like that.'

I ask the question and I ask it sudden.

'What about Mr Green?'

'I've already told you –' she fiddles with the candle '– I don't even know your Mr Green. He was never more than a – a silhouette in a car to me.' When she reaches across the remains of the pizza, the hand on mine is warm. It must be because of the candle. 'But I can help you find him if I accompany you to France.'

I tell her okay.

I'm only human.

Apart from which, having her along might help me to find Imogene.

Rube's detached herself from Mr Heartbreak for the afternoon and she's clutching a book and kneeling by two suitcases – one big and one small – in the aft companionway of the *Wooden No*. She looks better but looks can be illusory.

'This book's called France at a Glance and you'll need to read it during the plane ride, so it goes in the cabin bag. In the big wheelie bag I've packed nice, warm flannelette pyjamas, several pairs of socks, a toothbrush – and an electric razor. And here's the passport.'

The boat lurches as Rube flips open the little black book with the bird and marsupial on the front. I feel dizzy. It's strange existing, even if it's only temporarily and in the guise of someone else. Or maybe it's just the boat lurching.

'Arthur Halliwell,' Rube reads aloud. She looks up, comparing my face with the photograph. 'Not a bad likeness – except for the baldness. Who was he?'

I tell her what Ace wrote in the note accompanying the passport that found its way into Ruby's letterbox. Halliwell was a case of mistaken identity resulting in accidental death, courtesy of an Australian Federal Police hit squad. Too late, they discovered that Halliwell wasn't a terrorist at all, just a meek and mild suburban accountant who keyed bomb into his computer one day when he meant porn. No history, no family, few friends, so the death went unreported. Similar features to mine, except for the baldness.

Rube nods.

'I've also packed some nice grey suits, a grey cardigan and a grey Akubra. You won't know yourself.'

She shifts on her knees – the tube writhing under her jacket – and produces the kind of wallet an accountant called Halliwell might carry.

'Inside you'll find something to help with expenses.' I start to protest. 'Don't argue with me, Rainbow – think of it as an early inheritance. God knows, with my kidney the way it is there's unlikely to be a late one.'

'You're a long way from dying, Rube.'

'I'm not talking about me dying, I'm talking about you living.'

She shuts the suitcase as the boat yaws and the pump makes obscene noises in the bilge. Then she clambers to her feet.

'That closes that case. Now all you need concern yourself with is the one concerning the kid.' She glances over the railing like she's surprised to find we're still afloat. 'And don't worry, I'll look after the *Wooden No* while you're away.'

'And who's going to look after you?'

Rube grabs hold of a stanchion as a wave rocks us.

'Rory's offered. There's no need to grimace, he might be Rory, but he's – whatever he is. So keep your hair on.' She shoots me a wan smile. 'Or off, as the case may be.'

'Did your tame spook provide you with anything else?' Rube asks as my locks scatter.

I nod and the blades nick my right lug – the one Madam Lash missed in the Horses for Corpses caper. I feel the wind lick at the cut.

'Yeah, he came up with an itinerary. As for Lifar, he flew out yesterday on a Boeing 747 bound for Heathrow, London – business class.'

'Is that his final destination?'

'Ace thinks he's headed for France. Which makes it a match.'

'How do you know that's where Salina and the kid are?'

'Because Ace says so.'

Rube ditches the shears and switches to the buzz cut. 'Good old Ace,' she murmurs. 'But Lifar needed Salina and Imogene to fuzz-up his image. So their travelling separately suggests two things:

'There was no physical coercion on Salina and the kid to accompany him; and

'Lifar's nothing but a dumbstruck lover, after all.'

I cop another pinch, this time to the other ear, and this time from the buzzer.

'Maybe he just wanted to look different after he arrived,' I suggest. 'Remember, they're not expecting me to come after them.'

Rube nods and I duck, thereby avoiding further bloodshed. For the moment.

'Assuming they meet up in Paris, where will they go after that?' she asks.

'I'll have to work that out when I get there. With a bit of luck I can grab the kid and bring her home. Like I said, Salina won't be expecting me. She can follow me and Imogene back or stay where she is with Lifar.'

Despite my display of assurance, Rube looks worried.

'That ignores the attack on me and the bullets, Rainbow. I got mugged, remember? And a dancer got killed. What if this is more than just a simple abduction?'

I touch my integument and cartilage and my hand comes away spotted with blood.

'We play it by ear – if I've still got any left after you're done with them.'

But Rube's not interested in herrings, red or otherwise.

'You said we.' She waves her instrument of torture at the Harbour. 'Who's we?'

As an interrogator, Rube's got no equal. Torquemada would have had to wait in line if Rube was around during the Spanish Inquisition.

'You needn't come the detective with me, Rube, I –'

Her mouth tightens. 'Who's going with you, Rainbow?'

I take a deep breath. It's got hairs in it but no graces.

'Yeah, well, there's this dame called Hell and Damnation, see, and ...'

'Hell and who?'

The ship rolls and I roll with it.

'Yeah, well ...' Rube calls it my yeah-and-welling – when she hears me yeah-and-welling she knows that I'm stalling. 'It's pronounced Hay-leng Dah-mah-shong but I call her Damnation. She's the dame who taught Salina and the kid French and has been helping me with my inquiries. She'll change my profile.'

Rube examines her cutters.

'Just like Delilah did with Samson. Won't you ever learn? This Damnation's danger. The name's enough. You're not on some jaunt, you know. You're trying to find your kid.'

'She could have a tie-in with Lifar, Rube. And she speaks French. Plus she was at the ballet when the dancer was shot.' I don't quit while I'm ahead. 'Also I want her where I can put my hands on her.'

Rube's mouth forms a thin line, like she's in a great deal of pain and I've just added to it.

'You know how to speak French, Rainbow, remember?'

'Yeah, but she speaks it better.'

'I think you just want this dame where you can put your hands on her.'

I feel my eyes snow over and my worldview grow less bleak. 'Yeah, there's that, too.'

Chapter 15

PAY ATTENTION TO THE FOLLOWING

You become what you're wearing. And I'm wearing undertaker's smart-casual – grey daks, wide-lapelled jacket featuring too many brass buttons, shoestring tie, shiny black slime-ons – plus a grey Akubra with a brim so wide it could double as an umbrella. All of which turns me into an unassuming suburban accountant called Arthur Halliwell.

That, plus a suitcase full of the kind of possessions an unassuming suburban accountant might take with him to a double-entry bookkeeping convention in Paris, if he hadn't been occupying a plot in Rookwood cemetery. Which is what he's doing and how come I'm wearing his passport. Garbed in the unfamiliar clobber and possessed of an identity, I feel myself change – not just in appearance but in the way I think and the way I speak. Rube warned me it could happen. Me and the dame are on stand-by and I got Rube's tour book open at the section called 'Handy Travel Tips', which begins:

'You'll keep coming across familiar faces. But don't worry, it doesn't mean you're being followed ...'

The dame left me minding her bags while she went to the Ladies and now she's craning her beautiful neck checking the flight board for the plane we couldn't get seats on. She's dressed in what she calls the year-before-last Parisian chic – red silk scarf, cerise suit that highlights the colour of her eyes, and stockings you can hardly see at all, that really suit her legs.

Perched beside her is her wheelie case with the purple flowers on the outside and too many toiletries on the inside. I know because I checked while she was in the Ladies. The dame's clean. Or at least her suitcase is. I go back to the advice in the travel book:

'You're in luck, there have been two cancellations and the seats happen to be next to each other.' The woman at the check-in counter glances from me to Damnation and back again. 'Passports, please, and place your bags on the conveyor belt.'

We hand her our passports – one black, the other red.

'Mr Halliwell and Ms Dalmation.' The woman does her check. 'Father and daughter?'

'Just good friends,' I say, glancing behind us in case someone's listening.

'Are you all right, Rainbow?'

I frown Damnation into silence. 'You must be thinking of someone else,' I mutter. 'The name's Arthur Halliwell. In fact, anything other than the name you just said.'

Damnation colours. She looks nice, coloured. She looks nice in black and white, too.

'I'm sorry,' she whispers. 'But give me a break, Rai – I mean, Arthur. I'm still getting used to the baldness.'

The woman at the check-in counter smiles like she's thinking about anything else as she hands back our passports, plus two bits of cardboard that make us temporary owners of a pair of adjoining seats on a plane to Paris.

'Please go straight to the departure gate or you'll miss your flight. And that would be sad after waiting all this time for a cancellation, wouldn't it?' The check-in woman glances behind us. 'Ah, some late arrivals.'

An elderly couple step into our vacuum, smiling apologetically. Behind them is a man in black – wearing a hard bag and an even harder look – and I got to restrain Damnation because it's not smart to run at airports. Run and you draw attention to yourself. Run and you'll be dragged kicking and screaming to the interrogation room. Run and you'll be on their files forever, listed as people who are in the habit of running at airports.

When we reach customs and immigration, I take off my Akubra for a person in uniform, who asks, 'Business or pleasure?'

I reply that we're going to Romantasy-land at which the official smiles because officialdom's just like Salina and a lot more romantic than people think. He stamps our passports and we proceed along to baggage check, where I place my sober braces and sober shoes and even more sober hat in the plastic tray provided and hold up my hands so they can see if I wash under my armpits. And all the time I'm watching for anyone that might be becoming too familiar like:

The elderly couple behind us; and

The man in black.

Damnation touches my arm.

'We're through.' I give her the eyebrow-raise. 'I mean through the last barrier – not as a couple. We're almost on the plane. It's like we're entering a new world.'

I shake my Yul Brynner skull at her.

'There's no such thing as a new world, only more of the old. But if it helps to keep the fire alive, I'll come along for the bride.'

We've scored an aisle and an inner – the kind you've got to climb over everyone else just to get to the toilet. The man in black's in the seat behind me, taking up too much overhead luggage space with his oversized cabin bag.

Time for a position statement:

My ex has taken the kid;

They're in Paris; and

I don't know if I can trust the dame but it sure is nice she's here.

Chapter 16

CHARACTERS ON A PLANE

We stay on the plane for the Singapore refuel. The dame's got a nice line in patter. In fact, she's got a nice line, period. Also, she sleeps a fair bit, which allows me to do my homework. I've got no idea what Salina's up to, except more of the same. And I don't know what's happened to Imogene. Is Mr Green — alias Lifar — just an innocent lover? And how the hell do I find out? I've got half an idea, but sometimes half an idea's worse than no idea at all. I half-watch a movie about identity theft while reconstructing the evidence.

Salina ran off with Lover Boy and took the kid along for the ride. But if Salina wanted to be in the City of Love with her boyfriend, wouldn't it have been smarter to leave Immo behind? The kid was prevented from leaving a forwarding address, managing no more than one tape-recorded word and a cancelled ticket to the ballet. Which means that, after all the French lessons, it was a plain and simple abduction. But why would Salina abduct her own daughter? To get back at me? If so, why was Rube mugged? And what about the death of the ballet dancer?

I drag my eyes away from the movie and find myself staring at the safety pamphlet in the seat pocket in front of me. It's printed on nice, glossy paper — just like the stuff in the rats' nest behind the water heater at Salina's joint.

When Rube did jigsaws, she used to put the bits on a board so they wouldn't fly around. I retrieve the evidence bag from my pocket and set out the rat-chewed scraps on the safety pamphlet. People see what they want to see. That means the pieces will fall where I expect them to fall instead of where they belong. Beside me Damnation shifts in her sleep, bumping my elbow and knocking the letters out of position. A voice over the PA says, 'We are experiencing flatulence. Please return to your seats and fasten your seatbelts.'

Only it's not flatulence but turbulence. Spelled: T-U-R-B-U-L-E-N-C-E. I do what the voice says and the letters shift some more. For God's sake, Rainbow, Rube would say, you're seeing what you think you see. Look at what's there, not some pie in the sky. I steady myself. The word might be GRENE instead of GREEN. Or it could be ...

The plane lurches and the dame jerks upright.

'Wha –?'

A stewardess hurrying down the aisle leans down.

'It's all right,' she tells the dame. 'Have a great trip. Enjoy.'

A great trip. Enjoy. G-R-E-A-T-T-R-I-P-E-N-J-O-Y. That includes *TRIPE* and *JOY*. Take away ATTRIP and JOY and what's left? G-R-E-E-N. I'm like a blind man suddenly able to see. Because I'm not supposed to be looking at the letters I've got, but for the letters that are missing. Green's a red herring. Instead it's –

'What is it, Rai – Arthur?'

The main cabin lights have been switched off and my dinky little personal light is all that's illuminating the letters. Damnation wouldn't have seen anything.

'Go back to sleep,' I say. 'It's nothing – just some characters on a plane.'

I look down again and see what I've always seen – the word Green. But superimposed on that is the face of my daughter. The letters were in what the hostess said – GREeat trip ENjoy. But what I've got is different because the missing letters are different. It's GRE-something-E-something-N and maybe something else. The turbulence eases. I re-bag the scraps, pocket the bag, tilt back my chair, close my eyes ... and don't go to sleep.

Because someone's tapping my shoulder. I resist the normal reaction. Instead I turn nice and slow to find the man in the seat behind staring at me out of hard eyes.

'You just tipped back your seat, fella,' he says. 'And you made me spill my Fanta. You might have warned me.'

A scar bisects one eyebrow, giving his eyes a cross-legged look, his mouth's fighting a losing battle with a sneer, and his hands are knotting for a fight. Or maybe he just wants attention.

'Yeah,' I reply. 'Then again I mightn't have.'

He half-stands but a stewardess closes in and he sits.

'Next time,' he mutters.

'If you're not careful, pal,' I mutter back, 'there won't be a next time.'

While other kids were told stories from Dr Seuss, Roald Dahl and Hans Christian Andersen, Aunt Rube dissected cases of the Yank detectives called the Pinkertons, whose motto under an unblinking eye was: WE NEVER SLEEP.

The man in black's behind me.

I make like the Pinkertons and keep my eyes open.

Chapter 17

ON DEATH RUE

Horns blare and drivers scream, even though the WALK sign's the same colour as the park. It's springtime in Paris and Damnation's clutching my hand. She's got a stranglehold on my heart, too. We're in the colonnade next to the Rue de Rivoli – the boulevard beside the Louvre – and the traffic's exhibiting all the enthusiasm of a scorpion, just before his girlfriend eats him.

I'm keeping a close eye on the man in black who's been on the shadow since we left Charles de Gaulle aerodrome. He was behind us during the changeover from the aboveground train to the Metro then he turned up in our carriage where he pretended interest in everything but us.

After that, he took the same wrong turns we took, ending up behind us at Gare d'Orsay. He's mingling with the pimps, hip-swingers and deros like he belongs here, ambling when we amble, stopping when we stop, feigning interest in something – anything – whenever I look his way. He's just stopped and put his bag down on the footpath beside him and he's simulating interest in a bad copy of Rodin's statue The Thinker.

'Come on,' I tell the dame. 'We got a job to do.'

Damnation's reluctant.

'I know,' she replies, 'but ...'

'Listen to me: we're being followed so I want you to pretend we're lovers, okay? Be careful you don't dislodge the hat and whatever you do, don't look behind you.'

Damnation's sloe eyes shift like she's about to do what I just told her not to so I pull her to me and give her a smooch, the way lovers are supposed to in Paris, without taking my eyes off the man in black. Damnation turns co-operative, but she's also trying to turn around. 'Don't look surprised and don't look behind you,' I repeat. 'I'm going to let go. When I do, we're going to split up and I'll meet you in fifteen minutes at the first café on the Rue Saint-Denis.' The last I see of Damnation is a flash of red scarf swinging around the corner, our cabin bags under her arms and our wheelie cases trundling behind her.

The instant she's gone I hurl myself back onto the street of death they call the Rue de Rivoli. As I dive, I pull my hat down over my baldness.

Sometimes tails hesitate and sometimes they don't. This one doesn't. Without looking either to his left or his right like he should have, the man in black comes after me. I leap over a Smart car and land in an arabesque. From behind – above the roar of the traffic – I hear the yell of an onlooker that tells me I'm still being followed. I face the traffic. Holding onto my hat, I do a tumble-turn over the slippy-slide bonnet of a Citroën. From behind comes the screech of brakes and a series of sickening thuds.

I turn to find the road a mess of multi-coloured metal and people gesticulating. The Rue de Rivoli will never be the same again. Neither will the man in black. He's been hit by a car, thrown across the street and is now lying crumpled in a heap in the gutter.

Within seconds, sirens sound, but something tells me I should stick around. The cops arrive and one bends over the body in the gutter and lifts it up, checking for vital signs. But then he goes one step further. He reaches into the man's pocket, retrieving something that glints in the warm Parisian sunlight.

Chapter 18

THE CLAWED HAND

Following a serious traffic incident, the cops should be stringing out the coloured tape. But they aren't. They should be measuring skid marks. But they aren't. And they should be recording witness statements. Except they aren't doing that either.

Instead, they're handing out what look like business cards to the drivers involved in the pile-up and anyone else that happens to be passing. Keeping the brim of my accountant's Akubra well down I head back into the action. The fuzz in France are divided into local, state and what's known as the Sûreté Nationale. The Sûreté are the big boys and they're the ones handing out the cards. Traffic accidents don't usually involve them. A tow truck appears, along with Parisian street cleaners. A cop approaches. I clutch my chest with one hand, hold out my free mitt and receive a card.

After that I cross the road and head north, rough-translating as I go: *All this will be sorted. You do not need to contact an insurance agent. Nor do you need a lawyer. Your damages will be attended to. You will not be out of pocket. Just call the number below.*

When I reach the other side, I look to see what the cops are doing with the body. They're handling it – if not by the book or with kid gloves – at least carefully. But no-one's noticed the bag: it's still sitting where the man in black dumped it. I pick it up like it belongs to me, check the street cameras, get out of their range, bend and unzip the bag. Dirty clothes: scrunched-up shirts, ragged singlets, crumpled underpants, crushed daks. The man in black's bag's been through airport security so there's not going to be anything insecure in it. But there's nothing of anything in it. No books, no papers, no shaver, not even a toothbrush. I rezip it and

replace it where he dumped it while he was pretending too much interest
in a bad copy of Rodin's The Thinker. Before he stopped thinking and
leapt to his death.

Damnation's sitting on a cane chair at a cane table with a glass top outside
the café on the Rue Saint-Denis, her mobile on the table before her
and our cases on the footpath beside her. When she sees me she looks
concerned. I'm carrying a fresh bruise or two and my clothes could be
cleaner. Or maybe she's worried about something completely different.

'What happened?' she asks.

'Someone had a little accident. Must have been the food.'

She takes a deep breath. It reminds me of something. It reminds her
of something else.

'Do you know Les Halles, the shopping mall?' she asks. 'I need to buy
some summer clothes.'

But I've got other things on my mind besides fashion. I help myself
to her phone.

'Before we do anything I got to make a call. And after I've done that,
we got to find the flat.'

'I was just –'

I know what she was 'just', but I still check her call log, particularly
the activity since we split up, after which I enter the number on the card.
It's answered immediately and I'm put through to Special Branch, that
section of the French police dealing with unusual cases, so I sever the
connection and hand back the phone. I flip the garçon a couple of Euros,
grab the wheelie bags and head down the rue. Damnation's stilettos play
Bach's fugue in C-minor on the footpath behind me. Behind that again is
the echo of the body of the man in black being hit by a car. I don't look
back.

Seine is the name of the famous Parisian waterway. It's also the English
word for a dragnet to catch fish in. But I'm a long way from catching

anything as we reach the address Ace gave me – a Haussmann seven-floorer, if you count the bit they put in for the birds in the roofline just above the eaves. On the footpath outside, a Parisian beggar, almost totally hidden under a grey blanket, is sitting with an upturned cap beside him.

A pair of big doors – a doghole in one of them for when the doors are locked – open onto a courtyard. Inside, there are a lot of flagstones and too many doors leading off the flagstones. A dinky little button next to a doorway says: Artemis Bonnet, Concierge, Pressez. I pressez.

An elderly dame opens the door, bending to restrain the one-eyed goat beside her. The dame's got pink-tinted hair, rose-coloured glasses, a face like a gargoyle off the nearby Notre Dame cathedral and a mouth like she's had a bad day at the dentist's. The goat tilts its head because of the eye.

'Waddayawan?' she asks in French.

'Say what we want,' I murmur to Damnation.

Damnation tells the landlady what we want.

Forget Paris chic. The space above the eaves meant for the pigeons is rubbish and we're stuck with it for a week because that's how they let these joints. Except we won't be here any longer than it takes to work out where Salina, Imogene and Lover Boy have gone. Damnation looks about her.

'The concierge said this was where they stayed,' she tells me, like telling me might take her mind off the poky surrounds. 'There was a man, a woman who was headstrong and a girl. The concierge said the girl was cute.'

All of which I know already because I speak French. Only I don't tell Damnation that. I also know the landlady gave us a funny look when she handed us the keys. But maybe that's how she always looks.

'Well, the apartment's – different, anyway.'

'You wanted romantic.'

'Yes, but this romantic?'

There's a hallway, a living room, a kitchen, two bedrooms and a bathroom with a shower. A few downlights dot the tatty ceilings, seashell wallpaper decorates the walls and there are a couple of pieces of cardboard furniture. Also there's a window. The place is spotless. Just like Salina's.

'It could be the wrong apartment,' the dame says.

I shake my head. 'No, it's the right one, all right.' I've got myself up and onto the kitchen sink where I'm probing the gap between cupboards and wall with a coathanger I found in one of the cardboard wardrobes.

The dame's wearing her year-before-last clobber and shifting from one foot to the other in the doorway to the hall. 'So can I go shopping now?'

Chapter 19

SPRING SACRIFICE

Alot of stairways in Paris are corkscrew affairs and the one in our apartment block's no exception, its oak treads worn low by two centuries of sole-searching all the way to the ground floor, its balustrades as graceful as Marie Antoinette before she found herself at the wrong end of a guillotine.

As well as the corkscrew stairs there's a lift. Damnation takes the lift and I give her thirty seconds then take the stairs slow and soft while all the time listening to the lift. The lift doors open and the dame's footsteps emerge. I allow her time to reach the street, after which I step out into the courtyard. I feel eyes on me. It's the landlady, Artemis, craning to see as she bends to restrain the goat. I tip my hat. She doesn't acknowledge the gesture. Beside her the goat closes its one good eye and stares at me blindly out of the other.

I exit via the little dog-door, pass the beggar on the footpath, and head after Damnation.

Les Halles is in the opposite direction to the one she's taken.

Question 1: Why did she lie to me?

Question 2: Where is she really going?

Question 3: What else has she lied to me about?

There are more curves to this dame than there are in a Parisian staircase. But it makes her easy to tail.

All I got to do is follow the stares.

"

Because of the Revolution there's nothing left of the jail they called the Bastille. But as Damnation passes what's not left of the jail, I can still hear the clatter of the guillotine and smell the blood … before realising it's only the modern-day French enjoying the fruits of the Revolution – freedom and the demise of the hated aristocrats.

Meanwhile the stares tell me the dame's chucked a left followed by a right. In my suit I follow suit. She's not looking behind her, which means she's not aware I'm following her. Or else she's very aware and pretending she's not. I stay well back in case of either.

There's a lot of expensive shops in Paris but Le Printemps is the biggie, stretching over several blocks and selling perfumes, fashion and bric-a-brac that normal money can't buy. As I enter, a dame in a black frock disinfects me with gold-plated aftershave. Silver gee-gaws disguised as lobsters are a pinch at ten grand a claw. Tourists shove one another out of the way to get at the bargains. I keep my eye on the dame as she weaves her way towards the –

My legs suddenly go weak. In Le Printemps – which means spring – the French imagination has gone into overdrive. Over the PA they're playing none other than the Stravinsky ballet The Rite of Spring in the belief that most people won't make the connection. The Rite of Spring is about sacrifice and I no longer see shoppers but the heads, arms and outstretched hands of executioners –

Meanwhile I've lost sight of Damnation. There are no longer any people staring and telling me where she went because everyone's too busy shopping. I'm stuck in a Parisian orgy, a Bacchanalia, a Saturnalia, and the music's giving me the heebies. I got to escape, out of this bloody music of sacrifice, away from the memory of what was and the dread of what might be.

I stumble from the store but the music follows me, music depicting innocence in the face of evil – a child faced by impending death – and in my mind I see Pandora. As I reach the footpath outside, the music reaches a crescendo. The racket of the traffic hits me but compared to what I'm trying to escape, it's breath after asphyxiation, light after dark, life after death.

I hurtle back to the apartment on the Rue de Rivoli.

Chapter 20

WHAT THE CONCIERGE SAW

The sun's still shining and the beggar outside the apartment block's still begging, an indeterminate shape beneath a blanket. While in the courtyard, the landlady's watering her pansies in the company of her goat.

'*Tout va bien?*' she says.

She's asking how I am but I'm not supposed to know what she's saying.

'Sorry but I don't speak French.'

She does a sideways tilt of her head, much like the goat, and her eyes grow cunning.

'Oh, really?' she replies in English.

'Yeah, really.'

The goat stamps a curled-over hoof and lowers its horned head while the old woman looks like she's heard it all before and returns to her watering.

'Things can die from too much attention, Artemis,' I tell her.

She doesn't look up.

'Fifty euro.'

'I already paid the rent.'

She crosses to a tap shaped like a gargoyle to refill her watering can. All I can see is her hunched back and the bearded profile of the goat. I've got to strain to hear what she says over the noise of the traffic.

'I'm not talking about the rent.' She turns off the gargoyle, crosses to a cactus and continues negotiating. 'I'm a landlady in Paris. More precisely, I'm the ill-paid slave of the rich person who owns this place. Which means that, while I'm happy to pretend I'm stupid, me and Maria here still need to keep up with the cost of living. A hundred.'

'You just said fifty.'

'The cost of living just doubled.'

At the current exchange rate, a hundred euros is about a hundred and fifty Australian. I hand over the money while I can still afford it and it disappears down the landlady's cleavage like a rat down a rope. 'The woman and the girl arrived first,' she says with a crooked smile. 'The woman's French was basic but I let her struggle, pretending I didn't know English in the same way some people pretend not to know French.'

A truck rumbles past and I let the comment pass along with it.

'Your ex-wife thought she was in love. She was also clearly anxious about the girl.' The woman anticipates my next question. 'The girl didn't seem happy. I heard her say she wanted to contact her father.'

Imogene said that so the woman would hear her and pass on the information.

'What else did she say?'

Again the sly look. 'Nothing.'

'When did the boyfriend arrive?'

'A couple of days after the mother and daughter.'

The greedy look makes a return visit. She thought she'd fired all her bullets only to discover she's still got another slug in the chamber. The goat nuzzles her affectionately. Or maybe it's just scratching itself.

I palm her another fifty euros and it follows the rest down the rope.

'He couldn't keep his hands off her.'

'Were the hands caressing or restraining?'

The greedy look's replaced by a knowing one.

'In Paris, caressing and restraining mean pretty much the same thing.' I make like I want my money back. 'All right, the hands were strong.'

'That all I get for the extra fifty – that the boyfriend had strong paws?'

'I could invent things but you'd only find out.'

'What makes you say that?'

'Because you're not just a concerned father, you're also a private detective.'

'What about his face?'

'Like you, he was wearing a hat. So, like yours, his face wasn't there to describe.'

'What names did they put in your book? We wrote our names in a book so they must have, too.' She goes back into a room with a threadbare carpet lit by a barley-twist lamp, leaving the goat staring at me out of its one eye, and when she returns into the spring sunshine she's carrying a book with marbling on the outside and scribble on the inside. And what the scribble says is that one John Smith, in company with his wife Ann and daughter Annette, stayed in the selfsame flat we're in.

'No passport details.' I look up; the landlady's breath smells of garlic, or maybe it's the goat's. 'Don't you have to see passports?'

She shakes her head.

'The man paid extra not to show their passports.'
'How long did they stay?'
'He was in a hurry. Two days, but they paid for a week.'
'Did he possess any distinguishing characteristics?'
'His hands were beautiful.'
'Anything else?'
Then – but only after looking down at the goat, apparently considering whether she should do an Oliver Twist and ask for more – she replies, 'Yes, there was something else.'
'What?'
'The Monsieur was very interested in the beggar in the Rue de Rivoli.'

Chapter 21

NO VISIBLE MEANS OF SUPPORT

I'm about to ask Artemis to explain when – above the racket of the traffic and the sandpaper rasp of her hand on the even rougher horns of the goat – I hear the *tap-tap-tap* of expensive new heels on the pavement. I quickly palm the dame some more euros.

'This conversation never happened,' I say.

'Do I look stupid?'

I'm in the scullery when Damnation returns hugging enough parcels to send Santa Claus into early retirement. She looks far too innocent to be anything but guilty.

'How was Les Halles?' I ask.

'I didn't go to Les Halles. It's being rebuilt. I went to Le Printemps instead, the store that's not Galeries Lafayette ...'

I know Galeries Lafayette. I also know the dame's telling the truth. I came back via Les Halles and all I saw for my trouble was a whole lot of hoardings. Damnation glances around the flat before looking back at me and when she does her eyes widen.

'Have you been here all this time?'

'What did you buy?'

She shakes her parcels. 'Would you like a parade?'

I'd like a parade like I'd like a hole in the head that's not my nose, ears or eyes, but I tell her, Yeah, I'll go with the show. After she disappears into her room, I cross to the window overlooking the Rue de Rivoli. The beggar below is hidden by the sort of blanket Napoleon's soldiers might have worn on the retreat from Moscow – full of hard luck stories and holes and covered with stains that might be blood. No shape you could call a shape, its head tucked away like a cockatoo's on a bad night in Innamincka. The torso's parallel to the pavement and it's got no visible means of support.

'Why are you looking out the window when you should be looking at me?'

If I thought the dame was beautiful before, I was wrong. This is beautiful. She's dragged her hair back into a chignon to reveal her full magnificence – the sloe eyes, retroussé nose, soft mouth set in a half-smile, a neck that would be at home on a swan, and a body that might as well be naked. The dress is all but transparent, showing that – just like the beggar on the street outside – Damnation's got no visible means of support.

'Well, what do you think?' she asks.

I don't tell her what I think. Tell her what I think and the temple would collapse. I force myself to remember she's nothing more than a translator on legs and a profile changer. As well as possibly completely untrustworthy. So instead of telling her what I think, I ask, 'What did it cost?'

Her shoulders sag. 'Is that all you can say?' She glares at me but after a while she stops glaring. 'Oh well, I'll take it as an attempt at a compliment and show you more.'

While the dame takes a shower after the show – this time I don't ask where she's taking it – I return to checking out the beggar. There's something about his shape that's not quite right. It could be female but it's so far removed from the one under the shower, it could be an orangutan. I grab my hat.

'I'm going out!' I shout.

The steam coming from beneath the bathroom door has just reminded me of the smoke in the Rite of Spring, if I needed reminding. The Monsieur was very interested in the beggar in the Rue de Rivoli, the landlady said.

There aren't any clues in the flat as to where Salina and Imogene might be.

That just leaves the beggar in the Rue de Rivoli.

Chapter 22

THE BEGGAR IN THE RUE DE RIVOLI

I don't look his way as I climb through the dog-door. Instead I stare at the Parisian skyline like I'm surprised to find it's still there. After which I turn and head east, taking a line parallel with the river. A block later I find a tabac which has got a seat by the window with a view to the beggar.

One of Rube's lessons: The French are a naked tribe, their country exposed on all sides to their enemies. When people are exposed, they don armour. Or they wear attitude like it's chainmail. What's Latin for warm? Calere, I'd reply. Turn it into the negative. Noncalere. Now for the tot of rum, what is it in French? Non chalere? Close but no Bundy. It's nonchaloir. Which means non-heat, indifference, cool. And in English that becomes? Nonchalant. And that's what the clientele is when I enter the tabac: they pretend I don't exist. Which is fine by me because it's my natural state. It also leaves me free to examine the beggar up the road. Passers-by drop coins in the cap and the figure under the blanket doesn't thank the donors, doesn't even move.

Until, thirty-seven minutes into the surveill, a claw darts out to retrieve something dropped by a stroller: male, slight build, mackintosh, hat pulled down over eyes. Who afterwards crouches and disappears through the dog-door into the apartment block. I can't make out what was dropped. Just that the beggar picks it up and immediately resumes its posture while the dog-door flaps shut behind the raincoat …

Like I said, a lot of detecting's waiting. I wait until my legs go numb, my head's whirling, and I'm suffering acute caffeine poisoning. An inebriate bumps against me and doesn't apologise. This is Paris. Rude's *de rigueur.* The bartender wipes something red off a glass. It might be lipstick or it might be blood. The beggar moves.

At first it's no more than a twitch, the kind of movement a snake might make at the entrance to a burrow, barely perceptible to the rabbit unless the rabbit's looking. Which most of the time it's not. Another coffee arrives and the claw appears again. I'm too far away to make out the details, only that the claw comes out and an arm follows.

The arteries of the human body are positioned on the inner thighs in order not to be exposed. But whoever came up with that little idea didn't take into account surveilling. I been sitting too long for my legs to function properly and when I get onto the footpath I stagger. The weather's turned cold or maybe it's my apprehension. I work my way through the bloodlessness in my legs, drag my hat down over my baldness and start in the direction of the beggar.

There's too much traffic — motor and pedestrian — so I stick to the gutter. On my approach, the figure straightens and shucks off the blanket, to reveal:

The secret of how it defied gravity — a steel post sticking out of the footpath; and

That it's a he and he's around my height — just over the six-foot-two mark — but slimmer. He'd only weigh 160 pounds — 75 kilos — but his muscles are like steel cable. Most startlingly, he's dressed neck-to-toe in skin-tight white, his head and hands painted the same colour as the garb.

His head swivels and his snake eyes fix on mine.

Chapter 23

PURSUING PROTEUS

One minute he's there, the next minute he's gone. But he was there for a reason and that reason involved Imogene. It's difficult for a big man to hide. Paint him white and it becomes impossible. But he's *protean* – as in *Proteus*, the mythological being who could assume any shape he wanted. The beggar seems to change shape and as he does so he merges. And he's wearing his hurry-shoes.

I pound along in his wake, traversing the north side of the Rue de Rivoli while heading in the direction of the Champs Elysees, chasing a too-white figure with a too-white head bobbing above the rest of the pedestrians like a big white poppy in a paddock of pansies. It's peak hour so the traffic's at a standstill. There's no chance of another accident: there's not enough circulation. Besides, Proteus is too quick as he weaves towards the Louvre.

I hold onto my hat as I struggle to keep up with my quarry. He's already in the tunnel leading to the Louvre and I'm in there after him. He sends a busker flying as he reaches the queue to the glass pyramid.

I expect him to keep on in the direction of the Tuilleries but instead he slows and swerves into the pyramid. He doesn't show a ticket. It's like he's a ghost that no-one apart from me can see. People don't paint themselves white in order not to be noticed. It's only when they're trying to hide that anyone becomes aware of them. Meanwhile I'm wearing a sober grey suit, even more sober shoes and a grey hat. That makes me Security. Under the Code Napoleon the cops can chuck you in jail, throw away the key and go home to dinner laughing. The French embrace officialdom because they're afraid of it. And as I've just become officialdom, I walk unchallenged into the Louvre.

If Paris is Paranoia Central, the Louvre is its heart and soul. Watchers watch the watchers watching the watchers and the Louvre's no exception. The trick is to become part of the system. I cup a hand to the non-existent wire in my ear and wave away the guard demanding my ticket. He gives a Gallic shrug and ushers me through.

I head in the direction taken by Proteus. He's no longer hurrying. Hurrying attracts attention. I duck under a wing of the Samothrace Nike, lowering my hat under the probing eyes of the cameras. Marble heads of ancient busts stare from the walls and statues stand implacable. Real people get in my way, see I'm trouble and get the hell out of it.

But Proteus has disappeared.

The Louvre's a labyrinth: big when it was built and even bigger now. Artworks, sightseers, statues and guards mingle over several levels, in several wings, in several states of contusion. A uniformed guard approaches but I cup my hand to my ear again and tell him someone's acting suspicious around the *Mona Lisa* and he hurries off to check. The cameras are tracking me so I keep my hat down and my head down under the hat. I hurry through rooms followed by more rooms, corridors followed by more corridors, artworks followed by more artworks, stairs followed by more stairs. But I know what I'm looking for.

I also know where to find it.

I've reached the Balcony of the Gods. What did Rube once say about gods? *Gods were no more than humans writ large, not the other way around as with modern-day religions. Apart from exhibiting human emotions like jealousy, hatred, lust and revenge, they also possessed human shapes.*

Around me stand life-sized statues of Diana, Bacchus, Vulcan, Neptune, Zeus, Proserpine, Cerberus guarding the gates of Hell, Echo and Narcissus, Pegasus, the Minotaur, Ariadne and Theseus, Theseus's maze, Artemis and her goat ...Think! I tell myself. Try and remember. What belongs where? Mount Olympus had a hierarchy and it's mirrored in the Louvre. Gods were a family and, as with most families, its members hated each other's guts.

Diana with her bow. Hercules wrestling the serpent. Neptune rising from the waves. Poor little hobble-foot Vulcan. All roads lead to Rome but only one leads to Imogene. Before me stands yet another group of statues Napoleon stole on one of his campaigns. It occupies the middle ground of the balcony and they're the usual suspects – Zeus, Mars, Vulcan, Venus, Poseidon, Mithras, Diana …

A bunch of life-sized figures carved from marble – kneeling, standing, crouching, or poised to strike. While one of them … I turn away, hoping he hasn't noticed that I've seen him, fixing my gaze on the sculpted group of soldiers in the courtyard below.

He's good, I'll give him that. No, he's better than good. Street performance statues can hold their poses through thick and thicker, unmoved by kids kicking their knees and dogs peeing on their ankles, staying as still as crocodiles in a Northern Territory creek bed until …

By now, Damnation will have finished her shower and be garbing herself in her newly-acquired finery while wondering what's become of her private defective. I don't know who she is or what her game is or how she can help me find Imogene, only that she's …

Right at that very moment, Proteus makes his move.

Chapter 24

DEATH COMES TO THE LOUVRE

I'm trapped, my back to the balcony railing, while below me the jagged points of the spears of the soldier-statues are rearing upwards. I got distracted by thoughts of the dame. Rube warned she'd be trouble. You can't be distracted in this game. Proteus has got the drop on me and he's poised for the kill, snake eyes sharp as the tips of the spears in the courtyard. That's when the Fates step in, taking the form of a tall, stooped figure in a green-brown suit that might have been woven out of moss, and a small woman in tweed. They look like they'd be more comfortable in rocking chairs on a verandah in Matraville than wandering around the Louvre. They also look familiar.

It's like the Louvre goes into freeze frame, like the statues become the sightseers and the tourists become the tableau. Time stands still. So does Proteus, as the geezer in the moss-brown suit steps forward, peering up. The slightest of tremors runs through the statue as Proteus steadies himself.

'Please, Harold!'

The woman grabs the codger's arm below his elbow. 'But it shouldn't be here, Maud. I know this piece of statuary.' The man tries to shake himself free of his wife's grasp. 'Let me go. I need to get a closer look.'

But Maud only tightens her grip, restraining Harold from doing something even more foolish than usual. 'I realise you know all there is to know about such things, Harold, but this is the Louvre and the Louvre knows even more than you do.' She glances nervously about her then even more nervously back at her husband. But Harold moves closer to the figure that shouldn't be there – the beggar that became Proteus, the cuckoo in the nest – dragging his wife behind him.

When I was a child I drew squares in the dirt with sticks, topping them off with triangles and calling them houses. That's what witnesses do – they see the cliché. *The old man lunged forward while the old woman fell in front of him, tripping over one of the statues as she tried to steady herself. The old man was one of those statue-smashers. Why else would he be waving a hammer …?* While another onlooker, equally certain, insists someone else had the hammer and was going to whack the old man with it, except the old lady stepped in to prevent it. While a third witness –

Even I can't be certain of what happened next and I'm a trained watcher. It was all too fast for anyone to be sure of anything and too fast for me to stop it. The statue-that's-not-a-statue makes his move. The problem is the old man's in his way when he makes it, causing the statue to swear in very un-statuesque fashion as he trips over Harold with Maud clinging onto his arm. And in the absence of any means of support – visible or otherwise – the statue goes too far off the perpendicular to have any hope of ever recovering it.

The white-marble arms with the real flesh and blood in them flail as Proteus high-steps his way towards the railing separating the balcony from the courtyard below. The whole thing looks like it's been choreographed. The statue's face is contorted with rage. He raises one leg for a round-sweeping kick at my head. I switch my attempt to save the life of the statue into a sideways-roll to save myself.

My move throws him even further off balance. He looks around wildly for a handhold but there isn't one; he tries to steady himself but momentum's got a grip on him and he freewheels backwards. The back of his knees hit the parapet and he goes over, accompanied by a piercing scream. When I get to the railing, it's to see the points of the spears have got blood on them and the blood's coming out of a no-longer-white figure that was once a statue, and before that a beggar in the Rue de Rivoli, but is now dead.

Fate happens.

The tableau turns back into people and uniforms pop up out of nowhere. I hurl myself down the stairs. The wallet's a barely-perceptible lump against the man's now-dead heart. I'm gripping his neck like I'm checking the pulse as the guard arrives, hard-faced, grey-garbed and suspicious.

'Who are you?' he demands.

I wave the man's wallet like it's ID and it's mine.

'Gendarmerie, Organisation Anti-Terrorist Française and Chief Archivist,' I say. Through the museum's thick walls I hear the sirens. 'See to the body,' I order as the rest of the cohort arrives. 'And after that, see to your security – it's got gaps you could drive a bulldozer through. I will deal with it all in my report.'

The guard nods and begins doing his job, shepherding onlookers away as more people pour into the courtyard. I glance up. The elderly couple are staring down over the railing. I tuck the wallet away, jam down my hat and melt into the artwork.

Chapter 25

IN THE CAROUSEL GARDEN

I hurry along the Corridor of Angels, past Edvard Munch's masterpiece – the one with the man with the open mouth on the bridge screaming – around the Roman ruins, to the exit. I emerge from the pyramid, get around the fountain, past the mini-triumphal arch, and into the spring-green gardens next to the carousel, hard-edged as it turns slowly against the darkening sky. I take out the wallet and examine it.

No name, no brand – but I was expecting that. No money, either. I was expecting that, too. In fact, there's nothing that should be in it. I crouch beside a reclining bronze nude and look for anything that shouldn't.

But apart from a ticket to the Louvre, the wallet's empty. I rip out the lining. More nothing – no secret compartment, no microdots, no clues as to where I might find Imogene. I replace the ticket and chuck the wallet in the bin beside the nude as blue lights flicker on the archway, heralding nightfall.

To the west stand the golden statues of the Place de la Concorde, to the south is the Seine, and to the north the slow-turning carousel. But the east is where the action is. They've put up a police barrier, the queue's dispersing and 'closed' signs hang on the doors of the pyramid. Among the tourists around the fountain, I make out the figures of Harold and Maud, the elderly couple from Antiquities. And because they're sitting instead of standing, I remember where I've seen them before – behind me and Damnation at the check-in counter at Sydney Airport, and after that beside us on the plane.

You'll keep coming across familiar faces. It doesn't mean you're being followed. They're just people on the same journey …

A father's flying a plastic clitter-clatter bird for his kids, the lights on the carousel have become a rainbow against the sky, lovers kiss, traffic hums and a barge's tocsin sounds on the river. I put my head down as I make for the sunset, causing a little green garbage truck driven by a man in green coveralls to swerve to avoid me.

'Idiot!' shouts the driver. He shakes his head as he climbs down from the cab, crosses to a bin and empties it, still shaking his head.

I continue towards the gibbet they call la Tour Eiffel just as the sun's setting, marshalling the only facts that I'm sure of:

Salina took the kid

Rube was mugged and I don't know who did it

A dancer was murdered and ditto

I've got a few scraps of paper with letters on them that might spell GREEN

The man in black was known to the gendarmerie

The beggar in the Rue de Rivoli met with a grisly end. He didn't require a ticket to the Louvre.

Yet there was a ticket in his wallet …

I watch the little green garbage truck trundle away. Tidy lot, these Parisians. In half an hour all the bins in the Tuilleries will be empty. Tomorrow will produce more rubbish but that, too, will be swiftly dealt with. They've even got bikes with trunks on them to suck up poodle poo. They think of everything.

Just like I didn't. Because I didn't ask myself the one question I should have asked: Why would a man who didn't need a ticket to the Louvre have a ticket to the Louvre? The little green truck is beside the bin into which I tossed the wallet, compacting more rubbish. Gendarmes in SWAT gear are handing out cards. I break into a run.

'Hey!'

The cops look up and the cleaner straightens from replacing the insert.

'Wait!' I yell. A cop motions toward his gun. Rube on gendarmes: French cops shoot first and ask questions later. So if you must move in the presence of the gendarmerie, move slowly. Otherwise you might never move again. But I want to – need to – move again. So I slow to a walk and the cop lightens up. I gesture to the man in green standing beside the bin beside the statue.

'What's up?' he asks.

I indicate the truck.

'Any chance I can check your garbage?'

The man in green shakes his head.

'Ever tried opening a bottle without a corkscrew?'

It's like I just buried Imogene. Because whatever was in the wallet wasn't a ticket to the Louvre. It was what the passer-by tossed to the beggar and what the beggar picked up. The concierge told me Lifar was interested in the beggar in the Rue de Rivoli – the beggar who turned into Proteus before turning up dead. And the beggar in the Rue de Rivoli was interested in what the passer-by dropped in his cap before disappearing through the dog-door. It was my only clue. It can't have been anything else.

The cleaner's replacing the bin as I turn away. That's when I stop turning away. Because the cleaner's not replacing an empty bin but removing a full one. I spin, dive, grab the can out of his hands and empty its contents on the grass. I scrabble through the mess as the cleaner backs away. Nothing, nothing and more nothing. No wallet. No clue. No …

The cleaner opens his mouth and I expect a torrent of abuse but instead he says, 'It's not there.' He's got a little goatee, an awkward twist to the mouth behind the beard and a green canvas bag over his shoulder. I climb to my feet. He backs away, clutching the bag.

'What's not where?' I demand.

'In Paris, Monsieur, some people lose things while others find them. It's a perk of my profession – like the diamond ring a plumber comes across in a rich man's drain. One man's poison is another man's poisson. It's only a wallet …'

I stretch out a hand as well as the truth.

'Yeah, but it's my wallet.'

The street lamp's one of those wrought-iron affairs that earn Paris the title of The City of Love. A thin mist forms an oriole around the light, dimming it. But there's still enough illumination to show I'm back in the business of finding Imogene.

Because, just like I suspected, the piece of cardboard in the wallet isn't a ticket to the Louvre at all.

Chapter 26

THE RATS OF AGINCOURT

She's dead. Even in the absence of the one-eyed goat with blood in its beard I'd know, because I've been expecting it. The place is a shambles. A drinks cabinet has been upended, the barley-twist lamp's snapped in two, and while there's no light inside the unit, the curtain's torn from the window, making the street lamp outside just enough to see by. The blood's dried black and I calculate she's been dead an hour. Her torso's twisted under a reproduction Louis XIV settee while her legs form a vee that could mean victory. Except there's nothing to celebrate.

The tread of the goat's hoofs are muffled by the threadbare carpet as I pull the corpse straight.

The money I gave her in return for information is scattered over the carpet, which means robbery wasn't the motive. The killer wanted her dead and he wanted the death obvious. He wanted to stop her talking. He also wanted me – on the off-chance I survived Proteus – to know he'd stopped her, because it would warn me off.

I shove the notes into the pocket of the robe. It will help pay for the funeral. On the fridge is a magnet featuring a picture of the Arc de Triomphe and the words I heart Paris clamping a Post-It note to the fridge saying: FEED THE GOAT. I find a can labelled For the goat and empty its contents into a bowl. It should keep the animal away from the corpse for the night. I shut the door behind me. The lift's too slow so I take the corkscrew. But the door at the top of the stairs is locked. I put my shoulder to the door. The living room's empty.

'Damnation?'

She appears from the direction of my bedroom. 'Where have you been?' she asks. 'I was looking for you.'

'You had any visitors?'

'Not that I know of.'

I glance at her hands. No cuts, bruising, blood or splinters. 'Hear anything?'

'Not apart from the traffic. But where have you been?'

'It's not where I've been, it's where you were.'

'I wasn't anywhere. What happened?'

I've got to believe her. Correction: I've got to pretend I believe her. I tell her what she needs to know, watching her face closely while I say it. But there's no expression on her face, apart from what you'd expect.

'So what do we do now?'

'We sleep – you in your bedroom and me in mine. And after we sleep, we leave the premises and breakfast somewhere on croissants and coffee. Then I do a bit of research while you do some more shopping. After that we meet up again and get out of Paris.'

'I have to sleep in my own room?'

'Yeah, in your own room.'

'But how can I possibly sleep?'

'Just lie down, close your eyes and count corpses. It always works for me.'

As we leave, from behind the closed door of the landlady's room I hear the snuffling of the goat. We find somewhere for breakfast, after which I check out train timetables then look for a gun. But while there are plenty of gunshops in Paris, they all want ID. Showing ID puts Halliwell on a computer, telling the world he's someone with a gun. I don't want to end up on a computer, even as Halliwell. I trawl the dives and speakeasies at the sleazy end of Paris with no result until I bump into a Rasta outside a gunshop.

'What about good manners?' he demands.

This guy's as sensitive as a rat-trap.

'Go entertain the troops in Afghanistan,' I tell him.

'Hey, man, I'm talking about this.' He produces a little black gizmo about the size of a matchbox. 'It opens doors – hence the name: Good Manners. See? You place it against a lock, like this.' He places it against the gunshop's lock. 'Then you pull the trigger, like this.' He pulls the trigger. 'And – open Sesame!'

There's no explosion – just a nice, neat hole where the lock used to be. I buy the gizmo, plus the six-pack of charges that comes with it. After which I find myself a hole-in-the-wall internet joint and, using a dead man's email, check all the angles – slave trade, child porn, drugs and prostitution. But none of them fit. By the time I've finished, it's late afternoon. Damnation's waiting at l'Opera where I told her to wait, in the company of our cases and more shopping. I tell her to stuff the shopping in the cases, then I get us to the above-ground railway, via the apartment on the Rue de Rivoli. Where a policewoman's trying to entice the goat with the bloodstained beard into a paddy wagon, only it doesn't want to leave what's left of its mistress …

In Paris there are small stations and there are big ones and Agincourt's one of the big ones. Named after a battle, it looks like the war's still in progress as we drag our bags along the concourse towards the shops.

'Jesus, Rain – or Arthur or Neville or Bruce, or whatever you call yourself,' the dame says, 'I'm not a bloody – dromedary!'

She's dressed in what she must have decided is domestic travel gear – sharp-toed red shoes, a T-shirt so tight you can see her goosebumps, and jeans that look like they've been spray-painted on. She's right, she's not a dromedary. I shake my head.

'What have dromedaries got to do with the price of mangoes?'

'I mean I haven't eaten since – oh, I don't know when – and I'm ravishing.'

Her English could be better but the sentiment works for me. I make way for the marauders milling around us – a yelling, screaming mob all dressed up as rats: preening false whiskers, whisking fake tails, banging drums and waving helium-filled balloons in our faces.

'Who are these idiots?' I shout.

'It's the usual thing,' she shouts back. 'We French are children of the Revolution and if we're not protesting, we're parading. These ones belong to a rugby club called the Rats of Agincourt. But rats to them – I haven't eaten since breakfast and, as I said, I'm ravishing. I'm getting some food.'

I grab a part of her I'm allowed to grab without getting jailed for it.

'Sorry, Damnation. First we got to get tickets.'

I've checked and rechecked the destination on the beggar's ticket and I've also checked the departures board. The dame stops struggling so I let her go.

'Our train leaves at seven,' I say.

I get Damnation into the bureau and tell her to buy two tickets.

'Where to?'

I tell her the wrong place.

'Why me?'

'Look, we're up against professionals. Two of our followers have ended up dead and the concierge just joined them. On my calculation there'll be more and I don't want us to be among them.' I move her towards the counter. 'I didn't talk French before and I still don't talk it now. So you're getting us two one-way tickets to Perpignan.'

After Damnation's bought our tickets, I lead her back outside. After which we re-enter the office and line up again – only this time separately and apart. And separately and apart we buy two singles to Beguine.

Beguine was the destination written on the ticket in the beggar's wallet, the ticket the man in the Burberry dropped in the cap before slipping through the dog-door and killing the concierge.

And because I figure Beguine's where we'll find Imogene, that's where we're going.

Chapter 27

ESCAPE FROM AGINCOURT

There are half-a-dozen patisseries in the Gare d'Agincourt, but there are still too many rats. When Damnation sees there's a chance she won't be getting any food, she stamps a little foot with an expensive little shoe on it, like she's sick of Paris in general and me in particular.

'How long before our real train leaves?'

'Ten minutes.'

She gets her food.

I take the dame and our bags to the wrong platform and together we board the train to Perpignan. After which, using the door-forcer I bought from the Rasta, I force open the door opposite to the one we came in by, the one without a platform, drop the bags on the rails, get down after them, and get the dame down after me.

'What are we doing?'

'We boarded the wrong train and now we're boarding the right one. That means we got to cross the tracks and get ourselves onto the next platform and after that we get down on the rails again then up again and then we board the right train.'

The back door of the right train's locked, but the gizmo does its work again, after which I hoist Damnation up, followed by the bags. I do what I can with the door but it won't lock and the slightest of nudges is going to bust it open. When I straighten, I find Damnation watching me.

'This isn't what I signed up for.'

'You didn't sign up for anything, remember? You wanted to come to France and you wouldn't take no for an answer.'

'That was before and this is now and now I —'

That's as far as she gets before I realise we're being followed by a man in a coat who looks like a ferret, and he's making his way along the platform beside the train, sniffing because he's lost our scent. He could be dismissed as irrelevant. Except for the bulge under the coat, and the sniff.

The starter's whistle sounds. There's the sound of running feet as the train begins to move, the couplings taking up the slack. I get us into the next carriage as behind us I hear the rear door open and half-close. 'Go to the front carriage before the train picks up too much speed.'

After she's gone, I wait for the Ferret. But there's no sign of him — nothing but the hum of wheels gathering speed under us and the rocking of the carriage. He's staying in the back carriage so after ten minutes, I head off after the dame. I don't want a confrontation unless he forces one on me. As I make my way forward, I pass a boy with a balloon he must have nicked from the footy fans, and later on I see the old couple from the Louvre. They're just on the same journey … I find Damnation occupying a window seat in the car behind the engine and there's nothing else besides her in the compartment apart from the view, the patisserie and the luggage. I lift the bags onto the luggage rack.

'What was that all about?' Damnation says.

I've seated myself opposite her — I'm facing the way we're going — but only after removing my coat and parking it on the seat. It's smart to have everything secure. These trains go fast. This one starts going fast.

'Someone's out to get me, Damnation, and you invited yourself along for the ride. I don't care how beautiful you are or how upset you get or even how hungry you might become in the process, we're going to find my kid and I'll take care of any problems along the way.' I flick finger against thumb on the hand that's still got the thumb. 'Give me your phone.'

'Why?'

'Because I don't know you from a baguette. We're in the same boat and you could prove to be a leak.' I re-click finger and thumb. 'So — the phone.'

When she shakes her beautiful face, the expression on it is as inscrutable as the Mona Lisa's.

'I'm sorry,' she says, 'but I went to the toilet and the phone fell down the loo.'

Chapter 28

FOR EVERY ACTION ...

I asked for her phone because I want another look at the call log. She might still have the phone, then again she mightn't. Either way, nothing's to be gained from making a song and dance about it, so I keep my trap shut and resist the toe-tap. Instead I stare out the window at scenery that's rapidly changing from the concrete to the ephemeral – from city to towns to villages, from tall buildings to farms – at the same time as I'm keeping an eye on the dame.

I study the timetable they provided with the ticket. It gives the times between stations as well as a handy little diagram showing where the line swerves. Make sure you're seated on the bends, the timetable warns, as well as when the train accelerates immediately afterwards. I help myself to a crust. When Damnation finishes eating, she wipes her lips with a tissue from her reticule, brushes the crumbs from her lap, and her violet eyes make contact with my ordinary ones.

'I'm sorry about the phone,' she says. 'Losing it might seem an act of sabotage but I assure you it was an accident.' She takes a deep breath. 'Also I don't know if I ever said, but I'm sorry about your daughter.'

After she's got that off her chest, she leans forward and her hands alight on my knees. I don't move. The dame doesn't move her hands, either.

'And now you've got me where you want me,' she says, 'why don't you put me to use?'

'How do you know you're where I want you?'

'Two heads are better than one,' she says.

She takes another deep breath as her body sways with the train.

'I know I'm only here as a profile-changer and perhaps also because I speak French.' Her beautiful eyes fix on mine. 'But I could do a lot better than that.'

She takes her hands off my knees.

'I know you haven't said as much but I think that you like me, at least a little bit. You're awkward because I'm a woman. You're afraid of involvements. And maybe you're simply keeping me where you can see me. Yet when you searched my house you came up with zilch and ditto when you went through my bags. You're conflicted. You like me but you also suspect me. You want me to be trustworthy but you think I'm not.' She calms down as fast as she fired up. 'Please believe me, Rainbow, when I say it was a coincidence your Mr Green employed me as a tutor. It was also an accident my phone fell down the toilet. But it's no accident I'm here. You wanted me here, remember? But you won't tell me what's going on. For instance, what happened to the man on the plane who later turned up on the Rue de Rivoli? Where did you go while I was taking a shower? Why did we suddenly leave the flat? And what are we doing on this train? Whatever you believe to the contrary, I know I can help you find your daughter.'

It's a long speech and I can't handle long speeches, they've got too many words in them. When she raises her head, her eyes are brimming. Which means the speech didn't only contain a lot of words, there was also emotion. Even more than words, I can't handle emotion.

'What harm can it do?' she says.

I can fight the logic but I'm no match for the eyes. So I tell her about the death of the man in black and also about the gendarmes handing out the cards. I fill her in on the less gory details concerning the concierge, the beggar and the ticket in the wallet. What I don't tell her about is the paper that the rats chewed. Nor that I still don't trust her.

'So that's why we're going to Beguine,' she says. 'But what do you expect to find there?'

According to the guidebook, Beguine's an ancient town on the River Lot, four hours south of Paris. There are a lot of hospitals, a trick clock in the main square and, on a hill overlooking the town, a grand *château* – a big castle – whose owners don't like to be bothered by tourists. I take the question as rhetorical and don't answer it, so Damnation answers it for me.

'You're in two minds about your daughter's disappearance. Is your ex-wife just getting back at you or is this Mr Green up to something? They're not the same thing or even two sides of the same coin. But you know women.'

I don't know women but I nod anyway.

'You'd know, then, that if your ex-wife's intention was to take the child, she'd never signal she was going to do it. Warnings are a male failing, women just do things. So – thinking as a woman – you're right in believing your daughter's removal wasn't an act of revenge.' She pauses. 'Of course, there's always the romance aspect of it. But if it's romance, why take the child? That leaves a third possibility.'

'What possibility's that?'

Damnation shakes her head or maybe the train shakes it for her.

'You know the answer because it's your answer – that Mr Green took them for his own nefarious purposes.'

She looks uncertain – or maybe it's troubled – as if she's had second or even third thoughts about the wisdom of saying too much. There's something going on and I don't know what it is. It's always like that where dames are concerned but this is even more so. 'Your ex-wife – what's her name? Praline.' She says it pray lean; I correct her: Salina. 'All right, Salina. Well, she's a mother, not a monster. Which leaves a fourth possibility: that Mr Green's escaping something – maybe an ex-wife – and, like you, he simply needs a profile-changer.'

'I'm sorry, Damnation. Green cleaned both the house in Sydney and the flat in Paris too well to be anything but a pro. Also we've been followed too well for this to be anything other than a pro operation. My aunt was mugged, a dancer was killed and three more corpses have followed hard on the heels of the first.'

'It still could be just a coincidence …' she murmurs.

I trot out my hard line. 'I don't believe in coincidences.'

You rely a lot on reflection in this game, which is why I'm facing the way the train's going. Everything in the corridor is reflected in the wall behind the dame. That's how I see the figure and that's why I hurl myself into the corridor. Only to find – nothing. Nothing apart from the lurching corridor of a high-speed train plus the certain knowledge that a moment ago someone was standing there. I wasn't going after him unless he came after me. But now …

'What is it?' the dame asks.

It's an eight-car train and it's no more than five minutes to the next station so I don't reply. Instead I head back through the train. By the time

I reach the second car, there's only three minutes, thirty-seven seconds left to check the final six carriages. Some cars are compartmentalised. The others are in a two-by-two seat-conformation on either side of a narrow aisle. It's not easy staying balanced. An unexpected corner could land me flat on my face. Ditto unexpected braking and acceleration. In the second car a student's reading about the 1986 destruction of the nuclear reactor at Chernobyl while a nerd's peering through thick-lensed glasses at the kid with the balloon.

The train accelerates suddenly. I've anticipated it and brace. Predictably the kid topples onto his mother while the balloon escapes from his grasp. But unpredictably the balloon doesn't float to the ceiling. Instead it slams against the back of the carriage.

'Incredible!' the nerd says. 'A perfect example of Roemer's Law of Relativity. When the train accelerates, the balloon doesn't hit the train. Instead the train speeds forward and hits the balloon!'

But the mother's got her own law.

She whacks the kid.

Chapter 29

... THERE'S AN EQUAL AND OPPOSITE REACTION

The third and fourth cars are full of innocence. Passengers sleeping, passengers talking, passengers reading. There could be nothing or there could be anything. And I'm prepared for anything as I work my way through the carriages, carding my way into locked toilets when I have to and remembering to grab the overhead rail well before the train takes a turn for the worse at 200 miles an hour.

The old folks from the Louvre are asleep in the fifth car. The dining car's closed. In the sixth is a man in a wheelchair. One carriage and one minute, fifty-three seconds to go.

I enter the last car.

Gripping the overhead rack I glance around. Three passengers occupy the carriage.

First passenger: seated halfway along the carriage to my left, empty bottle between legs. Correction: not sitting – sprawling. Red-faced, faded-pink scarf around neck, no marked characteristics and seemingly dead to all around him. Not the Ferret.

Second passenger: further along the carriage, occupying a seat on the opposite side to the red-faced man. Younger, paler, sneering. Smaller than the first man and therefore in the ballpark. I consider taking him but before I do that, I check the last passenger. Always check the last passenger.

He's the last man standing, a small, thin figure in a gabardine overcoat at the other end of the aisle, his back to the door that we all entered the train by – the one that won't lock properly because I blew a hole in the lock. As the train slows for a corner, he grabs the back of a seat with one hand, while the other hand reaches for the bulge in the Burberry. My man.

Ninety seconds before the train docks. One and a half minutes before the Ferret can discreetly slip off the train after murdering me and just as discreetly slip back on again. One minute, twenty seconds.

The aisle restricts movement. There's no room for fancy footwork. And I'm not armed while the Ferret is. I couldn't carry a gun on the plane because it's not allowed and I couldn't buy one in Paris because it would put me on a computer. And being on a computer is like being at one end of a carriage on a high-speed train with a killer at the other end going for his gun. There's not much future in it.

In this game you expect the unexpected. And the unexpected is the young man with the sneer leaping to his feet as the train emerges from the corner. I mistook the look. It wasn't a sneer but a look of apprehension. He's holding one hand to his mouth while the other hand's scrabbling for a hold. Only there isn't one. He's on the loose, the thrust of the train's post-corner acceleration sending him skidding down the aisle towards the Ferret, and for a nanosecond the Ferret's distracted. The aisle skims under the sick man. I do a demi-plie and take to the air. The acceleration does the rest. It's the law of relativity in motion. For once, I go with the law.

The revolver the Ferret's gripping is a Manurhin MR73 – a French-made .357 Magnum – short and sweet and much favoured by the gendarmerie as well as by marksmen the world over. But the best's not good enough in a high-speed train bearing you swiftly towards an airborne attacker. The Ferret's slugs go wide, ricocheting off the chromework and into seats. I count three. That leaves three, four if there was already one in the chamber. The Ferret doesn't get a chance to unleash the rest. He utters a sound like a knifed tyre as the train thrusts his face into my fist and his back against the door that we came in by, the one that no longer locks ...

I grip the toilet handle as the back door flies open on a vista of high-speed train line fringed by hay bales. The rails reach up as hungry as Death. With my free hand, I make a grab for the Ferret as he scrabbles to stay alive. The gun clatters to the floor and the Ferret's mouth is a gaping hole. But like the man in the painting in the Louvre, no sound emerges

as the Ferret flies out and bounces once, twice, three times, and the hay
bales around him scatter like straws in the wind.

I turn to find the young man being sick and the red-faced man
waking, his empty bottle rolling forward as the train slows for the next-
to-last station. The toilet door opens and a surprised face peers out. I nod,
retrieve the gat and pocket it, then make my way back through the train.
The old couple in the fifth car are still asleep. And in the third, the kid's
contemplating a scrap of blue plastic, all that's left of his balloon.

Chapter 30

BEGIN THE BEGUINE

When I get back to Damnation she still looks beautiful. She also looks guilty. I shift my coat off the seat, at the same time as I reach for the guide to Beguine.

'I don't suppose you're going to tell me where you were,' she says.

She's too calm, an expletive in the making. Never excite the expletives.

'Just seeing a man about a dog.'

Guilt and calmness are dangerous bedfellows.

'I've always thought that to be such a stupid expression,' she mutters, pulling her legs up on the seat under her. 'It's so illogically English – or in your case, Australian. Oh, I know it means you've been to the lavatory. But why a dog, for heaven's sake? Why not a horse or a cow or a – a ferret?'

The violet eyes are guileless. Gripping onto the book, I look out the window as the crops, cows and pasture grass hurtle back in the direction of Paris.

'Anyhow,' she goes on, 'you were gone too long for a toilet run, and one of your hands is swollen. So you didn't go to the loo. You wanted to escape. You find me an encumbrance and a nag.' She glances at the suitcases then back again. 'I'm just another piece of baggage and you wish I weren't here.'

'If wishes were dishes I'd be working in a scullery.'

The nonsense gets Damnation smiling but she refuses to go along with the smile.

'Another one of your stupidities.' She leans forward. 'But tell me – before you went off to do whatever you did, you were saying that you believed your daughter was abducted ...'

Some questions aren't what they seem and this is one of them. The conversation isn't about the kid, it's about me. 'I'm playing it by ear.'

'Another one of your stupid expressions.'

Daylight's fading. So, too, is hope. Why was Imogene taken? I could be on a wild-goose chase. The kid mightn't be in France at all. And even if she is, we're headed south when she could be east, north, west, or north-by-northwest. But – the man in black was after me when he got hit by the bus, the dead beggar had a ticket to Beguine, the Ferret killed the concierge after she blabbed, and I know –

But what do I know? Little more than the fact I've got to park the paranoia. They were only cops handing out tickets. And the Ferret mightn't have been tailing me – just another tourist on the same journey. No, no and no again. I'm headed for the right place all right. It's just a matter of what I'll find when I get there. I tear my attention away from the castle, the one whose owners don't care to be bothered by tourists, and open the guidebook.

When they begin the Beguine
It brings back the sound of music so tender,
It brings back a night of tropical splendour
It brings back a memory ever green …
It's not what's written in the guidebook.
But it's what I read.

When we arrive at Beguine the rain's set in with a vengeance and I can see a troop of what look like soldiers working its way through a vineyard towards the château. They must be hunters because this is France and people hunt here. I drag my eyes away, shove the guidebook back in my pocket, retrieve the cases and climb onto the platform after the dame. She's nervous and the nervousness features in her word placement.

'Do you get the follow we're being feelinged?'

'You mean the feeling we're being followed.'

She glances behind, shivering.

'So you're experiencing it, too – that follow?'

Among our fellow passengers, the two old folks are struggling with their bags while further off a figure darts behind a bus with TOULOUSE written in its destination window. He could be anyone or nobody. I've turned one shadow into a corpse. All that's left now is a bunch of tourists, among them the old couple, Harold and Maud. A helicopter swings across the evening sky, heading north. The rain's hammering down and as we head uphill towards town, Damnation's dainty new parasol affords as much protection as a periwinkle in a deluge.

'Where are we staying?' she asks.

'Not at a hotel for a start.'

'Why not at a hotel for a start?'

'Because hotels put your passport details into a computer. And when they do that, people know where we are – that is, if they don't know already.'

Damnation tries to avoid a rush of water from a drainpipe but isn't quick enough. 'So-where-are-we-staying-if-not-in-a-hotel?'

The guidebook says Beguine's on a pilgrim track and that there's plenty of suitable accommodation. Tell that to the cherries. Because apart from the hotels there seems to be nothing. Until a voice behind us says, 'We know somewhere.'

I push Damnation out of the way, drop the cases, go down on one knee and go for the gat. But it's only the old couple – Maud clutching a big red, white and blue umbrella, while Harold's in charge of the bags. I leave the gun in its garage and help Damnation to her feet.

'Where?'

'Jaqui's place.'

It looks like the journey we're on is about to get even more similar.

Chapter 31

LETTERS ON A TABLECLOTH

The bike's an old Birmingham Small Arms Sloper – commonly known as a BSA – the kind that despatch riders rode between trenches when wars were wars, with the familiar girder fork straddling the front wheel, a wide saddle seat, arm-stretch handlebars and a sidecar. It's standing outside a tall, skinny joint that, if it were any taller and skinnier, would qualify as a chimney.

A sign says BUTTERFLIES ARE BEAUTIFUL and a ring on the bell brings us Jaqui, a dame with a voice that's swing-song. And while Damnation brushes herself down and the codgers stand around looking gormless, I check out our surroundings. The ground floor's one room. It contains a table, the beginnings of a narrow staircase, and too many walking shoes smelling of gruyere. Apart from the dame and the shoes, there's a gnome on the grave-side of ninety wearing a forage suit and a limp. For some reason he zeroes in as soon as he sees me, rapping my chest like he's tapping ashes.

'Listen up stranger and listen up good. Jaqui's my granddaughter and anyone wanting to mess with her climbs over my dead body to do it. Plus the bodies of my friends and the bodies of their friends. Read me, stranger?'

He smells of past apprehensions and incipient madness. I tell him I read him like a Tin Tin comic.

Jaqui interposes. 'Why don't I show you to your rooms? Don't mind Grandpa,' she adds as she precedes us up the stairs. 'He's got certain – passions. He hates aristocrats, for instance – or anyone who thinks they own people. In the Second World War he was in charge of the local Resistance. His wife – my grandmother – was killed by the Germans in retaliation for his activities, leaving a tiny baby – our mother. My sister and I are rather precious to him – hence his behaviour.'

She changes the subject abruptly.

'As to the accommodation,' she lowers her swing-song voice, 'we normally only put up people like the old couple, so there are no double beds.'

I tell her that suits me fine. Jaqui leaves the codgers on the third floor and takes us past a share bathroom to the fifth. Our room's the size of a dishrag and Jaqui knocks against me during a tight manoeuvre. I wince and she looks down, her eyes widening.

'Oh dear, look at your poor hand. How did that happen?'

I tell her I cut myself shaving.

'But it should be seen to. My sister's a nurse ...' Her eyes turn shifty and she stares at me confused while her hands flutter to her face like a pair of waterlogged butterflies.

'I'm sorry, sometimes I get nervous and talk too much. Here I am blabbing all the town's secrets when you could be anybody.'

She's scared of something. It might be the old man. Then again, it mightn't be. I treat her apology like the soup the town's famous for and park it on the backburner.

After the dame leaves, Damnation gets a look on her face that says the room's small. 'The room's small,' she says, as if the look mightn't be enough; she makes one of those gestures people make when a room's small. 'For instance, where am I supposed to change?'

'Try the share bathroom. From what I saw, right now it's not being shared.'

She opens her case, grabs some clothes and flounces out the door, and when she gets back we go out for something to eat.

Anywhere else but in France, the eatery the swing-song dame directs us to would qualify as a hole in the wall. It contains a small table, a red gingham cloth on the table, and a candle on the cloth. I decide on the wine and the dame opts for a confession.

'While you were seeing a – man about a dog, or whatever it was – I happened to look in the lining of your hat. Where I discovered – this.'

She's changed into a little blue number with a neckline so low it stretches the definition, not to mention the neckline. She produces from the neckline the rat-chewed scraps of glossy paper bearing the letters that might spell G–R–E–E–N.

'Why were you looking in my hat?'

'What's sauce for the gander –' She pauses midstream and decides to paddle back. 'Please don't be angry. After all, you did search my house in Sydney and after that, my case. And when I went shopping in Paris, you followed me.' As if to distract attention from what she just said, she leans forwards and taps the paper. 'I saw you examining this on the plane. What's so important about it?'

The wine comes and we order our meal – oysters in the natural for Damnation and leek soup for me. She forks up an oyster. There were local numbers on her call log when I checked it in Paris. But she's French so it could be family. Apart from which she's beautiful. So over the soup I tell her about the rat paper and when I finish she's nodding over her wine.

'When I found the paper I knew it was significant or you wouldn't have hidden it. So I spread it out and thought I – saw something.'

'What was that something?'

The restaurant's dark but I can still see her expression and it's troubled. She shuffles the pieces of paper around before glancing at me out of her beautiful eyes. 'What's the difference between boys and girls?'

I know what it is but figure Damnation might have her own angle. I'm right. She does.

'The difference is that, while boys are outside smacking the heads off daisies, girls are inside playing with bits of paper.' When she sits back the candlelight resumes its dance on the parts of her that aren't in the dress. 'When I was a little girl I used to do origami. I know my way around paper.'

She's ordered frogs' legs and paté – the mashed-up liver of force-fattened geese – while I've got the salad. She deals herself a forkful of paté. I pour her more wine.

'So what does the paper tell you?'

'It doesn't tell me anything – yet. I'm simply saying that it might. For instance, I know where the letters were and how many spaces there were between them. And knowing that gives me a clue to the words.' She absorbs more wine and her violet eyes become even more violet as she shuffles the paper.

'Even with the pieces separated,' she continues, 'I can see that three of the letters were consecutive ones in the same word. Which gives us G-R-E.'

I munch on a lettuce leaf.

'That leaves two letters unaccounted for.'

'Yes, the E and the N.' Damnation sits back. She's finished her oysters, frogs' legs and paté and demolished a fair swag of the wine, and now she's going to tell me about the E and the N. 'On my estimate there were six – perhaps seven – letters between the G-R-E and the last E.'

'Are you sure?'

She nods.

'Pretty sure.'

'What else are you pretty sure of?'

'That there wasn't much space between the last E and the N – if there was any at all.'

'So in the words of a crossword enthusiast, we got G, R, E, something, something, something, something, something, something, followed by something else. Then there's an E, maybe something, and finally an N.' I look up. 'Anything else?'

'I'm sorry but if there is something, I can't see it.'

I rake up the scraps and put them back in the hat before Damnation can swipe them again. She's a help but she's also no help at all. I can trust her and I can't trust her in the slightest. Over coffee, I don't know what else to say so I deal her an aphorism.

'In this world, all that people like me have are the scraps left by the rats.'

Chapter 32

WHAT THE NEWSPAPER SAID

The moon cuts a swathe across the room and the gap between our beds is an unbridgeable chasm. I've never slept with this dame before and I'm not sleeping with her now. Sleep's out of the question. She's muttering too much, her voice competing with the moon and the moon coming light years second.

It's like she's doing battle with the Devil and the Devil's got all the ammunition. I feel sorry for her but pity's not going to rescue Imogene. Then I get a brainwave, courtesy of what she's muttering: What if the words aren't English – but Latin, Double Dutch or Swahili? I try half-a-dozen languages and I'm still trying when the village bells toll the angelus and the dame stretches, revealing the fact that she sleeps in much the same state as her oysters.

'I had such a wonderful rest,' she says, smiling across the chasm separating our beds.

I'm pleased that somebody did.

A brace of triple-smack coffees puts me right, or as right as I'm ever going to be after a night like that. I've reshaved my head and I'm wearing what an accountant might wear, while Damnation's got on a Galeries Lafayette T-shirt with the words *Le Sacre du Printemps* – Rite of Spring – scrawled on the front and jeans that are even tighter than the T-shirt. We're seated in the usual cane chairs at the usual cane table on the usual potholed French footpath when she squeals, causing me to look at her even more closely than I was already.

She's clutching a copy of the local rag – *Lot-Matin* – and from where I'm sitting there's a photo of someone presenting the local Mayor with a cheque. Next to it is another story entitled: WHERE ARE THEY NOW? And that's the story I study while Damnation holds up the paper. 'A man fell off a train yesterday,' she reads. 'A farmer fossicking on the tracks found him. If he hadn't stumbled across him, the man would still be lying there, unattended.'

I shake off a bad feeling. What do they mean – unattended?

'Where's the body now?'

The dame rustles the paper for a better look. The story's just letters but they're letters that are joined together. 'What body? There is no body – at least not in the sense you'd use the word. The man's still alive.'

'How can a man survive a fall out of the back of a high-speed train?'

When Damnation looks up from the newspaper, she's frowning. Maybe it's the sun.

'It says he owes his life to the presence of some hay bales beside the track …'

I remember the hay bales.

'Where is he now?'

'In hospital, why?' The dame takes a beautiful hand away from the blatt and brings it up to her mouth. 'Oh, my God! He fell off our train, didn't he?' She stares at me. 'And you did it! You pushed him!'

She drags her eyes away from mine and back to the blatt.

'They even say as much: Police are looking for a man who eyewitnesses say was on the train at the time. There's even a description of the gun – a Manchurian something-or-other. If seen do not approach. Instead contact the following number.'

'What's the following number?'

Damnation tells me but I already know what it is. It's the one on the cards the cop was handing out in the Rue de Rivoli. The section that handles business that's too hot for the rest of the gendarmerie to handle. Like armed assassins getting chucked out of high-speed trains.

'There's even an e-fit or com-fit or something of the suspect. And if it's not you, it's your daily double.'

The sick passenger mustn't have been so sick and/or the red-faced man so wasted that they … Then there was the face coming out of the toilet. Together they must have come up with a description.

'Do they mention you?' I ask.

'What do you mean?'

I take it slower.

'Do they say this suspect of theirs might have been in the company of a woman?'

Damnation shakes her head like she can't shake anything else, so I shake it for her.

'That means we're stuck with each other, Damnation.' I don't wait for her to object. 'They're looking for a big, bald joker and you're a profile-changer. Of course, you could get away from me and blab but then they'd just make you an accessory before, after or during the fact. So sticking with me is your only option.' I leave the words hanging. 'Where did they take him?'

'To the hospital.'

'Do they say which hospital?'

Damnation shakes her head.

I settle my hat on my bald pate, climb to my feet, drop a handful of euros on the table and, just as I turn to leave, glimpse a shadow near the monkeys in the joke clock in the square.

'Where are we going?' the dame asks.

'To see a woman about a hospital.'

Jaqui knows enough and she's prepared to share it. She's naturally chatty. It's like it's only the presence of the old man that turns her into a clam.

'There are a number of hospitals in the area, all catering for different needs. Patients come here from all over. You might have noticed the helicopters – they fly patients to and from Paris. Among the facilities are the Beguine General, the Silicone Private and the Mon Dieu Hospice for the Dying. Not to mention the Infirmarie Speciale.' She pauses as if considering what she's saying before rushing on. 'There's even a suggestion that the château ...'

'What château?'

The swing-song voice turns cautious.

'The – château that you – might have seen from the train. Grandpa says ...'

'What does Grandpa say?'

Like a small yacht in an unpredictable wind she changes tack again.

'He says that – loose lips lose wars ...'

'What wars would they be?'

'Grandpa's own personal war, I suppose.'

She's trying to tell me something other than what it looks like she's saying.

'Where do they take people who fall out of trains?'

'My guess would be the General.'

Me and Damnation take a lunch of baguette, cheese and the local black wine high into the limestone hills by the river. Across the river, past the town, the château stands proud upon its hill. The General Hospital's in the valley, a road leading down to it from the château. I examine the road and the castle, followed by the hospital. The spring sunshine's warm. The dame takes a nap and after I finish my examination of the landscape I join her in La-La Land. It's late afternoon before we get going again. We take a circuitous route, one that takes us past the castle, and when we finally reach the hospital, Damnation's carrying her new shoes and there's only an hour to nightfall. I nod towards a bunch of rosebushes.

'If we get separated, we meet back here.'

There's three ways of playing this. I could send the dame on a reconnaissance, we could make like we're part of the scenery, or I could take my chances. I still don't trust her and I'm too big to merge, so I chance it, nodding to doctors, patients and nurses as I push open the doors, motioning Damnation to follow.

'If anyone asks, we're just visiting,' I say as we enter.

'Why? What are you going to do?'

I don't tell her what I'm going to do because I still don't trust her. Part of me says I'm going to find out what the Ferret knows, while the other part – the part with brains in it – tells me there'll be too many police around to get the chance.

It doesn't mean I'm not going to try.

Chapter 33

RUNNING INTERFERENCE

Hospitals are hospitals and the General's no exception. We pass a lot of doctors, a couple of guards and too many signs. There's something wrong.

'Where's the Emergency department, Damnation?'

'Along there somewhere – I think …'

She's both right and wrong at the same time. 'You might think you're right,' I tell her. 'But my feeling is it's not that way at all, it's along here.'

We go through a doorway and are immediately accosted by a guard.

'What do you think you're doing?'

I'm pressing a nerve at the side of his neck, that's what I'm doing. And after I've done that I pull one of his eyelids back to check how long he'll be asleep and calculate we've got ten minutes, give or take an eyelid flutter. I shove him in a laundry cupboard.

'Merde!' the dame says.

It comes out sounding like 'murder'.

We're in a corridor that's wide enough to drive a bed through, with too many doors leading off it and too many cops at the other end. I pull Damnation into a room containing fresh linen and bedpans, to the accompaniment of a sound like thunder. 'What's that?' Damnation asks.

'A helicopter. We're in a hospital where they bring patients from Paris, and after they've fixed them fly them back again.' I grab her arm. 'Now listen, you're going to run interference.'

'Murder,' she says again.

I grab her arm. 'Know what that is?'

'Yes, it's when people interfere with other people, the way you're interfering with me now.'

I let her go.

'It's an American football term referring to a ploy whereby a player distracts another player or players, enabling a fellow team member to score. Interference is when you get in people's way.' I indicate the cops at the other end of the hallway.

'You're going to get in their way; you're going to faint in front of the fuzz.'

'I could faint right now.'

'Hold onto that thought.'

I grab a handful of pamphlets out of a dispenser on the wall for cover, and step out of the room as Damnation heads down the hall. I watch her crumple.

The cops yell simultaneously and simultaneously they go to her rescue. But there's too much French gallantry and they fumble the catch and the dame goes down, creating enough confusion for me to get along the corridor, cramming the pamphlets into the pocket with the gun in it as I go, following the signs to Casualty. In the first room I draw a blank. The second contains a kid. Room number three produces a dame that looks like she's got the plague. Four's empty. Five's my man.

There are two beds. I get myself to the one containing the Ferret. He's got cuts and contusions from head to toe, his head's bandaged, and he's got as many tubes coming out of him as Aunt Rube. His eyes stare from gaps in the bandages. Killers don't like being on the receiving end. He knows who I am and the fear in his eyes is palpable. I lean over him to maintain the fear.

'Can you talk?'

'No,' he says.

'Then you're going to die.' The tubes wriggle as he shakes his head, while from outside comes the sound of the gendarmes trying to breathe life back into the dame. I grab one of the tubes.

'No!' the Ferret says again, only this time with more feeling.

'Then tell me where I'll find my daughter.'

Confusion replaces the fear.

'What daughter? What the hell are you on about? I don't know any daughters!'

His voice possesses a nasal quality, partly on account of the tubes, but mostly because of the fear.

'Why did you kill the concierge?' I demand. 'And why were you following me, armed with a gun?'

He ignores the first question – which means he's not denying it – but answers the second.

'Because they paid me to follow you.'

'That's not good enough.'

The bruise over his eye has turned a nice shade of yellow and someone's daubed the wound down his cheek with gerundial violet. I rip out a tube.

'But that's all they told me!'

I reach for another tube.

'Who's they?'

What I can see of his forehead creases until it looks like a condensed version of the tracks he landed on and his carved-up mouth trembles.

'I don't know, honest I don't! The organisation's big and they keep us in what they call information cells. I know only what they think I need to know.'

I'm having trouble making sense of what he's telling me past his fear, the noise of the machine and the efforts of the gendarmes in the hallway.

'And what did you need to know?'

'I was to report on your movements. After you left Paris but before you got to Beguine.'

'Why did you do it?'

'For very big dough.'

Hoofs hammer our way. The cops can smell a rat. I lean over the Ferret.

'Sorry I nearly killed you.'

He looks relieved.

'That's all right.'

'You misunderstand me. What I'm saying is I'm sorry I didn't succeed.' The lines on the screen on the machine beside him say I came close. 'My being sorry can be taken two ways.'

He nods but it's the end of the interview. I dive into the other bed and I've just pulled up the covers as the gendarmes enter.

'He's still here,' one says, looking at the Ferret.

'And still alive.'

'We'd better get back to madame.'

They get back to madame. Only she's not there when they get back to her. Instead, she's where I told her to be, huddled among the rosebushes.

'Nice faint,' I tell her.

She manages a ragged smile.

'That's because it was real. What have you got in your pocket?'

I pull out the pamphlets.

'I picked them up as cover while you were fainting.' She takes the pamphlets while I squint at the building. 'How many floors are there?'

'I don't know. Why?'

'Because something's not right.'

Chapter 34

THE SCARLET LETTER

We're in a ditch beside the vineyard on the same hill as the château. There's just enough light to see by. In the distance I hear sirens. I consider our position. We can't show our faces in daylight because someone might recognise us. By now, the Ferret will have told the cops I tried to murder him a second time. My description's in the papers and before nightfall will also be on every gendarmerie computer in France – in company with a description of the dame. Headed: *The Bald and the Beautiful.*

'Listen to this!' Damnation's staring at one of the pamphlets. 'Human organ transplant has come a long way since Christiaan Barnard performed the first successful heart transplant in South Africa fifty years ago. Surgeons are now at the cutting edge of achieving it, it's just a matter of ethics and finding suitable donors.'

I've got a stone in my shoe. I bend to get it out.

'Listen!' Damnation's out of the foxhole, thrusting the pamphlet in my face and shouting. 'It says here: *Greffe du rein.* Now tell me the meaning of *greffe du rein.*'

I'm no longer pretending I don't know French. 'It means kidney transplant.' I say it slow. 'That's what my aunt needs. So what? I can't see what that's got to do with –'

But the dame's on a rock 'n' roll. 'Look at the heading again,' she urges. 'The first three letters in particular. Then skip five – no, seven – spaces. Now – ignoring the letter i which, typographically, is so narrow that it hardly counts – and what's left?'

The foxhole's suddenly claustrophobic. I'm finding it hard to breathe.

'G-R-E-E-N.' Even then I don't budge – I made much the same

out of what the air-waitress said: GREeat trip ENjoy. 'It could be a coincidence ...'

Damnation shakes her head.

'I thought you didn't do coincidences.' She grabs more pamphlets out of my fist. 'Look at this! *Greffe du poumon* — that's lung transplant; *greffe du foie* — that's liver, what I had for dinner last night; *greffe* whatever you want; *greffe du tissu* — that's human tissue; *greffe du coeur* — that's —'

But she doesn't need to say any more. WHERE ARE THEY? ran the newspaper heading. And while we sat in the sun and Damnation read about the Ferret falling out of the train I was reading what could be Imogene's last testament and obituary: To date, 73 residents of Beguine and surrounds are unaccounted for. Too many are missing. It's as if a flying saucer comes out of the sky and carries them off to Mars ... The sirens grow louder. Soon there'll body-heat detectors, tracker dogs and a bunch of hunters like I the ones I saw from the train. It's only a matter of time. But we haven't got time. I grab the pamphlets, tracking the words in each one to the bitter end. And at the end is the face of an ordinary-looking man whose distinguishing feature is his handsomeness — that plus the hand that's passing a cheque to the mayor like he's never stopped handing out cheques: a strong hand. I drag out the rat scraps and place them over the kidney pamphlet. Even the paper's the same.

I ball up the scraps as a helicopter clatters overhead. There's none so blind as those who can't see what's right in front of their noses. The chopper's lights are on, revealing that it's a stretch job. I haven't come to the wrong place at all. *Au contraire*, I'm right at the heart of the right place. The question is whether I'm too late to do anything about it.

'I've got to go,' I tell the dame.

'I'm coming with you.'

'I'll be faster without you.'

'It's not just about fast. You're a man on the run and I'm a profile-changer. I know now that you know French but I can still help you. And you're going to need all the help you can get. Where are we going?'

'To see a man.'

'About a dog?'

'Not this time, Damnation. This man's got a lot more going for him than just a dog.'

I finally get the stone out of my shoe. But as we get ourselves back to town, I'm thinking I should have left it where it was, and worn it like a hairshirt.

Chapter 35

WHERE LOYALTIES LIE

The motorcycle's still outside the Butterfly House and Le Patron's still old. He's also still angry.

'You – foreigner! Why do you insist on hanging around my girls?'

I hold up my hands, palms outwards to indicate the absence of weapons.

'I'm not here for your family,' I say. 'I'm here for you.'

On the wall behind the old man hangs a sepia photograph of half-a-dozen young men – some in rough uniform, one wearing roll-legged shorts, all grim-faced for the camera, clutching an assortment of weaponry – squatting in front of or leaning against the selfsame bike that's outside the Butterfly House. The old man sees what I'm looking at and laughs.

'Yes, that's me. I'm the young one in the middle wearing the officer's cap and holding the .303. And while my body parts might have been of use to you then, Monsieur, they are no longer. My organs have been well and truly shot to pieces by my very great age and the war.'

I shake my head.

'I'm not after your organs, Patron. I'm after your assistance.'

'Resistance?'

'That, too. Trust me, I'm not with them, I'm against them. And I believe you can help me.'

I wait while he computes what I just told him. He won't have seen the WANTED poster. When you get to a certain age, news ceases to be of interest. But not everything doesn't interest him and when Damnation smiles her encouragement, the old man finally relents.

'All right, I believe you're not one of them,' he replies. 'But if you're not, who are you, why are you here, and what do you want from me?'

He's asking questions within questions, like he already knows the answers but needs to be sure I know what he wants me to understand. And suddenly I sense something about this old man I haven't realised before. It's not just the quizzical expression on his face. We're talking French but it's not that, either. It's the sense that there's something terribly wrong with him. But it's too late to turn back. So I answer the questions.

'I'm a detective who's also a father looking for his daughter. You said they. Well, we both know who they are. They're the people who've taken my daughter, threatening to do to her what you've always feared they might do to Jaqui here. I've got to rescue my daughter and I believe you can help me do it.'

'How much do you know?' the old man asks.

He listens intently while I talk and at the end he seems to trust me. A lot more than I trust him.

'All right, I'm satisfied you're not one of them,' he says. 'Now I'll tell you who they are because I don't think you fully realise.' He pauses, during which I see him glance at Jaqui. 'They're people who think some lives are worth more than others.' He pauses again, as if there's a complex idea to get across and he wants to ensure he gets it across right. 'It's what we fought against in the Revolution, and it's the same thing we battled in the 1940s. A sense of superiority.' Stray thoughts seem to pass and re-pass through his mind. 'Now we have these people. They call themselves Hearts and Minds, a euphemism for the illegal obtaining and transplantation of body parts. And just like the aristocrats in the Revolution and after that the Germans in the war they'll stop at nothing to attain their ends.'

There are wheels within wheels here – like with the monkey clock in the town square – a merging and coalescing behind the simplicity of the hands telling the time on the face of the clock. It's like a multiplicity of ideas is all mixed up in the old man's head, driving his obsession.

'Our enemy does transplants. In the safety of our homes we laugh and call them The Organ Grinders: those, nice, innocent little musical-perambulator people you see in the street. But outside our homes we don't dare to call them anything. We have families, you see. It's just like it was in the war. Our families are under constant threat.'

The old man clasps and unclasps his useless-for-transplant hands while his mind undergoes similar convulsions.

'They get their product – their organs for transplant – on the black market. People sell themselves or they sell others to put food on the table. Or the Organ Grinders just help themselves …' The old man's mouth twists and lines cross and recross his face like lasers with too many targets. 'Donors are kidnapped in America, Europe, Africa, Asia – yes, even in Australia. A potential donor is identified and, after that, if approved either by the recipient or the recipient's family, their organs are – I believe the word's *harvested*. If the transplant results in the death of the donor, the remains are discreetly disposed of.'

The old soldier's mouth trembles. He's at war again. But it's like he's at war with himself.

'Do you understand me? The closest parallel is when aristocrats exploited the peasants before the French Revolution in 1789.' He seems to be struggling to untangle different thoughts. 'Sometimes the donors are tricked into co-operating. There are so-called "honey traps", in which people are offered sex or free plane tickets to La Belle France. The victims don't realise the tickets are one-way until too late.'

When the old man pours himself another coffee, a lot ends up in his saucer. And when he drinks from the saucer, even more spills on the table.

'Organs can be removed in situ, to be shipped off to their destination in suitable containers. Or bodies are sent complete – that is, drugged, duped or already dead. The business requires the connivance of powerful people, whose loved ones receive free transplants. Or they just get money – there's a lot of bribery and corruption of police and politicians. It's like it was in the Revolution and again in the war – we no longer know who our friends are.' He pauses. 'In the end, what we cling onto is what's best for our families.'

After that there's silence – too much silence. Which is finally broken by Damnation asking, shakily, 'But all this buying of organs and bribing must cost millions. Where does the money come from?'

'We're talking about a multi-billion-euro-a-year industry. On the white market in Australia alone doctors pay $10,000 for an aortic valve. But on the black market it's far different, because they're no longer buying generic. Select kidneys sell for 100,000 euros while handpicked hearts go for as much as a million. You see, people like to keep their loved ones alive …'

There's still something horribly wrong about what the old man's saying and the way he's saying it. Like there's something he's trying to convince himself of.

'You're a detective, so you'll already know that many people around here have gone missing. That's why I keep a close eye on my girls. When you turned up I thought you were one of them. There was no trust in the Revolution or again in the war. It's the same now. In your grey suit, big hat and tie, you clearly weren't a tourist. So I had you tailed from the moment you arrived.'

'Was the man on the train one of yours?'

'If you mean by that the one in the hospital, no. He's one of theirs and he was meant to stop you.'

'How do you know that?'

The old man's eyes waver before hardening.

'I learnt a lot in the war, Monsieur, just as I did from reading about the Revolution. And first and foremost I learnt the importance of survival – of oneself but also the survival of one's family.' He shunts back to the main line. 'Worldwide, traffickers harvest 20,000 kidneys annually. Apart from kidneys, bodies contain lungs, livers, pancreases, bones, tissue and hearts. Transplants occur in the US, Spain, Russia, Serbia, Kosovo – and here.'

'And where are these operations performed, in France?'

The old man glances at Jaqui, who quickly looks away. He turns back to me and, as he does so, he takes a deep, quavering breath. It's like all his past and all his future and all his family's past and future as well as the past and future of the whole of France are in that breath.

'At the château.'

Chapter 36

TONIGHT JOSEPHINE

For a long time after the old man finishes speaking, silence reigns. Clearly distressed, Jaqui excuses herself and goes upstairs, leaving the old man gazing lovingly after her. After which he collects himself. He seems to have come to a decision.

'Very well, Monsieur,' he says. 'We will help you.'

He limps to a cupboard, pulls it open, lifts out an old-fashioned military field telephone, and brings it to the table. He dials a number, someone answers, and he speaks softly into the mouthpiece.

'Hello, darling? It's Grandpa. I need confirmation of what you told me earlier … I thought so. Very well, we must move. The castle … Yes, I said the castle.' I sense resistance at the other end but the old man's adamant. 'He's a detective and we've got no choice … Yes, they've got his daughter … I'm doing what I believe is for the best … You will activate the phone tree and afterwards come here … Yes, all of them … I love you, ma cherie.'

When he's finished, he carefully replaces the handset and resumes our conversation as if the phonecall never happened. 'Because I'm egalitarian – all right, a communist – I hate castles and all they represent. I hate the transplant people for much the same reason. Both these hatreds are now combined in the one target. It's ironic.'

The old fighter might be speaking French, but he's wrong in any language.

'Not ironic,' I tell him. 'The word you're after is coincidental.'

I don't believe in coincidence. But what I believe no longer matters. The old man might be all over the shop but I've got to accept what he says and go along with him – otherwise Imogene is going to die.

'D'accord, let's not quibble ...' The old man's voice tails off as the door opens, and when he speaks again his tone has softened. 'Hello, my darling,' he murmurs.

'Hello, Grandfather,' replies the figure in the doorway.

'Josephine's my other precious granddaughter,' the old man explains. 'And she is a crucial factor in our enterprise.'

She's big and soft-faced and, like Jaqui, in her forties. She's wearing an aqua-coloured uniform with a white collar, and her blonde hair's crammed into a white nurse's cap. After double-kissing the old soldier and Jaqui – who has returned downstairs – Josephine positions herself next to her sister.

'Josephine works in the – castle.'

I note the hesitation. There's a lot the old man's not telling me and a glance at the sisters confirms it.

The nurse's face is pale and Jaqui's eyes won't meet mine. She's staring at her grandfather but addressing me when she whispers, 'The castle's owned by a family that's the closest thing France still possesses to royalty. Nobody likes them. They're snobs. They ...'

The old man glares her into silence before returning abruptly to me.

'Where this terrible business is conducted has always been a closely-guarded secret. I know because I have my spies, while Josephine only knows because she works there. Very few others – including quite clearly Jaqui here – know what goes on in the castle. The aristocrats are behind it, as they are behind everything. Their philosophy's the same as that of The Organ Grinders – that is, that some people are better than others, and deserve to live while others can die. The two groups – the aristocrats and the organ-exchange people – are natural bedfellows, which is why –'

The old man shuts up as the old couple, Harold and Maud, drift down the stairs, smiling uncertainly around at everyone before disappearing out the door. Not until the door closes behind them does the old man resume his discourse.

'Who are they, for instance?' he asks as their footsteps recede along the street. 'And what are they doing here?'

'They say they're pilgrims,' I tell him.

He shakes his head. And oddly, I get the impression he's shaking it, not at what I just said, but at Jaqui. He turns back to his other granddaughter, the nurse.

'While we're waiting, Josephine, please tell Monsieur about the – castle.'

Josephine hesitates. It must be a family trait, this hesitating.

'All of it?'

The old man frowns at her. 'Just what he needs to know.'

The nurse might be discussing organ grinding but that doesn't mean she minces her words. Yes, the operations take place in the castle. The relevant wing of the – again the hesitation – Hôpital Grand Château contains three sections – Storage, Dissection and Transplant.

'We nurses view it as being like a body possessing three primary organs, with the corridors as its veins and arteries.'

She's suddenly even more hesitant, like she fears someone might contradict her. But no-one does. The old man's fielding phone calls while Jaqui's eyes are fixed on the photo on the wall. Josephine seems troubled but continues anyway. Like the other locals who work there, she goes on, she's confined to the so-called good section: Transplant. No-one acknowledges the other two sections. Organs appear as if by magic, after which the nurses help the surgeon to transplant them.

'Oh, I'm sorry,' she murmurs, glancing at the old man. 'There's a fourth section – Live Transplant. Of course, no locals work there either.'

'Do you know when ... I mean who ...'

I can't utter the words but Josephine knows what I'm trying to say.

'Grandpa trained me to observe,' she says quietly. 'That's why I always check.' She pauses and glances across at me. 'Could you give me a name?'

I tell her Simon Peter. Then, in response to her non-knowing look, add, 'He's a dead dancer.' But she's still unknowing, so I try Janus King. Still the blank look.

'Also known as Vladimir Gregorovich.'

'Ah, Gregorovich,' the nurse murmurs. In the semi-darkness, her fingers tangle in her blonde hair like she's trying to remember the proprietary name of a medicine but can only come up with the generic. She glances at the old man and when he nods she continues.

'There is a Gregorovich on our list, but the first name is Natalie, not Vladimir. A little girl desperately in need of a good heart to replace her bad one, the faulty heart she was born with. Not to mention several other organs which ...'

She needs a prompt and I provide it.

'You use the word *desperately*. Does that mean –' I can't bring myself to say it. It's a long while before the nurse answers my non-question. Like an artery, time can stretch until it seems like it's going to burst, only it doesn't. I finally manage, 'Has she had her operation yet?'

'The little girl was waiting for a match but I understand she's no longer waiting. The match must be your daughter. And I understand the operation will be tonight.'

I play it rough. It's the only way.

'Understandings can lead to misunderstandings, so which is it: not tonight Josephine – or tonight?'

After a final glance at her grandfather, Josephine nods.

'Tonight.'

Chapter 37

OLD SOLDIERS NEVER DIE ...

At her words, the photo on the wall seems to turn three-dimensional, as if the young men want to leap into action because their war has restarted. Jaqui grips her sister's arm while Damnation takes hold of mine. Jaqui's staring at me with what looks like mute appeal while the nurse seems to be having trouble continuing. I sense her hesitation and so does the old man.

'Have you checked the surgeon's log?' he asks Josephine.

Josephine nods.

'That's what you trained me to do, Grandpa.'

'Then tell him what it says.'

Her eyes fix on the photograph on the wall behind the old man, like she might find comfort there. 'I'm not scheduled to assist in the operation because it's what's called a simultaneous transfer. That's when they remove organs from one live patient and insert them in another ...'

The old man's voice cuts across Josephine's, 'How do they perform this transfer?'

Josephine takes courage from his intrepidness. But her voice is a whisper so I've got to strain to hear what she's saying. 'The surgeon removes the organ or organs while the donor's still alive. A simultaneous transfer enhances the chance of success because ...'

Her voice fades to nothing but the old man's remorseless.

'Does the log give the time?'

'Twelve-thirty tonight. The donor's death will occur upon removal of the spare part.'

I force myself to speak.

'Which part – which organ?'

'The heart.'

'Then we can get on with the plan,' the old man says, 'in the full knowledge our friend here is in command of all the relevant facts. The troops will be here soon.'

'What troops?' I ask.

It's like he's been expecting the question ever since France's General de Gaulle disbanded his beloved Resistance. 'You Australians have a saying – Old soldiers never die, they just fade away. Well, here we don't die either. But neither do we fade away. Instead, we take a leaf out of these people's book. In other words we perform a transplant.'

Jaqui seems anxious to absolve herself of something. It could be guilt.

'What Grandpa means is –'

'What I'm saying,' the old man interrupts, 'is that the Grafted Bush – as we now call ourselves – has gone on recruiting. There are a couple of us old ones left, but mainly they are all new, young ones. The new men are taught to shoot and to hunt …' I remember the soldiers I saw from the train, near the château, like they were practising for something. 'Above all, they learn about explosives. So we're ready for any threat.'

'Or any excuse?'

The old man glances at me, sharply.

'I see it more as an opportunity, Monsieur. And in answer to your next question – just as I recognise that opportunity, I'm more than ready to grasp it.'

'But why are you doing this?'

A tap at the door relieves the old man of the need to reply.

Chapter 38

... THEY JUST FIND ANOTHER WAR

One by one the new recruits enter, crushing into the small room between me, Damnation, the two sisters and Le Patron.

'Thank you,' the old man says, turning to the last arrival, an old man like himself. 'Especially you, Philippe, because I know how hard it is for you to get around these days.'

Philippe nods. He looks even older and more decrepit than Le Patron, and appears to be struggling for breath. But his comrade's already moved on to the others – big, raw-boned farmboys, pimply clerks, an academic or two from the local university.

'Tonight's the night,' he says. 'And, pardon my Shakespeare: Screw your courage to the sticking place!'

One of the sisters – I think it's Jaqui – has lit a candle. The old man surveys the room in its dim illumination.

'Welcome to Operation Clawheart.' He holds up a hand for silence. 'Don't cheer – the walls have ears. This might be the time for action but it's also the time for discretion.'

'But who's the enemy? Who are we fighting? And what's the target?'

The old man glares the interjector – a young man who seems a lot smarter than the others – into silence.

'You're too young to understand, Martin. Suffice to say, the enemy's the same one it's always been. We needn't go into that. All you need to know is that body vultures are at work in Beguine. What you don't know is where they're operating. Well, I can tell you now because it's tonight's target.' He pauses for effect. 'It's the castle.'

Surprise greets his words. Only Philippe, as if he's suspected all along, stays silent. Someone – again I think it's Jaqui, like she's having trouble keeping still, like something's bothering her – has cleared the table, enabling the old man to spread out a map.

'We're going to rescue this man's daughter from the body snatchers. But at the same time we will blitz the joint so it cannot happen again.' He glares around. 'Anyone who doesn't want to take part must speak up now.'

Martin relapses into silence, staring at his hands while Le Patron nods.

I make like I want to speak but Le Patron gestures me into silence. Like any good commander he knows his men. This is the new generation of fighters, brought up on the twilit flictures of the killing of Saddam Hussein. They're sick of virtual reality. They want nice, big, fat, real explosions. One or two glance in my direction. 'We'll take the blitz,' one of the recruits says.

The old man frowns the speaker into silence.

'You're not being given a choice. You'll follow orders. Now we're limited by two factors – the balance of opposing forces and the consequences of our actions.'

It's as though someone – it must be Martin – has distracted the old man, causing him to use terms that belong only in a textbook. He quickly corrects himself like he's redirecting an errant missile.

'As I said, this man' – he indicates me – 'wants his daughter back. Plus, as I understand it, his ex-wife. This is our chance to show an outsider what we can do. We have to get it right. First, we need to evacuate the innocents.' He spreads his hands. 'Because, unlike the enemy, we're not in the business of random slaughter.'

I want to argue. I'm not here to blow up castles. I just want to save Imogene.

He jabs an arthritic finger at a few faint red lines on the old map.

'These are tunnels into the château and they're our points of entry. We will form into four teams. I'll lead the bomb squad. Jacques will lead the rescue team. Martin will be in charge of the guards. The fourth group will go to Transplant, where this man's daughter is. They'll be led by Philippe here, with the girl's father and Mademoiselle Dalmation along to make the necessary identification.'

Josephine interrupts. 'The child might require attention,' she says falteringly, like she's not sure what she's asking but might be expected to ask it. 'Therefore, I should be with –' she indicates me '– this man.'

The old man shakes his head vehemently.

'A definite No to that.'

'*Au contraire*, Grandpa – it must be a definite Yes.'

'I said no! Those are my orders, Josephine, and you will obey them. If not, you must stay behind with Jaqui.'

'Very well, I will accompany you.' There's a strength in the nurse that's unexpected. 'I will be there.'

'Very well. But you will stay by my side at all times. And after we have set the bombs, you will return with me.'

'Very well, Grandpa.'

As Le Patron barks his orders, there's something else on my mind. When I snap out of my reverie he's already checking an ancient timepiece.

'All right, men, synchronise your watches. It is now 10 pm. H-Hour— that is, the time of the assault – will be midnight.' He turns to me. 'And in response to your earlier question as to why I'm doing this. It is because, Monsieur, we are fathers together, you and I, isn't that so?'

When we arrive at the château, the Ferret's gun's in my pocket next to the lock banger. Everyone with the exception of Le Patron, Philippe and Josephine has come on foot. Le Patron's parking the BSA motorbike nose-out in a bramble bush, steadying the machine while Josephine alights from the back and Philippe gets out of the sidecar. Then – with the aid of a walking stick and with Josephine trotting obediently by his side – he limps in the direction of the bomb unit, which is already at work in the shadow of the château. Even as I watch, I see the nurse slip from Le Patron's side and scramble down the hill towards us. Le Patron's too absorbed in the bomb-laying to notice while Philippe appears too old to notice anything much at all. As she joins us, the nurse nods without speaking while Damnation grips my hand. We huddle at the tunnel entrance while, several paces away, I hear the young man Martin murmuring to his handful of guards. Somewhere in the distance the rotors of a helicopter start up. Outside the tunnel, we get down on our hands and knees and the old man's boot moves against my skull, followed by an urgently croaked, 'Go! Go! Go!'

Chapter 39

THE RED HERRING

A sign at the tunnel mouth reads: UNSAFE ACCESS. Crouching, I follow Philippe. Behind me is Damnation, followed by the nurse. Pick-and-shovel squads have cleared away the bushes that have successfully hidden the tunnel for seventy years. Philippe's cracked voice filters back through the dust. 'The limestone's stable but a cave-in's always possible. Stay close. We don't want to rescue the wrong boy.'

'Girl,' I correct him. 'We're rescuing a girl.'

It's as if he doesn't hear. But it doesn't matter. Just as I find myself thinking and talking like an accountant, I weigh our chances and gauge the tunnel with the mind of a bean counter. The tunnel measures a metre by a metre. There are no struts, no timberwork, no supporting structure as far as I can see. I spit out the lime dust kicked up by Philippe. Time and again I find myself bumping into his boots, hearing him gasp for air before moving on.

Some vague thought's niggling at me, only I can't place it. It's as if all my detecting facilities have been replaced by the accountant I turned into when I put on these clothes. At first I put it down to my childhood fear of confined spaces, courtesy of the schoolyard bullies that locked me in sports bins. But it's not just that. It's more to do with these two old men – the madman that's leading us and the geezer gasping for air just ahead. Plus the memory of that odd, halting interplay between Le Patron and his granddaughters back at the Butterfly House ...

We inch forward in a silence broken only by the clatter of falling scree, its shards scratching my hands, the scrabbling of Damnation and the nurse behind me, and the ragged, laboured breathing of the old man ahead. There's little air. At times it feels like there's none at all. The walls of the tunnel close in. Like the old man, I start to struggle for breath. I stop to wipe the lime-greased sweat from my eyes and by the dim light shed by my headlamp, I check the time.

12.11 am.

They'll operate on Imogene first — cutting the arteries and slicing around the tissue to remove her heart and placing it in a dish of ice. There's to be no life-support system — it's not intended that she live. After they remove the recipient's defective heart, tying off the arteries and placing her on an artificial fibrillator before preparing the chest cavity, Imogene's heart will be —

If Josephine was telling the truth, it's only seventeen minutes to the operation. If ... I damn Le Patron for not scheduling our run earlier. We're in danger of being too late. I wish ... Then I hear Rube saying, If wishes were dishes, and fight back my fear. It's too late for recriminations. Le Patron's done his best, hasn't he? But will it be enough? The hill seems to crumble and the limestone turn to dust while all hope of saving Imogene seems to be turning to dust with it. If Josephine was telling the truth ... I shake my head and my head bumps against a boot. That's when I realise the old man's no longer moving.

'Hurry up!' I shout. 'For God's sake, man, get a move on, will you!' But his boot dangles immobile in the torchlight. 'Move!' I shout again. His boot's a sclerotic lump in an old artery, blocking circulation. I fight for breath. A voice wavers behind me, beyond Damnation, falteringly.

'What's happening?'

'I think he's dead.'

But there's no think about it. Death is a profound stillness and Philippe is profoundly still.

'This is a bad sign!' Josephine cries.

The voice reaches me as if from a distance, like a stray thought in the mind of an amnesiac. Terror plunges me into darkness and it takes an act of will to come back from it, to realise the nurse's voice is high-pitched and hysterical as she screams that something's a bad sign. But if Philippe's death's a bad sign, what's it a bad sign of ...?

It's then that the elusive memory — no, three elusive but interconnected memories — cease to be elusive any more. It's the word *sign* that launches the process, making me sweat even more than I am already. The first memory is of the signs in the hospital when I was looking for the Ferret. One sign read: Transplant. Not down there, Damnation said: It's this way. The second memory is of Jaqui saying: His wife – my grandmother – was killed by the Germans because of Le Patron, in retaliation for his activities in the war. And the third memory is of Le Patron's passionate denunciation of privilege: Just like aristocrats or the Germans in the war, these people will stop at nothing …

This is not about Imogene at all.

How can it be?

Imogene's not even here.

'The time!' I shout back to the nurse. 'Did you give me the right time? Or did you lie about that, too?'

I don't hear her reply. It could be because my fear has shut out all sound. I just manage to hear Damnation relaying the nurse's answer.

'She says the castle was a red herring: the old man wanted to blow up the castle and he also wanted you out of the way. It's because he doesn't want what happened to his wife to happen to Jaqui and Josephine. He's working for –'

I cut across her, 'But if Imogene's not here, where is she?'

I hear the murmur of question and answer behind me, then Damnation saying, 'In the real hospital.'

My heart sinks and with it all hope. My sight blurs but I manage to read the time on my watch and – still accountant-like – do the necessary subtraction and addition. Only eight minutes to go. We're in the wrong place at the wrong time. I'm tangled in my fear and Philippe's feet. The feet are stopping me moving. But I must move for Imogene's sake. I yell out, 'Tell Josephine to head back!'

They move and I move with them. Le Patron went to elaborate lengths to fool me. A final warning, he said before we left, looking me straight in the eye. When you get to the end of the tunnel, you'll find the door opens towards you. It's a strategy dating from the time of the ancient Greeks, making fortresses that much harder to break into.

A red herring, a sop to Sir Boris as Rory would say, a totally irrelevant detail meant to mislead. It was never intended we save Imogene. The old man just wanted to save his girls and at the same time blow up the hated castle. And now, if Josephine has at least told the truth about the time of the operation, it's only seven minutes before they remove Imogene's heart.

Desperation and lime dust turn my tears to paste as Damnation and Josephine shuffle behind me and I shuffle as fast as I can back after them.

Chapter 40

INTO THE VALLEY OF DEATH

Around the side of the hill, the silhouettes of toiling figures are outlined against the night sky. I hear the sound of heavy, homemade artillery being moved into position and the urgent commands of Le Patron.

'We're not going to make it!' Damnation whispers. 'It took us a long time to get here from the hospital, remember.'

'But we were on foot then.'

The motorbike's still where Le Patron left it, the glint of its handlebars and the glimmer of its paintwork barely visible through the bushes. One of Martin's men is on guard but he's distracted by the bomb layers and softly whistling the French national anthem. I cut him off mid-whistle, finding the appropriate pressure point, pressing it, and afterwards helping him down to the ground. The handlebars are cold. The key's in the ignition but I don't use it to start the bike. There are helmets – old, black, dull-painted affairs – but we're not using them, either. I wheel the bike into position. Someone's coming towards us.

'Damnation, get astride the petrol tank. Josephine, you're in the sidecar. Let's go!'

Clutch-starting a pre-war BSA with two dames aboard is no stroll in the vineyard. I put it into third, raise the valve lifter and push. Someone starts shouting. I depress the valve lifter. The Sloper's engine catches, dies, catches, dies and catches as the bike lurches down the hill. The front wheel twists and the bike threatens to fishtail but I manage to wrestle it straight. From behind us come more shouts. Martin and his guards are almost on us – I feel a hand clawing at my coat – as the engine rattles into life. I thrust away the hand and leap aboard, straddling Damnation, while giving the engine as much throttle as I can find.

The bike twists and turns as the engine splutters, roars, dies, roars again. The old man wanted Josephine out of the way before the bombs went off. She'll be out of the way all right, but not in the way the old man intended. He wanted me gone so he could satisfy his masters, the transplant people. Beyond the running feet I can hear him shouting. But he's not shouting at us. He's ordering the bomb layers to get on with the job. He must have decided that Josephine's safe and is making the best of a bad job. The guards' shouting fades and the running feet fall back. I glance behind as I manoeuvre the bike onto the road.

As our speed increases, my accountant's brain calculates that, despite the load, we're capable of achieving something like 60 kilometres an hour. My suit coat flaps like the wings of Samothrace and the night wind freezes my shaven head. Damnation's soft against me while the moonlight illuminates the balled-up paper by the foxhole we occupied earlier in the day. The engine hammers, the racket echoing into the valley as we head for the hospital, the sidecar bouncing like it's attached to the bike by rubber bands while our single yellow light probes the darkness like a scalpel. I twist sideways, shouting so the nurse can hear me.

'You've got three minutes to tell me everything, Josephine! And this time make it the truth!'

Grandpa made her do it, she tells me. He didn't want − wouldn't allow − what happened to his beloved wife to happen to her and Jaqui. In the war he fought against the Germans and as a result of his activities his wife − their grandmother − had died. But he was smarter now. Now he worked for the enemy. He was in charge of the transplant people's security.

Which was how he'd known of my arrival. When I turned up at Beguine he suspected that I must be one of the organisation's hunters and gatherers. A suspicion that was confirmed by my arrival at the Butterfly House. He knew he couldn't trust the people he worked for. They could still abduct his precious girls if they weren't happy with him, or even remove their organs if someone offered enough ... He hated aristocrats as much as − perhaps more than − the body farmers. So he decided to kill two birds with one stone. Blowing up the castle meant the end of a much-hated symbol as well as the death of any aristocrats who happened to be there at the time. With the help of police and politicians the organisation bribed he might even have got away with it. As for the bomb layers, they were only following orders. They wouldn't know what it was all about anyway. And my involvement would distract me from the real centre of operations while also ensuring my death. And meanwhile Le Patron would win favour with the enemy – which was the whole point of the exercise. And unlike his wife, his precious girls would be safe.

Josephine's voice is sober.

'You and Hélène were supposed to die in the blast while old Philippe was expendable. I wasn't meant to be with you. Grandpa was to bring me safely back on his bike. But I – couldn't abandon you, knowing what I knew. After all, I'm a nurse. But until Philippe died I didn't know what to do. I decided my dying would somehow atone for my part in the death of your daughter …'

Then Philippe died and the nurse saw his death as a sign. As we bump along the potholed road, she's clearly distressed.

'And my daughter?' I demand, my eyes watering with the combined effects of the headwind and the fear we'll be too late. 'What was supposed to happen to her?'

The answer's a long time coming. What did my old mate Harry Hopman like to say? That there are no winners in this world, only losers, and all anyone can do is attempt to limit their losses. 'This is a story about fathers and daughters, isn't it?' Her words are clear because she needs to get across what she's saying. 'Gregorovich is a father and it was your daughter's life or that of his daughter. His daughter needed a heart and your daughter had one. It was the same with Grandpa. He'd lost his wife but he still had us. And he was trying to protect us in the only way he knew how.'

We've reached the valley floor. The clouds seem to be hung out to dry and the river's gleaming in the moonlight. The clatter of the bike is all-pervasive as the hospital looms. Guards peel from the doors and sprint up the road towards us, the moonlight glinting on dull-painted barrels. It's no longer Le Patron's ragtag-and-bobtail group of recruits. These men are professionals, their weapons F1-Famas bugle assault-rifles, modified for nightwork.

'Stop or we'll shoot!'

'Hang on!' I yell to my passengers.

The impact should have derailed us but they made these machines from good old British steel. There are a lot of screams as we smash through the doors. Bodies bounce away from us and the glass shatters into spring-storm raindrops as the bike crashes through.

'The corridor! We won't fit!' Damnation shouts.

'We'll fit all right! Hospital corridors are wide enough to turn a bed in!'

As we skid to a stop, I twist to confront Josephine, who's still occupying the sidecar.

'Where are they? Are they on the floor that doesn't exist?'

Viewed from the outside, the number of hospital floors never added up. I've been thinking like an accountant and all the signs suggested the hospital had four storeys while my eyes insisted there were five.

Josephine nods and I aim the bike for the lift. But a sign says *En Panne* – Out of Order.

'I forgot – they decommission the lift when they ...'

I don't wait for her to finish.

'Fire stairs?'

She shakes her head. 'They lock the door to the fire stairs at such times.'

It's a heavy-duty door with steel reinforcing, built to resist most forces. But the bike's built that way, too. I ram the gear selector into First and twist the hand-throttle for the run-up. The corridor's not only wide enough to turn a bed in, it can take a lot of bike, too. I straighten the machine and bring the old 500cc engine up to its full 3000 revs.

'Stand back!' I yell.

Damnation dives to one side as I unleash the clutch. There's a bit of nonsense as the wheels look for purchase and we're sideways-on to the direction I want us to go when the tyres finally grip. The motor's screams ricochet off the walls and the sidecar becomes a Catherine wheel as it gets tangled up with a fire extinguisher. The building shudders as the BSA makes contact with the door, over which a sign shows a little green man running up a set of stairs accompanied by the words FIRE ESCAPE.

The bike rams into a concrete step and a sharp pain rips through my leg. I'm dazed as Damnation hurries towards me, followed by Josephine. It hurts but I manage to stagger to my feet. The bike's opened the fire door part of the way. I shove it the rest of the way. The stairs lead to the floor that's not there ...

'Give me a hand!'

I'll need them – the nurse anyway. For the kid, if not for me. The two women prop me, one on each side, as I drag my disabled leg up the stairs. The last door is what Le Patron said we'd find in the tunnel.

'It opens towards us!' Josephine yells. 'But it can't be locked from the inside because of fire regulations so it's open!'

The door leads to a high, wide corridor on the fifth floor, the level that doesn't exist. There are no more signs. Just the corridor and too many doors. I glance at Josephine.

'Which door?'

'I've never done a simultaneous transfer.' I'm prepared to believe that much at least is true. 'But I've done the other operations.' She points shakily. 'So, by a process of elimination, behind that door is your daughter.'

She's indicating a door at the end. I hesitate, nursing my shattered leg. We can't afford to get it wrong now, there's not enough time.

'We're down to the wire, Josephine. Are you sure?'

'Yes,' she assures me. 'They do their operations one at a time,' she goes on as she helps me along. 'We're talking millions of euros per procedure. It's not an assembly line – it doesn't have to be. They only do one operation a night. They're here all right.'

We head along the corridor, Damnation on one side and the nurse on the other. A faint sound of music emerges through the door.

'The door's pretty well soundproof,' Josephine whispers. 'They take every precaution. And it'll be locked.'

'Stand back!'

I bring out the lock killer, place it against the keyhole and the explosion's no more than a rat's squeak.

As I push open the door and we go in, we're hit by a blast of music.

Chapter 41

DANCING WITH BRICKS

We find ourselves in a room behind a high, wide insul-screen featuring a lot of little Beatrix Potter rabbits disporting themselves in a garden that – the screen, not the garden – muffles any noise we make upon entry. That and the music. No-one appears to have noticed us, anyway. Beyond the screen, I count five figures – three female, two male – wearing plastic gloves, shoe covers and surgical masks. A sixth is curled on a bed. And in the far corner a seventh stands slight and shadowy, closely attending to what's happening under the harsh arc lamp, under which lies a small, still shape, raised high on the operating-table as if for sacrifice.

And always the music. Over which booms a voice.

'*Mehr narkose, Herr Anästhesist!*'

'He's speaking German,' Josephine murmurs beside me. 'Grandpa made me learn German, it was one of his obsessions. The surgeon's German and he's asking for more anaesthetic, which means ...'

But she doesn't need to tell me what it means – either the words or their significance. I know German. I also know the figure on the operating table's Imogene.

'Not that it matters as far as the donor's concerned,' the surgeon continues, shouting to be heard over the music. 'But an anaesthetic gives us a happier heart.'

I'd been expecting French, because this is whatsisname: Green, Serge Lifar, Lover Boy – the man with the hands. Nosey Nora said he was French. And Aunt Rube agreed. After all, Rube decided the word on the tape was Merde! But Rube wasn't her usual self – instead she was looking for easy answers when there never are. The word wasn't Merde!

I also recognise the music. It's Tchaikovsky again but this time it's his

1812 Overture – the one with all the cannons going off at the end. I slip off my coat and hand it to Damnation, setting the screen rocking as I do so. Somehow above the music the surgeon hears the screen rocking. If the music was any louder I could wear it as a coat, yet Lifar heard the screen rocking.

'What was that? Don't you morons realise that – apart from the music – I require absolute silence?'

It's an assistant's job to reassure and an assistant reassures. But Lifar isn't satisfied. He demands someone check for the source of the noise. Footsteps approach and an aqua-coloured gown stops on the other side of the screen. The figure comes no closer – it mustn't be in the contract to peer around screens. But the nurse is close enough for me to assess her rate of respiration. It's a long way from normal.

'It's nothing, doctor.'

'But I tell you I heard something!'

That's when a third voice – one with a heavy accent – interposes. It's Russian – more specifically one of the six Slavonic languages, possibly Ukrainian. I identify the speaker as Gregorovich, the father of the recipient, the dancer who agreed that my daughter would make a suitable donor when Lifar produced her for inspection.

'What are you, Lifar, some kind of prima donna? This isn't ballet, you know. You're a defrocked morphine dropkick who lost his licence and I'm paying you a fortune to do a job. Now do what that fortune entitles me to and remove the heart.'

'But to do that I require peace and quiet.'

'You have a lot better than that, Lifar – you have the music of a great Russian composer. Remove the heart.'

In awkward counterpoint to the crash of cymbals, someone starts singing. I recognise the voice as that of the surgeon. The addict tremor is pronounced. Despite the language, I recognise the song. The surgeon's sub-conscious has kicked in and the result's not pretty.

'Gott sei dank fur kleines Mades …'

'He's using regional German,' Josephine whispers. '*Mades* is another word for *Mädchen* – it means little girls! He's singing …'

The word on the tape was *Mades*, not *Merde* …

Up to now I've been reluctant to move. I was worried I might hurt Imogene. I was in the kind of nightmare where all will is stripped away, as if some all-powerful force pinioned my arms, a nightmare I couldn't wake from.

Damnation's got my coat while Josephine's checking the upside-down dial of her nurse's watch. And when the nurse looks up and her eyes meet mine, the eyes are appealing. She crooks a finger at me, indicating half. Thirty seconds to deadline.

As I hobble around the screen I hear the father cry out in anguish: *Nyet! Nyet!* But it's him or me, his daughter or mine. And it's my daughter's heart. I forget my leg, go down hard on my good one, and leap across the operating theatre.

There's a moment – the briefest of nanoseconds – when the surgeon, blade in hand, stands, wide-apart eyes staring out of the handsome face familiar from the photograph. It's like he's seeing what he once saw in his drug-fuelled hallucinations. He tries to get out of the way but he's too late. Bone crunches against bone as my heel catches him full in the face and his head jerks backwards. The surgical assistants scatter in a pale-green blur as the scalpel clatters to the parquet. Lifar lies still. He's no longer singing.

Josephine's suddenly beside me. I push her. 'See to Imogene!' I yell. She moves but I've been distracted. Damnation calls out from the screen, 'Look out!'

I go into the half-pirouette, using the good leg to take all my weight. On the turn I find the Russian in centre stage. He's abandoned his attempts at English and is swearing above the music in his native Ukrainian. I sink to the half-crouch but the dancer's lithe figure follows mine. It's like we're linked by the piano wire of a garrotter. Before I can move again, Gregorovich pauses to gather up the scalpel. The blade flickers in his hand and the eyes in the broad Ukrainian skull fix on mine like a snake's.

He's no longer dancing to save his daughter. With the surgeon dead, she's no longer got any hope of a new life from that quarter. He's acting out of unrequited hope, dancing for vengeance. I see it in the forward thrust of his body and in the way he's holding the knife. He comes at me high and wide with his head back, legs together and arms spread. I've got nowhere to go. As the dancer's arm slices down, I'm hampered by the corpse of the surgeon behind me, the tray of instruments on one side, the nurse leaning over Imogene on the other, and my bad leg.

I'm a body in the making, and if a dancer knows anything, it's body language …

Chapter 42

DANSE MACABRE

I smell the stifling stench of disinfectant and the thick, galling odour of anaesthetic, feel my body crushed in a dust-filled tunnel to nowhere, blinking in the half-light, tasting what I think must be limestone until I recognise the bitter-sweet bile as the dancer descends. All in slow motion, as if time's stopped. Fine dancers can do that and Gregorovich is a fine dancer. With the music hammering in the background, I try to shield my daughter by standing between her and the dancer, awaiting the death stroke. It's all I can do. But it's not all Josephine can do.

Uttering a strangled half-cry, she spins from the operating table as the death dealer descends, interposing her big body between mine and the dancer's. Their combined weight thrusts me onto the surgeon as − above and beyond the music − a shot rings out. I'm expecting the knife of death. Instead the dancer's doing the puppet dance from *Petrushka*, arms flailing, body twisting, legs jerking, head thrust back as he soars for an instant above me before finally crashing down.

The knife plunges, but not into me. Josephine's big, heavy body sags against mine and lies still. And on top of her, the dancer Gregorovich is no longer moving. Past them both, I make out the figure of Damnation, my dark-grey accountant's coat crumpled beside her, Parisian jeans-clad legs wide apart, arms extended in front of her. And gripped in her two fists is the gun that once belonged to the Ferret.

I try to extract myself from the tangle of bodies but can't. I need to check on the kid but the bodies and the bad leg prevent me. My sight blurs and I hear a roaring in my ears. At first I think it's the cannons in the music only it's too soon for the cannons …Damnation knew where the gun was, the Manurhin MR73, .357 Magnum that was in my pocket. She also knew her way around the coat because she's been there before. It was simply a matter of ... But how did she know how to fire the thing ...?

One of the bodies moves. It's Josephine. Someone's still alive in this mess and it's the nurse. But looking at the blood leaking from her, I know she won't be alive for long. She wasn't the target, she just made herself that way. I settle her on the floor, cradling her head in my arms.

'Is your daughter ...?' she whispers.

I nod.

'She would have been safe if I'd told the truth,' she murmurs. 'You could have got here in – plenty of time.' She tries to raise herself but falls back. 'Don't be hard on Grandpa. He made me lie but it was only because he didn't want what happened to his wife to happen to me and Jaqui. So this time he was on the side of the enemy. He wanted to protect us even if it meant putting your daughter in the firing line.'

Her fading eyes seek mine.

'Ironic, isn't it?' I don't correct her because she doesn't need correcting. 'Grandpa sold his soul to the Devil in order to protect us. Yet I'm going to die because of it.'

'You'll be all right.'

Josephine manages a pain-racked smile. 'It's nice of you to say so, only it's – not true. It's like the lies I told you. In the end my lies cost me my life and it looks like your daughter has gone the same way ...' Her voice wavers as she sags in my arms. 'Even more ironically, someone could have had my organs but now there's no-one here to ...'

Her voice fades and I feel something within me fade with her. I'm lowering her down to the floor when, above the racket of the Tchaikovsky, I hear a crash and look up in time to see a group of men with blackened faces explode into the operating theatre. And far off, in some twilit world beyond the music, as consciousness leaves me, I hear a series of explosions.

Chapter 43

THROUGH A GLASS, DARKLY

Strong hands pinion me. I panic as I feel a needle enter my arm. Immediately afterwards – or it could be days or even weeks – I hear the clatter of what might be helicopter blades. Or maybe it's just the music. There are more explosions and I nod to myself. It must be the music. The music must be helping the replacement surgeon as he attempts to bring Imogene back to life …

I struggle but shadows fall around me. To the east – it must be the east because that's where the sun rises, even in France – I make out the glow of a beautiful dawn heralding the promise of a new day.

Followed by darkness.

'Careful!'

And dimly, as if from a great distance, the same voice, 'What do we do with him now?'

It could be a dream, a dream in which words make a half-sense that's worse than no sense at all. I sense a logic but it's the logic of Alice in Wonderland. Shapes approach and recede. The voice is soft yet it batters my soul. The words make a great deal of sense yet they make no sense at all … But it's not a sunrise, it's the castle. Le Patron has achieved one of his crazy aims, he's destroyed the château. Below – it must be far below, the drugs have warped my perception of distance – the castle's no more than a series of scattered fires and piles of dust. Le Patron thought I'd be there, that in killing me he could make amends for the death of his wife by saving his granddaughters. He was only half-right. Jaqui might be alive but Le Patron's efforts have resulted in the death of Josephine.

That's irony.

My mother was a drug-crazed madwoman who wanted to take me – her five-year-old son – on a roundabout-ride to death. But in the end she took only my sister because I hid, hearing her croon as I did so: *Come to me, my little rainbow, Rainbow by name, rainbow by nature, come to me ...* At a fair I was given a toy after failing to hook seaweed out of a horse trough. The toy was a kaleidoscope – a small, tube-like affair which showed pretty much what my mother saw when she gave birth: a rainbow. Me and my sister thought we could see a magical future in that explosion of colour – the gyrating circles, the refracting and diffracting spectra. We believed we were seeing the Utopia that our parents ranted on about. We decided it was our own special angel's portent, as if the future might bring us a wondrous beauty, instead of ... My mother dead.

My sister dead.

And now my only daughter ...

But when I became a man, I put away childish things.

For now we see through a glass, darkly.

What I see now through the fog of whatever they injected me with is another flash of multi-coloured light – the goddess Aurora spilling dew upon the earth to bring life to all things. But there's no life here, no wonder or wisdom and little joy. Instead, rocks and bodies spew into the early morning sky and the flames are hellfire. I feel the helicopter pitch and shudder, rise and fall and rise again. I struggle but my heart isn't in it. I've lost my daughter. I feel the jab of another needle followed quickly by another and the pain in my leg fades. And for a long time after that, all I see, hear, feel and experience is nothing. Nothing at all.

The chopper is more stable now and I'm grateful for that. I try to open my eyes but something's forcing them shut. Cramp gnaws at my guts like hungry rats. I struggle to remember the significance of rats, but like everything else on the edge of my consciousness it eludes me.

Amnesia is an anaesthetic. They must have injected me with amnesia.

The helicopter's falling from the sky and my guts lurch and my eyes swim. A voice orders me to fasten my seatbelt. I hear the scream of engines and feel the chopper pitch and shudder. The leg's hurting again, my mouth's dry, I can't open my eyes and my gut's been chewed to pieces by rats.

I'm in a wheelchair trundling along a walkway. The air's cold, much colder than it ought to be. I run a hand over my skull. No hair. No hat, either. I must have left the hat in the tunnel along with ... What tunnel? I remember a body blocking my way and the words of the nurse, followed by the terrible realisation that —

I must be somewhere in France yet the voices around me aren't French. And dimly through those non-French voices I hear a small, reed-thin one saying, *'He's waking. Get out of the way and let me wipe his eyes, they're full of gunk ...'*

And I know I'm dreaming because it's Imogene's voice and yet Imogene's dead.

Chapter 44

THE KID IN THE QUEUE

Fingers gouge into my corneas and water dribbles under the collar of my shirt. I force my eyes open and a familiar face swims into my vision like an image refracted in a goldfish bowl. I'm a goldfish. Because, while I'm opening and closing my mouth and saying nothing, the human outside the bowl is speaking. And the image and words make no sense, no sense at all … *'You're not who you think you are. You're not Mister Rainbow but Norman Halliwell and you're returning from – where?'*

It's a test. I can do tests. Rube taught me how to do tests. I concentrate on my answer.

'France,' I hear myself say. 'I'm returning from France.'

'Correct. And what is your name?'

'I am Norman Halliwell. I am a bald accountant and my name is Norman Halliwell.'

I turn to face the man in uniform checking my face against something I can't see hidden behind his counter. I rub my hand over my head again. Someone's reshaven my skull. What else have they done? But I can't wonder about that. I've got my work cut out just remembering who I am. Because I've given Norman Halliwell not only my heart but also my body. Norman Halliwell exists because I brought him back to life. Norman Halliwell is me, I am Norman Halliwell. The man in uniform looks like a grinning satyr as he gives me back the passport, the one with someone else's photo in it.

'I note from our files that you left Australia hale and healthy, Mr Halliwell. Yet you've come back in a wheelchair. Are you sure you're who you say you are?'

It might be an attempt at a joke but I'm not laughing.

Anyone can see I'm not myself.

'Where's your luggage?' Customs wants to know.

'There's no luggage,' Damnation replies. 'It must have been mislaid en route.'

As we pass out into the free world, I crane my bald head to see who's pushing me. And suddenly I'm in the tunnel again and unable to breathe again. Because the person pushing my chair looks like Imogene.

'Who are you?' I ask.

'Come on, Daddy!'

'You're Imogene,' I whisper.

'Right! And for that you get a tot of vodka.'

Damnation told me later that Imogene wouldn't let anyone else near me. She even had a little joke about it — that if anyone was pushing her father around it was going to be her. She laughed as she said it — laughed because she's Imogene, laughed because she's happy, laughed because she could, because she's alive.

She who lives last, laughs best.

'Come to Mummy, darling.'

It can't be but it is. The dream was a nightmare that turned into real life then back into a nightmare again. Salina must have been the figure on the bed in the operating theatre, lining up to have her organs extracted as an add-on extra after they'd finished with Imogene. And now she's walking next to Imogene like nothing ever happened — not a marriage, not the birth of a daughter, no divorce, no wild-eyed escapade to France in which Imogene nearly lost her life, not even any happy returns. I feel the grip on the chair handles tighten.

'I can't. Because right now I'm looking after Daddy.'

Imogene plonks the chair at the head of the taxi queue like it belongs there and I recall that when you're disabled, even in Sydney, you go to the front of the queue. Other memories come back, too ...

'What happened to the dancer's daughter?'

Damnation answers. She's on the other side of the wheelchair from Salina, wearing this year's Parisian chic and looking as beautiful as ever.

'After I shot the dancer in the operating theatre and while you were out to it – they had to give you injection after injection because you thought Imogene was dead, and apart from that were in great pain from your leg; were in fact, in my humble opinion, stark, staring mad – I visited the room next door to deliver the bad news to the would-be recipient.'

There's a long wait for a taxi that's configured to take a wheelchair. But this is Sydney.

'Am I alive now? the little girl wanted to know,' Damnation continues. 'Daddy promised me I'd be alive after the operation.' Damnation takes a deep breath. 'I told her, Yes, she was alive but there'd been a bit of a hitch and there had been no operation. The little girl actually looked relieved. That's good, she replied. Daddy said no-one would die giving me organs but I couldn't see how that could be, not when one of the organs was a heart. Was Daddy being true to me?'

It's my turn to take a deep breath.

'What did you say to that?' I ask.

'I replied that daddies were always true but some daddies were truer than others.'

I have trouble getting my brain around what she's said. 'What happens to the little girl now?'

'She returns to the back of the queue.'

Which we don't have to, because just then a cab with a bubble back arrives. And as Imogene wheels me into it, preparatory to getting into the cab herself, I spot the old couple, Harold and Maud, conversing quietly together at the back of the queue.

Chapter 45

THERE WAS A CROOKED MAN ...

I stay in the chair in the back of the cab as Sal and the kid decant themselves at 21 Castanet Close, the shack uncurtained and unwelcoming. The kid leans in and asks if I'm all right and I lie through my teeth and tell her yes. After which the hack drives me off and dumps me in Darlinghurst beside a twisted wheelchair ramp cobbled out of old bits of plumber's pipe and splintery scraps of second-hand marine ply. I recognise Rory's handiwork.

Rube answers my Mike Hammer, tugging open the door with a twisted wire coathanger she's affixed for the purpose and for a long while we look at each other from our respective wheelchairs. There's got to be something to say but neither of us can say it, so in the end, Rube lets me in in silence, wheeling herself down the hall ahead of me to the living room.

'Where's the machine?' I ask.

'What machine?'

'The one that was keeping you alive, the kidney pumper with all the bells and whistles.'

Rube chucks me a sly look.

'I no longer need it.'

'Why is that?'

'Because I've got a new kidney.'

'Where did you get a new kidney?'

'From a live donor who was more than willing to ...'

'Come on, Rube, I might have a broken leg but –'

'All right, you like clues so I'll give you one: the donor was brain dead.'

'Good old Roarer! So that's why he wasn't at the airport! He's convalescing!'

Aunt Rube's wound must still hurt because when she shrugs she winces.

'It's not good old Roarer at all. I'm grateful for what he did but he didn't do it for me. According to the Knock-Kneed Church of the Born-Again Idiots, donating an organ means you hit the eternal jackpot. Rory might have lost a kidney but, in so doing, he scored a first-class ticket to heaven.'

'Coincidence?'

'No, Rainbow, irony.'

I change the subject. 'How's the boat?'

'As you might say yourself, Rainbow, Wooden No. I've been too busy keeping myself afloat to worry about boats.'

I spend a few days with Rube. I don't go into detail about the trip to France, and in return she brings up nothing about me trusting Damnation. Instead, with difficulty because she's in a wheelchair, she makes up a bed on the couch and I go to sleep to the sound of drug addicts screaming at each other and wake to the refrain of traffic. It's good to be home but when Rube reckons I've had enough fun, she kicks me out. On the way she hands me an envelope. I open it on the bus. It's brief and it's in French.

Dear father of the little girl. It was very sad losing both my sister and Grandpa in the one coup. The explosion was terrible. Because he couldn't walk very well, Grandpa couldn't make his getaway without his bike so he went up with the castle. Many others also lost their lives. There is to be no inquiry however. The papers said the explosion was caused by a gas leak. I hope me giving you the warning about Grandpa helped in some way. He was wrong, I know. But in his defence, he believed he was acting for the best. He just wanted to protect us and because we were his granddaughters we had to obey him. He was our Grandpa, after all. I was happy to hear your daughter survived everything. The operations have stopped and now the top floor of the hospital is devoted to the victims of bomb blasts. In closing I am going to marry Martin, the man who put you in the helicopter. He's a good man. Jaqui

I'm out of the chair and we're standing in the Pitt Street mall, a piece of roadway clawed back from Sydney's traffic. I ignore the busker eating fire, focusing instead on Damnation. It's not hard. She admits what I suspected all along – that the entire operation was a fit-up. Flax was hand-in-surgeon's-glove with Lifar. While Lifar acted as spotter, surgeon and general factotum, Flax was the fixer and Damnation the go-get girl.

She pauses, emotion rendering her momentarily breathless, leaving me to fill in the gaps.

'Your friend Lifar spotted Imogene,' I say, 'befriended Salina, then paraded Imogene before Gregorovich, who approved of her as a donor. Lifar arranged a medical for Imogene to ensure compatibility. Lifar then focused on getting Imogene and Salina out of the country – the organisation deciding they could use the mother's organs as well. You agreed to teach them French. Everything was hunky-dory until in a swollen-headed moment – maybe they were in a relationship – Gregorovich blabbed the story to Simon. Which made Simon a threat that had to be eliminated.'

She holds up her hands like she's trying to ward off the truth.

'Honestly, I – I didn't know what they were up to. To me it seemed to be something – oh, I don't know – exciting. I didn't know it involved abducting and killing people. I just thought – Oh, I don't know what I thought. I just felt it was – well, romantic being a little bit on the wrong side of the law.'

My new hat's too big because I'm anticipating hair regrowth so it wobbles when I shake my head.

'Except there's no such thing as being a little bit on the wrong side of the law, Damnation.' The eyes are still beautiful and she's still gorgeous but something's changed – it must be the eyes of the beholder. 'After we arrived in Paris you kept Lifar informed of our movements – I discovered that from your call log. You took me for a ride but somewhere along the line you changed your mind and tried to change trains.'

Damnation gazes at me sadly out of her no-longer-so-sloe eyes, like she knows what's coming.

'I – I fell in love.'

I let it pass. You've got to let a lot of things pass in this game.

'Okay, so while you're still in love tell me this: was it Flax that duffed the dancer?'

After the briefest of pauses, the dame nods. She's in truth-telling mode and it hurts.

'When Simon became a threat, Lifar gave Albert the job of

– eliminating him. I didn't know at the time – I only worked it out afterwards.' She pauses. 'Remember my telling you Albert was an ex-Olympian? Well, it was the truth – he was a gold-medal marksman who didn't mind getting his hands dirty. His father was a politician. Two of the tickets were meant for Albert and me. Lifar bought a third – the child's one – but that was just a red herring: he always intended cancelling it. But your daughter must have guessed it might be significant so ...'

So Imogene hid the ticket in her music box, along with the mini recorder. Beside us the busker survives his ordeal by fire, and the crowd chucks a few coins in his cap.

'So Flax attended the ballet to deal with the dancer that knew too much,' I say. 'But wait on – you and Flax were in the dress circle and it was a loge shot.'

The dame shrugs. 'Albert told me he needed to stretch his legs. It's something old people do.'

'What – shoot people?'

'No, stretch their legs.'

I let it pass, along with the foot traffic.

'And when Flax returned after stretching his legs, did you ask where he'd stretched them?'

Damnation shakes her beautiful head.

'Albert paid my bills. I didn't want to upset him by asking too many questions.'

'Talking of shots, you had your place shot up, didn't you? In order to look like you needed my help. The shooter was in the room when he took the shot when I was there, exiting by the window afterwards. I know because the broken glass was outside the house instead of inside. That was Flax, too, wasn't it?'

'Look, I can explain ...'

'Where is he now?'

Damnation's face indicates sadness.

'He had a stroke when he heard what happened. He left everything he had to some political group in memory of his father.'

It's peak hour and the sky's a glowering masterpiece over the heads of people scurrying to work in order to earn enough money to return to work tomorrow. You might be able to make sense of it, I can't. I start in the direction of Circular Quay but Damnation follows me.

'Please, I only knew what I needed to know! There was a lot they didn't tell me. The helicopters at the hospital, for instance – one of which Jaqui's friend Martin commandeered for us to escape in. I didn't know about them or anything else, really. I was in my own little compartment, like you and me on the train …'

The busker's doused his flame and it's like the fire's gone out in me, too. I watch the crowd disperse. There's something familiar about the busker. But he couldn't be the same person. That was Paris and this is Sydney and besides, Proteus is dead. I turn back to Damnation.

'You even told them I'd worked out the beggar was with them. That's why you dropped your phone in the toilet, so I couldn't see who you'd called. But after you dumped your phone you couldn't call anyone any more. And then there was the major clue that you were on their side – when the Ferret killed the concierge, he left you alive.'

'But it's not what you think,' she cries. 'Not in the end anyway. Oh, Rainbow, I fell for you and I've still fallen for you. Which is why I helped you, don't you see? I switched. I worked out what GREEN meant, didn't I? And I was able to kill Gregorovich because Albert had taught me how to handle guns. Everything came out all right in the end, didn't it?'

I'm back to the old non-identity, together with the old clobber – pink jacket, yellow-spotted shirt and whitesides – and somehow it feels right. I'm my old non-self again and I'm thinking again. I doff the new fedora.

'See you round, Damnation,' I say.

She's standing stock-still as the busker departs and I continue on to the wharf, the lemmings scampering around me.

'But you won't, will you?' I hear her reply, faintly.Or maybe she didn't say anything at all. Perhaps it's no more than the murmur of too many soles clattering on the footpath. I catch a glimpse of her reflection in a shop window as I make my way up Pitt Street, an island of loneliness in a sea of commuters.

Chapter 46

BULLETS AT THE BALLET

When he telephones – I don't ask how he got my number – I pass what Damnation said on to Ace Mollema. Ace says he knew about Flax, which confirms my suspicion that he knew a great deal all along. I bring up the matter of Harold and Maud.

'Look, Rainbow, mate ...' he begins.

'Don't mate me, mate. I was set up by Damnation and the body farmers. But it was a set-up by you as well, wasn't it? So you could use your old mate Rainbow – the kid that once saved your life – to do your dirty work and break up a body-parts ring at the minor risk of killing my daughter.'

'Come on, Rainbow, you're too suspicious. All right, so I might have organised a couple of late cancellations so you and your lady friend could make that flight to France. But I promise that the man in black, the beggar and the gunman on the train were on the other side. We only added the old couple to the mix for your protection. But I'm not hearing any thanks for that.' Mollema simulates being hard done by. 'For God's sake, Rainbow, Harold and Maud saved your life in the Louvre. I could have abandoned you with no protection at all. I –'

I interrupt his self-justification.

'In which case, you wouldn't have got your result. You needed me alive, Mollema. And while you were safely back here, my kid was at the pointy end of a killer op. Harold and Maud were instructed to protect me, and also to get me to Jaqui's place so I could make contact with that madman, Le Patron. For all I know, you could have organised my daughter's abduction as well.'

'Jesus, mate, credit me with a little –'

But I'm not crediting Mollema with anything, other than a lot of guile and total bastardry. If I was still Halliwell, with recourse to an add-up book, he'd occupy nothing but the debit column. I might be paranoid but I've got a lot to be paranoid about. It's called survival.

'Feel free to contact me if you need anything,' I hear him say.

I click him off and chuck the dead-man's mobile in the Harbour.

Last time I was at the Opera House they put on a tragedy. But tonight's different. For a start the Bullets at the Ballet case is done and dusted. And for a finish I'm here with Imogene. She's wearing a neat little pale-green number with her hair pulled back, making her look far too grown-up in my opinion. But I don't care how she looks, I'm just happy she's alive.

'I'll have a champagne, please, Daddy,' she says, looking around at the other ballet goers. 'And make it Moët' – she says it right: moh-ette – 'I believe it's the most expensive drink they have.'

I do like she says even though I shouldn't, and when she takes the glass she doesn't slop it, which is more than I don't do with my beer.

'I guess this is the appropriate time to ask you the question, Immo. Why did you hide the ticket?'

She smiles over her expensive champagne.

'You taught me to beware of Greeks bearing gifts, Daddy, and all by myself I decided that might extend to other nationalities as well. I figured the ballet ticket might be important and I decided I was right when Lifar became very angry when he couldn't find it.'

'And the mini recorder?'

'It had one word on it that would help identify Lifar, regional German for "little girl". How was I to know you'd think he was saying something else?'

'How old are you, Immo?'

'Old enough not to take nonsense from you any more, Daddy, even if you did save my life.' She sips her champagne and when she hands back the glass it's empty. 'Now, let's go in, shall we?'

I haven't had time to read the programme but it doesn't matter with ballet. All I need to know is that, as we listen to the band do its knees-up, I feel for the first time in a long while that it's nice to be alive. And as the lights go down and the darkness closes around us I also get the feeling that Imogene's safe — at least for the duration of the performance.

But that's before the gun goes off.

It's a whipcrack of a sound. I'm thinking Colt .45 — one of the long-barrelled ones — or maybe a Smith & Wesson .38. At the second *crack!* I make a dive for Imogene. It's an awkward move due to the crook leg and the seats, so I'm a little less balanced than I'd like to be. The music rises to a crescendo as I drag Immo down between the seats while the ushers make a beeline in our direction. Imogene takes a round-arm swipe at me — accidental or otherwise, and I suspect it's otherwise — as she struggles to her feet.

'What on earth are you doing?' she demands.

'A gun went off! Don't say you didn't hear it?'

Imogene shakes her head.

'Daddy, a gun was supposed to go off. The ballet's Mayerling and in Mayerling guns go off in every act. The ballet's about this aristocrat who
—'

But the ushers are almost on us so I grab the kid and shove her in the direction of the exit.

'Fill me in on the details later, Immo. Because right now we've got to make ourselves scarcer than a legitimate body part.'

The kid goes quiet and I cover my scant regrowth with the new fedora as we leave. In a nearby concert hall someone's churning out Tchaikovsky's *B-Flat Piano Concerto*, and as I hobble past I hear them working themselves up to the fast bit, where the music goes into overdrive. And if you can't hear the menace behind the music, you haven't been listening.

MISTER RAINBOW

C.S. Boag

in the Case of the Cock Robin Killer

Who killed Cock Robin?
'I,' said the sparrow,
'With my little bow and arrow,
'I killed Cock Robin.'

– Traditional nursery rhyme

For my brother John

Chapter 1

BLOOD ON THE LABORATORY FLOOR

Queen's boat bumps alongside the old tub I call home – the *Wooden No,* as in, *What's she called? Wooden No* – disturbing the early morning calm along with my equipoise. He's called Queen because his real name is Freddie and the outboard powering his clapped-out boat's a Mercury. 'Here's your *petit dejeuner*, sweetie!' he sings. Something flops at my feet. *'Buon appetito!'*

He's off before I can thank him which is fine because I don't intend to. I finish my exercise routine, do the ballet warm-ups, prime the pump that keeps the *Wooden No* afloat, rinse my armpits with bilge water, clean the flounder and weigh myself on the scales – the ones from Vinnies, not the piscatorial kind. Then I strap on the shoulder holster while the fish sizzles on the Port-A-Stove, preparatory to keeping my appointment.

A dame in her distracted fifties directs me to the basement of the townhouse in Alexandria. The joint's a mess and the broad behind the professor is blonde, beautiful and in a state of disarray almost as bad as the laboratory. She adjusts her lab coat as she bends over a cage containing a two-metre diamond python while the professor – a grey-haired joker with blood on his collar – produces a big smile and an even bigger handshake. I accept the smile but not the handshake.

'I'm Professor Ransom and I called you in because the police – or at least the representative provided – seemed much more interested in my assistant than the break-in.'

The prof's assistant is what's known in the trade as a buxom wench

– the body in the coat's like air trying to escape from a balloon – and she straightens as much as a dame like her is ever going to straighten, smoothing the coat while her lips form the shape of a Petrie dish.

'I'm Grace Metalious,' she says, holding out a hand like a wish-fulfilling prophecy. I accept both the hand *and* the wish.

'As Professor Ransom's assistant,' she goes on, 'I attend to all his needs – experimentally speaking. I see you've noticed the door off its hinges …'

Yeah, I noticed the door off its hinges. I also noticed a lot else besides: the overturned work bench, the smashed rodents' cages, the overfed snake, the scattered remains of the lab mice, and the blood. Especially the blood.

'Must have been quite a party,' I say.

Ransom shakes his head. 'It was no party. My lab adjoins the marital home and on Thursday night I heard what sounded like a break-in so I hurried down to investigate.'

'The marital home being that of you and Miss Petrie Dish here?'

Ransom does a nice impression of a laugh. 'Oh, no, no, no and no again! I'm a happily married man while Grace here's my laboratory assistant.' I find myself wondering if Grace here could ever be nothing but anything. 'Having said that, I must add that she's very good at what she does.'

'Which is?'

He's a grown man but he still colours.

'I'm a behavioural scientist researching high-rise home units: why people buy them, what people like in them – basically what sells. Like me, Ms Metalious is a Pavlovian – I'm sorry, I should explain: Ivan Pavlov was a scientist who worked out why dogs dribble –'

I've strung him along enough. 'How much time elapsed between the lab being broken into and you investigating?'

'Well, I'm fit for my age.' He glances at the dame, presumably for confirmation. 'So it couldn't have been more than a minute or two.'

'Where was your wife at the time?'

'Asleep, I presume.'

'Don't you know?'

'We sleep separately. That is, in separate beds, in separate rooms, on separate floors. There was no noise from Mavis so I presume she was asleep.'

I leave his words dangling like a body on a roadside gallows in a high wind before doing the follow-through.

'And when you arrived you found all this damage?'

He nods. 'It was absolute chaos.'

'Who has keys to the laboratory?'

The grey eyebrows rise; he's a scientist; he's worked it out; why can't a detective?

'Why ask about keys?' He indicates the door. 'After all, the place was quite clearly broken into.' He shrugs. 'I'm sorry, the answer to your question is: Grace and I.'

'What did she do?'

'Who – Mavis?'

'I'm sorry, did I say she? I meant they – the vandals.'

'Oh.' The scientist frowns. 'Well, they released our experimental rats and Betty – that's the Morelia spilota spilota, the diamond python we keep in order to dispose of used rodents – ate them. It's pointless vandalism.'

'What – feeding rats to a snake?'

'No,' the Professor replies. 'What the vandals did. We had almost completed our research when it happened. Our records were stolen, which means we'll have to start again from scratch.'

That must be the scratch that resulted in the blood on his collar.

'Which, of course, will take time,' I say. 'Who do you think did it?'

'You tell me. After all, that's why I called you in.'

'Hazard a guess.'

He shrugs. 'Kids maybe; or someone who hated either me or the developer who employs me.'

'Who knew about your research?'

'Just Grace, Mavis, me and the developer.'

'Who's the developer?'

'Ivan von Franck.'

All I know about von Franck is what I read in the papers. But if what I read is only half right, it narrows the suspect list to just about everyone else in Sydney.

Chapter 2

NINE TIMES OUT OF TEN
IT'S THE WIFE

I switch tack or tack switches, however you want to play it.

'Tell me about the marital home.'

The boffin waves a white-clad arm past the broken-down door. 'It's where I live with my wife.' I nod; the wife would be the dame who directed me to the lab while wringing her hands like she was doing her husband's dirty washing. 'We've had thirty good years together and – thanks to this work and the fame and fortune it will bring – we can look forward to a good thirty more.'

'That's nice.' I glance from the assistant to the snake to the blood. 'But it must be tough on the rats.'

He frowns while the assistant goes on straightening the empty cages.

'It's for the greater good.'

'What – flogging expensive apartments to punters that can't afford them?'

'I'm a scientist, with a scientist's values. What people do with my findings isn't my concern – my interest lies solely in the research. Now if you can't help me –'

'Oh, I can help you all right. It's just a matter of whether you're going to fully appreciate my help or not.'

'What do you mean by that?'

'I mean I've worked out what happened. But before telling you my findings, I'd appreciate payment up front.'

The scientist has brought cash like I instructed him to and, while he's extracting it from his laboratory coat, I spot something on the floor of the snake cage, step across, open the door, pick up what I saw, pat the overfed serpent on the head, and close the door again.

'I'm something of a student of human behaviour myself,' I say, 'only I don't need birds to arrive at my findings.'

'But we don't use birds.'

'What's this then?'

I hold up the red feather I found in the cage and the scientist puts on a set of half-moon specs before whipping them off again because they make him look older than he probably wants to in front of his assistant.

'Why, that's a feather from the sternum of a male of the species Erithacus rubecula — otherwise known as a robin redbreast.' He frowns. 'It's a native of Europe although there are some in Sydney, having been introduced by the early settlers. Where did you find it?'

'In the cage with the anaconda.'

'But this is a scientifically controlled environment.' His frown clears. 'But, of course — the bird flew in after the door was knocked down, only to be eaten along with the rats. What are you implying?'

'Something different from what I was about to suggest — but only marginally. You see, at first I thought — as I was no doubt meant to think — that the break-in was committed by someone who didn't have a key.' The professor and his assistant exchange glances. 'Which would rule out both you and Grace here because you both have keys. Which means I was supposed to think that the break-in was done by someone else, someone who released the rats and the snake, leading to the wrecking of the lab, and afterwards departed with your findings — all before you got down here a minute or so after you heard the break-in. Which would have been extremely smart of the intruders.'

The scientist looks uncertain. 'Yes, it would, wouldn't it.'

'Not only smart but also impossible,' I continue. 'You see, Professor, you were too quick off the mark. Unless, of course, the destruction occurred before the door was broken down, having been carried out by someone who had a key.'

'Wh — what do you mean?'

'I mean I believe I was supposed to think that your wife — after learning of your affair with Grace here — broke into the laboratory and —'

'What affair!' the professor shouts. 'This is preposterous! Really, I'm not paying you to —'

'— discover the truth? But I thought that's just what you were paying me for — you being a scientist.' I indicate Grace. 'She's beautiful and that stuff on your coat isn't blood, is it?'

Absent-mindedly, the professor rubs at his collar.

'It's not what you think. I don't employ Ms Metalious for her beauty. She's a highly intelligent woman with a string of letters after her name as long as –'

'... as long as the snake I'm supposed to believe your wife let loose after breaking down the door and destroying your work and taking your records in a fit of pique over your affair?'

'It would be the end of our marriage if she did,' the professor says.

'Yeah, it would, wouldn't it? Under normal circumstances – given this little triangle is in any way normal – you wouldn't have left your wife in a fit. Because like most husbands in your situation, you think you can have your cake and eat it – keep both nooky and cookie. But Grace here didn't agree, so – hoping to prolong her employment as well as the relationship – she took matters into her own hands, let herself in with her key, wrecked the joint, and afterwards broke down the door to make it appear that ...' I leave it there; the prof's a bright boy; he can work it out. 'Grace is certainly big and strong enough to bust down a door, whereas your wife ...'

He's ashen-faced. I like them ashen-faced – it means I might have put out the fire.

'Grace here was relying on that old chestnut: Nine times out of ten it's the wife.' I hand the boffin back the dough-ray-me. 'Under the circumstances I can understand if you want to let the matter drop and under the same circumstances you can have your money back.'

I don't have to open the door because there's no door left to open. So I just tuck the feather in the holster next to the gat, straighten my chapeau, give the anaconda a parting nod and make myself scarce.

Chapter 3

I WANT SOME RED ROSES ...

I put his height at close to the two-metre mark and he's in our way like he belongs there – a mountain of muscle in a dirty singlet, pink shorts and mismatched thongs. When you're that big you don't have to worry about fashion. Once, Aunt Rube would have taken him with her eyes shut. But once, too, this was public land covered with gum trees instead of skyscrapers and you could see where you were going without using a periscope.

After I arrive at Rube's – the aunt-cum-detective who took me in and taught me how to be a private eye – she unhitches herself from her kidney machine and we go for a walk through the Botanical Gardens.

'They want to develop all this,' she says. 'Which means there'll be even more ghastly hotels and visitors' centres and no doubt yet another casino.' We cross College Street and enter Hyde Park, bearing westwards. 'They call it progress,' she continues after a while. 'The Hotel Australia once stood there with its glorious staircase and stained-glass windows, and men with manners in the vestibule instead of the thugs you see today. Buildings had awnings to protect you from the elements and gentlemen doffed their hats when they met you. Just there was the Hotel Metropole, catering for the sons of graziers in town for the Show.'

'So what happened, Rube?'

'Greed and corruption happened, Rainbow. I'm not saying things were better, they were just – different. It was easier being a detective back then because there was a well-defined line between good and evil. But that line started to go fuzzy until now there's no line at all. It's the same with development – people seem to build anything they want wherever they want.' Aunt Rube's sigh advances all the way up from her corn-cob toes.

I shrug. 'Where's this taking us, Rube?'

'The walk or the talk?'

'The talk.'

'Well, I've taken on a case, see, and …'

Rube used to be the scourge of every bent cop in Sydney, plus anyone else unlucky enough to cross her path. She was the best at tracking down errant husbands, exposing blackmailers, locating stray kids – solving anything from petty theft to murder. But detecting is a hard game and Rube's no longer young. And since the kidney problem resulting from getting thumped in the Bullets at the Ballet caper, she's had to keep herself pretty well caseless.

'I thought you'd hung up your gat.'

'It's just a little job for Madam Blavatsky.'

When Dad dumped me after Mum topped herself – taking my sister with her – Aunt Rube taught me the basics of detection: induction, deduction, abduction, gunmanship and dance. Yeah, that's right, ballet – to get me out of those tough places private eyes can find themselves in – and my dance teacher was Sydney's belladonna of dance, a refugee from the eastern Caucasus, a mammoth dame who gave lessons on the top floor of a terrace in East Sydney, just around the corner from Aunt Rube's hovel.

'I didn't know Madam B was in the building game.'

'She's not,' Aunt Rube replies. 'Nor does she want to be. But someone's trying to force her to sell her place in order to complete a zillion-dollar development block, only Madam B won't budge. Which puts her in the shooting gallery. Let's say there have been threats.'

'What kind of threats?'

'The usual. It'll escalate into pillage, arson and murder, but at the moment it's still in the gentle preliminary stages – people following her, threatening phone calls, anonymous messages, the odd visitor.'

'So Madam B asked you to –'

'Madam Blavatsky didn't ask me to do anything. I just happened to be playing piano for one of her dance classes when a rock came hurtling through the window. The window was closed at the time.'

'Why were you playing piano?'

'Because Madam Blavatsky asked me to. Which reminds me – I can't play tonight. Could you fill in for me?'

A song's stuck in my head: *I want some red roses for a blue lady/Need them for the sweetest girl in town.* The words don't fit the situation but it doesn't stop the music. In the armpit-sized nursery called *The Greenhouse Defect* the stench of crocuses mingles with the scent of the recycled animal remains they use for fertiliser.

'Hi, Bone,' I say to the dame lurking behind the aspidistra.

Bonnie – that's her real name, the distaff side of Bonnie and Benito, sometimes known as Bonnie and Clyde but to me just plain Blood and Bone – smiles.

'Hi, Rainbow. I take it you want some roses. You got woman trouble again?'

I like Bone. She's got a cross-painted mouth and her dress sense is right up the spout, but she calls a watering can a watering can and doesn't take nonsense from nobody, and that includes me – only cash.

'You could say that.'

'I just did.'

The Greenhouse Defect is an oasis in the desert, a verdant refuge among too many coffee houses atop Darlinghurt Hill. They used to hang ten-year-olds in Darlinghurt just for pinching handkerchiefs. Now spaced-out art students lug bedraggled canvases, prostitutes try to look alluring, and mad buggers with knives roam the streets looking for an excuse to rob people. I blame the coffee.

'I'm after a couple of dozen long-stemmed reds, thanks, Bone – with the thorns off.'

'It's that bad, eh?'

I discovered Bone when things started going wrong with Salina, the mother of my fifteen- – or is it seventeen-? – year-old daughter Imogene. In other words, right from the opening salvo of our relationship. I bought a lot of flowers and as a result got closer to Bone than an assassin to the heart of darkness.

'It's worse,' I reply as she gets to work with the paring knife. 'You see, I took this dame to France and –'

'That'd do it.'

'It was work, Bone.'

'That'd do it even more.'

There's a conspiracy among women and – nice as she is – Bone's part of it. Dames latch onto an inconsequential fact and, like a dog attached to a postman, there's no shaking them. All I did was take a beautiful dame called Hell and Damnation – sorry, that should read Hélène Dalmation – to France to help rescue my daughter.

'You missed a couple of thorns, Bone.'

'Why don't you just forget them?' she says, wrapping the roses in cellophane the colour of blood. 'You know, after too long in this game I've come to the conclusion that some men are cut out for relationships and some aren't. And you're one of the ones that aren't.' She hands me the flowers with a soiled hand and an extra big question mark. 'Forty bucks for you, Rainbow.'

'How much for anyone else?'

'Twenty-five.'

'Put it on the tab, would you?' She starts to take back the flowers; I flick her a fifty. 'Just kidding. You can keep the change.'

Chapter 4

... FOR A BLUE LADY

Darlinghurt used to be my playground. Rube lives there and I attended the primary school there, until she hauled me out because of the bullying. It doesn't pay to be a kid with a name like Rainbow in a place like this. Madam Blavatsky's dance studio is in East Sinny, a suburb that lies buttock-by-*gluteus maximus* with Darlinghurt, but it's half an hour until I play piano. My friend Annie does volunteer work in the Men's Refuge in Sanctuary Lane and it's dinnertime. I need to pay her a visit.

You're asking for trouble carrying flowers in Darlinghurt. Hannah is astride the wall outside the old Christian Science Church on Liverpool Street and chucks me a smile overcut with cocaine, swinging a bare tootsie at the end of a leg that doesn't seem to have any top to it.

'Who's the lucky girl, Rainbow?' she purrs.

I shrug. 'The way I see it, having me in the frame makes her unlucky.'

'I wouldn't mind putting my shoes under your bed.'

'You haven't got any shoes.'

'Doesn't stop me not minding.'

The Refuge reeks of booze, sweat and long-dead marsupials, a cross between a ferret house and a collective of camels. A couple of hundred deadbeats slouch at plastic-coated trestle tables while volunteers dish out the food. One of the volunteers is Annie, the pretty little number who once upon a time was my squeeze.

'You got a moment, Annie?' I ask, the flowers behind my back.

She's wearing a pink apron over khaki coveralls and the expression she puts on is somewhere between Who are you? and Go to buggery. She pushes past me bearing a tray of sausages and I follow, gripping the flowers. A dero lunges for the food, but Annie holds the tray over her head and frowns even more than she was already.

'Are you drunk, Tony?'

'Me?' The derelict grins around the room before returning his mud-stained eyes to Annie. ''Course not.'

'Because if you are I'm not serving you – you know that, don't you?'

It's like she's talking to a baby – a baby with devil-clawed fingers, cadaverous cheeks and random rows of stumps for teeth.

'Yeah, Anno Domini,' he answers meekly. 'I know that.'

'Then you'll also know to take your hand off my tray.'

The drifters are squid adrift in a sea of helplessness, the dregs of the heady concoction that goes to make up Sydney society, the muck that everyone pretends isn't at the bottom of the barrel.

'I'm sorry, Annie.'

'It's better not to do bad things than have to say you're sorry.'

She hasn't changed her tone from when she was speaking to the dero, or even her words.

'But what did I do?'

'Everything you've ever done is what you do, Rainbow. You come into my life, disappear out of it, then turn up again expecting everything to be normal. Well, you're right, everything is normal. Because normal's when you're more interested in your cases than in the people close to you, and I've had enough.'

I wave the flowers around Hell's waiting room; life-wrecked faces stare back like fledgling birds wondering where their next worm's coming from.

'But this is what you do and I've never complained about it.'

'Why do you think I do this, Rainbow? Have you ever thought about that?'

'What's there to think?'

It's the wrong answer in the wrong place at the wrong time. Annie turns her back again and this time it's a rock wall. The last I see of the rock wall is it crashing through a pair of faux-bar doors into a steam-filled kitchen full of ghostly and barely discernible figures, among whom Annie also becomes ghostly and barely discernible herself.

The steam makes the flowers wilt and my eyes mud.

As darkness creeps over the mean streets the world changes and it's not for the better. Druggies stare out of ice-crazed eyes, night girls scream and drunks urinate in doorways, while the over-rich cruise by in their black sedans taking what's in it for them. Next to a green-baize door in a terrace islanded in a lot of vacant land surrounded by chainwire looms a large sign reading *BLUEBEARD DEVELOPMENTS*.

Bluebeard was a serial wife killer which makes the name especially disturbing. There's a disturbance on the stairs, too, as I let myself into Madam Blavatsky's. I toss the flowers, go down on one knee and drag out the gat – the blow-back, single-action Beretta – the only kind of squeeze I've got these days. A 40-watt bulb lights up a lump on the stairs. I can't hear any feet shuffling on the floorboards above, there's just the figure under the blanket with nothing to show for itself but a pair of Nikes. I nudge the lump with a whiteside.

'I'll pay …' it mumbles.

Yeah, you'll pay all right, I tell myself, if you haven't already. But I don't say anything out loud as I gather what's left of the flowers, step over the figure and hurtle up the stairs, the gat switched to SHOOT NOW AND ASK QUESTIONS LATER. The ground floor's derelict; the second's where Madam Blavatsky lives; and the top floor's the studio where she teaches dance. I hear her voice, shelve the gat, push open the door with the mitt that's not holding the flowers, and go in.

The wide, bare dance floor's still ringed by two wooden barres with an old, cracked washbasin in one corner. There's the old wraparound mirror and a bunch of leotard-clad kids that once included me sitting cross-legged on the floorboards. The baby grand's a Steinway and Madam Blavatsky's perched on a chaise longue.

'I escaped from a terrorist regime,' she's saying, 'so I know that life's no more than a temporary respite from death. I want you to carry that thought with you when you dance.'

Madam B's the heavy metal of ballet. When these kids go to bed tonight, all bar the most insensitive are going to have nightmares. The parents won't be happy but Madam B doesn't care what people think.

'This is Mr Brown, girls and boys. He's an ex-student and tonight he's going to be playing piano.' She frowns. 'And while it's nice of you to bring flowers, Mr Brown, they look much like most of these kids dance – terrible.' She sighs and takes the roses across to the basin. 'But I'll put what's left of them in a vase.'

What's the difference, the Steinway asks, between a buffalo and a bison? Answer: You don't wash your hands in a buffalo ... I like Steinways – they speak to you. And what this one's saying – apart from the bad joke – is: People might be temporary but some are more temporary than others. It's a thought that accompanies the riffle-raffle of kids getting ready to dance to the music of Strauss.

'All right, children,' says Madam Blavatsky, placing the vase with the roses in it on the piano, 'it's dance time. Raeleen, take off those silly earrings – this isn't a fashion show. Harold, extend your fingers. Position, position, position!'

I crack my knuckles over the keys as Madam B raises her arms. It's hard to tell if she's about to belt the kids over the head or conduct them.

Just then the door bursts open. Immediately, I go into a crouch and haul out the gat. But it's just the figure who was curled up on the stairs – I can tell by the shoes – checking to see what all the fuss is about. And after he takes it all in, he shakes his head and wanders off again. But not before I see the look on Madam B's face – the kind of look a kid might get when the Gestapo come for her father.

Chapter 5

THE PIANO PLAYER

I go back to playing the piano and the kids finish their *arabesques*, *battements* and *pliés*. Some are good and some are terrible and nothing will ever change that, no matter what Madam B does. After the kids pack up and leave, Madam B collapses onto the *chaise longue* like a stabbed tyre, like everything's suddenly got too much for her.

'Are you going to tell me what this is all about, Madam B?' I mean, you're talking death to the kids; then there was your overreaction to the figure at the door –'

'You mean our overreaction.'

'I'm talking about your problem, Madam B, not mine.'

She shrugs. 'And it's just that, Rainbow – my problem.'

'I might be able to help.'

'I don't need your help.'

It's the attitude of someone who's made her own way in the new world after making her way out of an old one that consisted largely of blood, hate, organised suspicion and sanctified crime. I indicate the empty piano.

'Where is she?'

'Who?'

'Your piano player.'

'She broke her arm.'

'She wouldn't have done that playing Chopin.'

But I'm not getting anything out of Madam B so I take a gander at her address book under the pretext of helping with the clean-up. Under Piano Player I find a name – Gertrude Match. It comes complete with the honorific Miss and an address that's almost as bad as the name. I realise Madam B's behind me – she moves quiet for a big dame.

'What are you up to?'

'Just helping with the clean-up, Madam B.' I flick the address book shut and get myself to the door where the remaining rose petals look like blood. 'Be seeing you.'

She chucks me one of her looks, the one with a lot of suspicion in it. 'Not if I see you first, Rainbow.'

The figure's no longer on the stairs but as I move along the street I'm conscious of a shadow. All right, East Sinny's all shadows but this one's got substance to it – probably a prohibited one. I turn my back – one day I'll deal with Pandora but not yet – and on the turn I see the sign.

Your eyes play tricks on you around here. People think they see daemons with clawed fingers and monsters with humps on their backs and wild-eyed devils wielding pitchforks when all it is is other people just like you. I got it wrong. The name of the developer's not BLUEBEARD but BLUEBIRD.

It puts a whole new construction on things.

Piano players aren't the sharpest notes on the keyboard so it doesn't surprise me to find Gertrude Match occupying a hovel in Miller's Point – that's *Miller's* with an apostrophe, whatever the name changers say – a suburb that once harboured the Black Plague but has graduated to being a refuge for indigents and indi-ladies.

The figure behind me ducks behind a wall as I open the rickety gate leading onto a verandah, find what looks like a malignant skin mole with the word PRESS on it and do like it says. After a few seconds, the door opens revealing a dame with multi-coloured eyes, a shapeless frock made of sky-blue calico, and a plaster cast stuck out in front of her like a forklift.

'Miss Match?'

She peers at me through the fly-wire. 'Who's asking?'

I want to say Mister Perfect – in which case we're a perfect match – but instead I palm her a card through a hole in the fly-wire. The card tells anyone who wants to know that I'm a private investigator called Harvey Flite, contactable at harveyflite.etcetera.com.au or by leaving a note at Harry's Bar, allowing seven days for a reply – unless it's an emergency, in which case it'll take longer. And at the end:

No Case Too Heavy for Harvey/Don't Take Fright – Get Flite

'The name's Rainbow.' I give my real name because Miss Match knows Madam B and at some point they're going to compare notes; but the dame's already reading the card so I explain the discrepancy. 'Okay, so the name's different and the contact details are someone else's but the word INVESTIGATOR means what it says and I'm here on behalf of Madam Blavatsky.'

The face on the other side of the fly-wire looks only marginally gayer.

'Why would Madam B need a detective and what would a detective want with me? All I do is play the piano.'

I indicate the forklift. 'Correction: used to play the piano.'

When the dame shrugs, her prong rears up like it's operated by hydraulics.

'I was hit by a bus.'

'Yeah, and I just got hit by a suspicion.'

'Which is … ?'

'That if you were hit by a bus, Mismatch, you'd be covered with bruises and contusions, and you'd have at least one broken leg and a couple of broken ribs to go with the leg. Yet there's no sign of any damage other than your arm. Which means you've not only got a selective injury – you're also selective with the truth as well.'

'Wow – you *must* be a detective.'

'And you must be lying. Are you going to let me in, or do I make like Santa and come down the chimney?'

It gets me the shadow of a smile. It's a start.

'Why should I let you in?'

'Because I can help.'

'I don't need help.'

'That's not how it looks from the outside.'

'But there's not enough room in here to swing a cat.'

'That's okay, because I'm not here to swing cats.'

Chapter 6

A DISTURBANCE IN THE STREET

Due to the presence of a spinet, a stand containing a music book and a marker pen, and half a cubic inch of air between us, it's standing room only in Mismatch's house, so we stand. But after a while she loosens up enough to park herself on the piano stool while I make my own arrangements – sitting on a chair that would benefit by being chopped up for firewood.

'Sorry if I interrupted your rendition of Rachmaninoff's Second,' I say.

'You recognised the tune!'

I indicate the stand. 'No, I read the name on the music.'

'Oh.' She looks disappointed; she also looks like she's changed her mind. 'I'm afraid I don't have anything to drink …'

I drag out my flask. 'That's all right: I travel armed. All we need is drinking bowls.'

She goes into the kitchen and returns with a couple of jam jars. 'Very well, I'm ready for the interrogation, Mr Whoever-you-are. What do you want to know?'

'How you broke your arm,' I say, pouring her a double.

'I fell.' She glances at me, then down at her jar, before changing her story. 'All right, it happened in East Sydney; people get their arms broken in East Sydney.'

'No one's ever broken mine.'

'That's because you're male and you're lucky.'

'Like I said, Mismatch, yours is a selective injury. So what I'm guessing is that someone broke your arm and at the same time issued you with a warning: Don't go to the cops or anyone like the cops – meaning people like me. Which is why you look nervous and also why you're not telling me the truth. Make sure Madam Blavatsky knows about it, they would have added. But the merest whisper to anyone else and it's your Last Waltz.' I apply the heat. 'Someone followed me.'

The dame's face turns whiter than her plaster cast. 'Who?'

'If I knew that, I wouldn't be here.' I lean forward – that way she can see the gat. 'The jokers that broke your arm were standover merchants – push-men for someone with a lot of pull in this city. There's a sign outside Madam Blavatsky's that says DEVELOPMENT and it's not hard to see that her joint's in the middle of a development site. By itself, Madam B's place is worth no more than a slug in a week-old corpse – but as part of a building site it's worth a mint.'

'But why break my arm over it? It's not my property.'

'You came out of Madam B's. They might have thought you were her.'

'Come on, Mr Flite, she's twice my size.'

I shrug. 'Like the Bard said, The medium is the message. And your arm was the medium.'

'So it was a warning to Madam B ...' Mismatch's multi-coloured eyes contemplate my ordinary ones over the mug that tells me she's out of her depth. 'What do you want to know?'

'I want you to tell me who did it.'

'The little one.'

'Could you be more specific?'

'Only if you give me another smile-maker.'

I do like she says and after another swill or two she fills me in on the blind side of her ten-fingered concerto. She was playing piano for Madam Blavatsky when she was interrupted by a disturbance in the street.

'Come on, Mismatch, we're talking East Sinny. There's always a disturbance in the street. It would be disturbing if there wasn't a disturbance.'

The dame holds out her mug for another refill. 'Except that it wasn't prostitutes screaming or addicts howling at the moon.'

I top her up.

'What was it then?'

'The sound of music.'

'What kind of music?'

'A doof-doof kind of music, played fortemente – that means loudly.'

'So you went to investigate this loud music ...'

'I'm sorry, Mr Flite, but unlike you I'm not an investigator. The children were up to that bit in the ballet Les Sylphides where they dance off to church to the strains of Chopin. It's nice, gentle stuff, but because of the noise it was impossible to continue so Madam B called it a night and I left.'

'Just you?'

'We finished early and the children had to wait for their parents, so, yes, I left alone.'

'Even though we're talking East Sinny?'

The dame laughs. 'Oh, Mr Whatever-your-name-is, you're such an innocent! I was married to a brute which is why I live in a hovel. Compared to my ex, the streets of East Sydney are child's play. You can always escape from a mugging but ... Anyway, I left on my own, even though it was East Sydney.'

'Where did they get you?'

'In the arm.'

'I mean where were you – streetwise?'

Chapter 7

RHAPSODY IN BLUE

The dame suddenly sobers – but that could be the wrong word. 'Sorry, it was a foggy night so I couldn't see my hands in front of me. If I had, it would have been the last time for a while, I suppose – I mean, think … Anyway I was almost at the noise when I realised it was a recording. I thought it was a student prank. It was quite an elaborate setup, with witches' hats, plastic tape stretched between them and speakers the size of wire doors.'

'All this just to mug you?' I ask.

'I didn't – still don't – know what they were up to. But didn't you say they were after Madam Blavatsky?'

'Make that might have been. Describe them for me.'

As she talks I'm only half-listening because I'm imagining a surreal situation with the dame bright-eyed and innocent in the middle of something she couldn't possibly understand. And I'm also wondering how – with her arm like that – she manages to cook, eat, sew, clean house, undress herself and take a shower. Such thoughts are part and parcel of how a detective's mind works but right now they interfere with my hearing.

'What did you say?'

'As I said, there were two of them, a tall, skinny one and a short, fat one and they stepped out from behind the speakers and … It was dark and there was no-one else around. It was like the the locals knew what was happening. The small one wanted to know where St Vincent's Hospital was. When I asked why, he said someone's arm was broken and when I asked whose, he said mine …'

'How did you react?'

'I learnt not to scream when I was married.'

179

'How did they do it?'

'The big one stood behind me and held my arm out and the little one had a cricket bat ...'

'Did you see their faces?'

She stands, raises the seat, scrabbles out the drink that she said she didn't have, lowers the seat, passes the bottle to me and shakes her head. I knock the top off the bottle.

'In East Sydney, there are no street lamps because people use them for target practice. As well as that, as I said, it was a foggy night and ...' She takes a mouthful of the new malt. 'Also they were wearing masks.'

'What was their height?'

'Breaker Morant was small while the other one was tall.'

'Describe their voices.'

'The little one didn't speak.'

'And the other one?'

'His voice was unnaturally high. But in the end, all I got were the masks, a broken arm and a name.'

'What was the name?'

'Lofty.'

The one behind was tall; it figures; I still ask. 'Which one was Lofty?'

'The little one.'

After the attack, Mismatch returned to Madam Blavatsky's, who got her to hospital and after that ... But after that there's only one thing I need to know.

'How come you were playing piano when I arrived – considering you're wearing finger boards, a fact that would preclude your playing?'

She smiles her crooked smile and her bi-coloured peepers go crossed. 'I was wondering when you'd get to that, Mr Flite.' She spins the stool using her extensor breva digitora and glutea maxima and reels off a few bars using only her feet. 'This spinet doubles as a pianola – it contains a roll of paper which is turned by the foot pedals which acts on a mechanism that activates the hammers. All I have to do is pump the pedals.'

After a while we exchange seats – a difficult manoeuvre given the limited

space but somehow we manage — and, using my hands and not my feet,
I play George Gershwin's *Rhapsody in Blue*, that nice quick-slow, soul-
sinking number with the emotional kick in the middle. Before I go, I
pick up the pen from the music stand and — in letters much like those on
the sign outside Madam Blavatsky's — I write: *Somewhere there's a bluebird of
happiness* and sign it: *Rainbow.*

Chapter 8

OUT IN THE COLD

The cicadas are humming as I climb off the omnibus but clouds are gathering. After I cover the remaining two kilometres to 21 Castanet Close the cicadas have shut up and the first drops of rain are falling. The door's as tight as a miser's wallet, and the footsteps coming down the hall possess all the enthusiasm of a eunuch at an orgy. The door opens and my ex-wife Salina – also known as Aetna because she can erupt without warning – is staring stilettos at me. I make the request before the eruption.

'Could I see Imogene, Sal?'

'She's not here.'

'I just thought me and her might –'

'No, no, no and no again!' She grips the door and her eyes are bullets. 'If you expect me to be grateful because you saved Imogene, you've got another come thinking.' The word placement tells me she's upset, if I didn't know already. 'I only went to France because I was desperate to escape from you. Which means it was your fault Imogene was ever in danger.'

It's not the way I saw it – Salina went off to France with her lover and took Imogene with her. But like the good book says: There's a time to be born and a time to die; a time to get and a time to lose; a time for logic – but this isn't one of them. Sal warned me away from Imogene; this is my first visit to Castanet Close since the Bullets at the Ballet caper.

'We would just have a little patisserie ...'

Salina's knuckles whiten while her attitude darkens. 'I don't want Imogene anywhere near that tart of yours.'

'If you're referring to Annie, she's no longer on the scene, she ...'

'So what are you going to do – go to the police and tell them you're

Imogene's father and want to see your kid? They'd just say: We hear a voice but we can't see anyone. It must be the stress of the job, all these ghosts.' Sal shakes her head and my confidence along with it. 'You haven't got a leg to stand on, Rainbow – or arms, body or even a head because, by your own wish and volition, you're a non-person. "I've got no birth certificate, no licence of any kind," she mimics, "therefore I don't exist …"'

She pauses for breath. Even Salina's got to breathe sometimes.

'But if I call the cops, suddenly you will exist,' she continues. 'You'll have a face and they'll put a name to it and you'll be thrown into jail for not existing. You mightn't be aware of it, Rainbow, but people aren't allowed not to exist. You're breaking the law by not existing and can only get away with it by remaining a non-person. Because once you come in from the cold – which you'd have to if you want to see Imogene – they'll get you. Which means, of course, that you can't.'

'But, Sal … !'

'I'll tell you one time, Rainbow, and one time only: you might be the father but being a father is pretty much an irrelevancy these days, more so in your case. You're as substantial as the phenomenon your dopey mother named you after – nothing but coloured air. But you still need to hide from the cops as well as everyone else. You think not existing is a kind of freedom and maybe it is. But that freedom's got a price, just like everything else.' My ex-wife pauses – as much for breath as for effect. 'And that price is your daughter.'

I check the hallway behind her but all I can come up with is memories.

'You can't see her because as far as you're concerned she's not here – metaphorically, literally and in every other way. You don't exist, so how can your daughter? And if you try to exist – if you try your trickery-dickory surveillance routines or a kidnap – you'll end up seeing nothing but the inside of a jail.'

There's one last thing. There's always a last thing.

'But you still have to pay for her upkeep. Whatever society might say, she's still your child, and children don't come cheap.'

I start to say I never intended not to pay but Salina's already closing the door. On the about-turn I'm greeted by the ice-cold reality of rain.

These days, you can't do much without a phone, besides which I want to see Rory. But by the time I arrive, the rain's hammering on his newly-renovated hovel – a façade of speckle-brick cardboard over common-and-garden fibro, an imitation-tile roof and a front garden fresh out of *Reader's Dingbat's Confused Homes* – complete with fake crazy paving and gaily-painted gnomes. Rory doesn't take off the security chain when he opens the door so I keep my side of the dialogue bright and breezy.

'Hi, Roarer – long time no see!' He stares like I'm a disease; I force a grin. 'I need a phone, Roarer. Hey, it's cold out here – are you offering an old mate shelter from the elephants?'

Rory frowns at the rain.

'What elephants?'

'As in: *Nor rain, wind, thunder, fire, are my daughters: I tax not you, you elephants.* Although it's really elements … it's from King Lear.'

Rory's puzzled, but Rory's always puzzled. 'From what?'

'Shakespeare's King Lear.'

'I thought a Lear was a jet.'

'He was also a king.'

'No,' he says.

'What do you mean, No?'

'I'm not offering shelter to an old mate.'

'Why not?'

'Because we're not old mates.'

'Come on, Roarer – we could hardly be described as young mates! Which means –'

The head above the hand behind the door nods.

'You got it – it means we're no longer mates.'

I know the reason but I still ask.

'Mind saying why?'

Behind Rory I can hear Janet – behind every ex-hitman is his missus. Rory met Janet in The Hood with no Hands caper and it went downhill from there: he got hitched and found God – not necessarily in that order – and Janet sees me as the Devil incarnate which means that Roarer does, too. Which also means that the door doesn't open any further than it has to, while Rory launches into a diatribe.

'You use the word mate like it's some kind of Open Says-To-Me but that only works if we're mates. But we're no longer mates so the key no longer fits because I've changed the locks. I donated a kidney to your Aunt Rube which gives me a direct projectile to Heaven but I'm not resting on my barrels. There's going to be no more killing. And we're no longer mates.'

I shrug like it doesn't matter. 'I still need a phone.'

The voice behind Rory bounces off the new furniture that goes with the new house in much the same way as the rain goes with my mood. 'Dinner's ready, Sweetie-Pie!'

'I'm coming, Sugarplum,' Roarer sings back and when his eyes return to mine they're deader than his erstwhile victims. 'Try the morgue. Tell 'em Rory sent you, ask for Goldilocks and say you want the usual.'

Chapter 9

ANOTHER STIFF RECEPTION

It could double as a public inconvenience – a grey blockhouse crammed between a Toyota showroom and a developers' club in the inner-city suburb of Glebe – and the sign above the door says anything but *MORGUE*. A blonde eyes me out of a goldfish bowl, in a room with a washable floor.

'You Goldilocks?' I ask her.

'No,' she replies, with even more suspicion than she had when I arrived. 'You a delivery?'

I shrug. 'I was told to ask for Goldilocks.'

If you weren't dead when you arrived here you wouldn't have long to wait. The air alone could kill you. This is Death's tradesman's entrance – unpainted bricks, a cracked ceiling and the barely breathable stench of uncut formaldehyde. There's too many doors, the arse-end of an air-conditioner and a room labelled RELATIVES WAITING – forget the apostrophe. A black-haired joker with too many pens in his shirt pocket emerges from behind one of the doors.

'Who are you?' he asks.

'I'm whoever I am – what about you?'

'I'm Goldilocks.'

There's no point asking about the hair and how it fits in with the name; I'm an in-and-out kind of guy and this is an in-and-out kind of place.

'Rory said to see you about a phone.'

The waiting room's an alcove, a short hall and a room with a stiff in it. The stiff's seen better days – one eye's missing, her throat's been slashed and her lipstick's crooked. She's got nothing to say for herself and even less when Goldilocks reappears carrying a sack over his shoulder, which he dumps on the corpse's feet.

'Don't mind the stiff,' he says. 'It hasn't got anything to do with anything. Corpses come and go.'

'Rory said ...' I begin.

'Good old Rory,' Goldilocks replies. 'Did he say how we met? I was standing in York Street contemplating suicide when a bus mounted the footpath. I thought – make that hoped – I was a goner. You see, according to my religion, suicides don't go to heaven. But if I happened to be taken out by a bus I was hopeful I'd be categorised a non-suicide ... In that brief moment a lot of thoughts went through my head – none of which involved survival. But that was before Rory saved me with his crutch.'

'The brand of phone doesn't matter,' I tell him.

'I wasn't grateful.' He settles the sack and makes himself comfortable; like the stiff, Goldilocks looks to be settling in for the long haul. 'You see, suicide – and I'm a suicide counsellor, so I know – requires a great deal of courage. But courage is a quality I don't possess. The bus took out a blind man and a dog, yet I survived. I wasn't happy and when I was finally able to speak that's what I told Rory. Do you know what he replied?'

'I'll pay cash.'

'He said: Think of the paperwork you saved.'

'Any age, any brand, any condition,' I carry on, oblivious to his story. 'As long as it's got a few kilometres left on the clock.'

'It was like Rory knew what I did for a living. If you could call this a living.' He pauses. 'Anyway, when Rory said that, I just about cacked myself. It was a long time since I'd had a good laugh. I'd been scammed of my life savings, my wife had left me and my pet cat had carked it, so me and laughter were strangers. Then this bloke says: Think of the paperwork. Later, after I'd got to know him, I realised what Rory was saying – which was that, while life's serious, you've got to have a bit of fun while you're living it. But that was before I discovered what Rory did for a living!' Goldilocks shakes his head.

'One's plenty,' I tell him.

He looks like he's just noticed me. 'Of course, you want a phone.' He rummages in his sack. 'These are all legit, by the way – cops give them to me and I find them on corpses like Madam Slash here.' He palms me a fistful of Telefunkens. 'Ah, a watch with a compass in it – you might as well have that, too.' He rummages some more. 'And here's the piéce de resistance.' He's brandishing a near-new Samsong I-Spy. 'It's one of those clever phones that does everything but dance the tango and whistle Dixie.'

It's pink and there's a patch on it that might once have been blood.

'This is a death from unnatural causes,' I say. 'Mind telling me how it happened?'

'The subscriber stopped breathing.' Goldilocks shrugs. 'Does it matter?'

'It might.'

Goldilocks checks the tag on the phone. 'I remember: it was a murder that the police weren't interested in, which is how we ended up with the phone − the case, you might say, was dead and buried.' He checks to see if I get the joke; I do but I'm not encouraging him. 'There was a suspect but she was never charged.'

I sense that the phone's trouble. I could say No to it, but for some reason I don't. 'Any other details?'

'It belonged to someone called' − he rechecks the tag − 'Cock Robin Fahey. From memory there was something odd about it all.' Goldilocks fiddles in the pocket with the pens in it. 'Here, take this in case you want the file.' He hands me a card that says SUICIDE COUNSELLOR along with the mobile. 'I switched off the phone to save the battery and also the contract's still got legs on it.'

There are contracts and there are contracts. The phone's cold. So is the joker's hand.

'How much do I owe you?'

Goldilocks shrugs. 'Like I say, everything's got its price, but for a mate of Rory's −'

I cut across him. 'We're no longer mates.'

'All right, for an ex-mate of Rory's everything's got its price. But what I'm giving you happens to be free. I should add that the story I told you is a load of baloney − due to the nature of my work I tend to romanticise. I really met Rory when he delivered one of these.' He gets off the cot he's been sharing with the stiff, hefting the sack after him. 'I'm a trained shrink, by the way, so feel free if you're ever in need of counselling.' He winks. 'Just joking.'

I pocket the phone and decant myself from the morgue before I die laughing.

Chapter 10

THE PHANTOM CALLER

The strand of cotton is still stretched between the hatch and the top of the jamb, and the right-hand corner of my well-thumbed copy of *Crime and Punishment* is exactly where I left it – on the *Wooden No*'s map table in conjunction with the first point of Aries.

I swill out the bilge; clean, fuel and restart the pump – remembering to top up the oil; check the hull for fresh leaks; and wipe the bird dung off the bow. Then I haul out my new pink Telefunken and switch it on.

Immediately there's a machine-gun rat-a-tat-tat that's got me hitting the deck before I realise it's some smart-arse jim-crack's idea of a ringtone. I hit Speak – and get silence. The little window says it's a silent number. It figures.

'Yeah?' I say.

More silence. I got a connection but that's all. Then beyond the throb of the pump and the yelp of seagulls, I hear a noise that sounds like sniffling – which in turn is drowned out by what sounds like the beginning of the end of the world.

'Who's there?' I ask, abandoning my phone rule of not speaking unless spoken to.

But there's still no answer – just the tail-end of the noise that sounds like the end of the world and, closer to home, the sniffling.

I got two choices – ditch the phone or keep it – and I feel some connection to the phone so I keep it. No-one knows I'm the new owner – no-one, that is, except Goldilocks at the Morgue. But I've still got the feeling I'm covered with fleas – the kind of itch I get when I'm being followed, the feeling that someone's out there that shouldn't be out there, when in all likelihood …

Stalkers are a constant companion in this game: disgruntled husbands, thwarted lovers, killers crossed in the course of an investigation, the cops, other private defectives – as well as, in my case, my nemesis, Pandora. So I do what I always do: make a security sweep – checking the superstructure for hidden cameras, the cabin for listening devices and the rest of the boat for sensors of any kind. And after I find nothing, I take a bottle of Glenfiddich onto the *Wooden No*'s roof, pour myself a double and ask myself if it's worth it – to which the whisky replies in the affirmative.

That's when the rat-a-tat-tat begins all over again.

At first I think it's the chopper that happens to be passing overhead. But the rattling continues long after the whirly-bird's gone and I realise it must be the phone. Left to its own devices, the mobile lapses into silence. I watch a launch chug towards the open sea, the sunset turn Sydney Harbour into a bloodbath and pour myself another whisky – only to drop the bottle when the phone rings again. The phone belonged to a corpse. Who'd call a corpse? I click on.

'Who's … this?' a querulous, female voice asks. Dames of a certain age say Who's that? not Who's this? which suggests she's young. There's a nasal quality to the delivery, so she's got a sinus problem. Apart from which, there's no rising inflection, which means she's sure of herself – except for the hesitation.

'I'm someone answering a phone,' I reply. 'Who are you?'

'I asked you first.'

Most of the time when the wrong person picks up – and as far as this dame's concerned I'm the wrong person – they say, Sorry, wrong number, and click off. Instead, the voice on the other end of the line wants to know who I am.

'Like I told you the first time,' I say carefully, 'I'm someone answering a phone. Who are you?'

'I can hear sea noises,' the phantom voice replies, 'water lapping against a hull, seagulls …'

I get that feeling again. But as well as checking the boat, I also checked the phone and there's nothing in it that shouldn't be. Then I remember what Salina said, and after that, what Goldilocks said: everything's got a price. And I find myself wondering if the caller might be a dead subscriber who's suddenly realised she's got time left on her phone, ringing to ask for her money back …

'I don't need to know who you are,' I lie.

'Nor do I have to say who I am, because I'm not the person with the phone.'

'What difference does that make?'

The voice doesn't say. Instead it asks, 'How come you've got it?'

Everything's got a price. And in this case that price could turn out to be death, except the phantom caller doesn't sound like a killer. But like Aunt Rube and experience have taught me, killers come in all shapes, sizes and voices. Killers don't have to sound like killers.

'How come you're asking now?'

'Because the phone's been turned off but now it's turned on again.'

Which means the caller has been trying this number regularly, often, frequently, which gives me the answer to the question of who she might be – if not why she's calling. Which means I know pretty much what I want to know and, by leaving the phone on, I'm only giving her the chance to get what she wants – whatever that might be. So I switch off, pour myself a triple, and try to enjoy what's left of the blood on the water.

Next morning, with the Harbour as flat as I feel after a night on the hops, I stare at the cabin wall and try to put a face to the voice on the phone the previous night. It was low-slung, soft as silk but with an edge to it – like the silence a knife makes after it hits the wall next to your head. The boat swings 180 degrees and a shadow crosses the cabin. I climb out of the bunk, get up the companionway, blink into the harsh light of a new day and make myself a coffee on the Port-a-Stove. And after I bail out the boat, fill the pump with fuel and oil and restart it, and the position of the sun over South Head tells me *normal* people are heading to work, I grab another phone and dial the number that Goldilocks gave me.

'Death-watch beetle here.'

Like the man said, you got to laugh.

'You said you could get me the court records that go with the pink phone.'

'Pick up or delivery?'

I tell Goldilocks delivery.

'What's your interest in all this?' Harry asks.

I shuffle the newspaper out of the way so he can park the bucket of sludge he calls coffee where it can do the most harm. Then I tell him about Rory, Goldilocks, the phone and the phantom caller. He puts on his you-got-to-be-kidding face.

'Except it's not about the phone, is it, Rain? This isn't about a damson in distress or some anonymous caller or the desperate need of a modern-day Don Quixote crusader-detective to right wrongs, because right now you haven't got a wrong to right.'

He pours himself a cup of coffee out of his personal squeezebox.

'You're interested in this whole caper because you need the distraction, right?' He rubs the table with a rag even dirtier than the table. 'Your aunt's crook, maybe dying; Rory's told you to go to buggery; Little Orphan Annie's given you the brush-off; and your ex-wife's acting up even worse than usual. You're conflicted and that's the real reason you want those records.'

'Ever thought of turning detective, Harry? With those eyes of yours and that razor-sharp mind you could be another Perry Mason – all they'd have to do is cut off your legs.'

'I'm just saying you ought to stick to cases that come your way, not go shopping for them. You don't know what you're letting yourself in for.'

I'm happy to take my chances. Just like I'm prepared to take a risk with Harry's coffee, even though there are some things you shouldn't do if you want to stay alive.

Chapter 11

THE LAST WITNESS

A headline distracts me but I feel like being distracted. It takes up most of the front page:

SYDNEY IN THE DOLDRUMS
Developers to the rescue
Exclusive by JOHN CURTIS
'First they complained about Barangaroo — that magnificent development soaring proudly from the old Sydney docks on the western edge of the city. The same wimps and fairies that want to live in the Dark Ages got up in arms about plans to develop the Botanic Gardens and the Domain. After which there was all that fuss about developing the disused dog track at Wrigglesworth Park. And now ...'

I continue reading because it's a distraction.

'... Sydney would still be a backwater containing nothing but gum trees and kangaroos if not for our far-sighted developers. Men like Ivan von Franck are the modern-day explorers — the Burkes and Wills and Leichhardts and Edward John Eyres of the 21st century — men who risk their very lives ...'

There's more in the same vein — the sort of vein that, if it was in your wrist, you'd slit it. A codger goes to sit at a table but Harry waves him away, sags into the chair next to mine and hunches over his *cross-ant* and coffee. I tap the blatt.

'What's this about von Franck risking his life?'

'Ivan von Franck has crossed more people than your average priest has crossed either himself or the line into moral turpitude. As for him risking his life – well, this is the building industry where most of the time the only thing on the level is the floors, and even then ...' He wipes a crumb from his mouth. 'Some unionist got up von Franck's nose and died and people reckon von Franck was responsible.' He flaps a hand at the blatt. 'That journalist,' he adds, indicating Curtis' byline, 'is an honourable exception.' He pats the pocket of his apron. 'I nearly forgot – someone left this for you.'

The court papers are court papers and the people in them say what they typically say. It's not the truth but a coroner's court is a court of law and a court of law isn't interested in the truth so much as in people's ability to avoid it. I try to put myself in the minds of witnesses but it's like a play with no surprises because the dialogue goes according to the script. And at the end, the coroner rules:

I believe that the police in this case – particularly Detective Sergeant Richard Richardson – did their best to determine the identity of the murderer. But so far they have been unsuccessful. I am therefore bound to find that the deceased met his end at the hands of a person or persons unknown ...

I go over the cast of characters and always and forever come back to the same name. For a start, it belongs to one of the few dames in the case. And for a finish, she appears to be one of the few jokers in the pack who actually want to solve the murder.

Please tell the court your full name and address.
My name is Carmen Maria Blenkinsop and I live ...

I half-expect her to be told the correct word is *reside* but if there's an interruption it's not recorded. Instead, she's asked:

What was your relationship to the deceased?
I was his wife.
Would that be in the traditional sense or de facto?

I'm sorry?

Were you or were you not actually married to the deceased?

As I said, I was his wife.

Magistrate (intervening): You're being asked if the arrangement was a common-law union or one espoused by the Church.

Does it matter?

Yes, because this is a court of law and we are concerned with the truth.

Then I suppose we weren't actually married …

We have to steer clear of suppositions – were you or weren't you?

We weren't but aren't we trying to find out who killed –

That's enough, witness. Next question, please.

There's more of the same – too much more of the same – but none of it gives me that nice, warm feeling I get when I'm learning something worth knowing. Why, for instance, did the dead man die? Who killed him? And who was my phantom caller? I've got a name but no idea if she's short or tall, fat or skinny, likes cats or possesses a squint. She's as much a mystery as the identity of the person who killed the husband who wasn't a husband, and the only surprise is the witness who makes his appearance near the end of the proceedings.

Please state your full name and address.

My name is Ivan von Franck …

Chapter 12

MAKING A KILLING

If a name crops up twice in one day it's not because the elements have conspired or the planets are aligned or the cat ate the canary – in my book, there's got to be a reason. Also, there's an address for the dame – courtesy of the court papers – so I catch a blue Government bus with grey-speckled windows so that outsiders can't ID the passengers. The bus driver's radio is tuned into someone called Shockman Jock.

JOCK: We've got Trevor from Verdant Vale on the line. Thanks for joining us, Clever Trevor, it's great to have you with us. We're interested in your views on people who – ha, ha – make a killing in the building industry.

TREVOR: Yeah, well, people should be allowed to make money, shouldn't they? I mean this is a free country with free entry-prizes and everything ...

JOCK: That was meant to be a joke, Trevor – I was talking about all the murders.

TREVOR: All what murders?

JOCK: Thank you, Trevor. (Hangs up.) Bloody idiot. Now we have Mavis from Matraville. What do you think, Mavis?

MAVIS: I agree, yeah, Trevor's a bloody idiot.

JOCK: I mean what do you think about all the killings?

MAVIS: Hasn't there only been one?

JOCK: I'm speaking journalistically, Mavis. We might have heard of only one but where there's smoke there's sure to be some arson around – that's a joke, Mavis. What I'm saying is: Should there be an inquiry into the building industry?

MAVIS: No, let the bastards kill each other. Just the other day, Tony was at it hammer and thongs with another dog and –

JOCK: I don't see what …

MAVIS: – and there was no way I was going to interfere, know what I mean? It's the same with these bathplugs. Let them rip each other's throats out. They're a bunch of thugs, if you ask me, and –

JOCK: Thanks, Mavis, but I didn't ask you. We now cross to someone with an opinion that is worth listening to – Mr John Curtis, of Sydney's *Daily Terrorgraph*. How are you, John … ?

I get off the bus in the middle of Peter from Parramatta saying they should bring back the lash and hoof it to the address given by the dead man's widow, a hovel next to a billboard featuring a cop with a camera promising: *MORE COPS, MORE CAMERAS, MORE CHANCE OF GETTING CAUGHT*. I knock on a door that's about as welcoming as the billboard.

'Is that you, Arnold?' comes a voice from within.

'No, I'm someone doing a survey. I –'

'And I'm the Duke of Edinburgh. Look, if you want money, I haven't got any. And if it's furniture you're after, there isn't any of that left, either. So bugger off and leave me alone.'

I wait.

'Look,' comes the voice again, 'I know you're still there because I can see you through the peep-hole. But I'm not opening up so you can bugger off.'

The stone step's rough and there's an even greater roughness to the voice behind the door; a roughness that says she's had enough; a roughness that implies that, under normal circumstances, she might be a nice person, but otherwise she's got a gun; it's also the wrong voice, so I do like it says and bugger off.

On the way back to the boat – a walk, another bus trip, a ferry ride, and finally a cross-country trek to where I beached the coracle – I switch on the pink phone and ring Aunt Rube. And Rube says that, while it's nice I phoned her, she happened to be enjoying a kip for the first time in weeks and I woke her. No, she's not interested in how I'm going with her case, just in sleeping. After which I'm even less reassured than I was before and my mind's a long way from where it should be as I return the phone to my pocket, flip the row boat right-side up, drag it into the water, find the oars and start rowing.

Night does strange things to boats and I've had too much to drink which makes it worse. Somewhere between waking and sleeping I find myself detached from my personal moorings, like I'm floating in space. And because my feet aren't on *terra firma*, I could be upside down or sideways or drowning. Distant noises seem close and the water lapping against the hull could mean I'm on a lake on the moon. I feel my consciousness drift with the boat. Fate laughs as something nudges against the bow. It could be a shark or a mackerel or a lost dolphin but the next bump's none of the above …

I hurl myself out of the bunk, drag on my pants and grab a gat – it turns out to be the Hoopla and Cock-a-Doodle .38 – and get up the companionway. As I make my way through the main cabin, I make out a shadow on the wraparound deck. There's too much cloud to see any detail but the way it moves tells me it's a dame. And in the absence of evidence to the contrary, I figure it's Pandora, my nemesis, who's been after me for as long as I can remember.

As I ease myself towards the hatchway, I've got the gun out but I'm also faced with the usual conundrum: what to do when we find ourselves face-to-face. I can't kill her because I don't know who she is and she hasn't hurt me – yet. But if she runs true to form she'll be carrying a knife. I don't know how she found me, and neither do I know what she'll do in a shoot-out. All I know is there's a figure on the deck and from its size and weight and the way it moves, it's no seagull …

I crouch beside the map table as I work my way through the possibilities. If it's not Pandora, it could be a drunk, a thief or a vandal. Like drowned crews, lost souls come and go on boats moored in Sydney Harbour, and with a bit of luck this one will go. Unless she's something to do with one of my cases – past or existing – someone I've crossed in a long history of crossings, or –

The figure's on the lee side of the boat – I can see its head against the night sky. The *Wooden No*'s an old flat-bottomed ferry which means that when she's not sinking she's stable and the tub doesn't move when the figure does, just continues to sway at its mooring, impelled by the movement of the sea. Weight of interloper, 130 pounds – 65 kilos in the new measure; height: five foot six, maybe seven; and she's slow but not scared – just careful. She reaches the back hatch. I make my move.

You die every day in this game. The trick is to watch your back and try to stay out of trouble. But that means applying logic to an illogical business. I'm sleep-stupid but that doesn't excuse the mistake. I'm on home territory but I forgot the bottle, the empty I dropped last night on the way to my bunk, the one I tread on now, my foot twisting to one side and my arms coming up like I'm surrendering.

A light as sharp as a stiletto cuts across my eyes and a banshee starts screaming. Suddenly, the figure's leaping down the companionway towards me. An instep gets me where I don't want to be got and I go down. The figure's above me and to my right and the light's full in my eyes. But she's an amateur. I lunge, my fingers find what feels like a calf, and I bring the interloper's leg up and sideways. The torch clatters to the deck and goes out, the figure goes down and I'm on top of her. She's soft and there's the strong smell of –

I don't do lights on the *Wooden No*. Show a light and it's an invitation to crash the party. So as my mind goes, I do what I do by feel. Hair – long and wet and done up hard against the skull; head neat and smallish – confirm it's a woman's; arms strong for a dame; waist a woman's waist, hips ditto; and the kind of thighs you don't muck around with unless the owner consents. This isn't a fight I want to be in and for a moment I ease off and a wave of nausea sweeps over me as I recognise too late the sweet-sour smell of the chloroform and feel myself go under.

Chapter 13

THE CONTROL FREAK

I come to trussed like a marrow, the early-morning sun cross-eyed against the *Wooden No*'s salt-encrusted eastern windows. I'd think it was a nightmare – except for the ropes and the dame seated on the wraparound bench opposite me.

She's not looking my way but gazing out at the bushland fringing the Harbour. Most of the tension is in her hands, one of which is clutching my gat while the other's holding the pink phone she filched from my pocket. She must have sensed me looking because she turns and for the first time I notice the nose. With her kohl-ringed blue eyes, golden hair and skin that looks like it would melt at a touch, hers would be a face of radiant beauty – except for the nose: at some point it's been broken and not reset properly. It should make her look bad but it doesn't – it just accentuates her beauty.

'We've decided to wake up, have we?' she says.

It's the voice on the phone, the one accompanied by the end-of-the-world sounds and the sniffling, the one that belongs to the dame in the coroner's court. Past the dregs of the chloroform I try to recall the name. Caramel – no. Carmel – no again. Carmen. Yeah, that's it, Carmen. Carmen Ready-Or-Not – Carmen Maria von Blenkinsop. No, not von. Just plain Blenkinsop. An unlikely name and an even unlikelier dame to have it.

'Carmen Maria Blenkinsop isn't your real name, is it?'

'No, I'm Minnie, and – for reasons that wouldn't be immediately obvious – they call me Skinny Minnie. Carmen Maria Blenkinsop was the name I gave the court.'

'Which leads me to ask the following question,' I go on. 'Why give the court a false name? It was only a coroner's court, nothing but a preliminary inquiry into a death, not a murder trial. Why lie about your name?'

'I was acting on advice.'

'You mean someone told you to commit perjury?'

She shrugs. 'As you said, it was only a coroner's court.'

'Who advised you?'

'Just someone.'

'Why didn't you answer the door?'

'What door?'

'The door to your house.'

'Why should I answer the door to my house?'

'Because I knocked on it.'

Skinny Minnie looks fazed and then quizzical – then we both pause. It's called a freeway standoff, when people find themselves on a median strip in the middle of an expressway with traffic speeding past in both directions and no way of getting to the other side without dying. The end-of-the-world racket on the phone was a plane taking off while the sniffling was … Yet neither of those factors pertain to the address given.

'No-one knocked at my door.' She looks confused. 'People never knock at my door …'

'So as well as giving the wrong name, you also gave the wrong address?'

The dame nods. Something's not computing for her either.

'Again acting on advice.' She frowns. 'But the question I need answering is: why did you kill my husband?'

'What makes you think I killed your husband?'

She holds up the pink phone. 'Because you had this.'

It's the mobile from the morgue, the you-beaut pink phone with all the fancy trimmings, the one that Goldilocks assured me didn't have a price on it. Only now I'm discovering that it does.

'How does having your phone make me a murderer?'

'How else would you get it, except off his body?'

'I can explain …'

'Can you?'

I struggle against the bonds but it's no good – the dame knows the ropes.

'How about untying me?'

'And let you kill me the way you killed my husband? That wouldn't be too bright, would it?'

'Except I didn't kill your husband.'

It's daylight and the Harbour's waking – a boat robber rows past looking for a boat to rob and a ferry thumps by going in the direction of Manly. The early-morning oar-splashers have come and gone, but the dame's still with me.

She looks determined, I'm trussed like a rooster, and she's got my gat. And if I don't give her what she wants, she'll most probably strap an anchor to me and chuck me over the side, and no-one will be any the wiser. That's the downside to not existing – you can't kill a non-person because he's already dead.

'You work for von Franck, don't you?' she asks me.

'No, I don't.'

'But if you don't work for von Franck, who do you work for?'

'I'm a private investigator.'

'A private investigator who does contract killings on the side …'

'No, I'm a private investigator full-stop. I right wrongs. And deaths on the side are wrong so I don't do deaths on the side. People might die but I'm not the killer. What I do is solve cases.'

'Like finding out people's names and where they live. Only you didn't do that very well, did you?'

'That was because my starting point was a lie.'

'As they say in the computer world: GIGO – Garbage In, Garbage Out,' Skinny Minnie murmurs. 'But while your old-fashioned methods didn't work, I tracked you down using modern technology.'

'So it was the phone …'

The dame nods. 'My husband was a control freak. He bought the phone and installed an app on his computer so he'd always know where I was.' She shrugs. 'It's just a blinking light. And as soon as you turned the phone on and left it on, I had you. All I had to do was go where the LED light led me.'

I've already worked that out. What I haven't worked out is why the dame's leaning sideways while I'm sliding across the splintery deck towards the bow. A wind's sprung up and something's banging against the side of the *Wooden No* but that's no reason for the tub to –

Chapter 14

NOT ONLY
SLEEPING DOGS LIE

Skinny Minnie's making like a gimbal – one of those gadgets you use when you don't want your drink to spill – staying upright while the bench tilts under her. At the same time I feel myself slide and when I look out the window the trees are leaning and the horizon's at an angle it shouldn't be.

'We're going under!' I yell. 'There's a hole in this boat bigger than Fate and the pump's stopped. You've got to untie me so I can restart the pump.'

The dame shakes her head but the gun stays still. 'If I let you go you've got me. You're bigger and as a private detective you're undoubtedly far more unscrupulous. I'm not untying you, which means you've got to tell me how to stop us sinking or we'll both drown.'

So I tell her what to do and she puts down the phone and the gat, gets herself out on deck, lowers herself over the side, and restuffs the hole like I told her to. After which, I hear her refuel and restart the pump and I feel the old ferry begin to right herself as the dame returns, even wetter than she was before.

'You'll find something in the aft locker,' I say. 'You'd better change or you'll die of pneumonia.'

'What's it to you?'

'It's the normal concern of one human being for another. Also I'm trussed, remember.'

I look out the window and when I look at her again, Skinny Minnie's dressed neck-to-knee in oilskins, scraping her hair back and working out where to take it from here. She picks up the gun but I can see her heart's no longer in it.

'Where were we?' she asks of no-one in particular. 'That's right, I was accusing you of killing my husband and you countered with the accusation that I was following you. In the course of which it turns out you're a private detective who uses old-fashioned methods to find someone and fails.'

'I only went to the wrong address because you lied.'

She shrugs. 'Detection should be above lies.' She pauses. 'But as it turns out, you're right – I shouldn't have lied. If I hadn't lied, I could have got on with my life, secure in the knowledge that my husband could no longer attack … me.'

'What difference did lying make?'

'It made me vulnerable all over again.'

'Yeah, vulnerable to the person who told you to lie, the joker who's trying to seduce you – at a wild guess, I'd say it's the cop in charge of the investigation into your husband's murder.'

She turns wary. 'How did you know?'

'Old-fashioned detection methods. Only one person knew you were lying and that was the person who told you to lie. And he not only told you to give a false name and address – a lie that could get you into serious trouble, by the way – but also to dream up an alibi, because he believed you were the murderer. His motive being to save you or put you in his power or both. Your adviser wouldn't have been your lawyer because – going by the court records – you didn't have one. That leaves the investigating officer – from memory, one Detective Sergeant Richard Richardson.'

For the first time, Skinny Minnie looks at me with interest. 'You're more than just a pretty face, aren't you? Which is just as well because you're not all that pretty.' It's an attempt at humour but I don't laugh. 'I suppose I should have got on with what was left of my life.'

'So why don't you, instead of hunting down people who happen to have your phone, in the belief that they might – just might – be your husband's murderer? The bloke might have been a dog but now he's a sleeping dog, so why not just let him lie?'

'You'd like that, wouldn't you? Seeing you're the murderer.'

The boat's on the level and it's about time we levelled, too.

'Look, Minnie, we could go round in circles like a boat at a swing mooring but you've got to get back to your baby.'

I've surprised her again and her eyes grow even darker than they were before.

'How did you know I had a baby?'

I shrug.

'There were three clues: the crying I heard on the phone; your hesitation when you said your husband could no longer attack me – you were going to say us: that is, you and your child; and your increasing anxiety as feed-time approaches.'

A vertical line forms between Skinny Minnie's eyes like she's just thought of a possibility she hadn't considered before.

'You're not only a detective,' she muses, 'you're a good detective ...'

I can see where this is headed.

'No way,' I tell her.

'You're hardly in a position to argue,' she replies. 'Given this tub's going to sink, you'll drown if I leave. Which means you'll take on the case if you want to live. But before I employ you, how can I be sure you're not the killer?'

I take a deep breath and tell her the truth. 'Because I've got an alibi.'

Skinny Minnie grimaces. 'According to my late and unlamented husband, wrongdoers have alibis because they need them, while innocent people –'

'The transcript gives a date of death. Your husband was killed on –' I say the date. 'But it so happens I was overseas at the time, trying to save my daughter.'

That was in The Bullets at the Ballet caper; I was in France, something that's easy to prove – even using the outdated methods of an old-time defective.

'And before you suggest I might have employed someone else to do my dirty work, think about it. If von Franck contracted me to do the killing, I'm hardly going to use a sub-contractor, am I? It puts too many people in the loop, when the aim at such times is to keep things as close as you can.'

The dame waves the phone with the hand that's not holding the gun. 'So how come you had this?'

'It's a long story, Minnie. But cutting it short, my usual supply dried up so, acting on advice just like you did, I visited the morgue where I found no-one particularly interested in your late husband's belongings – including that whizz-bang Telefunken. So I scored the phone, a watch with a compass in it – and a widow.'

Chapter 15

GREY CLOUDS IN A BLUE SKY

Truth takes longer to sink in than the *Wooden No* takes to sink into the Harbour and the dame's stubborn, so I leave the sentence hanging along with my fate. I feel the boat lurch, which means the plug's already working itself free again.

'If I let you go, will you look for my husband's killer?'

'Have I got a choice?'

'You could promise, then break that promise after I untie you.'

'Which means you haven't got a choice, either, Minnie. Because:

You've found yourself a detective;

You need to feed your kid before it dies of hunger; and

If you let me go, the three of us have got a chance but if you leave me to die, at least one of us hasn't got any chance at all.'

She comes to a decision, parks the gat, unties me, steps back while I restart the circulation in my arms and legs, then picks up her pink phone but leaves the gat. After that, I row her to shore where she changes back into the jeans she left under a bush – along with the purse containing her fare home. She returns my wet-weather gear but hangs onto the phone.

'I'll be interested to see if you keep your side of the bargain, Mr Sailorman.'

I nod, concentrating on getting the oars in the rowlocks. 'You'd better give me your address – and this time make sure it's the right one.' I nod at the phone. 'Also you could leave that – I might need it.'

The explosion's one I'd prefer not to have witnessed – a *Whoomph!* followed by a lot of smoke and a sheet of flame. There's no time for fancy knots to secure the dinghy – nothing more than a hasty half-hitch over the stanchion – as I hurl myself onto the *Wooden No*, fighting my way to the heart of the conflagration: the pump. My first thought is the dame did it, while the second is I'd better put out the fire.

The heat sears my skin, lifts the paint off the hull and gets far too close to the fuel tank for my liking. By the time I get the extinguisher going, the fire's blazing. Other sailors keep away: it's the maritime code – if someone's in trouble, stay away until it's safe to help. By which time you should be even further away.

After the fire, the *Wooden No*'s even more of a wreck than it was before – black where it once was grey, charred where it used to only be rotten, and in imminent danger of ending up at the bottom of the Harbour. I check for signs of a bomb but there aren't any; look for a fire-starter but there isn't one of those either; then I examine the remains of the pump, to discover the dame didn't top up the engine oil when she refuelled – either because she didn't know or was distracted. Either way, I'm up for a new pump.

It takes forty-eight hours to recalk the old hole, patch the new ones, scrape off the burnt offerings and repaint the hull so the aqua-cops don't get me for being in possession of a shipping hazard, and find a replacement pump. After which I switch on the pink phone. Almost immediately it does its machine-gun *rat-a-tat-tat*.

'I knew you wouldn't show.'

It's the familiar voice with the familiar attitude and the familiar noises in the background.

'The trouble with conclusions, Minnie,' I reply, 'is that people jump to them.'

'You let me down.'

'Everyone gets let down in this world – it's called self-preservation. People never match up to other people's expectations – half the time we don't even match up to our own. But be patient and be there and eventually I'll be there, too.'

'So you're still taking the case?'

'Did I say I wouldn't?'

Harry's in. It doesn't mean his shop's open, just that he's in, the outline of his hunched form barely discernible through the steamed plateglass window. He opens the door but shuts it again immediately I'm inside, the *CLOSED* sign's facing out, and I risk death by saying *Yeah* to a coffee.

'What else do you know about von Franck?' I ask him.

Harry brings a couple of mugs out of the microwave. He stinks of pre-loved nicotine.

'He's king of the developers. If there's an inch of Sydney capable of being built on, you can be sure von Franck's been sniffing around it – the Botanical Gardens, Hyde Park, the airspace over the Harbour Bridge. He makes self-interest look like sacrifice to the ultimate benefit of Sydney when it's just a way of making more money.'

'He sounds smart.'

'He sounds like a greedy bastard, if you ask me.'

'Got anything else?'

Harry tells me that when von Franck arrived in Australia, all he had was his ambition and one Romanian ban – the monetary equivalent of a cent – and apparently he's still got it. He came when Sydney was ripe for the plucking and he plucked it. He got into the funeral business and then building – he made influential friends, then he made a motza.

'So he's not popular.'

'Come on, Rainbow, he's a foreigner. On top of which he's successful, and Australians hate success – particularly successful foreigners – unless it's to do with sport. Women fall all over him.'

I look through the steam-fuzzed window at a passing stranger, a black dog, grey clouds in a blue sky.

'Anything else?'

'Not concerning von Franck.'

'They say he killed Cock Robin.'

Harry shrugs.

'Know anyone who might know more?' I ask.

'John Curtis comes to mind.'

'The journo who wrote the piece on the building industry?'

'That's him – the only person who'll give you an opinion on von Franck not laced with arsenic.'

'How come?' I ask.

'Because he's an old-time balanced reporter. I believe there are still some around.'

I cross to the door.

'Thanks, Harry. Also could you get me a list of Cock Robin's enemies?'

'People that hated him enough to kill him? Apart from von Franck, that is?'

I nod, open the steamed-up door, and leave.

Chapter 16

THE PILGARLIC

I find Curtis where you'd expect to find a balanced reporter – propping up the bar in an inner-city pub nursing a bruised ego and a schooner of Old. I know the beer's Old because the sign on the bar says it's on special and I know the scribe's the worse for wear because that's what he's telling the barmaid. I pull out a stool, order a double-sour upside-down and check out my surroundings.

Journalists' drinking holes once made workingmen's pubs look like milk bars. Their most-favoured pastimes being to smoke, drink, curse, fornicate and bash the other bloke senseless before he did it to them. Sometimes they used words but mostly it was fists.

But that was then and this is now. These days, Murdoch's Muckrakers and Fairfax's Flunkies might sound like football teams but they're namby-pamby sweethearts compared with the Hannibals that once hurled typewriters at editors and evil-eyed epithets at everyone else. Now boys and girls come out to play in the quaintly named Dickens Inn, sipping shandies in a non-sexist, smoke-free environment while discussing what they read in the social media, and ping-pong.

I count fifty, most of them wearing earphones like they're electronic tracking bracelets; spending more time on their techno props than in face-to-face contact; ninety-eight per cent of them staring at tablets, while the remaining two per cent is John Curtis.

'I'm the only journo in town writing without fear or favour. So why do they treat me like shite?' The barmaid's sympathetic, producing a murmured tut-tut whenever she manages to get a leg over. 'There are a thousand yarns in this city but does anyone want them? No. And d'ye know why? Because this is Sydney, Australia, and it's up to its neck in corruption. And why? Because of advertising – income stream, money, profits, filthy lucre. What happened to good old-fashioned journalism?' A jerk of a blunt thumb over his shoulder indicates the sewing-circle behind him. '*That lot* happened.'

The scribe's a pilgarlic – that's bald, as in peeled garlic – shaving his head for reasons best known to himself while also pretending to be drunker than he really is. From the next room comes the ding-a-ling of a pokie promising the next spin of the electric wheels is going to be a winner.

I turn back to Curtis.

'What kind of stories?' I ask him.

He gazes at me while I do the same back. He's wearing a red chequerboard shirt and stained jeans; the drunkenness is a front or he'd be off his stool as well as his face; and from the accent he's as Scotch as pot-stilled whisky from Speyside. He doesn't ask: Who are you? He's an old-fashioned journalist who knows the best way to get a story is by feigning disinterest. He doesn't ask questions, either; instead he looks drunker than he is and, rather than asking for news, volunteers it.

'Take this Balangalulu project.' He touches the side of his nose with a slab-of-beef hand and winks like he's got the palsy. 'There's more to that than there are pigs in a sty, laddie. Then there's the proposal to develop the Brewster Block – money changed hands on that, too. And the fire in the old Macquarie Barracks the cops say wasn't deliberate. Well, I know better, don't I ...' He takes a swig of his beer but when he puts the glass back on the bar, the level's the same as it was before. 'There's more mischief in the building world than you or I ever dreamed of – or there are stories in a skyscraper ...'

'Tell me about Bluebeard Constructions.'

'You mean von Franck's outfit?' He looks at me suspiciously. 'Why drag him into this?'

I tell him I'm not dragging anyone into anything and he seems to relax.

'It's Blue-bird – not Bluebeard – and von Franck's an exception to the rule: he's straight. My exposés always expect – sorry, ex-cept – Ivan and for good reason. He's as clean as the proverbial – the only stories I'll credit about him are good ones, despite what you read in the papers.'

I drain my glass, get the scribe another beer to go with my second, and keep up my side of the pretence. 'It sounds like you've known this Vladimir character a long time.'

'It's Ivan,' he corrects me; I like it when they do that – it means they're listening. 'And, yeah, I've known him for – hell, it must be going on for thirty years.' He abandons his old drink and picks up the new one and it's my turn to feign disinterest. 'Early in my career I was asked to do a story on immigrants because I was one myself, and Ivan von Franck was one of my stories.'

'Still keep in touch?'

Curtis takes another swig and the level stays the same. 'We're in the same business. Why?'

I shrug. 'I'm a private detective and I hear that he kills people.'

There's a pause – the kind that a person makes before deciding against throwing something and afterwards changes channels. Curtis goes into thinking mode.

'While it's a tough game, I don't think Ivan would kill anyone,' he says at last, taking a swig – and this time the level does change. 'How about you?'

'I don't kill people, either – unless they cross me. But getting back to the hard drive: would you call von Franck a good hater?'

'Why?'

'Like I said – because I hear he kills people.'

'Come on, this is Sydney, Australia and von Franck's a tall poppy.' I've upset the scribe and the lapse back into brogue is the result. 'So, aye, a' course there's aggravation and from plenty a sources but that's towards Ivan, not away from him. Take this Cock Robin character, for instance ...'

'The joker that was murdered? The union organiser?'

'Union dis-organiser more like. Cock Robin set up strikes and took bribes to settle the men, only to immediately foster more dissatisfaction. Over the years he caused von Franck no end of grief, so, aye ...' His voice grows careful; von Franck's rich and alive so the libel laws that favour the rich and alive still apply. 'But the coroner didn't finger anyone who might have killed Cock Robin.'

'Do you know who killed him?'

Curtis shrugs – or maybe he's just keeping his beer close to his chest. 'I'm a journalist – which means I don't pay attention to rumours.'

'Given that Cock Robin's dead, who does von Franck get aggravation from now?'

'You say you're a private detective ...'

I nod and hand him a card – the one where BERT SMITH'S MATRIMONIAL INVESTIGATIONS is crossed out and JOHN JONES, SPECIALIST IN MISSING PERSONS inserted in its place.

'... In which case, you'd have a story or two you could put my way'
– he checks the card – 'Johnnie ...'

'I might do,' I say. 'Meanwhile, you were saying no-one actively dislikes von Franck – what about the other way round?'

'You mean who *likes* him?'

'No – I mean, who does von Franck actively hate.'

'Clean Fill.'

'Clean Fill? The stuff that builders put in holes in the ground?'

He allows himself the shadow of a smile. 'Aye, that's the essence of the name – if you Australians are clever about anything other than sport, it's names. It must be because you're antipodeans but most nicknames are upside down. Clean Fill – real name, Phillip McLean O'Hare – is anything but unblemished.'

'You sure got a way with words, Curtis.'

He laughs – I've made him happy. 'Nicknames are bynames, hypocoristic, cognomens, pen-names, pseudonyms and briquets – I particularly like briquets because it sounds like brickbats.'

I've fed his ego. I down the rest of my sour and place the empty on the counter.

'So what's he do, this Clean Fill joker?'

'You must live under a rock, Johnnie-boy. Clean Fill was once a shyster – that is, a crooked lawyer.'

'What does he do now?'

'The general populace. He's a crooked politician – the Minister for Development.'

'Where would I find him?'

'Down by the seaside – in white man's country.' Curtis smiles; it's an interesting smile – full of bonhomie but at the same time guarded; he touches the side of his nose again. 'So come on, now it's your turn – what d'ye have for me?'

'I'll put my mind to it,' I promise.

That's when he asks who I really am and who I work for and I tell him the answer to the first question's Bob Brown and to the second, the general good. After which I straighten my fedora, climb down off the stool and make my way out of the pub to breathe once more the foetid air of the city.

Chapter 17

TWO-BIT CHARMER

Flea: *a wingless, bloodsucking insect of the order* Siphonaptera, *a parasite of man and other mammals which – by sucking the blood of rats and then of humans – is capable of spreading disease ...*

As soon as I'm aware of their presence – there's a shadow between me and the deep-blue nausea and another by the *Vincentia* – I haul out the Smith & Double-Yew and take refuge behind the burnt-out wreck that was once a Toyota Corolla. The Good Book says: *There's a time to be born and a time to die; a time to kill and a time to heal; a time to stand and deliver and a time to duck for cover.* I do like the Good Book says and stay behind the Corolla.

My mind's on holiday or they wouldn't have got me. I was too busy brooding. There's two of them – one tall, the other short – and they're onto me before I know it.

Crooks take stuff that isn't theirs – cars, CD players, reputations, a life. In Sydney they're like fleas on a dog and I'm the dog that every second flea in Sydney wants a bite of. I'm wearing the sunset-red jacket and it makes me a sitting duck for whoever wants to take a pot at me. Which might be Pandora, the cops, a random player, or someone completely new to the game – like the two jokers who have just offloaded themselves from the Reserves bench and into my life.

I go into a whirlygig from the ballet Petrushka – half of it by intent, the rest by chance – but these two know their business, and the kick to the side of my skull is by the book while the thump in the ribs isn't for medicinal purposes. I go down and see the rest of the world go by – a dame in Givenchy; a pack of schoolkids; and a couple of surf heroes. None of whom stop because clearly I deserve it. The tall one's boot comes for my face. I avoid a direct hit but it grazes the side of my head and my left ear starts playing Waltzing Matilda – the version with the didgeridoo improvisation as background and the side drums in the refrain.

It must be the surprise element but the old dame wielding the umbrella appearing like Boadicea on a winning streak sends the tall thug into the camellias while the smaller one reassesses his priorities. I manage to find my feet – it's not easy when I don't know where they are – and my head feels like it's been taken off and not put back on straight again. A cop appears, the small thug helps the big thug out of the bushes and they disappear.

'You from around here?' the cop asks. I shake my head; I'm trying to change tracks; I've never liked didgeridoos; the cop takes it as a No. 'Then get the hell out of my beautiful, idyllic suburb and take your problems with you,' he adds, dispersing onlookers while I make my own arrangements. Which don't involve leaving.

It's like they haven't changed the use of the joint so much as updated the menu, a fish-and-chips sign still visible under the palimpsest on the sea-rusted awning reading: *ELECTORAL OFFICE OF PHILLIP McLEAN O'HARE*. The door's got a red waratah painted on it to prove this is NSW and opens onto a big room containing a counter and a dame sitting behind it.

'Why, hello!' she says like we're married but haven't had our first argument yet. 'What happened to your face?'

'I fell by the wayside.'

She looks nonplussed. 'What can I do for you?'

'I'm after the incumbent.'

'The what?'

'Is your father in?'

'Do you mean the Minister?'

I'm trying to turn off the recording; I can still hear the didgeridoos. Her look takes in the battered hat, rearranged coat and smacked-together features – after which she reaches under the counter like she's been taught when confronted by people like me.

'Do you have an appointment?' she asks.

'I don't need one – I'm a constituent.'

'A what?'

'A member of the electorate, an ordinary Joe, a voter: one of the people who put your father where he is.'

'Oh, one of those!'

She changes her mind about the button and a voice emerges because she's got the Telefunken on Loudspeaker when the dialogue should just be between her and her progenitor.

'I thought I told you to hold all calls, Molly.'

'But it's not a call, Daddy, it's one of those what-do-you-call-them – persistents.'

Sigh from the other end of the phone. Then, 'Did he give a name?'

The dame puts a hand over the receiver like she's seen it done in the movies. 'What's your name?' she whispers.

'Mr Jones.'

She takes her mitt off the phone. 'It's a Mr Smith.'

Sigh from the speaker; the voice softens – she can't help being what she is. 'Very well, tell him I can give him five minutes and send him in.'

He's not what I expect but they rarely are. I pictured him as a broad-shouldered brute but instead he's a two-bit charmer in a two-bit charmer's suit with a face like a dummy: small build, narrow shoulders, close-together eyes, and the proud possessor of the family squint. Talking of two-bit: something glimmers on the floor – I place a foot over it as I take a seat.

'Don't worry about the girl,' he says. 'She means well. She just let two others in she shouldn't have and I roused on her for it, so she's a bit twitchy.' The squint settles in for the long haul as he examines what's left of my face. 'Do I know you?'

'No. But you know Ivan von Franck.'

An expression darts across his face like a frightened rabbit, before disappearing back into its warren. 'Are you telling me Ivan sent you?'

'I'm not telling you anything except that I need to know something.'

'What's this all about?'

I hand him a card – the one that says I'm Simon Templar and I'm a saint. 'I'm a journalist doing stories on important people.' All right, so the idea was inspired by Curtis. 'I'll be getting around to you before long but at the moment I'm doing a piece on von Franck.'

Chapter 18

THE CAT THAT BARKED

He looks up from the card. 'It says here *Without Flair or Flavour*. What the hell does that mean?'

It was a phrase Curtis used – before the machine on the railway station spat out the card and before the misprint; it sounded good at the time but doesn't bear scrutiny now.

'It means I'm not afraid of the truth.'

'Who is afraid of the truth!' Clean Fill tries for a grin but it only accentuates the family resemblance. 'That was a joke, Mr Templar. So tell me: who do you tell the truth for – who's your employer?'

'I haven't got one, I freelance.'

'Which means you've been sacked by all the major players and now work for some two-bit street rag promoting some social issue or other, produced on a Romeo-machine somewhere in downtown Chippendale.' He flips the card like he knows where it's from. 'All right, on the off-chance that – as well as being unemployed – you're also a constituent, and therefore possess a vote, I'll allow you five questions. But first: why me?'

'Because you know von Franck and also because you're the relevant Minister.'

'So what's your first question?'

'What's he like?'

'He's a top guy.'

'Why do you say that?'

'Because of the laws of libel.'

'So you're afraid what you really want to say might land you in trouble?'

'I didn't say that.'

'All right – you're the Development Minister and von Franck's a builder. Did von Franck donate to your slush fund and afterwards demand favours – or issue threats if the favours didn't happen?'

'No comment.' He shuffles some papers. 'Okay, that's it – you've asked your five questions.'

'One was for clarification.'

'All right, I'll allow one more.'

'Going back to the fear thing, what are you afraid of? The law of libel – or the law according to von Franck?'

'That's two questions and my answer's No comment to both.' He presses down on the desk and raises himself like a crane on a building site. 'Now if you've got any more questions you can put them in writing.'

'I also want to ask about Robin Fahey – Cock Robin.'

'Why – is he unemployed, too?'

I reach down like I'm tying my whitesides and when I straighten the shiny thing on the floor has made its way into my pocket. I'm a bowerbird for facts and this is a fact.

'Cock Robin's dead.'

Unlike the dud hand Minnie dealt the court, the second address works. It's a pretty little joint in inner-city Camperdown – she must have rung from the airport just to throw me – with too many coloured windows, too much pink paint and a bunch of knives that jangle at a touch. When she throws open the door she's clutching a gizmo with a flashing light on it and she's not happy.

'For God's sake shut up, I've just put Fiona down!'

I follow her inside past a phone table with a picture of a man, a woman and a baby on it; a set of stairs; through a living room containing too many flowers; and end up in a ploughed field containing a garden chair, a clothesline full of nappies, a stump and a shed with a gate beside it. The dame sits on the chair, leaving me in charge of the stump.

'I see you use real nappies,' I say, to break the ice.

'I do it for the environment. But we're not here to talk about the environment.'

'So why are we here?'

She shrugs. 'I suppose asking you to take on this case seemed like a good idea at the time. I tracked you to your boat in the belief that whoever had that pink phone killed my husband. Only to find that you were nothing more than a detective with a dead man's phone.' She shrugs. 'I thought you could help but I see I was wrong.'

I climb down off the stump. 'I'll let myself out.'

'He was such a bastard!'

'He being your late husband Cock Robin, the joker in the picture in the hall?'

Smiling for the camera but still nasty-looking. I wait and after a while the dame continues.

'He was a thug who went out of his way to hurt people – especially me.' She touches her nose. 'For years I put up with his violence thinking it was normal. I actually thought I was lucky because I had a man.' She shakes her head. 'I thought parenthood might change him but it only made him worse. One night he shook Fiona and when – when he did that I – all right, yes: I wanted to kill him.'

I get myself back on the stump. 'So did you?'

She nods her head and shakes it all at the same time. 'That's exactly what the police – specifically Detective-Sergeant Richard bloody Richardson – decided when they found Cock Robin's body. I actually heard one of them say: Nine times out of ten it's the wife. But how could it have been me when I thought you did it?'

'Look – I'm sorry, what's your real name?'

'Maxine – Maxine Grant.'

'Okay, Minnie or Maxi or whoever the hell you are – the kind of logic you just used says that if a cat thinks it's a dog it must bark. But let's take a Jail Pass on the logic and stick to the questions: where did the killing take place, what was the cause of death and did they ever find the murder weapon?' Court transcripts can be misleading – deliberately or otherwise. 'And I need to hear it from you, even though I've read the transcript. So tell me about the murder.'

Chapter 19

SUCKLING BABES TELL NO TALES

The gizmo in the dame's lap burps and farts and starts chattering; at first I think it's talkback radio until I realise it's a back-to-base alarm and the kid's hungry. The squawking fades and the dame manages to focus.

'The killing was done with what the police called a blunt instrument. They never found the murder weapon even though a lot of men in blue singlets spent several days digging up my backyard.' Hence the potato field. 'They found his body over there.' She shudders as she waves towards the shed. 'When I came downstairs and saw his body, a great wave of sadness washed over me, when I should have been relieved he was gone.'

'You mean you were actually on the premises when Cock Robin copped it?'

Minnie nods. 'I was upstairs feeding Fiona.'

I raise my voice to be heard over the racket coming out of the gizmo. 'Did you happen to hear anything?'

The dame shakes her head – the noise has risen to a crescendo but she still wants to answer the question. 'As I said, I was feeding Fiona. There could have been a world war for all I knew.'

'Not much of an alibi, is it? I mean you could hardly get little Fiona to swear she was using you as a milkbar when her father was murdered. You could have come down, whacked your husband over the head when he wasn't looking, disposed of the murder weapon, gone back upstairs and finished feeding the kid – all before dialling 000.' I glance at her. 'I assume you called Emergency?'

She nods wanly. 'You think the same as them, don't you? But I tell you I didn't do it. And I can't say I wouldn't have asked you to take the case if I was innocent because you'd just say …'

Whatever argument she's got wouldn't stand up in a court of law, which means she was lucky she didn't stand up in a real one – only a coronial inquiry. But the question remains: why wasn't she charged? She answers without being asked.

'The long and the short of it was that Detective-Sergeant Richardson couldn't take his eyes off me. And all his questions steered me away from culpability. You loved him, didn't you? he asked. You're not a strong woman, physically, are you? You heard a noise as of someone entering the house while you were upstairs and when you came down to investigate …

'All his questions were like that; he put words in my mouth. I suppose a lawyer might call Richardson's questions leading. And because I was scared, I let myself be led.'

'And where did he lead you?'

'Not into his bed, if that's what you mean. That's what he wanted to happen, of course. A woman knows these things.'

'But you must have been grateful that he got you off the hook …'

'Yeah. Off one hook and onto another – off a murder charge and onto Sergeant bloody Richardson's Most Wanted list. I felt like a – a fish that takes a bait when it thinks it's being thrown a lifeline. He wanted me obligated so I became obligated. It didn't mean I had to oblige him. Not in that way, anyway.'

'So what did you do?'

'I said No, of course – except that Richardson wouldn't accept No. He seemed to think I was playing hard to get. The fact I'd put up with my husband for so long somehow worked against me – Richardson thought he was Mr Wonderful by comparison.' She shrugs. 'He's a very persistent man. You saw the flowers in the living room – pots and pots of them? Well, they're from him. It's as if he thinks I'm an epitaph on a headstone he can wear down if he thrusts at me enough. And behind all his thrusting is the very real threat I'll end up convicted of a murder I didn't commit if I don't – and where would Fiona be then? Robin warned me police can plant evidence proving beyond reasonable doubt that someone did something they didn't. And it wouldn't be double jeopardy because I was never tried, was I? Besides, Richardson really does seem to think I'm guilty …'

'Which is why you want me to prove you're not.'

The kid's screams are close to Force 9 on the Bo-diddly scale and the waves are starting to turn into spindrift. Minnie gets up.

'Will you try to prove my innocence or not? I know you know I didn't do it, which means it must have been von Franck. When he was in the witness box saying how he much he admired my husband, I knew he could kill his own mother. Anyway, I need to feed Fiona.' As she disappears inside she calls over her shoulder, 'Can you wait till I come back?'

Workshops are like mausoleums and the shed at the end of Minnie's garden is no exception. Light creeps through a window like a burglar, cobwebs dangle from rafters, and sawdust hangs off the cobwebs. Electrical tools are lined up like an identity parade while a grease-stained workbench squats under a shadow board. Before he became a corpse, Cock Robin was a do-it-yourselfer.

I push back the hat, pull out the torch and send its beam for a stroll among the cobwebs. Rusty pipes lie on the rafters; sky glimmers through holes in the roof; and the bin contains offcuts. The workbench is cluttered and a tool's missing from the shadow board.

They call them shadow boards because the shapes of the tools drawn on them look like shadows. And this particular shadow says what's missing is a 24-inch Blackbird Carrington monkey wrench weighing in the vicinity of five pounds – more than enough to qualify as the kind of blunt instrument that can kill someone. If Richardson had organised a proper search – instead of getting his glorified gravediggers simply to plough up the yard – he might have found what he was meant to be looking for. Only he didn't find it because he wasn't looking – hence all the flowers.

'Where are you?'

I'd forgotten nursing mothers do it in public now and that's what Skinny Minnie's doing. I dowse the torch, step across to the shadow board, select a short-handled sledgehammer that would weigh about the same as the wrench, belt a nail halfway into an offcut, and head back outside.

I hold up the block of wood. 'Could you finish hammering this nail in for me?' I ask.

Minnie frowns. 'Why?'

'Call it a whim. I'll hold Philomena.'

The dame can't swing the hammer – even when she holds it near the head – and I'm experiencing much the same problem with the kid. We do the swap back. Minnie didn't kill her husband.

Chapter 20

VOICES IN THE HALL

She's gone back to feeding the kid so I heft the hammer. 'A couple more questions. The first being: who else, apart from von Franck, had it in for your husband?'

'A lot of people, because he was so nasty.'

'Enough to kill him?'

'That's different. To do that, you'd need to be a particular kind of person. Plus there'd have to be a particular reason to do it.'

'Not necessarily – having a bad temper would be enough. But putting those two factors together – the right person and a sufficient motive – can you think of anyone?'

Minnie shakes her head. 'No-one – apart from von Franck. And if people don't just kill people, then I suppose intense dislike wouldn't be enough ... ?'

'So why do you think it was von Franck?'

Just then, the knives on the front verandah make the same kind of noise they made when I hit them.

'You expecting anyone?' I ask her.

She shakes her head. 'I never have visitors apart from ...' She frowns and her eyes get that scared look. 'It must be him.'

'Okay. He's just a man in a uniform, a public servant that happens to carry a gat.' The words ring as hollow as the cutlery chimes; I keep talking; sometimes there's nothing else to keep. 'Cops might be cops but they're still no more than cops. Just act normal. Tell him I'm your brother, John Peel, and all you got to say then is goodbye.'

I park the hammer and take the babe – she's got her hands full without having a built-in diner. The babe arches its back and screams as the dame pads past the pots of flowers, down the hallway and opens the door. I bounce the babe like I've seen it done on television but the babe still howls.

'You took your bloody time,' says the visitor.

'I'm … sorry, but my – brother's here.'

The babe strains in my arms and there's a rush of activity in its nether regions followed by a stench you could grow roses on. The kid relaxes. I've got the magic touch. Voices in the hall.

'Your husband's not even cold yet,' Richardson is saying, 'and you've already got lovers crawling all over you.'

'It's my brother.'

'So I'll just come and meet him. By the way, I brought you something.'

The two sets of footsteps advance up the hall – her bare ones and his booted ones – and when she appears she's clutching yet another flowerpot while the bull's staring at me like it's only a matter of time before he makes the arrest. He's short, maybe five-ten, but he's built of much the same material they make grenades from. His smile's annealed steel and the eyes could blow up a safe.

'Ah, the baby minder,' he says softly.

There's no number on his chest because he's not wearing a uniform. But he's still a bent cop from the soles of his shiny black boots to the top of his frizz-cut hair.

'What's the matter – cat got your tongue?'

'I'm Minnie's brother, John Peel.'

Chapter 21

WHEN THE MUSIC STOPS

He narrows his eyes until all that's left is slits. 'As in: *D'ye ken John Peel with his coat so gay?* Yeah, it figures.' Richardson turns back to the dame like I'm expected to know who he is. Rhomboids, deltoids and triceps ripple under his coat as he hunches his shoulders, feet wide apart like he thinks he's bigger than he is. 'New evidence has come to light.' It's like I'm not here. 'The result of some over-keen constable sticking in his bib where it's not wanted. Turns out that your DNA's all over the —'

'But I tell you I had nothing to do with it!'

'Then you've got nothing to worry about, have you, my pretty?' His rough voice turns smooth as he shrugs his shoulders. 'But if you ever are worried, you've only got to say the word and I'll come running.' The dame's gripping the flowerpot like the blooms aren't roses but belladonna. 'Mind you water those flowers or they'll die – everything dies.' Richardson turns so he's facing me again but this time he's up-close and personal. 'Do I know you from somewhere, Peel?'

'I don't know,' I reply. 'Do you?'

He holds out his right hand. 'Show me your licence, smart guy.'

'I don't drive.'

He flicks his fingers. 'Some other ID then – Medicare card, library ticket or life membership of the Phantom Club.'

'I don't get sick and I don't read.'

'You telling me you've got no ID?'

I don't tell him I don't exist. Tell him I don't exist and he's got the arrest he wants while I get the arrest that I don't. The dame steps between us.

'My brother's helping with the grieving process.'

Richardson lowers his fist. 'Is that what they call it now? The way I see it, you're only too happy to be shot of your husband so you can play up. So happy, in fact, that people might be excused for thinking you knocked him off.'

'But you know that I didn't!'

That's when he turns on her and that's when the dame looks scared all over again.

'That's the funny thing about the law – it can find people guilty when they're innocent or innocent when they're guilty. Criminality's a moveable feast, with guilt reliant on the rules applying at the time. The trick is to make sure the rules don't apply to you when the music stops. Think about that while you're grieving.' He prods my chest; I don't like jokers that prod my chest; but I already don't like this joker. 'I've got the strongest feeling we're going to meet again, Phantom Man.' He indicates the dame with a nod of his steel-wool head. 'In fact, I wouldn't be surprised if you're still around when I return to arrest Little Miss Innocent.'

'I'm so glad you were here,' Minnie breathes once Richardson's gone. 'He'll be back, though. What am I going to do?'

'You got any friends, Minnie?'

She pats the babe. 'Cock Robin was a control freak. I wasn't allowed to talk to another man and it was pretty much the same with women – he felt threatened by everyone.'

'There must be someone.'

'I suppose there could be one person ...'

'Who?'

Minnie takes a deep breath. 'Her name's – Tsunami.'

'Are you sure of the address?'

We're in the bush – in Sydney the wilderness starts as soon as the money runs out – in the kind of place where killers dump corpses knowing that only lost people end up here, never to be seen again. The cabbie dumped us at a sign reading NO ADMITTANCE and left as soon as I paid. It was a seventy-buck ride but he didn't stay to give me the change from a C-note. The light from the sickle moon's fighting a losing battle with the clouds while the leaf canopy takes care of the rest.

'There never was an address as such …'

'So walk me through it again.'

'As I said, Cock Robin didn't allow me to …'

The bush noises are the sounds of nightmares – the sharps and shreds of untuned violas, rustlings in the undergrowth, the flapping of wings that could be the etiolated skins of dead men, and the rush of unseen creatures fleeing the bloodstained claws of Doom.

'The technology he installed in my mobile was the same as that used for tracker bracelets.' The babe starts whimpering again, its tremolo at one with the rest of the bush. 'There was no way I could maintain a proper friendship – much less an improper one. Robin used to go through my call log.'

I look at the bush. No-one's home. There's not even a home for anyone to be home in.

'This acquaintance of yours – would you describe her as a friend?'

'I don't know all that much about her. You asked for a name and hers was the only one that came to mind.'

'Except you didn't give a name. Tsunami's not a name – it's a death-defying leap into the unknown, a natural phenomenon that kills people.'

Chapter 22

THE VOICE IN AISLE 16

'Her real name's Sue Mahoney but it sounds like *Tsunami* so that's what I call her. She'd come around and we'd have tea and talk. One day Robin arrived home unexpectedly and – it was weird – looked taken aback when he saw Tsunami. I thought there'd be fireworks but I was wrong. Tsunami had been coming around for a few weeks before he saw her and – he, well, after that, he stopped hitting me. But while Tsunami would come to my place, I never went to hers: he wouldn't let me.'

'So as far as you knew, Tsunami lived in a hole in the ground.' We've got to move but when we do it's got to be in the right direction or we'll join all the other corpses in the forest. 'How did you meet?'

'I had little freedom but of course we had to eat so Robin let me go to the supermarket and that's where I met her. She was a voice in Aisle 16. I was reaching up for a box of breakfast cereal when I heard someone say: Don't touch that crap, it'll kill you! It was like the shelf talking. I went, Who's that? And Tsunami appeared.'

'Did you consider the possibility she might have been lying in wait?'

'Why would she do that? No, our meeting was accidental: we were two lost souls in a supermarket.'

'How did she strike you, this fellow lost soul?'

'It was – strange. It was like being with a man but without the tension. I've forgotten what we talked about but it seemed as if she was – well, flirting. She was – handsome, in a way. She had a strong personality while I'm more maternal. So, yes, she was mannish, both physically and in the way she dressed. That first time she wore men's trousers and a man's shirt, her hair was cropped short, and she had no make-up on. She just stood in the breakfast section with her feet apart.'

'Did she tell you anything about herself — like what she did for a living?'

'We didn't talk about anything in particular and what we did talk about I've forgotten. But I committed the directions she gave me to memory because I knew I might be in need of a bolt hole one day: Take the Workhorse Parkway, turn off at so many clicks, you'll see a fire trail, go another so many clicks, then head north, and after half an hour switch to north by north-east ...'

'Does she walk fast?'

'Like a gazelle.'

I check the watch with the compass in it I got from Goldilocks at the Morgue and do the calculations. If Minnie's memory's good we're twenty minutes from our destination.

'Any hint of a profession?' I ask as I bash through the undergrowth. 'A surgical smell that might suggest nurse? The physique of a dancer or the translucent pallor of a nun?'

'She smelled of cement.' Minnie pulls a twig out of her hair. 'I met an abattoir worker once and knew immediately what he did for a living, due to the smell of — it was a sort of barbecue smell. Well, Tsunami had a cement smell.'

I put two and two together and don't like what I come up with. I've got a lot of questions but I don't ask them. Instead I recheck the compass and head north by north-east and the dame follows.

'Where are we going?'

'North by north-east.'

Through the trees I make out a small block-shaped affair, little more than a box on wheels. It's painted dark but I can't determine the colour, only that the caravan sucks in light like a black hole. A small set of steps sticks out from under the door and a yellow light gleams from a small window set high in the side. The ground around it has been cleared but there are still a few trees. By the window light I note the overhead branches have been stripped away. Whoever lives here knows their bushcraft. Probably eats berries, roots and leaves ...

'Are we there yet?' Minnie asks.

I hold out an arm and hit soft.

'Stop!'

It's old fashioned in these times of lasers but it's still effective and if I hadn't been looking I wouldn't have noticed because the trip cord's completely buried, except for where a wombat, a bush turkey, a fox or a feral cat unearthed it: an innocent-looking wire that must go right around the clearing. I motion to the dame to stand still.

'This would form concentric circles an irregular distance apart.' I put down Minnie's suitcase, kneel and scratch at the dirt around the wire. 'They'll be connected to a battery which would power an alarm. The system would be so sensitive the slightest touch would activate it ...'

Chapter 23

A CASE OF MISTAKEN IDENTITY

I've never met Pandora, I don't even remember when or where I first heard the name, or if the name's imagined or real. But for as long as I can remember, the deadly and significant *idea* of Pandora has been lodged in my mind.

I spent my first five years on the funny farm – that's what we used to call the hippy commune in the north of NSW – it was a loony bin, a madhouse, Bedlam, in which the smell of dope eclipsed the scent of eucalypt.

The adults – I realised in my own adulthood – were always half-stoned and forever in and out of each other's wigwams. Half the time we didn't know if we were Arthur or Martha or even who our parents were. I could have been spawned by a wombat. Then one night with the sky ablaze with scorpions my mother immolated herself. She was high on a burning windmill and even higher on dope and she took my little sister with her screaming into the night. I was five at the time and scared and hid behind a totem pole. I can still see its Easter Island face with its grinning lips and flattened nose, the three great scars on each of its cheeks angled upwards. But most of all I remember its eyes because there weren't any – just two empty holes in the gleaming white carapace of the skull.

That was the night Pandora entered my life. Since then, I've often seen her, half-hidden behind buildings, a vehicle or a tree. I've sensed her evil, tried to apply logic to her and failed. I grew up knowing she could be around the next corner. It helped me survive. Because I knew if I relaxed for a moment, Pandora would get me, so I never relaxed. No logic to it, I just – knew.

I've left Minnie-Ha-Ha, the babe and the suitcase and I'm halfway up the steps to the caravan. The gat's shelved because we're not in enemy territory and the clouds have parted company with the moon, turning the trees and caravan silver. My knocking echoes on emptiness like I'm banging on a bongo. There's no sound from inside, just the pale light from the window and the whispers of the bush and I'm starting to think it's going to be a long walk back to town.

I'm concentrating on the van. My weight makes the springs creak but – apart from the echoes of my knocking and the sounds of the bush – it's all I can hear. On the boat there's always the familiar fart-gurgle of the water, but here it's different – the whisper of the wind, the rustle of land animals and the hoot of an owl. Familiar sounds if you're familiar with them but I'm not.

My first thought is for Minnie and the babe. They're a long way back and exposed. Death moves quiet in the bush, no more than a shadow on the periphery of your consciousness, until suddenly you're no longer alive.

I don't know how I become aware of the danger because there's no noise: it's – just – something – visceral. It could be a movement of the clouds, a shift in light intensity, the flicker from silver to –

Or it could be my febrile imagination. Because when I look back, Minnie is still there, a moon-glossed figure hugging her babe while – a short distance away from her – the suitcase looms large on the ground. Except that –

At first I don't notice because my attention's on the dame and the babe. They've become one, a solitary shape in the moonlight, their shadow seemingly more substantial than they are. From the vantage point of the steps, I quarter the area. My footprints are stones in amber and sticks lie stark among the leaves while the place where I rooted out the trip wire looks like snout marks made by a boar. The bag moves.

Your eyes do that – suggest movement where none exists. But while such phenomena are common at sea, in the bush they're –

The suitcase *moved*. It wasn't much of a movement but it moved. In the normal course of events bags don't move – unless someone moves them. Or unless they're not bags at all.

That's when I see that the black shape – what I thought was a suitcase – isn't a case at all but ...

Almost as though it senses that I know, the shape moves, lengthens

and becomes –

I've never seen Pandora – only her outline, her shadow, the *idea* of her –
but I know what she looks like. She's a figure in black – a *female* figure in
black – lithe and dangerous, with an ill-defined face and carrying a knife.
She wears figure-hugging clothes – the one garment stretched thin, like a
second skin, black. And that's what rises before me now, a figure in black
with a knife and Minnie and her babe between us – all of them bathed in
the snow-white light of the moon.

I'm quick but the figure's quicker, feinting to the right before diving
the other way and I hear the whang! of a knife as it nails my fedora to the
van. And when I look again, the figure's already got another knife in its
hand. I hurl myself down the steps. The knife will go through my chest
or pierce an eye but the dame and the babe will survive, I try to reassure
myself, because I'm the one that Pandora's after …

I awaken cushioned in lava, blinking upwards, to see a curved ceiling and
below it the face of a concerned Minnie. I'm dead and in heaven. Except
that Rube always said that there wasn't a heaven and Rube only ever dealt
in facts.

'You're alive,' the angel murmurs.

My head hurts and when I try to raise it, it hurts even more. 'Pandora
…' I murmur.

The van's the usual home-away-from-home – a crumpled mattress,
sink, fridge, stove, bench, table, and not nearly enough air. Minnie's
shaking her head.

'What is it with this Pandora? While you were out to it she was all
you could talk about. And now you're awake you're still talking about her.
Who the hell is she?'

'Where's Pandora?'

'There you go again,' Minnie says, bewildered. 'Who?'

That's when I realise that the apparition with the knives only looked
like Pandora – looked like Pandora, dressed like Pandora, acted like
Pandora and nearly killed me like Pandora might one day kill me. I shake
my head – to clear it but also because I'm confused.

'The dame in black — the one that tried to kill me ...'

It's Minnie's turn to shake her head.

'I presume you mean Tsunami. She heard us coming and when she saw you she threw the knife. After that she knocked you out with a kick to the head. Then I called out and ... Anyway, she's gone for a walk — she said she needed a bit of space to think. Look, I'm grateful, Mr Peel, or whoever you are, but ...'

My hat's on the table and there's a hole in it and the dame's grateful? She shrugs.

'Tsunami acted in self-defence. She didn't mean to kill you. In fact, she aimed to miss.'

'Did you know she could handle knives before she aimed to miss?'

'Well, no, actually, but I ... she —'

The door flings open and there's Tsunami. She doesn't look happy. She looks dangerous, menacing and beautiful, but not happy, and her words suit her looks.

'I've thought it through.' She's looking at Minnie, not at me. 'Cock Robin's dead and his murder survived the cops, an autopsy and the coroner. You're in the clear, Minnie. So why come here? And why' — a jerk of a thumb in my direction — 'bring him with you?'

'Because of the cops in general and one in particular.'

'What cops in general and which one in particular?'

The babe's on the bed, grumbling but asleep. Minnie tells Tsunami about the cops in general and Sergeant Richardson in particular and while she's talking I check out the dame who almost killed me.

Chapter 24

WHO KILLED COCK ROBIN?

There's something disturbing about her, like she has two parts and neither of them fits. She's strong but she's also ephemeral as if – like the wave that Minnie named her after – she could destroy everything in her path but afterwards become nothing. She has dark hair cropped short, black eyes, mobile lips, sinuous body and intelligent eyes …

'So while this big, brave detective is working out who killed Cock Robin, you need a refuge from a cop, is that what you're telling me?' she asks Minnie.

'It would only be me and Fiona.'

'And what happens after I give you refuge, Minnie? Do you move on or move in? And if it's the latter, how long are we talking?'

'Please, just until Mr Peel finds the murderer. I know Richardson will never give up as long as he thinks there's a chance of getting me into bed and that will be for as long as he can frame me. He won't rest until either I give in or we find the killer. I – thought I could stay at your place.' Minnie looks around dubiously. 'But there's not enough room, is there? How was I to know you lived in the bush like a wild animal … ?'

Tsunami examines a bootee. 'Don't worry, I'm not turning you out, sweetie. I happen to like my privacy but I have another home.'

'You mean a proper home?'

'I only come here when things get too much for me. I gave you directions to the van without really thinking you might try and find me.' She shrugs. 'You can stay at the other place – but only on one condition.'

It was my hat she nailed. I've got a right to butt in. 'What's the condition?' I say.

It's the first time she's looked at me since she threw the knife.

'That I'm going to help you find Robbie's killer,' she replies.

'Why would you want to do that?'

'Let's just say I have a vested interest.' She nods at the dame. 'I saw what Robbie did to her and I can guess what the cop could do by way of a follow-up. Isn't that enough reason?'

Yeah, it's enough reason but I don't know if it's the right reason. But in the end there's no option but to agree because I need to park the dame while I get on with the job.

Balmain's a poodle stretched out in the sun, its paws in the water. Tsunami's home away from home is a picturesque little joint overlooking a picturesque bay with a picturesque ex-oil refinery in it and Minnie's standing in the doorway like she's waving her boyfriend off to war — except that there are two of us, and one's a dame.

We're in a pub — Tsunami's idea — and we're nursing a couple of triple-strength rums — my idea. Tsunami could be a bloke, perched on her stool with her trouser-clad legs so far apart she might be trying to split the atom. I prefer to operate alone but I need to know what her game is — if she's in love with Minnie or killed Cock Robin or both. My money's on both, only I don't tell her that. I want her where I can find her and if I tell her what I think, I won't see her for the dust.

'What's your real name?' she asks.

'Brown.'

'So what do you know, Brown?'

When I tell her I know that the prime suspect's von Franck, the arched eyebrows in the beautiful face become even more arched. 'You don't mean *the* von Franck?'

'How many are there?' I finish my rum, catch the eye of the barmaid with the cherubic lips and order two more. The pub reeks of perfume, sweat, garlic and — nearer at hand — a cement smell. I ask the question.

'You in the building game, Tsunami?'

'I'm a vet.'

'You mean you look after animals?'

Tsunami shakes her head. 'Haven't you noticed all the scars, Mr Brown – together with the way I talk and my attitude? Plus the fact that I can afford a nice home in an even nicer suburb due to an interest-free loan, yet prefer to live in a caravan? And what about that hole I put in your hat?' She shrugs. 'Forget animals, I'm a veteran-type vet – ex-Major Susan Mahoney, Australian Engineers – skilled in the martial arts as well as in engineering. Someone who served in one war too many and can't forget it; seen too many deaths and can't forget them, either; and craves excitement because she's reached the point where she can't live without it.'

'Is that why you want to hunt down a killer?'

'It's one reason.'

'Last time I looked, being a vet wasn't a full-time profession. You're young, bright and attractive, so why not do something useful?'

She laughs her deep laugh and somehow it's no longer masculine. 'As well as being a war vet I'm also a civil engineer. It's why I was in the army – I build bridges. And before you ask – civil in this context doesn't mean I'm not a criminal or polite. It just means that I know my way around buildings – what holds them up and what lets them down.'

'You've got some connection to Cock Robin. What are you – an ex-wife?'

'Cock Robin was a cock-of-the-walk, a bully and a toad. When I first met Minnie, she told me how she came by her injuries, and my soldiering instincts told me to go in.' She realises she might have said something she didn't mean to. 'That is, I felt I had to help her.'

'By bumping off Cock Robin?'

'*Who killed Cock Robin?*' she quotes, because sooner or later someone had to. '*I, said the Sparrow, with my bow and arrow, I killed Cock Robin.*' She downs the rest of her drink and clicks her fingers for more without checking if the barmaid's looking; because she knows she is – just like she knows more about Cock Robin than she's letting on. 'I'm sorry to disappoint you, soldier, but unless you haven't noticed, I'm no sparrow.'

Chapter 25

I, SAID THE SPARROW

I've got three suspects now – Skinny Minnie, von Franck and Tsunami – and I've met the first and the last and there's still one to go. But when we turn up at the site of von Franck's latest and greatest skyscraper, a familiar-looking gorilla wearing a hard hat and an even harder expression tells us the boss is too busy to see anyone. Tsunami shrugs and bends to peer through a hole in the wraparound hoarding marked *FOR THE FOOTPATH SUPERINTENDENT* while I occupy the hole next door. The structure's a concrete skeleton rearing from a giant's grave.

'Like boys the world over,' Tsunami murmurs, 'von Franck's got to have a bigger car, a bigger cannon, a bigger cockle-doodle-doo. This thing's 300 metres high – a thousand bloody feet – nearly as tall as the Sydney Tower and more than twice the height of the Bridge. A thousand apartments and not nearly enough parking places, because von Franck's bought someone off. Average price of units when they're finished: $2 million. Twelve lifts. And views to die for. It's so big, von Franck had to get clearance from Sydney Airport to build it. He's taken the usual short-cuts.'

'What usual short-cuts?' I ask.

'There, there and there.' Tsunami points. 'The foundations aren't deep enough – that would represent a hundred grand to a building inspector – and the concrete contains too much sand. A lot of the ties that bind – that is, the reinforcing – are missing. Von Franck would argue that the requirements are too severe.' She shrugs. 'Which they are, of course – this crapheap will be standing long after we're gone. But it's still got all the integrity of a toy tower built by a kid. Clever boy! Mummy says. And what else did Miss Phipps teach you today?' Tsunami shakes her head.

'I call it kinder-construction – worth a gold star until the family dog brushes up against it and it topples over.'

'And will it?'

Tsunami shakes her head. 'There'll be leaks and cracks and the paint will peel off but it's safe, so, no, it won't fall down.'

I squint around. The usual nice-suited denizens going about their business. Plus the not-so-neat joker coming out of the building site – the giant nodding to him like he's a friend – smiling.

'Well, if it isn't the private detective,' says the pilgarlic. 'The one obsessed with von Franck!' He doesn't notice Tsunami. 'And now you're on his doorstep. Does that mean you've got something on him?'

'No,' I reply. 'Have you?'

The pilgarlic laughs and he's still laughing as he goes on his way.

'Who was that?'

'A journo called John Curtis, who's proving very helpful because he knows the main players in this case as well as a lot about the industry and he's prepared to share it. I want you to lead the questioning.'

'Why?'

'Because you said you wanted to help.'

The pink phone rings. I check the window. It's Skinny Minnie. 'Hello?'

'Oh, Mr Peel, it's –'

Phones are like guilt in a court of law, a jailable fact until someone proves otherwise.

'What can I do you for?'

'I need more nappies for Fiona, she's run out.'

'Do you want me to see if they'll throw in some baby powder and pins?'

'No, just nappies. Meanwhile, how are you getting on with –?'

I cut across her. 'Yeah, it is nice weather.' I click off and repocket the Telefunken. 'She wants nappies,' I tell Tsunami.

'What kind?'

'Just nappies.' I pause before adding, 'For a baby.'

'But does she want them for a crawler, an infant or a toddler? And would they be night-time ones with plastic on the outside or day-time ones without; compact or comfortable; high-capacity or fine-line; medium, large or small; girl or unisex; washable or disposable …?'

I shrug. 'She just said nappies. And she's okay for powder and pins.'

He's the same giant Rube and I came across on our walk-and-talk and we get past him by the simple expedient of me pressing the relevant nerve in his neck while he's distracted by Tsunami tying up a non-existent shoelace. After which we head down the steep track towards a white-painted structure in a corner of the building site. I put on a helmet and yellow vest from a pile near the steps to keep it quasi-legal and Tsunami follows suit. At the other end of the walkway is a door with a *KEEP OUT* sign on it. We go in.

He's seated behind a desk flipping a coin in front of a calendar featuring a heavily underdressed dame hugging a tall building. He doesn't look up as we enter — just goes on flipping the coin: flip, spin, catch, flip, spin, catch and flip again.

'This is all I had when I came to this country,' he says. 'Just this one coin and I've still got it: a Romanian ban with 1952 — that's the year of my birth — on one side and sheaves of wheat and the sun rising between mountains on the other. It's a symbol of my success, Mr Brown, what's yours?'

By using my current pseudonym, he's thrown me, but that's what he wants to do — a rough-cast man with a face carved out of granite who knows the name I gave the pilgarlic. Flip, spin, catch, flip, spin, catch and flip again.

'Success only comes at others' expense,' I tell him. 'Meanwhile, I don't do symbols.'

Tsunami steps forward with a wiggle in her catwalk. 'Look, we haven't got time to frig around, von Franck,' she says.

When he looks up, the hard eyes don't soften. 'That's fine because I don't either. What do you want?'

He doesn't ask how we got in because he's worked it out; he doesn't ask why we're here because the pilgarlic's already told him; and he's leering at Tsunami, who consequently colours and loses her place in the directory. I step forward.

'I want your thugs to stop harassing Madam Blavatsky.'

'Who?'

It figures — it's a big business: Madam B's no more than a small Rorschach blot on a very big bit of paper. I switch to the main drag.

'Where were you on the night of …'

I tell him the night Cock Robin copped it and when von Franck smiles it's like rock splitting.

'Let me guess – that's the night that uppity little unionist was killed, right? And you're on the case because the cops have other fish to fry, am I right? Well, it wasn't me.'

Harry's right: von Franck's personable – for a rock. I shrug. 'That's an answer but it's an answer to another question. What I asked was –'

'I know what you asked but not who you are or who sent you. You're a thug in a red coat in the company of a dame on her way to a fancy-dress ball, accusing me of committing a common-and-garden murder and you expect an answer?'

'Why not, if there's nothing to hide?'

He stops flipping, wraps the coin in his stone fist and when he looks up it's like I'm being measured for a coffin: hard eyes in a hard face, the kind of eyes used to being obeyed, and not far behind them a clever mind doing cartwheels. He shrugs his couldn't-give-a-damn shoulders.

'I knew some idiot might ask so I checked my movements. But after I tell you where I was, you're going to leave and you'll take your girlfriend here with you. That a deal?'

I nod.

'All right,' he says. 'I was walking my dog.'

'Where were you walking your dog?'

'Where I always walk him, in Waverley Cemetery.'

'Any witnesses?'

'Only dead ones.'

'Not much of an alibi, is it?'

'It's enough for a man as rich as I am who no-one's charging.'

He starts flipping the coin again – flip, spin, catch, flip, spin, catch and flip again – and he's still flipping as we leave.

Chapter 26

THE DAME ORDERS RISOTTO

The next morning finds Harry's collar crooked and his hair in urgent need of a Hoover. The tables are full of yesterday's plates and silence takes over as someone switches off a lawnmower.

'You got that list I asked for, Harry? The one containing the names of jokers that might have hated Cock Robin? I also need food-handling gloves, if you possess such a thing, as well as a five-pound hammer.'

'Why would I have a five-pound hammer?'

'You've got scales, haven't you? You mightn't have decent coffee or a milkshake machine but you've got to have scales.' Harry nods a reluctant Yeah. 'Okay, so I want something that weighs the same as a small dog.'

I slip the list that Harry palms me into the lining of my hat, just below where Tsunami's knife went through it, then do my bit to help by taking the elastic bands off the blatts. The *Terrorgraph*'s front page says:

The city that Jerry built − 9 out of 10 Sydney buildings shonky: Royal Commission into construction industry
Exposé by John Curtis

Accompanying the headlines are photographs of new buildings with cracks in them. Unnamed builders pay unknown politicians big potatoes to get zonings changed. Councils accept bribes to overlook deficiencies. Labour providers threaten disruption if builders don't use their workers. Building materials are stolen and replaced with rubbish …

'Hi!'

I only recognise her because I'm trained to see past the obvious. And the obvious is that Tsunami's exchanged the cat-suit for a nice little number in bloodbath-red with a key hanging off a Magiclip attached to the frock. Even her hair looks good and there's enough black on her eyelashes to induce muscle fatigue in her orbicular palpebrae. Behind her stands what I thought was a motor mower – a dinky little 125cc Honda step-over motorbike, a set of crash-hats growing out of the side like carbuncles. I lower the paper.

'You must be somebody's beautiful sister.'

She grunts like she's heard it all before.

'So where are the flowers?'

Harry's ogling from behind his steam-smeared window and I got no riposte worthy of the name.

'What flowers?' I ask.

'When a girl's invited to breakfast on a romantic autumn morning, naturally she expects flowers.'

Harry rushes out and props a menu in front of Tsunami before bending to scrape a dog turd off the footpath. He's done his hair in a comb-over.

'Thank you, darling,' Tsunami murmurs to him, fluttering her mascara, and Harry's dribbling as he leaves; she turns back to me. 'You'll be pleased to know that I solved the nappy problem by buying all twenty-seven varieties. However Fiona needs clothes so we have to go to Minnie's for them.'

I don't know what to say, so I don't say it.

'Cat got your tongue?' Tsunami picks up the menu. 'I hope this dump's better than it looks.'

With the clouds scudding across an azure sky and the leaves on the street trees turning orangey-yellow before fluttering to the footpath, it's a romantic day. But that's not what we're here for. I take a deep breath. 'Look, Tsunami, we've got to –'

'I'll have the risotto.'

I've put the list that Harry produced, along with the two sets of sandwich gloves, in the inside pocket of the orange coat next to the gat; I've got a five-pound window-weight under one arm; and I'm wearing one of the powder-green helmets so as not to attract attention. That's not the case with Tsunami, who's hitched her skirt high enough to cause a pile-up, and if I had any say in the matter I wouldn't be in Bathurst Street on the back of a motor scooter with just enough *oomph* in it to power a ladies' shaver.

'Where am I taking you?' Tsunami yells back to me.
'To see Hunk Waller.'
The first name on the list.
'Who's Hunk Waller?'
'An ex-labourer.'
'Where do we find him?'
'In the Woolloomooloo Refuge for Rogues and Vagabonds.'

I'm shouting to be heard but also because I'm nervous and it's not just due to the dame's driving. The refuge is the soup kitchen where Annie – my ex-squeeze – does voluntary work and I'm going there in company with a dame who, if she looked any sexier, could be arrested for it. Annie dumped me out of hatred but tell that to her subconscious.

'What are you doing here?' Annie's lugging a bucket of soup and, when she sees Tsunami, looks like she wants to throw it at her. 'And who's the tart?'

'Come on, Annie, I can explain ...'

'I'm sure you can.' Annie's lips go thinner than a three-legged greyhound's chances in an open sprint as she turns her back on me. 'Only I won't be listening while you're explaining.'

'I need to see someone about a case.'

'With you, Rainbow,' she says over her shoulder, 'everything's a case. And if it wasn't, you'd make it one.' She nods at Tsunami. 'Just like you made her.'

'It's not like it looks.'

'Nothing's ever like it looks,' she says. 'But whether it's like it looks or looks like it isn't, it doesn't change what it is.' She relents; I don't like it when they relent; it's a down payment on misery. 'Who do you want to see – in company with your case?'

'Waller.'

'You mean Hunk?' Annie nods towards an emaciated-looking joker sucking a straw. 'Hunk's jobless, broke and friendless, so go easy on him, or you'll make him cry and you and your case will have to leave.'

She moves among the tables while I approach the man of straw.

'You Hunk Waller?'

When the skinny man raises his head, he's drooling – much like

Harry did over Tsunami – and the bags under his eyes could double as button mushrooms. 'Are you from Jobs-R-Us? Does that mean you got a job for me?'

I tell him no to both questions and he goes back to looking dejected.

'Why are you here then? You look like a gangster and his moll, so go ahead, kill me – you'd be doing the world a favour.'

Chapter 27

IN POTEMKIN'S CLOSE

'I'm not here to kill you, Waller, just to ask you a few questions.' I show him a fistful of fivers. 'You get a couple of these now and the second lot if I like your answers.'

A crafty look appears in his eyes. 'What sort of answers?'

'That's not how it works, Waller – I want fact, not fiction.' I palm him a couple of notes followed by the first question. 'What do you know about Robin Fahey?'

'Robin Who?'

'Robin Fahey – also known as Red Robin, AKA Cock Robin.'

Waller shrugs. 'I know he's dead.'

'How do you know that?'

'There was a celebration at the Put The Boot Inn.'

'What were you celebrating?'

'His death, of course. Cock Robin was a bastard. Among other scams he ran an employment agency called Work-R-Us.' Waller sucks at his soup. 'But he only ever found work for people who paid him – never mind any skills they didn't have – and I've never bribed anyone so I stayed jobless. Employers went through Cock Robin or they lost building contracts and workers had to go through him or they didn't get work.' Waller shrugs. 'I tried to get a job without using him and ended up getting bashed.'

'Did you kill him?'

He looks at the money. 'Is that a question or an accusation?'

'A question.'

'Do I get the extra dix if I say yeah?'

'That's not the way it works, Waller. I don't want the right answer, I want the truth.'

His eyes hang off the money. 'All right, nah, I didn't kill him.'

'Do you know who did?'

He nods. 'Yeah.'

'Who?'

'Someone that hated him and also had the guts to do it.'

'Why might anyone hate Cock Robin?'

'Does my answer get me another tenner?'

'No.'

Waller grimaces. 'He was a bully. For instance, everyone knew he bashed his missus.' He gets the thought long after everyone else got it. 'Hey, she probably done it!'

'Got any other names – apart from the wife?'

Waller gives me a few more names and most of them tally with those on Harry's list but I give the down-and-out the second dix anyway and make like I'm leaving before pretending to remember I forgot something and hand him the window sash. 'Hold this for a moment for me, would you, Hunk?'

He goes to take the weight but drops it. He tries to pick it up but can't. It wasn't him.

The shots go wide. I like it when shots go wide. They're big ones, the kind that come out of a Taurus Raging Bull Magnum or a Colt Python. We're scootering down Liverpool when the first slug whistles by, I yank the dame off the bike with the hand that's not holding the window weight and the bike does a cartwheel and smacks into a wall. I give Tsunami the twice-over and by the time I get around to the gunman, he's gone. I can't see Tsunami's face because of the visor but I can tell she's not happy.

'Are you hurt?' I ask her.

She struggles to her feet, tugging her torn skirt over her thighs as she rips off her helmet. I can see her face. I was right, she's not happy.

'You don't know the half of it.' She checks the bike: the fairing's cracked but the front wheel's still straight and when she presses the starter, the thing still goes. 'Know what? Being with you is like being in a war zone. You owe me a dress.'

We're in George Street outside the Queen Victoria Building, opposite the Hilton. A couple of years back someone planted a bomb here and now someone's shooting out of the hotel. Going by where the slugs landed, the angle of fire was 30 degrees off horizontal. I check the relevant windows but see nothing but pigeons. I turn back to the dame. She's still not happy.

'Anyone hate you enough to take a potshot at you, Tsunami?'

'I'm just a girl, soldier. Otherwise I'm an engineer in the building industry – which means no-one likes me.'

'Anyone in particular?'

'No,' she says, and I know she's telling the truth because she's still angry. 'Now, you owe me a dress.'

Darkness is falling as the dame swings her leg off the bike and if I hadn't ducked I'd need to make an unscheduled visit to the dentist. The street sign says we're in Potemkins Close but for my money the name wears an apostrophe. I check out the street and discover too many hovels, none of them wired to the free-for-all soporific, Foxtail. I can't see Pandora and, if the gunman's nearby, I can't see him either. Just two stray dogs doing what stray dogs do, a cat, and a yellow Transit van, the writing on the side telling anyone who wants to know that it can be trusted.

'Bugger, hell and damn,' Tsunami mutters.

'What's wrong?'

'I've lost the bloody key, that's what's wrong.'

Chapter 28

THE ANGRY SHADOW

'Come on, it's not the end of the world.'

'But how can we get into the house without a key?'

'We break in.'

The figure in the van isn't a cardboard cut-out which means going in by the front door could be fatal. I take the pencil torch out of my pocket but don't switch it on until we get to the garbage lane. If you don't want to attract attention, always take the garbage lane. In any situation, I'm careful; when jokers start taking potshots, I'm even more careful; and when I'm entering a joint where someone's been murdered, I'm more careful still. I stuff the butt-end of the torch in my mouth, get myself in the workshed, and recheck the shadow board.

After that I take the torch out of my gob and head up Minnie's garden path, one hand gripping the weight and my arms out and slightly forward like James Cagney in every movie he ever died in, while the dame's my angry shadow. Still the same cop-ploughed ground; still the weeds; and still the bench where Skinny Minnie sat feeding Fiona. I tuck the weight under my arm, palm Tsunami a pair of sandwich gloves, jam the torch back in my cakehole, put on my gloves, do the necessary with the fuses, and picklock the door.

'Why all this cloak-and-dagger stuff?' she asks.

I remove the torch and heft the weight. 'Because I'm a cloak-and-dagger kind of guy. Also I want to stay alive. We've come for baby things but, going by the van parked outside, we could end up with a lot more than we came for.'

The scent of the flowers the cop brought Skinny Minnie hits me like a smack in the kisser as we enter the loungeroom. Dust, mould, the stench of flower-pot soil and the scent of flowers. No-one's disturbed the length of cotton I taped across the hallway when I last visited. Which doesn't mean nobody's been here.

There's no such thing as luck — luck's for lickspittles. Outside of comic books, Superman's not flying to the rescue if I make a mistake. Trust to luck and you might as well sit on a plastic duck, sucking your thumb on a merry-go-round in a fun fair. Cock Robin's been murdered, Pandora's after me, a thwarted cop's keen to make an arrest, I've been used as a punching bag, a gunman's taken a potshot at us, and a Foxtail van's parked in a street where no-one's got Foxtail …

'Wouldn't it make our lives a lot easier if we turned on the lights?' Tsunami asks.

'If we turn on the lights, there's a good chance we'll no longer have lives. A van's out there with someone at the controls and the writing on the side says it shouldn't be. The driver doesn't live next door because: a) the equipment in a Foxtail van is too expensive to leave in the street and b) the van wouldn't be parked outside Minnie's if the driver lived next door.'

'But who'd stake out an innocent little townhouse?'

'First of all, this joint ain't all that innocent. And second, the driver could be one of too many people with both the motive and the resources to do a stake-out. So ask yourself who —'

'It's the cop who's trying to crack onto Minnie, isn't it?' she says. 'The reason why Minnie's at my place instead of here.'

The scent of flowers is a reminder of the strength of the cop's motivation as the front door crashes open, followed by the click of a light switch that doesn't work, followed by the click of a torch that does. Boots crunch up the hall.

'Wh — what do we do now?' she whispers.

I chuck her the penlight. 'Hang onto that and keep it turned on — it'll tell me where you are.'

'But it'll tell him where I am, too.'

I drag the window weight out from under my arm.

'Yeah, that, too.'

There's acting in self-defence and there's stupidity and hitting a cop with a five-pound length of cast iron is stupidity except when you've got no choice. As Richardson hammers up the hallway, the beam of his torch illuminates the dame. It's enough to distract him and I get him in the ribs but the weight's no good for closer combat so I chuck it, Tsunami screams and the pencil torch flies through the air and lands at my feet, while the cop goes for his Glock. I dive.

I got three advantages:

I'm bigger than he is;

I may have fractured his rib; and

He's distracted by Tsunami.

But fights don't always go with the advantage. Richardson's got his gun out and he's holding it near my ear – which makes this a matter of lithe or deaf. I roll away, see a flash by my left eye and hear a deafening report as he fires. On the roll, I remember Richardson held out his right hand when he asked for my ID, keeping his left hand free in case he needed to go for his gat. So I go for his left arm – his gun arm – and my grappling fingers find a wrist, followed by the gat. I try to get a grip on it, remembering too late that cops put carbonitride on their weaponry to counter corrosion, which makes them slippery. Also I'm wearing condom gloves. Richardson gets his arm free and the second slug plays follow-the-leader with the first …

Chapter 29

POTSHOT

In the eternal battle of good versus evil there's no smart money on who'll win. There's fear but no favour and the results are random. I've got my hands on the gun but the cop's out to do damage, the sounds emerging from his throat the sort of noise you'd expect from a predator – a bestial shriek, a bellow from a cave, a roar as the creature sinks its fangs into the neck of its victim. I tear myself free only to find myself on roller-skates. A whiteside finds the pencil torch and I go down, my head hitting the floor and momentarily putting me out to it. But a moment's all he needs. I'm flat on my back and when I open my eyes, he's standing, legs apart and knees bent in the firing position, arms straight out in front of him, hands knuckle-white on the gat, torso forward to deal the death blow, face uplit by the torch, which shadows his eyes and mouth, turning his face into a skull.

A .45 GAP slug's only short but when fired at close range from a police-issue Glock it leaves no room for manoeuvre. At a distance, cops go for maximum body mass. But I'm not at a distance so he's aiming for my eyes and I'm staring down the barrel as his forefinger squeezes the lock-lever before going for the trigger. Even before they hit I can feel them – the bullets, the blue beans – as the gun's mechanism reaches tipping point. I close my eyes to death: Imogene, I hear myself murmur, Aunt Rube, my dear little dead sister, Dad, Mum, Annie …

Followed by a crash, a scream, then terrible silence.

The cop's gun hand is empty and his eyes are emptier still but somehow I'm still alive. I roll the dead weight off me, find the little torch and jam it in my mouth. The flowerpot Tsunami chucked shattered when it hit him. I work my hands over his body to find a lot of dirt, the remains of the pot and wetness. An artery is pumping Richardson's lifeblood out of him and signing my death warrant. You don't kill a cop in this city and get away with it. After this, I'll be lucky to be mining opals in Coober Pedy. The light comes on; I spit out the torch.

'There are some things upstairs called Magiclips,' I tell Tsunami. 'They'll connect anything to anything and you'll find them with the kid's things.'

I fight to recall the relevant section of Gray's Anatomy: the sheath of the artery should be divided to a sufficient extent to allow for the introduction of the ligature, but no further ... I find the severed ends of the artery, press them together and the blood slows. Behind me, I hear Tsunami. She hands me the clips. I transfer the two ends of the severed artery into one hand and seal the ends off with the Magiclips.

'Did I kill him?' Tsunami asks.

I feel his pulse. It's as lively as a dead rat. 'Not yet.'

Richardson's eyes are fluttering, his arms spread out like he's offering absolution — or begging for it.

I jerk my head at the phone. 'Dial 000, Tsunami, and dial it fast.' I hear her pad down the hall, pick up the handset, tap out the numbers and rap out the necessary details, before hanging up and returning.

'Now get the nappies,' I tell her.

It takes a lot of nappies to stanch the bloodflow but there are still some left after I manage it. Only then do I sit back.

'We got to get out of here.'

When I turn up at Harry's next morning, the play bike's already outside, the dame's already seated and Harry's already hovering. She's wearing a little silk number that barely covers her shoulders, there are dark smudges under her eyes that didn't come out of a beauty case and she comes straight to the point.

'I had to throw the flowerpot, Brownie.'

'It's all right.'

'I didn't know it would kill him.'

'He's not dead yet.'

'I'm sick of being a babysitter.'

'I didn't ask for your help.'

'I don't mean looking after you, I mean Philomena, or whatever her name is.'

'Look, I'm more than happy to go it alone from here,' I say. 'You came in handy last night, chucking that pot, but ...'

'Richardson was just another enemy and it was just like throwing another hand grenade.'

'... but you could get yourself killed. Apart from which,' I add hopefully, 'you must have a lot of work to do.'

'So I'll put in an appearance at the office. But I finish what I start,' she adds and the sun ricochets off her bare shoulders like shot silk.

She pauses while Harry serves the coffee – a nice, clean little cup with a heart carefully worked into the froth for Tsunami; a dirty, cracked mug with slops in the saucer for me. I take a slug of the muck and shove it aside. I like coffee but this ain't coffee.

'That's not how I run a case. Solving a murder isn't some kind of social outing. The cops have let someone off but are now busy framing someone else. Which means that somewhere out there is a killer.'

Tsunami looks downcast. It must be the coffee.

'But surely I can help.'

Like I say, waves change. Tsunami's like an idle surf licking at a sandbank – frothy driblets caressing the shore while the big thumper's building up its killer load far out to sea. I pick up the *Terrorgraph* to give me time to think, only it doesn't do anything of the sort. Because the front page – as well as several more pages inside – feature a stoush between von Franck and the politician known as Clean Fill, the main entry reading:

A Fill and Franck Exchange?

Chapter 30

IF YOU PRICK US ...

A billboard reading *BLUEBEARD* – make that *BLUEBIRD* – fills the background while the two combatants are down and dirty, a lot of onlookers trying to pull them apart. One picture shows Clean Fill attempting to run, with von Franck in pursuit. Another shot shows them slugging it out to a backdrop of a passing bus with *WELCOME TO SYDNEY* on its side.

It takes a lot to keep people happy in this burg but this story should help: a billionaire and a politician down in the gutter with the rest of the *Terrorgraph* readers – proof positive that jokers at the pointy end of our plutocracy are no different from the rest of us. The big type says: WE PAID A QUARTER OF A MILLION DOLLARS FOR THESE PHOTOS AND THIS IS THE REASON WHY ... Followed by a lot of frothing-at-the-mouth articles – with only one in exculpation:

A FRIENDLY STOUSH

A Pair of Not-So-Ordinary Men Reveal their Human Side

JOHN CURTIS reports:

They've been mates since attending school together. As friends they've had their ups and downs but who hasn't?

There's the mandatory journey down memory lane before the piece winds up with:

Just another blue

The two blokes in this stoush – the cabinet minister and the developer – might be tall poppies. But in the end they're just like the rest of us – a couple of knockabout guys giving vent to their feelings, simply because they have feelings.

They might be down today but they'll bounce back tomorrow, role models for the rest of us. Take the word of one who knows: this bit of biffo is news simply because of who these men are — a pair of Aussie success stories. And in the end, all it proves is that they're human. As the Bard said: 'If you prick us, do we not bleed?'

I look up. Tsunami's eyes are on me. She shrugs. 'I saw it on the late night news while trying to get Fiona to sleep. Von Franck's our man all right, while the rest of those names on your list are no more than Caution's bedfellows. I knew it when we confronted him and I feel it again now. Just look at that face.'

The face in the photo's contorted with rage. But a face doesn't determine guilt. If von Franck killed Cock Robin, what was the motive? Would a successful man risk a lifetime's work in a moment? And if he was angry with his old schoolmate, what could have been —

Tsunami gives voice to my thoughts. 'What could have upset von Franck enough for him to ...? It must have been something that this mate of his — what's his name ...?'

'Clean Fill.'

'... said.' Tsunami shrugs. 'But people say things ...'

I find myself thinking aloud.

'What about the photographer? What was he doing there? Good photographers don't grow on trees, Tsunami, and this was a good one — a quarter-of-a-million smackeroos good, going by what the *Terrorgraph* paid. The question is: how come this good photographer was in the right place at the right time?'

Harry returns. Harry does that — he returns, like bad food. I note the photo credit: Peter Parkinson.

'Want anything more?' Harry asks, looking hopefully at Tsunami.

I follow his gaze. Tsunami's an amoeba — seeming to change shape, attitude and sexual orientation as quickly as a rabbit. I stand.

'See you around, Tidal Wave,' I say. 'I got a couple of jobs to do and — like you said — you got to go to the orifice. I'll give you a bell in a week or so.'

'Why not sooner?'

'That's not the way it works.'

Because the way it works is that I go back to the *Wooden No* and get the toolbag. After that I don a pair of grey workingman's overalls from Vinnie's, pick up a yellow Port-a-rail from a building site and hoof it to Bondi, where I locate the relevant phone hydrant, set up my little fence and, using the tools from the boat, remove the cover. I flick through the connections until I come to von Franck's, attach the buzz-cock then replace the cover. And after that, I pay a visit to the photographer.

Parkinson's office is in The Rocks, a hole in the wall at the top of a set of stairs next to a souvenir shop flogging genuine artefacts made overseas. I pull the fedora well down over my eyes and Parkinson doesn't look up as I shove open the mottled-glass door with *DONT ENTER* written on it and enter. A window produces just enough light to reveal a top-of-the-lion digital camera with a snout on it like an elephant's bo-diddly. It's sitting on a desk that contains one too many knotholes, together with a notepad, pencil and phone.

'Can't you read?'

I shrug. 'Why waste time reading when I can look at all the dirty pictures? Are you Parkinson — as in the disease?'

He's big and of a certain age and uncertain temperament and when he finally looks up he's not smiling. 'That's my line, mate. Yeah, I'm him — what's your excuse?'

'I'm a private investigator.'

'I can see how that could be a problem.' He tilts back his chair and considers me over his gut. 'What have you got for me, Mr Gumshoe? A nice little old-fashioned slab of adultery? An insurance scammer hefting pianos? A peasant poking a princess?'

I feel dirty just being here, like the air's foetid and crawling with maggots. I square my shoulders and come to the point. 'How did you get ringside tickets to the von Franck–Clean Fill bout?'

The paparazzo's face gets a stonewall look to it and filters come down over his piggy eyes. 'Who wants to know?'

'Like I said I'm a —'

'Yeah, I know what you said you were — what I haven't heard yet is who.' He reaches for his camera, the one with the long-range snout on it. 'More important, who you're working for.'

He's picked up the camera and he's got it up to one piggy eye with his finger on the danger button when I reach across and snap it out of his hands before he's got a chance to snap me.

'You'll get it back when you tell me why you were there.'

'That's theft!'

'So is taking people's pictures when they don't want you to. Who told you there'd be a fight?'

Chapter 31

... DO WE NOT BLEED?

Parkinson's sitting and I'm standing and I've got a firm grip on his livelihood. My hat's well down over my eyes so the eye-spy positioned at 11 o'clock in the ceiling can't see my face and I'm capable of anything. Who knows with private defectives?

'All right,' he mutters. 'I got a tip-off.'

'Who from?'

His eyes go even craftier than they were before and he goes coyer than a virgin in a harem. 'A little bird told me.'

'Heard of the Marquis of Queensberry Rules? That's when you get three-minute rounds, there's no hitting below the belt and if you stay down long enough they call it a knockout. Well, that's them and this is me: I know no rules – apart from the facts. And the facts are that if you don't give me a name on the count of three you lose your Box Brownie and a lot more besides. One –'

His eyes shift to the door but it's an old trick so my eyes don't shift with his. Instead I bring the camera over my head like I'm about to throw it.

'Two –'

When he drags his eyes away from the door, there's a scared look in them.

'All right, I'll talk.'

'Of course you will. And it'll be the truth, too, because otherwise your expensive little camera goes out the window.'

So he tells me, only what he tells me isn't the truth. And I know it's not the truth because his eyes go walkabout to the door once more as he slings me a story about von Franck being a playboy who playboyed Clean

Fill's wife and when Clean Fill's daughter found out about it she told her father who got angry with von Franck and – he winds up, like I'm still wet behind the ears – the rest is history …

'His-tory or your story, Parkinson? Because what you left out is what I want to know. Namely how you knew the fight was on. You've got one last chance: Who told you?'

But Parkinson doesn't reply because he can't. There's an old saying that the only good paparazzo is a dead paparazzo which is what Parkinson's just become – a third eye appearing in the centre of his forehead about the size and shape of a .45 slug. I pirouette and drop, my gat transferring itself from the under-shoulder holster to my fist as another bullet wings over my head and a figure I only see the tail-end of disappears out of the DONT ENTER doorway.

I close the two of the dead man's eyes I can do anything about, remove the tape from the closed-circuit television camera, gouge the photo device out of the extra knothole in the desk, tear the top sheet off the pad by the phone, and flip the sign on the doorknob so it reads *DO NOT DISTRUB* as I make my departure.

In these days of hi-tech surveillance, people forget the imprint of a telephone message remains on the undersheet of a writing pad after the top page is removed, and that's what I subject to the necessary treatment on board the *Wooden No.* And what I come up with mightn't be much – no more than a four-letter word – but it's enough to give me a lot to think about as I row back to shore and take a bus into the city.

BLUE, the word says. But is that blue as in stoush? Or blue as in mistake. Blue as in sad maybe … What about blue as in Once in a blue moon. Or blue blood or university blue or blue movie or true blue – the last being a reference to butchers' aprons which, because of their colour, somehow manage to hide bloodstains … Blue beans are bullets, a blue fish is a shark. What about the flag that departing ships display – the Blue Peter? Or blue ruin, as in gin; blue talk, as in indecent language; or …

Blue is as blue does and in the end all I'm left with is the fact that BLUE means both too much and too little and I put it to one side and get on with what I've got – which is little more than a fine day and a listening device attached to a phone hydrant.

I set up shop at a bus stop where I pretend my big white earphones are playing Beethoven's *Fifth*, the first four notes of which represent Fate. *Dah-dah-te-daaah* … I wave my arms around, conducting as I hum – it keeps the flies away. *Dah-dah-te-dah* … A couple of surfers give me a wide berth and an old dame smiles uncertainly as she hobbles past. *Dah-te-dah-dah; dah-dah-te-dah* …

But all I'm really hearing is the kind of noise allegedly made by rice bubbles – a snap, crackle, poopedy-scoop – until a voice comes out of the stratosphere, saying:

'That you, Elephant?'

'Who else would it be?'

'Pesto wants more.'

'Pesto always wants more.'

'That's why they call him Pesto – you know, as in pest?'

General laughter. Von Franck – he must be Elephant – gives the relevant instructions and there's a click followed by silence. Paranoids reckon intelligence agencies bug everyone but we're assured by those same agencies that they only collect metadata – who rang whom and when – and then only when those calls involve people the spooks believe are menaces to society. In which case, von Franck's in the clear because he's clearly too rich to be a menace to anyone. Dah-dah-te-dah-te-dah-dah … Another call:

'Hey, Maestro!'

'Dithyramb!'

'Guess what? The Premier's come good – we got the okay for the western subdivision.'

'How much did that cost?'

'Nowhere near what it'll earn.'

More general laughter. Von Franck and his mob are a merry little gang of toadstools but they've got a lot to laugh about – the happiness that comes with making a lot of money for themselves and misery for everyone else. More of the same, a morning – make that mourning – of more of the same. But I'm not here to hear about corruption, I'm here for –

'Mr von Franck?'

The voice is respectful, verging on sycophancy.

'Who's this?'

'This is the Minister for Development's secretary, Mr von Franck. The Minister says he'd be delighted to accept your kind invitation for a cruise aboard *The Holy Profit* to show quote there's no ill feeling over our little contretemps the other day unquote. Is there anything he should bring?'

'No, only something he shouldn't – his conscience.'

General laughter. After which:

Secretary: 'I'm sorry but could I have that date again?'

'Why do your own barking when you own a dog? Here's my personal assistant.'

The PA comes on; she's got a sweet voice, honey mixed with an overdose of strychnine, and Yes, she says, the cruise is next Thursday – 7 pm to midnight – and I commit the date and time to memory.

After which I doff the earphones, unhitch the bug and call Tsunami.

Chapter 32

FIGURES IN A LANDSCAPE

The tide comes in and goes out again. Annie still doesn't want to know me and neither does Rory; Salina still won't let me see Imogene; and Ruby's still crook. 'Forget about me, Rainbow,' she said the last time I called. 'Bury yourself in your work …'

Rube's right, so I keep on with the early-morning exercise regime; do the ballet exercises and the laps at Bondi; overdose on Harry's coffee; watch the high-rise buildings rear ever higher on Sydney's skyline; patch the boat until it becomes patches on patches; and watch the to-and-fro of *The Holy Profit* – von Franck's cruiser, a modest little vessel roughly the size of the *Titanic*.

The following Thursday night, clouds cover the moon and Tsunami's a black shadow under a streetlamp as she settles her bike on its haunches on the inner flank of Bondi's Campbell Parade. I quarter the area – the sparkle of the main drag, the cold stretch of the promenade, the black sea – but apart from the gentle flip-flop of the surf on the night sand and the murmur of lovers on the swings, there's nothing but the sound of Tsunami sniffling as she draws near, and the strong stench of camphor.

'You can still change your mind,' I say.

'Why?' She hauls out a baby-wipe to stifle a sneeze as she glances at the lovers before bringing her eyes back to me. 'After tending to a sick kid all week, this is a walk in the proverbial.'

'All right, there's a good chance we're going to meet up with dogs and/or armed guards and you're reeking of a highly aromatic sinus-clearer because you happen to have a cold. They'll know without looking that they've got company. Which means you've either got to take a rain check on this outing or ditch the medication.'

Once we're sorted, I go over the plan. We're here for a reason, which is to link von Franck to the killing of Cock Robin — or not, as the case may be. The murder mightn't have been committed by von Franck in person — like he said: If you've got a dog, why do your own barking? But he's smart enough to know that the more dogs he uses the more there'll be to bite him.

Bondi used to be the kind of suburb where punters slipped out of their trackies, kicked back on the sand and relaxed. But that was before von Franck and his mob built hotels for *über*-rich tourists and the toffee-nosed coffee houses followed. Now all you got to do is pay and the garb's Givenchy.

Von Franck's place leans so far over the beach that it looks like a potential suicide. I've supplemented the misinformation from *Home Incredible* with the plans that Blueprint Eddie (add *blueprint* to the list of things blue) filched from Council. Which reveal that, in addition to the six bedrooms, there's a 32-seat movie theatre, a games room, a sauna and a heated indoor pool that Samantha Ricecake would feel at home in — plus a guardhouse in a bunker under the billiard room.

The tide's in and the waves are licking at my rubber duckies as I stuff my hat in my backpack, don the balaclava and abseil up the cliff with Tsunami behind me. It's a long way up, Tsunami's coughing by the time we get there, and her coughing's attracting attention — as I coil up the rope ready for a quick departure, somewhere in the house a dog starts barking.

Our presence has also activated the sensor lights. I park Tsunami by the lights, put on the night-vision glasses, move to a window that's well within range of the cameras, tape a fist-sized section of glass next to the window lock, do the cut, remove the glass, then lead Tsunami around to the front door. She clears her throat.

'I thought you didn't do front doors,' she says.

'I still don't,' I reply. 'But the guards will be attracted to the window and when they are' – I waggle my gat: a Chinese-made BBQ-901 general-anaesthetic gun – 'I feed them the sleep juice.'

'Are we looking for anything in particular?'

I keep my eye on the hole in the window. 'A pair of kingsize plimsolls complete with garden mud from Minnie's on their soles would be nice.' I hear two sets of footsteps – one heavy, the other light. 'Failing that, whatever's on offer. But first we got to neutralise the guards.'

The moon's on holiday but I'm wearing the head-mounted Gen-3 ATN PS15-21 night-vision binoculars and they pick up the guards as they round the corner to the tune of the dog barking inside the house, two figures showing up in my Gen-3 lenses coloured blue.

Not possible, I tell myself. But anything's possible, even the appearance of the pair of goons that thumped me outside Clean Fill's, who would also fit Mismatch's description of the thugs that broke her arm – one big, the other small. Both are wearing the same kind of head-mounted Gen-3 binoculars I'm wearing, the tall one's got a gun and the little one's wielding a cricket bat – but at a guess, I'd say he's not looking for a nice little game of elevenses.

That's when Tsunami sneezes and that's when the tall one's head flicks our way.

'There he is!' High voice. 'The window was a trick – pincer him!'

'What do we do now?' Tsunami asks.

'We keep our balaclavas on.'

As directed by the tall man, the small man – Lofty, Piano Girl said he was called – stays where he is, while the tall, skinny one – by the same logic, he's probably Chubby – goes around the side. I could anaesthetise the bat-wielder after which me and Tsunami could escape down the cliff before the tall one reaches us, but I don't like failure – never have. I motion Tsunami with the Barbecue.

'Get out there with your hands up.'

'But he'll shoot me!'

'Not with a cricket bat, he won't.'

'But –'

'Remember your training, soldier!'

'What the –!' cries the little one. After which, he yells, 'Watch out, Fat Lady!'

Chapter 33

DEEP BLUE

at Lady? The barking inside the house goes up a couple of notches as
the little man hesitates, a tailender at the crease with the light fading
who's desperately in need of a six. I shoot him with the anaesthetic gun,
he goes down and the bat drops from his hands.

'Gotcha!'

The voice is too close for comfort. I stand my ground.

'Drop the gat!' says the voice belonging to the figure that the small
man called Fat Lady.

When Tsunami cracks her over the head with the bat, the Fat Lady
goes down like a foot-long sandwich. I check their pulses; they're both
as slow as Rory's thought processes. With Lofty anaesthetised and the Fat
Lady counting canaries, we've got ten minutes, fifteen tops.

Whatever door the guards came out of, it's closed, so I reach through
the hole in the window and flick the latch. There's a growl, followed by
a black-and-tan bloodhound and just enough time to unleash the sleep-
maker before it gets me.

There's something wrong with this scenario but there isn't time to
work it out. I've got enough in my sugar bowl without working things
out. The lights in the house are on and there's no need to turn them off
because both the guards and the dog are accounted for. But the cameras
are still operative so I remind Tsunami to keep her balaclava on while we
search the house. Upstairs are the promised en suites, which gives me just
under two minutes a room; I hear the dame moving about downstairs as
I check walls, floor and furnishings. Nothing, nothing and more nothing.

When we get outside again the dog's just coming to and the salt air's
shimmering over a building that didn't feature in the blueprint – a small,

blocky structure situated on the northern boundary of the block, its door open. Tsunami looks nervous.

'How long before they wake up?'

I move towards the open door. 'Couple of minutes.'

The headlamp doesn't work when deprived of starlight so I use the pencil torch. There's the usual electric appliances plus the usual workbench with the usual tools on it.

'Ah!' I murmur.

Tsunami squeezes in beside me. 'What have you found?'

I shine the torch on the tools. A faint glimmer shines back.

'What do you see, Tsunami?'

'Just some tools.' She shrugs. 'But von Franck's a builder – you'd expect him to have tools, wouldn't you?'

'But what do you notice about them?'

'That they're rusty because the door's open and the salt air's got to them.'

'Except' – I hold up the wrench that's on top of the pile of tools – 'this one's not rusty.'

'That means that it doesn't belong here, which makes it the murder weapon,' says Tsunami. 'Case solved, end of story.'

'Sorry, but it's only the beginning.'

'Why? Doesn't it mean that von Franck did it? All we have to do now is tell the police where we found the wrench, Richardson will no longer have a hold over Minnie and she can go home.' Tsunami reaches her climax. 'And take her bloody kid with her.'

I heft the wrench. 'While I'm pretty certain this is the murder weapon, I'm equally sure I'm not judge, jury and executioner. And going to the cops won't work because: a) We're somewhere we're not meant to be; b) von Franck's protected by his wealth and; c) I can't go to the cops.'

'Why?'

'Because I don't exist.' I recall Salina's words. 'I'm a non-person – proof of my existence being either non-existent or destroyed. And if I go to the cops I'll exist and that'll be the end of the line.'

'Why?'

'Because I'll be thrown into jail for existing. And after that – after I exist – I'll be at the mercy of everyone I don't want to be at the mercy of – the cops, the taxman, bill collectors, assorted mercenaries, and Pandora.'

'All right, what do we do now?'

'We get the hell out of here before the dog, the Fat Lady, Lofty or all three wake from their sleepy-byes and come after us. And we dump the wrench on the way.'

At least the tide's out as we get ourselves down the cliff and along the rock platform. As we hit the platform, I chuck the wrench out to sea.

The wind rock-and-rolls the *Wooden No* and through the porthole I make out the Harbour, the Bridge, the real estate of the Eastern Suburbs, the Botanic Gardens they're talking about developing, the Opera House which probably ditto and the inevitable flock of cranes dragging the city ever higher into the unknown.

The boat lists and I get myself into the bilge and start doing the bail-out. It's like lightning's split the sea and the deep blue hole under the boat goes on forever.

The phone rings.

'Brownie?'

It's Tsunami.

'Could be,' I say.

'Something's happened.'

'What?'

'It's all over the news. You wouldn't want me to say on the phone.'

'I'll be right over.'

There's a pause as I hear a voice and a baby crying in the background. 'Minnie wants you to get some nappies on the way.'

'Would that be crawlers, infants or toddlers; the night-time ones with plastic on the outside or day-time ones without; compact or comfortable; medium, large or small; girl or unisex; washable or disposable —?'

'Just nappies — and hurry.'

Chapter 34

ARTERIAL MOTIVE

No paper boy cycles down to the shore with the early-morning newspapers, singing sea shanties as he rows among the boats, chucking rolled-up *Terror-diddlies* down gangways. I like it like that — there's enough trouble in the world without having to read about it. But, forewarned, I buy a newspaper from the inconvenience store where I get the nappies, reading it in the back of the Deluxe Blue hansom cab on the way to Tsunami's.

DETECTIVE DEAD
HERO HACKED
MAGICLIP MURDER
ARTERIAL MOTIVE?

I work my way through the contorted phraseology to find what the paper's saying.

A hero has died, the victim of an apparently motiveless slaying. In the course of his duties, Detective Sergeant Richard Richardson was attending a house that was the scene of a recent murder — only to fall victim to possibly the same mystery slayer himself.

The recipient of a Police Medal for Bravery after an incident on a building site, Sergeant Richardson was allegedly subjected to kinky sexual practices as he lay supine on the murder house floor. Bullets recovered from the crime scene show that he tried to defend himself, but to no avail.

Responding to an emergency call from an unknown caller, detectives and paramedics discovered the police hero lying in a pool of blood. Portions of a shattered ceramic pot were allegedly found, along with a number of nappies and two pins known as Magiclips.

Detective Richardson was rushed to hospital but died shortly after admittance. Investigating police are looking for …

The cab drops me outside Vegan Nirvana in Balmain and I complete the rest of the journey on foot. When I arrive I palm Minnie the Disposable Girls Reversible Dri-Tots while Tsunami hands me a mug.

'Is that how you like it?'

'If it's coffee I like it.'

She lowers her voice and raises it all at the same time. 'They're trying to pin this latest murder on Minnie as well. It's in all the news and the cops are buzzing around like sex-crazed hornets. They're calling Minnie a gangster's moll.'

Sunlight gleams on the French-polished furniture, Skinny Minnie's perched innocently on a daybed feeding Fiona and from somewhere outside come the sweet strains of an étude by Chopin.

'They don't really think it's her,' I say. 'Blaming her makes it look like they're doing something while at the same time the real killer – that is, of Cock Robin and maybe also the photographer – relaxes and maybe makes a mistake. If that's all they're doing, then Minnie's safe – at least for the moment.'

I speak with an authority I don't feel. If Minnie was in trouble before, she's in double trouble now.

The coffee's better than Harry's – then again, anything's better than Harry's – and if Tsunami's face was any more drawn, she'd be a charcoal sketch by da Vinci.

'So what do we do now?'

I nod at Minnie. 'I'm going to see a journo about a hero.'

'What about me?'

'You've got to stay here and keep an eye on Minnie.'

I find the pilgarlic nursing a beer on the other side of happiness in the bar of the Scribes' Swill in good old downtown Slurry Hills.

'Top cop dies – nursing mother suspected of second slaying,' he says. 'Only the good die young.'

I order a first for me and a fourth, fifth or tenth for Curtis.

'Tell me about Richardson being good.'

'He –' Curtis looks cunning. 'You got something in exchange, Mr Private Defective?'

I hand him the beer. 'Here's a down payment on sorrow,' I say. 'Tell me about your hero.'

While he talks, I figure the scribe for a Pollyanna. Despite the hardboiled act, he only ever sees people's nice side. Von Franck is Mother Teresa, Richardson was the Messiah and Curtis doesn't tell me anything I couldn't have read in the *Terrorgraph* – but then, he probably wrote it.

'Richard Richardson,' he says, 'the recipient of a Police Medal for Bravery after an incident on a building site, met his tragic end at the hands of an assassin bent on …'

It's like listening to a talking typeface but I still hear him out. And after I hear him out, I buy him another lip-loosener and ask the question I really want answered.

'Tell me about the incident.'

'What incident?'

'The one in which Richardson was a hero.'

On the turn, Curtis knocks over the glass with the outline of Australia and AHA on the side. Once the letters might have stood for Australian Hotels Association but now they just spell Aha! The barmaid mops the beer off the bar-top and I order a new one.

'What's your particular interest in all this?'

'I'm not particularly interested in anything – except a chat. I'm at a loose end due to the End-of-the-world Financial Crisis and I'm just trying to make ends meet – you know, as in End, I'd like you to meet End.' I stand. 'Okay then, I'll get out of your hair.'

Goal number one in journalism – even before the truth – is to hold onto your contacts. He grabs my elbow.

'You have to understand I – just lost a mate.'

I spread my hands like I'm the Pope or the Daily Llama. 'I didn't realise Richardson was a particular mate.'

Curtis bows his head over his beer. 'Us old-time journos were put through the hoops – that is, we did the rounds. When I was on Police Rounds, Richardson and I hung together. So, do you want to know about the hero?'

'Only if you want to tell me.'

Chapter 35

UNDER COVER OF LIGHT ...

Several years ago, Richard Richardson was just another young constable when he got his big chance.

'It was a time of great unease in the building industry,' Curtis says. 'There'd been the so-called Green Bans, but when they stopped, the unions became irrelevant again – they were rebels without a cause who had lost public sympathy. Then along came a man who was half-crook, half-saviour. Due to his politics, they called him Robin the Red or Red Robin – but eventually he came to be known as Cock Robin.'

I finish my drink and order several more for both of us.

'As General Secretary of the Building Labourers' Federation, Cock Robin organised a strike on one of von Franck's building sites. But von Franck, being von Franck, fought back and negotiations ended in fisticuffs. Iron bars that were meant for reinforcing – there's irony for you – were produced. It was striking workers versus scabs. Then Richardson rode into the mêlée ...'

'And won himself a Police Medal for bravery. Is that when he turned crooked? You know, Under cover of light, darkness reigned? And that union trouble – did Richardson foment it?'

'Ferment?'

'Fo-ment – as in heat, excite, encourage, cause.'

Curtis smiles. It's a nice smile, one that once must have once got him that extra scoop of ice-cream – and later on, just scoops.

'I'm having you on, laddie – I'm a journo, remember, born with printer's ink under my nails. No, if anyone caused the problem it was Red Robin. It was his style to cause trouble, which was why he was called Red ...'

There's more of the same but I stopped listening when Curtis upended his glass. There was a lot in it – what he was saying, as well as the glass.

'Okay, I've got a story for you,' I say finally. 'But before I tell you, who hated Cock Robin enough to kill him?'

Curtis takes a swill and this time it's a real swill. He nods like he's come to a decision. 'This is strictly off the record,' he warns. 'If anyone asks, I didn't tell you. Do I have your word on that?'

I tell him Yeah and he holds out his hand and I hold out mine and our hands miss but he still takes it for a gentleman's handshake in an era when there aren't any gentlemen. Then he lowers his voice because this is confession time and what he's about to say needs to stay in the confessional.

'I can't name names but my guess is it was someone in the industry.'

'That's it?'

Curtis touches the side of his nose. He might be trying to pick it or it might be a sign. I take it as a sign.

He rubs his shaven head and considers me.

'You're a detective – you work out the rest. Now tell me your story.'

I tell him a story.

A unionist's death can be swept under the carpet but kill a cop and the world turns upside down. I tell Minnie and Tsunami to keep a low profile while I keep myself to myself – no swims at Bondi, no trips to Harry's caff, no drinks at the speakeasy. Queen delivers my breakfast and I accept it without demur. I keep my boat clean and my nose cleaner. If my profile was any lower I'd be dead. The world spins on its axis but I don't spin with it. Call me quiet or don't call me at all.

I make a few calls but my ex-girlfriend Annie and my ex-mate Rory won't give me the time of day. I accept the usual rebuffs from my ex-wife Salina when I ask to speak to the kid. I call Aunt Rube but it's like communing with the dead. Finally there's the inevitable lull in the newsworthiness of the cop killing and it's time to return to being a telephone repairman. People nod as they pass. I get to know Mary with the cocker spaniel, the geezer in the Walk-a-Chair, and the postman. I'm a technician in a grey combination overall with writing on it on a street corner in Bondi and most of the telephone conversations are about as exciting as beached eels.

Von Franck's secretary to girlfriend: She's having an affair behind his back — can you believe it?

Why, that's terrible!

Yes, isn't it? But understandable under the circumstances …

Another call and more exclamation marks — this time courtesy of Mrs von Franck.

Yes, of course we'd love to come to dinner! Your place at eight? Should I bring anything? Just Ivan? Doubt enters the voice. I'll see what I can do …

Later, another call from the wife:

I'm sorry but Ivan can't make it. Do you still want me to come? Shall I bring anything? Just myself? I'll see you on Friday …

I note the day, time and details in my logbook. But what I note most of all are the clicks on the line that tell me someone else apart from me is bugging von Franck.

When you're on a boat, the world's reduced to a narrow compass — the turn of the tide, ships that pass in the night and passing thoughts. Curtis's words churn in my brain: *You're a detective — you work out the rest.* What was he referring to — and why? If it was the occupation of Cock Robin's killer, so what? The pink phone rings. I click on. In the background, the baby's crying, while in the foreground, Tsunami's screaming.

'Calm down,' I say, 'and tell me what's going on.' To hell with confidentiality. 'And this time without the wisteria.'

Tsunami takes a deep breath. The newspapers, television — even the social media — have got their knickers in a knot over Richardson. No-one liked him when he was alive but he was a cop and now that he's dead the cops have to solve his killing. It doesn't matter who they pin it on, as long as they pin it.

'I went to Minnie's to pick up more baby things but couldn't even make it to the door because of the cops. So I left — but not before I saw them with the — what's it called?'

'Shadow board.'

'That's right, the shadow board. Anyway, they're serious now. They're after Minnie and it's only a matter of time before they find her.' There's a significant pause. 'There's something I didn't tell you. I —'

It's time to postpone the dialogue. 'Hold that thought, Tsunami — I'll be right over.'

When I get to Tsunami's, pools of sunlight are strewn on the floorboards like autumn leaves. Tsunami shuffles into the room in espadrilles. That's when I see the resemblance and also what she didn't tell me. But I ask anyway.

'So what didn't you tell me?'

'It – it was no coincidence I met Minnie because I was lying in wait for her. They say a man's good dies with him but there was never any good in Cock Robin. Some people are born bad and there's nothing anyone can do about it. Cock Robin started life as Little Robbie, became That Little Bastard, then – because he was adept with a bow and arrow – Robin Hood. Until finally, because he was a cocky little bastard, he became Cock Robin.' Pause. 'He bashed me until I learnt to fight back. That was what gave me my taste for the Army. Then I discovered Minnie was copping it and I had to protect her.'

'You mean … '

'That's right, he was my brother.'

Chapter 36

THE CANARY IN THE MINE

This either sheds new light on the killings or no light at all.

'Why do you feel this information is important now?'

'Because the cops are after Minnie and she's here. And now they're investigating in earnest they're sure to come up with the fact that Robin had a sister and they'll find out where I live. And when they do, they'll have their killer on a plate – even if she didn't do it.'

The two dames and the babe have become a responsibility. They're no longer a way of forgetting my problems – they've become problems themselves. Skinny Minnie and the babe look like The Pieta and Tsunami needs help.

'I think I've worked out who killed Cock Robin and the photographer,' I say. 'But I've got to make it stick. Meanwhile, you're spot on – the cops will find you and, through you, they'll find Minnie. Which means you'll have to go somewhere they won't find you in a hurry ...'

The spider's in his parlour and it's the long-legged variety that wraps up flies and parks them in its web to eat at leisure. Which is why I feel vulnerable when I tell the dame I've come to see Clean Fill. She gives me an unwelcoming smile.

'He's not in.'

'So I'll wait in his office till he gets back.'

She gets the sort of look on her face that people get when things are moving in the opposite direction to the one they want and reaches under the desk. I could stand around waiting but if I do that long enough, Clean

Fill will leave via the tradesmen's exit, so instead I step past the dame and throw open the door to find Clean Fill already climbing out of his comfort zone. He reseats himself like he wasn't really thinking of going anywhere. He's still carrying the scars of the fight – a black eye, swollen lip, political embarrassment.

'Nice to see you,' he says.

'Can't say the same.'

'It's still nice to see you,' he repeats. 'How can I help?'

I shut the door. 'By keeping a couple of friends of mine out of the meatworks.'

Clean Fill reaches for the telephone. 'If you don't leave immediately,' he says, 'I'll tell the police.'

'And what will you tell them? That someone's accusing you of the murder of a unionist and a photographer?' His hand comes off the phone and a wary look comes into his eyes. 'I don't know what your game is, O'Hare' – I use his real name, it sounds official – 'but I've got a fair idea. It's called Making Money – you go round and round the merry-go-round with a bunch of crooks and the one that ends up with the most dough wins. But your first problem is that I'm not interested in money.'

'And what's my second problem?'

'How you're going to get out of this. My bet is you'll go for the trifecta and play me in with the dames.' Clean Fill looks relieved; I like it when people look relieved – it's called narrowing the field of inquiry. 'Where were you the night Cock Robin copped it?'

The politician recovers his equilibrium, along with a little black book with APPOINTMENTS inscribed on the cover in gold. 'I'll need a date and time,' he says.

I give him a date and time and after he flips through his little black book he comes to a page that makes him smile. It's not a nice smile, more like the rictus you find on corpses. He fingers a little badge that reminds him he's been honoured by prosperity.

'I'm sorry to disappoint you, but I have what you might call a cast-iron alibi. The day in question was my daughter's birthday and I was helping her celebrate.'

Clean Fill's still smiling as I leave. It doesn't mean much. Or maybe it means everything.

'Happy birthday,' I tell his daughter as I pass.

She smiles her unhappy smile. 'But my birthday's not until next month!'

I take a cab and the circuitous route via The Hills to lose any tails I might have picked up, either courtesy of the cops or in remembrance of things past. The telephone hydrant's where I left it – a grey protuberance with nice views of the sea – and when I park myself back in the bus shelter wearing the two headphones – one for the phone, the other for the bug I installed at von Franck's the night me and Tsunami paid our visit – it's like listening to sounds in a conch shell. I hear noises that might be the sound of waves, except they're accompanied by too many clicks. Followed by:

Mrs von Franck: I'm sorry, Maisie, but Ivan still can't come.

Maisie: What a shame. But what could be more important than me?

Mrs von Franck: I have to be honest with you, I don't know. He'll either sit around doing crosswords or be off on one of his walks with Sherlock – sorry, that's his bloodhound. Anyway, it'll be a lot more fun without him …

I've put two and two together and come up with a canary, the kind they put down mines to see if people can stay alive when the air's poisoned – and when the canary dies they know that they can't. Nice birds, canaries – they sing and give up their lives for you. The only trouble is that – looked at from the point of view of the bird – you generally end up with a dead canary.

I go and see Annie. She's serving tarts. 'I see you're serving tarts,' I say by way of conversation.

'Speaking of which,' Annie says, 'You didn't bring yours with you this time, the one with the big, you know – tickets on herself.'

'She's just an acquaintance, Annie.'

Annie smiles, only it's not a nice smile. 'Just like these are just tarts,' she murmurs.

By the time the Mercedes rolls out of von Franck's – the silver one that runs on fifty-dollar bills as opposed to the husband's, which is still in the garage and prefers C-notes – I'm positioned in the shadow of the stink chimney, the one that vents methane from the raw sewage piped out to sea. It must be the guards' night off because I can't see them, which means von Franck must be all alone in his mansion with his dog, himself and his money.

Chapter 37
WHERE THERE'S A WILL ...

I've trawled through his past – backwards, sideways, upwards and downwards – and come up with all the disclaimers. Von Franck arrived in Australia with nothing but that coin: a single, solitary *ban* – which he was at pains to show me he still possesses – starting out as a mortician's assistant and quickly becoming the principal of *FRANK FUNERALS*. Nice name and even nicer business. Von Franck perfected the simple send-off and business prospered.

Meanwhile, his private life – again according to my sources – was what might be called interesting. He had a lot of relationships with a lot of dames that were famous and a lot of dames that weren't, blonde and not so blonde, beautiful and not so beautiful. I'll say this for him, he didn't discriminate. Then he met and married the woman that's just gone out to a card game and became a builder – making an even bigger fortune than he had already. Along the way there were the usual *contretemps* but that's the way it is in Sydney – ordinary people like lying on the beach and talking down anyone who doesn't.

I stay glued to the stink chimney.

Von Franck still doesn't go out.

I feel like a ferret at the wrong hole. What if the burrow's empty and the rabbit's in the next warren but one? But the Mercedes is still in the garage and von Franck's hardly likely to have clambered down the cliff. It's cold – which means there's a temperature inversion – and the chimney stinks.

Von Franck killed Cock Robin – that's the view according to Minnie.

He had good reason to hate Cock Robin and – with or without the help of either his guards or Clean Fill or both – he also had the motive to frame the victim's widow. The fact that Richardson wanted it otherwise would have played into von Franck's hands. It should have been: Exit, widow, in direction of Long Bay Jail. All very neat – too neat. Because it doesn't explain where Clean Fill fits into the picture or why the photographer copped it. Nor does it explain the clicks on von Franck's phone.

Von Franck still doesn't go out.

Solving a case is a matter of discounting prejudices. In the Laboratory Case, where the snake ate the rats, I figured I was pointed in one direction, while what really happened occurred in the house next door. What if von Franck and/or Clean Fill *didn't* kill Cock Robin and are also innocent of killing the photographer – what then? All our technology and the best we can come up with is shit in the sea.

A figure detaches itself from the chimney and for a moment is silhouetted against the night sky. It's either Pandora or someone else. Von Franck still doesn't go out. I abandon the surveil and go back to the boat.

Murder most fowl. When I was a kid, Aunt Rube used to trot out that phrase and afterwards I'd have nightmares about dead hens. And while the modus operandi varied – the killer might be a fox, a man with an axe or a dog – the result was always the same: there'd be a lot of dead chooks and I'd wake up screaming.

'Murder most foul,' Tsunami's saying now. 'There's no TV in the caravan but the kid wouldn't sleep so I was doing the social media thing when the news went viral.'

The Balmain house is crawling with cops but Tsunami and Minnie are holed up in the van. I'm visiting to make sure they're all right, only to find that – while Minnie and the kid are asleep – Tsunami's as agitated as hell.

Clean Fill was alone in his office when the killer struck. Neighbours heard raised voices but didn't come to investigate. Police described the scene as one of carnage. The photographer's death wasn't worth developing but the cops have linked Clean Fill's with that of Cock Robin and also of Richardson, which means it's gone straight to the darkroom. The latest killing has thrown my theory – that Clean Fill was the murderer – into a cocked hat.

Suddenly I find it hard to breathe. I throw open the door and stumble outside to find the predawn drenching the leaves with dew and the rising sun a threat. I reach into my pocket and feel the coin I found at Clean Fill's; I also feel the cops breathing down my neck.

Tsunami appears behind me. 'If they find evidence linking the deaths,' she asks, 'won't that put Minnie in the clear?'

'Unless they're madmen, murderers kill for a reason. That reason might be money, fear, hatred or revenge. So tell me this: why would someone go out of their way to kill your brother?'

'It wouldn't have been money because he didn't have any – he spent everything he had on what idiots always spend their money on: fast cars, even faster women, drugs and gambling. He was feared but there wasn't all that much fear; and while he was hated, he wasn't all that hated.' She glances past me at the sunrise. 'So by your reckoning, that leaves revenge …'

'A dish best served cold, just like this case is getting.' I know the answer but I still ask. 'So do you know anyone that felt vengeful towards your brother?'

'I can't think of anyone who didn't.'

The baby starts crying and as Tsunami heads back to the caravan I tell myself that asking people leading questions limits their imagination – ask why they hated their mother and the question assumes the answer. I follow Tsunami back inside – Skinny Minnie's there but she's not there.

'There are now four victims – Cock Robin, the cop, the photographer and the politician. And the cops are saying at least three of them are linked.' I'm thinking aloud. 'We know they're the wrong three but we still know there are three: Cock Robin, the photographer and Clean Fill. If we believe the cops, what's the common factor in those three deaths?'

Tsunami thinks aloud, too. 'Ivan von Franck.'

I'm back listening to bugs. Bugs have an ambient noise – cicadas chatter, flies buzz, mosquitoes whine and the one on von Franck's phone clicks. Why is someone else besides me bugging von Franck? More importantly – who? It could be a rival, the cops, or just someone who …

Click.

Mrs von Franck: Thanks for the other night, I did enjoy myself. Frankie can be so sullen. His public image might be rosy enough but that's not the way he is at home. I sometimes wish …

Maisie: But that's just what we were saying when you were here, isn't it? The more money there is, the more misery …

Mrs von Franck: Yes, but murder?

Silence, apart from a flurry of clicks. Then:

Maisie: What do you mean?

Mrs von Franck: Oh, Maisie, I have to tell someone. You know how Ivan's not interested in me any more? Do you think there's another woman – a woman he's serious about? And could it be linked to these deaths? Does that mean I might be next?

Maisie: Sheila!

Mrs von Franck: What am I going to do?

Maisie: You can pull yourself together for a start. Because if you leave him you won't get anything …

Mrs von Franck: But if I stay I could be next. Is money worth dying for?

Maisie: If there's enough of it. I'm only joking, Sheila. Seriously, though, is there a will? Remember where there's a will there's a way. I think you should see a lawyer …

I find Curtis in the pub.

'I need your newspaper's files on von Franck.'

The light shines off his head while the chatter of the other journalists ebbs and flows around us like hot air out of a hairdrier. I could go to Wackipedia but all it's going to tell me is that von Franck's successful and likes the ladies and I already know that. Except that Wackipedia might give me a clue as to which lady …

'Electronic or solid?' Curtis says at last. 'Let me explain. Newspaper libraries used to be known as morgues.' He raises his glass and this time he drinks from it. 'That was because they were places where articles went to die. You see, journalism's got a very short shelf life. Once they're published, stories are no more than corpses, doing what corpses do — turning yellow and rotting. But that was in the old days — modern records are computerised. Which ones do you want?'

'Both.'

Curtis demolishes the rest of his beer. In the time I've known him, he's never done that. Like any good journo, he'll sip or he'll knock his glass over but he'll always stay sober — even while he's busy pretending to be as drunk as a monk. A pokie next door goes ker-chunk and Curtis comes to a decision.

'All right, why not?'

Chapter 38

... THERE'S A WAY

The computerised files – that is, the ones on the memory stick – get me back as far as the 1980s, when newspapers switched from the clunky past to sweeping modernity, and I need to go beyond that. But apart from the memory stick, Curtis also gave me a mountain of yellowing newspaper clippings in a lot of dusty manila folders contained in what used to be brown and called a *kitbag* but is now bright yellow and rebadged *stuff sack*. He handed me the yellow sack – together with the USB – in Hyde Park where there was no-one to witness the transaction – no-one, that is, apart from the two shadows behind the Moreton Bay fig, a couple of trees down from the War Memorial.

'I didn't give you this,' he says, glancing around. 'It fell off the back of a truck when the driver wasn't looking. I won't ask what you're after but I assume it's to do with the murders. I'll need it back. Few people worry about old-time newspaper morgues any more but it's the principle ...'

'Thanks.'

'Don't mention it. And I mean that.'

I know I'm being followed because – after crossing Elizabeth Street and heading along Park before turning down George by the Woolworths Building then right into Chinatown, after which I double back towards the Semi-circular Quay – they're still there: the two that broke Mismatch's arm, thumped me outside the politician's office and later turned up as guards at von Franck's. I duck into the Queen Victoria Building and telephone Tsunami from Victoria's Basement.

'Where are you?' I ask.

'At work – I need a break from that bloody kid.'

'I've got a job for you, Tsunami.'

'What kind of job?'

'A decoy job. You'll need to dress up for it.'

'Do I get shot at?'

'Not necessarily.'

Pause. It's a soldier's pause, the kind that soldiers make before accepting a mission they suspect might end in their death. 'What do you want me to do?'

I tell her what I want her to do and after she chews it over for a moment, she's prepared to oblige. Not happy, just prepared to oblige. I click off, disentangle myself from the shop's cut-price saucepan section and head back towards Central Railway Station, and the only old-time army disposal store the developers have left standing.

It's late afternoon by the time I meet Tsunami on the corner of Sussex and Park. I've taken the long way round to shake the tail and I'm wearing army-surplus jungle greens and carrying two bags – both apparently full: one brown, the other yellow – and Tsunami's wearing pretty much what I had on before I changed: a bright red coat, blue strides, trainers that from a distance look like my whitesides, and a hat pulled down over her short-cropped hair.

'Where did you get the clothes?'

My doppelganger shrugs. She's even got the shrug right.

'I bought them at one of those pop-up shops. I asked for the worst clothes they had and ended up looking like you.'

'Give me your phone and take this one.' I switch on the pink phone and hand it to her. 'They'll have tabs on it so they'll pick you up in less than a minute, but as long as you stay in full public view you'll be safe. Stay away from nooks and crannies and keep walking. Meanwhile, I've got some homework to do. I'll call you when I'm done.'

I stay in the Limited News doorway on Park as Tsunami swaggers off towards the Cross, doing a more than fair imitation of my walk. She's carrying the yellow bag and she's bulked out her shoulders and the hat and the coat and the way she's walking do the rest. If I wasn't me I'd swear that she was. On cue, the thugs who witnessed the transaction between me and the pilgarlic fall into step behind her.

As long as they think she's me they'll be careful to stay where she won't see them and also not try anything on until they're certain they won't be seen. Which means that as long as Tsunami does what I told her, she won't get hurt. I board a bus, get off at Cammeray, hoof it to the shore, turn the coracle right side up, put the brown kitbag in the stern, push the boat into the water, and row out to the *Wooden No*.

Dusk is clamping its iron fist over the mouth of the Harbour and the brown bag is a veritable Pandora's Box. A boat drifts past making the *Wooden No* rock at her mooring, swirling in the bigger vessel's whirlpools. I make out the distinctive superstructure of what must be von Franck's boat, bigger than death and even more stupefying, and as I stare through the porthole, plague flies and disease-bearing mosquitoes fill the cabin.

Everywhere I look cries out von Franck: the city skyline's von Franck; a billboard on North Sydney's highest tower says BLUEBIRD ENTERPRISES; the deaths are linked to von Franck; and the files in the sack on the chart table are full of him — file after dusty file going back decades. I drag the laptop out of the sail locker, plug it into the 240-volt outlet, switch on and insert the thumb drive in the port featuring the menorah.

The gun's uncomfortable so I remove it, placing it on the map table next to the files. If von Franck ever did anything wrong, you didn't read it in the *Terrorgraph*. Because for years Curtis has not only been covering industrial rounds, he's also been covering for von Franck. The memory stick takes me back to 1987 but that's not far enough so I switch my attention to the stuff sack.

A heading in *The Sydney Morning Horrible* says: WILL THIS BE THE WORLD'S FIRST CONDEMNED SKYSCRAPER? And the story starts: So far investigators have found 137 faults in the tower ... I flick through the rest of the files.

The movie Aunt Rube screened on the wall of my childhood almost as often as the Jimmy Cagney gangster flicks was the 1930s creak-and-groan monster classic, *Frankenstein*. It was all about thunder and lightning, dark nights, lonely moors and a mad scientist's slash-and-burn laboratory. Legs and arms, a head, eye of toad, leg of newt. *Why am I showing you this?* Rube would ask. *Because you're as mad as a mashed potato,* I'd reply – but not out loud. *Because you want to frighten a little orphan boy half to death, because you're a crazy old spinster with nothing better to do than show scary movies to kids* …

A scientist created life out of death and thought he was God. Except that the life he created was a monster. Why am I showing you this? Rube would repeat. Because you're bloody insane! I replied to myself. But all I said out loud was: I dunno.

Then think about it, Rube would say. Because there's a reason …

Chapter 39

HERD IT ALL BEFORE

There's a reason for von Franck, too. He was a poor little immigrant boy who found refuge in Australia and struck it rich. Like the monster in the movie, he was born fully grown. There was another birth thirty years before but that didn't count because his real birth was in Australia in the early 1980s. That's when the media discovered him so it's when he was born. The birth notice appeared in the *Terrorgraph*, accompanied by a photo of a thirty-year-old man flipping a coin.

NO BAN TO SUCCESS

Ivan von Franck grew up in the shadow of death. Romania's Ceausescu regime killed off his parents, sister, aunts, cousins, friends – a start in life that would have destroyed a lesser man.

But since finding sanctuary in Australia, Ivan von Franck has forged a meteorically successful career. In just a few short years, Frank Funerals became synonymous with death. Then von Franck branched out into building. He's just landed a major government contract. We asked Ivan von Franck a few questions.

(Here the journalist adopts a pose of wide-eyed astonishment.)

JOURNALIST: Mr von Franck, from graves to building in a single bound!

VON FRANCK (flipping his trademark coin): What's the surprise? Building's just another hole in the ground that needs filling. That makes it the same as burying, but without the grief.

JOURNALIST: So tell me about that coin.

VON FRANCK: It's all I came to this country with – a 1952 Romanian penny, what they call a ban – that's not a green ban, by the way! No more than a gram of cupronickel but to me a symbol of my success.

There's more of the sycophantic same – too much more. That's von Franck, the story winds up, an enigma wrapped in a puzzle who only answers questions with more questions. And why not? The only thing not to query, in this humble reporter's opinion, is that von Franck will reach the stars he's so clearly aiming for.

The story's a set piece where the journalist asks questions the interviewee wants to be asked. It's called *absentee journalism* because journalist appears to be absent. And the name at the end is …

So the two go back that far. I skim through the rest of the files and von Franck's life's like a movie in which a plant grows at lightning speed. A shoot pops out of the ground and takes a look around, leaves appear, there's a bud, the bud unfolds, and suddenly, lo and behold! – there's a flower. Media-born in 1982, by 2014 von Franck's a rip-roaring success. One of the mobiles rings. I click on.

'Brownie?'

'Yeah?'

'They're closing in.' It's a voice from a war zone. 'I feel like a sheep being herded by a pair of kelpies.'

'Where are you?'

'Where you and I were before, at von Franck's project. I don't know if I was aiming for it or if my followers herded me here.' The old herd-it-all-before trick. 'I thought it was a through road but it turns out to be a dead end. They bury people on building sites, don't they?'

'Can you get inside the building?'

'I think that's what they want me to do.'

'Is there anywhere else to go?'

There's a pause, during which I hear the sounds of the city – the revving of engines, horns blaring, the whisper of footsteps. Tsunami comes back on the phone.

'No,' she whispers.

'Then you've got no choice. As an engineer, you'd know your way around construction sites, while the chances are your followers don't.'

'Okay.'

'Stay alert and stay alive.' I get myself up on deck. 'Hold them off as long as you can. Chuck that bagful of nothing at them if that's all you've got. But get in that building and start climbing. I'll be there as soon as I can.'

I'm halfway to shore before I remember the gun. It's still on the map table beside the stuff sack. I've got the folder but I forgot the gun. Only it's too late to turn back.

I row to shore, beach the coracle and hoof it to the shops, where I flag a cab. Using my pen torch to study the file as the taxi weaves through the North Sydney traffic before crossing the Bridge, I learn how von Franck's life reconstructed itself like a skyscraper, story upon story. Cuttings files consist of articles that have been dated, arranged according to subject matter, pasted onto sheets of A4 paper, and filed. I riffle through 1985, 1984, 1983 – there are white spaces where cuttings have been removed from their backing sheets but otherwise it's all yellowing newsprint: von Franck in front of his third tower, his second, his first; coloured pictures from women's magazines: von Franck squiring a beautiful blonde; von Franck with a brunette; von Franck with … The cab hits a bump and a picture slides out from behind another one – unglued, an orphan, and therefore overlooked, showing von Franck with yet another dame, a dame who's gazing up at him adoringly; a dame that's somehow familiar. I remove the picture and slip it in my pocket.

I pay the cabbie, open the door and get out, keeping the photo but leaving the rest of the folder in the cab. It'll find its way back to where it belongs. The phone rings again like it never stopped ringing. I click on.

'Where are you, Brownie?'

'Where are you?'

'Where you told me to be, up the tower.'

'How did you get onto the site?'

'Like any good soldier, over the top of the hoarding.'

'Where are your followers?'

Chapter 40

A VOID DANGER

Why do you think I'm showing you this movie? Rube would ask. *I dunno,* I'd reply.

'They can't be far off, Brownie,' Tsunami says.

'Stay away from the edge.'

I start running.

Somewhere there's a blue bird of happiness … The words are from a song and the song's from a play by a joker called Maeterlinck who believed happiness comes from within. Clearly he didn't have much of a hold on reality. *Why do you think I'm showing you this movie?* Rube would ask. *Who do you think is the monster?* Finally she answered her own question: *The monster's in all of us, Rainbow — we're the monster …*

I'm in front of the big, wide door that — when things are running smoothly — provides access for trucks. But the trucks are idle, the signs say KEEP OUT – NO ENTRY and the door is locked. A sign reads A VOID DANGER. It's got a concrete base and in normal circumstances I wouldn't be able to move it. But these circumstances aren't normal. I pick up the sign, swing it around my head, let go on the turn — and the gate is suddenly splinters. The roadway slopes down to the building site, its surface scarred by trucks. I slide into the abyss, prop, look up.

Three hundred metres is nearly a third of a kilometre and that's how high the building's framework is, the top floor too far away to see it. I seek and locate the unclad building's backbone — the lift well, its bank of buttons glowing blue. I hit the Up button and a mechanical voice says:

Enter. I do like the voice says and after entering turn and face outwards, just in time to see a shadow — or is it two shadows? — move across my field of vision. It might be my imagination. Then again it mightn't.

The doors close and, apart from the blue-lit buttons, I'm in darkness. The lift's padded because during construction it carries building materials and when it moves it's with the grace of a wounded alligator. Now and again there's a lurch and a scraping sound like a grounded vessel trying to free itself from a reef. I hear a sound that could be that of another lift but it might be my imagination.

A cold wind slams into me as I step out onto the rooftop. Dull halogens illuminate the roof while, halfway along the bank of lifts, I make out what looks like the feeble gleam of another torch. The torch — if it *is* a torch and not an aeroplane or a star — stays still for five, maybe six seconds before moving on again. There's no sign of Tsunami but I didn't expect any. She would have heard the lift and decided it must be the tail. The light over the lifts flickers and goes out.

Hard hats, high-vis jackets and building materials — tiles, tins, bags, timber and steel mesh — are heaped about indiscriminately. A frayed length of rope — there's not much life left in it — is coiled loosely around a battered wheelbarrow while a couple of portable toilets are parked near a stack of bricks, the rope end winding aimlessly between them. The safety fence is little more than knee-high, propped up by star posts. There's concrete, then there's no concrete — nothingness ending in the glittering fireflies of office buildings across the road and, far below, the slow-moving headlights of toy cars. A crane stands idle, its hook dangling like the noose of a gallows.

At three hundred metres, darkness eats light. I step back from the abyss. To my left is the beginning of the stairs and next to them the lifts form a squat, square block against the night sky. I hear footsteps. This is danger time and I'm in it.

Killers don't think like the rest of us. They're wild dogs, focused on one of three things — sleep, the nearest bitch or their prey. These two are the goons from von Franck's. Their shadows split away from the fire escape.

I haven't got my back against the wall because there's no wall to have my back against, just a poor excuse for a safety rail with certain death a third of a kilometre below. The goons are doing what they know to do, splitting up to deprive their prey of a single target, in case there's any fight left in their prey. I hear nothing from the shadows, just note their signals. And after a while, the small figure disappears behind the lifts while the tall one heads directly for me.

This isn't a cat-and-mouse game because there's no hole to hide in. I hear the small thug scuttling behind the liftwell. The torches aren't lasers or Gobi-lights or G3 whizzbangs – just common-and-garden head-mounted lamps. But they're enough. I'm unarmed and Tsunami wouldn't be carrying, either. The halogens bang and fizzle and go out, leaving the rooftop in darkness except for the pinpoint glow of one headlamp. Three hundred metres is too far to jump. There's the rope but that would get me three floors at most before it frayed completely and snapped. And first I've got to find Tsunami.

The Fat Lady's only ten paces away, partly obscured by the bricks. Off to my right, I hear the soft-shoe shuffle of the small thug, Lofty, as he approaches. If I move my head slightly I can see the stairs, the lifts, assorted junk, the barrow and the dangling hook of the crane – but no Tsunami.

Chapter 41

IT'S NOT OVER TILL ...

All my guns are on the boat – the three Smith & Wessons, the two Brownings, the Glock, the five Specials – one on the map table while the rest are neatly wrapped in plastic bags and inserted in the fake S-bend of the head, the lavatory. It's not much of a hiding place but, despite what they say in the movies, searchers gloss over dunnies.

That's when the penny or the pfennig or in von Franck's case, the ban, drops. Tsunami's in one of the Port-a-loos because there's nowhere else to hide. Before long the goons will kill me and after that they'll work out where Tsunami is and kill her, too.

I've got to think like them, put myself in their Nikes and put it fast. Don Bradman's got a bat while the Fat Lady's carrying a Uzi. I've worked out where Tsunami is but I'm behind the bricks and the 8-ball. Think like them, I tell myself, they're after a kill – which means I've got to provide them with one. I hear the building creak. Then I realise it's not the building at all but a lavatory door opening. The rope's loose-coiled between me and the Fat Lady and the barrow's on top of the coil. The dunny door swings open and I reach for the end of the rope ...

Animals react to whatever makes the greatest movement. A dog will take on a rampaging bull rather than a mouse because the bull's bigger and therefore poses the greater threat. The Fat Lady's got a choice between a squeaking door and a barrow that suddenly rears towards her. She ignores the door and takes out the barrow.

It doesn't take long to empty a 32-round magazine at a cyclic rate of 1900 revolutions per minute and that's how long it takes the Fat Lady to turn the barrow into a sieve. There's the familiar clatter-click as she replaces the empty magazine with a full one. Tsunami's still got the yellow fun bag like it contains the crown jewels instead of a lot of wadded-up newspaper, and together with the red coat, the hat and the daks she's a beacon. I reach out, grab her and drag her behind the bricks. I haven't got any tricks left and now they know where we are.

'Wha —' she starts.

She's interrupted by another burst from the Uzi that sends brick fragments flying over our heads.

'Take off the jacket!' I whisper.

Lofty's coming down one side of the rooftop while the Fat Lady's coming along the other. Tsunami shrugs herself out of the jacket and hands it to me as another magazineful of slugs unleashes itself into the bricks. I count thirty-two then chuck the coat. It lands on the hook of the crane and the beam of the Fat Lady's lamp swings around to greet it. She sees the red coat and remembers that's what she's here to kill. She changes magazines. Then she kills the coat.

The brick's heavy but I learnt to dance with bricks, pirouetting with one in each hand in order to develop the requisite poise, strength and balance for ballet. I bring my arm back and step out from behind the bricks. I'm throwing blind but I'm rewarded with a scream that doesn't hang around and a bat skittering across concrete. I figure Lofty's gone over the edge but there's still the Fat Lady and she's the danger man. Another magazine clicks into place.

'Come out,' the Fat Lady orders.

Beside me, I feel Tsunami shiver. 'We're going to die, aren't we, Brownie?' she whispers.

I shake my head. 'Like they say in the classics, it's not over till the Fat Lady sings.'

I can't see the Fat Lady but I know where she is by where all the grunts are coming from: primordial noises, the sound a fox makes on a lonely hillside at night or a dingo makes as it moves in for the kill. *Confronted by a wild dog, you have to put yourself in its place,* Rube used to say. *Which means you need to react like a wild dog.*

But if I'm going to die, I'm going to die rational. If I die it's got to be for a reason and right now that reason's Tsunami. There's no such thing as luck, no *force majeure* appearing out of nowhere when the crisps are down. Fortune á la Rube: You need to make your own luck in this world, Rainbow.

The Fat Lady's only three paces away and she's got the Uzi lying along the *radius* and *ulna* of her left arm with thirty-two nice, bright, shiny new rounds in the magazine. The first and second phalanxes of her index finger are tucked inside the trigger guard and death – our death: mine and Tsunami's – is imminent. She's stopped speaking because cunning's cut in – she knows that any noise she makes now will give away her position.

We could be hiding from a spectre, a ghost, a shroud, a miasma. Tsunami huddles in close, shivering like a featherless bird. The world's suddenly gone quiet because the hunter's suddenly gone smart. A crocodile lies as still as a floating log as it awaits its prey and a spider hangs immobile in its web. I've created a diversion but all that's done is told the Fat Lady where we are. I replay the snapshot of what I saw last: the top of the liftwell, the pile of bricks, the lime and mortar, the barrow that's now a sieve, a length of rope, a shot-up coat, the cricket bat. I could chuck another brick but this time the Fat Lady will be ready and close in for the kill. The cricket bat …

There was nothing to stop Lofty going over the edge – from the sound the brick made when it struck it was a skull-shot. I do the physiology. At the moment of impact, all tension leaves the body. It's like a baby falling – the muscles and ligaments turn to cheese, knees relax, toes unclench, the arms fly out in a post impressione gesture as the body's forced backwards while the fingers unclench from whatever they're gripping.

But a bat's not part of the physiology. So what happened to the bat? I remember the twang as the fence snapped which told me Lofty must have gone over. But what happened to the bat?

I ease a brick out of the stack like I'm removing a slug from a still-beating heart, hand it to Tsunami and indicate by dumb show where she's to throw it – afterwards miming a rat-a-tat-tat to remind her the Fat Lady's armed. Tsunami nods and when I hold up my hand, fingers spread, she understands that, too. Five seconds to go and the countdown starts – now!

I'm holding the hand up on the turn, folding one finger down as I go:

One! I step to the other end of the pile and another finger comes down: Two! I locate the bat, black against the moon-white cement: Three! I visualise grabbing the bat and swinging it: Four! I glance behind me – Tsunami's already bringing her brick arm forward as I dive, grab, swivel and swing: Five!

I hear the brick rattle and roll followed by the *rat-a-tat-tat* of the gat. But two things happen that aren't supposed to happen – the machine-gun burst isn't long enough and Lofty's got hold of my leg because he didn't go over the edge at all and by the time I'm within swinging distance of the Fat Lady, Lofty's hand's attached to my ankle like a limpet and the Fat Lady's swinging the snout of the Uzi towards me and I know it's still got bullets in it because I counted and …

I've got the bat but the Fat Lady's got the gun and it's aimed at my head and I'm done for. But Tsunami isn't. I see her rise up behind the Fat Lady and she might be unarmed but she's got surprise on her side, as well as a sound knowledge of unarmed combat, and the cutting edge of her hand catches the Fat Lady on the side of the neck, the headlamp goes flying and the Fat Lady goes down. I give Lofty a whack with the bat and he goes sleepy-byes.

Tsunami finishes wrapping up the small man with some twine she's found and is retrieving the headlamp as I secure the Fat Lady's legs with the rope. Tsunami shines the lamp in the Fat Lady's face as she comes round and her pupils roll like a pair of dice as they take in her surrounds – her trussed-up mate, the bricks, the barrow, Tsunami and the rope.

'Where's von Franck?' I ask.

'Don't tell him!' It's Lofty, awake and straining against his bonds; his voice is as squeaky as the Port-a-loo door but I can still make out what he says. 'The bastard hasn't killed us yet which means the chances are that he won't; you don't have to say nothing.'

The Fat Lady looks at Lofty with contempt; it's been a long time coming, this contempt, probably a lifetime. 'Your logic's not even as good as your English, little man,' she says. 'Don't you see? If I don't tell him what he wants to know, we're dead; but if I do tell him, we've still got a chance.'

Chapter 42

... THE FAT LADY SWINGS

A look passes between them and it's not a nice look. There's something happening here and I'm not sure what it is. But what I *do* know is that Cock Robin's dead; after that the photographer; then the politician – not to mention the cop – and me and Tsunami were supposed to be the follow-up act.

'There's been enough deaths,' I say. 'So where is he?'

'What will you do with us after I tell you?'

'This ain't a debate.'

'You'll hand us over to the cops, won't you?'

'Come on, you're a couple of standover merchants that have had their day – the cops have got better things to do with their time than bother about you, unless you're the killers: like extortion, drug-filching and general mayhem. Where is he?'

'He's ...' she begins.

'Don't tell them!' Lofty shouts.

The Fat Lady shrugs; she looks defeated.

'I have to tell him, Lofty.'

'No, you don't, Bruce, you –!'

For a moment the Fat Lady reminded me of Madam Blavatsky but that was before Lofty said what he just said. In the light of Tsunami's torch I examine the Fat Lady more closely and when I do I see what I should have seen all along – that the Fat Lady's waist is too low and the hips are too narrow and that she's shaped like an inverted triangle instead of an approximation of an hourglass. The Fat Lady's not only not fat she's not even a lady. But what does that mean except that people are tricky with names? And what does it matter anyway? Because what matters is –

'Who's Lofty so afraid of?'

The Fat Lady shakes her head – either in the negative, or just to clear it.

'It's –'

Killing's like lime milkshakes – once you start, you can't stop. And Death must have been Lofty's constant companion because he knows how it works: after they report failure to whoever they work for, they'll die in our place. It's called clearing the decks and it's what Lofty's about to do as I urge the Fat Lady to finish what he started saying. But if I thought the Fat Lady would sing like a canary, I'm disappointed. He's said something but he hasn't said enough and he could be playing the wrong tune anyway. He wants to live and that's a good sign but it looks like there's zero hope of an encore.

'Who?' I urge.

But it's too late – Lofty launches himself and his head catches the Fat Lady in a place where it hurts because the Fat Lady's no lady and his legs might be trussed but his hands are free and he grabs Lofty and hugging each other they roll together towards the safety fence that isn't a safety fence and they go over, the knot on the end of the rope tied around the Fat Lady catching under the bricks and the rope tightening as, three floors down, the entwined bodies thump against the side of the skyscraper once, twice, three times before the Fat Lady must have realised that, even though he's not fat and his accomplice is only small, their combined weight is still going to be too much for a frayed rope, and as the rope snaps, I hear the Fat Lady's swansong in diminuendo as he takes his last dive.

It's not over till the Fat Lady swings.

And the Fat Lady's just swung.

By the light of the lamp I find my coat. It's shot full of holes, just like the case. There's still some material in both, but not enough, not nearly enough, and when I drape the coat around Tsunami's shoulders, it doesn't stop her shivering.

'Who was she talking about? I thought that …'

Her voice trails away. You just shot the messenger, a little bird tells me. But if the Fat Lady was the messenger, what was the message – and who sent him? The Cock Robin case started in a scientist's laboratory with an escaped snake, too many dead rats and an eternal triangle, and I saw only what I was meant to see. What I've got to look for now is what I'm *not* meant to see.

The *Wooden No* rocks at her moorings. I've taken Tsunami back to the caravan where she can look after Skinny Minnie and made the return trip in the cab, the cab driver's voice an annoying murmur: *Look, I know it ain't none of my business but you just dumped a dame in the bush.* And I tell him, *Yeah, you're right, it ain't none of your business* ...

A ferry's hooter blasts, sharks fade in and out of rocky crevices, deadly blue-ringed octopuses search for prey and dangerous currents swirl. When we left the building site, two bodies lay smashed. Someone will complain to the coroner: We warned people it was dangerous by way of obligatory signs that said A VOID DANGER. And leave it at that.

Except I can't leave it at that. I go over the evidence:

Someone broke into a lab

A unionist was murdered

A photographer was shot

Followed by a politician

And there's only the one clue: Blue ...

Common factor Number One: Ivan von Franck. Other common factors ...

I usually have Rube to bounce things off, or Rory, or Imogene, or Annie. But one by one they've gone over the edge leaving nothing but echoes. Like the cab driver said: I know it's none of my business but ... Other common factors –

Who are the suspects? Nine times out of ten it's the wife. In the case of the lab break-in, everything pointed to the wife – although my money was always on the assistant. With Cock Robin, everyone thought it was the widow while the widow insisted it was von Franck. When the cop died, the finger of suspicion returned to Skinny Minnie, Cock Robin's widow. Then there was the fight and Clean Fill was killed and again von Franck looked to be the guilty party. Except that would be a coincidence and I don't do coincidence. But it must have been someone connected with Cock Robin – or von Franck. There was the death of Clean Fill, immediately following the brawl, and before that the death of the photographer. Nine times out of ten it's the wife ... Think, dammit, think!

The scientist was working for von Franck – so could the lab wrecker have been von Franck himself? But if so, why? Because there's always got to be a why and where there's a why there's a will. Seriously, though, von Franck's wife's friend told her: where there's a will there's a way. I think you should see a lawyer …

I'm wearing the coat, the one I wore when I visited Clean Fill and before that, the lab, the one that the Fat Lady who wasn't a fat lady at all shot full of holes, and as a result I'm shivering. But who says my shivering's the fault of the holes? Couldn't I just be shivering because … What's intuition if not a barbed-wire entanglement made up of prejudices? What if I'm presupposing too much?

What I take to be von Franck's boat sails past, rocking the *Wooden No.* The monster's as big as Fate and, silhouetted against the city skyline, I can make out the funnels – except suddenly I see that they're not funnels at all but the jumble of skyscrapers in the city behind the boat. I bring out the night scope to discover that it isn't even von Franck's boat but one of those cruise ships that takes revellers for jaunts around the harbour. I only thought it was von Franck's because that's what I expected to see and I expected to see it because my mind was full of von Franck.

I drop the binoculars and dive back inside to the map table and what's left of the files, the sackful of stories Curtis got me. The answer's been staring me in the face all the time. There are none so blind as those that will not see, as Rube would have said. Or, she might have added, as those who were tricked into looking in the other direction. I go back to the beginning, the year the all-new Ivan von Franck was born. And this time I'm not looking for what I'm supposed to be looking for. Instead I'm looking for the other side of the coin.

Von Franck's wife answers on the tenth ring and I remember Rule One, where all this started – that nine times out of ten it's the wife.

'Mrs von Franck?'

'Yes, this is she. To whom am I speaking?'

I tell her to whom she's speaking and, although it isn't the truth, it'll have to do.

'Look, it's very late,' she says. 'Can't this wait until morning?'

'Not if you want to help your husband,' I reply. 'Do you in fact want to help your husband, Mrs von Franck?'

'Of course I want to help my husband,' she snaps. 'Doesn't every wife?'

'Okay, if you want to help him, tell me where he is.'

'Who did you say you were again?'

I tell her who I said I was again.

'And why do you want to know where he is?'

I tell her it's a matter of life and death; I don't say whose life or whose death; but it seems to satisfy her. 'Well, there is one place that comes to mind.'

Chapter 43

GRAVE RUN

It's a two-man operation and Rory's no longer available so I call Vertical. Vertical's a back-up man who's called vertical because something's wrong with one of his legs, so he leans.

'It's 4 a.m. in the bloody morning!' he says.

'Death doesn't wear a wristwatch, Vertical. You got wheels?'

Too right he's got wheels. In fact, he's got a 1956 FJ Holden, beautifully restored, re-ducoed in the original black, with red upholstery, its big spidery steering wheel complete with red-nose horn, white-walled tyres with lion-and-ball hubcaps and a heavily-chromium-plated front grille – a car to die for. I cut across his encomium.

'Spare me the details, Vert, and meet me in North Sydney in half an hour.'

The car's at the kerb. I adjust the Smith & Double-You and climb in.

'There's no air-conditioning so the back windows have to stay open if you want to breathe,' Vertical shouts above the burble of the speared muffler as I scratch around. 'And you can stop looking for a safety belt because there isn't one. This is an old car so belts aren't mandatory and for the same reason there's no headrests or airbags. Where do you want to go?'

'Waverley Cemetery.'

'Why do you need me?'

'To drive the car.'

'I mean after that.'

'For back-up. But we'll cross that bridge when we come to it.'
'You mean the Sydney Harbour Bridge?'
'Yeah, that, too.'

The cemetery's gates are locked and above the burble of the Holden the Tasman is hammering against the cliff like it's demanding entry. Otherwise the place is as quiet as the grave. It figures.

I tell Vertical to park the jalopy in front of the Mercedes, cut the engine and shut up. Plastic flowers perch on sandstone- and marble-covered plots in fond memory of the dear departed. We take the easterly path – down dale and uphill, away from the row of mausoleums and towards the sound of the sea. The graveyard smells of new-mown hay and a pair of lovers is murmuring sweet nothings to one another in the little stone shelter overlooking the Tasman. I give them a wide berth.

'Christ, this is spooky,' Vertical mutters. 'Why can't we do this in the daytime?'

I tell him daytime will be too late. We zig-zag past graves. Stone angels vie for elbow room with marble cupids. Some plots contain nice-tended gardens while others are miniature forests. The moonlight reveals inscriptions rewritten by Time: PEST IN PEA, WE'LL NEVER FORGE HIM and MUCK LOVED BY AL. Ivan likes to walk the dog there by moonlight, von Franck's wife told me. He says that, given his harsh beginnings, death inspires him.

She could have been mistaken – she might even have deliberately misled me. Or else von Franck has come and gone – only I don't think that's the case because his Mercedes Benz is still parked by the gates. We complete the round-tour but find nothing but more graves and we're back near the shelter shed to find the lovers are no longer whispering sweet nothings to each other but instead appear to be arguing.

Vertical tugs at my arm. 'This ain't none of our business, Rainbow,' he says. 'So why don't we just clear out and come back in the morning?'

It's hard to make out what the lovers are saying over the noise of the waves. It's like the worn-out R.I.P.s on the headstones – I've got to fill in the gaps made by the elements, try to make sense of what otherwise makes no sense at all, plug the holes where the missing letters and words should be …

Voice 1: '… It …'

Voice 2: 'Look, I know we were once homaláu but that was long ... never ought ... you've been ... all these ... ears ...'

You imagine lovers' voices to be forever young but these ones are old, one angry and the other tinged with sadness, a voice used to negotiating minefields, whatever form they might take, while the other ...

Voice 1: grudge ... when someone's ... after all these ... justice is what ...'

Voice 2 (laughing, but without mirth): 'You're like securitatea ... secret police ... justice for imagined wrongs ... justice when they really meant ...'

Voice 1: '... real enough ...'

There's two things wrong with this lovers' tiff:

Voice 1 is vengeful while Voice 2 isn't a lover's voice at all but sounds like it wants to walk away, yet for reasons best known to itself is staying. And they're not lovers at all, at least not any more.

The word revenge hangs in the air like a shelf of rock after centuries of wind and waves have hammered away at it. I try to see what's under the overhang but all I can make out is darkness. It's not like the chiaroscuro of the paintings Aunt Rube failed to get me to understand, vague images of pots and pans and other loose ends under a bed, or a dog by a fire. Dog? What dog?

The wind's risen and with it the racket of the waves. Which means not only can I no longer make out many of the words, it's impossible to make out which one's speaking.

Voice: In ... Faustus ... the Devil ... his due ... because ... Devil's deal ... day of reckoning ...

When someone talks about a day of reckoning – whether it's the prey or the stalker – it's time to act. Because the day of reckoning is settlement day, when people fulfil their destiny and pay their accounts. Like they say in the Litany: In all the time of our tribulation; in all the time of our wealth; in the hour of death and in the Day of Judgment, Good Lord deliver us ...

Voice: Nelu, Nelu, nu fi prost ...

I know enough Romanian to know those words mean: Don't do it! Which means it's time to do something because neither the Good Lord nor anyone else will be doing anything, unless it's to deliver Death. I haul out the gat and motion Vertical one way while I go the other. But I stumble, the gun flies out of my hand and, after I manage to steady myself and look down to see what I tripped over, I see it's the dog, the bloodhound I silenced at von Franck's all those aeons ago, the one with the tired-looking eyes that will never be tired-looking again because the dog's tongue's lolling out and its eyes are closed forever. It slows me. The death of a dog always slows me. But you can't afford to be slowed in this game and I'm only halfway to the entrance when I hear the shot – in the confines of the shelter it sounds like a cannonade – followed by another, then a shout, then several more shots, followed by silence, apart from the sound of the waves.

The figure's heading up the hill towards the gates, making a transverse section across the graves, a grey shape against the sharp white of the marble pillars, stumbling over ankle-high wrought-iron fences, ricocheting around sandstone angels and racketing along a path before reaching the fresh-cut grass. At least one unburied body – two counting the dog – lies on the consecrated ground behind us. After all those years of smouldering hatred, Voice 1 has had its revenge. Only it didn't pan out the way it intended, not the way it intended at all.

We're not leaping tall buildings at a single bound but it's something like. It's called parkourse or something like it and involves running in a straight line, despite impediments – much like life. The figure vaults over a gargoyle, hurdles a grave plot, swings around a statue that's too high to leap over, and I follow. I've got to catch the figure because if it gets away, the chances of ever pinning anything on it – even several deaths – will be next to impossible.

Revenge is a dish best served cold, the old saying goes, and this particular dish has been years in the making.

Chapter 44

A CAR TO DIE FOR

The Holden's unlocked with the key in the ignition and it starts first go because Vertical's done a nice job on the resto. The gears crunch as the driver wrenches the column lever into reverse and through the gate I see the car back and fill. It's not a clean fill because on the way back it crunches into the front of the Mercedes. I leap the fence as the driver slams the gear lever into first. There are three paces between me and the car and the distance is growing rapidly.

Madam Blavatsky taught me the sissonne fondue – a leap from both feet ending in something as close to unpowered flight as mankind can manage – and my *demi-plié* landing should be soft and pliant only it isn't because I slam into the back of the car and I'm hugging its smooth roundness and the car's gathering speed as it heads uphill, swaying wildly as the driver tries to dislodge me.

I feel myself slide as the car lurches. I hug in tighter as my fingers encounter ...

There's no air-conditioning so the back windows have to stay open, Vertical said. I work my hand around with little more to hold onto but hope, waiting for the lurch that will hurl me to my death.

There's a moment when all my weight's hanging on the little triangular window at the side of the car and my life's hanging by a thread as I find myself wondering how much filler gunk Vertical used to patch up the rust hole in the door and under my weight the door clicks onto its security latch as if debating whether to swing open completely and lose me or stay shut as the driver swings the steering wheel with the horn in the centre in an attempt to dislodge me. I'm too big to fit through the window, even if I could smack out the triangle of glass, but it doesn't matter because there's no headrest to the driver's seat, just as the car hasn't got seatbelts or airbags, and although my whitesides are dangling and the car's already up around the 50 mark – that's miles per hour not kilometres – I manage to get both hands around the driver's neck and hang on, which means he's going to die if he doesn't pull over because my fingers are around his trachea. The car's spinning to the left as the driver takes his hands off the wheel in an attempt to unloosen my grip at the same time as – by transverse reasoning – his right foot goes down on the accelerator and I see the brick wall rear up and there's nothing I can do but hang on. The house behind the wall behind the fence reaches out for the Holden's nice chrome-plated grille and there's nothing I can do about that, either, nor about the car smashing through the brick wall into a bedroom full of pansy-coloured furniture, nor about the dame sitting up in bed, hands up over her mouth and her eyes wide open as ...

The car's sideways on in the bedroom, hard up against the bed. I yell at the dame to get the hell out before the flames reach the petrol tank, drag out the driver and lay him on his back on a flowerbed. It's several days since he shaved and his head-hair's sprouting nicely.

He's staring up at me, his face drained both of blood and of revenge.

'You figured it out, didn't you?' he murmurs. 'I took you for an idiot which is why I gave you those files. But you're smarter than you look ...'

He gets all his words and phrases and tenses right as you'd expect an old-time journo to and he's still a tough-looking bugger but now he's a tough-looking bugger who's dying, his creased shirt collar awry and his face ashen while a portion of the big, chrome-plated FJ Holden steering wheel is sticking out of his chest and I tell him, *Yeah, I worked it out,* and his head falls back as his mouth and eyes fall open and he looks like he's talking to the moon.

'I thought I had it sorted ...' The words emerge in dribs and drabs, like the blood leaking from his chest: there are no Magiclips available and they wouldn't be much use even if there were, he's too far gone.

'It was a good disguise, pal – the best,' I tell him. 'You were no longer The Loved One – the little wife – but the nice, warm face of well-balanced journalism. And you were no longer someone who hated von Franck – you became his best friend and greatest admirer. What was clever was that in the intervening years you never tried to harm him, never showed how much you hated him, right up to the end. Instead, when you finally made your move, you killed other people in the belief that von Franck would be convicted of their murders. But Cock Robin's widow got blamed for his death.'

I keep talking, like it might somehow prolong life.

'When the investigation started to fade, an anonymous call from you alerted the cops to the significance of the shadow board and the possibility that von Franck was involved in Cock Robin's murder. The death of the cop ramped up the investigation but pointed it in the wrong direction. To make matters worse there was no evidence because I got rid of the wrench you planted at von Franck's. You set up that fight between von Franck and Clean Fill, with the idea of killing Clean Fill and framing von Franck for it. The photographer had to go because you were the one who told him about the fight and he was about to tell me ... Then, of course, it was Clean Fill's turn, complete with the coin on the carpet that you got Lofty and the Fat Lady to leave there to point to von Franck's involvement. And all the time you pretended to be von Franck's greatest admirer – which wasn't all that hard because you still loved him ...

'Meanwhile, I was busy removing your planted evidence and wrecking your attempts to frame von Franck – although at that stage I didn't realise who the murderer was, only that evidence was being planted. The Fat Lady and Lofty tried to frighten me off. When I came across them at von Franck's I thought they were von Franck's guards until I realised they weren't – because they were outside the house while the dog was inside. Then there was ...'

'Until I did what I should have done all along,' Curtis croaks, 'and gone for the jugular – his jugular – forgetting all about subtlety. Framing him didn't work because he was too lucky, too rich and too powerful, and also because you ...'

Like an ebb-tide, his face is fading from ash-grey to white; it won't be long; it had better not be long because the whole world's got mobile phones and soon all the neighbours will be taking photographs. Technology's the enemy of anonymity.

'The girls,' he says. 'I'm sorry, my good friends, the Fat Lady and

Lofty, did their best, but it wasn't enough, was it?' He frowns. 'Where are they now?'

'Dead,' I say.

'I thought they could be.' Every word's an agony but he still asks: 'How did they die?'

I tell him how they died and he winces.

'They did their best … they were good friends who deserved a better fate than death.'

'Everyone dies.'

'Yes, but not by falling from the top of a ninety-storey skyscraper. I loved those two like the ex-lovers they were because we parted amicably. Unlike that other one' – he can't even say von Franck's name – 'The bastard who I loved with a passion, even after he dumped me, the man I called Tiny because he was big, while I was –'

I nod.

'Yeah, I know: Blue. I worked that out, too, Curtis.' I haul out the pretty-coloured picturegram he overlooked in the files and smooth it out, holding it up so that he can see von Franck and the dame with the red hair gazing into each other's eyes the way lovers do. 'He liked to be seen with women because in macho Australia it was good for business – he surrounded himself with nudie calendars and still made eyes at women but only for effect. Which is why he married Mrs Anonymous – because it looked good – and went on to fame and fortune while his ex-boyfriend – you – shaved off your lovely mop of red hair that resulted in your being called Blue and von Franck's naming his business after you – and you became bitter, twisted and vengeful.'

'Revenge is a dish best served cold,' Curtis murmurs.

Chapter 45

THE OTHER SIDE OF THE COIN

I lower Curtis's head until it's resting on the rosebushes. He won't feel the thorns.

'What about the coin?'

'Ivan's only coin?' He manages a last smile and tries to reach in his pocket but fails. 'I can't,' he murmurs. 'Can you …'

I drag out a green bag. It's heavy – I assess its weight at maybe a kilogram – and when I upend it, hundreds of small, glittering coins spill out.

'He always said he only had one coin but he actually had hundreds. I got the Fat Lady and Lofty to seed Clean Fill's office with one of the many that Tiny gave me – in order to link von Franck with Clean Fill's coming murder. Except you took it, which meant there was nothing apart from the stoush and that wasn't enough …'

'Yeah,' I add as he pauses, 'a 1953 coin, recognisable because it was copper-coloured, while the 1952 coin – von Franck's one and only real coin, the one he habitually flipped – was more of a gold colour.'

'So you noticed that, too. He was too rich and powerful, wasn't he? And the police too slack, my luck too bad and you too smart for anything to stick. Leaving me with just the one option and that was to kill him myself and hang the consequences. I'd already bugged his phone to keep track of his movements – an old journo's habit – but you knew that, too, didn't you? You realised there was some other bugger …' He allows himself another smile but it's weaker now. 'But how did you work out where we were?'

'The Fat Lady sang and after that I telephoned von Franck's wife for confirmation.'

Curtis sinks back for the last time. It's just as well because the sirens are almost upon us.

'What about Tiny? Is he –? Did I –?'

But it's Curtin's last byline.

I'm wearing the same coat I wore at the start of this caper as I swing by the lab. Through the mottled glass in the new-mended door I make out two figures. It's time to eat humble pie so I knock and after a while the boffin opens the door just far enough for me to see he's still big, still handsome and still smiling – although now there's something different about the smile.

'Ah, Detective,' he says. 'What a great time for you to call. I'm at a decisive stage in my latest experiment, having just made the discovery that logic, incorrectly applied, can be terribly misleading.' The red mark's still on his collar but I see now that it's ink. 'All my experimentation with rodents has gone to hell because rats don't buy flats ...'

We all make mistakes.

'Don't worry, Prof,' I say. 'Because I was wrong, too. Which is why I'm paying you a visit. You see, I deduced from all the available evidence that your assistant was to blame for the broken door and the mess, both in your lab and in your personal life, when all the time it wasn't her but a man named Curtis.'

I stop. The boffin's thrown open the door and the smile's still on his face and it's still a different smile but now I can see the mousy little woman – his wife – and she's smiling, too, at the same time as she's advancing towards me, her outstretched hand full of money.

'It's nice to see you,' she says, thrusting the dough at me. 'I wanted to thank you for what you did. If it hadn't been for you sowing the seed of doubt in Arthur's mind regarding that Jezebel, a hands-off relationship could have flowered into a hands-on one ... As it is, not only are we closer than we've been in thirty years of marriage, but – after sacking Miss Anorexia – Arthur made me his assistant.'

Arthur's arm around his wife is protective and he's still smiling, only no longer at me. 'My lovely little Gorilla,' he murmurs.

I take it as my cue to depart.

I don't visit Annie – I've got to move on, unlike von Franck's boyfriend, John Curtis, who, before shaving off his red hair, was von Franck's lover and – because of the hair – was known as *Blue*. I drop in on Aunt Rube to make sure she's still alive and after that pay a quick visit to Madam Blavatsky, the tinkle-tankle of Tchaikovsky greeting me – but no longer the *BLUEBIRD CONSTRUCTIONS* sign, which someone has replaced with a sign saying *FOR SALE*.

Upstairs I find Mismatch thumping away at the Steinway. Twenty or so grommets are scattered about the dance floor, going through the motions of dancing, while Madam B is shouting: 'One-two-one-two!'

Mismatch is too engrossed in her task to look up, Madam B's got her back to me and the kids are too disciplined to tell her there's a man with blood all over him at the door, so I head back down the stairs.

He's sprawled at one of his customer-free tables, his legs outstretched and the bright sun of a new day lighting up his craggy features as he contemplates a fresh-minted copy of the *Daily Terrorgraph* while a mower rackets away in the background. Harry's Caff is a hole-in-the-wall with wall-to-wall disservice and coffee you drink only if you're tired of living. Harry believes in not doing any more than he has to and doing it often.

'So what's news, Mr High Energy?' I ask, sitting down.

He doesn't look up because that takes effort. Blood all over me? I could be a headless zombie for all Harry knows. He shrugs his coathanger shoulders, keeping his eyes on the newspaper.

'Just another corpse in a graveyard,' he replies. 'Someone this rag refers to as vertical even though he was horizontal – if that makes any sense.'

'Nothing makes much sense in this world, Harry.' 'You of all people ought to know that.' The sound of the mower dies down. 'Was there just the one corpse?'

Harry shakes his head – or he could be trying to dislodge a fly.

'No, there were thousands. But in terms of fresh ones, no. Correction: there was one other body, with a steering wheel embedded in its chest, discovered not far from the cemetery – in an accident involving a bedroom, a dame and an FJ Holden. But it appears that the cops are treating it as an unrelated death while someone – there's a picture of him, a big man with his face deliberately pixilated and his name undisclosed because he can afford a good lawyer – is being held on suspicion of the murder of the man in the Holden.'

Harry looks up finally and notices the blood.

'Did you cut yourself shaving, Rainbow?'

I shake my head and at the same time, something – call it conscience or call it hope – makes me look towards the kerb where a dame is climbing off the pillion seat of a motor scooter cradling a babe while the rider's busy setting the bike back on its haunches. I turn my attention from the passenger to the pilot.

She's garbed entirely in black: flesh-cramping black tights, a black T-shirt that could be a first skin, a pair of high-polished black elastic-sided boots and a black full-face helmet, the visor turning multi-coloured as it swivels towards me, making my blood run colder than a lifetime of vengeance.

It's not just Harry's coffee that can kill you.

C.S. Boag

MISTER RAINBOW

in the Case of
the Morgue
the Merrier

For Alan Mills – writer, guide, friend

He was an – an – extremist.
Heart of Darkness, Joseph Conrad

Chapter 1

THE KID

He's tall and bony and he's hopping about the Camellia pier like he's high-stepping over hot sand in a Bondi heatwave. He's wearing long socks, sandals and a carnation-coloured T-shirt with a horseman swinging a polo mallet on its left bo-diddly – the kind of outfit jokers wear when they believe everything the fashionistas tell them – and the legs below his Great White Hunter shorts are matchsticks.

He called while I was minding my own business. My own business being non-existent at the time I agreed to meet him.

'It's like they're *stalking* me, you know?' he says.

'No, I don't know. But why don't you take time out from your tap dancing to tell me.'

He raises his peepers from his iPhone.

'I was attacked by a bunch of thugs but was rescued by these men who asked if I was *disaffected* with Western society. When I said *yes* – remember, I'd just been attacked – they said if I wanted to do something about it they could provide the necessary arms, ammunition and training.'

'Where?'

He ducks his head to his iPhone.

'At a camp in a secret location on the outskirts of Sydney.'

'I mean where did the incident occur?'

'Near home.'

'Where's home?'

'Vaucluse.'

A market garden for growing money.

It was late at night and he was alone. Four kids stepped out of the cover of darkness and demanded his wallet and anything else of value.

When he refused they attacked him.

'Why call me?' I say.

'You came highly recommended.'

'By whom?'

He makes the kind of gesture rich men's sons make when conversations aren't going their way.

'Oh, you know, by heaps of people – I don't remember *who*.'

'Describe them.'

'How can I when I don't remember them?'

'I'm talking about the jokers that tried to recruit you.'

'Oh. They were of Middle Eastern appearance – the kind you avoid on a dark night.'

'Why would you avoid them just because they looked different?'

'It was more than that.'

It's like extracting bullets from the victim of a shooting – you got to probe and there's a lot of blood and afterwards you think it might have been better to leave the slugs where they were.

'Okay. What's your name?'

'Bertie – Bertie Thomas.'

'Bertie, let me tell you something. It's like I asked you to describe a bunch of nuns and you said they were *devout*; or that a group of boy scouts were *small, pimply-faced and helpful*. Your words don't ring true. *Of Middle Eastern appearance?* Give me a break. Next you'll be saying they were bearded and their heads were wrapped in tea towels.'

'But they were!'

I glance at the yachts bobbing about on the Harbour; you don't have to be bright to live in a place like this, just greedy. I look back at bright-eyes.

'I can't see the problem,' I say.

'I said *no*.'

'I still can't see the problem.'

He shakes his head. 'Come on, mister, people have known about this for years. If it's not al-Queda, it's Hamas, Hezbollah or the Islamic Jihad. These people are terrorists preying on disaffected kids. When I said *no* they felt vulnerable. They threatened me. I've no doubt they'll make good on their threats. I want you to frighten them off.'

'Why not go to Daddy or the police?'

The kid consults his iPhone. It's getting to be a habit.

'Before I said *no* I went to one of their meetings.' He looks up. 'Which makes me involved, too, doesn't it? I'll be on the books of the security agencies, my phone will be tapped, Daddy will find out and my life will be hell.' He sees me contemplating the expensive boats and the even more expensive houses. 'My father's not the kind of person who'd be happy having a terrorist for a son. So, yes, I need help. And don't worry, I haven't spoken to anyone else.'

I hunch my shoulders; he's given me the dough-ray-me; I suppose I need to go through the motions of earning it.

'Describe the meeting.'

'They showed us a movie called *Unbeloved Infidel*. It was blatant anti-Western propaganda with scantily-clad women flaunting themselves, men staggering around drunk and a lot of people getting up to no good. It ended with an explosion in which people were killed. When the lights came up, one of the men said they were recruiting for ISIL – he spelled out what the letters stood for. He said we could fight either here or overseas.'

'Where did this occur?'

'In some kind of hall. I don't know where it was because we were blindfolded.'

'Where did your journey start and how long did it take?'

'They picked me up near home –' he hesitates '– and the drive took an hour ...'

I keep the questions coming like I'm a one-man firing squad and the kid's got his back to the wall.

'You said *we* – how many were there?'

'About six jihadists and the same number of recruits.'

'What do the letters ISIL stand for?'

When Bertie glances down again, the eye movement's barely perceptible.

'Islamic State.'

I knock his iPhone into the water.

'There are four letters in ISIL – you only accounted for two.'

'Islamic State, Islamic Land.'

He's lost his memory or I just lost it for him.

'Try *Islamic State of Iraq and the Levant*.'

He looks like he's about to cry.

'Are you saying you don't want to take the case?'

I finger the nice, big, crisp lettuce leaves he brought me all the way from Vaucluse where they grow them.

'Bertie, I wouldn't not take this case for quids.'

Chapter 2

THE SMILEY MAN

The search engine in the computer café coughs up *Thomas, Bertie – student*, then the name of his father, which is different to his but that doesn't prove dishwater. The addresses tally and although the kid's story's far-fetched I can't see any reason why he'd lie.

Farewell to old England for-eh-eh-vah
Farewell to my rum coes as well
Farewell to the well-known Old Bay-ee-ly
Where I used for to cut such a swell.

We're in my old school gym, the curtains are purple and – to the background of the convict song containing too many incomprehensible words – the latest generation of kids is milling among control-freak teachers, bemused parents and assorted ex-students. *It's really indigo,* Rube murmurs, *the colour of memory.* The Principal is at the front of the stage, people find their seats and a kid with a mouth organ gets in one last squeak before fading into silence.

'This isn't the real thing,' the Principal says. 'But the children need to rehearse before a live audience. We'll be staging the play proper on the Friday following the Australia Day weekend. I do hope you'll all be able to make it. In the meantime – enjoy.' She claps, sits and the kids try the next lot of incomprehensible words:

The curtain rises on a rabble of undersized convicts straggling across a stage strewn with papier-mâché rocks, lugging picks filched from Dad's garden to a backdrop of gumtrees, complete with koalas.

'Speaking of colour,' I murmur, 'it looks like we've finally grown up as a society. Those kids are from every conceivable background – a couple of them are even wearing burqas.'

'They're *hijabs*, Rainbow,' Aunt Rube says. 'Plus there's a shayla and maybe an al-amira or two. Not that it's important because we can only call ourselves civilised when we start judging people on who they are instead of what they wear. People aren't Australian, American, African, Asian, Jewish or of Middle Eastern appearance, they're people.'

Aunt Rube can be about as comfortable as a bunch of burrs in your Y-fronts. I scan the audience and a face leaps into high relief – that of a small man, smiling. He waves and I dredge my memory. But all I remember are hours in dark cupboards, getting beaten, being tied to active ant hills and suchlike. I don't recall any small, cheery kid. Beside me Rube winces. It's either the quality of the acting or her kidney.

'I'd better get you home, Rube.'

She shakes her head. 'You heard what the dame said – shut up and enjoy.'

So I shut up and what I see is a bunch of kids acting out Australian history the way too many people imagine it happened – a nice Captain Cook claiming an unoccupied land in the name of a distant King; a couple of fine Governors; intrepid explorers; Rum Corps soldiers swigging cold tea out of Coke bottles; awed Aborigines; and a lot of hard-working white men. Now and then one of the convicts waves to his parents.

When it all goes up in smoke I'm down on the floor with my gat out in a nanosecond. Vapour fills the air, lights flash and chain-gangers tumble left, right and centre. Over the top of the commotion a voice booms: *To forge a way across the Blue Mountains, workers used dynamite. Casualties were many but work that was vital to the opening up of the Western Plains continued until ...*

I take in the crowd. The smiley man's still there. So, too, is a shadow that might be Pandora, the nemesis that's been after me for as long as I can remember.

'Get up off the floor, Rainbow – it's only a stage effect,' Rube murmurs. 'Remember our lessons on explosives?'

I put away the gat and climb back into my seat. Yeah, I remember. Aunt Rube taught me how to handle live rockets, defuse time bombs and disable detonators – we even dabbled in nuclear technology.

'I haven't forgotten a thing you taught me, Rube.'

'Notice everything's *terrorism* these days? It's like those little faces they call – what is it: *motor-cons* …'

Me and Harry go back to when he was a bookie with his life in front of him, long before he got into the brawl with the crooked gamblers that persuaded him to retire to this hole-in-the-wall caff in Cammeray. We got no secrets from each other, me and Harry. He even once showed me his distinguishing marks – in case he copped it and needed to be ID'd. *You won't get killed, Harry,* I assured him but he shook his head. *Everyone cops it one way or another, Rain.*

'It's emoticons.'

'That's what I said – those things that save people thinking. Like words such as *terrorism* that people use as shorthand for *Don't Trust Anyone.* The way that the letters *L.O.L.* stand for *Little Old Lady.*'

'It's *Laugh Out Loud*, Harry.'

But Harry's on a roll.

'Terrorism means different things to different people. To politicians it's votes; to some, it's an outlet for their insecurity; to others, it's a man in a balaclava doing a beheading. Know what I mean?'

Chapter 3

INSIDE THE BLUE BALLOON

'No, what *do* you mean, Harry?'

'I mean that everyone has the potential be a terrorist – whether they're husband, wife, sister, brother or just someone that pushes past you too hard in the street.'

He goes back in his hole-in-the-wall caff while I flap the wrinkles out of the newspaper. Sometimes it's hard getting things straight at Harry's. The table wobbled when I arrived so I propped up one of its legs with a serviette only to find the same problem with another leg so I levelled it with a bottle top but that only made matters worse. Take that caper far enough and you end up with a stairway to heaven, to discover when you get there that the table still wobbles.

'Hey, Harry!'

He emerges looking like he's been mauled by a pack of dingoes. 'What?'

'Ever consider getting three-legged tables?'

'Why?'

'Because it's a scientifically proven fact that you can't level four-legged ones. Ever hear of the sixth law of dynamics?'

He frowns, suspecting a trick.

'Maybe.'

'Then you heard it too late. Science has moved on since Einstein. Now it's the Convergence of Unrelated Phenomena – or *COUP*, for short.'

'You been drinking, Rainbow?'

'No, I've been reading the *Daily Terrorgraph* which is the next best thing. It's the usual blood-letting: an editorial on how our society's obsessed with sex – with a photo of a near-naked dame on the front page to prove it; a totally unrelated story about the convergence of unrelated phenomena; all wrapped up in a piece saying that our Australia Day spectacular will be, well, spectacular.'

'In my humble opinion, Rainbow, the *Terrorgraph* presents a greatly oversimplified view of things.'

I start on my burnt mushrooms.

'There's nothing simple about the convergence of unrelated phenomena, Harry.'

'So explain.'

I take a stab at the toast but it rejects the knife, the table wobbles again and the newspaper slides to the ground.

'It goes something like: *While one action doesn't necessarily follow another, in the end it probably does. Which doesn't mean that things that seem totally unrelated aren't.*'

'Aren't what?'

'Totally unrelated.'

Harry drags out a seat and sits down like everything's suddenly got too much for him.

'I'm glad you explained that, Rainbow.'

It's one of those days when a clear sky arches over the city like a blue balloon and shadows exist where they shouldn't. Maybe it's the table, maybe it's Harry, maybe it's the newspaper, but more than likely it's the totally unrelated convergence of all three.

Harry leans forward.

'Some bastard broke my window.'

'Who?'

He shrugs.

'Either a gang, a window-fixing company or a bunch of those terrorists we were talking about.'

That's when Tsunami shows up and asks what we're eating.

I'd told Tsunami – that's Sue Mahoney, pronounced Sue *Mah-nee*, hence the moniker – that we might catch up one day, meaning never. And to prove that I meant what I said when I didn't, I wrote Aunt Rube's address on one of Harry's table napkins, which Tsunami immediately attached to her scooter. So what does she do after that? She turns up at Harry's for breakfast. Which today consists of Harry's undrinkable coffee, a couple of rounds of toast carefully burnt around the edges, and coagulated sugar in a bowl the size and weight of an eight-inch cannonball.

They're on the other side of the road dismantling a bus stop, five of them – male, clean-cut and young.

I turn to Harry.

'Are those thugs over there somehow connected to you?'

He indicates the broken window. 'They're the ones that did that. They must be waiting for you to leave.'

Harry's wrong on one count – they're not waiting for us to leave. Because they're already crossing the road, shoving each other around and shouting on the approach. They're wearing a kind of uniform – red T-shirts teamed with leather jackets, jeans and lace-up boots.

'Why?'

Harry shakes his head as if to clear it.

'I must have upset them somehow.'

'Describe the *somehow*.'

'I got the scimitar that I keep behind the counter and told them if they didn't clear out I'd dice them and serve them for dinner.'

I turn my attention back to the gang.

'That'd do it.'

Chapter 4

A DANGEROUS MISTRESS

'What did you learn tonight, Rainbow?' Rube asks as I walk her home
after the rehearsal. As we pass the old Darlinghurt Jail I hear the clanking
of the treadmill, the stretching of the rack and the moaning of the wind
where the gallows used to be. I learnt: *Don't expect nothing from nobody and
you'll never be disappointed.* But I don't tell Rube that.

'What do you mean, Rube?'

'Come on, I know you like I know Rumsford's *Rules of Evidence.*
Something's got to you.'

I tell her about the terrorist case I'm on – courtesy of Bertie – and I
feel her glance at me.

'That's a coincidence because I'm looking into terrorism, too.' She
frowns. 'Be careful. Certain people don't like my being involved. There
have been threats. And if you're not careful, you might come under sway
of the same logic.'

'What's the nature of the threats?'

'Death threats to me personally – using my name, on my computer,
in notes and by way of graffiti – calling me an *infidel pig* and saying I'll die
in the name of Allah.'

'Jesus, Rube, why didn't you tell me this before?'

She shrugs. 'Because I knew you'd get hot under the collar, Rainbow,
just as you're doing now. Come on, private eyes get threats all the time –
you of all people should know that.'

'What did you mean about *indigo* being the colour of memory?'

'The word's been on my mind. Life's like being lowered into a
bottomless pit. In the first flush of youth you have all the hot colours – the
reds, oranges and pinks. But as you grow older and the pit gets deeper, you

get your greens and blues – what I call the *shadow colours*. Until in your twilight years everything's indigo. Are you listening to me, Rainbow?'

Maybe I am and maybe I'm distracted by the shadow by the old jail that could be Pandora because it's too substantial to be a wraith and too ever-present to be coincidental. The lights of a passing car cut a swath through the mist while from the Harbour comes the echoing boom of a foghorn.

'Yeah, I'm listening. And what I'm hearing is a lot of death talk.'

'What if it is? People like me don't live forever. I'm a private detective – long and happy retirements are for others.'

The thugs are still coming our way.

'These people don't look like your regular clientele, Harry.'

Under his nine o'clock shadow Harry's become a whiter shade of pale.

'I haven't *got* a regular clientele, Rain. After a long and generally unhappy life I find myself with few compensations apart from this place. I'm alone and as far as possible I'd like to keep it that way. Consequently, I do my best to repel boarders.'

Drivers are afraid to go forwards or backwards in case they hit one of the mincemeats and get sued for it. I count four of the thugs before looking away. Which is when I spot the fifth – busy examining Tsunami's scooter like it's a species of cockroach. Even as I watch, he takes something off it before kicking the bike into the gutter. It's like a signal – his cronies leave off their game with the cars and start towards us at a trot.

Harry slips into the chair next to Tsunami – like getting up close and personal to an ex-marine might make for greater security but Tsunami immediately shifts away from him. She also picks up the cannon-ball sugar bowl. I get out of her line of fire. The writing on the nearside arm of the lead boy says:

TEROR 4 EVA

Five sets of shoulders hunch and I read their intentions as easy as I can read the words on the kid's arm but without the spelling errors. Tsunami brings back her arm like she's waving.

Cheap sugar dispensers are heavy and this one's no exception. It arcs through the air and hits one kid and the shrapnel takes out the boy next door. I roll from my chair and take out the next two in the assembly line with what I call my *Nutcracker Sweet*: smacking a couple of heads together before grinding them like dried berries in a pepper mill with the setting on *COARSE*. Which leaves one thug standing – easy pickings and we pick him.

Harry tenses for the follow-through but there isn't one. The thugs break camp, helping each other off the canvas and back into the bleachers while a stray dog fossicks for scraps. I set my chair back on its feet.

'It looks like we need another breakfast, Harry.'

'Thanks for that,' Harry says as he brings out more burnt toast and more undrinkable coffee.

I dust off my hands. It's only a gesture – I hardly got them dirty.

'Don't mention it.'

Harry shakes his head. 'Irony's too subtle for you, Rainbow. I wasn't thanking you in the traditional sense. In plain English, you and your girlfriend have just put the *UNDER NEW MANAGEMENT* sign up on my caff.' He nods towards the retreating gang. 'Jokers like that see resistance as a gilt-embossed invitation on which the letters *R.S.V.P.* stand for *Really Severe Vengeance Proposed*.'

I feel sorry for Harry but *sorry* doesn't buy nobody a suit of body armour so me and Tsunami clean up while Harry telephones the glass people. Going by the wait they're starting from scratch.

'Have you dealt with this lot before?'

'The thugs?'

'No, the glass people.'

Harry shakes his head. 'This is the first time. The old ones folded – they couldn't handle the transparency-in-business laws.'

The glass people arrive in one of those tent-backed trucks they use for carting glass around in, *A GLASS ACT: all pane, no pain* written along the side. They lift the glass into place with suction cups and slap their sticker in the bottom left-hand corner so they can be called when it happens again. By which time I'm no longer paying attention. Which is why me and Tsunami head off into the sunset together aboard Tsunami's scooter.

'Where are you going?' I call through my visor.

'Where you're going.'

'I'm going home.'

'Where's home?'
'The boat.'

I steady the dinghy as she climbs aboard, a sassy, hourglass shape in figure-hugging black easing herself onto the wraparound deck of the *Wooden No* (*What's your boat called?* Nosey Parkers ask, to which I reply: *Wooden No*). Once we're aboard, I get my half-hitch in a knot and by the time I reach the stateroom she's found the Glenlivet and when she hands me my jar her fingers are electric eels fresh off the charger.

Time for a cautionary shot across the bows.

'Loneliness is a dangerous mistress, Tsunami.' I could be warning myself. 'Which is why you got to drown your misapprehensions before they grow into cats and scratch your eyes out. After which I'll row you ashore and you can go home.'

Without waiting for a response I make my way down to the bilge. Starting the pump isn't just to keep the boat afloat – it's to keep my head above water as well. I hear a sound like thunder and to distract myself I murmur: *Remember the engine oil.* Because in the Case of the Cock Robin Killer, Skinny Minnie destroyed the pump by forgetting the oil.

Chapter 5

NOT EVEN CLOSE

When I get back to the stateroom I find the cause of the thunder. Tsunami's dragged the mattresses out of the cabins and lashed them together and now she's busy covering them with canvas. I stay by the hatch, a place of relative safety.

'Let's go,' I say.

'Where are we going?'

'It's not where *we're* going, Tsunami, it's where *you're* going – back to your home in Balmain.'

'Oh, really?'

It starts bad and ends worse. Tsunami tries to get drunk and fails. Then she takes off all her clothes and lies down, patting the mattress beside her and inviting me to join her. When I refuse – saying what she's got in mind is the worst idea since the invention of money – she gets upset. After which she falls asleep, leaving me to consider her scars.

About midnight, she opens her eyes. I look up from the scars.

'What happened?'

She takes a deep breath. 'They're war wounds. A bit of shrapnel and I was knifed once. That one's my appendectomy.'

'I'm talking about the other scar – the one that no-one can see.'

She looks away.

'Enemies can be anything from bona fide soldiers to kids armed with rocket launchers and axes – some even used forks and bottle openers out of the knife drawer in the kitchen. Wars aren't parlour games, Rainbow.

After I was taken prisoner, my captors behaved in the way captors have
behaved since time began. And since then I –'

I don't say anything. It's not deliberate. I don't know what to say.

'It doesn't matter,' I tell her at last.

'What *does* matter then?' Her voice is bitter – she's staring at the
shadows criss-crossing the ceiling. 'Does Harry matter? Your Aunt Rube?
Your daughter? Do *you* matter for that matter? Does *anyone*?' She shakes
her head. 'You think I'm selfish, that there are a lot of people worse off
than me – that the inability to be intimate isn't the end of the world.'

She moves away the way she distanced herself from Harry – all that's
missing is the sugar bowl. Not because she wants to but because she can't
help herself and when she speaks again she's talking to spectres.

'You knew I couldn't bear Harry being close to me and would have
guessed it wasn't just him. That's why I was a successful soldier and also
why I chucked the sugar bowl as hard as I did, nearly killing that kid in
the process. I translate my fear into violence just like those kids do. Do
you know what was done to me?'

'I can guess.'

She shakes her head.

'You wouldn't even come close.'

Because of the darkness, I know where the water is only by its resistance
to the oars. A vessel black as Fate passes, making me pause in my rowing.
But as soon as the water settles I start up again and when I beach the
coracle, Tsunami's reluctant to disembark, like she thinks she might be
stepping onto quicksand.

'You should have let me face my devils, Rainbow. I know I can beat
them. Can't we at least give it a go?'

I shake my head in the darkness. 'Imagine yourself on a permanent
war footing, Tsunami, and you'd have some idea what it would be like
being with me.' I remember Rube and the threats. 'A private eye never
knows if he'll see tomorrow.'

She's lost the ability to feel, she says. After growing up at the mercy
of a born-to-kill brother, the Army offered a chance to escape. At first it
worked – being a soldier seemed to enable her to feel again. But in the end
it only made matters worse.

I try to reassure her.

'It's not just *you* that life doesn't fit, Tsunami. Existence isn't made to measure — life's the hand you're dealt; it's off the hook, one size fits all.' I think of Imogene. 'Apart from which, attachments make people vulnerable.'

A weariness overcomes her. She climbs out of the boat, clambers across the rocks and scrambles through the trees to her bike. I hear the little motor putt-putt to life as I get the coracle back in the water. The echo of my reply keeps time with the oars as I row back to the hulk, as if rebounding from the walls of a labyrinth: *vulnerable, vulnerable, vulnerable* …

Early the following morning a mobile rings — one of the unsafe ones. I pick up but don't answer.

'That you, Rainbow?'

I don't exist — I got no property, no bank account, no Medicare number, no email, no licence of any kind and no name to speak of. Which makes me no more than a careless word on an unguarded phone away from outage by negligence. But sometimes Rory forgets.

'You got the wrong number — this is Mother Teresa.'

'It's still Mother Teresa,' I answer when the phone rings again.

'Hello, I —' But it's not Rory this time, it's Tsunami. 'This *is* you, isn't it?'

'It might be. Then again it might not.'

'I —' There's a pause; there's always a pause. 'You haven't changed your mind, have you? About us, I mean?' When I don't reply, she continues. 'Look, I know not to use your name and I also know not to call you. But the other phones weren't responding so I …'

The *Island Princess* is sliding through the Heads flanked by a couple of tugs. The big boat's got to go where the tugs take her and it's the same with Tsunami.

'Are you still there?' she asks.

'Yeah.'

'I'm afraid.'

'We're all afraid,' I say. 'It's called life. Where are you?'

'In the office.' Her voice descends to a whisper. 'Only I can't concentrate because of this fear. And it isn't *that* kind of fear. There's someone … I'm not imagining it, someone really is —'

'Describe the *someone*.'

I hear shuffling on the other end of the Telefunken, like Tsunami's picking up pens and putting them down again, aimlessly.

'I – can't.'

Which means she only *thinks* that someone's tailing her.

'There's either someone or there isn't.'

'It's not as simple as that. As a soldier I learnt to ignore this sort of thing at my peril. People die for less. There's someone out there.'

Chapter 6

SPEAK HARD, SPEAKEASY

'There's someone out *where*?'

'Around the next corner or behind the last one, how should I know?'

'Is there something you haven't told me?'

'Only that I have to be on my guard.'

I know the feeling.

'So what is it?'

'I don't know. But I thought you'd care enough to check it out, to make sure I'm safe, I –'

'I'm a long way from where you are. By the time I got there, whoever it is will have gone.'

'Isn't there anyone you could send in your place?'

'No.'

The moment she hangs up, the phone does its *rat-a-tat-tat* again. It's Rory coming out of the queue.

'Why didn't you pick up?'

'What do you want?'

'I want to apologise for my behaviour that time. I was short.'

There's two counts and Roarer's right on both of them – he's five foot nothing and in the Cock Robin caper he wouldn't let me in out of the rain.

'Is that all?'

'No, I got a call.'

'And?'

'I can't say over the phone.'

I've bagged the empty whisky bottle and found myself a half-full one, the sunlight's sparkling on the Harbour, the job the Bertie kid dealt me can wait and before this it was shaping into a beautiful day. I sigh – like I told Tsunami, life doesn't come complete with a tape measure.

'Okay, we'll meet at the usual place. But before that, there's something I want you to do, seeing as you're feeling contrite.'

'Anything you want, mate,' he says. 'Just say the word.'

So – using code – I say the word.

The speakeasy's having one of its speak-hard days – there are a lot of cops while honest-to-goodness, bona fide, card-carrying criminals are thin on the ground. I enter under a sign saying *EAR* instead of *O'LEARY'S* because this is the Cross to find Hank the barman behind the counter but no sign of Rory.

Hank hands me a glass of green stuff with a little pink umbrella sticking out of it.

'If you listen hard enough you'll hear that drink talk. It's saying how nice it is you teamed the electric-blue jacket with the polka-dot tie, the orange hat and the snarl.'

I play along; there's nothing else to play. 'Why does it say that?'

'Because it's complimentary.' I don't laugh and Hank keeps talking to cover his contusion. 'I expect you're looking for Rory.'

'He said he'd be here.' I nod in the direction of the clientele without looking; it pays to keep your head down even in O'Leary's; make that *especially* at O'Leary's. 'What's with all the fuzz?'

'Ever since that latest jihad incident, politicians of all persuasions have joined the fight against terrorism. People are afraid and politicians are anxious to translate that fear into votes. This' – he waves his cloth at the room – 'is the cutting edge of the fight against terrorism.'

I told Rory to do a job after which I'd meet him at O'Leary's but somewhere along the line he got side-tracked. I climb down off the stool.

'If Roarer shows,' I say, 'tell him I couldn't wait.'

In the Cock Robin caper, Tsunami was there when I needed her so I owe her one. I unstable the Heckler & Coalesce as I mount the stairs to the third floor of the refurbished brothel where she keeps her office to find a door with a black-and-white sign on it saying:

SUE MAHONEY

ENGINEERING – CIVIL

BUT ONLY IF YOU KNOCK BEFORE ENTERING

I don't do like the sign says. Do like the sign says and I could get knocked *after* entering – given the panic in Tsunami's voice when she telephoned; the fact that Rory didn't keep our rendezvous; and too much silence behind the sign to be good for anyone. I kick open the door, swivel and hit the floor on the dive.

If I say I didn't know what to expect I'd be lying. I knew what to expect only it's not what I get. Instead, there's a suite of offices got up like an army barracks – white as far as the eye can see, nothing on the white-painted walls and not much more in the way of furniture. No Rory, no Tsunami and not even the breath of a whisper they've been here. Just a desk with an electronic recorder on it which I pick up and switch on.

There's stuff about engineering, Tsunami dictating letters and writing reports – interspersed with Tsunami talking to herself. A lot of technical jargon before – out of the blue or the purple or the indigo or however you want to play it – the following: *Adults are no more than children writ tall.* The voice is indistinct; I can only just make out what she's saying. *What we become is engraved in our psyches right from the start. Don't talk to me about trauma – I've had enough to last a lifetime.* Silence, then: *This isn't what I signed up for. I thought I could have something with Rainbow but it's like he's running away, just like I am.*

It makes a lot of sense and it doesn't make any sense at all. There's a noise at the door and I swing round only to find it's static coming out of the recorder along with a voice saying the one word: *Rude.* It's Roarer with his phone-voice on, talking into his phone. *Rude,* he says. Then Tsunami to no-one in particular: *We have to go.* Followed by silence.

It takes me a while to work out the buttons. These things ain't like they used to be – a spool behind a window wearing a tape that you wind this way and that. Instead there's a lot of electronic buttonry. More snatches of Tsunami agonising about existence, more engineering specifications then, just when I'm about to give up, Roarer saying that one word again: *Rude.*

Only it's not *Rude* but *Rube.*

Chapter 7

HIS AND HEARSE

When I get to Rube's, I find a hearse at the kerb, the front door smashed in and the hall wearing eau-de-cologne. The torn-out pages of books – Dupont's *Blasters' Handbook* circa 1934, *The History of the Decline and Fall of the Roman Empire*, a *King James Bible*, R.B. Samuelson's *Detection Methods* and Roger Rogerson's *The Compleat Cabinetmaker* – litter the lounge. The safe's wide open and empty. The coffee table Rube took so much trouble to make is intact but the carpet's up and several floorboards have been prised away.

This was where Rube reared me on old Jimmy Cagney movies, ballet and detection methods after taking me out of school when the bullying got too much. It's also where she died. I know this from the silence, from the busted banisters and because – after her kidney transplant – Rube never went upstairs again. But she's upstairs now.

'Roarer?'

Silence.

'Roarer!'

More silence.

Then, 'I'm up here, mate.'

I take the stairs three at a time. The joint never looked lived-in but right now it looks died-in. Through the bathroom doorway I make out a dragged-down shower curtain and traces of blood. I straighten the black-framed photo of a group of kids in the hall. Rube's bedroom's at the end.

Her body's still warm. At the time of death, she was wearing a black T-shirt and jeans. I'm aware of Tsunami behind me as I turn to Rory.

'How did you know about it?'

Rory's as shaken as a bad martini.

'She rang just as I got to the dame's. Apparently she tried calling you but you were busy so she –'

'What did she say?'

'Something like –'

'The exact words, Roarer.'

Tsunami's looking from me to Rory and back again, anywhere but at the figure on the floor. She's seen death before but not like this – all her deaths wore uniforms.

'She said –' Rory frowns; he's used to killing strangers, not downloading obituaries on people close to him. 'She said, *Is that you, Rory?*'

'Jesus, Roarer …'

'You asked for her exact words and that's what she said.'

I resist killing him; one death's enough.

'Go on.'

'I said *Is that you, Rube?* And she repeated: *Is that you, Rory?* And I said: *Yeah.* Then there was a lot of noise after which she said –'

'Describe the noise.'

'A door getting smashed in and a couple of shots.'

'What kind of shots?'

'.25 slugs out of a Baby Browning.'

Rube toted a Baby Browning because – along with the matches for the stove and her handkerchief – at just over four inches, the peashooter fitted neatly into the pocket of her apron. Under the circumstances it would have been as useful as a popgun against Godzilla.

'What did she say after you confirmed your identity?'

'I could only make out one word – it started with *N*.'

'That's it? An entire conversation and that's all you remember?'

The colour drains from Rory's face. 'It wasn't a word I was familiar with. It sounded – foreign. Besides which I had to move fast and the dame insisted on accompanying me.'

I check my watch.

'Rube's been dead over an hour. The cops respond slow but eventually they'll turn up and we don't want to be around when they do.'

Downstairs I straighten the hall table, write Imogene's name, address and phone number on the back of her photo and remove the camera. It comes out easy – the *obscura* one in the middle of the wall, not the obvious one sitting up and saying *Take me*, which is what the intruders did. The coffee table comes apart the way Rube designed it to. I slide out the pegs holding the outer cover in place and discard the top until what I'm left with is a filing cabinet – a lightweight box made of three-ply timber about the size and shape of a baby's coffin.

We're pulling away from the kerb when the TV crew arrives. A TV crew?

'Couldn't you have chosen something a bit more obvious than a hearse, Roarer? Why not a screaming-pink van with a loudspeaker sticking out of the top announcing: *We're speeding away from a murder, come and get us?*'

Rory's got the lights on – or maybe the lights come on automatic in hearses – and traffic's lining up obediently behind us. I tell Tsunami to get on the floor, after which I pull my fedora over my eyes and slide down in my seat. Rory shrugs or maybe he's just having trouble with the pedals.

'How was I to know there'd be a murder? This hearse is my daily drive and the fact that I'm driving it is – what's the word – no more than continental.'

'Coincidental.'

The answer's automatic because my mind's elsewhere. What's with the TV people? They must have been just around the corner sipping lattés. I try to block Rube's body out of my mind. *You can't solve cases through a vale of tears,* she'd say. Or maybe it was *veil. You have to stay objective – check my wounds; close my mouth; cover me if I'm uncovered; destroy the hard drive; write the kid's name and address on the back of her photograph; and take the little wooden filing cabinet built into the coffee table in the middle of the room where everyone can see it and take it for granted – take it for granted and therefore not take it …*

Roarer's still banging on about the hearse. 'It's bulletproof, there's two rows of seats and it holds two coffins – it's even got a place for your tinnies.'

'But why a hearse?'

'When I gave up killing, the Singalong Church gave me obsolescence for my sins in return for my life's savings, leaving me with nothing to survive on but my wits.' I don't say anything. 'A man's got to make a living.'

'How can you make a living driving a *hearse*?'

We're taking the back roads. There are still cameras but they're not so prevalent.

Roarer shrugs. 'I buy and sell old American cars: Dodges, de Sotos, Buicks, Chevrolets, Caddies ...'

'Is it legit?'

'It doesn't pay that good so it must be.'

Chapter 8

PLAY IT AGAIN

Rory's place is where it's always been – on the wrong side of the tracks in the wrong suburb at the wrong end of a wrong city. The driveway contains a black Buick Electra, a pink Chevrolet Biscayne, a grey Olds and a purple-and-green Lincoln Continental. The furniture's covered with cobwebs and black mould's giving a come-as-you-are party on the southern elevation. I set Rube's box on the lounge-room floor.

'Where's Janet?' I ask.

Roarer shrugs. 'She found religion.'

'I thought she'd already found religion.'

'All right, she ran off with the minister.'

That's why he wants to be friends again.

'You mean that fat bugger who hitched you?'

Roarer looks uncomfortable. Roarer always looks uncomfortable but right now he looks like he's playing host to a plague of fleas.

'When I caught them at it he said it was no more than a *laying-on of hands.*'

I leave it at that; there's nowhere else to leave it.

'You got a machine I can watch a video on?'

Rory leads me to a hole under the house.

'This was our little joke,' he explains. 'Janet didn't like me under her feet.' The entrance is via a crawl-hatch from the side path and there's an air vent I can see the street through. 'So I ended up under her feet – how erotic's *that*?'

'You mean *ironic*.'

'That's what I said.'

I change the subject. 'What happens to the house?'

'The Church is selling it off which means I got to excavate.'
'When?'
'They're taking the furniture today.'
Tsunami appears in the hatchway, beautiful in black.
'I got to get back to work. Can someone call me a cab?'
'You're a cab,' Rory says. When no-one laughs he shrugs. 'I'll take you in the hearse.'

Rube's box contains details of all her cases, recorded in handwriting as precise as her mind. From the very first words of the first entry – *MISSING PERSONS* – it's like she comes to life again: *A runaway's like a soldier absent without leave: a look of bewilderment on the parents' faces, suspicion in that of the lover, confusion among friends and – nine times out of ten – a couldn't-careless attitude on the part of the police. There's no body, no crime scene, no murder weapon, no suspect and it's a big country. It's as if the person never existed ...*

I flick through to the file labelled *ERRANT SPOUSES*. First page: *The politicians promised that infidelity would end with no-fault divorce but it simply means people like me no longer burst into cheap hotel rooms telling people to smile for the dicky-bird. Straying husbands and wives are as prevalent as ever ...*

I'm kneeling among the ruins of Rory's marriage surrounded by my Aunt's files when a shock runs through me. *Pay attention to those feelings,* Rube said. *They're the warnings that an animal gets before an earthquake, subliminal sensations we so-called civilised beings ignore because we think we're above them.* The file marked *PERSONAL* starts like one of those signs on the backs of cars that read: *If you can read this you're too damn close.*

If you're reading this it's because I no longer exist ... The words conjure up hard-to-handle memories because – just like the sign says – I'm too close. A note falls out. *This little filing cabinet – overlooked because it was right under my killers' noses – contains details of all my cases. Among the notes you'll discover who killed me. I don't know who it was – if I had known, I could have prevented my death. I'd rather you moved on, Rainbow, but knowing you, you won't. Apart from which, if my prognosis is right, they'll be after you, too. Which means you'll have to do what's necessary to protect you and yours. But first watch the video.*

In the hole in the wall under Roarer's joint I insert the cassette and hit *PLAY*. Enter, *Left*, Rube, wearing an apron. She moves out of shot towards kitchen, returns, paces up and down like she's forgotten the cameras or – like any good actor – is simply pretending they don't exist.

Beyond her, the door's still where it's meant to be.

Suddenly she frowns. I stop the video, wind back – watching her jerk about like she's being volted – and start the tape on its forward progress again. As she frowns, Rube glances down. I pause the video on the downward flick of her eyes, note the time in the bottom right-hand corner, then hit *Unpause*. Rube bends, picks up the receiver from the telephone in the hall, speaks into it, listens, speaks some more, listens some more, then finally hangs up. *Note facial expression.* Hit *Play.* She seems to consider something then come to a decision. She feels in her apron for the gun.

I force myself to keep watching. Rube disappears. To reappear five minutes later clad in jeans and T-shirt and carrying a basket. An hour later – I've fast-forwarded – she returns through the front door with her basket full of goodies. I can only see what's on top of the basket: a half-pound of Sourco butter; d'Aura coffee; a newspaper – Rube loved her newspapers – folded to show part of a headline that starts *TERRORIST THREAT TO …* while a baguette's dangling over the side of the basket like it wants to escape.

She disappears in the direction of the kitchen and I fast-forward the tape before bringing the speed back to *Normal.* I'm not looking for clues because the killers haven't arrived yet. Watching the video is a means of keeping Rube alive, like calling my daughter to tell her I've got a new phone number, on the off-chance my ex-wife will let me speak to her. But I'll never hear Rube's voice again.

The cloth on the hall table rises like a ghost's lifting it – the barest of flutters. But it's the breeze before the tornado, the flutter of butterfly wings that ends in a storm, a presage of doom. Suddenly, the front door's on the floor and figures are swarming across it. Rube goes for her mosquito-blaster but she's too late – she's slowed since the kidney transplant – and the lead figure catches her by the arm so that her pea shots go wide, smacking harmlessly into the jamb and the wall beside it while leaving the intruders intact.

I wind back and play it again – only this time on *Slow.* Again the cloth flutters, again the door bulges and again Rube goes for her gun. I shift attention from Rube to the intruders. To find they're wearing anonymous clothes while their faces are pixilated – hair covered, noses squashed, ears crushed and eyes and mouths the vaguest of shapes – by the cut-off feet of panty-hose.

My mind's between the morgue and a hard place when I hear the sound of a motor being cut, doors slamming, feet on the front steps, a key turning in the lock and footsteps on the floor above. I stop the video and peer through the peep-hole. From the lounge room comes the slip-slide of furniture being moved, the footsteps heavier now because they're weighted by their load, then the soft thud of a couch hitting a wall. *The Church is selling the house so I got to excavate. When? They're taking the furniture today.* The Telefunken rings and I click on before the removalists can hear it. The voice at the other end is querulous.

'Daddy?'

Once I had more than one kid. Before I discovered that two were fathered by a telephone repairman while the fourth was a concoction of my imagination — a vain attempt to resuscitate my dead sister.

'Yes, darling?'

I call her *darling* because — after all these years — I can still get the name wrong. Just the name — not the kid. Because I know who it is, can see her broad as daylight, my little girl — make that grown woman because Imogene must be all of eighteen now, or maybe twenty — clutching the phone and sobbing, 'Daddy, Auntie Rube's dead!'

Chapter 9

BETWEEN THE MORGUE
AND A HARD PLACE

I don't tell her I already know and that *she* only knows because I wrote her name, address and telephone number on the back of a photo on the hall table I left for the cops.

'Are you still there, Daddy? They said someone killed Auntie Ruby and Mummy was awful about it – shouting at the police because she thought they were only here because of you. Daddy?'

'I'm still here, sweetheart.'

'Why are you whispering?'

'The news must have affected my vocal cords. Go on.'

'They took her to the – you-know-where – and as next of kin they want me to identify the body. Can we meet somewhere?'

'I can't go to the morgue because of the cops.'

'What about afterwards?'

'Where afterwards?'

She tells me where afterwards, in code.

God moves in mysterious ways but there's no guarantee He'll do it quiet. Upstairs, the crashing and banging says the removalists are getting on with their removalling and through the vent in the wall I can see a pantechnicon with the words *SAVOES DEPOT* on it, the back door's open and a man wearing a tag that says *TED* is loading a chair.

She's wearing faded blue jeans and a fashionably ragged top and with her hair cropped short I barely recognise her. Standing on the other side of Parramatta Road, her eyes fixed on the hedge, she doesn't look like her mother – which is a blessing. But neither does she look like me – which is even more of a blessing. She's got one foot forward and her arms out like I taught her and her face is pale because she's just come from seeing Aunt Rube.

The morgue's at the back of the Coroner's Court in a suburb with no trees called Forest Lodge. Through the hedge, I see cops barging through the automagic doors. Inside, they park their bo-diddlies in the lockers provided and – after giving evidence to the Coroner – retrieve their gats, return to their cars and drive away. Other players include lawyers, witnesses, clerks, secretaries, suspects, hangers-on and – on a big day – TV crews. This must be a big day.

Imogene crosses the street just like any other kid except instead of having wires sticking out of her ears she's busy noting age, sex and danger level of fellow pedestrians – ever-ready to reach into her open-necked casement bag for the pepper pot.

That's when she sees me and that's when her eyes light up and she forgets all her training and starts running. And for a moment I forget everything I ever learnt, too, and suddenly she's in my arms and laughing. 'Daddy!' she cries. 'My little girl,' I say back ...

Only that's in my imagination. Because in reality she looks right, left and dead centre, after which she walks slowly across the road and – while still a pace away – stops and we shake hands like strangers.

Pandora could be behind the tree by the oval or secreted next to the hedge. Rube's dead and even if Pandora didn't do it, it's like the blade's already between my scapulae and I don't know how I'm still on my feet. Imogene stares like I'm a mirage and I take one of those breaths that mirages take.

'We should spend more time together, kid.' That's as intimate as it gets. 'Did you do the ID?'

She nods. 'It was Auntie Rube all right. She always said it could happen.' Again the stare. 'You knew before I called you, didn't you?'

'I couldn't identify her without revealing my own identity, Immo – a faceless man can't do IDs.' I change the subject. 'What's with all the cameras?'

'Something to do with terrorists. They wanted to interview me but I gave them the slip.'

'How's school?'

Once more, the stare. 'You know I've left school, Daddy.' Imogene hurries over the implications of my not knowing. 'I'm eighteen now, which means I can make my own decisions.'

Yesterday she was a babe in arms, today she's making decisions.

'So what are you up to?'

'I'm ... at uni.'

From the moment they're born you wonder what will happen to them. Imogene was never going to be nothing. I can't keep the complacency out of my voice when I ask, 'And what are you studying – at uni?'

'You'll be upset.'

'I don't get upset.'

'It's not university in the *traditional* sense.' She can't meet my gaze. 'I've enrolled in the – I'm attending the Police Academy in Goulburn.'

The traffic on Parramatta Road ceases to exist and I struggle to breathe. It wasn't my worst fear because it was never a possibility.

'You mean you got to study for *that*?' I'm on the side of the angels but nine times out of ten the angels aren't; my job's to fill in the gaps left by the cops and sometimes the gaps are chasms; I step back; it's not a conscious act but that only makes it worse. 'For God's sake, Immo – *why*?'

She's got a lot of reasons – too many. Foremost among them is Rube's death; Imogene had already pretty much decided when it happened but Rube's death made it a certainty. Somewhere amid all the explanations is the need to do good and while she's talking I find myself thinking: *I should have stayed with the mother, toughed out the marriage, been there to protect the kid.* Except that maybe it was me Imogene needed protecting from. She's still explaining when I cut across her.

'You got nothing to apologise for, Immo. But I suppose if they knew you had someone like me for a father ...'

'You are what you are, Daddy.'

What did I expect – harps and fairies? I hunch my shoulders and make the best of a bad job.

Chapter 10

THE CASE MAN

'Let me give you a piece of advice, Immo. When you're –' the words stick in my throat '– when you're what you're going to be, you got to stay on the side of the angels, do you hear me? You don't have to do me any favours – never mind I'm your Dad. Lesson number one in law enforcement is to avoid bias – no helping family, knock-ons for friends or kickbacks to chance acquaintances. Crookedness starts with good intentions and ends in evil. There's no such thing as *half*-bent.' I think about that. 'At least you're not turning criminal, Immo.'

She smiles a wan smile and her eyes are glistening but it's still a smile. 'I forgot to tell you – that's next.' The smile fades. 'Don't worry, I'm still me. And when you finally come to terms with what I'm doing, you'll realise you're partly responsible.' I imagine her in uniform, complete with gun, hit-stick, stunner, handcuffs and the walk – especially the walk. 'What do you want to do now?'

I'd like to stay friends, that's what I want to do now. Which means that I got to work out how I won't be an embarrassment to her – but only after I find out who killed Rube.

'Like they say in the song, Immo: *You go your way and I'll go mine; now and forever till the end of time.* I'll just finish this case I'm working on, after which I'll …'

Imogene interrupts. 'I never told you this, Daddy, but that was my name for you – *The Case Man.* It's what I called a doll I had. The doll had a tough face and I dressed him in the sort of clothes you wear – you know, kind of crappy – and went to him for advice. I asked him about becoming a cop.'

'And what was his reply?'

'He said what you want to say, Daddy, but can't – *Go for it, kid.* So that's what I'm doing. What's the case?'

'I need to find out who killed Rube.'

I don't tell her about the other case, the one I'm doing for the Thomas kid.

'But that's police work!'

I shake my head; the body in the morgue used to be Rube. 'To the cops, Rube's death is nothing more than a difficult case closed. They never liked her because she exposed their shortcomings. So all they'll do is punch their fists in the air and shout *That's one for the goodies!* I got to do it, Immo.'

'But isn't that what you've always told me to do, keep the *personal* out of what should be objective – don't do things for family, et cetera?' She hasn't even started and she's already struggling. 'Can't you give up detecting? I want you to live. I've just lost Rube – I don't want to lose you, too.'

My mind's on the clock and I know the kid knows because even as we're talking she's moving further away – both physically and emotionally. Growing up's another way of saying *growing away*. And all the time Pandora's behind, beside or in front of me, awaiting her moment because she knows it's getting close.

'Just this one last case, Sweetheart.'

But Imogene's already turned her back and – slinging her bag casually over her shoulder but always ready to reach into it for the spray – is walking out of my life and into her own.

Like I told Harry, everything's connected. Which includes the headlines screaming: *TERRORISTS STRIKE AGAIN, Well-known Female Investigator Struck Down in Blind Jihad* and *HOW LONG MUST WE COP THIS LOT?* When I get back to Rube's, the blue-and-white tape's in place and the door's nailed shut but there's something cursory about it, like they've just gone through the paces, because it's only the death of an old woman.

In the photograph she's leaning against a lamppost with her arms crossed, frowning into the sun. 'She walked like it hurt and she was wearing a T-shirt and jeans and carrying a basket.'

The café proprietor's got better things to do with his time than look at pictures of old women.

'When was I supposed to have seen her?'

I shrug. 'When you saw her.'

Black shirt, blacker look and he couldn't give a damn about anything except making coffee and money.

'If it was lunchtime I was busy.'

'She was murdered.'

'I was still busy.'

I indicate the waitress behind him. 'She might have seen something.'

'She's working.'

'That makes two of us.'

The overblown barista taps his watch to show who's in charge and his frown warns the waitress: *Take more than five minutes over this and you're out on your sweet potato.*

'What's your name?'

'Jane.'

'Have you seen this woman before, Jane?'

'Of course I have. That's dear old Rube. Why, what happened to her?'

'Why should anything happen to her?'

'Because you're showing me her photograph and you've got that look on your face. Besides, I *knew* something might happen because I saw this man and had a flash of implication.'

'You mean *insight.*'

'Whatever it was I had a flash of it. He seemed interested in Rube.'

'Describe him.'

'He was leaning against the wall of the old jail. I knew he wasn't a local because his shoes were clean.'

'What did he look like, under the clothes?'

'A cross between a lawyer and an assassin. You still haven't told me what happened.'

'She was murdered.'

Hand to mouth, eyes wide with horror – passes reaction test.

Final question. 'Do you recall the expression on her face?'

'She looked worried. I only say that because –'

'– usually she never looked worried?'

Bone, the dame in the flower shop on the corner, The Greenhouse

Defect, remembers Rube hurrying past with her head down while a dero saw a late-model black BMW outside the laundromat. The woman in the deli thought Rube seemed preoccupied – she had to remind her to buy butter. And the phone records indicate that, just before she went shopping – I don't know the details, my contact could only provide the metadata – Rube had a 1 minute 21 second conversation with a stranger.

Chapter 11

THE HUNTSMAN

The past's a huntsman. Huntsmen are spiders that finagle their way into penny-slot gaps to become part of the furniture. Until one day you open the door and they fall on your face when you least expect it.

'Imogene's gone,' Salina says through her tears.

'Yeah, she said.'

'Police officers get killed in the line of duty which means she's going to die.' I'm standing well back so she can't hit me. 'And *you're* to blame.'

'Come on, Sal, you know I hate the fuzz.'

'That's why she signed up, out of rebellion against you.'

I'm not going to argue. Arguing with my ex is like wrestling with glue. We're up a side alley with too many spiders in it.

'Look, Sal, I'm not here to talk about Imogene; I'm interested in Clint.'

Clint was the telephone repairman who came to plug in our phone and ended up plugging Salina. At the same time, he was also making connections with several other women – a fact that Sal discovered after obtaining his phone records from another Telco employee.

'Clint's dead,' she says bluntly.

The fact that Clint had been boffing Salina while she was my wife gave me a hold over him – enough to get the phone records that helped nail a killer. The only problem from Clint's point of view was that he was killed in the process.

'Rube got a phone call just before she died. I need to know the identity of the caller; your contact – the one who obtained Clint's phone records – could tell me who it was.'

My ex-wife considers me through her tears. 'And after I tell you, will you leave me alone?'

I tell her *Yes.*

'Her name's Marianne Merriman. She's got a social conscience.'

The dame across the table is smarter than she looks but that's because I'm the one doing the looking. She takes a swig of her expensive wine and when she glances around at the equally expensive diners, I can make out the indentation left by the headset.

'All these rich bastards.' Her peepers swivel back to me. 'Why do you want that telephone number?'

'It'll help solve the murder of a little old lady.'

'What you're asking me to do is illegal.'

'Most of life's illegal, Merriman.' She's bright, bored and possessed of a social conscience; I gamble on the character assessment. 'Do you play chess?'

'What's chess got to do with the price of a good feed?'

'Chess is about good versus evil. Sometimes black wins and sometimes white loses but in the end it always comes down to good versus evil.'

'It's only a game.'

'Not when you're playing. When you're playing, the pieces are real, their removal from the board is real and – win or lose – the game's for keeps.'

She looks up from her chicken.

'You talk about pieces – bishops, rooks and the rest. What about the pawns?'

I've told the waiters to keep the food coming and it's the kind of joint where they do what you tell them as long as you pay. I hunch over my salad.

'Look at these big spenders and remember that – unlike them – me and you and people like us are no more than those self-same pawns, only able to move one square at a time. Unless, of course, you're smart enough to take a piece *en passant* – that is, move more than one square and take out a big one. That's what I'm offering you – a chance to strike a blow for the little man – sorry, *person.* A call was made, someone died and that someone was my aunt – a white pawn who took on the army of the night and lost.'

Merriman can tuck it away. But she can also listen because it's her job to listen. 'How do you know I'm not one of the bad people?' she says.

I shrug. 'Good and bad are in the eye of the beholder. That's why there's so much trouble in the world – everyone thinks they're right. And the more right they think they are, the more dangerous they become.'

Marianne Merriman smiles, nods, mops up the rest of her gravy, cleans up her ice-cream and palms me the number.

You got two choices when you get a number like this – you can either chuck it in the nearest bin and forget about it, or you can die. I call the number.

Immediately a voice says, 'You're ringing from an untraceable phone. I can respond only after you advise me of your identity.'

'You'll respond if I tell you my call concerns terrorism.'

'How do I know what you're telling me is true?'

'Because of today's headlines. I'm on the side of peace and I need details of a conversation.'

I give the name of the *callee* – Rube – plus the date, time and duration of the conversation.

'Sorry, but we're bound by law to collect no more than the dates and times of calls and who called whom. Which appears to be information that you already have.'

'Tell that to the birds. As it happens, I'm not the birds.'

The voice doesn't miss a beat. 'Where do you want to meet?'

If you're playing a Grand Master, you need to think several moves ahead just to stay in the game. I do the equivalent of crossing a river in flood in order to shake off a pack of tracker dogs.

'The Martin Place memorial in half an hour. Bring what I want and come alone.'

'How did you get my number?'

I click off.

The ordinary-looking joker in a grey T-shirt and even greyer jeans is in place. So, too, are the three snipers – one on the roof of the Uncommon

Wealth Bank, one in the Post Office clocktower and the third mingling with the populace. The Grey Man's head shoots up when I ring him.

'You're calling from another untraceable phone.'

I ignore the protest. 'I told you to come alone.'

He thinks quick but that's how he's paid to think.

'I didn't invite him – the back-up's the Agency's *default* option.'

'Nice try but I count at least three of them.'

'Yeah, well, like I say, I –'

'Next stop Centennial Park.'

'But that's several hundred acres of parkland!'

'Wait by one of the gates. I'll find you. You'll get further instructions on arrival. And this time, no shooters.'

Chapter 12

MURDER BOYS

Roarer's driving a stolen Fiat.

'Does this mean we're mates again, Rain?'

'No, it means I need someone with a stolen Fiat.'

The Grey Man's opted for the Lang Road gates because they provide plenty of hidey-holes. There's no sign of back-up but that just means the gunmen are better hidden than they were last time. I watch as he clicks on and read his lips as he mouths the word *Ready!* into his wristwatch.

'I want you standing by the kerb, Grey Man,' I say into the phone; he takes a step, all the time looking about him. 'Closer – so close you might be stormwater on your way to the Harbour.'

We come at him from the eastern end, Roarer slowing just enough for me to scoop up the Grey Man and hibernate him. After which Rory accelerates as the wolverines come down from the fold.

I've relieved the Grey Man of everything right down to his recorder pen; his tracker bracelet's at the bottom of the Harbour; and we've ditched the Fiat. I didn't need to remove his powers of conversation because he never had any.

'I chucked all your belongings in the Harbour.'

'Then you've just signed your death warrant,' he says. 'Australia's counter-terrorism powers are second to none. We'll work out who you are and track you down, even though you're hiding your identity behind a hijab.'

I consider him through my peep-hole. 'It's a burqa not a hijab. And you can't trace me because I'm an unknown quantity. And when you fail to find me you'll look even worse than you do now.' I shrug. 'But I'm prepared to give you an alibi if you drop the *mucho-macho* and give me what I want.'

'Which is?'

'What I asked for – the transcript of a conversation.'

'It's in the sole of one of the sneakers that you chucked in the Harbour.'

I produce the sneaker; it's empty.

'Nice try but I didn't and it wasn't. Your latest lie leaves me no choice but to make you look even more stupid than you do already. You, the great protector of people's freedom, have been abducted. Do you want to be tarred and feathered as well and left in the middle of Bondi? It'd be the end of a promising career.'

'I committed the transcript to memory.'

I produce his recorder pen and click on.

'So now you can uncommit it.'

After we dump the spook, Rory says he wants another job so I tell him to keep an eye on Harry. Then I get back to the boat where I pour a Glenfiddich, take out the spook's recorder pen and hit *Play*. The voice is *tremolo* but otherwise the words flow nice because the Grey Man's got no cause to lie. While he's talking I conjure up the image of Rube looking worried.

*TRANSCRIPT OF CONVERSATION BETWEEN AGENCY AND OCCASIONAL AGENT R***:*

MALE VOICE: I have an urgent message for you.

*R***: Who's this?*

VOICE: You know who it is.

*R***: Why are you breaking cover?*

VOICE: You've helped us in the past so now we're helping you.

*R***: What's the message?*

VOICE: They're coming to get you and we cannot – repeat cannot – come to your aid. Which means that you're on your own. Leave immediately and do not return in the foreseeable future. Go shopping or fly to the moon but leave and do not return. I repeat: we're powerless to help you.

I play it again till I've got it by heart. After which I drop the recorder over the side for the fishes to listen to. Important phrases: *we cannot come to your aid; you're on your own; we're powerless to help you.* It's not necessary to analyse the voice – I know who it is. I watch the Harbour go about its innocent business – ferries, yachts, seagulls – under the so-called protection of our counter-terrorism agencies. Since when were such people *powerless*? More to the point: what could make them that way?

I put on the flak jacket under the coat and because someone's tailing me take the long way. When I arrive, I make two phone calls; the second one's to Rory. I keep to code and Roarer responds in kind.

'Does this mean we're mates again?'

'No.'

When he arrives he's behind the wheel of the hearse and he's sweating a dog's smile; I shove aside his crutch and climb in.

'What's the news on Harry?' I ask.

'He's going about his business.'

'No sign of trouble?'

'Not that I could see.'

'Keep watching.'

But Roarer's mind has moved on; it's not much of a mind but it moves. The last time I needed help he slammed the door in my face.

'Look, if you're still cranky about that door business, Rain, let me just say I didn't have any choice.' We're heading south by south-west. 'I was trying to make my marriage work and you were a good part of the reason it didn't. You got to learn to turn the other lip, Rain, because God moves in mysterious ways, his blunders to perform.'

'It's *wonders* not *blunders*, Roarer – which is another way of saying that people don't need to worry because Someone Else is picking up the pieces.' I shake my head. 'God or Allah or Jehovah or whatever He calls Himself twigged early on to the fact that knowledge is power – which is why He operates on a *need-to-know* basis.'

Rory changes gears, his one foot flying, his face frowning. 'I did all that church stuff but I still don't get it. Maybe it's because I've got gunfire-induced industrial deafness. I only realised afterwards that the fat bugger in the bullpit –'

'Pulpit.'

'– was saying *God willing*, not *God killing*, and that the song didn't go *Murder boys* but *Gird her loins*.' He taps the wheel. 'I guess people hear what they want to hear.'

'Right.'

'I know I'm bloody right, Rain. When that fat bugger started adulterating Janet …'

'I said *right* as in *turn right*!'

Rory flicks the wheel and veers in front of a truck that clips the sign on the back of the hearse reading *FUNERAL IN PROGRESS*. The funeral was nearly ours.

Chapter 13

THE CEMENT MEN

The sign above the gate reads *HEA-VAN ON EARTH* but grass won't grow where grass won't grow and at some stage they called in the cement men. The joker behind the counter pretends to check the books – they always pretend to check the books – and when he looks up he's in lockdown.

'No vacancies,' he says.

I'm wearing the bright blue coat with the gold fleck in it, the tough expression and the hat. If I was him I wouldn't have any vacancies either.

'I'll pay double.'

Suddenly he's got a vacancy.

Going by the prices, the cement's rolled gold but the caravan's a roof over my head and he didn't demand any proof of identity.

KEEP QUITE and *ELECTRICS EXTRA*, the signs say. Along with *WATER TO BE PAYED FOR* and *CLEAN BOG AFTER USE*. I open Rube's file on the little flop-down table under the light I'm paying extra for to find three clipped-together sheets of A4 paper in a sealed, clear-plastic sleeve marked *WILL* and *WON'T*. The testament's short and there are no surprises. You can't make bequests to people that don't exist so Rube left everything to Imogene.

I hear movement but in caravan parks there's always movement – people arriving and people *de*riving; relationships breaking up and relationships breaking in; drunks drinking; lovers loving; residents showering or using the lavatory; dogs, cats, possums and mothers-in-law doing what dogs, cats, possums and mothers-in-law do. Except that whoever's outside is no mother-in-law – he's too furtive. Rube's dead and her killers were never going to leave it at that.

The other thing about caravans is they haven't got escape hatches. There's a little round sink; a table and seat that convert into a bed; a stove; a refrigerator; and a cupboard. And someone outside.

I check the cupboard but all it contains is an iron, an ironing board, a lot of mould and the usual ragged pile of *Phantom* comics. To satisfy the law, vans have got wheels. Which means they tend to bounce in response to movement so I stay where I am. Whoever's out there saw me come in so they know what I'm wearing. A change of clothes will give me a lifesaving moment of uncertainty.

I take off my hat and coat but keep the flak jacket. *Coming ready or not.* Because if I stay where I am, bullets will find me. All the gunman has to do is rake back and forth until he hears the screams that say he hit me. After which he'll hit me some more.

I think it through like Rube must have thought it through, but without the flak jacket. When I open the door he'll have a target and it'll be my chest and that's what he'll aim for – the biggest and brightest of all available targets: me in the brightly lit doorway, all dressed up like a shish-kebab. And if he's a good enough shot there's a chance I'll live because he'll hit the flak jacket. I shovel the *WILL* and *WON'T* back in the box before hauling out the Heckler & Cock.

Instead of taking the paces I do a jeté. I hear rustling as I throw open the door that tells me I've got surprise on my side. The volley – it comes late but it still comes – finds its mark. The gun's an AKS-74U – I know that because the bullets are 5.45 millimetre, not 9s. I hurl myself down and sideways out of the van, taking my weight on my left forearm while keeping my gun hand well out of trouble before turning the movement into a roll and ending up on my stomach in the prone-fire position.

Only there's nothing to prone-fire at. *When you're caught by surprise, don't move* – that's the code of the professional shooter and this shooter's nothing if not professional. The cement's making more movement than he is. Another rustle as a creature heads for some nocturnal rendezvous but otherwise –

I roll to the right – hard and fast – as a new batch of slugs seeks their target. We both know he outguns me; we also both know there's nothing to hide behind. The night scope means he can see everything except my thoughts.

CLEAN BOG AFTER USE. It's the only building of any substance – built of breeze blocks, low-flying but high enough to do the job if I can make it. But he knows where I am, the bullets will reach me before I'm halfway to safety and there'll be a levy on the surviving residents to pay for the clean-up. So I dive in the opposite direction. Feint and dive, then feint and dive some more as the salvos find their mark. Only it's the wrong mark, a bush halfway between where I was a split-second ago and the ablutions block.

The shooter forgot to kill the lights. Also too late, he realises that, while the power-saving bulbs are weak, they still shed enough illumination for me to see by. And also too late he finds out I'm armed.

He throws himself sideways. I could go for the kill but the sirens are closing in at fifty paces a second and when they arrive I don't want them to find a corpse – the shooter's or mine. So I clip his nearside capella and it's enough to make him scream but not so bad that he won't be able to escape. Which he's intent on doing because he knows he's missed his chance and will have to wait for the next one because he can hear the sirens, too.

Ten seconds – five. It doesn't matter about the bag but I've got to get Rube's box. I shelve the gat, get myself back inside the van, grab the little plywood coffin and I'm away just as the squaddies squeal through the gates.

The hearse is in shadow – a long, dark shape with Rory at the wheel.

'What are you doing here?'

He shrugs. 'Mates aren't something you put on and take off like your underpants, Rain. I thought you'd need help – call it a killer's *premeditation*.'

Tsunami's wearing men's pyjamas, she's been watching the television news and she doesn't seem all that surprised to see me.

'There's been a terrorist shootout in a caravan park,' she says. 'They're interviewing the manager now.'

'He was a terrorist, dead set, I knew it the moment I set eyes on him.'

The moron's saying what he'd want to hear if he was watching. *'I only* let him have the van because I knew he'd kill me if I didn't. When I heard the shots I immediately called the police.'

He likes his world to look secure even if it isn't; his park's been shot up but that's not what he's on about.

'I was concerned for the residents — clearly they were in danger. Who knows with these people?'

The residents of the *HEA-VAN ON EARTH* caravan park were no longer slide-bys but so many law-abiding citizens.

'That's why I called in the cops.' The camera pans to the shot-up van. 'And what did the police do?' the reporter asks. 'Were they able to make an arrest?'

Tsunami switches off the TV. 'Nice to see you again,' she says. 'Where have you been?'

'In a caravan park.'

There was the Tsunami I first met — acting like she owned the world — who became a figure in black who might have been anyone. All I knew about her was that she was an ex-marine who understood trouble. Then she was on the boat cringing from too many ugly memories and after that, a lonely voice on a recorder. And now she's a dame in pyjamas.

She asks if I'll be comfortable before making herself scarce. This is Balmain where noise is cushioned by so much money that, however loud the noise, it still sounds like autumn leaves falling on lawn. No-one followed the hearse. Which should be a comfort, except that the one thing I'm sure of right now is that I can't be sure of anything. The world might stop but sooner or later the music will start again and the world will start turning again and — whether I like it or not — I'll have to move right along with it.

Rube's file still says: *RAINBOW — FOR YOUR EYES ONLY.* And after that: *If you're reading this it only means one thing and that is that I'm dead. I know I had it coming. But you'll have to find the people who did it because they'll be after you now. You'll have seen the CCTV but if these people run true to form, the cameras will tell you nothing.*

Later: *Some people see death as an end while for others it's only the beginning. But to me death's the start of what I like to call 'death duties' — the corpse's responsibility to those left behind.*

And still later: *Taking you on wasn't a burden, Rainbow, I don't want you ever to think that — it was a privilege. You offered the chance for me to change my life for the better. Maybe I only made things worse but I tried. It was no chore — I had fun, my little James Cagney, a great deal of fun ...*

It's only words but they're almost too hard to bear.

NOTE: From time to time I do work for the Agency. I've been in touch with them regarding the present case. They say there are wheels within wheels as they always do in such cases and I'm not sure that the right hand knows what the left hand's doing. They owe me but there's nothing in writing. They did promise that when I was in mortal danger they'd warn me but what's that worth when you're in mortal danger?

Chapter 14

DEATH IN THE AFTERNOON

I stuff Rube's *PERSONAL* file in an inside pocket, pick up the box and when I open the door the peace of Balmain sweeps over me like sweet-scented balm. Tsunami's huddled next to me in a green woolly dressing gown. I explain why I'm leaving but she isn't listening.

'I thought you came here to – you know – make up for last time,' she says.

I clutch the box.

'I just needed a temporary haven, Tsunami. I'll get out of your hair.'

'When will you be back?'

For a moment, during which my going doesn't seem necessary, I decide to leave the detective business, settle down in a little house with Tsunami and have marzipan for tea. But that's before I remember I don't exist and that, if I try to settle down, Tsunami won't exist either. Because they'll find me – the ones I know, the ones I don't know and Pandora. Why am I thinking about sweet-scented balm? I've got a case to solve.

'I won't be back, Tsunami – at least, not in that sense.'

'Then you can go to hell.'

I don't know how long they've been tailing me but after I cab it from Balmain to Likeheart, I find a bus stop with a bus in it by which means I hope to lose them. I want to put as much confusion between them and Tsunami as I can but the bus driver's decided I need help with the confusion.

'No coffins on government buses, pal,' he says, indicating the box.

367

'It's not a coffin.'

'You got a ticket?'

'I'll buy one.'

'You can't buy tickets on government buses any more – you need a prepaid card.' He gets a look on his face. 'That's two strikes against you – the coffin and the card. And if we had dress regulations you'd score the trifecta.'

Argue the toss with this joker and he'll call the cops. Which is how I find myself taking the back streets and that's when I see them again. They've cut me a bit of slack but I know a reverse-tail when I see one. There are three of them – big boys, young and broad with a bit of fun to them: the kind of fun that in childhood takes the heads off flies and in adulthood graduates to decapitating humans.

I break into a trot, hurrying into a lane where I remove my coat and sling it over my shoulder to mess with the profile, but the box is a dead giveaway so they're still with me when I reach Cleveland, laughing and joshing but still keeping pace as I head across the park to Central.

Once upon a time Prince Alfred Park was down-at-heel tennis courts, bedraggled trees and people sleeping off whatever people go to parks to sleep off. Then money got in the way and now it's got a fancy-pants swimming pool and acres of green grass infested with joggers playing tag with personal trainers. I head for the fence behind the oleanders. *When you want to hide something,* Rube always said, *put it where everyone can see it. And when you got something to protect, use it as a weapon.*

I sling the coat into the bushes, do the coffin-swing and get the first joker on the side of the toboggan with a sidekick from the whitesides, á la Nureyev. Then, using the box as a counterweight, I catch the second with a back-kick to the capellas. One to go. I put down the box and prance forward to meet him, arms out with fingers extended. Only to find he's no longer there. There's two thugs dancing on the path with all the grace of a pair of legless centipedes but the third one's vanished. I pick up the coffin and coat and get the hell out of there.

The boat's a fine and private place but none I think do there embrace. The *Wooden No* still rocks at its mooring and it's still in danger of sinking but I'm not feeling so good. *When you feel bad,* Rube said, *bury yourself in your work.* So

I do like she said and bury myself in cases she's both solved and not solved over the years. *Correction:* I don't bury myself – I go through the cases methodical in the hope that I'll find what I'm looking for.

People's memories come to a grinding halt with accidents. One minute they're in the passenger seat chatting to the driver, the next they're in hospital with their neck in a brace and the driver's dead, and they can't remember a thing. A mobile phone rings but it's a long time before I answer. I know it's a long time because by the time I click on, the voice at the other end is up to the expletives.

'Jesus, Rainbow, I thought you were dead!'

Roarer's still caught up with his guilt, still trying to shift the blame. I click off. He calls back.

'Mate, I just need to know if you're still alive. I was going to call around and, you know …'

'Well, don't call around and you know.'

'I thought you might have a job for me.'

'Anything else?'

'Thingo copped it this afternoon.'

'Who's *thingo*?'

'I can't say over the phone because you'll only hang up. But you know because you've been expecting it. That's why you asked me to watch him. Well, when I went round he …'

Roarer's hard enough to understand at the best of times but through the filter of security he's an enigma tied up in a question mark wrapped in a tiger blanket. But I've worked out who *thingo* was. I only hope they didn't hurt him too much before they killed him.

'Also, I remembered the word,' he adds.

'What word?'

'The one that the other you-know-what said – the one starting with N.'

I take the risk because it's important.

'What was the word?'

'Indigo.'

'But *indigo* doesn't start with *N* …'

'It does when you think about it.'

Chapter 15

US AND THEM

I stay away. They – *someone* – will be expecting me so instead I work through Rube's files. *Don't get caught up in detail,* I tell myself. *There isn't time.* The bottle's empty so I find myself a full one and start it on its way to emptiness. It means there'll be fire in the guts and foolishness in the brain but suddenly I'm in urgent need of both. First Rube then Harry – with Tsunami and the rest of them lined up waiting on the gangplank. Foolishness first … A phone rings. I find out which one from the selection in the bilge and click the thing on. The voice is like the whisky – still maturing. It's Bertie, the kid from Vaucluse.

'Have you discovered anything yet?'

Suddenly I'm sober. 'Yeah – I've discovered that these friends of yours mean business.'

'They're not friends and they're still after me.'

'Then you'll have to go into hiding. Work in an ashram in India or something.'

'I don't think Daddy would approve of that.'

It's Rube's computer and therefore dirty but at least it's traceable only to Rube and no-one can hurt her where she's gone. I open Gargle, come up with Bertie's email and – after a lot less than the usual trial and terror – find that his password is the same as his name. Also that – apart from the expected emails to friends and relations – there's nothing even faintly suspicious. Nothing, for example, linking him to terrorist groups like Hezbollah or al-Qaedar or Khalid Sheikh Mohammed or the deaths of Harry and Rube. After that I try *Father of* and after that chuck the computer in the water. I'm not as innocent as Bertie.

He's a name from Rube's files under the heading *Security Adviser*, he's big and he's wearing the kind of expression that a ghost might wear on his day off. I can't see through him – just where the bookshelves covering the back of his office stop on one side of his suit and come out the other. He's frowning over my card – the one that says I'm a vice-president of something or other in an obscure concern that might or might not be important.

'What did you say you were interested in?'

You don't need a fake moustache or a funny accent to change people's perceptions of you – just a change of clothes, a self-effacing manner and an all-purpose chuckle. I do the chuckle.

'Please don't take too much notice of the card, John – you don't mind if I call you John, do you? If we can do business we'll do it and if we can't, we never met.'

He persists. They always persist. 'What kind of business are you in?'

'Security.'

'That's a big word, security.'

I keep my hands still – that's a large part of the secret, keeping your hands still – and look at him like he's a cross between Steve Irwin and the Dalai Lama.

'You're a shrewd man, John. And yes, security's a very big word, which is why I'm here. I'm not trying to sell you anything or even buy something from you. As a newcomer to your country, I simply need the answer to a question, and that question is: *Is Australia safe?*'

'Economically, politically or socially?'

I get the impression I'm looking in a mirror, that I'm as fake as this joker representing himself to me as a security adviser.

'That's a very clever question and of course the three are connected.' I do the chuckle. 'I guess what I'm saying is: should I invest here?'

'That's another big word, *invest.*'

He looks at his watch – he's got a couple of minutes, no more: it's time to cut to the chase.

'But neither *security* nor *invest* is the key word. The key word's *control.* And the answer to your question is, *Here in Australia, yes, we are in control.* Our two main political parties might represent themselves as Whig and Tory but in fact they're one and the same. Which makes us *safe* in every sense of the word.' He shoots me his Steve Lama look. 'So, yes, everything's under control.'

I find what I'm looking for towards the end of the second bottle, a thinner file than the rest because the case was incidental, worked on only when Rube had time and spread out over a number of years, starting when I was eight. The file's vague, no doubt intentionally so:

1. Because Rube hadn't had time to collect all the data; and

2. In case someone other than me found it.

It's called *THEM*, it contains no more than a few pages and those few pages contain nothing that could be called even vaguely coherent. *When doing a crossword,* Rube wrote, *you need to put yourself in the mind of the setter. That's the key, the clue, the thread – the code, if you like. You need to work out the compiler's mindset, see if they like anagrams or acrostics or spoonerisms or just mucking about with the mind of the solver. Because once you've worked out their mindset you have a chance of solving the crossword. Indigo,* Rory said. Rory who wouldn't know *indigo* from *impetigo* or a hole in the ground … I stare at the empty bottle. How come it's empty? A ferry rocks the *Wooden No* and the pump stops. I'm inclined to let it stay stopped but after a while I go down and get it started again.

The moonlight shining through the porthole's from the same moon that shone on the world when life began. Then it stops shining and the cabin's dark. The moon that's been shining forever has gone because the *Wooden No*'s swung on her mooring. *THEM*, the file's labelled. And in it is what Rube worked out over a number of years. Did it ever achieve the status of *Case*? Rube wrote beneath the heading: *Is this important?* To which there's no reply, just the same silence that's filling the cabin now – the plash of innocent wavelets against the hull and the tick of the old tub's chronometer marking off measured increments of time.

In the middle of the night, Roarer rings again.

'It might have been something else.'

'What might have been something else?'

'That word I told you – it might have been *in-he-go.*'

'Thanks for that, Roarer.'

'Don't mention it.' This time he's the one that clicks off.

Chapter 16

DIS IS DE NIECE

The café's so much charred wreckage ringed by the usual blue-and-white plastic tape. In the pallid light of the setting sun, the blackened benchtops are broken, plastic plates reduced to Dali shapes and the words chalked on the footpath read *NEVA X US*. It's been a fine day but not for Harry – his corpse is in the morgue and his home's in Cammeray.

I'm loitering on the other side of the road pretending to read the *Terrorgraph*. I don't know why they still produce the *Terrorgraph* – how many private eyes need a tabloid blatt to hide behind while waiting to gain entry to an apartment? Photos of the burnt-out caff accompany the story, together with a grainy head-and-shoulders of an old but very dead friend.

YET ANOTHER DEATH
CAFE MAN KILLED
When will this carnage end?

An old dame's having trouble getting out of the block of flats because she's tangled in a walking frame so I help her before the security doors shut, keeping the gat closeted because there's no need for armoury – it would only frighten the pigeons. In the foyer there's the usual ragged carpet and peeling paint, the stairs creak and the smell alone could kill you.

Harry's door's open.

Inside the flat the carpet's heavily patterned, the walls were last painted fifty years ago and a woman's foot is dangling from an unmade bed. It's the stuff that mantraps are made of so I stay where I am. The building contains twenty bedsits with a lot of punters hanging around in the daytime because they got nowhere else to go. Above the muted roar of traffic there isn't a sound and the foot on the bed keeps swinging.

The trick to detective work is to stay out of range – be a fly on the wall instead of an active participant. But it doesn't always work that way. The door next to Harry's opens, a gorilla emerges and I make out I belong here, push Harry's door open all the way and find I'm no longer a fly on the wall – instead I'm in the middle of a tableau containing chintz curtains, a few scraps of furniture with Harry's stamp collection on one of the scraps, in the presence of the dame belonging to the foot.

She's in her early twenties and she's supporting her nicely distributed weight on one hand while she's got a gat in the hand she's not leaning on. The gun's a Para-Ordnance Warthog, a handy little number with a sharp-release hammer which makes it highly accurate – not a good thing if you're at the pointy end which is where I am. I wave my arms in the hope that it looks like I'm either a very close friend or surrendering.

'Don't shoot,' I plead.

'I won't,' the dame replies. 'At least not yet.'

Her black hair's done tousled, her face is pale, her eyes are minus the epicanthic fold and she's wearing a loose dress without much support to it – but who needs support when you're holding a Warthog? Her foot's still making like a metronome and her expression's somewhere between suspicious and suspicious. After a while her foot stops swinging, her lips tighten and I decide against jumping her. The gun's too steady and the gaze hasn't wavered from my sternum.

'I've been waiting for you,' she murmurs.

'There must be some mistake.'

'Yes, there must, mustn't there?'

I could stand here forever swapping pleasantries only I haven't got forever. I came to look for clues – apart from the expected ones – only to be confronted by the totally *un*expected ones.

'You're either Harry's niece or his daughter. One thing's for sure – you ain't his mother.'

The dame laughs. At least I think she's laughing because the almond eyes crease and the mouth twitches like there's a fly on it but the gat doesn't move so maybe I'm wrong.

'That's two shots, mister, both of them wide of the mark.'

'That's too bad,' I reply, 'because I've already decided you were an interloper which is why I called the cops.'

That's when her eyes waver and that's when I take her. A ballet move always fools them. Instead of diving, I do the splits. Then instead of staying split I do the kind of roll Margot Fontaine would have been proud of, followed by a grab of the metronome foot and a twist that puts the dame on the floor a millisecond too fast for her to reorganise the gun. I relieve her of the firepower, get to my feet, close the door and switch on the light. And with the light on I rebadge her. She's small, aged twenty-five going on fifteen and the lips in the Hepburn face – that's Audrey not Katharine – are set in a snarl that stops a millimetre short of beautiful. She's about to speak but I get in first.

'So what's it to be – *sister, niece* or *daughter?*'

'I was Harry's girlfriend,' she says, a sad expression clouding her face.

'You got a name, girlfriend?'

'Yes, I do,' she says.

'Mind telling me what it is?'

'Yes, but I'll tell you anyway – it's Denise.' She smiles at a memory. 'Harry always introduced me to people as *de niece* but to my face it was always *Babychino*.' She glances at me shyly or maybe it's slyly – it's hard to tell because of the eyes. 'I know who you are – you're Rainbow.'

'Where were you at the time of Harry's death?'

She doesn't miss a beat, segueing from grief to reliable eyewitness in less than an eye-bat.

'I was going to meet him,' she says straight from the hip, 'but by the time I arrived it was all over. Harry was in a bad way but he still managed to say something.'

'What did he say?'

'He said: *Life is only froth and bubble.*'

'Did that mean anything to you?'

She nods before answering. 'It meant that he recognised me even though he was dying. I used to – I still do – shoot off at the mouth. And when that happened Harry said I was living up to my name of Babychino: frothy. Then he'd mess with this quote and say: *Life is only froth and bubble/ Two things stand like stone/Blindness to another's trouble/Cunning in your own.*'

'When did he say that?'

'All the time. But he didn't really mean it.'

'Is that all?'

'Isn't it enough?'

Chapter 17

THE BIG BOY

'It depends whether I prefer milk with my coffee or like it straight. Going back a couple of stanzas, Bubbles – you said you were hurrying. Why?'

'Because –' Babychino glances away '– Harry was under threat.'

'Who was he under threat from? Debt dealers? Junkies? Standover men after his property?'

Babychino moves to the door where she pauses with her hand on the handle but her mind elsewhere.

'After you and that woman rode off on the scooter, the terrorists came back to the café, wanting to know where you lived. Harry wouldn't tell them. There were too many people around for them to do anything but they threatened to return.'

'Where were you when he copped it?'

'I told you – I was on my way to see him.' She's got her composure back from wherever she parked it and she's tugging at the curtains, moving furniture, adjusting bedcovers – all the things a person does who's familiar with a joint – pausing only long enough to add, 'This was our love nest.'

'When did the cops arrive?'

'While I was kneeling beside Harry.'

'Were they real cops?'

'What kind of question's that?'

'Did they ask who you were?'

'Yes.'

'What did you tell them?'

'I told them we were lovers.'

I think back to Aunt Rube.

'Did they invite you to do an official ID?'

'Yes.'

'What did you tell them?'

'I confirmed it was him.'

'Why did you call them *terrorists*?'

'Because that's what they must have been.'

'Did the cops ask you about any identifying marks?'

'Yes.'

'Did you show them the birthmark in the shape of a boat on his right ankle?' I say it quick so there's no time for evasion.

'It wasn't a birthmark, it was a scar; it wasn't on his right ankle, it was on his left side; and it wasn't a boat, it was a bird.' She gives me one of her glances. 'Do I pass?' She shivers. 'It's like reliving it all over again. But they say you have to relive things if you're going to cope.'

It seems like Harry had good taste in everything except what he dished up to his customers.

They've cemented over the dirt, the gym's been turned into a theatre and the demountables have been replaced with permanent classrooms. A sign reads *BE NICE TO YOUR NEIGHBOURS* while a second one warns students to *REPORT UNUSUAL ACTIVITY*. It's Sunday, so the school's deserted, but I people it with savages.

When I was a kid, if you reported 'unusual activity' you became part of the unusual activity. Like Harry, I had a girlfriend — or what passes for a girlfriend when you're ten. I even remember her name and what she looked like. The corrugated-iron toilets have been rebuilt in expensive new brick and the gallows tree's still standing except that now it's fenced off with *STRICTLY OUT OF BOUNDS* signs hanging from its branches. I climb over the fence.

I need faces, shapes, bodies and attitudes to go with the names that I haven't got and they swarm all over me. The footholes are still in the trunk and I can still hear the shouts and feel the hands dragging me through the foliage. The marks of the rope have filled with lichen but they're still there and the bloodlust echoes through time.

I crawl out on the branch. Rube calls it — make that *called* it — *method detecting*. I see the chanting kids like they're still there, feel the tightening of the rope and — just before passing out — the anxious face of Ariadne Indola behind the willow-switch form of the Headmaster as he hurries towards us, waving a pair of scissors and shouting, *You little brat, why are you doing this to me?*

I pleaded with Rube not to make a fuss. But after she was satisfied I was okay, she visited the Headmaster. He was on the defensive – he'd saved her brat, who'd brought it on himself by not mixing more easily with the others. *Be assured,* he told her, *the ringleaders will be expelled.* Rube was aghast. *Can't you see what that will do?* she replied. *They'll come after him!*

Back aboard the *Wooden No*, I crack a bottle of J&B and continue sifting through Rube's files. Despite what she told the Headmaster, she thought it was just Darlinghurt being Darlinghurt and it took her a while to figure out what was really going on. She set traps, caught some of the transgressors, gave them a kick up the bum and life returned to more-or-less normal. Then – years down the track – the persecution started again. Only this time it was more like drip torture – subtle, not so easy to pin down. Whispers in the crowd, items missing from the house, nasty little notes in the mail. All of which Rube took in her stride because she'd lived with such things all her life. It wasn't until she put two and two together that she started the dossier.

Something happened to make it start all over again but it's not clear what. I find nothing in Rube's files apart from the single question: *Why?* Apart from which, I never noticed anything and people change. All I remember is that the ringleader was a big boy. Somehow Rube came by the names, only I let them get stolen before I had the chance to commit them to memory.

A ferry passes, the *Wooden No* rocks and the empty bottles roll with her. By nightfall I'm rolling with the boat because I'm as drunk as a day-old newt. A ship's hooter bleats and over a distance of thirty-five years all I've got is a fistful of six-by-four-inch cards, each containing little more than nothing – a few vague references to a bunch of bully boys, one of them – the ringleader – big.

I don't do vengeance; this isn't a vendetta. Rube's dead and nothing I can do will bring her back. I stare at the screen. The figures on the CCTV weren't middle-aged like they should be – middle-aged men move careful and at least one of them would be stiff-backed with care. How can I find out, how can I *know*? Rube knew – which was why she went to the trouble of keeping records. It's also why they came after her. So surely –

Chapter 18

LOOKING FOR ARIADNE

Something whangs against the hull and nausea assails me as I ease myself up from my bunk, assume an approximation of the perpendicular and stagger out on deck. A fish flops at my feet.

'Ahoy there, me hearty!'

Queen the Sailorman's strutting around the stern of his boat wearing Gucci. Breakfast is flathead. I try to stare him down but can't because of his bonhomie and the sun. There's a time for everything and this isn't one of them. I toe the fish back in the water.

'Sixteen men on a dead man's chest!' he sings as he throttles away; someone ought to throttle Queen. 'Yo, ho, ho, and a bottle of Calvados! Row, row, row the boat! Sixteen men ...'

The echoes recede as I crawl back to my bunk. *Sixteen men,* Queen's singing. I can't remember sixteen men — make that *boys;* I can't even remember one.

What do you know when you're a kid? You know how to survive and after that you know what you like and what you don't like and you do something about it. And what I did — at least once every schoolday — was I held Ariadne Indola's hand. The one and only thing I hated about my deschooling was that it meant leaving behind the girl of my dreams.

On the computer at the internet café, for plain and unadorned *Indola* I get the infernal question: *Do you mean Indolent?* But as well as the question, I also get a couple of *Indolas* — namely *George, Simon* and *Marguerita.* Even after I apply the acid test – *parents of* – I still come up empty-handed. Around me, kids watch porn and social misfits harass other social misfits. A virtual life is no life at all and I can't find Ariadne.

Because the machine is logical, the computer asks: *Do you mean Indole, Indolo or India.* I try what they suggest followed by a few things completely different. Then I insert a couple of asterisks. Finally, *Bingo!* There's the name change – to *Indox* – while the first name remains the same. The girl of my dreams is still Ariadne – the only offspring of a couple that was once Indola but somewhere along the line changed their name, for reasons best known to themselves.

They supported polar bears in Alaska, muskrats in the Ukraine, set up a fighting fund to stop oil mining in the North Sea and sent their only child into the jaws of death – namely Baisson Primary – in accordance with their principles regarding equal education for all. But I already know that because, apart from holding hands, me and Ariadne Indola also talked. What I don't know is what she died of. Because Ariadne Indox – née Indola – apparently no longer exists.

Until I scroll to the end of all the good deeds of the Indolas – make that *Indoxes* – to discover that she does.

The joint's one of those pleasantries that God inducted and Man constructed – a tower of ice-cold marble with forty floors of pastel-tinted windows smiling back at the sun. The foyer's an introduction to infamy and there's a thug standing guard.

'What do you want?' he snarls.

Not *How can I help you, my good man?* Or *Good morning, sir, isn't it a nice day?*

'I'm a friend of Merz Sidonia's.'

He doesn't even make the call, just comes at me like a loaded howitzer. You don't negotiate with loaded howitzers so I thump him. Blame an imbalance of derivatives.

Money does people's dirty work for them. Here it locks down the building, sounds an alarm and calls in the heavy artillery. Before I can hit *Rewind* I find myself cross-stitched to a chair in a small room undergoing the kind of interrogation that can only result in a great deal of pain.

'The police will be here in –' The security boss stretches his long legs under the desk and consults his imitation Rolex '– twenty minutes and fifteen seconds. They always allow us a bit of leeway.' With his grey eyes he could be a film star with a bank account in the Bahamas. 'During that leeway, we have free rein to do anything we like, short of killing you.'

He's got my gat on his desk and he's studying it, along with the contents of my pockets.

I try again. 'Like I said, I'm a friend of Merz Sidonia's.'

'And I'm the King of Siam.' He assumes a smile about as real as his watch. 'I suppose you're going to tell me you're here to give her the gun?'

'The gat's no more than part of the wardrobe, a fashion accessory that means nothing and does even less. I'm here to see Ariadne.'

The security boss puts down the Smith & Double-Yew, raises his eyes to mine and suddenly they're not so much grey as overcast and threatening.

'The point is –' he checks the calling cards that he filched along with the gat '– Mr Green or Orange or whatever you're calling yourself today – you can't see anyone. How do we know who you are? You come here armed to your broken teeth and when you find entry difficult, knock out my concierge. Which means you've just bought yourself a one-way ticket to the cop shop – and after that court, followed by jail. Unless you can come up with a far more convincing explanation for your visit than the one provided.'

That's when she appears. Ariadne was only a girl when I last saw her, with shiny hair, big opossum eyes and skin like caramel ice-cream. A hand you needed to hold and a smile that lit up your life. Thirty-five years later I'm strapped to a chair and not in a position to disbelieve anything. But what I see puts a lump in my throat. Thirty-five years after my last sighting, my lovely little girlfriend advances into the room.

'It's not – it couldn't be … Rainbow?'

Since the age of consent I've been supporting the whisky business and last night was no exception. I've had my ears mashed and my nose broken and the cut over my right eye gives me a permanent expression of malevolent quizzicality. Add to that the missing thumb, too much musculature and the op-shop wardrobe and – like they say in the classics – I leave a lot not to be desired.

'One and the same. Except that – like you – I'm all growed up now.'

Ariadne walks to where the sunlight can pick up any imperfections she's collected over thirty-five years. Gone is the little white dress, to be replaced by a sheer-silk number in iridescent mauve, reaching sedately below her knees and covering most of her shoulders but having difficulty covering subsequent developments. Of course she's taller. Otherwise she is as she always was, just older.

'Make that,' I add, '*not* just like you.'

Chapter 19
THE GIRL OF MY DREAMS

I manage to grind the thug's foot into the marble before following Ariadne into her private Otis elevator and halfway to heaven. You meet someone out of the mockery of the past but you don't see them – what you see instead is yourself as they see you. And what I see through Ariadne's eyes as she seats herself behind a desk big enough to waltz on is a gaudily dressed pug with a face hacked out of misfortune, twisting a battered hat in his ham fists, and shifting from one foot to the other like he needs to go to the toilet.

'Remember when we used to hold hands?' I say. 'Except you'd always let go when that bully-boy appeared, I suppose in case he hurt me for consorting with you.'

'I remember.'

'Do you also remember the one about the three wells?'

'Well, well, well ...' she murmurs, smiling at the memory of what used to make us laugh while I try to get used to an office big enough to double as a launch-pad for an Airbus. The bank of telephones before her is a private army and the view from the window is pretty much what Gurgle Earth would get from a satellite. I turn back to Ariadne – you can only get so far on satellites.

'Speaking of *well,*' I say, 'you look great.'

She shrugs. 'Mum and Dad looked like teenagers well into their sixties; I didn't have children; I'm cushioned by wealth; on top of which I keep fit by stroking in a women's rowing team. All I need to worry about are taxes and the Troubles and neither is going to prematurely age me because I've got everything covered.'

Because I'm a detective, like the character in the Notre Dame book I get hunches. And my hunch right now is that – apart from finding out

the present-day identity of the boy that used to bully me – those *Troubles*
might be worth knowing.

'What Troubles might they be?'

She smooths her hands over her arms like she might be able to iron
out perfection.

'As I said, they're nothing I can't handle. In fact I only really became
aware of them after James died' – she waves a beautiful arm at the desk,
the launchpad and the view – 'leaving me this.'

'Could you be a bit more specific?'

She shakes her beautiful head. 'What are you?' she asks. 'Oh, I know
you *used* to be Rainbow but what have you become? You might be from
the Tax Office or one of those TV shows that do exposés or from a spy
agency or the police. Having all those business cards suggests you might
be far more than you appear to be. I know *who* you are – what I don't
know is *what*.'

'I'm a private detective.'

'And are you here to investigate my business or me?'

I shake my head to indicate reassurance but in reality to stop my mind
buzzing. I'm interested in who she remembered from school only to be
sidetracked by talk of the Troubles and her beauty.

'I'm here for something else entirely.'

'How do I know that?'

'Because I came in by the front door.'

She plays with the little replicas of trucks, scale models of edifices,
bundles of share scrip and gold ingots that litter her desk and when she
looks up she's come to a decision.

'I'm sorry if I seem suspicious, Rainbow – it's the nature of business
that people are out to get you. It's one way of winning – by hobbling the
opposition. I wasn't brought up to money or I'd never have been at that
school. As a late convert to wealth I tend to be over-protective of it. But
I trust you because of our past so I'll do my best to help. What do you
want to know?'

'We could start with the Troubles …'

She puts down a model of a dredger. 'Not to put too fine a point on
it, James – that's my late husband – was paranoid. He thought there were
two threats facing business – one from within and one from without:
traditional workplace problems that have always been there plus a new
one – which, for want of a better word, he called *terrorism*. It was the latter
he was most worried about. So he set up a department to study what he
perceived to be a very great threat, thereby providing himself with the

wherewithal to deal with it. He called his department *Watchdog*. At the time, I didn't know the background or what he did with the information.'

She looks across her airfield desk to see if she's got my attention; she has.

'I use the word *paranoid* but it seems that there *was* something to my husband's fears. Among other things we dabble in coal-seam gas and it was assumed that a series of disasters was the work of eco-terrorists – that is, well-intentioned do-gooders we could bundle off to court and be rid of, relying on our PR people to stop us looking like bullies. But Watchdog found there was more than that. Which is how we became mixed up in politics –' She stops like she's just remembered something. 'But enough of my problems – what happened to you?'

'After those bullies nearly killed me?' I shrug myself into a chair. 'Against my will – I was only a kid, remember – my Aunt Rube took me out of school. She was my sole care and consolation.'

'You talk as if she's –'

'Dead? Yeah, that's why I'm here. Rube taught me to be a detective and that's what I became. I'm looking for her killer – or killers.'

'Who do you think killed her?'

'I don't know. It could have been the kids from school, the ones that nearly hanged me, evolved from schoolboy bullies into murderers. It might be someone else entirely. Or it might be your terrorists.'

When Ariadne's smile fades, the lights go out. She picks up a little clock and taps it like she wants to stop time.

'You do know, don't you, that your incident with the bullies was my epiphany? I don't mean I had a vision but afterwards my life changed. Because up to that time my parents wanted to bring me up according to their lights, which meant keeping me at that school.' She glances across the tarmac at me. 'Is this too much of a side-bend?'

'There's this theory doing the rounds that everything's connected,' I say. 'So go on.'

'Although my parents were moderately wealthy, they sent me to Baisson Primary because of their beliefs, even though it had to be the worst school in Sydney. But after the incident in the playground there was no way their precious Ariadne was going to swing for their principles so they took me out, changed their name to Indox and fast-tracked me through the kind of education that led to finishing school and ultimately marriage to a rich old man.' A wave of her hand takes in the room and the view and ends up with me. 'While it appears that you –'

Chapter 20

KICK PRO QUO

I shrug.

'Yeah, I went to *unfinishing* school and ended up going in the opposite direction.' I clamber to my feet. 'I won't take up any more of your precious time, Ariadne. I just thought you might be able to help.'

'Is this some kind of vendetta?'

I shake my head. 'Someone killed my Aunt Rube and I thought it might have been the kids from school with *their* vendetta. No, it's not a vendetta because I don't do vendettas. I just thought that, because you knew those bullies, you might also know where I could find them.'

She takes her eyes off the clock.

'I can't help you with any of that. But as I said, I have friends in positions of power. You can read it in any newspaper but as it happens I donate. And the people I donate to have much the same interests as my business does. They want employment – we give them employment. They want income from workers' taxes – we give them such income. And they're as concerned about terrorism as we are. From what you say, the death of your aunt might be the work of terrorists. And while I don't know any of your bullies, I do have political contacts who might be able to help.'

She writes something on a scrap of paper. As if acting on impulse, because that's the way it plays, I come around the desk to show that I still harbour some feelings towards her. But she's too quick and presses a button under her desk. There's a knock at the door and without waiting for an answer the thug enters, like he's more than anxious to take up where he left off.

'Yes, Miss Ariadne?' he asks.

'Our visitor's just leaving.'

I plant a kiss on her cheek – it seems called for – and in return she hands me the scrap of paper.

'I'm sorry I can't be more helpful,' she says. 'But if you think of some way in which I might be, please don't hesitate to call. Our Headmaster's name, by the way, was Jonathan Hercule.'

Visiting Ariadne was a long shot and, in the way of long shots, all it's left me with is memories. I'm still no closer to finding Rube's killers. Added to which is the fact that I'm wondering how things might have been if I'd stayed at school and faced the music – even if the lyrics didn't say *murder boys* but *gird her loins*. But like Rube said: *Might have been – schmite have been: what didn't happen can never be regretted. All you have after the past is the here and now. Unless, of course, something happens to change it – like the future.*

Irving Morris is a big man in his bitter middle years who looks like he might know a lot more than he does. We're in the headquarters of some political party and the office looks like it could double as a storeroom. I let him make the play.

'This isn't my room. Mrs Sidonia didn't say *who* you were nor did she say *what* you wanted to see me about. Besides which, what would I know?'

It's a good question but I go through the motions anyway.

'Why would she direct me here if she didn't think you could help?'

'Would you like a cup of tea, Mr, er –'

'Brown – Terence Brown. You wouldn't have anything a bit stronger, would you?'

No, Morris says, and even if he did he wouldn't know where to find it because – as he's already pointed out – this isn't his room: someone far more powerful than he is lent it to him.

'Can I speak frankly, Mr – er – Brown?'

'Is there any other way?'

'Mrs Sidonia told me that your visit had to do with that anti-terrorist department of hers, a department that reminds me of those signs saying green for safe, amber for maybe and red for high fire danger. Her department happens to be remarkably similar to the one I head up for the party – as a matter of fact we work hand in glove. According to Mrs Sidonia – and I don't think she'd mind my saying this – Australia's going through a period of high fire danger. It's like global warming – no-one will admit it doesn't exist because it would disaffect too many voters. But society has to be kept safe. And that department of hers, in lockstep with mine, helps keep society safe. Do I make myself clear?'

It's like a secret handshake. And while he's using the kind of code these people use I've got an idea I know what he's saying and I've also got an idea I don't like it – the crazy, red-eyed view of politics where the secret of life is to make a lot of money and if anyone gets in your way, kick them in the teeth so they don't do it again. I terminate the interview.

After my meeting with Genghis Khan, I need a breath of fresh air so I telephone Imogene. She might be learning how to be a cop but that doesn't mean she's not still my daughter. It's easy to reach her now she's no longer living with my ex-wife, her mother.

'Hello, darling? I'm ringing from a phonebooth that somehow still works which means there's no chance of a bug – from my end, anyway. What about yours?'

My ebullience is met with silence. Maybe I could have been more tactful, tactical, played it as it lays. I try again.

'I just rang for a chat, Chickadee. How are you?'

'I can't talk just now, Daddy, I'm in a lecture. But while you're there, could I ask a favour? Could you not call me so often? It makes life *difficult*. They give us heaps of homework and also there are lectures, tutorials, PE, drill and as well as that I ...'

'It's okay, Chickadee. Goodbye.'

'Goodbye, Daddy.'

I've put a lot of coins in the slot in anticipation of a long call but there's still a lot left after I hang up. I hit *Return* but nothing comes out. Faulty phone.

Chapter 21

CRUSHED BONES

Jonathan Hercule's wearing a moth-eaten pink cardigan and his spectacles are growing out of the top of his head like an afterthought.

'Are you calling on behalf of a charity, did I win the Lotto or are you here to assassinate me to get your hands on the tinful of out-of-date banknotes under my bed?' He peers at me; his breath smells of dirty socks. 'You look familiar.'

I'm standing on a concrete verandah belonging to a block of flats that could double as a high-security prison.

'I was one of your students at Baisson Primary.'

'Which one were you?'

'The quiet one.'

The head on the end of the long neck bobs until it looks like it could fall off.

'I remember – you were the boy who was always being bullied. Caused me no end of trouble. You had an aunt.'

'What do you mean – *had*?' It's the chance he's been waiting for.

'My tense was preterite rather than pluperfect. That is, while I knew you *had* an aunt then, I do not know if you still possess one *now*. The tense employed does not presume the demise of your aunt.'

'As it happens my aunt *is* dead, which is why I'm here.' Searching the darkness behind him is like trying to see into the past. 'Mind if I come in?'

I follow him into room that, if it was any bigger, would qualify as a sarcophagus. A plate edged in yellow was lunch and gunshots are rattling from the television. The old man fumbles a pointer and the gunshots cease.

'I don't normally watch television,' he says. 'But because it was about religion I made an exception. I was just about to have a cuppa – would you care to join me, ah … what did you say your name was?'

'The name's Rainbow.' I'm at school again and I don't want to be at school again. 'And I'm here to find out what you remember.'

My ex-Headmaster spoons too much tea into a teapot the size of a thimble – most of it goes on the floor – before adding water, most of which goes the same way as the tea.

'Next to nothing, I'm afraid. A lifetime spent trying to educate numbskulls like you tends to drain one – sometimes I even have trouble remembering where I put my glasses.' He hands me a cup I can see through. 'But I'm still a teacher – which is why I provide the following information: the material your cup's made from is called bone china because it's made from crushed bones.'

'Something like blood oranges.'

'It's not at all like blood oranges.' There's a frown but it clears; he's been around kids all his life and is up to their tricks, even when they're not tricks. 'It's nice of you to drop by, if only to ask questions.'

'I'm not nice and neither are my questions. Do you remember a hanging?'

'Is this a joke? Are you trick-or-treating? Has that infernal pumpkin time come around again?'

'It happened in the schoolyard – a girl called Ariadne went and got you and you ran to my assistance. You were carrying scissors.'

He frowns into his bone cup, staring at the worn carpet, then looks at me as though through a cottonwool shroud.

'If what you say is true I shouldn't have done that – run with scissors. It sets a bad example. I've expelled students for less.'

'Like you expelled that boy over the hanging.'

'You should have said: "*As* you expelled that boy over the hanging". *Like* is used to introduce a simile – but you wouldn't know a simile if you tripped over one on a night as dark as ashes.' He shakes his head like – as though – he wants to rid himself of the cottonwool but can't. 'What hanging?'

'My hanging. I was hung. From a tree.'

'*Hanged.*' The correction's automatic. 'Pictures are hung, people are hanged. Didn't you learn anything?'

'What was his name?'

'Whose?'

'The boy you expelled.'

After a pause, he says, 'I believe it was Parkinson. He used to sit up the back and tease the girls.' He looks confused. 'But why would he try to hang you? And what tree?'

I turn to go. 'It's *which* tree. And if you're looking for your glasses they're on top of your head.'

In 1930s Chicago, speakeasies were outlets for hooch – illegal grog distilled by sweatshops called *alky-burners* and distributed by gangsters like Al Capone. But the prohibited substances of today wear names like crack, ice and gammahydroxybutyrate – fantasy or liquid ecstasy – shortened to *GHB* because its users can't manage to say more than one syllable at a time. And because the drugs are illicit, speakeasies like O'Leary's pull in starlets looking for excitement, common-and-garden addicts, plenty of cops and Sydney's usual crop of colourful identities. Roarer's propping up the bar.

'I'm getting screwed,' he says. 'It's like prostitution after they brought in free love – us professionals lose out to over-enthusiastic amateurs. I ask you, where's the justice?'

Hank the barman hands me a Pink Whizz with a maraschino cherry in it and a smile.

'Justice is where it's always been, Roarer – under the jewel-encrusted jockstrap of the nearest politician. When will you learn that it simply isn't for people like us? It's to safeguard the rich and powerful which is the reason why it was invented in the first place. There's nothing you can do about it so have another beer.'

Roarer hunches over his hooch. All he knows is that his missus left him, after which he left the Church, which leaves him free to go back to killing.

'It's a bastard about Harry – he never hurt anyone, except when they deserved it. Got another job for me? I can do toecaps, kneecaps or the single shot to the back of the head for no better reason than someone smiled at someone else's missus. I don't charge GST and there's only a slight adjustment for inflation. Cash on the knocker – or should I say *knock*.'

After leaving Hercule I got to work on the White Pages and found too many subscribers with the surname Parkinson. But upon inquiry, most were the wrong age, two were dead and several belonged to the wrong sex. But one in Manly filled the bill: *Parkinson, T.F.* It might be him or it might just be an innocent bystander.

'Yeah, I got a job. Only it doesn't involve killing.'

'What *does* it involve?'

'Finding out who someone is, what they do and who they consort with.'

'A yawn job in other words. Are you sure you don't want them dead?'

I think of Rube and Harry. Sure I want them dead – only it's not what I do.

'It's not what I want, Roarer. It's what's got to be done.'

Chapter 22

THE WOMAN IN RED

We're battling the *elephants* along Manly's Corso, the parade within a parade without a single bikini in sight, looking for an address spat out by a computer. Sydney's having a weather moment, the kind when Scotsmen wish they'd worn underpants. The wind could sink the *Wooden No* but I haven't got time to worry about boats. I got my hands full with Rory.

'You sure it's just a watch-and-wait job? Because if not, my crutch is loaded and ready to go and ...'

'Like I said, Roarer, this ain't a death job.'

Most of my words are blown away before they reach him and I don't know which words but it doesn't matter because I've just seen the shadow that followed us onto the ferry and is still there – a black shape, lithe and dangerous-looking, flitting between buildings. It could be a garbage bag blown by the wind – if the wind wasn't going in the opposite direction. I drag Rory into a piece of prime real estate labelled *MENS*.

'Our target lives in that block of flats across the road, the one with the balconies,' I tell him. 'You'll enter by the usual means – that is, by holding the door open for an old lady and, while she's turning herself inside out saying *Thank you,* you go in. You'll make your way to his floor – the unit number will be on a letter box in the foyer alongside the name Parkinson.' I check my watch. 'By my calculation, you won't have to wait long. And remember, no shooting – you're only here to observe.'

'Observe what?'

'His salient features.'

'His *what*?'

It's like briefing a cistern.

'What he *looks* like, Roarer – his build and facial characteristics, his *appearance*. Got your mobile?'

'You want me to call him?'

It's not like there's a glut in the job market but surveillance is a niche industry and however the economy's doing you got to be happy with what you can get.

'Repeat after me, Roarer: you got your mobile – right?'

'Check.'

'Subject will appear at door of said apartment.'

'Check.'

'You'll photograph him and text me the image.'

'Isn't that insecure?'

'I'm insecure, you're insecure, the whole world's insecure. But my phone's traceable only to the morgue and I'd say the same thing applies to yours.'

'It's prepaid in someone else's name, if that's what you mean – what they call a *burner*, because after you've finished with it –'

'I know what a burner is, Roarer – it's what I'll turn on you if you blow it.'

The Manhattan began life as the tallest building in town but that was way back in the sixties. There are bigger buildings now but the Manhattan's still the one with the prestige – more pot plants per floor and a concierge that pre-revolutionary France would have been proud of. I'm wearing overalls with *PREMIER PLUMBING* on the bib and carrying the kind of attaché case a plumber takes to the most prestigious address in Sydney, if he wants to be invited back.

'Foul weather, friend,' the concierge says as he lets me in. 'And you're –?'

I point at the bib. 'Premier Plumbing. I'm expected upstairs.'

He hands me a card with a pin through it reading VISITOR. 'You'll need to wear this. Also I'll need some form of ID.' I give him the fake passport I used in the *Bullets at the Ballet* caper, the one featuring me as a baldy, a pilgarlic. 'Hair today, gone yesterday,' he says and I laugh because he expects me to while explaining I was never really bald, it just looks that way due to the stocking over my face, and he's still chuckling as he escorts me to the lift.

The first rule when you're somewhere you shouldn't be is to avoid the cameras. I exit the lift and step into the Gents just as Roarer's images arrive on my phone.

It's not him. That's my first thought as I study the snaps under a sign above the gold-plated taps. The man with the beard's big but he's too young. It could have been the wrong address, Roarer could have gone to the wrong door or it mightn't be the right Parkinson. I climb out of the overalls, jam on my fedora, stuff the overalls in my case, decant myself from the Gents and head for Suite 66.

'I'm from Ace Security,' I tell the receptionist, handing her the card that says I'm from Ace Security. 'We're doing a random check to make sure everything's in order, security-wise.' I keep my head down under the hat and hold up my all-purpose attaché case to prove I'm who I say I am. 'I'm looking for the office of a –' I pretend to check '– Thomas Parkinson.'

'I'm afraid Mr Parkinson's not in yet,' the receptionist says, smiling the smile of the bored while I nod the nod of a man who knows Mr Parkinson isn't in yet.

'When do you expect him?'

She glances at a clock on the wall. 'In ten minutes – exactly.'

'Is Mr Parkinson reliable?'

'You could set your clock by him.'

'Then I'll be all done and dusted in nine minutes – exactly.'

Rube taught me how to look like I'm doing one thing while doing another. Keeping the hat well down over my eyes I pull on the gloves, carry a chair to the corner and unfocus the camera while appearing to check it – five minutes. After that, I make great play of patting down the office – checking bookshelves, running my hands under the desk, picking up the receiver of each of the three phones like I'm inspecting them, while all the time doing something completely different, which is checking the contents of the drawers. Five of which yield little or nothing while the sixth … I keep my eye on the time – six minutes.

When you steal anything, always leave room for doubt – take the money but leave the jewellery. The sixth drawer contains a small black notebook and wads of cash. I pocket the book, leave the cash and relock the drawer – all the while looking like I'm nowhere near it. Seven minutes.

I snap a shot of the photo on the desk. Eight minutes. Nod to receptionist on way out – nine minutes.

Right on the ten-minute mark – after a trip to the Gents, I'm back in the plumber's overalls – he exits the lift accompanied by a woman in red and for a nanosecond the Joker ceases to exist. She's blonde, her legs are straight off the lathe and the red frock clings to her like a rejected lover. Looks like a red herring.

'But darling,' she's saying to the man beside her, 'isn't that too high a price to pay for innocence?'

'No price is too high if you want something badly enough …'

He stops, frowning at the figure before him in the overalls.

'Your plumbing's fine,' I tell him.

It's nice to see the Woman in Red's cheeks dimple.

But she still looks like a red herring.

Chapter 23

THE CLUE

It's stopped raining and Rory's got his wet-weather gear strapped to the crutch that isn't a gun while using the other crutch to keep him upright. The roadway's glistening like shot velvet as we head down Macquarie Street towards the semi-circular quay.

'Spot-check time, Roarer. You went to the fifth floor, right?'

'Check – fifth floor.'

'And you waited outside the flat with your mobile up to your face like you were talking into it.'

'Check.'

'And the geezer came out of Flat 524.'

'Don't try to trick me, Rain.'

'Okay, 514 then. And he had a dame with him.'

'You didn't ask for a shot of the dame.'

'Just because I didn't ask …' A thought strikes me. 'Describe her.'

'Dumpy, dowdy and frowzy.'

Which means I got a case within a case within a dilemma because, like the Bard said, *Post hoc, ergo propter hoc* – a presumed cause might be an effect but usually isn't. Because when a lark appears, it doesn't mean it's summer – the sun might have come out anyway.

As we board the *Wooden No*, Queen yells a greeting. 'Ahoy, me hearty!'

'What do we do now?' asks Rory, climbing aboard after me.

'Kill Queen,' I reply. 'After which we go into deep surveill.'

After Roarer decamps and Queen ferries him back to the wharf, I check the little black book I filched from Parkinson. It's one of those diaries that isn't: from random notes on what the cat ate for dinner to a brand new recipe for bratwurst. I chuck it overboard and check the mobile pic of the desk photo. Beard, accompanied by dowdy wife. No sign of a dame in red or anyone else for that matter. He's a happily married man with no antecedents. I check an image from Rube's CCTV against Rory's shot of Parkinson and the one from the desk, freezing the frame when I get all three together.

There are no features on the CCTV because the faces are squashed under stockings and the image isn't all that crash-hot because the figures are moving. *There's something in the way they move.* I shuffle the images of Parkinson emerging from his flat and the snap from his desk with the still from the CCTV. No relation. Even under the stocking I'd notice the beard. I try the next image, followed by the next and the next. Still nothing – apart from suspicion.

Crime-scene tape's stretched across the pavement outside Rube's, the door's nailed back into position and there are too many gawkers. I avoid looking anyone in the eye as I make my way round the back. The kitchen stinks of mould and the hall's still redolent of eau de cologne.

I check the lounge where nothing's changed and the hall *ditto*. After which I head upstairs, fighting off the memory of Rube's body as I dust and photograph and dust and photograph some more. I take the group photo in the hall upstairs out of its frame and pocket it. The CCTV told me nothing and the relevant file's gone. All I've got is a name, a blurred photograph and Rube's thoughts. The bathroom cabinet contains pretty much what I expected – Rube was never the lipstick-and-scent type.

I could be on the wrong track entirely. Who says it's the gang from school or derivatives thereof? And why can't it be terrorists? Why does everything need to be what it appears *not* to be? Rube's Lesson No. 34: *You have induction, deduction and abduction – if one doesn't work, try one of the others.* Inducting from that: *Why shouldn't it be simple, straightforward, common-and-garden terrorism?*

I used to consult Harry but Harry's dead. Failing Harry there was always Rube but she's dead, too. Asking Rory would be like asking why dogs scratch themselves – he'd only come up with something like: *Why limit the question to dogs?* My old flame Annie might as well be on the other side of the moon, I split with Tsunami before anything started and Imogene's studying to become a cop. Which leaves just one person.

'I'll make coffee.'

I watch her move to the corner of the room. She told me to get in touch if I needed help and I need help. We dined on pie and peas at Jake's Café de Wheels in Woolly-Moo-Loo and afterwards made poetry out of the clouds and talked about old times.

'I learnt a lot,' Ariadne says.

'So did I – I learnt that people like to hurt people.'

'Not everyone, Rainbow.'

Clouds roll over the Harbour and there's lightning in the air. I've got the feeling that Pandora's nearby but I force myself to focus on the dame beside me. There's danger in that, too.

'Why did your parents call you Ariadne?'

'As a Renaissance couple my parents were interested in Greek legends.' It's too dark to see but I sense her shrug. 'According to mythology a king named Theseus was upset because a bunch of people called Cretans were sacrificing children to a bull-headed beast called the Minotaur. So Theseus offered himself as a sacrifice.'

'He must have wanted to die.'

Lightning flashes across the sky. In its glare the surface of the Harbour turns from printer's ink to shot silver while the shadow by the finger wharf stays black.

'No, he just wanted to put an end to the bloodshed.'

'He killed the Minotaur only to die anyway because he couldn't find his way out of the maze?'

'No, he escaped from the maze.'

'How did he do that?'

'A princess called Ariadne provided him with a clue.'

I know but I still ask. 'What do you mean?'

'The word *clue* doesn't mean what people think it means. *Clue* means *thread* and that's what Ariadne gave to Theseus – a ball of thread. *Unwind it as you go,* she told him, *and after you kill the Minotaur follow the clue.* That's how he escaped.'

'Then they lived happily ever after.'

'We need to find a shop, Rainbow.'

'What kind of shop?'

'A convenience store. We're about to rent a room in a sleazy, two-bit pub. To make up for it, at least we can have a real cup of coffee in the morning.'

Chapter 24

INTO THE MAZE

I shake my head.

'Mind if I call you Princess?'

Under the red, green and yellow of the shop's neons the dame smiles her *Giaconda* smile. 'You can call me anything except late to bed.'

'You're a fine memory and I'd like to keep it that way. I'm nothing but a gumshoe – a flash of lightning, a drum roll of thunder, too much darkness and too many clouds. Relationships don't go hand-in-hand with detecting – all we can ever be is friends.'

Ariadne shrugs; her mind's elsewhere. 'That's all very well, Rainbow, but I'm going shopping.'

A tall, bony dame in a frock that could have belonged to a pygmy is sprawled on a bench while a joker behind a cast-iron grille with a sign above it that used to read *NO SMOKING* but now reads *NO POKING* rolls ball-bearing eyes over Ariadne before asking the eternal question: *Hourly or weekly?*

I tell him all night, he names a price and I lean in to make sure he gets an eyeful of the gat. 'We're just renting a room,' I tell him, 'not buying the building.'

He replies that he spends his whole life dealing with smartarses which could account for the error. What he meant was that the aforementioned room's no longer available but he might be able to manage a smaller one at double the price. Ariadne shifts from one foot to the other like she's about to take over negotiations so I pay before he doubles again. He chucks me the same key he's been holding all the time.

We're assaulted by the smell of dust, too many years of bodily interaction and the ever-present promise of death. Too many stairs, followed by corridors piled high with dirty sheets and nowhere near enough illumination. I throw open the door to Room 231.

Welcome to Paradise.

The room's five paces long and six wide and reeks of industrial-strength disinfectant. There's a sideboard for making coffee without – as Ariadne predicted – anything to make it *with*, and a half-open package on the table next to the bed with a picture of a dame on it that might be a packet of after-dinner mints but isn't.

Ariadne places her purchases on the bench.

'You sure know how to spoil a girl.'

From the silence I deduce she's asleep. The storm's waned and the moonlight through the uncurtained window illuminates the sheen of her caramel skin, her tousled hair and a pair of wide-awake eyes staring back at me.

'I saw Irving Morris.'

'I trust he proved of assistance.'

'He didn't tell me anything I didn't know already.'

'He's chairman of his party's think tank, *The Way Ahead* committee, and has co-operated with Watchdog in our research into terrorism.'

'I need some information.'

'What about?'

'Going back to those *Troubles* …'

She shifts as far from me as she can without falling out of bed.

'Is this why you asked me out?' She lapses into silence and it's not the silence of the lambs. 'I thought you wanted me for myself – or at least for old times' sake.'

'Don't be like that, Princess.'

'I'm not being like *anything*. And stop calling me *Princess*.' She pauses; considers; decides. 'Very well, I'll tell you what you want to know.'

'It can wait until after.'

'Until after what?'

Until after what happens next. Which involves a lot of this and a little more of that which adds up to nothing in particular or something of everything, depending upon your point of view.

The next morning Ariadne is holding two mugs of fresh-brewed coffee out from her body so she's not in danger of burning herself. I notice the zig-zag marks on her stomach.

'You've had kids.'

She stops on her way to the bed. 'There was a child but it wasn't my husband's. I was in a relationship with someone else before we married. Actually my pregnancy was why James and I married. The father already had a wife so he wasn't available even if I wanted to marry him, which I didn't.' She changes the subject. 'What about you?'

'I got hitched, we had a kid and I lost both because I wasn't fit for husbandry.' My turn to change the subject. 'Ready to talk about the Troubles?'

She shrugs. 'It was industrial sabotage – with a twist.' She reaches the bed, stops, hands me the two coffees and climbs back under the covers, after which I hand her back her coffee. All of which takes time but I need time, in order to work out where this is going.

'What's the twist?'

'I told you – *terrorism*.'

Chapter 25

THE HOLES IN THE WALL

What's with the convergence of unrelated phenomena? Harry wanted to know. To which I replied: *While one thing doesn't necessarily follow from another, in the end it probably does. Which doesn't mean things that seem totally unrelated aren't.*

'What's *terrorism* got to do with anything?'

Ariadne takes a sip of her coffee.

'The popular view is men in masks doing beheadings, suicide bombers at embassies, hijackers, the Munich Olympics and people flying planes into tall buildings. But it's not as simple as that. You don't build businesses the size of ours without being different and James was – different. Before becoming a businessman, he was an officer in Vietnam in charge of supplying arms and ammunition. He diverted weaponry to people in the Middle East. He supplied well and they paid well.'

'Did you know this when you married him?'

Ariadne shakes her head so hard her coffee spills.

'Only afterwards when it was too late.'

'So things went bad after that?'

'On the contrary, things went extremely well. I learnt to live with it and by the time the war was over, James was filthy rich. He bought goldmines and other lucrative enterprises and put the rest of his money into industry. As part of the money-making process, he financed politicians who helped him to become even richer. By then, politics had discovered a natural bedfellow – terrorism. Which meant that James had to tidy up his past or – despite his donations – politicians would cease to be his new best friends.'

'In other words he needed to cut the thread that linked him to his mates in the Middle East?'

'He was in deep. He made a lot of money and they expected a lot back. When he tried to break from them, they reacted badly. These extremists – they can't be called religious fanatics because they're not religious at all: they only use religion as an excuse for killing – declared a jihad on him. He became a marked man. That was when he set up Watchdog, to keep up to date with developments in terrorism. He passed on Watchdog's findings to the politicians. After his death, Watchdog continued.'

'Do the terrorists still bother you – now that he's dead?'

Ariadne nods. 'Don't they bother everyone? In our case they did things like cut brake lines and laid bombs. They shot the manager of one of our mines but we couldn't do anything in retaliation, even if we'd dared.'

'How did James die?'

'They shot him.'

'How come no-one heard about it?'

She takes a deep breath. 'The object of terrorism is to terrify people and there wasn't an election at the time so it was hushed up. If jihadists could kill a rich and powerful man they could do anything. Terrorism thrives on terror and the government didn't want people terrified. Not just then, anyway –'

The small, black hole in the wall between our room and the room next door seems to appear *after* Ariadne's mug shatters. I roll her onto the floor and grab my gat from under the pillow. The hole looks like one made by a 0.40 which most likely makes the weapon a Para-Ordnance Tac-Forty.

'Stay where you are, Princess,' I tell her. 'They're listening for movement and if they hear any we're done for.'

I get out the door quiet and take the stairs three at a time to make as much height as possible as fast as I can. On the way, I loose off a volley that splinters the door of the adjoining room and brings an immediate shot in return.

The rest of the doors – I count eight – stay shut and all is silence because the punters have paid for an easy roll rather than a hard death. If Ariadne does what I told her she'll stay where she is. But she's not used to being told to do anything which means there are no guarantees. I get myself to the next floor, hotfoot it to the service stairs and start down again.

He's small and he's armed and when I burst through the paper-thin wall into Room 233 he spins around gun-first. But he isn't expecting a house call from a wall, making him a split-infinitive too slow. I've got time to do a swan dive, which I'm about to follow up with a knee to the groin when –

I thought he had more than one gun or was a quick reloader but there was a third option and that was a second gunman. He's on the other side of the little man and his Tic-Tac-Toe's aimed at my ear. I've just got time to yell in the direction of the far wall, *'Run for it, Princess!'* before the slug gets me in the only part of my anatomy he can hit because the first gunman's in the way.

'Don't move!' screams Number Two.

I wipe the blood off my ear. There's a style about these two I haven't seen before. Or if I have, it's buried deep in memory – a coolness under fire that doesn't go with street thugs. The guns are high quality and matching – a combined 15.2 inches of death. But if you obey killers you're a dead man so instead of doing what I'm told I grab the first gunman, swing him over my head like I'm a principal *danseur* and he's a *danseuse* and chuck him at the second gunman just as he unleashes the follow-up.

Half a dozen slugs at close range are always going to find their mark even if the mark isn't their first choice and the little man's body jiggery-pokes like a puppet with its strings cut. He hits the floor as I dive for where I last saw the second gunman. But he's already out the door and I hear his feet clatter down the stairs as I turn to what's left of his mate.

He's lying face down, no more than a bale of hay, a dead dog, a colander with six 0.40 holes in it – which is six too many if you want to live. I roll him over and go through his pockets to find that his clothes – apart from the flick knife in the shin sheath and the mobile phone in the silver case, both of which I take – are even emptier than his body.

Chapter 26

GOODBYE SWEETHEART

I get back to our room to find Ariadne already dressed.

'It's not enough to bring me to a brothel!' she shouts, shaking her head while gripping the doorknob with a hand even whiter than her face. 'Someone has to shoot my coffee out of my hand and –'

She's interrupted by what at first sound like violins but turn out to be sirens. I shrug on my clothes.

'If you try to leave by the front door the cops will arrest you on suspicion of whatever comes to mind. Also at the front door will be photographers which means that in the morning you'll find yourself staring from the front page of the tabloids and it won't be in company with a story about your community spirit. You'll go down in your shareholders' estimation and your company's shares will go down with it. The front door isn't an option.'

People don't like losing money, particularly when they can afford to. Ariadne hesitates. She who hesitates is raspberries. I grab her by her uncertainty and head for the fire escape.

That's how it goes in this game – from sin to rivalry to love and affection then back again in one easy lesson. In this case via the rear window of a brothel above a strip joint in a lowlife part of town clutching the hand of a memory with the cops after you. In places like this the law stops at the front door – like there's gold-plated armour between a brothel and the rest of the world. The Tax boys never visit, safety regulations go out the window along with people's morals and anyone can kill anyone else as long as they dispose of the body. We're two floors up and the fire escape's so rusty it wouldn't hold a rat.

'Was it a trick, what you said about share values?' Ariadne asks.

'Want to find out?'

'I'd rather not.'

'Then it's like I said, Princess – you're a slave to wealth and we got to go back inside.'

Back into the stinking corridors that are the dwelling places of sad secrets. *When you need to hide, make for where they least expect you.* I drag Ariadne through the warren of corridors and finally out a fire door at the rear of the building. I offer to accompany her back to her office but she declines.

It's between the hatch and the jamb on the deck door, a white envelope with nothing on the outside apart from the words: *CARE OF RORY.* I don't open it until I restart the pump, untangle the mooring rope, straighten my emotions, uncap the high-shouldered bottle of Glenlivet Number 18 and take a long swig as well as a deep breath. Only then do I thumb open the envelope.

Dear Daddy, I'm trying to put into practice what you taught me but it's not easy. Our teachers are rigorous about ethics, the same as you were. Along the driveway to the Police Academy stands a row of plastic posts with the words Excellence, Trust, Honour, Impartiality, Commitment, Accountability and Leadership on them. As you will have worked out, the initials spell ETHICAL. You'll be pleased to know I excel in shooting and thanks to you I'm not doing badly in other areas as well. But I'm not writing to brag – it's about a certain line I can't cross. They say any cadet crossing it will be thrown out.

So I can't help thinking what they'd say if they knew you were my father (in my application I wrote what's written on my birth certificate: Father Unknown). I know you'll understand, Daddy, and also that I'll always love you. But if I'm to succeed here I need to break with you. I'm not a little girl any more. Which means I have to make my own way and that way must be without impediment. You're tough and you've dealt with a lot of people a lot tougher than I am so you'll cope. I'm seeing another cadet and he helps me make the hard decisions, of which this is one. You always wanted me to play it straight. What I'm saying is that we can't be in contact. Please respect my decision and don't try to call. Imogene.

Impediment. Even in code, the word jumps out at me. The kid –

But I can no longer call her that because – like she's been at great pains to tell me – she's no longer a kid, she's a *woman.* And the woman that used to be my daughter knows what an *impediment* is because I taught her: it's from the Latin *impedimenta,* meaning *unwanted baggage – something that gets in the way, a load too great to bear, a hindrance, an obstruction,* in other words ... The day's stolen from me and all I'm left with is a blood-red sunset, a sinking boat and a set of unmatched fingerprints, courtesy of the gunman's phone and knife.

A death rattle wakes me and I drag myself out on deck to find the pump's stopped, it's late afternoon, Queen hasn't done his rounds and one of the phones is ringing. I fumble it out, click on and the death rattle ceases.

'What do you know?' says a voice.

I don't recognise the voice so I don't reply. The Harbour mirrors my feelings – a grey sky over a leaden sea that goes all the way down to Hades. I'm not thinking too clear and the voice on the other end of the phone doesn't help with my thinking.

'You still there, Sailor Boy?'

Chapter 27

MEET ME AT THE MORGUE

'What do you want?'

'It's not what *I* want, it's what *you* want,' the voice replies. 'Your own life mightn't be worth much but what about your nearest and dearest?'

'I don't know anything.' I choose my words careful, the way a drunk focuses on walking a straight line after a bad night. 'I thought I did but I don't. And I'm no longer investigating those deaths because nothing can bring those people back to life.'

'In other words you'll let sleeping dogs lie – a stupid policy, if I may say so, which could result in more innocent people dying. Anyway I don't believe you.' Pause. 'This will be death number – I've lost count – let's call it death number three. Look to windward.'

The voice clicks off and I'm left staring at a dead phone in a silver case which I recognise as the one belonging to the gunman in the brothel, which explains how they got onto me. I drop it like it's come out of a crematorium before doing like the voice said because I was never going to do anything else, and look to windward.

Grey cumulus clouds are sweeping in through the Heads. And aimed straight for the *Wooden No* is a familiar boat – a fishing smack of shiplap construction with a fisherman's gantry sticking up fore of the superstructure, a prow like a Roman nose and cadmium-yellow marks on the hull. A boat that – if it keeps on its course – will ram the *Wooden No*, sending it finally and forever to the bottom of the Harbour.

'Hey, Queen!' I yell.

Putt-putt-putt. The motor's throttled back to *Dead Slow* and it looks like a dead man's boat, empty of life, a ghost ship. It's no more than five fathoms distant and closing fast. I get myself to the railing, keeping an eye on the *Flying Dutchman* as I scrabble for the boat hook. Only it's not there because it's where I left it after untangling the mooring in a drunken stupor last night. Two fathoms. Ten feet. Eight. Five.

I heave myself over the side, brace myself against the rail, grab the Roman-nosed prow and lock my arms around it like a lover. Setting my shoulder against the hull I heave, feel Queen's craft start to turn, reluctantly letting itself be diverted. The *Wooden No* shudders as the smack hits her. I force my legs straight, feeling the veins in my temples bulge as timber shrieks against timber, using my ebbing strength to straighten, before pirouetting onto the smack as she slides by, at the same time scrabbling for the tiller. To find a length of wire twisted around it while the throttle's held in position with gum. I untangle the wire, strip off the gunk, haul at the tiller and cut the engine. The unmistakable smell of eau-de-cologne fights the stench of diesel but that's Queen, who's curled in the foetal position next to a couple of lobster pots, looking like the overgrown schoolboy he is.

Correction – *was*. Because Queen is no more. I find an anorak covered with fish scales, tuck it over his body and turn away. The tragic Harbour's just turned more tragic. Rube's gone, then Harry, now Queen. I climb back on the *Wooden No* just as the phone rings. I check the little window as I switch on. It's the same number.

'I'll do whatever you want,' I answer before the voice has a chance to put the question; I think of Imogene, Rory, Ariadne – people close to me who are still alive. 'Just stop the killings.'

But all the voice says is, 'In forty-five minutes, you're to meet me at the morgue.'

Rain's churning the Harbour to sandpaper as I hammer the coracle shoreward. I'm halfway there when I ring Roarer.

'Yeah?'

'You're still alive.'

'Thanks for letting me know.'

'This ain't a joke, Roarer, or I wouldn't be on an open line. Has anyone asked for a meet?'

'As it happens, yeah, someone called about a job.'

'A contract?'

'What other kind of job is there?'

'Anyone we know?'

'Only another low-life that had it coming.'

'I'm talking about the *client* not the corpse – is the *client* someone we know?'

'No, just someone with a rough voice, plenty of money and a grudge.'

'When and where's the meet?'

'At Victoria Park in half an hour.'

I'm due at the morgue just after that.

'What's the deal with the rock spider?'

'What rock spider?'

'The one that looks like you.'

'You mean Hertz?'

Diego Hertz, a creep that's hurt more innocent children than anyone wants to know; who's avoided jail only by dint of good lawyers and bad judges; someone even the *Terrorgraph* hasn't been able to get.

'Roarer?'

He comes halfway out of his stupor. 'You know what I think about Diego, Rain – people like that should be –'

'How quick can you contact him?'

'I know someone who knows someone who knows his number. So, yeah, pretty well straight away.'

'And how quick after that can you get him where we want him?'

'Depends where we want him.'

'At the swimming pool at Victoria Park.'

'Give me an hour.'

I give him an hour.

Chapter 28

THE WRONG DEATH

After I've dealt with Roarer I phone and ask the Voice for extra time and he seems happy to oblige, almost too happy, the rough tones going into overdrive and coming out even rougher.

'You just made a telephone call. Who to?'

'Santa Claus.'

'Laugh while you can, Rainbow. How long do you want?'

'Two hours.'

'I'll give you one.'

'I need two,' I reply. 'I got to get to shore, walk to Cammeray, wait for a bus, change at Town Hall and after that – well, you know what public transport's like.'

'One hour.'

'Two,' I repeat grimly.

'Ninety minutes tops.'

I note the flash of high-powered lenses as I row. The watcher's on a vessel not of these waters, a small cadmium-yellow speedster that – because of the paint marks on the hull of the fishing smack – has to be the craft they used for the Queen job. The watcher's watching to make sure I follow instructions. I pretend not to notice. But who do I think I'm fooling?

The rain's stopped and the sign at the entrance to Victoria Park says skateboards, bikes and dogs are unlawful but there's nothing about murder. Me and Roarer watch events unfold – a couple of innocent picnickers minding their own business under a Moreton Bay fig.

'Any problems?'

Rory shrugs. 'My contact gave me the number of a screw who sold me Hertz's details and when I spoke to Hertz I pretended to be that other paederast – Mollie something or other. I told him I knew a kid who liked one-legged men.' Rory pulls a face – just talking to Hertz had to have hurt. 'I told him to dress like me and the bastard could hardly answer for excitement.'

The sun comes out and its light nestles among the indigo-coloured kale in the garden beds. The wet trees glisten like fresh blood while kids scream happily behind the chain-wire fence around the swimming pool. The bench by the path outside the fence is vacant. Rory gets a thought; it's rare but it happens.

'You're sending this guy to his death, Rain. I know he's bad but I got to ask: have you lost your moral compass?'

I shrug. 'Life's complex, Roarer, and death even more so. It was either you or Hertz. And every day he's dead means another kid escapes his clutches.'

'Since when did you become Mr Retribution?'

'It's not about killing Diego. It's life that matters, not death. They were going to kill you – we're giving them someone else in your place who happens to be a bastard.'

'Why don't we just kill the killer?'

'Because we're dealing with a Hydra-headed monster, Roarer. Chop off one head and we'll end up with a whole lot more. We're up against a force we've never fought before. We got to kill the beast and make sure it *stays* dead. I'm hoping your *apparent* death will lead us to them.' I can see by the faraway look in Rory's eyes he doesn't understand and never will; I try again. 'These are the people who killed Rube and Harry and almost certainly will try to kill many more.'

I haven't told him about the latest murder so I tell him now.

'Queen's dead. I told the Water Cops which means Queen will be at the morgue and news of this latest apparently motiveless killing will be all over the media. We're deep in the labyrinth and if we lose the thread we might be lost forever.'

Just like Rory's lost the thread – but that happened long ago. I get in before he does.

'It's a case of better thread than dead, Roarer.'

The shadow's at ten o'clock high, up by the cutting edge of the university – an etiolated, bleak figure at odds with its environment, accompanied by the quickest of movements and the flash of a knife. But I can't let Pandora distract me. I look back to the pool. He's sitting on the bench reading a newspaper.

He's someone I've never seen before, tall but sufficiently well-trained to know he's got to compensate for his height in order to appear innocuous, a phone wire doubling as a hearing aid sticking out of his left ear as he sprawls on the park bench, his weight on his coccyx and his long legs stretched before him, conversing with his hearing aid while he pretends to be reading his newspaper.

I'm close enough to read the front page heading:

ANOTHER DEATH

Terrorism Tightens Noose

I'm also close enough to see the figure in the grey tracksuit – one pants leg pinned up – swinging across the park on crutches. And seeing him, I do a double-take, the sort of take you do when you see someone's double – in this case, Rory's.

I can just make out that the figure on the bench behind the newspaper is cuddling a Heckler & Koch USP – the Universal Self Loader – a pistol with pretty fair accuracy coupled with an extended barrel designed to take a suppressor. To a background of happy cries of unmolested children splashing in the sunlight and the stentorian shouts of teachers trying to shush them, the man on the bench shifts slightly and immediately afterwards a puff of incandescent smoke appears above the newspaper. The one-legged man's crutches spill silently onto the grass and the paederast follows.

It's five minutes before the arrival of the ambulance – during which time the teachers must have been informed of the killing and the kids herded out of the pool into their respective change rooms for the usual post-assassination counselling. The cops drive over the wet grass and the even wetter garden beds because they don't respect anything, not even death. It's only when they've got their crime-scene tape in place and the death van drives off with the body of the dead paederast, that I realise my error.

'They weren't cops, Roarer.'

'What do you mean? They were wearing uniforms, weren't they? And they were driving cop cars. Plus they were doing what cops always do after a crime.'

'That's just it, Roarer, they *didn't* do what cops do after a crime. For a start they were too quick and ditto the ambulance. Where's Forensics? And what happened to the police photographer? Cops don't take bodies to the morgue immediately after they become bodies – anything but. They leave things as they are and they look for clues and ask witnesses questions like: *Did you see anything unusual?* Someone's doing the cops' dirty work for them in order to keep the real cops out of the way.'

'But they *are* looking for clues.'

I look to where Rory's looking. There are five of them and they've got their Glocks out and they're prowling along the pool fence, poking at bushes and treading all over the garden beds.

I shake my head.

'They're not looking for clues, Roarer – they're looking for me.'

Chapter 29

THE FAVOUR OF THE MONTH

*T*errorism Tightens Noose, the heading read. They were smart enough to kill Ruby, Harry and Queen and after that, via me, locate Roarer. They were also clever enough to see through my ruse. Which doesn't happen unless someone's a past master at second-guessing – a past master at staying in business as well as alive. They knew it wasn't Rory but went ahead anyway because another death – any death – would still serve their purpose.

'It's time to go, Roarer.'

'Why don't we just pot them?'

'Because potting people isn't the answer to everything – right now it's not even the answer to anything.'

Students are pouring out of the university in preparation for becoming an integral part of the workforce. As me and Roarer work our way into the crush the students come into sharp relief. Thin faces, young faces, a worried face, a happy one – tall, short, fat, skinny, male and female. Which reminds me that the world isn't some amorphous crowd but a collection of individuals. It matters. The lights change and we stay with the crowd as it makes its way along Glebe Point Road, keeping our heads down.

'Look, I get what you said about the pedo copping it instead of me,' Roarer says, swinging himself along on his crutch-gun as the students chatter around us. 'What I don't get is why I'd be a target in the first place.'

'Because you were associated with me in the first place.'

'So why doesn't whoever it is get rid of the middle man and just pot you?'

'Because these jokers …' Something's bothering me; I bother Rory

417

with it. 'Look, I got a question, Roarer – did anyone get in touch with you after we spoke?'

'No.'

'Was there any way someone might have *overheard* you talking to Hertz?'

'Only the bloke outside the phone booth.'

'What bloke? Which phone booth?'

'The guy mending the road and the phone booth outside my place, the one that –'

'You got to go into hiding, Roarer.'

'Before or after we go to the morgue?'

I tell him we're no longer going to the morgue.

WILL WE EVER BE SAFE?

I flex my trapezia under the gabardine coat and bury my head behind the headline in the giveaway newspaper as the train clatters out of Central. The reason I wear bright clothes is because I disappear into obscurity when I'm not wearing them and I'm not wearing them now. I've put Rory into hiding as much as you can hide a one-legged assassin with half a brain but the old mortuary station just outside Central is a reminder – if one's needed – of what might happen if I become complacent.

I didn't identify myself but Imogene must have guessed who it was because she wouldn't come to the phone. Going to see her was my second option but I change my mind when confronted by the headline. There's a pattern here and I don't like patterns. I get out at Redfern, find a public telephone that works and call Ariadne.

'Ms Sidonia isn't in.'

'Tell her it's a matter of life or death.'

'She's still not in.'

I break every rule in the book. 'Tell her it's Rainbow.'

Once we were kids but now I'm a two-bit detective and she runs an empire. I had my chance and I blew it. It's not just a desk between us – I'm trying to bridge an abyss.

'I thought we weren't going to see each other again,' Ariadne says stiffly.

'That was then and this is now. Something's happened.'

'Apart from my getting shot at in a brothel?'

'My daughter's in danger and I need your help.'

'I've already helped by putting you in touch with Irving Morris. But Irving said you didn't seem interested.'

'Irving Morris was more concerned with pushing his own barrow than helping me with mine.'

'You wanted an *in* to the Troubles and he was it.'

I change the subject. 'Remember when I saved you from Parkinson?'

Ariadne looks uncomfortable. 'We were kids. It was a long time ago.'

'It was near the bubblers. He had you in a headlock and you were crying. I managed to get you away and paid for it afterwards.'

'What you're saying is that it's my turn to help.'

'It's just something I remembered, Princess.'

Chapter 30

THE RED HERRING

'What do you want?'

A weak man kills, an honest one lies and the pacifist goes to war – you don't play tiddly-winks with fortune when your kid's life's at stake. After I tell her what I want, Ariadne reaches for the red phone nestled between the green and yellow ones and dials.

'This is Ariadne Sidonia. Is that Minister Caxton and is this line secure?'

'You have my word.'

'I don't want your word, Caxton, I want a secure line.'

'I'm sorry, yes, the line's secure.'

'Okay, listen. I'm calling in a favour – one of many, incidentally, that your party owes me.'

'It's real nice to hear from you, Ariadne. How can I –?'

'It's Ms Sidonia.'

'I'm sorry, Ms Sidonia. How can I help?'

'I need you to send a police officer to Mars.'

'State or Federal?'

'State.'

She glances at me. I nod confirmation. The politician chuckles ingratiatingly.

'Been speeding again, Ms Sidonia?'

'None of your business. Just do it.'

'But it's a State matter and I'm a Federal minister, remember.'

'And *you* remember that I'm Ariadne Sidonia.'

'I'm sorry. What are the specifics?'

'I need a police cadet sent to the Outer Hebrides.'

'Name?'

I tell Ariadne and Ariadne tells the Minister. 'And Caxton?' she adds.

'Yes, Ms Sidonia?'

'You're to call the NSW Police Minister *now*, he's to contact the chief of the police academy *now*, the transfer to the secret location is to be immediate and if anything goes wrong you're out on your neck, got me?'

It's Baisson Primary coming out in her.

'Very well, Ms Sidonia. In return, I have some news for you.'

He's a dog begging. Ariadne switches off *Speaker* and while she's listening her face goes white and when she hangs up it's translucent.

'It's going to happen.'

'What's going to happen?'

'What I feared. Something terrible.'

'Can you give me a clue?'

'That's just it – there *are* no clues. ASIO are checking it out but Caxton wants to know what Watchdog can discover.'

'Is there a *when, where, what* or *how*?'

Ariadne shakes her head. 'Just *when* – tomorrow, Australia Day.' A thought strikes her. 'Why – what are you going to do?'

I tell her something other than what I'm going to do.

The *Wooden No*'s where I left her but that doesn't mean she's safe. I stop rowing, tap into the onboard Secur-A-Cam from the safety of the skiff and scroll through the day's imagery. No sign of untoward activity: the pictures are grey-filtered nothingness – scenes of an innocent Harbour tilting this way and that as the boat sways; of moored vessels ducking and weaving; of ferries passing; scullers sculling; dads taking their kids for a sail.

There's been no visitors apart from gulls and cormorants but that doesn't mean there won't be. I climb aboard, restart the pump, find the paper with Babychino's address on it plus the first-aid kit, load Rube's box of tricks into the coracle, do a final check, get the oars back into their manacles and set about putting as much distance as possible between me and the *Wooden No*. She doesn't explode.

'Who's speaking?'

It's tomorrow and the voice is distant but my life's made up of distant voices. Also I'm no stranger to the clicks saying someone's listening in on the conversation.

'I can't say.'

'Oh, it's you.' Silence for a moment. 'What do you want?'

'The use of your second residence – the caravan in the forest off the Workhorse Parkway.'

'I like your hide asking.'

'I like my hide, too – which is why I'm asking.'

One day intimacy, hatred the next. I don't ask Tsunami what she's done since our last meeting – the less said the better because I don't want whoever's listening to suspect I'm deliberately feeding them information.

Tsunami fills the silence. 'Make sure you leave the van clean.'

'That goes without saying.'

But all I'm talking to is echoes and a series of clicks. I call Roarer on the same open line. Which means the same closed party will be listening.

'I need to go to a caravan in the forest off the Workhorse Parkway. I'll be outside the burger palace at the Cross in ten. Repeat our arrangement back to me.'

Rory does what he's told and whoever's bugging us can't fail to make the connection.

Chapter 31

THE MANEATER

Rory's in one of those American cars without a back that was here one day, gone the next – cream-ducoed with tiny windows behind the rear seat and a sidestep walkway – a 1940-something de Soto. I chuck Rube's box inside, climb in next to Roarer and glance in the rear-vision mirror. They're in a Hummer, black, with tinted windows. High vehicles, Hummers.

I turn to Rory. He's a mess. 'Pull yourself together, Roarer.'

'That's easy for you to say but I been trying to tidy up my private life. Janet won't leave the Fat Man, I'm in debt up to my bald patch and I'm having difficulty breaking back into the death game because I'm no longer in the Yellow Pages. Apart from which, word-of-mouth's telling would-be clients I've retired.'

'Where's the hearse?'

'I sold it. Where are we going?'

'*Not* to the caravan in the forest. I want you to head in that direction, lose the tail and end up *not* going to the caravan.'

'And after that?'

I don't want to overload him – his brain must be close to bursting.

'I'll tell you after you lose them.'

I'll say this much for Roarer, he can drive. One-legged or not, half-brained or with no brain at all, he's got the tail acting like the ball attached to the racquet I gave Imogene for her eighth birthday – or was it her tenth? Where we go, the Hummer follows. We turn right, the Hummer turns right; we exit City Street, so does the Hummer; we slip up a side road, the Hummer slips straight up after us.

'I'd prefer you not let them know that we know they're following us, Roarer.'

'How do I do that?'

'You can stop all these Dixie little manoeuvres for a start.'

There'll be at least three thugs in the Hummer and three into two won't go. We could waylay them but we need to stay alive. I peer through my half of the de Soto's split windscreen.

'What are you looking for?'

'A supermarket.'

'Are we going shopping?'

'Ever wonder why you never see Hummers in supermarket car parks? It's because they're too big. That thing behind us happens to be a 2006 model complete with balloon tyres which put it well over the two-metre mark. Know those signs in supermarket car parks that say *HEIGHT 2 METRES*? Well, what we're looking for is a sign that says –'

'I'm not stupid, Rainbow.'

It's getting on for lunchtime, the newspapers say we're headed for the greatest Australia Day ever and Babychino's still small, still oversexed and still having trouble with her tear ducts.

'This might sound silly,' she sighs, mopping at her beautiful eyes with a handkerchief big enough to sleep in, 'but every time someone knocks, I think it's Harry.'

The joint's a doll's house – a two-up, two-down, dunny-out-the-back terrace in North Sydney. I swing to cover the figure by the back door, gat uncocked and a slug already on the launch pad, only to find it's only a department store dummy dressed like Harry. A photo of the lovers making cats' eyes at each other is sitting on a record machine. I garage the gat.

'It looks like you miss him.'

'It's not just looks.' Babychino slumps on a sofa. 'Harry treated me like a queen and you ask if I miss him!'

'Did he leave you anything?'

'Apart from the memories?'

'Apart from the memories.'

'Yes, this house.'

'Anything else?'

'A life insurance policy worth a million.'

'A *million*?'

She nods, unaware of the irony in the eyebrow raise – or if she isn't unaware, doesn't show it. 'As you probably know, Harry was a successful bookie before he got into the hospitality industry. Yes, he could look after me and he did. He also made me laugh – eleven times out of ten his jokes were at his own expense.'

'Have you had any trouble since his death? Thugs heavying you, anonymous phone calls, men with shaven heads standing over you in buses?'

Babychino shakes her head. 'Harry was careful. He kept me hidden like a genie in a bottle – he didn't even tell you about me because he said you attracted criminals like flies to a sheep's bum.'

It doesn't sound like Harry. Also I could think of better ways of putting it.

'Do you know who killed him?'

'I never saw his killers.'

'Was he scared of anyone?'

'Harry was scared of his own shadow.'

Time to put the real question. 'Were you involved in his death?'

She doesn't even pause for breath. 'Harry made me laugh.'

Which is why she's crying now. I change the subject. 'I need somewhere to stay.'

'You can stay here – I owe that much to Harry.'

When the phone rings, the dame answers and afterwards she shows me to a bedroom the size of a broom cupboard.

'I don't want to profit from others' misfortune,' she says, naming a figure even more generous than her own. 'I need a deposit for the key but you can come and go as you please.'

I hand over enough moolah to rent the main hall of the Sydney Opera House, park Rube's box and see Roarer off the premises.

'You okay?' he asks.

'Why shouldn't I be?'

He glances behind me. 'Because she's a man-eater and you're a man.'

Chapter 32

PATIENCE AND
SHUFFLE THE CARDS

It's not hard to get information when people owe you favours. Wills are wills and someone's got Harry's. The ring-around takes ten minutes by the end of which I've learnt what I already suspected – Harry left nobody nothing. I set the index cards aside and open Rube's diary to the first entry. Music floats up the stairwell – Babychino's playing Doris Day playing at singing. Rube was tough but her diary reminds me she was also human.

There's a quote from Cervantes: *Paciencia y barajah*. Rube taught me enough Spanish for me to know this means: *Patience and shuffle the cards*. So I do like the quote says and work out the cards are pointers to Rube's cases, in alphabetical order and cross-referenced. *Allbricht, Arthur; cross-references: Murder; Corruption, Police; Horder, Lillian … Amhurst (company name); cross-reference: Drugs; Murder; Corruption, Police … Aperville (location of Hooligan HQ)*, cross-references: *Conrad, James; [a list of names]; Drugs; Murder; Corruption, Police; Terrorism …* One of Rube's sayings was: *Never discount connections.* Which is why I don't discount what must be close to the last word she ever uttered – *indigo* or *indiquo* or … I go back to the Cervantes quote. *Paciencia y barajah – Patience and shuffle the cards.* What's *indigo* in Spanish? Or what sounds like *indigo* in Spanish? Another song starts and I picture Babychino teeny-bopping to the music as she tries to cope with the memory of Harry.

Rube's diary again: *Don't discount connections.* But the evidence is only *circumstantial.* Which in Spanish is: *indicios vehementes* which gives me *indicio* which looks more like *indigo* than it sounds, but Roarer was the filter. The music switches to ABBA while I try to make the connection. *Indicio* means *clue*. And what, long ago, did someone say about *clue*? Without warning the music stops.

It doesn't just stop – it comes to a screaming halt in the middle of the song that brought ABBA to prominence, followed by a crash, a scream, then silence.

The cards scatter as I head for the stairs. I came here for refuge but that's not what I'm getting. The stairs turn into a slippy-slide as the front door slams and a motor starts. Not one motor – two. The word's stuck in my head: *indicio*. What's it mean? *Thread*, that's right, it means *thread*. Where's Babychino, the dame who said she had a million good reasons to mourn Harry's passing, but hasn't? Going by the mess downstairs, she's gone straight into the loving arms of a death worse than fate.

I get myself into the street, find nothing and return via the back door – always return via the back door – to find two of them, young, fit, of medium height, one pale, the other swarthy. I'm not expecting them but they're expecting me even less. Swarthy's on the ground floor clutching Rube's box while Whitey's coming down the stairs with a high-velocity Tac-Five automatic in his belt, staring at the broken-down front door where I'm supposed to be.

It's an impossible shot, one-o'clock high through the banisters with the gramophone blocking my sightlines, so I leave my gat where it is and opt for the dive, bringing my knees up to my chest, grabbing my shins, curling my head into my sternum and hurling myself over the gramercy, uncoiling myself just as Whitey reaches the last step but one.

The trouble with weapons is that when people are carrying they forget their natural armoury – hands, elbows, knees, shoulders, feet. Instead they think they got to go for the gun. And while Whitey's going for his gun, I grab his foot, twist and lift and he goes over the side like a bleached tomato. *Keep him alive*, I tell myself. *Live men tell tales and I need tales.* I reach for Swarthy but he steps up and back, at the same time hurling Rube's box. It catches me in the chest, knocking me towards the broken-down door.

Like the tag-team in the brothel, these jokers know their way around brawls. While Swarthy gets ready for the follow-through, his mate kicks the record player out of the way and brings up his gat. I got the light behind me. Whitey blinks as he tries to adapt his peepers. I feint and his

eyes follow as I go into a *plié* like I'm about to fly but instead stay on the
ground and do a *glissé*.

The Para-Ordnance has the capacity to inflict maximum lethality in
minimum time. Which is what it does as Whitey unleashes all nineteen
slugs where his half-blind eyes tell him I'm headed   into the air where his
mate is. Caught by the volley, Swarthy drops at the designated acceleration
of thirty-two feet per second per second. I hurtle over the body to where
I last saw Whitey to find that he's gone, leaving nothing but the upturned
record player plus the stench of cordite and eau-de-cologne. I set the
machine upright and it picks up where it left off.

My *Telefunken* rings.

'Yeah?'

'It's Rory.'

'What do you want?'

'It's a good thing I stayed.'

'Stayed where?'

'At the dame's. You told me to go but I didn't. It was a good thing I
didn't, wasn't it?'

'Why?'

'Because I was able to tail them. They went through the lights at
Cammeray and –'

'Where's Babychino?'

'She was in the car with the remaining hood. They got tangled in
traffic, the offside rear door opened, the dame jumped out, the traffic
cleared and the hood had to clear with it.'

'And you followed the car rather than sticking with the dame?'

'A man with one leg's as good as the next man only if he's armed or
he's driving.'

'Where are you now?'

Rory tells me where he is. There's nothing I can do for Swarthy. On
the way out I pick up the photo of Babychino and Harry gazing into each
other's eyes because they're so much in love. Maybe too much in love.

An hour north of Sydney, gum trees unfurl into a vista of water dotted
with islands. TERRIGAL, I read on the station sign but somehow it
comes out *Terror-gal*. It could be paradise but the outer-Sydney suburb

of Bridgetown is more like a murder house – looks nice but no-one in their right mind wants to live there. There's only one cab and the driver's asleep. I wake him.

'What's the quickest way to the shops?'

He blinks up at me. 'Depends whether you're going by cab or walking.'

'I'm walking.'

'That's the slowest way.'

I let him have his little joke because all I wanted was for him to remember the man with the wooden box asking directions. I find a speedboat called *Loverbuoy* bobbing at the end of a wharf with a dinghy beside it, while the pair of lovers that belong to it gaze into each other's eyes in the Pierless Restaurant. I double back to the station.

They call them *cells*, Ariadne explained. *For greater efficiency, terrorists divide themselves into cells. At least they used to but our research says that they're changing tactics. More and more, they're acting in pairs or alone. We think it's due to the 'bikie laws' the government brought in, making it an offence to associate with known criminals. But it seems that was the way the terrorists wanted to play it anyway.*

Rube, Harry and Queen are dead and Rory was set to join them. At least they can't get at Imogene. There were two killers in the brothel and, after that, another pair visited Babychino. To all intents and porpoises, the actions were spontaneous – ad hoc, arranged for the purpose, special. *The anti-terrorism people describe it as their worst nightmare,* Ariadne went on. *When they operate as individuals or in pairs it means there are no mass text messages, emails or phone-outs; there's no planning to eavesdrop on because there's no planning – just the intent to kill, followed by the kill.*

Chapter 33

IN THE COUNTRY OF THE BLIND ...

The de Soto's half-hidden by scrub a hundred paces from the cluster-pack of Mercedes, BMWs, Lexuses, Audis and the Hummer with the crunched roof, while Roarer's slumped so far down behind the wheel only the top of his head and the tip of his crutch are visible. The joker limping towards the de Soto is carrying a Giandoso TZ45 – a different weapon to the one he had in the caravan park but it's the same knee. A swarm of ants finds me.

The day the bullies at school smeared me with treacle and tied me to an ants' nest I was saved by the fact that the small ants behind the gym – unlike these bigger ones – were more interested in the treacle than in me. These ones are already under my trouser legs and rapidly moving north.

Option 1: Ignore the ants and take the gunman.

Option 2: Dislodge the ants.

There's no choice so I take it. I drop Rube's box and hurtle towards the de Soto, shouting as I run. The gunman calls on me to stop because he's seen too many movies, his warning's followed by a single shot and the shot's followed by silence.

Turns out Rory wasn't asleep.

He's a good shot, Roarer. Knows where it kills, where it wounds, where it's only going to hurt. The bullet's found its way through the tendons, bones and veins like a grub through a rotten apple. The limping joker with the Giandoso TZ45 will walk again, talk again and pick his nose again.

I haul out the first-aid kit, tourniquet his arm, apply mercurochrome, bandage the hand, then do the wrists-and-ankles back-truss, gagging him in case he feels the urge to scream. Then I sling him in the boot of the de Soto along with Rube's box. The boot's got built-in air holes – if he dies, it won't be the fault of the manufacturers.

A set of worn sandstone steps leads to double doors, across the top of which a faded blue sign reads: *STRANGEFELLOWS' HALL, 1881* – printed at a time when the world still acknowledged apostrophes. The joint's white with a green corrugated roof and pointy windows, set high.

'What are *strangefellows*?' Rory asks.

'The name's ironic – they were pillows of the community.'

'What are they now?'

'Dead.'

'Why are we here?'

'Because Rube, Harry and Queen are also dead and at the Victoria Park swimming pool you nearly joined them.'

We let the air out of the tyres by depressing the valves instead of knifing the tubes because that would make too much noise and right now I happen to like my privacy. We don't do the Hummer because its oversized tyres are wearing valve locks and disabling the alarm would take more time than we got.

'What do we do now?'

'We shut up.'

'After we shut up.'

'We go round the back.'

As well as working alone and in pairs, terrorists still also use cells, Ariadne said. *There are dozens throughout Sydney and each one's a stand-alone – which means the right hand doesn't know what the left hand's doing. They've redoubled their efforts since we followed America into its latest war and – like the Irish Republican Army and any other terrorist group you care to name – they have one aim and that is to cause as much terror as possible. As a safeguard, the cells work independently of one another.*

I haul out the gat and motion Roarer to follow as I work my way along the side of the building. The windows are too high to see through, the path's cracked and a steel fence screens the hall from its neighbours.

There are no spider webs, the electrical board's been read recently and the trip wire's close to invisible. I warn Roarer before high-stepping over it. If anything's going on inside the hall I can't hear it. What did I expect? The sound of goose steps? Rifle fire? People cheering a beheading?

Behind the hall, the trees are carved, the lawn's mown and the smell of fresh-cut grass takes me back to Hopesville where I met the dame of my dreams, Salina, and convinced myself that my Aunt Rube was weird, my dead mum and hippie dad were aberrations and detective work was for the birds. The feeling lasted as long as it took to realise that the real aberrations were marriage and the lawn.

The roses covering the trellis are nicely tended and the table's clear of leaves. Beyond the fence with the panel missing the jungle takes over. But here, birds sing and the window throws back a double reflection, the kind that usually only comes with cheap mirrors.

The sun's at a bad angle but I haven't got time to wait for a good one. While Rory parks his crutch, I look at the reflections – of Roarer and, behind him, the well-tended lawn. After my eyes stop doing gymnastics, I make out that the figures on the other side of the double-glazing aren't doing gun drills or learning how to make bombs or being harangued by a demagogue in a kaftan. Instead, a couple of dozen suits are focused on a speaker.

He's small, smiling and somehow familiar. Dark hair, small head, tight mouth and even from here I can see the calculating expression in the bright little pinpoint eyes. Because of the double-glazing I can't hear what he's saying but there's more ways of killing a cat than covering it with yak fat and baking it. I read his lips.

'To quote the master,' he's saying: *'You should not deviate from what's good if that's possible but you should know how to do evil if necessary.'*

He pauses to show that he's finished quoting but also to make sure that he's got his audience's attention. He has. He's got mine, too.

'Remember: Increased terrorism means greater surveillance – more tapped phones, less secure internet communication, more cameras; the power to arrest and confine will increase exponentially; the government might arrogate to itself the right to expel an entire community. Are you ready for tonight?'

I don't need to lip-read to know that on these last words the room erupts – the vibrations are enough. The faces as they turn to their neighbours are radiant and the hall shakes with the stamping of feet. Young feet and young faces, with nice haircuts like the lawn, close-shaven cheeks pink with emotion. *The master?* Who's *the master*? Or did little

Mephistopheles say *martyr*?

'Don't move!'

The scene in the reflective window shifts like an amoeba. We got company. 'Turn slow or don't turn at all,' the company says. 'The window's bulletproof as well as soundproof which means I can send any number of slugs your way and after they've gone through you they'll bounce harmlessly off your reflections. And you can take your hand away from that piece you're carrying under your jacket.'

I turn, slow. Sex: *male;* Age: *25–27;* Description: *medium height, stocky build, brown hair cut respectable, blue eyes;* Clothes: *cabbage-tree hat, baggy pants thong-tied below the knees, coated with dried grass-mush and held up with braces, collarless shirt.* Conclusion: *what I should have guessed but didn't – that a big, nice-tended garden means there's a tender. Or maybe not so tender.* Add-on extra: *machine-gun with silencer, held professional in the big hands, pointed at me but light in the nozzle meaning it's also aware of the existence of Roarer.* Further information: *confident smile – too confident.*

I could go for the gat but that wouldn't be clever. He's dappled in shadow but there's nothing attractive about the holograph because of the gun. It's what the Birmingham Small Arms people dubbed the *Essie –* short for *Silent Sten,* due to the integrated muffler – and its hollow stock's tucked into his waist, one big, gnarled hand's on the silencer and the other's around the trigger guard. The black hole at the end of the barrel's pointed at my chest. The Essies were discontinued because of the tendency of the silencer to melt under sustained fire but the gun still kills.

'I said *don't move.* That means you, one leg, as well as the oaf in the Akubra.'

'We're looking for Pete,' I tell him. 'But we must have the wrong address so we'll give our apologies and get out of your hair.'

The bullet takes out the toe of my left whiteside, the smell of gunpowder mingles with the scent of roses and the expression on the gardener's face doesn't change because there's no expression.

Chapter 34

... THE ONE-EYED MAN IS DEAD

'Let's go for a little walk.' The gardener flicks his weapon at Rory. 'Pick up your crutch.' Rory does like he's told and the gunman flicks the Sten back at me. 'Now take the gun out of its holster and drop it. Slowly.'

I go to reach inside my coat but the gunman waves *No* at me with the Sten. 'The other hand.'

My Smith & Wesson clatters to the pavers; the gunman jerks his gun at Rory. 'You, too.'

'I don't carry.'

Rory lifts his crutch-gun and suddenly there's much more expression in the gunman's face than there has been up to now, a sort of inclination of the head that could be quizzical, what looks like a laugh in the region of the mouth and, in the middle of his forehead, a hole that looks like an eye.

'You haven't lost your touch, Roarer.'

Nothing goes according to plan, especially when there isn't one. Unlike the Sten, Roarer's gun doesn't possess a silencer and its blast could waken the dead. Boots clatter along the walkway which means that, as a means of egress, it's no longer an option. I head for the arbour.

'Shake a leg, Roarer!'

'It's all I got!'

The ants I had up my trousers are nothing compared with the mob pouring out of the hall, led by Mephistopheles. It's going to be touch and go – if they touch us, we're gone.

'Want me to mow 'em down, Rain?'

'They're not grass and we ain't gardeners, Roarer!'

Our pursuers are only thirty paces behind by the time we reach the car. I download the joker from the boot – he's still alive – and grab Rube's box as Roarer gets behind the wheel. I start across the road.

'Aren't you coming with me?'

They're almost on us but with Rory you got to explain everything. 'I got a previous engagement. You know what to do.'

He guns the motor; it sounds like a bunch of tin cans doing the Watusi; yeah, he knows what to do.

'I lead 'em a merry dance.'

'And if they catch you?'

'I shoot 'em.'

'Wrong answer – the right answer is you won't *let* them catch you. Now *go!*'

The speedboat's still at the far end of the pier, its dinghy bobbing by its side. I get myself into the restaurant, lean down and take Lothario by the arm.

'Sorry to interrupt your little tryst,' I tell him, 'but I'm taking you for a ride.'

He puts up a fight but I tell the waiter Lothario's my best friend and we always do it this way when he's drunk. I drop an extra fifty on top of the bill by way of compensation and a half-Nelson on my new best friend does the rest. The dame gets a fit of the giggles and she's still giggling as we board *Loverbuoy*.

'You've kidnapped us because you think we own this boat when we don't,' she gurgles. 'Which means you have to let us go. It also means that the *real* owners are going to realise what you've done and before you get halfway down the coast the cops will stop you.'

Like I said, nothing goes according to plan – even when there is one.

'I guess you're some kind of terrorist,' she goes on. 'Which makes you halfway exciting, which is more than Bombshell here is.'

I throw myself on the mercy of the Fates; there's nothing else to throw myself on.

'Got any ideas?'

'We could take my ute.'

She leads me to a battered Falcon, which she gets started and up the road to the highway. I tuck Rube's box between us, the wireless is playing *Deep Purple* and the dame's swaying to the music like she's at sea.

Babychino's got the door back on its hinges and the innocent look back on her face. 'Where did you go?' she squeaks.

I ignore the question because I've got a few of my own. 'How did you escape?'

'The car was held up by traffic and my abductor wasn't looking so I took off.'

'Do you expect me to believe that?'

'What do you think happened?' I don't tell her what I think happened; tell her what I think happened and I'll alert the Cookie Monster and I don't want to alert the Cookie Monster. She gives up on that question and asks another one. 'Are you staying?'

'What happened to the corpse?'

'What corpse?'

'The one full of bullets I left sprawled at the foot of the stairs.'

'I don't know what you're talking about.'

Chapter 35

OUT OF THE FRYING PAN ...

Tsunami's in. She's dressed in black and I sense rather than see the dame that's as high as a kite on ecstasy behind me peering across from her ute.

'I need you for a job.'

'What if I say no?'

'Like they say in the song, Tsunami: you're just a girl that can't say no, not when lives depend on it, not when your country's calling you.'

That gets me a half-smile. 'And what's my country saying?'

I tell her what her country's saying and after she says she's not having any more to do with me, I climb back in the ute where it's the drug dame's turn to ask questions. She's just started to ask them when Tsunami trots across to me. I wind down the window.

'All right, I'll do it,' she says.

'Why the change of heart?'

She shrugs. 'I've always had a heart and that's my problem. Like you said, life's not a bowl of cherries and you have to eat what's put in front of you. Well, you're in front of me and —' she peers in the car, '— who's she?'

I do the introductions but it's like I never spoke. There's a lot of silence until we reach Cammeray, where we part company with the drug dame, I tuck Rube's box under my arm, and me and Tsunami go the rest of the way on foot.

We can't stay at Babychino's because I no longer trust her and we can't go to the *Wooden No* because they know about the boat and I don't want to compromise Rory by going to his place. There's only one position vacant and after we finagle our way through the front door, we find the lift out of order and have to take the stairs to the fourth floor. I pick the lock and we're embraced by the cold, dark flat that used to be Harry's.

Tsunami looks around like she's back in the Army in a house with a bomb in it. 'Why are we here?'

'We got to hole up somewhere for a couple of hours and this is it. You can catch up on your beauty sleep.'

We're in the middle of a blackout, shadows flickering on the walls like the place is suffering early-onset dementia. By the light of my torch, I rework my way through Rube's files, after which I return to the diary. Like someone once said, misfortune's not necessarily the beginning of the end, it can be the end of the beginning. Rube, Harry and Queen are dead and nothing will change that.

Why didn't Harry tell me about his squeeze? Babychino said Harry told her it was because I attract trouble like flies to a sheep's bum but what's that got to do with March hares? We were mates. I haul out the picture. There they are, gazing into each other's eyes, proof-positive they were lovers.

It's an old photograph because Harry hasn't yet acquired the scar that happened about ten years ago. So they been together that long? She must have been no more than a babe in arms when they met. I stare at her baby face. Still the same damp eyes and pouting lips – in ten years she hasn't aged at all when she should have. I look back at Harry – no scar, which means the photo was taken *before* the window was broken, the window behind Babychino with the sticker in the corner.

Harry's stamp collection's still on the old sideboard and with it his Sherlock Holmes magnifying glass. I hold the magnifier over the sticker: *A GLASS ACT – all pane, no pain.* But how could Harry have a new window but not the old scar?

I examine the photograph more closely and that's when I see it – a carefully photoshopped join between the dame's new face and Harry's old one.

They were never together.

I hear the sound of the lift rumble into life. *How can a lift work in the middle of a blackout?* I wake Tsunami. It's a two-metre leap to the downpipe, the kind people made before they realised downpipes didn't need to last beyond the next generation. The lift stops and the doors open as we shin down.

If indigo's the colour of memory, it's also the colour of the darkness in the courtyard. Four floors above us, I make out the flicker of torches.

They'll see the open window soon enough and know where we are. I give Tsunami a leg-up over the wall and get over after her, my whitesides sloshing in the ripe fruit of a mulberry tree. I move but I move slow, hampered by the weight of Rube's box, the mulberries and the implications of the photo of Harry and Babychino.

Ariadne's wearing the face of someone forced to drink hemlock.

'I'm a person of great importance to the Australian economy, Rainbow – it's unfair to ask me to risk my life on business that's properly the province of the police. You know the old saying: *When I became an adult I put away childish things.* Well, we're adults now, we're grown up, we're different.'

I shake my head. 'Childish things have a habit of bouncing back into contention, Princess. We're the same as we always were – we just wear bigger clothes and carry more burdens.' Her face is pale in the moonlight. 'You've tried every other angle – paying their ransom demands, bowing to blackmail. Even, I suspect – on the basis that if you can't beat 'em, join 'em – working alongside them, doing their bidding so that your business will prosper.'

Ariadne hasn't taken to Tsunami, who's got her own thoughts, and I'm still trying to work out Babychino. Why did she make out she was Harry's lover when she wasn't? Why the elaborate photo set-up? She couldn't have come up with that on her own, which means she's working for somebody she shouldn't be. The cab winds its way out of Ariadne's labyrinth and along New South Head Road, the Harbour on our right and the money on our left. It's not until we reach Rushcutters Bay that Ariadne speaks.

'Who's she?'

'She's a professional and we're going to need a professional.'

'Why do you need me, then?'

'I think you know the answer to that.'

The night looms and I hear the cackle of what sounds like Pandora's laughter. Nothing's changed and everything's different. Ariadne stares out the window. What she's seeing might be anything and the laughter no more than the sound of silence.

Chapter 36

... INTO THE FIRE

Because of the fireworks, Sydney Harbour's a no-go zone. The barriers are up and the cops and security people are marshalling the foot traffic – families out for a picnic, lovers, schoolkids, groups from old people's homes, drunks. There's to be two lots of fireworks, both on the Bridge – the first in an hour's time, the second at midnight.

Ariadne glances at Tsunami then back at me. 'We really should be calling the police, Rainbow. I know these people. Didn't you hear me tell the Minister to have your daughter moved to a safe house? I know the police commissioner and God knows who else. Just a word from me and –'

'And what?' We're out of the cab; I hustle her through the crowd and Tsunami follows. 'There had to be a time in your life when your power hits the wall and this is it, Princess. We're not playing Happy Families, this is for real. The world as we know it is set to end and somehow we got to see it doesn't.'

In daylight, people inhabit an oasis. The city stands four-square to the Harbour and the shadows of tall buildings are somehow comforting. People hurry to and from work and the traffic edges sedately around them. The light's a safety net.

But right now the city's a hellhole. The traffic's stopped at the edge of the Criminal Behaviour District – the CBD – and everything's reduced to shadows. The Bridge is hostage to darkness. Now and again a face looms out of the shadows but just as quickly looms in again while the voices around us wear padded shoes. If the crowds go where they're told they'll be lambs to the slaughter. It's a bad image and I try to dispel it but can't – we're beasts in a holding yard and the only way out is via the abattoir.

'We gotta talk, Princess.'

'We've already talked.'

'Then we gotta talk some more.'

Images shuffle through my head but they're not the right images. Because all mixed up with them are suicide bombers, Guy Fawkes preparing to blow up London's Houses of Parliament and planes flying into tall buildings in New York. Why us, why innocent Sydney – innocent, at least, of offending on the international stage? *Because we declared war on Islamic State*, Ariadne explains. *We're the mouse that roared and it appears that someone was listening.* Tsunami's silent.

'Let's go through it all again, Princess, only slower this time. You're hand in glove with the politicians, right?'

'It depends what you mean by *hand in glove* ...'

'This is no time to be coy. Something's about to happen and you're the only one with anything that might be called a clue to what it will be. Let me get this straight: there's your Watchdog department and then there are the politicians you've got under your belt. You led me to believe –'

A firework goes off. It's like a light going on over my head. *You led me to believe*, I said ... Like Rube always said, *Magicians get you to look in one direction when you should be looking in another.* I was *led* to believe. Like it says in the law of the convergence of unrelated phenomena, everything's connected. The early fireworks burst into life around us.

'You shouldn't have trusted me,' Ariadne says. 'What do you want to know?'

'Everything. And fast. There isn't much time.'

'Once it was easy but now –' A bursting anemone turns Ariadne's face green. 'Economies can't expand forever, the money has to come from somewhere. Once it was taxes – when a king needed money he'd just dream up a new tax. It's no different now. The only ones who don't pay tax are crooks, the very wealthy and the churches.'

'So you don't pay taxes?'

'Hardly any.'

'What do you do in return?'

'We pay politicians.'

'Is there anything else? From either side?'

'Yes – silence. We indulge each other and then look the other way afterwards.'

'It looks like you can't look the other way any longer.'

Ariadne shakes her head and when she speaks her voice is a whisper. 'No, I suppose I can't …' Fireworks have taken over the world.

The first shot has the three of us sniffing the asphalt and the second shot has me going for my gat. Beside me, Tsunami's crouched behind a car, while in front, Ariadne's lying on the ground as still as death. Around us is the sound of stockaded animals milling towards the abattoir. There's a third shot and I scan the surrounding buildings to see where they're coming from.

'Don't move, Ariadne!' I say.

'But a stone's sticking in my back!'

'Be grateful you're alive to feel it.'

I've worked it out: the shots came from our left and the weapon was big, in the order of a .45. I look for a gunman but all I can see are more fireworks, courtesy of a bunch of kids who came by their crackers courtesy of the internet. I haul Ariadne to her feet. Tsunami never stopped standing.

'It's only kids with a bunch of bungers.'

Ariadne tries to dust herself off but Gucci doesn't clean good. 'Where was I? That's right, I discovered that politicians, far from being cornerstones of our society, are very often the whackos of the world. Most of the ones I dealt with took my money and crept off into the night, hoping I wouldn't ask any favours in return.'

'But you did?'

'Of course I did. That's the way it works, Rainbow. You give people money and in return they do you favours – development approvals I didn't deserve, licences I shouldn't have got, contracts that should never have been signed. Politicians are the grease that enables the wheels of industry to turn without squeaking.'

'What about your research people – this Watchdog committee? What did they find that they shouldn't have?'

It's a long time before Ariadne answers and in that time the little family beside us – mother, father, daughter, dog – finish their picnic and, like the good citizens they are, clean up afterwards and place their rubbish in the receptacles provided. A lifetime passes – my lifetime, Ariadne's,

Tsunami's, Imogene's.

I try to keep my voice calm as I repeat the question. 'What did they find that they shouldn't have?'

Ariadne shakes her head. Maybe it's the fumes. Maybe she's just trying to breathe.

Chapter 37

PAWNS

'Elected representatives think they're all-powerful when they're nothing of the kind – members of parliament are no more than egocentric mouthpieces. The real power's in the people who put them there. And by that I don't mean political parties. Parties are made up of envelope stuffers, old women who make lamingtons, volunteers who man booths at election time and ambitious people who want to get into parliament. But they're nothing but pawns.

'The real motive force of political parties is the extremists. They're the ones with the enthusiasm, the drive to keep the Bib-and-Bub parties going. They might be *extreme* socialists, *extreme* capitalists, *extreme* environmentalists, *extreme* anything. Whatever they are, they'll do pretty well anything to achieve their ends. They're the real terrorists.'

I cut across her. 'What did Watchdog find out? And make it snappy, Ariadne – if there wasn't much time before, there's even less now.'

The early fireworks have been and gone and the world's reclaimed by darkness.

'As with all political parties, the one in power now is both informed and propelled by a cabal. All cabals have an agenda. And on the agenda of the cabal of the party in power now is increased defence, less social services, reduced business tax, denial of global warming, no asylum seekers – and hardline religious intolerance. Except they don't call it that.'

'What *do* they call it?'

'Counter-terrorism.'

At the Strangefellows' Hall I lip-read the Mephistopheles joker saying: *To quote the master, you should know how to do evil if necessary.* The quote's from one of the works Rube made me study – *The Prince*, by

Machiavelli: the *master* that Mephistopheles was quoting. Another way of saying that *the end justifies the means* – even if those means are as warped as the philosophy behind it.

'So their aim's to make people fear terrorism even more than they do now – be so fearful, in fact, that they'll accept *repression* in the name of security?'

Ariadne nods. 'That's only aim number one. Aim number two is to link terrorism to religion – as in: *some dogs bite, therefore all dogs bite*. And the third is to commit an act so shocking it will result in the banning of that religion.' She sees my look. 'Yes, they're *that* mad.'

'*Who*, Ariadne?'

'You already know the answer to that, don't you?' The night's revving up again; there's so much racket I'm back to lip-reading. 'Your Aunt Rube knew – her name came up on their radar early, which is why I wasn't surprised by her death. As I said, it's the nature of extremists that they'll go to any lengths to achieve their ends.'

She knows and yet she doesn't know; she's got nothing to do with what's happening and she's got everything to do with it; she's being loyal to someone she shouldn't be.

'They killed Rube.' I force myself to say it. 'And Harry and Queen. Then they went after Rory and were about to –' I stare at Ariadne. 'What did you do with Imogene? Was your phone call to the Minister a sham? Is my daughter safe?'

'As safe as she can be – considering.' Ariadne shrugs in the half light. 'They had the power to kill your Aunt Rube as well as the wherewithal to get away with it. Her death was part of a plan – all the deaths were. They could get rid of someone they needed to be rid of and blame it on terrorism.'

'It's Parkinson, isn't it? The real terrorist isn't some Middle Eastern bogey at all but a nice little Westerner called Parkinson. Who I had trouble recognising when I saw him because he was a big boy who became a small adult.'

'It's not as simple as that. Parkinson's only a foil. Didn't you tell me Harry said we were all terrorists? It's the system that's at fault. The system that our headmaster Mr Hercule and little Irving Morris are an integral part of. Under Nazism, no-one was guilty of any atrocities. Refugee children die but we don't kill them. Instead, we leave it to the workers in the abattoir. We see nothing, are responsible for nothing.' Her voice falters. 'It's the system.'

'What's he going to do now, this innocent foil of yours? What did your people discover?'

'It's like karma, the fate I brought on myself.' It's confession time. 'All those years ago when you imagined I was on your side I was really on Parkinson's. Remember the time you thought you were rescuing me? Well, you weren't at all – I was just bait. Tom – Parkinson – was clever, devious, if you like. He wanted to get you. There were other times you've probably forgotten.' I haven't forgotten. 'The only time I stepped in to stop them was when they were about to hang you.'

'At least you were on my side then.'

Ariadne shakes her head sadly. 'When I realised you might die, I was afraid I'd get into trouble. You could have been hung.'

'Hanged.' The correction's automatic. 'You mean you knew what they were going to do?'

She shrugs. 'They told me. I was their friend and yours, playing both sides against the middle. While all the time I was … just as I'm doing now, right up until –'

Rube was keeping tabs on Parkinson when she stumbled on what they were up to and decided to monitor them.

Meanwhile, the MC's speaking, his voice echoing over the Harbour.

Up until now we've kept the nature of tonight's 'reveal' a close secret. Well, now I'm going to tell you what that 'reveal' is to be. But not right away. Let's have a physics lesson first, shall we? Do we want a little physics lesson? Louder, I can't hear you. Do we want a lesson in physics to justify our being called the Clever Country?

It's what they call a warm-up on this dull, lustreless night under a heavy cloud of suspicion.

With our beautiful Harbour as the backdrop we are about to see a sound-and-light show. But first, what are the colours of the spectrum? Murmurs issue from the crowd. *Come on, you can do better than that – you'd better because the eyes of the world are upon us. The first colour, on the count of three, is – one, two …Red!*

Hey, that's really good! Now on the count of three, the second colour – one, two … Orange!

The announcer's spinning the thing out, giving me a chance to put two and two together. I turn to Ariadne, this familiar yet unfamiliar person I used to know who's reappeared as a stranger. We've forced our way through the crowd till we're near the south-east pylon and the acrid fumes from the early fireworks linger in my nostrils and sit on my tongue. Beyond us the all-trusting, all-unsuspecting spectators go on with their chanting.

Yellow!

Chapter 38

COUNTDOWN TO TERROR

Louder, cries the MC, like Penelope unplucking her cloth as Ulysses draws close to home. *I want you to wake the gods.* After a bit more of this, it's time for *I Still Call Australia Home, We are the Ones* and *You are the Wind Beneath my Wings* – like we're about to go to war on a heaving wave of patriotism.

Ariadne raises her voice to be heard or maybe she's just raising her voice. Suddenly she looks agitated. Maybe it's the music; or maybe at long last it's the truth. 'I was alerted to a plot. Remember these people's minds work differently from yours and mine. First, they're mad which gives them the kind of power we could never possess. Second, they have political protection. And third, they have a Machiavellian turn of mind that would take your breath away.'

The music stops and it's time for the announcer again. *Remember this is beaming worldwide, people ... millions upon millions are watching, which means we've got an audience to die for. So let's knock 'em dead, shall we? It's practice time again, so let's do our rehearsal. On the count of three in this rainbow nation of ours, the first colour is ...*

'I didn't go to the police because I – I was scared I'd be tarred with the same brush as the people we were monitoring. They'd think I was part of the plot. For the same reason, I couldn't go to the media. So I convinced myself that it – it couldn't happen here.'

'That *what* couldn't happen here?'

The Bridge looms above us, stilled of traffic. From where we're standing I can just make out the electric wires strung between the girders they'll use to set off the fireworks.

Ariadne's voice goes quiet. 'In a way I suppose I was part of it.' Under the hubbub I'm having trouble hearing her. 'The anti-terrorism people realised something big was planned but they didn't know what they were looking for.'

'And what *should* they be looking for?'

'I'm not – please believe I was never part of it. That is, I knew what they were planning but didn't think anything would happen – I thought it was all talk.'

Up till now, Tsunami's been silent, like she's been monitoring us, a black shadow among a lot of other black shadows – lithe and deadly beautiful. 'We're running out of time,' she says. 'From what I've heard, whatever *it* is will happen tonight. We have to cut to the chase.'

I turn to Ariadne. 'It's the Bridge at midnight, isn't it?'

'I promise, I didn't think …'

'Then for God's sake, Ariadne, think now!'

'It's meant to be a symbolic act, the destruction of a cultural icon. There are to be three linked explosions.'

'Why three?'

All right everyone, pay attention – the next colour, on the count of three, is … one, two …

'Why three?' I repeat.

Tsunami steps between us. She's the bomb expert, been here before, knows how it works.

'Anyone who's seen those old photos of the Bridge will know that an explosive device – even a pretty big one – would still leave the structure standing. There'd be some twisting but the Bridge was built to last and there'd be a strong chance it could be put together again, because each end's a self-supporting cantilever. I don't think they'd want anything to remain standing because it would water down the symbolism.' Tsunami says more because she knows more, after which I turn to Ariadne. 'So where are they – where have they put the bombs?'

Ariadne shakes her head, all the strength drained out of her. 'It's complicated. But basically, left, right and centre, linked by the same electrical wires they're using for the fireworks.'

'Do they want deaths or do they just want to destroy an icon?'

The silence is broken by the roar of the crowd: *Blue!*

'Our information is they wanted to *maximise deaths*. They said it was for the greater good.' Ariadne pauses. 'Extremists don't like half measures.'

'Where's the primary bomb and how will it be detonated?'

Indigo!

The word sparks something in me, the way a detonator sets off a bomb. It's the word Rube uttered just before she died. That was why they killed her – because she knew. She worked out the significance of what she'd discovered and was on the cusp of stopping them when she was murdered, her death made to look like the work of terrorists. She might not have known the *how, when* and *where* but she was well on the way to finding out when they killed her.

'As I said before, everything was on a need to know basis,' Ariadne goes on. 'There were cells and, while my spies were privy to some, they weren't to others. It's just become clear to me now.'

'Okay, how's the main bomb to be detonated?'

'They debated electric, electronic and impact but finally decided on impact. There was mention of *fulminate of mercury, chlorate of potash* and something called *tetryl*.' Tsunami's nodding, recognising detonators' constituents, what we're up against. 'There's a sort of "baby bump" on top of the bomb. According to our sources, the ones I didn't fully believe, they rehearsed. They used a chock of hardwood –' She points to Rube's box '– about the size of that. They lodged it next to the button to prevent the detonation. But that was rehearsal – there'll be no block of wood tonight. The impact will set off the bomb which will set off the other two bombs.'

Something – a noise, movement – makes me spin around. At first I think it's Pandora but it's only Tsunami, no longer afraid of being too close.

'You're saying a block of wood stopped it going off?'

Ariadne nods.

'Tom described it as "fail-safe". The bomb's impervious to impact from other directions – it had to be, he said, because he was working with amateurs. And, yes, a mere block of wood is enough to stop the detonator setting off the bomb.'

Chapter 39

SOMEWHERE PANDORA

'And where is it now – the bomb?'

The MC has led the crowd to the end of the spectrum, the dutiful audience has given the required responses and now he's speaking in the kind of voice used by Sunday school teachers explaining a Biblical passage – all-knowing, patronising and wrong.

Superimposed upon the Bridge will be an outline of our great country. One by one, we'll display each of the colours of the spectrum to symbolise who and what we are – starting with red and ending with violet. It will be a spectacular the like of which has never been seen before. Remember this show is being beamed live by satellite across the world and viewed by tens, maybe hundreds of millions of viewers – so make sure your noses are clean.

His captive audience laughs; Ariadne still hasn't replied.

'Where is it?' I repeat.

'At one of the meetings – Watchdog was able to record most of them – Tom made what he regarded as a joke. He said: *We don't want to blow this.'* Ariadne pauses, gathering her thoughts. 'Pyrotechnics are complex. It's not merely the effect, it's the practicality of realising that effect. A display has to be designed, co-ordinated – and safe. Installations are checked and double-checked – the security tonight is stringent.'

'Then how, where –?'

'Remember these people are in power, they're in charge. They control vital sections of our security organisations. They're here tonight in force. I remember a report saying they'll use those electronic bracelets they put on criminals, so that their central control knows where everyone is.'

The music starts again only this time it's not *Waltzing Matilda* or *Advance Australia Fair* or even *I Still Call Australia Home* but Hector

Berlioz's *Symphony Fantastique* – the mad bit where the man kills his lover because he no longer trusts her. The crowd settles. They feel secure. In their midst are security people, wired up and ready to act. Somewhere, too, is Pandora.

There's only a short burst of the Berlioz but it's enough, like the organisers decided too much culture can kill. It's replaced by the shanty song about a convict leaving old England forever and coming to Botany Bay. The madman behind the planned deaths of so many must have chosen the music.

'Don't hurt him, will you?'

'He deserves to be hurt.'

'I'm not talking about Parkinson, I'm talking about our son. He's only helping because he's obedient. And obedience is a fine quality.'

I remember the stretch marks. When they met, Parkinson already had a son who became the *bearded* Parkinson. But there was another, younger, child who must be *their* son – Ariadne's and Parkinson's – fathered by Parkinson before Ariadne married her billionaire. So Parkinson has that much of a hold over her.

'You were someone Tom could never be and he hated you for it. When your Aunt Rube took you out of school he more or less shifted his campaign onto her. But it was a casual, desultory sort of business and it only became serious when Rube discovered Tom's other activities – his right wing, not "think-tank", but "act-tank". In his drive to frame an entire people, Tom wanted to what he called *neutralise* both you and your aunt. And I knew because we kept in touch, both on a personal level and through our respective groups. Watchdog fed his act-tank and vice-versa. But I didn't want you killed, Rainbow. Getting you to investigate terrorism was my idea; it meant I could keep tabs on you ...'

Her voice fades as it's overtaken by the noise around us. I'd already worked out most of it.

'Parkinson grew up,' Ariadne goes on. 'At least he became an adult. Although he was a big boy he became a small adult, which was why you didn't recognise him. And he got to do what he liked doing best – hurting, even killing, people – at the same time as he was framing terrorists and, through them, adherents of their religion.

'He left clues at the scenes of his thugs' crimes to incriminate terrorists. It was my department that told him terrorists ritually cleansed themselves before killing, doing such things as dousing themselves with eau-de-cologne before setting out to commit their atrocities. Then there were the slogans ...'

I butt in. 'And Babychino, Denise, or whatever her name was. She is – was – Parkinson's squeeze, isn't she? I caught her going through Harry's apartment and she came up with some cock-and-bull story about being Harry's girlfriend. It was easy for her to get personal details – Parkinson's group must have "ins" everywhere: the cops, security, the morgue. It was Parkinson's bad luck that Babychino was a lousy actor. Where's the bomb, Ariadne?'

Her hands drop helplessly by her sides. 'On the barge under the Bridge. They'll hoist the main bomb into place at the last moment. No-one will notice – it'll just be another black object against the night sky, part of the scenery. My son will be there …'

'Describe him.'

Ariadne describes Bertie Thomas, the kid I met on Camellia Pier all those aeons ago, the one with the story I didn't believe about being set upon by a gang of toughs and later being approached by terrorists.

'And Parkinson – where's he?'

'On the barge. Rainbow, I don't have to tell you of Tom's – predilections. He's got the death wish that all sadists have. I think he wants to die a martyr to his cause. Ironic, isn't it? That makes him just like them.' She reaches out and clutches my arm. 'Please don't hurt Bertie.'

I remove her hand from my sleeve and step away. 'Sorry, Princess, but no promises.'

They've blocked the approaches to the Bridge but it's too late to take that route even if I wanted to. I can't alert anyone because they'd arrest me on suspicion of whatever they want to be suspicious of when confronted by someone that doesn't exist. A guard with a walkie-talkie is patrolling the foot of the pylon. Beyond him I can make out the outline of a dinghy to be used in an emergency. This is an emergency.

I could cut and run, in which case I'd be safe. But it would also mean hundreds – maybe thousands – of innocent people would suffer. What kind of detonation will it be? *Impact*, Ariadne said, but that's just her information and the information could be wrong. How big is the bomb? *As big as a length of thread. Wrong analogy*, I reply. Then, giving her Rube's box and telling her to stay where she is, I make for the guards, taking Tsunami with me.

Security thrives on patterns and hugging the cold stone of the Bridge

pylon we watch for this one. As my guard gets to the end of his patch –
the pathway that bisects the park – light sparkles off his belt, his gun, the
badge on his cap and his nightstick. He's not trying to hide because he
wants to be seen – it adds to the sense of security of anyone watching.
That's how I recognise him. It's also how I notice his companion.

I nod to Tsunami.

Chapter 40

ONE MINUTE TO MIDNIGHT

We're close enough to see the other guard and hear the contact words: *All quiet on the Western front?* Followed by the other guard's reply, delivered in a squeaky falsetto: *All quiet.*

Do not deviate from the script, warns the *Secur-A-Guard* booklet. *Safety lies in following the format to the letter – deviating will only compromise.* It's a short sequence because high security needs short sequences – it's no good discovering trouble half an hour after it occurs. In less than five minutes, the guard's back. Only this time I'm the guard – complete with cap, gun, nightstick and the right intonation – asking: *All quiet on the Western front?*

To which the response comes: *All quiet. What about you?*

My reply's already in my throat – *You're not supposed to say that* – when I remember the words of Thomas Jefferson, quoting someone else: *The price of liberty is eternal vigilance.* The other guard isn't the other guard because they've taken out the other guard just as they've taken out the rest of the security team. Which means the tall, thin man with the non-squeaky voice is not only the wrong man, he's also got orders to neutralise me.

Always get in first. Which is what Tsunami does because she's noticed him, too. He's a looming shadow with a job to do, only Tsunami does it better. He leaps in the air from a standing position because he knows his karate – correction, *tae kwon do.* I hear him say: *Metsuke no ezan – I'm gazing at the far mountains but can still see everything close at hand* as he comes at me in a flying side-kick. These boys play by the rules and he's not ready for Tsunami. Tsunami doesn't do rules. We find Ariadne still clutching Rube's box and make for the dinghy. More shadows, among them Pandora. I feel her presence, *sense* it with a terrible certainty. There's only one reality as I disable the second guard, unmoor the runabout, nod Tsunami aboard, load Rube's box in with her then – leaving the outboard motor up out of the water – tell Ariadne to use her rowing skills to get us out into the silver sea. At any moment a spotlight could slice across us. But right now we're a dark shape on darker water, moving silently.

It's three hundred metres from where we pushed out from Miller's Point to the Bridge's centre. The music's changed to something more up tempo because the organisers want to heighten the audience's expectations. There are hundreds of boats, the MC says, but only official ones are allowed under the Bridge. They don't want breaches of security getting in the way of festivities. Ariadne keeps rowing.

Only five minutes to go, folks. It's time to cast your minds back – at the same time remembering the traditional owners of this land – to that magical moment when Captain Arthur Phillip, our first governor, arrived at this historic site on this day in 1788 and declared it a colony in the name of His Royal Majesty, King George the Third. It's hard to believe, isn't it, that it all happened just a little over two hundred years ago. Harder still to imagine that not all that long ago the Bridge was no more than an idea in the mind of a man called Bradfield. It's like it's been here forever, one of life's immutables.

The world's reduced to the plash of oars in darkness, phosphorescence marking their tips before turing into flying fish, and our progress is that of a pregnant snail. The barge looms while the Bridge cuts a swathe through the stars. The barge is almost on us. So is midnight.

Only three minutes left, folks.

There's a lot of activity on the barge and the sound of raised voices carries down to us. Black figures scurry along the deck. It's only when we're almost upon them that I see the hook.

Two minutes.

It's dangling from a rope the same colour as the night sky, passed through a simple, manually operated block and tackle – a fiddle-block with two sheaves, one beneath the other – to ensure sufficient purchase. They can't use a motor for the same reason we can't use the outboard – there'd be too much noise. Everyone's meant to believe the bomb's part of the display, another rare device to be hauled into place at the last minute, the spotlights turned off to maintain the magic.

Speaking of the traditional owners, I'm sure you've all heard of the Rainbow Serpent. While we're celebrating the coming of the white man, we must also acknowledge the inherent belief of the Aborigines. Or should I say the Koori people. According to the Kooris, the Rainbow Serpent is where it all began ...

One minute to midnight.

I grip one ratline while Tsunami grabs another then draw the gat I took from the guard and hand it to Ariadne. Apart from the knife, I'm now weaponless, but where we're headed, the weight of a gun could be the difference between waking up tomorrow and dying.

'Two things, Princess. Hang onto this – you might need it. And with the other hand keep hold of the barge.' I turn to the figure in black poised beside me. 'Ready?'

Tsunami nods.

Five figures are hauling on the rope and they're all going to die, except they don't know it because it's a detail they haven't been made privy to. There's no other way it can work – they've got to get the bomb into place and they know too much to be allowed to live. Only two are meant to survive – Parkinson and his kid; the two are wearing lightweight divers' outfits while the rest ... The rope dangling from the Bridge is five-eighths abaca – good, strong stuff also known as Manila hemp – and it's hanging from the block and tackle under the platform below the Bridge forty-seven metres above our heads. The bomb's a giant Rubik's cube covered with plastic and innocent-looking – except for the giveaway bump at the top.

Forcing my eyes to adapt – *gazing at the far mountains while seeing everything close at hand* – I can just make out the steel baffle jutting from the platform designed to make contact with the lump on the cube. The men will have been instructed to haul extra hard at the end to ensure the impact-detonation occurs, although they won't know that's the reason. They'll have been told something else.

I work my way up the side of the hull, aware of Tsunami beside me. The barge is black and cold but it's a lot worse where we're headed. The

MC's begun his countdown. I ease myself over the rusty railing. Tsunami follows.

I hear Parkinson's last-minute instructions. 'We're hauling up a fireworks display and it *must* hit right on the button when the man says *indigo*. So that you remember, the sequence goes *red, orange, yellow, green, blue, indigo, violet* – got it? The timing's sixty seconds from go to whoa – from when the man says *red* to when he says *indigo*. The Bridge will light up with the relevant colour when the MC names it but don't be distracted. There'll be two seconds a haul and there are thirty hauls, just like in a tug of war.'

'What happens when the bundle hits the Bridge?'

'Like I've told you a million times, there'll be a surprise fireworks display spelling out the words: *SPARED BY ALLAH!*'

'All this for a sign?'

'Remember that we're not the crazies around here. We don't believe in death – we're far more civilised than that. We're just making a statement. And that statement is that thousands of innocent people could have died tonight. We want to make people afraid, make them sit up and take notice, allow the counter-terrorism people to finally take the appropriate action.' He pauses; he's said enough. 'Bertie will do the call. Heave!'

We could try to take them now but we'd never succeed. There's too many. The men are leaning into their task as I come around the side of the wheelhouse, five shapes bent low, grunting, and their words drift across to me like hammer blows.

> *I must down to the sea again,*
> *to the lonely sea and the sky,*
> *And all I ask is a tall ship*
> *and a star to steer her by,*
> *And the wheel's kick and the wind's song*
> *and the white sail's shaking*
> *And a grey mist on the sea's face and a grey dawn*
> *breaking.*

The words seem at odds with what they're doing until I realise it's the sailor's old-style drill to get the rope-haulers working in synch – sixty seconds they've got and sixty seconds is what the poem will give them. They're up to *sky* and me and Tsunami are on the opposite side to the men

as the chain attached to the rope rattles around the capstan. The bundle
lurches into the air and we creep aboard as Bertie, the boy in the long
socks, says, 'Remember, two seconds a haul, right on the button, no more,
no less – the secret's in the rhythm. *Haul!*'

Chapter 41

RUBE'S BOX

The men chant and the chain rattles around the capstan as I make my way up the side of the bomb. All the while Rube's words are hammering through my cerebellum: *Do you remember how to defuse bombs, Rainbow? It depends, Rube. It depends whether I've got all the time in the world or a matter of seconds; it depends whether I'm on the ground or swinging from a rope hundreds of feet in the air and making a rapid, jerky ascent; and most important of all, it depends if the bomb's detonated electronically and not through impact at all.*

The plastic tears under my weight, forcing me to scrabble for a new hold. The crowd's roaring *orange* and the men are chanting *by* as I abseil into space before slamming back hard against the load. The bundle's three metres by three metres and about the same height, but a lot of it's soft packaging behind a ribbed framework of steel bars. I manage to grab one of the bars just as the plastic gives way, hauling myself in again. Tsunami's beside me.

Yellow! yells the crowd.

Kick! bellow the men on the barge.

The Bridge will collapse inwards, 50,000 tonnes of steel crumpling as its weight bears the structure down. The men on the barge will be killed when the bomb goes off, followed by those in the nearest pleasure craft as the wave gets going. But I won't be around to see it because I've got fifteen seconds left — twenty at best — and there's no time for a cheerio call or to work out where I went wrong or how things might have been different. I've got to focus on the detonator — how it works, how to get to it, how to defuse it.

Far below I can make out the movement in the crowd as the security people start their surge towards the Bridge. They've finally noticed what's happening and it's confirmed their worst fears. To the north and south searchlights swing towards us then suddenly go out.

The load's swinging like a pendulum in a coffin clock as we draw close while I'm tearing at the plastic like a boy with a Christmas present to see what's underneath. When I needed it, the plastic tore; now, when I don't, it resists to the end; I pull out the knife I took from the gunman in the brothel and start cutting. No-one on the barge has noticed us – they're too intent on their task. Placing the knife between my teeth, I continue climbing.

I'm looking for the button designed to hit the platform under the Bridge and send the Harbour Bridge sky-high; a button and a bunch of wires. I'm also looking for the fail-safe, the standby device they always install in case the impact detonation fails. It's the first thing a defuser looks for – the fallback, the second detonator, the pointer being the aerial saying it's electronic or a blinking red light which says there's a timing mechanism. Tsunami scrabbles alongside me, black and shiny as a shark, her eyes following my every movement.

Blue!

I feel like a suicide on a ledge with the crowd chanting *Jump!* Out of nowhere Parkinson appears. That's the thing about mad people, they can be relied upon to do mad things. *Why didn't you stay with him*, I asked Ariadne. *Because he's mad. I love him but he's mad. It didn't stop me loving him and doing what he told me to do but I could never have married him.* Besides, he had a wife who *could* put up with his madness.

He's discarded his oxygen pack, mask and goggles, he's swung himself onto the bomb and he's gaining on us. I wonder what death will be like, whether it comes complete with a kaleidoscope of colour or just blackness, a slow clawing at consciousness as my brains scatter. The impact ledge is closing in and with the shortening of the cable, the load has momentarily stopped. I hold my breath. The men below will shout *and a grey dawn breaking* and the bomb will hit the impact hammer and that will be the end of everything.

Faintly through the midnight air I hear – or think I hear – someone, somewhere, intoning the word *indigo* just as the men bellow *breaking* and suddenly he's upon me, my torturer of old, Parkinson, only now he's no longer twice my size but smaller and he hasn't got a lot of bully boys to help him. I'm the one with the upper hand but a lot of good it'll do me. The uprush of the word that will mean the final haul on the rope that will depress the plunger and detonate the explosive is rising in the throats of the men on the barge like the suction preceding the formation of a tidal wave.

Parkinson has the strength that comes with madness, the desperation of a man who believes in something strongly enough to die for it. I'm not going to succeed while he's all-powerful because that's what he's always been. He's a fanatic, an extremist, and this is his extreme mission. His hands grapple at my throat as the Bridge's underbelly looms. Around us strands of wires connect the fireworks to the glinting packages of installations. The bomb looks benign by comparison – safe, almost comforting.

I find his pressure points without thinking. I'm in the playground again but now I've got my torturer at my mercy. The load is surging upwards, taking me with it, and we're on the upward stroke of the hammer blow. Suddenly, I'm an animal acting on instinct. And my instinct is to raise Parkinson above my head and lodge him in the rapidly narrowing crevice between Bridge and bomb, ensuring he's out of the way of the detonator button but just to one side, a human buffer to prevent detonation as the crowd screams *Indigo!* and the crew on the barge separate the last word of their chant into *brea-* and then *-king!* and I hear the sound as a body crunches and wait for the explosion that says I've failed, that tells me instinct isn't enough, was never going be enough, even as I swipe the knife across the ropes in a final desperate attempt to stop the world exploding.

White air, silence. A figure grows wings and takes to the sky, hurtling into space. As the men below roar *-king* I imagine I see Tsunami smiling. Only I can't see Tsunami. Then comes the crunch. I look away.

There's no explosion.

As the fireworks go off, I feel like I'm suspended in space, the flat, black Harbour below me, the crowd a collection of broken rocks and the spotlights smoking ruins. Water, when you hit it after a fall from this height is as hard as diamond, and that's what I'm falling towards. The bomb has swung around until it's above me. I grapple to turn it and my hands find wires. I clutch at them and they come away. I wait for the explosion but it doesn't occur. Too late, I try to force the bomb under me. It must be too late – falling this far at an acceleration rate of thirty-two feet per second per second I'll hit the water and the bomb will land on top of me and afterwards my body will be borne down to the smoky depths of the Harbour. *Think like an animal. On second thoughts, don't think at all. Just act.*

I give one final, desperate heave as the water rushes to meet me.

There's no splash, not even the hint of one. Just, close at hand, the suspiration of splintering wood, the noise of exploding fireworks, multi-coloured lights shooting into the sky and breaking into flowering petals and fountains of light. And, far away, the faint roar of the crowd. I must have blacked out. Because when I can see again, I've surfaced, alive enough to make out an anxious face peering over the edge of the dinghy.

'Are you all right, Rainbow?'

I blink up. 'I've just fallen into the Harbour from the top of what must be the equivalent of a fifteen-storey building ...'

'Where's my son? Where's that woman? And where's Tom?'

I tell her I don't know times three as her hands grapple for me. She helps me aboard and immediately I hear the rattle of a motor starting.

'The bomb landed on the barge and you landed on the bomb and the bomb didn't explode because it was the right way up. The people on the barge must all have died but I didn't see the others who were on the bomb with you – that woman and Tom ...' There are tears in her voice but then Ariadne's all business. 'Lie down so you can't be seen.'

Boats are coming our way. There'll be police and security people, including, inevitably, anti-terrorism squads. I lie as still as I can next to Aunt Rube's box.

'Don't give anyone reason to suspect there's anyone in the boat apart from you,' I murmur.

'There isn't.'

C.S. Boag

MISTER RAINBOW

in the Case of the Nightmare in Nimbin

When Gregor Samsa awoke one morning from uneasy dreams he found himself transformed ... into a giant insect.

Franz Kafka, *Metamorphosis*

Chapter 1

FIX ME OR FRAME ME

'*Die, you bastard! Die!*'

'Wake up, Rainbow! Wake up!'

She could be anyone – even Pandora. I lunge at her.

When she tells me what I did, she's got the marks on her neck to prove it. They aren't pretty. Murder never is.

We're on the lanai of a mansion, eating a magnificent repast beside a sea that looks like used blotting paper. I'm pretending it never happened.

'I've got two questions,' I say to Ariadne. 'What's on the news and where's the whisky?'

She has her back to the view – she's seen it before, she'll see it again and she can afford to share it. After all these years, she's still easy on the eye. She's also as hard as a bullet.

'You're not having any whisky. As for the news, in the case you chose to call the Morgue the Merrier there were a few innocent deaths and a lot of guilty ones; police and security rounded up what was left of the perpetrators – with the exception of someone who sounded very much like you; and Australia's safe' – she glances at me – 'at least from terrorists. Meanwhile, you're in bad shape both mentally and physically and you'll do as I say.'

I slug down my third hard black for the day. 'I'll have another one of those and get out of your hair.'

Ariadne's my childhood sweetheart who re-entered my life when I needed her. But she's worth a motza and she's also a control freak and on either count she's not for me. A ship on the horizon is so small that its passengers could be microbes. I know how they feel. I climb to my feet but my legs are spaghetti.

'I've had you sedated,' Ariadne says. 'It was in the coffee. As a result, you're experiencing a sensation known as accidie – a feeling of sloth, dizziness and despair usually associated with the 'flu. I've made arrangements with a clinic I happen to own and they're making arrangements for your admission. You'll need to stay calm while we're waiting for the ambulance.'

When she pours me another coffee, her hands are as controlled as a clergyman's conscience. 'Look, I'm doing you a favour. Your boat's at the bottom of the Harbour, the police are after you and you not only need somewhere to hide, you need help – both medical and psychiatric. Left to your own devices someone's going to end up dead and I might get dragged into it.'

Her face is swimming above me like a fish in oil.

'That's *my* pigeon,' I mutter.

'Sure. But, more importantly, it's also mine.'

The shrink leans forward, tall and cadaverous. 'Tell me about this virago, chimera, succubus, wraith – this *nemesis* you believe is following you.'

'It's not a belief – I know that she's following me for a fact.'

'It sounds to me like a case of delusionary fantasy.'

One of Ariadne's medicos has seen to my wounds while the psychiatrist – trick-cyclist, head-banger, shrink, call him what you will – is an add-on extra. I didn't have any choice. It means sleeping over at the clinic but with my boat at the bottom of the Harbour it's better than dossing in a ditch. The certificate in the frame on the wall behind him says he's a surgeon as well as a shrink.

'It sounds like you've made up your mind,' I say.

'So help me unmake it.'

In the silence that follows I hear what sounds very much like a fight to the death next door. I get off the couch and make for the door.

Behind me the shrink says, 'It's locked.'

I unlock it with my shoulder and hurtle down the hall, to be confronted by three men in white coats. The door at the other end is too far away and the hall windows are barred like the ones in the insulting room. I take the only course open and neutralise the men in the white coats. Correction – I try to neutralise them. Because – courtesy of whatever they've been dosing me with – I trip over my whitesides, bang my head on the wall and end up flat on my face. Two of the nurses sit on me while the third asks, 'Want us to put a camisole on him, Doc?'

I feel like a baby's bum with the shrink's voice wafting down over me like powder. 'That won't be necessary, boys. You can return to normal duties.' Then to me, 'If you promise to behave, Mr Nowlc, you can get up.'

I struggle to my feet. 'I'm a free citizen. You can't do this to me.'

He shepherds me back into the interrogation room. 'On the contrary, on your own admission you're no kind of citizen at all. Which means I can do pretty much what I like with you. You weren't born and have no ID: no driver's licence, credit card or private investigator's licence – not even a Medicare number. All of which means that you don't exist. While Ariadne most certainly does. I follow her orders and her orders are to fix you.'

'Fix me of what?'

'Your physical injuries are superficial while your psychological ones are far more deep-seated.'

'What psychological injuries?'

'That's for you not to know and for me to discover.'

The window overlooks the garden to the east, north's the drop-dead end of the building, south's where they park the patients, while to the west is New South Head Road, Vauclues, the direction of freedom.

'I've managed up to now,' I tell Ariadne as we wait for the ambulance.

She shakes her head. 'You only think you've managed up to now. You're a pothole in everyone's road, including your own. You're resilient, I'll give you that – actually, it's a miracle you're still alive – but the fact remains that you're faulty and you need fixing.'

'Fixing or controlling? What do you see me as – damaged goods or a hostile takeover?'

She shakes her head while her butler positions himself for trouble. 'You're a loser, Rainbow. You lost your parents and you lost me. You also lost a marriage, your aunt, too many friends, a wife and your daughter. You need help and I intend to see you get it. Otherwise, you'll go down in a screaming heap and, despite all my power and my money, I'll be at risk of going down with you.'

A stepladder is standing in the corner, there's a violent altercation taking place next door and the muzak's Verdi.

'Nothing you say will go beyond these walls, Mr Nowlc,' the shrink's saying. 'Look around and all you'll see is an innocent consulting room. I'm sorry about the ladder and the half-painted walls but the clinic's a work in progress. It doesn't mean our services are anything but the best. As for privacy, I'm not taking notes. And, apart from the opera – incidentally, I hope you like La Traviata – we're not wired for sound. So. How many people have you killed?'

With his long hands clasped before him he looks like a praying mantis – make that preying. How many people has *he* killed?

'At last count, none. And I thought admission to joints like this was supposed to be voluntary.'

'You were signed in by family.'

'I haven't got family, apart from my daughter, and she's ...'

'She's what?'

I shake my head. 'She wouldn't do it. Besides which she's at the police academy learning to be a cop.' My mind de-clouds slightly. 'At least she was before Ariadne had her moved somewhere else. Imogene's got my best interests at heart so if you're saying –'

'That's precisely what I am saying – that you're here on your daughter's recognisance. Because, like Ms Sidonia, your daughter is concerned about your health – in particular, your mind. And in answer to your next question, yes, Imogene *has* returned to the academy.'

Chapter 2
THE WEAPON OF CHOICE

It's been a hard summer and the leaves on the trees outside look like so many little brown corpses. It might sound like I believe in signs. I don't. Once you fall for that sort of stuff you might as well believe in fairies. I'm a private eye. I deal in facts. And if you don't deal in facts, you're not dealing.

But corpses aren't all I'm thinking about as I lie on the couch staring at the manhole above me while getting an around-the-corner, side-on, how's-yer-mother third-degree from the shrink. They've drugged me but I can still hear the shrieks of the soprano – accompanied by the kind of sounds coming from next door that usually precede a murder. I imagine there'll be a wild-eyed dame waving the usual irrefutable evidence of adultery – a hotel bill in the name of Mr and Mrs Smith, a letter signed Cuddles, or a lipstick-smudged pair of Y-fronts – and a joker doing his unlevel best to deny the undeniable. A 'domestic', the cops call it, and leave it at that. Until someone gets killed and it's not.

'Mr Nowlc?'

The weapon of choice is usually a knife while the corpse is the one furthest from the cutlery drawer. The shrink's not a private eye, which would account for him not noticing. But I am and I have. The trouble is that the medication blunts my reactions.

'I'd appreciate your undivided attention, Mr Nowlc.'

Nowlc's not my real name but it's more than he's given me. 'How about telling me who *you* are?' I say.

'You don't trust anyone, do you? My name doesn't matter because I'm no more than a sounding board. But if you insist on a name you can call me Dr Caligari – as in the cabinet.'

'Could you repeat the question?'
'How long have you had this feeling?'
'What feeling?'
'The feeling that you're —' he pauses, a chair scrapes, the window slams and the sounds of the fight next door cease '— being followed.'

It's the umpteenth time he's asked me this question and I give him the same answer I've given him umpteen times before.

'It's not a feeling. Pandora exists.'

After the crypto-terrorists tried to destroy the Harbour Bridge in the *Morgue the Merrier* case, I found myself lying in a bed with a teardrop chandelier hanging over my head like a guillotine and Ariadne Sidonia contemplating me like Madam Defarge. All that was missing was the knitting.

'You're safe.' Ariadne might look open but she's as accessible as a Swiss deposit box; I knew she was lying because I'll never be safe. 'Do you want to talk about it?'

I could have said: Talk about what?; to which she'd answer: You know what; to which I'd respond, No, I don't; and she'd say: I think you do. After which the dialogue would spiral off into one of those confrontations like what's happening next door. It's all about control and I don't do control. I try to remember …

It was the night of January 26 — Australia Day — and the early evening fireworks had had their moment of joy and the crowd was baying for more. Me and the bomb-whispering ex-marine, Tsunami, were clinging to a bomb on the Harbour Bridge when the killer came at me. I fought him off and cut the bomb free, falling into the water with it. When I surfaced it was to find Ariadne staring at me like she's staring now with an outboard motor spluttering into life — followed by darkness.

The sun streamed through the expensive window.

'What happened next?' I asked Ariadne.

She frowned at her Rolex. 'Where's that wretched ambulance? The bomb fell on the barge. It didn't go off and you lived because you'd managed to get it under you, detonator uppermost. You were thrown into the Harbour. I hauled you onto the dinghy and had you brought here. And now you're – safe.'

'What happened to the others?'

'Although the bomb didn't explode, everyone on board the barge died – including my son. My ex-lover was among the dead. I don't know what happened to ...'

'Tsunami.'

Also known as Sue Mahoney, the beautiful ex-marine who helped me defuse the bomb.

'... but I imagine she died, too.'

She didn't seem all that sorry. I remember a body falling but couldn't make out whose – the bully that bashed me at school and grew up to become a madman who tried to frame the Caliphate, or the beautiful Tsunami. Which one depends on how much I wanted to fool myself. I shook my head; it was a rough night.

'What happened next?'

'As we sped away, a security boat intercepted us. But when they saw who I was, they waved me on without looking under the canvas. For several times the usual fee, a cab brought us to my house where my servants took over the heavy lifting ...'

Back in the insulting room, I figure I could take the shrink, but that would prove nothing except that I need treatment.

'Pandora exists,' I repeat. 'What makes you think she doesn't?'

'Ms Sidonia said you were trying to kill people in your sleep. You were yelling out Kill! Kill! and trying to strangle her. It's known as nocto-articulation – the revealing of hidden desires while comatose. Tallyrand once said, Speech is a faculty given to man to conceal his thoughts. But hiding one's thoughts is an unrealisable luxury when one's asleep, a time when Eliot – George, not T.S. – said, Light is shed on the depth of the unspoken.'

'You're quoting wrong and out of context.'

The shrink looks at me keenly.

'I imagine that would happen to you a lot. In the common argot, you appear to be as thick as wet cement but in reality you're not unintelligent.

Your success as a private investigator must be due in large part to your confounding people's expectations. But I suggest you look out or you might just outsmart yourself.'

'You're making dollar judgments out of penny rumours and this is a waste of time.' For several days I've been hiding their pills and the effects are finally wearing off; I test it by getting to my feet. 'I'm not sick, I'm leaving and you can't stop me.'

The shrink shakes his head. 'If you go now, your condition will deteriorate and someone will get hurt. In which case, you'd be letting down both Ms Sidonia and your daughter – not to mention the person you end up killing. What could possibly be wrong with your getting better?'

'I'm not sick.'

'Yet both Ms Sidonia and your daughter believe that you are. Let's do a deal. Pretend this is an away game and, if you play ball, I promise it won't go into extra time.'

'Would you mind translating that?'

'Your boat's at the bottom of the Harbour and any friends you ever had have either deserted you or are dead. You've pretty much run out of options. I'm offering you a new life.'

He knows where it hurts, where the pressure points are and how to press them. I lower myself back onto the couch.

Satisfied, he says, 'Let's start at the beginning, shall we?'

Chapter 3

THE DEATH NEXT DOOR

It's like I've committed a crime and when I speak I'm eavesdropping on my own confession.

I was born on a hippy commune just outside the northern NSW town of Nimbin, Australia's drug capital. I had an odd upbringing – I had no schooling and there was a total absence of parental control. I'm only vaguely aware of a great deal of what happened. When I was five my mother killed herself and took my little sister with her. But the memories are disjointed. Dad seemed unable to cope when Mum died so with me and his current girlfriend in tow, he drove away to Melbourne, dumping me on my Aunt Ruby – his sister – on the way. Rube was a private detective who sent me to primary school but took me out when the bullying got bad and brought me up on old gangster movies, ballet, the classics, fingerprinting, disguise and how to handle guns. I married, had a daughter, unmarried and went to live on a boat. I had a lot of enemies so Rube decided to safeguard me by expunging my existence from the public records. I became a private detective. I solve crimes.

'A nice little précis,' the shrink says when I finish. 'Except it hides a great deal more than it reveals. Let's go back to the beginning, shall we, back to your very first memory.'

'I was born in a dam …' That's as far as I get.

'I'm not a Jungian, Mr Nowlc, so I don't buy the concept of awareness in foetuses or the idea of an all-purpose common memory. You don't remember your birth so don't try to fob me off with received information. I want your first real memory – what you recall, not what someone told you.'

'We lived in the bush, my sister was a pest and I got measles.'

The shrink sighs. 'Real memories.'

I find myself talking; it must be the after-effects of the pills. 'I had a recurring nightmare. It involved fire, a giant figure in black and people chanting. I had trouble distinguishing dreams from reality.'

The shrink nods. 'Now we're getting somewhere.'

'*É strano! É strano! In core scolpiti ho quegli accenti!*'

The scream picks up from where the tragic heroine in Verdi's opera screeches, 'How strange! So strange! His words are carved upon my heart!' My guess is someone's lying in a pool of blood next door and nothing's being done about it.

'How about we deal with the elephant in the room, Calvary?' I say. 'There was a fight next door but when I went to investigate, your goons stopped me. Now someone's dead. Deals cut two ways. Let me visit the scene of the crime and I'll tell you anything you want to know.'

The shrink sighs. 'There was no fight next door because there is no next door. I'll let you see for yourself but afterwards you'll have to keep your side of the bargain and talk.'

The lawn's couch – *What else would you expect from a psychiatrist,* the shrink jokes – and I blink in the sunlight like a wombat. The shrubbery's lobotomised and the joint next door – it's a Federation house, dark and ugly – is locked, barred, shuttered and clearly deserted. I stare at it, disorientated.

'You remind me of the explorer lost in deepest Africa,' the shrink says. 'Tribesmen he came across said, We're the Fukarwee. To which our explorer said: Damn, I hoped you'd be able to tell me!' The shrink pauses for effect but there isn't any so he continues. 'This is an ex-boarding school. Ms Sidonia's having it converted into a research institute.' He allows himself a smile. 'It has bars on the windows and high walls. We call it Alcatraz.'

There was a scream and the sound of a body hitting the floor – there's a corpse in the kitchen.

'Have I got to bust this door down, too?'

The shrinkwrap hauls out his hardware – he possesses more keys than a grand piano. 'There's no need. But neither is there a need to investigate. The place is empty, I can assure you.'

'So now I'm hearing things as well as imagining them?'

'You said that, Mr Nowlc.'

'Open the door.'

He sighs, climbs the steps, crosses the verandah, opens the door, stands aside and I enter. They've taken my gat but I've still got my arms and they're out from my sides a la the late, great Jimmy Cagney. I feint to the right, break to the left and end up in the doorway of the death room. The hall's dark but the kitchen's darker. I flick the switch but I'm still in the dark. I haul open the shutters and throw up the window.

To find the room empty and the floor even emptier.

There's no corpse, no blood, no sign of a struggle – the joint's clean. A ring-a-rosy of green benches skirts the walls but the cupboards are empty while the floor's got nothing on it but tiles. There were screams but now there aren't even echoes.

The shrink's in the doorway, smiling.

'You see? It was nothing but your vivid imagination. And now it's my turn.'

'You got me, Calvados,' I say. 'Let's go.'

I'm in a straitjacket. Calvary's goons forced me into a neck-to-waist affair that encloses my arms, with a lock at the back that can only be undone by a second party. He didn't have any choice, he said, because I refused to take the pills. I lie on my back and contemplate the manhole.

'Let's start with free association, shall we? You know what free association is, I presume, Mr Nowlc?'

'Torture.'

'Clever answer. Second question: how did you feel when you witnessed the death of your mother?'

'Powerless.'

'What did you do?'

'Hide.'

'And afterwards?'

'I wanted to stop such things happening again.'

'One word.'

'Obsessed.'

'What are your feelings towards your father?'

'Blame.'

'Blame for what?'

'For the death of my mother and my little sister; for going off god knows where with a woman who wasn't my mother; for just about everything.'

'One word.'

'Abandonment.'

'What did you want to do to him?'

'I –'

'One word.'

'Death and transfiguration.'

'That's three words.'

'Rebirth.'

'Aunt Ruby.'

'Refuge.'

'Bullies.'

'Hurt.'

'Pandora.'

'Kill.'

Chapter 4

I, PANDORA

It's like trying to avoid drowning in quicksand by waving your arms about – you just sink faster. Days pass. I sleep in a dormitory to a background of the ravings of the other inmates and in the mornings return to the inquisitorial chamber for more of the same. Some nights Imogene visits – I know she visits because I hear her ask questions like: *Is he getting better?*

To which a voice replies: It's like doing a trepan. He clams up just as we think we're making progress. It's as if he'd rather die than divulge his secret.

What secret?

That's what we're trying to find out.

'Why can't I see my daughter when she visits?' I ask.

'What makes you think she visits?'

'Because I hear voices and one's hers.'

'You're imagining the voices just as you imagined Pandora and the death next door.'

'Does she or doesn't she visit?'

'I don't live here so I don't know what happens when I'm gone. Let's just say I think it highly unlikely. So, why don't you tell me about Pandora.'

'What's there to tell? Someone's following me and that's what I call her.'

'Why?'

'Why is she following me?'

'No – why do you call her Pandora?'

'When I was with Aunt Rube, I studied Greek and Roman mythology: Pandora released evil into an otherwise innocent world by opening a boxful of vices. The name's appropriate because I was innocent before she arrived on the scene. Besides which, I'm pretty sure that she said on one occasion, I, Pandora.'

'Just as you're sure there was a murder next door and you heard your daughter's voice?'

'That's different.'

'How?'

I open my eyes to find the shrink bent over his pad, scribbling furiously. 'I thought you said you weren't taking notes.'

Calvary doesn't look up. 'I'm not – I'm working something out.' He frowns for a moment and when he looks up he's triumphant. 'I've got it.'

I start drowning. 'Got what?'

'I noted early on that you're partial to wordplay – it's part of your strategy to avoid reality. You were word-playing when you made up your cryptonym – Nowlc being an anagram of Clown. And, consciously or unconsciously, you were word-playing when you named your nemesis.'

'But I didn't – she –'

'I, Pandora,' says the shrink softly. 'In an attempt to distance yourself from your problems, you came up with the kind of truth that usually only attends sleep-talking.'

'Now you're the one doing the imagining.'

'You're a most interesting case,' Calvados replies – so softly that I could be imagining that, too. 'It's a case of Where the fuck are we all over again, isn't it? Because, reshuffled, the letters in I, Pandora form a very interesting and significant word.'

'To whom?'

'To me, to you, to whomsoever you like. It's an old-fashioned word but you're an old-fashioned kind of guy.' He takes a deep breath. 'Psychiatry's come a long way since the bad old days when they locked madmen away in dungeons, chained to walls and left to grovel in their own excrement. And just as the treatment's changed so, too, has the language. Patients have become guests; we listen instead of turning a deaf ear; and we medicate them instead of beating them senseless. Where once we trundled through people's psyches in horse-drawn carts we now fly straight to the moon. What I'm referring to is a word derived from the Greek where para means irregular and noid is mind. Which adds up to a distracted mind.'

'I don't know what you're talking about.'

'Of course you don't. And I suppose you also don't know that I,
Pandora is an anagram of paranoid.'

Chapter 5

THE MARK OF A MADMAN

It's a long time before I answer. During which I recall the unseen visits of Imogene and the non-existent murder next door and, before that, Pandora paying *her* frequent visits – which always occurred at times of greatest stress. When I return to the present, Calgary's watching me closely.

'Pandora's real,' I say. 'What I call her has nothing to do with anything. Just because your name can convert into –' I think for a moment '– A1 garlic doesn't mean you scare vampires. The name Pandora's no more than a coincidence.'

The shrink gives me one of his looks. 'You think your phones are bugged and people are out to get you. Everyone's suspect and violence is the answer to everything. Put bluntly, you're a psychopath who might one day kill a loved one in mistake for the Devil. You describe your nemesis as "horribly scarred" one minute and "beautiful" the next. The reason for the discrepancy is Pandora doesn't exist. Pandora, I said, to which you replied, Kill. You need to be cured.'

'Only the sick need curing.'

Caligari sighs. 'And only the sane will admit they might be mad. You're sick and you need treatment.'

'Or I'm well, in which case everyone's happy.'

'That's a Band-Aid solution. And Band-Aid solutions tend to end badly, with madmen leaping off high buildings because they think they can fly or murdering a loved one because they think she's the Devil.'

He's wrong. He must be.

'There's another option,' I say.

'What's that?'

480

'We could cut a deal.'

He sighs again. 'No more deals, Nowlc.'

'If I am delusional, if you're right and I need treatment before I hurt someone, I'd agree to whatever it takes – pills, electro-convulsive therapy or a lobotomy. But give me a chance to prove I'm not.'

Caligula shakes his head. 'The thing is that we don't need your agreement to treat you. You don't exist. Besides which, you're basically behind bars. We can treat you however we like.'

'But what if you're wrong?'

'We can't take that risk. If Pandora is a figment of your imagination, you need treatment. And when I advise Ariadne of my diagnosis, she'll almost certainly give me the go ahead.'

'The go ahead for what?'

'Surgery.'

'But what if Pandora exists?' I persist. 'That would mean that I'm the one in danger. What if one day I wind up dead with a knife in my back? That wouldn't look too good on your record, would it?'

The shrink holds up his preying mantis hands. 'Only it wouldn't be on my record. You see, this is a private research facility and I'm accountable only to Ms Sidonia. You imagined the voice of your daughter, you believed you heard a murder next door and you think you're being followed. We're not talking about a neurosis here, some minor disorder. Yours is a full-blown psychosis. You could commit murder – so sure some innocent person's Pandora that you end up killing them.'

Aeons pass. Dinosaurs tread a ferocious planet and sabre tooth tigers roam bloodstained veldts; ice packs melt, the seas rise and there are islands. No man is an island. What if he's right? Hi, Immo, I'm going to kill you. No, no and no! Her life can't end like that. But neither can mine. Argument:

I'm a prisoner

The shrink says I need treatment

If he's right I'm a menace but if he's wrong I'm as good as dead

I don't want to die

I've got to find Pandora

But first I've got to escape.

I prepare the way. 'Okay, you're right. My aim's to protect society. Clearly I'm a danger to society and so I've got to be neutralised. I've got no choice. I agree to treatment.'

The shrink looks suddenly wary. 'Why the sudden change of heart?'

'Because I don't want to hurt anyone.'

'You're up to something.'

I shrug as much as the zoot suit allows. 'Who's paranoid now?'

It's late afternoon and streaks of cadmium orange dribble down the rungs of the ladder and onto the half-painted walls. I'm wearing a straitjacket, there are bars on the windows and the place is crawling with guards. It's a situation that would challenge Houdini. But I've got a motive, which is to prove my sanity, and I'm a great believer in motives.

The shrink's nodding.

'All right, we'll strike while the iron's hot. That's a blacksmithing term, Mr Nowlc — in order to be worked, a horseshoe needs to be malleable and at the moment you're malleable. I'll tell Ms Sidonia we're going to operate.'

'When?'

'Now.'

Description of room: six paces by six; low ceiling with manhole; barred window; one recently-patched door; couch; heavy oak desk; chair; and in the corner a stepladder. There's not much to play with but the game's on. The shrink's on the phone saying, I have good news for you, Ms Sidonia, when I hit him with the bad news in the form of a shoulder charge which upturns the desk. He can't say he wasn't warned. I'm a madman who could kill at any time and this is the time.

I knee the couch out of the way and, using my upper body, manoeuvre the ladder into place. When I was a swan in Swan Lake, my arms were pinioned by feathers. It's the same now, except they're no longer feathers. I lean into the ladder, climb, head-butt the manhole cover out of the way and I'm halfway into the ceiling when the door crashes open and I hear the pounding of boots. Hands clutch at my legs, my heels find a couple of heads and desperation does the rest. I twist onto my back and, using positional reflex, angle west across the rafters in the direction of New South Head Road, using feet, knees, shoulders, head and hands but not my arms because they're encased in the straitjacket. Alarms go off — thin, high and intermittent like drip feed in a torture chamber. From the sound of the feet hammering down the hall, they've worked out where I'm headed. I change direction.

The trouble with Plan B is that the other person ends up driving. And the trouble with *this* Plan B is that the other person's mad. I crash-land into a madhouse.

They no longer call it Bedlam. A big man's wearing a tea cosy on his head; a little dame's screaming obscenities at a photograph; two men are playing poker using make-believe cards; and two girls are arguing with their backs to one another. There aren't any nurses because they've metamorphosed into guards and are looking for me. The patients are screaming. Only one – a small man with Mickey Mouse ears – isn't.

'Are you sane?' I ask him.

He nods his head. 'I'm as mad as a hatter. I committed myself even though this place is so expensive you'd have to be crazy to be here. That's how they know I'm insane.'

If I've learnt one thing from Calvary it's the fact that the mad will never admit it; I turn my back on him. 'Unlock me.'

'Take me with you.'

'Sorry but I can't do that.'

'Then I can't unlock your jacket.'

There's no choice; feet are pounding down the hallway. 'All right, I'll take you with me. But hurry.'

The other inmates show no interest – it's as if by not acknowledging my existence, I'm not there. The coat comes off. I raise my voice. It's the voice of authority.

'I want all of you at the door on the double – now!'

They're mad but they're brainwashed to obey orders. There's at least twenty of them and when they're assembled at the door I raise my voice over the hubbub in the hall.

'Now we're going to play a little game.'

They nudge each other like kids in a playground – a tall man with wild hair nods, a young woman smiles and a little dame in a pinafore jigs her arms about like she's about to break into a foxtrot.

'Let's call it The Great Escape. When the door opens, run. People dressed as doctors and nurses will try to stop you but just remember it's part of the game. If you escape, you've earned your freedom. If you don't, you deserve to be here. Let's do it – ready, set –'

My newfound best friend tugs at my sleeve. 'It won't work. These people are all promise and no performance. It's the whispers.'

The man must be mad. 'Whispers?'

'Not whispers – Rispers. Risperidone. Hide in the broom cupboard and the screws will think you're not here and when they leave, I'll let you out.'

'What about you?'

'I'm madder than any of them. When the pills wear off, voices in my head tell me to kill people.' He opens the door to the broom cupboard. 'Get in.'

The only difference between him and me could be the ears. 'There's a lot of parts to what you just said and I only believe a couple of them. The trouble is I don't know which ones.' I turn to the assembled motley. '– Go!'

Chapter 6

NAMES FOR THE NEMESIS

The list takes shape and the shape's a Rorschach inkblot – the kind where you see things that aren't there. In the space headed *WHAT AM I LOOKING FOR?* I write: *Pandora*. For *WHAT DOES SHE LOOK LIKE?* I put: *Female, masked, dressed in black, carries a knife*. Then, *PROPENSITY: Murder*. *WHEREABOUTS: Unknown*. *SPECIAL INSTRUCTIONS: Avoid killing the wrong person*.

I'm on a rickety chair at a broken chart table on an unclaimed boat – one of thousands dotting Sydney Harbour – with birdlime on the superstructure, mould on the deck and angled in the water like a madwoman nodding her last. I've looked and there's no corpse, no sign anyone's been here in the immediate past or is likely to visit any time in the future. Nothing except for a notepad and pencil, an unopened bottle of port, a bit of kick in the ship's battery and a computer. I find an extension cord, rig up the computer to the 240-volt power system, take the wine and laptop topside, key in the password sticky-taped to the lid, press ENTER and uncork the bottle.

Under ANYTHING ELSE? I write: Suspect might be armed so approach with care. LIST OF SUSPECTS: Make it as broad as you can, Rube would insist – cast the net wide because it could be the person least likely. Don't omit any names – you need all the fish you can fry. Pandora's been around forever but you've got to forget the little matter of age and deal with that later. First work out motive and opportunity. Imogene.

485

My daughter is back at police school, Caligari said, but why should I trust him? Or is that my paranoia speaking? Paranoia's what makes me a good private eye — everyone's guilty until proven innocent. I try to shake the kid from my brainpan but I'm investigating a death and it could be mine. I've got to focus on the women in my life. First cab off the rank: Tsunami.

Word association washes up Tsunami but Tsunami's dead. The night on the Bridge a figure flew through the air and it might have been Tsunami but she could have survived. I Gargle *The Sydney Morning Horrible* and check the Australia Day deaths. There's no Susan Mahoney, ex-marine major, or anything like it. A figure fell from the Bridge and it might have been Tsunami but that doesn't prove rabbits. She could have slipped under the radar. I continue with the list.

Next suspect: Annie, my ex-squeeze, the heart-on-sleeve social worker. Strike one and two: she's the wrong size — too small — and too young. Only I've decided to forget young. Strike three: There isn't a bad bone in her. She still goes on the list. I take another swig of the hard-boiled and go back to the beginning, back to Sally, the beautiful surgeon who hired me in the case of the Hood With No Hands to check on her husband.

After that, in chronological order: Monica Best, the dame who helped me in the case of the Horses for Corpses — tall, blue-eyed, untrustworthy and capable of anything; Hélène Dalmatian — aka Hell and Damnation — from Bullets at the Ballet: amethyst-eyed and also as untrustworthy as stink; Tsunami … I complete the list but there's someone missing. Leave out nobody, however unlikely, Rube would always say. I add the name.

Dark clouds gather, thunder ricochets across the Harbour and rain starts to fall. The wine's sour but, like we sailors always say, any port in a storm. I rearrange the names in order of suspicion but it doesn't work that way so I apply reverse chronology to prevent the dice landing in any preordained order, all the time reminding myself that anything's possible. Result:

Sidonia, Ariadne
Mahoney, Sue
Best, Monica
Dalmatian, Hélène
Kane, Sally
My ex-wife Salina.

Ariadne Sidonia had me at her mercy. Question: Why would she want to neutralise me? She consorts with criminals but who in Sydney doesn't? They call killers *colourful identities* and make television series about them. Further motive – I'm a private detective who could stumble across something I wasn't meant to. A third motive is what she told me: *Left to your own devices someone might end up dead and I'd get involved.* She had the wherewithal to neutralise me, so why not use it? Fourth motive: She's Pandora.

Proof positive I'm a danger is a dozen madmen – including at least one psychopath – screaming along New South Head Road, Vauclues, with doctors, nurses and guards screaming after them and cops arresting the most likely. Ariadne will organise someone to come after me – she's got the resources. She's dangerous so I put her on standby and move on to the next.

I need to see Imogene. To my surprise, she agrees.

'How are you, darling?' I ask when I call.

It's a long time before she answers and, when she does, it's like she's talking to a corpse. 'I told you not to contact me.'

'I was worried.'

'Maybe there's cause to worry but you brought me up to look after myself so you'll have to trust me. We can meet one more time but after that you mustn't call again.'

A lump comes to my throat. 'Of course, it was just –'

But it isn't just and when she hangs up it's as unjust as it can be. Unjust because I'm her Dad and I love her and I haven't done anything wrong. Unjust because I forgot to ask my second question which was: Did you commit me to Ariadne's asylum and come around afterwards asking questions? But I can't call back. Besides which, she's agreed to a meeting. Besides which again, she's not Pandora and my job is to find Pandora. Like Rube always said: Bury yourself in your work.

Maybe I only *thought* I first met Monica Best in the case of the *Death of a Ladies' Man* – a woman on the high side of tall with beautiful eyes and even more beautiful lips. She pretended to be a coincidence but turned out to be an insurance investigator using me to do her dirty work for her. Nothing wrong with that, only I don't like being used. *How come you know how to hurt people?* I asked her. *I went to finishing school,* she replied.

Some people are hard to find and others are harder. Because of her height, Monica Best stands out in a crowd – I've just got to find the right crowd. She used to be in insurance but in Sydney no-one's ever what they used to be. Her size is the sticking point. Monica's well over the six-foot mark, while Pandora's more or less standard. But that could be in my mind and at the moment my mind's in question. However much I want to find Monica Best, it won't be a stroll in the proverbial.

Insurance companies are like sewers – they stink and the flow's all one-way. HOW – that is, Home Or Wealth, the company that used to – or still does – employ Monica Best, is as tight with information as it would be with payouts. But the voice on the phone is as smooth as strawberries and ice-cream.

'Helping people is our business. Is your inquiry business or personal?'
'Business.'
'And the nature of that business?'
'It's an insurance claim – to do with personal property and therefore private.'
'I can help you with that. Do you have a file number?'
'No.'
'A name?'
I click off.

The last thing I knew, Imogene was in the police academy. Now she's in front of me wearing a uniform several sizes too big for her but not carrying weapons, not even a nightstick. Something's wrong.
'What is it, Chickadee?'
She was a babe in arms who became a kid, then – all too quickly – someone who made her own decisions. One of those decisions was to become a cop. It hurt at the time but you learn to roll with the punches.

We're in O'Leary's and the clientele – drug pushers, hitmen, crooked coppers and general lowlife – are casting covert glances at this cop-avoiding private detective talking to a cop. The world's been tipped on its head; nothing's sacrosanct.

Imogene casts a look around. 'Can we go outside?'

The air in Patterson Street's foetid but it's sweet vermouth compared to O'Leary's. We head up Darlinghurt Road towards the Cross. Criminals pose as taxi drivers and you can't trust anyone, not even yourself. A spruiker bleats outside a strip joint, a prostitute does a jig for the passing trade and Imogene's got a problem. Correction: a problem's got Imogene.

'I can't say what it is,' she says, 'or you're likely to go off like that gun you once showed me – half-cocked. I'm no longer at the academy.'

Chapter 7

A MESSAGE FOR MONICA

'Do you need my help?' I say.

'From what I hear, you're the one needing help.'

'What have you heard?'

'At the academy we're kept apprised of any news involving the Force Field – that is, what's happening regarding the police outside the academy. One item caught my attention because Ariadne Sidonia's name was attached to it – a breakout from some psych facility followed by a hunt for the instigator. I don't have to be Sherlock Holmes to know the instigator was you.'

I can't pretend we walk on in silence because the Cross is never silent – sirens wail, tyres screech, people scream and you can hear the guns go off if you're listening. I cut back to the action.

'You tell me the academy's not going well.' I can't say I'm not pleased; I've never liked cops and I like the idea of my daughter becoming one even less. 'What's the problem?'

Imogene shrugs her shoulders. 'There was an incident, they're holding an inquiry and while they're holding their inquiry, I'm persona non grata.'

'C'mon Immo, give me a clue.'

'Giving you a clue is giving you the answer.'

I change the subject. 'How's Mum?'

'I'm not staying at home, if that's what you're asking. They put me somewhere but I can't tell you where it is. I tricked my way out to see you because I knew you'd make inquiries if I didn't.' She glances at her watch. 'I've been out too long, I need to get back.'

I've got to ask and I've got to ask fast.

'What do you know about Pandora?'

She looks at me strangely. 'Your so-called "nemesis"? Only that I've never seen her.'

She puts quotes around the word so I don't pursue it. 'At least you're still alive, Immo.'

'What's that supposed to mean?'

'Fathers worry.'

'There's nothing to worry about.'

Which tells me one thing.

And that is that there is.

My ex, Salina, opens the door and stares daggers at me. I imagine her *throwing* daggers at me and get in my two-bob's worth before she can reach for the weaponry.

'I've got a couple of questions, Sal.'

'What, like: Do you regret meeting me? To which the answer's a resounding yes. Or: Do I want you dead? In which case the answer's yes again. You're never going to get out of my life are you, Rainbow? It's like you're tailing me. Although I believe a better word would be stalking.'

'I thought that you might be stalking me.'

Salina stares at me for a good minute. A minute's a long time when Salina's staring at you. It's like being face to face with a psychopath — you begin the countdown to death. Salina's got sharp nails and maybe also somewhere there's a knife.

But instead of trying to kill me, she starts laughing. At first it's a slow laugh but then it gathers momentum and becomes a shrill laugh, a kookaburra's laugh, the kind you might hear in a ghost train, the kind that chases you to the grave, and she's still laughing long after I've gone. I know because I can hear her a block away, even though I've got my hands over my ears.

Bury yourself in your work and be thankful for large mercies — Imogene's alive and there's nothing you can do to help her unless she asks. The chest tags that HOW — the insurance company — issues to staff aren't rolled gold. They haven't even got feature measurements or fingerprinting — just a face and number. I bump into an employee, pat his chest as I step away from him, insta-camera his ID, return it without him being aware I borrowed it and take the result to Ace Mollema.

Ace was one of the kids on the funny farm – the name we kids gave to the collective at Nimbin – except that he left some time before me. One day he was there, the next he wasn't. He became a spook – a spy with Australia's intelligence agency, ASIO – and I last saw him when I needed a fake passport; last spoke to him when I discovered he'd dudded me. I ask him now to make a copy of the ID with my face on it. He still feels guilty so he does me the favour. He's also got something on his mind.

'Do you ever think about the funny farm?' he asks.

'Just the one copy,' I say.

'When my grandparents took me away, they called it a kin-nap.'

'How long will it take?'

'I'll have it ready for you within the hour.'

However much security people have got, it's always going to have holes in it and when I enter the HOW Tower wearing the uniform from the Prop Shop and waving my fake pass the guard doesn't take his eyes off his comic. And at the second hurdle – the one where you actually need to look like who you're pretending to be – when I display the brown paper parcel, the dame looks up from her crossword.

'What's Basic instinct, the crime of being someone else, in two words – eight letters and five?'

'It's id and robbery – the answer you're looking for is identity theft.'

She smiles as she clicks open the door. 'That gets you into the holograph.'

HOW rents floors number thirty-eight to fifty and I start on thirty-eight, entering the lift in the company of a bunch of workers saying, 'Parcel for Monica Best'. Which gets me frowns and shrugs all the way to the top, where I'm still saying, 'Parcel for Monica Best'.

An ugly little joker looks up from a sausage machine behind the cafeteria counter.

'You mean Monica West – as in: The men she rejects make Monica West the best? You're too late, mate, she's gone.'

I turn to go. Always turn to go. 'Sorry to have bothered you.'

'Hold on a moment there, Hotfoot.' He comes around the counter mopping his hands. 'Nice lady, Monica, despite her height – always a kind word for the little man. What do you want?'

'I've got a message for her – in fact, a parcel – and this is her last known address.'

'Last known to you maybe but not to me.'

The clock's running but I can't appear to be running with it because that's when they smell a rat. People are scared of rats. I start for the lift.

'I don't have to do the delivery.'

'Jeez – just a minute, will you?' I wait; he's keen to talk; always wait when they're keen to talk. 'Monica was beautiful and a top operator. Nice person, too. But she had her enemies. When things went bad, I overheard people in the lunch queue saying she deserved it.' He pauses. 'There might have been something else, too; the feeling she was – well, different.'

'I'd better go.'

'Her Waterloo was a disputed claim for insurance. The matter went to court but it was her word against the claimant's – a Greek woman whose husband was a conman.'

The sequel to Death of a Ladies' Man.

'It would have helped if a certain private detective had given evidence but he disappeared like he never existed, leaving Monica to pick up the pieces. The judge didn't give an inch. When he ordered the company to pay, Monica's fellow workers actually cheered. When she was sacked, she sued for wrongful dismissal but she got no support.'

'I'll mark the parcel Address unknown.'

'But other people's enemies are my friends so I gave my condolences and we kept in touch. She got a job but not in insurance because the company blacklisted her. What's in the parcel?'

'Money, I think.'

'I know where you can find her.'

'I'm a delivery boy not a private detective. It's not my job to find her.'

'You don't have to. I can tell you where she went.'

Chapter 8

THE KARATE KILLER

He's built like a Mack truck and comes at me fists first, a giant with a face that didn't evolve along with the rest of him. I dance to the right but that's when I discover he's a *dan* – a black belt in karate – his beautifully executed *mawashigeri* – roundhouse kick – catching me as I do the splits. He follows with a full-frontal kick – a *maegeri* – but I'm ready for that, too, and a *glissé* with arms transposed gets me out of the way. It's nice to see the kind of damage ballet can do to a *dan*.

'Kiai!' he yells, which roughly translates as: You bastard!

'The same to you,' I reply and headbutt him in the gut.

We're in Aces, the nightclub that lawmakers are always going to crack down on but never get around to because it's part of their investment portfolio. Its façade features nice people smiling sweetly at each other while inside it's wall-to-wall drugs.

All I did was mention the name Monica Best.

It's daylight so the joint's empty if you don't count the thug. He comes at me again, this time with murder in his eyes where before it had only been mayhem. But I'm ready for the ashibarai – the leg-sweep – making myself as small a target as possible for a six-foot-something detective. Bring it to a conclusion, I tell myself. You're looking for information, not for trouble. He's got his eyes on my chudan – my mid-section – which means he's got another target – my knees or my head – because he wants to finish it, too.

Always beware the gyakuzuki – the reverse punch. It's a short-travel hit, and delivery can occur from a standing position or with the deliverer retreating or advancing. Again he's looking elsewhere which means he's going to go for my midriff. The standard counter's the kick that weakens

the punchline. He's ready for it but that's all he's ready for. I do a grand
jeté, legs apart and arms spread like I'm flying – I can almost hear Hérold's
music for La Fille Mal Gardée, almost see the dancer Alain as I snap my
foot in the pug's face and he goes down. It's like kicking a habit – it might
be hard but it's well worth the effort. I pour water over him out of a
bucket from the bar.

'Where is she?'

'I don't remember.'

The pressure point's just below the ear, the one that results in paralysis
or – if I'm not careful – death. Just as fat men possess the same skeleton as
thin ones, the placement of nerves never varies. I remember the shrink's
warning: One day you'll kill someone you don't intend to. I don't ease off.

'What did she do here?'

'She bounced.'

'Why did she leave?'

'The boss's girl thought she was after the boss so she spread rumours.'

'Where did she go?'

'How would I know?'

'Because you want to live.' I fight back the urge to really hurt him.
'Where did she go, Spitgut?'

She got a job in a rival club, he says, but that didn't last long, either.
Where did she go after that? The thug produces a thug's leer. When you're
as tall a poppy as that dame, the only way to go is down. I thump him in
the guts and dump him.

You hear of ugly drunks ending up in the gutter but not beautiful
women. That's because by the time they're on the greasy slide to nowhere,
they're no longer beautiful. I decide to press two lemons with the one
squeezer and go in search of Annie.

Annie's a former squeeze but right now she's just another ex, yet another
dame who's better off without me. She tends to the homeless and I find
her in a park in Darlinghurt.

'Hi, Annie.'

She's crouched over a bundle of rags. She risks her life for others but
anyone could be Pandora and she's not about to jump at a voice she'd
prefer to forget.

'I'm looking for someone.'

She doesn't look up. 'You're always looking for someone, Rainbow. If it's not a suspect, it's the love of your life.'

I stretch the truth. 'This one's at risk of dying.'

'Everyone's at risk of dying – that's one thing I know better than anyone. But before you go, help me get Xavier into the van.'

Xavier's a bundle of dirty linen that stinks of hard liquor and grunts.

'Her name's Monica Best,' I say as I help with the lift. 'She's tall and very beautiful.' Already Annie hates her and Annie hates nobody with the possible exception of me; she slams the door hard in case my hand's in the way. 'The reason I'm after her is that she might be Pandora.'

Annie shoots me a funny look. 'Your so-called nemesis? Don't tell me you're still living in the threat of shadows and the hope of eternal love. When are you going to accept that Pandora doesn't exist and nor does the love of your life? No-one will ever commit to you, Rainbow, because you can't commit to yourself. Now if you'll excuse me I have work to do.'

She's wandered off the main track; I steer her back on. 'Where would I find her?'

'Who – Pandora or this Monica woman?'

'Either or both.'

'If I tell you, will you leave me in peace?'

'I promise.'

Annie climbs behind the wheel. 'She's at The Three Sisters.'

'Why would she be at a women's refuge? Monica's not afraid of anyone.' Annie starts the engine; there's time for one last question. 'Tell me it isn't you, Annie.'

There's time for the question but not for the answer.

She's already driven away.

If you're looking for a straight-line job, avoid detecting. Because in detecting the best way from A to B is mostly by way of Z. This is due to:

Red herrings – which distract the investigator because, like their name suggests, they're brightly coloured and stink; and

Baseless assumptions.

Watching Annie go leaves a hole in my heart as big as The Gap, the cliff at Watsons Bay that people jump off when they're in a bad way. We used to be lovers but we'll never be lovers again. Annie said I'm married to my work and maybe she's right. But going by what she said about Pandora, she left me because I'm a basket case. But that's a baseless assumption and finding Pandora will prove it. I hotfoot it down South Darling, up Cleveland to Broadway, past the City Morgue to the refuge.

Chapter 9

THE THREE SISTERS

I work my way to a spruce tree on a rise overlooking the refuge and while waiting for inspiration try to talk myself out of Monica Best. This is the *delusional phase* in detecting and goes something like:

She's too young – Pandora's been following me since before Monica was born

She's too tall and

She's got no motive.

Think positive. Forget her height and age. She was an insurance agent, hired to track down frauds. I came across her in the Death of a Ladies' Man, waiting for me behind locked doors. A strong dame who knew her way around self-defence, which puts her in the ballpark. Setting aside height and age, what could be a possible motive? She could hate men and this man in particular. But that's a stretch of the imagination and I don't do stretches of the imagination. Or she's mad and the mad don't need motives. Which is pretty much what the shrink said about me.

What bounces her out of the reckoning is her age. Monica postdates Pandora, which means that at thirty-something – even if she's pushing forty – Monica's still too young. But that's a red herring if not also a baseless assumption. So forget young and return to motive. Why would Monica follow me, haunt me, track me down and put me in fear for my life?

Why does anyone follow anyone? Why do stalkers stalk? Out of hatred, anger, jealousy? Whatever it is, they don't want the object of their affections to be with anyone else. I'd rather you were dead is the usual sentiment. Because their so-called love is a sense of ownership where the mate's regarded as a possession. But that's not why Monica would be on the follow. We've got no history, unless it's a history I'm not aware of. Apart from which, she's not the one doing the following – I am. Return to motive:

Love – discount love

I've hurt someone close to her or she thinks I have – an outside chance

Mistaken identity; I'm a six-foot-something private detective that dresses bad – discount

Anger – but at what?

Other.

I could be talking about myself. How can I not be a stalker when I'm hanging around a women's refuge in the middle of the night, looking for a woman?

Any one of those cars pootling along Grebe Point Road could contain Pandora. There are too many suspects and too little time. But cutting corners leaves holes in the net that could let in a shark. I've got to follow up all suspects – including the most unlikely – and I've got to do it thorough. If there's no Pandora, it means I'm mad. Monica's a suspect and there's someone behind the bush.

The bush is an oleander – pink-flowered and poisonous – while the figure's grey-tracksuited and even more dangerous than the bush. I don't have to be a mind reader to know what he's after. Which means it's business as usual at the refuge.

There's the familiar click-clack-click of bolt cutters as he severs the wires but no alarms go off because they're neutralised. He's wearing a head-mounted torch with its beam directed at the fence so I can't make out his features. All I know is that he's big. But at night, everyone's big, like the bats of my childhood. If they get in your hair, you have to cut off their legs, my mother warned. If you need the scissors, they're beside the bed. In my five-year-old mind, those bats were vampires.

My reaction's slow because I didn't expect him. I forgot the number one danger in detecting, the red herring. I thought the figure with the bolt cutters was a break-in because I was supposed to think that. I thought the target was someone in the refuge when all the time it was me. I was *meant* to be watching the man with the bolt cutters – that's why he was there. I'm a sitting patootie.

There's no time to respond. Thug number two's got me pinioned, his hands clenched at my chest, and I feel my stored air diminish as the figure at the fence starts our way. When you're caught by surprise you feign helplessness to make your attacker relax. But that's what the Squeezer's expecting because he's a trained attacker. Which means that he's ready for the relax ploy, I'll run out of breath and I'll be dead. But that's before anger takes over. Anger at my not realising what they were up to; anger at being tricked. And my anger neutralises common sense like the figure at the fence has neutralised the alarm. Instinct takes over. And that's what saves me.

I lock my elbows and the Squeezer's arms find themselves wrapped around steel. I twist out of his clutches but he's ready, his fist raised to deliver the death blow just as Fence Man arrives. All thought deserts me and I'm left with nothing but the blind, savage will to survive. Something tells me to duck as the bolt cutters scythe over my head, as big as a battleaxe and just as lethal. The Squeezer screams as the cutters crunch into his face. Then Fence Man's onto me.

At times like these your mind functions on two levels. On one level, I'm coordinating my responses to my attackers while on another, more conscious, level I'm trying to work out who they are. Because knowing who they are is how I'll survive. That's how I'll know if they want to kill me or just keep me for questioning. The answer decides the mode and ferocity of their attack and therefore my counter to it. I feint to the left, fall and slide down the slope as Fence Man comes after me.

This is not some random event – a raving lunatic and his mate after the maniac's missus. Nor is it a couple of passers-by who happen to be in the vicinity. The wire-cutting exercise was a warm-up while the assault's the main event. They were tailing me when I was with Annie – possibly before. They heard her direct me to The Three Sisters, worked out their plan of action, picked up a pair of bolt cutters if they didn't already have them, and were waiting when I arrived because they had wheels while I didn't.

But that doesn't tell me who they are or why they're after me. You're imagining things, the shrink said. Only I'm not imagining this. I'm on the ground, the Squeezer's somewhere in the spruce needles and Fence Man's coming for me again.

I get to my feet but the needle-covered ground's slippery and my footing's uncertain. My attacker's head torch has slipped about his neck, up-lighting his face. I don't know him, which means he's an out-of-towner. A bent cop? A crony of some crook I crossed? A hitman? He

could be any of a number of criminals or an accomplice. He's male so he's
not Pandora. So who is he and why is he after me?

When you're under attack, never over-think. Thinking's dangerous.
Think and you lose focus, think and you waver. The thug senses my
indecision and, grabbing me by the hair, drags me to the ground. With
the advantage of certainty he's astride me like the fifth horseman of
the Apocalypse, his raised arm outlined against the moon, half-lit face
triumphant. He's Death and he's got me. The arm begins its descent.

He's not keeping me for questioning.

Darkness is death, death darkness. There's a flash — the kind of light that
was there when the world began — then darkness. I manage to twist so the
slicing-down hand catches the point of my shoulder instead of my throat.
It's the best I can do. The shoulder goes numb and I roll further down
the hill. From somewhere come the strains of *Death and the Maiden* — the
string quartet in D minor. Did Schubert call it that because of its dying
fall — the death drop? I glimpse something between my attacker and the
moon. It could be my imagination or it might be a bat — there are fig trees
around here and bats like figs. I steel myself for the death blow.

Chapter 10

BODIES ARE MY BUSINESS

A cat's got nine lives but a private detective's got none. A gumshoe's a dead man walking, surprised to wake up in the morning and find he's still alive. He treads the shadows – a wraith, a spectre, a phantom. And I'm one step along even from that. I don't exist. And now I'm about to exist even less.

I'm held down by one thug while the third – the one outlined against the moon – arrives like pestilential rain. If they get in your hair, chop off their legs – the scissors are next to the bed. I grapple among stones, twigs, leaves – a child scrabbling for scissors – and my hand closes on the bolt cutters. I raise my arm to get the cutters between me and the figure coming at me out of the sky while trying to dislodge the figure astride me. He was clutching a pair of bolt cutters – he must have been breaking into the refuge when he was surprised. I feel the thud of a body, the bolt cutters crash onto my chest, then there's silence. Silence and utter darkness.

'Rainbow!'

Rainbow was the name my mother gave me when I was born and a rainbow appeared in the sky. It's a sign! she said, although she didn't have a clue what of. My little Mister Rainbow, she crooned. She must have been as mad as a tailless wallaroo even then. I hear the voice from the past croon, 'Rainbow!'

I'm dead and I'm hearing voices. Dying smells of blood, decaying leaves, rotten spruce needles and dirt. Let me lie here and decay, part of the Great Plan – death and configuration. Or should that be transfiguration? And if transfiguration, what does that mean? If rebirth, why not say so?

'Mum,' I hear myself reply.

'Rainbow!'

She's giving me the kiss of Death, her cold mouth pressed hard against mine like she needs to devour me. It's Pandora come to claim me. I struggle but Death's astride me, her weight too great for me to move. My shoulder hurts, my head, my chest, my face. My lungs are bursting because my mouth is blocked by this succubus crushing me. The pressure intensifies, unaccountably eases, then intensifies again. I sense a pattern here and I can do patterns. I count five-second intervals and realise what it means. It's the Silvester method of cardio-pulmonary resuscitation – CPR. Which means that it's not the kiss of death at all but the kiss of life. I open my eyes. It's her.

I didn't check face, clothes, pockets of the corpse. When there's a body that doesn't belong to you, you get away fast. Because when people find bodies they start looking for who made them that way. I ought to know. Bodies are my business.

I don't know how far she lugs, drags, half-carries me. One rib feels fractured where the Squeezer did his work, my shoulder aches, a leg defies straightening and my face is bruised. There's nowhere that doesn't hurt. Pandora's dragging me along a footpath when her foot catches on a root, a streetlamp or a bench and she stumbles and falls. That's when she sees one of my shoes and my fedora are missing. And that's when I see that my rescuer isn't Pandora at all but Monica Best.

'We can't leave any evidence,' she says. 'I need to go back.'

She's away for an eternity, during which I drop in and out of consciousness. Bats circle and I don't know if they're imagined or real. Footsteps hurry past and there are cars. I'm dead. Then I'm alive again as hands force the shoe back on my foot, cram the hat on my head and get me to my feet.

'Christ, you're heavy,' she says as she carries on dragging.

After a while she stops again. Next to us I make out a fence and decide that the world must be made of fences — fences to keep people in, to keep them out. Tall, short, wire, wood, corrugated-iron, stone or brick — fences, defences and offences. Monica's breathing hard, a winded animal, blown.

'Why were you at the refuge?' she manages to ask.

'I was following someone.'

'You were lucky I was there.'

'You were the someone I was following.'

Cases should be discrete — separate — but at least two have become joined: the hunt for Pandora and the one where someone's hunting me.

Early-morning workers hurry past wearing Hi-Viz jackets and carrying lunch boxes. Headlamps impale us and a cyclist wobbles off the footpath onto the road. You can't stagger about inner-city streets in the early hours of the morning looking like us without someone calling the cops. We get going again.

We're on a patch of grass overlooking Grebe Point Bay, the weak sunlight glistening on the oars of a rowing shell slicing through the water, a black dog galloping along the bank beside it, barking. *One-two,* the coxswain calls. *Yap-yap,* goes the dog. Monica gets her wind back.

'Why were you following me?'

Don't answer questions — ask them. 'Did you know me before I met you?'

'How could I know you before I met you?'

In Death of a Ladies' Man, a dame called Annabel Franklin was in danger and I rang the bell to another flat to gain access to her unit block. It turned out to be Monica's. As an insurance investigator, she was following Annabel so it was natural she'd be in the flat above. It was also possible she was lying in wait for me. But why would she save me now if she was Pandora? I put the question.

'Once you were a voice on the intercom, then — when you opened the door — a girl with a gun. Did you already know me? Did you have a grudge against me, as well as the gun?'

'You tracked me down just to ask me that?'

The dog splashes into the water but the scullers keep to their dead-straight line. Like the rowers, I mustn't allow myself to be deflected. 'Second question: why were you at the refuge if you weren't trying to escape from someone?'

'I was a guard at the refuge, not an inmate. I was on watch, heard a noise and went to investigate. When the man at the fence tried to get away I went after him and came across you getting killed.' She gives voice to my thoughts. 'Why would I rescue you if I was trying to hurt you?' Then, 'Who were they?' And, when I don't answer that question either, 'You need a doctor.'

'No way. A doctor would report me to the cops; the cops would link my injuries to the death at the refuge; and I'd be arrested, given an identity, charged, found guilty and do time.'

She interrupts, 'Make that deaths because there were two of them. Which reminds me – I need to get back before someone finds the bodies.'

I get to my feet. 'You've been following me, haven't you?'

She brushes the grass clippings off her jeans; she also brushes away my question. 'I thought you said that you were the one doing the following.' Her eyes return to the scullers – the dog's splashing back to shore, its barking reduced to yelps – then back to me. 'Seeing you refuse to see a doctor, I'll leave you with Mildred.'

Chapter 11

TOO CLOSE FOR COMFORT

Mildred's on the far side of sixty, limps and lives in a dungeon under Grebe Point Road. I don't ask where she got the limp.

'We have been in the wars, haven't we?' she says.

I know her profession by the number of the pronoun and the concern. 'You're a nurse, aren't you?'

'Lie on the couch.' She fills a bowl with water to which she adds gentian violet after which she kneels beside me. 'And in answer to your question, no, I'm not a nurse – I'm a double-certificated sister retrenched to make way for a kid who does nothing but sit in the corridor avoiding all patient contact and playing with computers. You don't know anything about hospitals.'

She applies the disinfectant. It hurts. She's right. I don't.

I haven't got long, no more than a pig's whisper. I've got to think fast at a time when I'm having trouble thinking at all. The shapes of pedestrians wobble over glass bricks in the ceiling and photos sit on the Radiola: old pictures, young pictures, sepia pictures – coloured and monochrome – and when Mildred leaves the room I study them. There's one of a young nurse, a middle-aged nurse, an old nurse – sorry, *sister*. But a different kind of sister to the one my mother killed. An older woman with a soul's curse on her, an *angry* woman. It's life in fast-forward – Mildred as a young woman in the company of an older woman who looks pretty much like Mildred does now; Mildred holding a baby; Mildred with a child; Mildred and

Monica. *Ashes to ashes, death and regeneration.* There's something about the background in the Mildred-and-child photograph.

But it's not Mildred's background I need to concern myself with – it's mine. I'm on the right track but I need to cover all bases. All the clichés. I rewrite my list. There are more suspects – a lot more if I don't scratch dark horses like Rory's ex-wife, Janet Q. Peters; Lisette Priée, the ballet dancer; the pianist with the multi-coloured eyes, Gertrude Match; and my old mate Harry's alleged or otherwise squeeze, Denise, also known as de niece – Babychino. And why shouldn't Pandora be someone I don't know, the unknown follower?

After Mildred leaves, I carry the photograph to the light. Behind the two figures are rolling hills. After that – day after day – I force myself to do press-ups – one-two, one-two – my legs and body straight and the threadbare carpet hard under my fingertips, screaming silently with the pain in my arms. One-two, one-two. As soon as I can, I start circling the dungeon like a prisoner, keeping track of the laps – doubling, tripling and quadrupling them. All the time marking off the days – one, two. And at the end of the seventh day calling a halt.

'I've got to go.'

'But you're not well enough.'

'No-one's ever well enough, Mildred, but it doesn't stop them going.'

The phone number's not perched on its hind legs begging to be dialled but I'm not a pet owner, I'm a detective who's run out of dead-men's mobiles so I use a call phone. A termagant answers.

'What do you want?'

'It's not what I want – it's who. I'm after Monica Best.'

The valkyrie's got a stock line and she uses it. 'There's no-one here of that name.'

'She's not an inmate.'

Another stock line, 'We don't call them inmates, they're guests.'

'She's not a guest – she's a guard. And I'm not a danger man – I'm a friend.'

'I'll see if she's here.'

'You're too close.'

I move away.

'I don't mean too close to me, I mean to this Pandora business.'

We're in a Likeheart coffee shop and the place is crowded. It feels like normalcy. I like normalcy. You can't get hurt in normalcy.

'And before you ask,' Monica continues, 'a jogger found the bodies and the police visited the scene. They questioned me but I denied everything. Despite my denials I'd be a person of interest except they weren't all that interested — either in me or in the bodies. The killers were members of the Irish Republican Army.'

I nod. 'In other words, they had no ID but Interpol had their fingerprints which they kindly provided to the local gendarmerie. But what on earth are the IRA doing in Sydney hanging around a women's refuge?'

'That's what I was about to ask you.'

I change the subject. 'What happened to the cops?'

'Sally — that's the name of the woman in charge at the refuge — wouldn't let them in without a warrant so I had to go out to them. They walked me over the crime scene — from the hole in the fence to the place where the jogger found the bodies. They said they had evidence that I was implicated in some way but they weren't interested because the men were IRA and dead. They still wanted to know why I didn't report it but I said there was nothing to report. They asked about you.'

'Why would they do that?'

I'm what's known in the trade as layering — superimposing what might have happened onto what the witness is saying. Monica was interviewed by the cops. Check — it's a fact not in dispute. But why were they there? First possibility: Monica contacted them. With that in mind, I superimpose a second layer: that the cops didn't ask about me — Monica volunteered the information. Third layer, following on from layers one and two: she's here to implicate me. Fourth layer: she's wired.

She shakes her head. 'I can read your thoughts as clearly as if your head were made of glass. For God's sake, I rescued you — you have to trust me. The police only asked about you because of your footprints.'

'Which means they must also have found yours. Which means you lied either to me or to them when you said that you didn't investigate.'

'I was trying to cut corners.'

'Whose — theirs or mine?'

'I'm not trying to entrap you, Rainbow. The cops aren't after you for the simple reason I didn't tell them about you. Look around — do you see

anyone suspicious? I lied to you once and now I want to make up for it.'
She takes a deep breath. 'There's something I haven't told you.' There's
always something they haven't told you. 'It's this.'

From her pocket Monica pulls a rough-cast affair the size of a glasses
case. It's a coarse-weave thing of violet-coloured cloth, roughly sewn
around a thatch of straw. When I turn it over, a face stares back at me, a
leering face with a patch of hair askew on its forehead, a crooked mouth
and criss-crosses of black cotton for eyes. The eyes make the doll look
unconscious or dead. Someone's slashed its calico chest. The doll brings
back memories but I don't know what of. All I know is that it's beckoning
me to my past. Monica's fidgeting.

I waggle the doll. 'Where did you find this?'

'At the scene of the crime – on the hillside outside the refuge. I didn't
tell you about it before because – well, because of what I said: you're too
close and this might make you closer. You could overplay its significance.'
She shakes her head. 'Look, it's just an innocent doll, probably dropped
there by a kid.'

I think back to the night outside the refuge – one body on the ground
and Monica in the process of making it two. It was too dark to see dolls.

'When did you find it?'

'I went out at first light to cover your tracks and see if either of us had
left any clues. I used to be an insurance investigator, remember, so I know
all about clues. I was smoothing down the soil and scattering leaves about
when I found it.'

'It's clean. Did you brush it? It would be a natural thing to do –
people like things to be clean.'

'No, that's how I found it.'

Chapter 12

BURN CITY

Simeon Samson's behind his desk with a gun at his head and it's my gun. With the sinking of the old tub the *Wooden No* along with all my weaponry, I've had to make do with the odd spanker from nefarious sources. The one I'm wielding is a Golightly – otherwise known as an Astra Cub 2000. There's no safety on the grip and it's pretty well obsolete but beggars can't write their own orders and it doesn't make much of a bulge in my jacket. There are a thousand ways to get past security and I only had to use one of them.

In trying to prove I'm not a psychopath, I've got to move a lot faster than usual. My old mate Rory's ex-wife, Janet Q. Peters, is worth a visit; the dancer I was brought up with, Lisette Priée, is ditto worth a visit. The pianist with the multi-coloured eyes, Gertrude Match, is a long shot but long shots can still hit the target; likewise Denise, also known as de niece – Babychino. Not to mention Hell and Damnation, the dame from the *Bullets at the Ballet* caper, real name – if anyone's ever got a real name – Hélène Dalmatian.

So like I say, in detecting terms I'm well over the speed limit – in this game you've got to go steady or risk kicking the ball into touch. But I've got no choice. Pandora exists – I've got to keep reminding myself of that fact or accept that I'm mad. I sense her around the next corner and behind the last, a dark shape on the edge of the crowd, a figure in an otherwise empty corner of my consciousness, an ever-present menace. I repeat: I've got to prove she's real or accept that I'm mad. The doll in my pocket's clean but that doesn't mean Monica Best is. She's still on my shopping list.

Sydney is Burn City, Nero's Rome, a place where punters have got to be pond hoppers just to survive. Hélène Dalmatian could have gone back to her native stomping ground – France – or simply changed her name and address and stayed. Which is why I'm visiting *Natality, Mortality and Misery Inc* – also known as the Department of Burps, Debts and Massages – and holding a gun to Simeon Samson's head.

'Why the gat?' he asks.

'Because I want information and you're reluctant to provide it.'

'Our superiors – not to mention Australia's security agencies – watch us like echidnas hang around ants and if we deviate from the norm in the slightest we're hauled off for questioning. They're not sympathetic to the leaking of information.'

'That's why I've got the gun – it makes me even less sympathetic than they are. Do it.'

Reluctantly, Samson fingertips his way into forbidden territory – like bugs are coming out of the computer and crawling over the keyboard. Password, the screen asks – he provides it. Then: Reason for inquiry – he provides that, too. After which: On whose authority are you asking? He types in a name. Followed by one last chance to stay clean: Are you sure?

He shakes his head. 'I'm dead.'

'We're all dead, get used to it.' I jam the barrel hard into his head. 'Find the name,' I say, a touch more savagely than I need to.

Everyone in Australia's on a grid called an IGU – an Intelligence Gathering Unit. The security people can deny it till they're pink, blue or violent in the face, but everything, and I mean everything – names, nicknames, friends, enemies, relatives, ages, interests, addresses, sexual proclivities, what you had for breakfast and the state of your kidneys – goes back to base. There's a bit of privacy but people with Samson's seniority can override it.

'Faster,' I tell him.

'Here he is: Flax – Albert,' he says. 'That's the name of the sugar daddy, right? Ex-Olympian, financier, deceased.' He leans back, wiping his palms on his trousers, job done. 'There's a heap of detail – awards for service to society, contacts with crooks, unproven allegations of this, that and the other, no relatives, blah-blah-blah, list of girlfriends, the last one being Dalmatian, Hélène – subsequently rebadged as Helena Dannazione. Satisfied?'

He's forgotten his fear in the thrill of the chase. He's also forgotten his brains.

'Not by a long shot, Delilah,' I growl. 'Tap dance your way to Helena Dannazione.'

In my book there's no such thing as coincidence. My legs are rubber as I leave the building, climbing the staircase from Samson's hidey hole, going down multiple corridors with little glass cubicles leading off them. I finally pass a security that's no longer interested because I'm leaving. Before saying bye-bye Samson I placed a bullet on his mouse pad – a .23 slug the size of a gnat.

'A little memento of my visit. So that when they're giving you the third, fourth or fifth degree for breeching security, you'll tell nobody nothing except that it was all your idea.'

The lawn's freshly mown, there's a sign on the newly-painted fence saying *BUY ME* and the joint looks as innocent as a new-born ferret. But there's someone inside – I know it for a fact because of the curtains. I'm dressed for anonymity – grey tracksuit, even greyer shoes, forage cap turned backwards. The curtains are open. I continue up the street without turning my head.

Sydney is all about real estate – call it real astute – which makes realtors the new elite. From being the dregs of society, they've risen to the top of the oil can because selling houses has become one of the black arts of success. And part of that art is keeping the curtains closed. That way no-one gets to see in without an appointment; buyers beg for admission; and the agents get their Lo and behold! moment when they throw open the curtains exclaiming, Let there be light!

At the end of the block I chuck a left and head down Prime. Due to the booming property market, Browntown's shifted gear from chugalug to second — there's no longer a lot of wrecked cars in the gutter, the dog poo's been cleared away and people pull T-shirts over their singlets before going for a walk. I climb the back fence.

It was meant to be no more than a house call. Rube's files — the ones containing all her cases, her diary, codes and advice — is in a filing box behind a pile of paint tins under Rory's house. But I can't get to it because someone's inside.

It could be someone after Roarer, it could be someone after me or it might be a random stranger. Rory's ex, Janet, has had the place made over. There's a strong smell of paint and there are no longer piles of rubbish in the backyard. I get around to where the path slopes down from the road and stand on my tippy-toes. In the bathroom a vase of flowers is sitting on the cistern and there's a tray of cosmetics by the door. I card the catch, ease up the bottom window sash and a hand-leap gets me inside, my right whiteside sending the flowers flying.

The vase shatters and the crash echoes through the house like cannon fire. In two strides I'm across the bathroom, my fist with the Luger in it thrust into the hall, but the opposition's faster. A sisal chop sends the gat flying and I feel my wrist gripped and someone starting to make barley twist out of my radius and ulna as my head comes into contact with the freshly painted jamb. The colour's off-white. I like off-white but not when it's wearing my blood. Something tells me I'm in trouble. It's not the astute agent.

Chapter 13

THE ASTUTE AGENT

I'm on one side of the door and he's on the other and my arm's in serious danger of breaking. At times like these, the brain works fast and my hypothalamus goes into overdrive. I run through the options. Top of the list is to die. After that comes breaking free by main force – impossible because his grip's too strong; following my arm into the hall – which is what he wants; or falling limp – the option of the obvious. The tray of cosmetics teeters on the edge of the bath as my knee hits it.

I feel searing pain in my arm as the pressure reaches tipping point. The elbow's the link between carriages and it takes up the slack as the train moves out of the station. The tray contains unguents, deodorants and astringents, plus a lot of active constituents, most of them carrying the suffix: DANGEROUS. I grab the nearest canister with my free hand – fingers and thumb around the can, forefinger on the button – and launch myself through the doorway, turning against the arm twist, the pain of it blinding as I press the button and keep pressing. At first there's no reaction but just as my arm's about to give way, the hiss of escaping chemicals is joined by yelling as the active constituents find my assailant's eyes – yelling accompanied by a loosening of the grip and the return of my arm.

He's big which gives me part of the edge because the hall's narrow. He's also in pain which gives me the rest of the edge. I keep the spray aimed in the general direction of his face. While he's yelling, he's tearing at his eyes. The poet said, Any man's death diminishes me. This isn't death but it's the next best thing and I don't feel diminished by it. Instead I exult in his pain. He's on the floor trying to escape but I keep the spray aimed at him. One day you'll go too far, the shrink said. You'll kill someone you don't intend to. I take my finger off the trigger and he stops yelling.

I switch the can across to the bad hand, bend and shove the thug on his back with the other, while elbowing his hands from his face so I can see his features. He's youngish, his hair's trimmed to sandpaper and one tooth is capped with gold. Mullygrub ears, eyes that right now contain more blood than pupil and his clothing's smart casual. He doesn't stop me going through his pockets because he can't. There's nothing in them. I step back.

'What's your name?'

He can't see me and it's like he's lost his voice. It could be a ruse and people have been killed by ruses. He's wearing a fawn T-shirt with I HEART SYDNEY on it, gabardine daks and a nice pair of light-brown shoes – the clobber of choice if you want to get lost in the crowd. Big biceps and steel pectorals. Clearly he works out – although nothing's worked out for him today. I find my gat, bag it, drag Gold Tooth to his feet with my one good hand – contrary to what people think, a man on the ground has the edge on a man standing – and get him into the loungeroom, knocking over a lampstand on the way. I shake him till his teeth rattle.

'Who sent you?'

He sucks in his breath, borrowing time to get across the pain, at the same time lulling me towards a space where he can take me. I drop the can, drag down the curtains and use them to secure him to a chair. I go through his pockets a second time. He's smirking.

'You won't find nothin'.'

He's right, I don't. No more than an attitude that says he's a particular kind of thug belonging to a particular part of my life – but which part? He bears more than a passing resemblance to the corpses at the refuge. The cops found nothing on them, either – a nothing that Monica said proved that the thugs were IRA. They could be triplets – the only difference being this one's still alive. I could beat him up but what would that prove? Only that the shrink was right and I'm a psychopath. So I resist, leaving the desirable residence in disarray and the thug tied to a chair.

I find Rube's box, tuck it under my arm and get away fast. There's nowhere else, so that's where I go.

'I thought you'd be back,' Mildred says. 'What is it this time – an ingrown toenail?'

'I need somewhere to stay.'

Mildred shrugs like she's seen it all before.

'Why not? Sure beats watching television.'

I look up Dr Sally Kane on the medical register, Gargle, the White Pages, everywhere I can think of but end up with a big fat zero so I ask Mildred to babysit Rube's box while I train it to Dashiell, Sally's hometown. It's the same country town with the same lazy shops and the same people wearing laughing-side boots and Akubras. I've rebadged myself – I'm wearing conservative dark-green daks, deep-brown velour jacket with a hunter's cut to it, a wide-brimmed Stetson in accordance with the mores of Dashiell, and whitesides – otherwise known as co-respondent's shoes, my usual footwear of choice. I'm packing a Pistolet Makarova – a gat with a long, heavy trigger pull to it but it'll have to do – as I make my way from the coach stop to the hospital known as Dashiell Basic.

I find a pumpkin at reception who's about as helpful as saltlick in a desert. Dr Kane might once have worked here, the pumpkin says, but she's here no longer. She might also once have lived at 48 Daisy Drive, Dashiell, but now she's nowhere.

'What do you mean nowhere? Brain surgeons don't just cease to exist.'

She doesn't say this one did but that's the subtext. 'Sorry but that information's privileged.'

'Why – because she's privileged and the rest of us aren't?'

The pumpkin reaches for the phone. 'I think you'd better leave, sir.'

Always check what they tell you, especially when the teller's a pumpkin. I find a fleet of Tonka toys in the driveway, mail in the letterbox addressed to someone else and the neighbours confirming that Sally Kane no longer resides at 48 Daisy Drive, Dashiell. The Royal Society for the Prevention of Cruelty to Surgeons has got no-one on their books called *Kane, Sally*, so after training it back to Sydney I find a computer café and roll back the flaps of time.

First stop: Australia, Surgeons, Brain, Female – but Sally's name isn't there, either. Second stop … Following the Hood With No Hands caper, a court case was scheduled and Sally would have been subpoenaed as a witness. It was a long time ago but courts, like the mills of God, grind slow. Because of who was involved – the Mafia – Sally would have been placed in a Witness Protection Program just like her husband. They're life-changers, WPPs. You can no longer be who you were or you'd be dead. The hood with no hands was Family, which means that an unfriendly witness — and Sally would be seen as unfriendly — would be marked out for the regulation bullet in the back of the head. Hank, the bartender at O'Leary's, the speakeasy, has got Rory's number.

'You only call when you need me,' Rory complains.

'When does anyone call anyone?' I cut to the action. 'I need an in to WPP, both here and in America.'

Rory parks his contrition. 'I got back in touch with The Dwarf when I was looking for work.'

The Dwarf's all of four-foot-eight, well over the mandatory height limit for dwarfs but still no giant. He was a big man in crime prevention before being found guilty of just about every crime in the book. Which means that he's a small man again — last heard of acting as the rear-end of a horse in a circus. But he kept up his contacts — which makes him handy for Rory, who's a killer.

'And?'

'So, yeah, I can do that for you. What's it worth?'

It's an insecure line but now and then I've got to park the paranoia so I give him Sally 's name, adding, 'But there's no payment, Roarer — we're friends, remember?'

Roarer sighs. 'When do you want the info?'

'The day before yesterday.' I remember the second reason for my call. 'Are you back with Janet?'

'Janet who?'

Chapter 14

DOWN AMONG THE TOMBSTONES

The parsonage is deserted but I find her near the cenotaph tending to the dahlias. When she looks up, the sun's in her hair and she looks like an angel. But she doesn't talk like one.

'What are you doing here?'

'I need information.'

Her hair's still red but her face is redder. Janet Q. Peters was never one of God's masterstrokes but now she's in serious need of a makeover.

'I'm not going back to Rory.'

I keep it smooth. 'Good decision, Janet. Roarer's a killer who'll never mend his ways. You did right to commit adultery with that preacher.'

She squints through her goggles. 'Are you having a crack at me? Because if you are –'

I cut to the chase. 'Look, when we met, you were working in a hospital in Dashiell and afterwards at the reception desk in an estate agent's. Where were you before that?'

'All over the place. My mother was a drifter.'

'Where did she drift to – specifically?'

'Northern NSW, Western Australia, Fiji – wherever her latest man led her.'

'Was she mixed up with magicians?' Her frown of incomprehension gives me the answer. 'Okay, next question: have you got it in for me?'

'Of course I've got it in for you! If it hadn't been for you I'd never have met that one-legged moron called Rory. Nor would I be trying to justify myself every second day to the preacher.'

'Is that all?'

'Isn't it enough?'

'Enough to kill me?'

Janet shakes her head. 'Being a pagan, you wouldn't understand. As a Christian I follow the path of righteousness.' She fumbles the spade, drops it, bends to retrieve it. 'Which means that every day I struggle with the desperate urge to kill people.'

'What about adultery?'

Pandora's quick on her feet but Janet's slow. She brings her spade over her head like she's about to whack me. The bees buzz and the birds twitter. Only in my wildest dreams could she be Pandora. But I'm a detective, not a dreamer. I haul out the gat – an old Roth-Steyr with rotating barrel but it does the job.

'Don't kill me!' she cries. If she were Pandora she'd be behind a tombstone or at my throat. I park the gat and raise the fedora.

'You're not the woman I thought you were.'

'What's that supposed to mean?'

'Neither more nor less than it does.'

It's nice to be back at the ballet. It's Lisette Priée's swansong – she's danced *Swan Lake* for the last time and she's covered in feathers and curtseying her final curtsey on a stageful of flowers. She returns my eyebrow-raise and nods in the direction of the forecourt like we're performing a *pas de deux* before the *entr'acte*. She's a wild card but I've still got to play her.

'I've got a question for you, Lisette.' Except for the nice little tutu-clad body, the pixie face and the feathers, she's all ears; when we danced together, Lisette seemed to like me but it could have been just another performance. 'And my question is: what's your next act?'

'Being a proper parent, just like mine weren't.'

'I didn't know you had kids.'

She shrugs. 'How could you? We haven't seen each other since the death of the dancer.' In the Bullets at the Ballet caper a dancer got shot. 'You're not part of my life but if things had been different you might have been.'

She's lithe enough and the right age and she can act. 'Did you resent me for passing you up?'

'I was the one who passed you up, Rainbow.'

'Did you want to kill me?'

She adjusts her feathers; they're ruffled. 'You're a strange person but, no, I never wanted to kill you.'

'Did you want to follow me?'

'Ha, not likely.'

It'd be easy to check the detail, just like it'd be easy to find out if she's a mother. But I've learnt enough. She's not Pandora.

'Happy retirement,' I say.

'I'm not retiring. I'm taking up martial arts, it being a natural corollary to ballet.'

She's still not Pandora.

Next cab off the rank is my dead mate Harry's might-have-been-but-never-was squeeze, the dame who fed me a cock-and-bull story about Harry loving her and after he died, leaving her a fortune. I find Babychino aka De Niece (or Denise) in Broadfoot Women's Reformatory, courtesy of an Identikit picture and someone who owed me a favour. She's wearing fetching Prussian-green coveralls like the rest of the inmates.

'Fancy meeting you here,' she says, all hard-faced candour. 'You always were a sucker for a pretty face and I had you fooled, didn't I?'

She's hard and she's fast and she could be Pandora except for her size and age – she's too young and too small. But instinct tells me to forget both. In my mind I replace the green outfit with black and put a knife in her hand. We're in a visitor's room with bars on the windows and I'm holding onto my strides because they took away my belt. Babychino's the original amoeba.

'How did you end up here, Denise?'

'That's not my real name but ultimately nothing's real – life's just a magician's trick. I had a scam going but the last jockstrap I tried it on turned out to be a copper.'

'What was the scam?'

'Getting suckers into hotel rooms on the promise of sex then hitting them over the head with a cosh and taking their money.'

'Subtle if not also highly original. How long have you been in the slammer?'

'Since the last time I saw you.' During which time Pandora paid me the odd visit, which means that Babychino's got the perfect alibi. 'Perhaps we could get together after I get out?'

She'd have to be Houdini to be Pandora. I tell her perhaps and clear out.

Next stop: Sally Kane.

Chapter 15

IN THE MUSEUM OF MODERN HEART

Nothing's secure if you know where to find it. According to the information obtained from The Dwarf, Sally Kane, brain surgeon, is still in Australia. Except that there's been a change of name, address and occupation so that now she's Sheila Keane, artist, presently living on the island state of Tasmania. After a great deal of to-ing and fro-ing, she finally agrees to see me.

I first came across Sally Kane in the case of the *Hood With No Hands*. She wanted kids but her husband, David, didn't add up, so she hired me to do the maths on him. At least that's what she *said* she hired me for. She was a bona fide surgeon who knew her way around acting and psychiatry and she was beautiful and bright and, as a result of my investigation, she and her husband parted company. After which Sally and I also went our separate ways.

She's got to be Pandora.

Of course, there's the stumbling block of age. She's older than Monica but all things being equal she's too young to be Pandora. But all things are never equal which means there's a chance that I only imagined the early Pandora – with Sally picking up the reality where the chimera left off. It's a long shot but it might be the only shot I've got. I can't work out a motive but that can wait.

Her lips barely move as she glances nervously around and says, 'Are you sure you weren't followed?'

Her hair's black where it used to be blonde and she's wearing paint-spattered bib-and-tuck overalls with paintbrushes sticking out of the pocket plus a pair of sunglasses with wraparound frames. She's lost weight and she should be carrying a scalpel instead of a brush but I'd still recognise her – if not for the posture. She hasn't stopped glancing around since I arrived and I get the feeling that I'm not the one being followed.

I've taken the usual precautions. I flew to Adelaide under an assumed name – what other names are there? Then I caught a bus to Melbourne, wearing a change of clothing from Vinnies – brown daks, black coat with an orange fleck to it and a purple straw fedora. I spent the night in a doss house in Melbourne. Someone there showed more interest in me than was good for either of us but I demobilised him and left. After which I ditched the hat, put on a grey wig and caught the ferry to Hobart. There was another joker on the boat but I shook him, too. Any other suspicious figures must have been in my imagination – ask the shrink. I envisage Sally wearing skin-tight black and armed with a knife. I'm wearing a roll-necked sweater, brothel creepers and cords and could pass for an artist myself.

'I'm always being followed, Dr Kane,' I tell her.

'Don't call me that. I'm Sheila Keane, I'm in fear for my life and I paint.'

'Why are you in fear for your life?'

She tells me what I know already and I check out the joint while she's doing so. We're in an art gallery that calls itself the Modern Art Derivative or MAD for short and the name fits like a tea cosy on the head of a madman. A giant Meccano machine is clanking away in a corner, a square of black is titled Preponderance of Virtues and a naked dame is perched on a tea box. They favour words like Live Art and Working Installations. Sally Kane, brain surgeon – sorry, Sheila Keane, artist – chose the venue. The main light switch is to the left of the front door. I make with the conversation.

'When is your case up?'

'I can't talk about it.'

Change of subject. 'Any of your stuff here?'

She waves her hand at what might be a self-portrait: an anguished face behind bars. There's no friendliness – in her gesture or in the portrait. 'We're not here to discuss art. Could you ask the questions you came here to ask and leave?'

'Okay. First question: going back to the Hood With No Hands, why did you employ me? You needed a gumshoe but why me when you could have hired anyone?'

'All those years ago I didn't tell you the truth.'

'From memory you rarely did.'

She shrugs. 'I could have dealt with David myself. But I had an ulterior motive.' She looks around and I look around with her; we're surrounded by more body parts than you'd find in a mass murderer's freezer. 'Why am I telling you this?'

'Because you want me out of your hair but you also know I'm not leaving until I've got some answers and the longer I'm around the greater the likelihood someone will draw conclusions. A series of unfortunate events led you here and you don't want them to lead any further. You've either appeared in court or you've yet to give evidence. Either way you're afraid for your life and you want me gone.'

Her face clears and for the first time this session — despite the hair, the overalls, the paintbrushes and the hunched shoulders — I see again the beautiful Sally. 'It's nothing personal,' she murmurs. 'I was grateful for your help but unfortunately it led to —' she shrugs '— this. And you're right — I don't want things to get any worse than they already are.'

I take a deep breath and it's full of inevitability. 'I'll leave after you answer my questions.' I glance around; she's got me doing it now. 'Why did you hire me?'

'Because I saw your ad in the newspaper.'

'A lot of gumshoes advertise.'

'Your ad was in the Personals and I was looking in the Personals.'

'Some people call them Poisonals.' I glance around again and that's when I notice him: he's wearing a black three-quarter length coat and a beard and he's carrying a gun held lengthwise under his coat. I position myself between him and Sally and speed up the questioning. 'You can't fob me off this time. You didn't pick me out of that paper by accident.'

She takes a deep breath. 'Okay, I — was already aware of you,' she answers softly; then because someone — an elderly woman — has moved in next to us, 'Isn't that a beautiful line?'

'Yours or that so-called painting's?' I shepherd her away from the gunman who's also looking for a line — a sightline. 'Don't fob me off with lines.'

'Being an artist it becomes a habit.'

We move and the man with the gun follows.

'So what's this other life you knew me from?'

'It was during my first posting as a neurosurgeon. I was called to an emergency — a man who'd been shot in the head. I removed the bullet and he lived for a few days but then he died. It was my first life–and–death operation and it was a failure. I was angry. I wanted to find the killer.'

I flip through my mental files, the ones preceding the Rainbow cases: twenty-something years of trial and error, error and trial – The Body in the Basement, The Widow Who Wasn't, The Guatemalan and the Gun, The Mob Manifesto, The Die-Hard was a Dame. I can't remember this particular death. 'And did you?'

'Did I what?'

'Track him down, find the gunman?'

We're out of the prank room and into another room too full of possibilities.

She nods. 'Yeah.'

Chapter 16

A SHOT IN THE DARK

'The victim was a crook,' Sally says, 'although his file didn't say it in so
many words. While he was still alive, crooked types came to visit him,
men in black coats who kept their hands in their pockets and didn't bring
flowers. A cop told me a *gumshoe* shot him — that was the word he used,
gumshoe. When I asked for a name he said there wasn't one. One day I
called in sick.'

We're standing before a giant potato with six eyes called Rebirth.
'Doctors are natural detectives. We've got organised minds and are taught
to classify and analyse. But the difference between us and people like you
is that, while doctors are dedicated to saving lives, people like you destroy
them. I wanted to track down this man who put bullets in people's brains
and I was prepared to put my job on the line to do it. It took me a month.'

'You're supposed to be a surgeon.'

'When you do it it's called detecting while I'm a meddler, is that it? I
followed a trail of blood that led from a man with a bullet in his brain to
a Sydney speakeasy with a heap of criminals in it. I came up with a name
— Rainbow. But I still had to find you.'

'And you did that via the Poisonal columns. After which you stalked
me.'

She shrugs. 'I was an actor, remember? I was never the same person
twice. Sometimes I was an old woman, at other times I passed myself off
as a man.'

'Did you carry a knife?'

'Are politicians liars? I'm a surgeon, remember.'

'Is that all you did? Follow me?'

'It was like stepping into a sewer. I didn't want to but I followed you.

But after a while work claimed me back. I no longer had time.'

'Until you needed a private detective and remembered me. You wanted an excuse and your husband provided one so you rang up the number you'd found in the Poisonals.'

The first shot takes out the fake brain – the skull shatters and the synapses fade and so, too, do the main lights while the rest of the *installations* – that's what they call them: audio, visual, tactile, olfactory and probably tasty – must have been on a different circuit because they continue their *clackety-clack*. The next shot merges with the background, ending up as no more than an echo in the overall assault on the senses, a natural extension of the whirring of electric motors, the rattle of old-fashioned destination signs and the hammer of waves on the rocks below: the report of a late-model .45 Canadian Para-Ordnance, the one with a stock made of cocobolo wood, a work of art that merges with the background like it belongs there.

The thin red line of a laser pierces the darkness, ending on the sinister temporalis of Sally's head like a tattoo telling a surgeon to CUT HERE. At such times there's no indecision. I grab her and we end up on the floor. Sally's livid or maybe it's the blood. She struggles to disentangle herself.

'They knew you'd lead them to me eventually and that's what you've done!'

'Shut up and keep your head down.'

Lasers possess a beginning as well as an end and I trace the beam to its source, making out a bearded face about where you'd expect one if it was attached to a thug holding a laser-mounted equaliser. It's a high-risk shot because there are too many people about so I hold my fire as I rib-crawl my way to the door. The main switch is to the left. I flick it and light floods the room. The gunman's searching for Sally and I just get a bead on him when someone shouts,

'Is there a doctor in the house?'

Nuns give themselves to Christ, cops swear allegiance to law and order and medicos vow to save lives. Sally identifies herself – however much she pretends to the contrary, she's still a doctor. I grab her again, another shot whangs over her head and by the time I look up, Laser Man's gone. My first thought is that he's Pandora and after me; the second, more accurate, diagnosis is that he's a Mafia hitman after Sally. Which makes him a two-edged sword and anyone could lose their head on the backswing. I scramble up but I'm too late. I turn back to Sally. 'We're leaving!'

But she's tending to the injured; she shoulders me away. 'No – you're leaving! Go away from me as far as you can and never come back!' Her voice turns suddenly tender. 'Don't move, darling.'

The last words aren't directed at me.

You see a shadow behind the installations, so you go after it. Only to find when you get there that it's gone. I hurtle through the gallery, gat at the ready, but it's like they create this stuff to hide killers. The gunman's gone but not forgotten because you never forget a gunman. This one was short, bearded and black-coated. Only next time, the beard will have gone and he'll be wearing something different. The sirens become ambulances, fire engines and cops as I pass a bunch of empty beer cartons. Or maybe they're works of art.

Her address is in the White Pages – *Sheila Keane, Artist, So-and-so Street, So-and-so suburb, Hobart*; her home's a converted barn; and I find the documents under a flea-bitten couch with a paint-splattered sheet over it. The papers confirm that she's a surgeon with a certificate in acting from NIDA and a degree in psychiatry. But the appended list of operations doesn't include a man with a bullet in his brain. I return the papers to their hidey-hole. Sally's career is shot to pieces but she still wants to stay alive which is why she made up the story about the bullet. At least that's a reason I can accept. Someone's arrived outside; I make myself scarce.

Someone who knew me and Sally were linked followed me and now I've left her exposed – tending to the victims of a shooting. There are two reasons to return to the gallery:

Sally could be Pandora and

I don't want to be responsible for her death.

I'm greeted by what they call in the classics a scene of chaos – meaning cars all over the place. Relatives and friends have arrived, along with TV vans, investors worried about their investments, artists wringing their hands over the fate of humankind plus the usual ambulances, cop cars and fire engines. And maybe also the killer.

I never trusted Sally and now I trust her even less but I got her into this mess and now I've got to get her out of it. A cop confronts me but he's overworked and under-brained so he lets me past. I count two bodies along with another one that could end up that way. Sally's arguing with a fat man waving a stethoscope.

'This is a small town on a small island,' the fat man's saying, 'where everyone knows everyone else. I'm a doctor who's also an art lover and you're Sheila Keane, artist. You're not a doctor so you can't tend to people.'

Sally's caught between her oath and a hard place. 'People are dying, as in sharp nose, hollow eyes, collapsed temples, ears cold, contracted and with their lobes turned out, skin about the face rough, distended and parched, colour greenish or dusky.' She glares at the fat man. 'If I wasn't a doctor, how would I know the Hippocratic facies?'

'I don't know what you're talking about. Officer!'

I flash a badge. Any badge. They never look. 'Inspector Moriarty at your service. What's the problem?'

Chapter 17

SISTER PSYCHOLOGY

The fat man waves his stethoscope. 'This woman's a fraud, spouting nonsense about *faeces* while pretending to be a doctor when she quite clearly isn't.'

'Thank you.' I grab hold of Sally's arm. 'I'll take it from here. Come with me, ma'am.'

I shepherd her past bodies with real doctors tending to them, real policemen not blocking my way because I'm just another cop doing his job and the job's hard enough without having to deal with fools.

'Let me go!' she says.

'The gunman could have come back,' I tell her. I nod to a constable. 'I'm AFP. I found this woman posing as a doctor and I'm taking her in for questioning. As if we haven't got enough on our plate without charlatans.'

She's still struggling. 'I swore an oath to save people and I'm going to save them if it kills me!'

I shake my head as I usher her out the doors. 'Right now you've only got one job and that is to stay alive. Have you got your driver's licence on you?'

'I drove here, so, yes.' I get her behind the wheel of her car; a battered VW; she starts it then pauses. 'This means we're going back to the mainland, doesn't it? That's why I need the licence – not just to drive but in case they ask for my ID.' She thinks some more. 'If I ask questions, you'll only lie. It's like a doctor asking a patient if their appendix needs operating on when it's really their leg. I realise you have to take me because my cover's blown but first I have to collect some clothes.'

I shake my head again or the road's shaking it for me. 'If you go home all you'll collect is a bullet. They're waiting for you. These people want you dead.'

She nods.

'Where are we going?'

'To the bus terminal and from there to Adelaide.'

She nods again. 'That means the airport and Sydney.'

We dump the car and cab it the rest of the way. I call Roarer and tell him to meet us.

Back in Sydney, Roarer drives us to the caravan belonging to Sue Mahoney – Tsunami – the one that's hidden in the bush off the Bratwurst Parkway. Tsunami's missing, presumed dead, so she's unlikely to have any further use for it.

'This is your home for a while,' I tell Sally.

'How long's a while?'

'As long as you want to stay alive or until they work out where you are – whichever comes first. The stove works, there's food in the cupboard and cutlery in the drawer under the sink.'

The key to the caravan was on the tyre but that's not the key I'm after. It's been staring me in the face ever since I started interviewing the dames. Janet Q. Peters' father figures; Lisette Priée with her talk of parenting; Denise's father fixation; my own haphazard relationship with Imogene. Back at Mildred's I go through Aunt Rube's files again. The heading on the one I want reads: *THE COMING OF RAINBOW.*

It was a shock to the system. Here I was, a middle-aged private investigator, a bachelor girl from way back, suddenly lumped with a kid. Not a lifestyle choice I'd put up my hand for but what else could I do? My brother's a bastard and the kid's probably one, too …There's more of the same – Aunt Rube is as eloquent on paper as she was in life. I was five and can't recall much of what happened but Rube revivifies it – the trip from Nimbin in the Kombi with my father and his latest blonde; me half-stunned because my mother and sister had just gone up in flames before my eyes; while the grieving widower – a word that at five I didn't even know – was acting like he'd swatted a fly; arriving in Sydney, the first home outside a hut that I'd known; and my father telling me to bugger off.

What does it eat? One thing I do know — the father won't be back, not in my lifetime. At least he gave me a last-resort address ...

The files are ordered, annotated and indexed, complete with a number of cross-references. It takes all of my narrative detecting skills — the application of search theory Rube taught me, as in: use a logical approach, be bold, use the grey matter, persevere. Thanks to my acrobatics in the gullery, my left arm's pretty well useless and it will be a while before it's fully operative again. The light in the Hobbit hovel's penumbra and Aunt Rube's files are spread out before me on Mildred's rust-sprung couch.

There's nothing in the diary so I switch to the case files going back fifty years. I give each batch of papers a good shake but no handy scrap falls out. I turn to the file labelled CONTACTS, the one I've been avoiding because I haven't even got a name. I know that even from the grave, Rube won't make it easy for anyone rummaging through her affairs. Any names and addresses will be for my eyes only, which means they'll be in code.

Somewhere in the 1980s the coded contact details are joined by email addresses. Criminals rub shoulders with police commissioners, spies with terrorists, politicians with spivs. A lot of the time it's hard to tell the difference. Reinvented names are accompanied by tags consisting of two, three, four or five letters. I cast my mind back. *You must have at least one language in reserve,* she drummed into me — *a language confined to a restricted group of people. There'll be times when you'll need it.* This is one of those times.

Rube had a great many codes but I dispense with the ones where numbers are substituted for letters or the alphabet's inverted because they're far too simple for this exercise. Rube used French, Latin and Greek derivatives; Morse code; algebraic symbols; and complex combinations thereof. I'm still trying to find a name and address when Mildred returns. She reminds me of Rube.

'You need a wife,' she says, bustling about. 'Fancy a grown man like you getting about on your own. Dinner's tofu curry — vegan, which I believe is to your liking. A lifetime in hospitals has taught me how bad food can be. Would you select a wine? And what are you up to?'

When I get to my feet I'm suffering near-paralysis from vein clamp and can smell the sweet-scented mixture of turmeric, apple blossom and garlic. I uncork a Corbiere vin de table as Mildred repeats her last question. I let the genie out of the bottle.

'I'm looking for my father.'

Night's fallen and Sister Mildred should open a restaurant.

'Nursing's not all badinage and bandages,' she says. 'To a great extent, recovery depends on Sister Psychology. And Sister Psychology tells me you're in a pickle – you've told me little or nothing, much like my daughter.'

We go on eating in silence – if that's the right word when there's a continuous roar of traffic outside, low-flying planes rattling the roof tiles and a pack of wildcats loose in my brain. Rube numbered her codes from one to fifty and the relevant code could be any one of them. You've told me little or nothing, Mildred said. It's the same with the address file.

Mildred continues, 'Nurses get used to talking to themselves. I tended to wounded soldiers from Vietnam, you know, old men with hip replacements and women with the kind of complaints that women get. And Sister Psychology worked every time. What worries most patients isn't what you say – it's what you avoid saying.'

'I thought patients were called guests now.'

She sips her wine. 'Yes, and don't those code words make everyone feel so much better? Modern hospitals think that meaningless phrases are cure-alls. That it's not what you say but how you say it – which is usually the opposite of what is. All you need is to find a euphemism and you've found the cure. As if someone on the point of dying can be healed by words.'

Chapter 18

THE MAN FROM LOTTO

All you need is to find a euphemism and you've found the cure. It's like the Rosetta Stone unlocking the mysteries of Egypt. I've got to work out what the words mean on the surface then set the hieroglyphics beside them and track down their opposites. While Mildred clears away the plates I recheck the relevant ciphers: *Gentle Violence* which several codes along the track becomes *Gentian Violet.* Which transposes into *Prater Violet* which becomes – I recheck the code – *Peter Violente.*

Now for the address. The Dark One, plus a street name and number, also in code. By a process of elimination, the suburb becomes the obverse of what it appears – you see what you want to see – just like Mildred said. That means Dark becomes any one of Light, Clear, Unshaded, Illuminated or multiples thereof. Followed by One then the seemingly misspelt Minuse – when Ruby never misspelt anything. Which makes it One Minus-e. Which could be anything but includes the very real possibility of Brighton, Melbourne. Using Mildred's computer, I log into Gargle Earth and enter the suburb, street name and number my father gave Rube and Rube subjected to her elaborate code.

At Tullamarine I buy a ticket for the big red bus plus a travel card. At Southern Cross station I switch to a blue and silver train that's *not* going to Brighton and after that catch a train that is. I get out where the railway intersects Bay Street, head north, switch to a side street, then swing east. Big houses, high walls, lots of ivy – just the place if you want to hide and the cops are subservient. I'm unarmed because they don't let you take gats on planes, which is no bad thing if you're psychotic.

Weeds poke through the fence and signs say NO ENTRY. Number 53 Cornucopia's begging to be put out of its misery, the U-lock on the gate's an easy pick and the path's heaped with snail-chewed mail. I imagine what it looked like when my father arrived here forty years ago. The house would have had the sparkle of new paint, the weatherboards wouldn't have broken away, tiles wouldn't have slipped off the roof and the weeds would have been lawn. And my father would have had the sparkle of adventure in him – he was in his thirties, his wife was dead and he had a new dame on his arm. A dog barks, something slithers under the house and I go in.

Dust and desuetude, darkness and death. My checks showed the joint's owned by someone called Gambetta. A yellowed letter says the water and power were disconnected years ago and never reconnected. No-one's lived here for ages – Gambetta being too old, too rich or both. The mould in the fridge is hardcore and the floor's pulp. I start at the back of the house because you've got to start somewhere.

I would have missed it except that I was looking, treading on the lines of nails indicating the position of the bearers because the floorboards are unsafe. A flock mattress lies in a corner, a cheap earring lies next to the mattress and a faded photo of the Delhi Banana hangs askew on the rose-print wall. I get splinters under my nails digging the thing out from behind the skirting – time and the elements have worked on it like they have on the mail. I brush it clean, pocket it and move on.

I've got none of my tools of trade apart from intuition but that'll have to do. The wallpaper in the front room, east, is Laura Ashley, circa 1980. My father would have arrived here in 1974, before the wallpaper. I peel it away where mould has begun the work for me to find more of what I'm after. Above the phone jack in the hall are names, phone numbers, addresses and squiggles, as well as a lot of cryptic messages and lazy thoughts that would have made sense at the time but make little now: Protest makes perfect; When the mouse is away, the cat sleeps; Ice Queen; a heart with P.V. arrow A.G. on it – heavily pencilled like the person who did it was under the influence of something, call it delusion. I'm used to it now – it's my father's handwriting.

It takes me a day – a day in which seconds turn into minutes and minutes into hours. I find a public telephone and punch in the numbers only to come up with nothing because, over time, phone numbers change. It's easy to find the addresses that once belonged to the numbers but they turn into stone walls. All bar one, that is: 7 Lucretia Avenue, Ophelia. A late-model Jaguar's sitting in the driveway and an old maid opens the door.

'I'm from Lotto, the government gambling institution you can trust. I want residents' names.'

The old maid peers at me with suspicion while restraining a cross Alsatian-mastiff. A very cross Alsatian-mastiff. 'What do you want?'

'If I knew what I wanted I wouldn't be here. How long have you been in residence?'

Pride overcomes suspicion. 'I'm an old family retainer – forty-one-and-a-half years.'

'Who else lives here? Starting with the name and occupation of the head of the house, like in a census.'

The maid's going to get into trouble whichever way she bounces; somewhere behind her a baby's crying and somewhere else a newsreader's saying there's been another earthquake in Nepal. The maid takes the line of least resistance; she wants to hear the news or settle the baby, most likely both. But before she can do anything she's got to answer the question.

'Dr Jonathan Gambetta, Queen's Counsel – the Victorian Government changed back from Senior Counsel because people like Dr Gambetta complained – is in his chambers and Mrs Gambetta's having her hair done.'

The maid starts to close the door but I put my foot in it.

'Would that be Gambitta with an i?'

'No, with an e. And a double-t.'

The baby's wails have increased in intensity, the news goes into overdrive and to add to the maid's anxiety a jug's boiling over. Old mansion, ancient jug.

'Are we talking about the same person? What are Dr Gambetta's antecedents?' I take it slow – it makes them jittery and keener to talk to get rid of this unwanted intrusion so they can deal with the primary source of their anxiety. 'Mother, father, grandparents, uncles, aunts.'

'I only know the name of Dr Gambetta's maiden aunt – Annita. And, yes, she lived here.'

'Age?'

'She's dead.'

'What age would she have been, had she lived?'

'I don't know – sixty? No, wait a minute, I know exactly – sixty-one.'

'What did she die of?'

'A broken heart. Look, I'm a bit busy, would you please leave?'

The initial's right, the age is in the ballpark and so is the broken heart. I please leave.

She remembers something as she closes the door. 'Does Dr Gambetta get the prize?'

'I'll come back,' I reply.

And I do.

Chapter 19

A ROLAND FOR AN OLIVER

I've changed into a snug-fitting black tracksuit courtesy of Vinnies and I'm carrying a torch but I don't quite know what I'm looking for. As a precaution, I sedate the dog, disable the alarm and climb in through the pantry window of Number 7 Lucretia Avenue. I learnt as much as I could on the first visit. What I'm looking for now could be in the study, which should be on the ground floor, well away from the nursery. Which, going by the screams I heard earlier, is off to the right. I go through the pointers that say this is the right place:

My father had a low female-attention span and was sick of his blonde

The initials of the blonde's successor were A.G.

One of the phone numbers, adjusted for time, match this address

A resident was one Annita Gambetta – right initials

Calculating back from age sixty-one, in 1978 Annita Gambetta would have been twenty-one – which for my cradle-snatching father was pretty much the right age.

The study's not on the ground floor, the stairs squeak and the floorboards in the hallway are bare. I've put the pooch in dreamland for twenty minutes, which means I've got fifteen minutes before it starts calling in its IOUs. I switch off the torch as I move past a roomful of snores. The baby's whimpering and the study's at the end of the hall.

I ease the door shut and turn on the light. The walls are covered with books, complete with designer footstool to reach the upper echelon; while in the middle of the room is a desk containing a gilt-framed photograph of a man in a wig who must be Gambetta, a green telephone and a silver letter opener. There's the usual array of fine chairs and an ancient-looking book in a display case by the window.

I already know that my father was – is – not a nice person. Aside from dumping me, he hived off with a blonde the moment Mum dissed herself. Everything points to his soon thereafter abandoning his blonde for a dame with the initials A.G. Working forward, one Annita Gambetta had an affair, relationship, *connection* with my father while her nephew – whose study this is – was a kid. My dad was an opportunist. What I want is here somewhere.

Going by the instructions on the packet containing the sedative I fed the pooch I've got thirteen minutes left and valuable time is always saved by analysis. Good lawyers – and going by the signs, Gambetta's good – leave little to chance. If there's anything of significance, it won't be sitting up on the desk with a smile on its face saying Take me. The prints on the wall are of things legal and for show while what I'm looking for is quasi-legal and private. Official documents would be in his chambers but I'm not looking for official documents. I'm after unofficial ones.

If there's a safe in his chambers – and there would be – a safe here would be an unnecessary duplication. What I'm looking for doesn't have to be all that secure – just away from the prying eyes of a maid. The desk drawers are locked but it would be logical not to keep anything of value in the desk. Any one of the 5000 tomes on the walls might be fake, with the words Blackstone's Law of Torts on the outside and pornography within. But that would be too obvious. So where is it? Anything hidden would be personal – love letters, children's drawings, the odd obscene postcard. I calculate the size of such a collection and come up with a bundle slightly smaller than the quarto-sized book in the display case.

The volume is Foxxe's Book of Martyrs and it's open like a pair of innocent hands. The cabinet's a fish tank minus water, its lid locked but not secure. I ease it open with the letter opener. Gambetta's got little sentiment – he's a lawyer, after all – and although the book's a rarity it's been gutted. What I'm looking for is in the left side cut-out.

I could take it all but I don't need it all. I only need what's mine, my inheritance – the letter with the name and address on it. The faint odour of women's perfume wafts from a scrap of tear-wrinkled paper; a sepia photograph of a woman in a bikini smiles for the dickey-bird; a child's drawing reveals a liking for elephants; there's an interesting document signed by a well-known criminal, deceased; and a one-page note in a hand I recognise – addressed and dated. I check my watch. Five minutes to go. The dog growls. So much for the promise on the packet. I pocket the note, replace the book, close the cabinet and straighten to find Gambetta in the doorway, holding a gun.

'I could shoot to kill,' he says. 'However, were I successful I could be deemed to have used undue force as defined in obiter dicta in judgments on trespass. I could shoot to wound only I might miss. I find myself caught between Scylla and Charybdis, a rock and a hard place. Either way' – here he waves the gun, a pretty little Steyr M40 automatic with triangular sights – 'I imagine you'd prefer this little chap not to go off, particularly with you at the pointy end of it.'

In wig and gown in a courtroom and waving a sheaf of papers, Gambetta could be impressive. But with his hair all over the place, wearing a loose-tied paisley dressing gown and waving a gun, he looks and sounds like any other two-bit criminal – of unsound mind and dangerous.

'I must be in the wrong house.'

He advances on the desk with the phone on it. 'Yes, you must, mustn't you?' He waves the gun even more. 'Stand back.'

I stand back, he picks up the handpiece and I make like I just thought of something. 'But just in case I'm in the right house, I'm here on behalf of Peter Violente, who I believe is an old friend of yours – or at least of your aunt.'

He drops the phone like it's hot. He's big and well-built but I could take him, even with the gun, because he's off-guard. But I don't have to. I've got his attention, which is what I'm after.

'I beg your pardon?'

'It was a matter of blackmail and settlement – I expect you'd regard it as a contract.'

'You're not making sense,' he says.

I translate it into legalese. 'Although the two principals on your side are dead, it still looks bad. Bad enough to lose you your membership of the Melbourne Club – I believe they're still particular about such matters.' It makes me no better than my father but he didn't have a gun at his head. 'Your father did something illegal and my father found out about it, via pillow talk with your aunt. The contract showing payment by your father to mine is tantamount to an admission of guilt.'

'What do you want?'

'My father's most recent address.'

The dog's barking; next thing the baby will start crying; followed shortly thereafter by the appearance of a wife or the maid.Gambetta's eyes flicker to the door. 'Is that all?'

'That's all.'

The lawyer considers his response, weighs it against the alternatives and decides in the only way he was ever going to. 'Your father was in touch with me only recently – after even more money. I'll tell you where he is if you return what you stole from me and tell him I'm not paying any more.'

When I reach into my pocket, he flinches; I'm a burglar after all, as well as the son of a blackmailer and clearly no slouch in that department myself. 'Don't worry, I'm not armed.' I place the note on his desk. 'Now you can either tell me where he is or shoot me; I strongly recommend the first option.'

'His last-known address was Hamilton Street, Prahran, in Melbourne – number seventy, I think.' Gambetta pockets the paper. 'It's a men's refuge as far as I know. Which would mean that he'd fallen about as low as he could go when he last demanded money, which wasn't so many months ago.'

He flicks the gun like he's seen it done on television.

'And in my book that's quid pro quo – which is Latin for, It's all you're going to get in exchange for that piece of paper. In other words, a Roland for an Oliver. You have nothing in writing and I haven't written a cheque so this didn't happen – it's just momentarily embarrassing.' He levels the gat. 'Now if you'll fulfil your undertaking and leave, I'll fulfil mine and not shoot you.'

Chapter 20

THE MYXO MAN

Skid row's skid row, whether it's in New York, Paris, London or Melbourne. It's no particular street in no particular part of town, more an attitude – a figure under a blanket, a shape in a doorway, a wraith, usually with its hand out. I'm my father's son and should want what's best for him. But looking at the figure before me I feel nothing.

I never really knew him. There was a young man who abandoned a small boy but memories need reinforcements and I didn't even have any photos. He could have been short, tall, fat, thin, handsome or plug-ugly and anything might have happened since. The old man shuffling along Chapel Street before me could be anyone. His feet are black, his hair's scraggy and his crumple-legged, shiny-bummed pants are held up with twine. If it's my father he's not just my past, he's also my future.

He goes to cross the road but a tram dings its warning bell, causing him to stumble back onto the kerb. To attract all those women, he must have had something. But that would have been no more than ersatz, bravado and charm. Because he would also have been fearful – fearful of what he'd done to my mother, fearful of losing what little there was left to him, fearful of what was to come. If I'm paranoid, this is where I got it.

When the old man's eyes wander my way, I see myself – the same mashed-in features, the same nose, same chin. When he finally notices me, he assumes I'm a mugger or a cop and veers away. I'm no more than a corpse's length from him. Close enough to smell the stench, close enough to not want to be here. You're too close, Monica Best warned. When I was a kid on the funny farm, I chased rabbits with myxomatosis – the disease that makes their eyes bulge and eventually kills them. That's what I'm following now – a sick animal staggering towards death. I feel myself recoil, wanting to get away. Then I touch the objects in my pocket. Apart from which, there was the writing on the wall.

It was stupid chasing those rabbits – even as a kid I knew that. They were good for nothing because they were diseased. When you caught one, what did you do with it? I stare at the figure before me. Can he think, talk and perform the functions necessary to survival? I don't want to be anywhere near him. I let him draw away. You're too close, Monica warned.

I turn and when I look back he's gone. The sun's a burning ember in a grey sky and there's an alternative. I could forget Pandora, forge a new life for myself and let my father rot in the sun. Then I hear my mother shrieking as she went to her death, together with my sister Sophie. And Pandora. That's when I remember what I'm here for and what I've got to do.

I break into a run. A boy on a bike passes, a woman smiles, leaves flutter from the trees. When I reach the corner of Watson and Chapel I still can't see him – there's too many shoppers, too much traffic. He's got away. I found my father only to lose him again.

Then I make out the figure on the bridge and hurry towards it before I lose him forever. When I grab his arm, it's a matchstick and the stench coming from him is overpowering. He tries to pull away but he's too weak. He's smaller than I thought and the whites of his eyes are yellow. I've made a mistake.

'Leave me alone, you bastard, or I'll …'

It's an empty threat, a parrot's curse. He's been on life's receiving end for too long and there's no strength left in him. This can't be my old man. Whoever it is has decided I'm a cop.

'What law am I breaking, tell me that! Can't a man be left alone? Who do you think you are?'

'I'm your son.'

The wretch cackles. 'Which son? Jesus, there are hundreds of them.' He rubs his head. 'That's what they always said about me – that Lothario's got kids all over the place.'

I followed the directions Gambetta gave me, a social worker at the hostel directed me to the old man's haunts and after a day and a half searching the streets of Melbourne I've come up with this. Only to find that I'm most likely wrong. In my desperation to find my father, I forgot to be a detective. The thing before me is what I feared my father had become, I'm seeing what I expected to see, twisting this old man to fit some childish image from an Identikit. I need proof.

'You're not Lothario, you're Violente – Peter Violente.' I can't say more, mustn't muddy the water; what I need is some further confirmation apart from the smell – proof positive that this is my father. His eyes go dead, his body sags and I grab him before he falls. 'Who are you?'

'I told you — I'm Lothario.'

It can't be him because I can't bear it to be him. My father's a strutting dandy waving an ebony cane with a silver handle on it, a rich widow by his side – healthy, strong and in charge of his life.

'Does the name Annita Gambetta ring a bell?'

He pulls away, trying to free himself. 'Who are you?'

'I already told you – I'm your son.'

'I haven't got a son.'

'But you just said –'

He peers out of the fug, his watery eyes hooded. 'Who did you say you were?'

'The name's Rainbow.'

He shakes his head. 'What kind of name's that?'

I let go his matchstick arm and turn away. It was a futile exercise, a wild goose chase, a madman's impulse. You're too close, Monica had warned. While the shrink said, You need treatment before you kill someone. A tram rattles past, the racket rearranging the old man's words until they're no more than an echo.

'My little Rainbow!' It's the voice of my mother. 'He's so pretty, this little son of ours. Oh, we must have another and another ...' The parrot's mimicry ceases, to be replaced by a harsher voice, the voice of reality. 'There was only one choice and I took it.'

I can't believe it's him. In some dingy dive somewhere this derelict overheard my real father say those words and he's imitating him. He's of unsound mind and doesn't know what he's saying. One last try.

'I want one-word responses.' If he's who I need him to be, he would have gone through the routine many times. 'You've played the one-word game?' He nods, interested despite himself. 'All right, I want the first word that comes into your head. Children.'

'Burden.'

'Wife.'

'Victim.'

'Blame.'

'Sex.'

'Home.'

'Nimbin.'

'Pandora.'

The old man's eyes hood even more and he shakes his head – to clear it but also because he doesn't want to acknowledge that he knows the name. 'There were a lot of women in my life but I don't know anyone called Pandora.'

I haven't got all I want but you never get all you want. Get all you want and you stop looking.'Why did you say Nimbin?'

The guarded look returns. 'It was just a game. Life's a game.'

'Don't try to take refuge in stupidity.'

'What else is there to take refuge in?'

It's what I'd say; it must be him; I take his arm. 'You're coming with me.'

'That's what you think.'

This time I hang on. 'No, old man, it's what I know.'

But at Tullamarine airport the dame in the cobalt-blue uniform has other ideas. 'I'm sorry but we can't take him.'

I've arranged for Roarer to pick us up at Mascot and through a Melbourne contact of Ace Mollema's I've obtained IDs for me and the old man that say we can drive. A gold driver's licence for me and a silver one for the old man. We're Sammy and Bert Smith, father and son – I'm Bert and this is Sammy. At the Salvos I got him a pair of sky-blue daks, an orange shirt and a pair of sneakers to cover the feet but he's still got the beard, he still stinks and the dame in the uniform comes around the counter and draws me aside.

'I'm sorry, sir, but we have strict regulations. There are other customers to consider and we'd get complaints.' The old man's too close to her; she edges away. 'Dementias can cause havoc.'

'He's not a dementia.'

'Then what's wrong with him?'

'His wife died.' It's not a lie. 'I've got to get him to Sydney.'

'Can't you go by train?'

'The train's too slow.'

The airline dame considers her options and realises she hasn't got any. She takes one of those breaths without any options in it.

'Do you have any baggage?'

'Only my dad.'

Chapter 21

NO TIME FOR MOURNING

After we touch down I park the old man with Roarer. They're two of a kind, last seen heading towards the Cross in an iridescent-pink Shangri-la coupé discussing the cross merits of dames. I cab it to the caravan off the Bratwurst Parkway, hand the cabbie a C-note and tell him to wait. Sally opens the door. She doesn't invite me in. I come straight to the point.

'We're going on a little journey.'

Her colouration indicates a state of excitement which would impede coherent thought. 'I'm not going anywhere except away from here. I'll contact the witness protection people and tell them I want out of their stupid program. Anything's better than a life on the run. I'll go back to medicine. Those thugs won't dare touch me.'

I hitch the gat. 'Have you got a preferred funeral parlour? I'll be happy to make all necessary arrangements.' She considers me while the alizarin crimson in her cheeks fades to pink; even angry, she's beautiful. 'I really don't like you, Rainbow,' she says at last. 'Where are we going?'

'You'll know when we arrive. In the meantime I'm taking you to town where you'll buy three autumn-coloured tracksuits — sizes big, medium and small; black leotards and tights for night-time wear for yourself; a first-aid kit; torches; and backpacks for three. Plus a pair of binoculars. Oh, and some stuff from a theatrical supply shop that turns hair white.' I hand her a wad of dough. 'That should cover it. We'll meet under the clock at Central.'

'Is that all?'

I repocket my wallet. 'No, it's just the beginning.'

She's no longer Hélène Dalmatian. Instead, she's Helena Dannazione, a barista in an eatery called Discord in Concord. I ease my way past too many black shirts, white suspender braces and hard looks and at first she doesn't recognise me. Memories belong to contexts and when she last saw me I was bald and we were in France. Change the context and you forget who was in it.

'Rainbow!' she says finally. 'Hang on, that should be – what should it be?'

'Arthur Halliwell. When you last saw me I was a bald accountant, everyone's favourite non-entity.' There are a few familiar faces but there are always familiar faces – what's important are the unfamiliar ones. 'But Rainbow will do. Got a minute?'

'I guess so.' A figure looms behind her and I slip my fist under my jacket; this would be Sugar Daddy No. 3 or maybe it's No. 9, and he might be dangerous; she changes her mind. 'I mean, no, I haven't got a minute, I'm busy. Coffee?'

'Three shots and black like my conscience.' A few years back she was a waltz in the moonlight, an unnecessary evil who became a necessary one. Her watch waggles on her wrist as she taps the used coffee grounds from the ladle and replaces them with fresh ones; the figure behind her drifts away; the one I've got to watch is the one by the door. 'I need some information.'

'I know nothing you need to know.'

'You knew me before you knew me, didn't you?'

'That doesn't make sense.'

'Nothing and nobody makes sense. Were you ordered to come into my life or did you happen upon it by accident?'

Her lips tighten but she's still got those beautiful eyes – amethyst-coloured, the shape of sloes, berries to die for, like I nearly died for her. She yanks her hand away from the machine. It might be guilt or it might be the steam.

'It was an accident,' she says.

'What – coming into my life or burning your hand?'

'Both.'

'Lie and I'll stay, Dannazione. But tell me the truth and I'll leave.'

She lowers her voice. 'And when you do, do you promise to stay away?'

The figure by the door is moving towards us, his hand in his pocket – evil is as evil does and it's a living. I flick the safety to Off as I turn back to the dame.

'Answer the question – were you in my life before you were in it? Did you know me before I knew you? Were you tailing me?' 'All right, yes!' She's hissing like the coffee machine now. 'Someone told me to follow you.' It must have been Arthur Flax, her then sugar daddy, who was hand-in-glove with a bunch of crooks but is now dead. 'I know what you're thinking but it wasn't Arthur. It was –'

The gat's in my hand in a microsecond. Silencers make a sound like a coffee machine and that's what this one's like – helium escaping from a balloon, a puff of breath, the hiss of a snake. As Dannazione slides to the floor, she's got what she wants – she'll never see me again and this particular sugar daddy will be her last. The figure who was by the door has nearly reached us while half-a-dozen other gats are also aimed in our direction, most of them made in Italy.

When I hit the floor, my gun barrel's smoking and Hell and Damnation – born Hélène Dalmatian but rebadged as Helena Dannazione – is staring sightless at me under the counter. There's no time for mourning. I snake-belly my way to the back door, through the cucina, into the gabinetto and out into the lane, accompanied by the usual fusillade. Not all the gats are muffled and some are cannons. Dannazione might be dead but she's still in the PANDORA PENDING file as I upset the wheelie bins. When there are guns after you, always upset the wheelie bins.

Gertrude Match looks innocent but she's always looked innocent – a lightweight beauty with a heavyweight smile. But innocent or guilty I don't want her dead. Which is why I covered my tracks after leaving the death caff and why I don't hang around now. I put the question to the background of Madame Blavatsky banging out the fairy dance from the *Nutcracker* like a Death March while little feet shuffle on the bare wooden floorboards of the ballet parlour like the cloven hoofs of Fate.

'Where did you come from, Gertrude?'

'Just now I was playing piano for Madame Blavatsky.'

She's a sweet potato but when potatoes go bad, they stink. 'No – forever. You turned up in my life with a broken arm but you existed before that. Everyone's got antecedents — what were yours?'

The dancing feet are as innocent as rain on a roof. 'I was a good girl who married a bad man only to escape and become a piano player. It's not a story you could make a novel from.'

I feint to the right, followed by a quick-switch play, right arm down, left up, then the pirouette, watching her all the time. There's no reaction, nothing but a look of wonder.

'Madame B said you could dance but I had no idea!'

There's no other response, no attack move, no knife. She's nothing but a nice girl with her arms by her sides, amazed at this exhibition of ballet by a 200-pound private detective. I half expect her to ask for an encore. I've still got to put the question.

'Who else is in your life, Match?'

'No-one good. But no-one bad, either. Since escaping from my husband, I've kept away from men. Which means I lead a sequestered life — I get all the kicks I need out of playing piano.'

I'm inclined to believe her; then again I'm inclined to believe anyone — especially when they're beautiful. 'Does the name Pandora ring a bell?'

Match half-closes her multi-coloured eyes. 'I know a musical instrument of that name — also called a tambora. Or do you mean the chain of jewellery stores?'

'It's neither a musical instrument nor a shop but a person. Someone's been tailing me and I thought it might be you.'

'How long have they been tailing you?'

'About forty years.'

When Gertrude Match puts her hand on my arm, it's a pianist's hand and the touch is legere. 'I'm thirty-seven, Rainbow. How could I be this Pandora of yours?' After the meaning of life and the best age for whisky, it's the only question that really matters. 'Tell me, have you thought of visiting a psychiatrist?'

I leave without saying goodbye.

Chapter 22

THE DAY OF THE DOLLS

Too many hours north of Sydney, the town of Casino's a damp squib and the bus is a slow boat to China. The old man's drunken snores are the grunts of a warthog and Sally can't stop fretting about the chain of events that's landed her where she is. The bus is packed with tourists.

'I feel stupid, exposed and downright angry,' she says. 'Remind me again – why are we going wherever we're going?'

'Because I used to live there but also because you're in danger and I made you that way.'

She nods at the old man. 'What about him? Why bring him?'

'Because he could be the answer.'

Sally turns away. 'If he's the answer, I'd hate to know the question.'

The exhaust system's shot and the bus rattles like a cryptful of bones which means we've got to shout to be heard.'I'm with her,' the old man mutters. 'I'm here against my will. I wanna go back to Melbourne.'

Sally's gone back to looking out the window. What she sees is verdant countryside but for me there are two landscapes – the one outside the bus and the one in my mind. Trees claw at a manganese sky, the kind that innocence swims in, and pearls fall out of the air. But in my mind it's forty years ago, in a wilderness through which blind memories swirl in a torrent.

I don't know the town because I was never in it. I was five when my dad spirited me away from what we kids called the funny farm – the so-called *collective* of hippies situated somewhere outside Nimbin. We lived in a world without fences, real or imagined. We never went to town.

Town is a narrow, pot-holed, tar macadam road lined with a lot of multi-coloured shops, a sign above one of which reads: THE GRASS ON THE OTHER SIDE IS ALWAYS GREENER – WELCOME TO THE OTHER SIDE. As we collect our haversacks, Sally says she's going to stretch her legs and the old man shambles away after her.

'Don't let him near alcohol,' I say. 'He's no good to me drunk.'

She turns and gives me a queer look. 'So now I'm his keeper as well as yours?'

I think I know what she means as I watch them go – the graceful figure of Sally and that of the old man shuffling beside her. Welcome to Paranoia Central.

Someone's playing guitar and I chuck him a couple of coins at which he jumps to his feet and hugs me. 'Wow, thanks, man!' he says with far more enthusiasm than necessary. A sign reads: THIS IS WHERE THE RAINBOW CAFE WAS BEFORE THE FIRE. Stray dogs, more nondescript shops, more hippies pointing guitars at me like machine-guns and a couple of kids in ragged caftans, their hair in tangles and their thoughts even more tangled.

'Why are we here?' the kid says.

'Because we're dreaming,' the girl replies. 'None of these people are real. We only see what we want to see.'

'What if we don't want to see anything?'

'Then we're not here.'

Nothing makes sense and everything makes complete sense. My fingers close on the dolls in my pocket – the one that Monica said she found at the refuge and the one I found in the house in Melbourne. The kids smell of sweat and the sky's the colour of oxidised slate. The boy nods, I nod back and the girl hugs me. The old man and Sally are dots in the distance.

Notes are sticky-taped to shop windows like magnets on fridges – the Moon's in the ascendant, a guru's doing tea-leaf readings on Tuesday and the reason for all the tourists is the approach of St Valentine's Day. Which to me means a massacre on 14 February 1929 in Chicago, presided over by a thug called Al Capone, while to everyone else it means love. The only pub's full and so are the bed and breakfasts. A newspaper flaps against my leg. I pick it up. It contains details of St Valentine's Day celebrations – market stalls, maypole dances and love-ins. While another story's headed ANOTHER DEATH and one of the advertisements for fortune tellers features a picture of a doll much like the ones in my pocket. A joker I ask for directions nods at the paper.

'Valentine's Day is death day,' he says. 'They reckon those deaths are suicides but I know better.'

'I was looking for the fortune teller.'

'You'll find her next door to Luscious Fruit.'

'You're not a believer,' the fortune teller says straight off the bat.

If I hoped she had a wart on her nose and looked cadaverous, I'm disappointed. She's small and full-figured and looks like everyone's grandmother, except for the eyes. We're in a room behind a trinket shop with a sign in the window that says ASTROLOGY, NUMEROLOGY, MEDITATION AND SPIRITUAL HEALING. Dolls are scattered around the room, while a green-baize table stands between me and the necromancer. She's busy trying to set out her cards in the shape of a cross and nearly succeeding.

'What's with the dolls?' I ask her.

'What dolls?'

The dolls that are sprawled on chairs, lying in corners and scattered all over the floor. 'The ones in your advertisement, all these.'

She doesn't look up. 'Oh, I've ceased to be aware of them except as background to the main event. And they're not really dolls, they're whatever you want them to be.'

'What if I don't want them to be anything?'

In the end it's the eyes – the rest's just bone structure. They're the connie agates of my childhood – the pale-green marbles other kids didn't want because they were too ordinary; eyes that stop her from being a grandmother.

'Choose a card,' she says.

I choose a card. She doesn't even look at it.

'You're a stranger in town and you're searching for your past.' Her fingers touch a card featuring a skeleton; one of its corners is creased. 'It's not what you think. The Death card doesn't mean death – it stands for regeneration.'

'You've got to say that or risk getting sued.'

'Do you want me to go on or are you just going to sit there making smart comments?'

'Go on,' I reply.

'I see a killer. A killer who's about to get his comeuppance, his just deserts, what's coming to him.' She pauses, frowning. 'That's funny, the cards also say that you don't exist, there's no —'

'Aura.'

'You're making fun of me again, just as you made fun of the dolls. You might come to regret that.' She shakes her head. 'Meanwhile you're not computing. Are you sure ...'

I play along. 'I'm not sure of anything. That's why I'm here.'

Not death but regeneration. Where have I heard that before?

'You had a troubled childhood.' She shivers. 'I hear screams, I see death.' She pales. 'I'm sorry but I can't go on.'

'How about trying?'

The agate eyes close, the mouth opens and I wait for the shaking that will tell me she's in the hands of a Greater Force than her. Instead she murmurs, 'I see a lot of dancing but it's not happy. People die.'

'I thought you weren't supposed to say stuff like that.'

She opens her eyes without looking at me, gathers the cards and shuffles them. 'I can say whatever I like. Including making the prediction you'll meet a tall, dark stranger and go on a journey.'

She's smiling as she says it but the connie agate eyes don't look up as I leave.

Chapter 23

ALPHA AND OMEGA

I'm outside the pub with two empty whisky glasses before me and nursing a third when a shadow falls across the table with the suns and moons all over it and a hand lights on the back of the chair beside me.

'Anyone using this, my friend?'

A nice, deep voice, the kind that might be owned by a tall, dark stranger but turns out to belong to a small, fat man in crumpled brown corduroy trousers, a green-and-white T-shirt, beige linen jacket and nicely shone shoes with dimples in them. The hair's grey and I put his age at around sixty. There's no hug. Instead he's holding out a hand and smiling.

'The name's Malcolm Booby and I'm a guide.'

A passer-by greets Booby and he flashes his nice, bright smile at them before turning back to me. His hand's so soft it could be a soufflé.

'Hubert Brown,' I murmur.

A drink appears like he conjured it out of thin air. 'You from around here, Herbert?'

It's a test; I correct him. 'It's Hubert. You?'

He no sooner finishes his drink than another appears. 'I've been here since the Devil was a girl – call me Mr Nimbin. It's a great place, full of mystery, beauty, soul, energy and health – Paradigm Lost, I call it. You didn't answer my question.'

'No, I didn't.'

The smile jumps out at me like it was lying in ambush. 'I see, you want me to guess. Very well, in your grey tracksuit and windcheater, you've dressed down for the occasion but you're still not from Nimbin. Also I saw you getting off the bus.' He smiles out of his nice grey eyes; the second drink disappears; someone else greets him; he nods in reply then returns his gaze to me like it never went away as a third drink arrives – plus a whisky for me.

'It's a nice day.'

I'm not here to talk about the weather. 'Know where we can find a bed, Booby?'

'How many of you are there?'

I'm about to say, I'm a detective, a father, a son, a paranoid schizophrenic, an ex-husband, a non-person and a misanthrope – which would make it about seven, but think better of it. And while I'm thinking better of it, Sally and the old man roll in like a Bondi thumper. Booby's on his feet in an instant.

'You must be Mrs Brown.' He glances at the old man. 'While you'll be –'

The old man slumps in the chair that Booby just vacated. 'I'll be stuffed,' he says. 'Where's me beer.'

'You're not getting one,' I tell him. 'You're drying out.'

'All right, a fag then.'

'No.'

'Who do you think you are?'

'He's been pestering me for a drink ever since we arrived,' Sally says. 'Much more interesting drugs were on offer but he didn't have any money.'

The old man turns on her. 'And you wouldn't give me any.'

Booby intervenes. 'How long are you staying?'

The old man glares at Booby. 'And who the hell –'

He suddenly seems to think better of it, shrugs like it's not worth the candle and Booby calmly continues like the old man hasn't spoken, like he isn't even there.

'I only ask because if you haven't anywhere else to go you can stay with us. And if you're here for the weekend, you might like to attend our little St Valentine's Day celebration.' He waves aside any protests before we can make them. 'We haven't got the phone on so I can't ring my wife to warn her but as long as we don't arrive too early I'm sure it'll be fine.' He speaks like he's done this before but also as if he's trying to reassure himself. 'That gives us a couple of hours. How about a spin in the Maserati?'

The 'Maserati' is an old Ford Transit van with BOOBY'S TOURS in black on the side but it gets the old man away from the pub. Booby waves through a dusty window at a park with a rainbow-coloured building in the middle of it. 'That's the community centre and next door's the radio station.'

'Fascinating,' Sally says like it's not fascinating at all.

The candle factory's well worth a visit, there's a place called the Nowhere Café, a lot of interesting shops and even more interesting people, all set in Nature's wonderland. Which brings us to Nature's wonderland. The old man stays slouched like a small boy with the sulks while me, Sally and Booby teeter on the edge of a cliff.

'Not so long ago, that valley used to be an ocean,' Booby says, his voice heavy with conviction. 'Over there's Mount Wollumbin – it used to be a volcano.' Molten lava's pouring down the sides and survivors are fleeing, their hair on fire, screaming. I hear screams, the necromancer said. I see death.

By tour's end, it's late afternoon and me, Sally and Booby are in the front of the van while the old man's alone with his devils in the back. He's not happy but he never is. Booby's pitching a yarn that's a mix of fact and fiction, pre-history and magic, with a bit of religion thrown in for good measure – an unholy trinity of Darwin, *The Golden Bough* and the Bible. He reminds me of the necromancer. He also reminds me of my mother.

At one point his mobile rings and he stops the van, climbs out and answers it. I hear his deep, sonorous voice murmur something but can't make out what it is. The tour and the commentary have brought it all back – my mother rattling on about spirituality, preaching about Earth Spirits and spouting random scraps of poetry ending in a row of dots like it meant something when it didn't.

'You've made quite a study of this,' Sally says as Booby finishes his call and climbs back into the van.

Booby inclines his head. 'When humans evolved from fishes, we climbed out of the sea. We mock the Aboriginal Dreamtime but that's only because the unknown scares us. We feel safer looking down on others' beliefs, just as we looked down into that valley back there. We need to confront our fears and burnish our spirit in the flames so we can renew ourselves.'

Sally changes the subject. 'Have you always lived around here?'

'I wouldn't live anywhere else.'

'Why?'

'Because this is the beginning and the end, alpha and omega, fundamental to both our existence and our non-existence. Only in

somewhere like Nimbin can we hope to get in touch with our real selves.'
He smiles gently. 'But I mustn't get too serious – I get the feeling your
husband doesn't approve.'

It's the third time he's married us but Sally doesn't correct him.

A car's following us. A pair of thugs attacked me at the refuge
followed by a second attack at Rory's, someone tried to kill Sally and Hell
and Damnation's dead. I don't know if I'm a killer or why all of a sudden
the old man's fallen silent or how long before the stuff I want out of his
addled brain is going to come to the surface. All I know is that I need
some information and need it bad.

We didn't get about in cars in my childhood – the ride to Sydney was
my first in anything other than a billy cart and the trip in Booby's van
reminds me of it. We can put you up, Booby said. It's an offer too good to
be true. But darkness is falling and it hasn't proved true yet.

'I'm sorry, I must be boring you silly,' Booby says, breaking the
silence. 'What about you? What line of business are you in, Herbert?'

This time I don't bother correcting him. 'Market research. I find out
how people vote, what they're interested in and what they buy.'

It's a conversation stopper; it's meant to be. 'Fascinating.' Booby turns
to Sally. 'And you?'

'I paint.'

'And you, old fellow who's so quiet in the back?'

But there's no reply from the old fellow in the back.

Chapter 24

BECAUSE OF THE BATS

Up to now the countryside's been lush greenery, the kind you could drown in – the chrome and viridian of mature gums and the peppermint of saplings darkening to the somnolent depths of Prussian-green mangroves. Lantana and morning glory weave among native plants like boa constrictors and now and again there's the paler green of camphor laurels.

But as darkness falls, the shades fade to earth colours – burnt madder, indian red, raw umber and violet. The ultramarine sky is shot through with flames like the volcano's suddenly become active again, molten lava spewing down its sides as the sun deals the landscape its parting blow, while survivors flee from the volcano with their hair on fire.

I open the window to dispel my thoughts and that's when I hear the squeaks. It's the sound of rusty wheels, of seized bearings, a multitude of rats. No, not rats – bats. Because there are suddenly thousands of them seemingly unleashed by the coming night, black ash against a pewter sky, a vortex soaring up from the Moreton Bay figs, the rustle of their wings the crackling flames of an inferno. Booby points out a stone formation rising above the trees.

'That's Nimbin Rocks.'

I'm back in my childhood, in the hut thrown together by my father – my father who's now the old man hunched up and silent in the back. I'm curled on my straw bed petrified, ready with the scissors to cut off the bats' legs, shaking with fear because – apart from my sister – I'm alone. It's Mum's special night, she said before she left, and any significance I apply to that now has got to be nothing but déjà vu. I was a kid, there were bats and I had to protect my sister.

A wooden gate hangs off its hinges and blackberries and lantana claw at the van's sides. I pull in my arm. The headlight – only one's working – cuts a swath through the darkness. Black shapes appear out of nowhere.

This is where Pandora dates from. The van's single headlamp illuminates a track as narrow as a monomaniac's thoughts. That night, I remember being grabbed by my father, stuffed in a van and taken on a journey something like this. Until we ended up at Aunt Rube's – me, the old man who's now behind me and his blonde. A truck hurtles past, interrupting my thoughts.

'How long have you lived in Nimbin?' Sally asks, picking up a conversation from a couple of kilometres back.

'Several years or several centuries, who knows? We call it Nimbin time.'

The track leads under the feature called Nimbin Rocks, the van's single headlight probing like the eye of a Cyclops. A fox slinks across the road, its red eyes glistening; a kangaroo bounces alongside; and something black – an owl, a bat or a pterodactyl – covers the windscreen with its wings before banking away. We've been on this road forever. Nimbin time.

Booby resumes his travelogue. 'As you may or may not know, a number of the old collectives are still in existence. They were all the go in the 1970s. We didn't aim to be great farmers – we wanted to create a new world. That's Nature Farm over there and the one over to your left is the Carbourne Collective.'

Black hills sweep away on either side. Nothing seemed aimed at when we were kids. When I grazed my knee, got a bunged-up nose or cut my hand, the stranger who happened across me would say something like: It was meant to be. And maybe take me home or maybe not. There were mantras and mandalas and talk of Nimbin time as though we inhabited another planet, a place where time didn't exist – just space and plenty of it.

'We're almost there.'

We arrive at an overgrown driveway, a rickety bridge, more bumps even than on the road; the tentacles of out-of-control blackberries, lantana and morning glory reaching out as we plunge deeper into the darkness. Sally's politeness underlines her hostility – towards me, towards Booby, towards the old man.

'It looks like a war zone,' she murmurs. 'What happened?'

Decrepit buildings appear in the beam of the headlight only to disappear again – crazy structures covered with weeds and once-bright graffiti; the tattered remains of tents and teetering things of wood; ancient caravans; concrete bunkers; a windmill with half its vanes missing; a house with oeil de boeuf windows, the glass shattered; rusty containers with the shapes of what might once have been solar panels dangling from their roofs. Booby's mobile phone rings but he doesn't answer it. Instead he stops the van, his fingers tightening on the wheel. His hands seem much older than the rest of him.

'I've been thinking.' He's staring straight ahead. 'What if I let you out here? It used to be some kind of hostel – what we used to call the Palais Royale.'

A long, low, ramshackle building stretches before us.

'Fantastic,' Sally says.

Booby shakes his head; he's changed his mind. 'No, a promise is a promise.'

He restarts the van, crunches it into gear and we drive on. As if on impulse, he takes a paper bag off the dashboard and hands around what he calls 'Nimbin lollies'. Even the old man takes one but he'd take anything. The sweets taste of aniseed. More dwellings – a few with lights on but most not; more blackberries; and finally a sedate structure with an old car parked out the front and, off to the right, a huge pile of garbage teetering under the weight of old tyres. I make out what looks like an agricultural experiment gone wrong – bars and boxes, rough-hewn poles, raised garden beds, scarecrows. The road ahead veers off to the left. The brakes screech as Booby pulls up.

'Now for the naked wife,' he says.

We climb down, stiff after the long ride. I go to retrieve the backpacks but Booby stops me.

'It wouldn't be a good look, turning up as if you expect to stay. We'll do it in stages.'

The house looks like it was designed before the invention of right angles – something between a backyard dunny and a cathedral. A bark roof sags over corrugated-iron walls supported by buttresses and surrounded by a makeshift verandah. Gothic windows throw multi-coloured light onto pavers while late violets bloom by the slab-wood door.

The old man hovers while Booby enters the house. 'Let's see how she blows,' he says.

She's not what I expect but we'd be something of a surprise to her, too, a large woman in her sixties, her grey hair blonded, wearing a bulky caftan.

'At least she's clothed,' Sally murmurs, then aloud to Booby, 'Aren't you going to introduce us?'

'This is Mr and Mrs Brown and' – he looks around – 'somewhere outside is an old man.'

Sally steps forward, smiling. 'Whatever Malcolm says, we're not married – in fact we hardly know each other. I'm Sheila, this is Hubert and the old gentleman outside calls himself Sam. We're visiting Nimbin because we had time to kill. It's very kind of you to put us up.'

The old man hasn't come in. If you run away when your wife kills herself, you're not going to return forty years later, laughing. Booby's wife has the look of an ageing hippy still trying to cling to her youth, her face is expressionless and her eyes are hard. She turns to her husband. 'Could I see you for a moment, Malcolm?'

They pass through an internal doorway, leaving me and Sally alone with adze-cut rafters, a wood-burning stove that doubles as a heater, a telephone which must be some kind of prop, too many bad paintings, a rammed-earth floor and the feeling we're not wanted. The place is in disarray – a chair's lying on its side, the table's skewiff and the floor's wet like it's just been mopped. The happy couple returns. Booby shuffles his feet while his wife glares at me.

'You've caused us a lot of trouble,' she says.

'Calm down, Marsha,' Booby says; it sounds like a warning.

She turns on him. 'Why should I calm down – or, rather, why should I pretend? We ought to be allowed to express our true feelings, there's far too much namby-pamby evasion in this world.'

Booby turns to us, his expression one of apologetic resignation. 'I'll drop you at the gate.'

As we leave, the phone starts ringing but stops when Marsha answers it.

Chapter 25

BODY OF EVIDENCE

I climb out of the van into darkness and open the side door while Sally retrieves the packs. Booby stays where he is – his hands on the steering wheel, staring straight ahead even though there's nothing to stare at. For some reason, the headline from the newspaper jumps into my head like a newly-opened pop-up shop: *ANOTHER DEATH.*

I'm here to find Pandora. Any other bodies are someone else's problem, someone else's unexplained deaths. My mother and my sister died on a burning windmill and the totem poles are where it occurred. I step back as Booby leaves in a cloud of dust. One of his taillights doesn't work, either.

I'm in a weed-infested outpost of civilisation with an old man who might be my father and a woman who dislikes me intensely, looking for a phantom. Don't leave the windows open or you'll get bats in your hair. My mother was mad and my father gutless. Your mother probably took drugs during pregnancy, the shrink said. Your enemies are all in your head. I should have left them there.

Sally's just about dead on her feet and the old man looks even more of a zombie than usual. It's too late to go back to town and there's nowhere to stay there anyway. I make for the nearest building, the one Booby called the Palais Royale. I'm not so far gone that I'm going in without checking. The sense of Pandora is strong – this is where it all began, in this hive of shadows. Booby drove off without a word, his single taillight bouncing like a scarlet firefly dancing. 'Wait here,' I say.

The moonlight illuminates an architectural horror story, a building that seems to have run as wild as the lantana. It's a long, low, negative shape outlined against a sky of ultramarine violet. A hundred paces from end to end, its crenate roofline is broken by onion domes, a pitched slate roof, iron skillions, the odd spire. There are no doors to the side, just glassless windows. A sign on a stump reads: PALLIASSE ROYAL. It's a haunted house, the motel from Psycho, the stuff of nightmares.

But that's a string of clichés and clichés never solved anything. I get a torch out of my pack and go in, the walls closing around me like tentacles. The rooms are linked by a series of drunken passageways, the place part crumbling concrete, part rotten wood, with some walls of hardened mud, while others are wooden slabs, rough-cut when the timber was still green and now separating. I run into a spider's web and something's got under my shirt. A small snake blinks in the smoky beam of the torch. On the walls swastikas mingle with peace insignia and stars of David. The torchlight flickers.

My mother might have been mad but she wasn't alone in her fantasies. Roughcast depictions of rainbows are everywhere – together with what might be spatters of blood, a tree, an arrow, a cross. Drawings that once might have meant something are incoherent daubings by Dali wannabes. The floor's broken concrete with weeds sprouting from the cracks. I make my way past broken cupboards, scattered pots, piles of clothing – emerging at the southern end where I call out to Sally. There's no response.

I hardly know her, only that she's that most dangerous of combinations – beautiful and angry. I don't even know the old man. I'm stumbling around in the dark with a pair of strangers and my voice is swallowed by darkness. What did I hope to prove by coming to Nimbin? That I'm not mad? I've proved I'm mad just by coming here.

'Where are you?' I call. 'Sally? Sheila? Old man? Sam?
Answer me, will you!'

But they've gone and suddenly I'm a child again. Bats wheel around my head, panic seizes me and dark things rear out of the darkness – half-memories, imaginings, fears. The windmill's turning again and my mother's screaming again – my mother and my sister. My head spins. Pandora.

I've no idea what happened. Only that I wake blinking in blackness. I must have tripped or the emotion got too much for me or I've had some kind of fantasy reaction to being in Nimbin. I can't feel any bumps on my head and I'm not bleeding. All I know is that I'm staggering to my feet and there's a strong sense that time has passed. I can't find the torch and my head's splitting.

Aunt Ruby: Anchor yourself. Think of what you know. Find a line of thought and follow it, untangle the knots, relax. But I can't do any of that. Because in my mind, Sally is suddenly tangled up with my mother, my sister, Tsunami, Gertrude Match, Ariadne, Hélène Dalmatian, Monica Best, Denise, Annie and Salina. And each and every one of them could be Pandora. You could kill someone close to you. I back away from the possibilities, switch thought lines.

What do I know about Sally? What do I know about any of them? I confronted all of them and they all claimed to be innocent. And how could any of them except Ariadne be Pandora? They're all too young. Like the shrink said, it's all in my mind. I'm mad. Pandora never existed. I reel away from the possibilities. In Nimbin, memories are the smell of lantana.

I blunder into a bush and my foot nudges against something soft. The odour's that of an animal. There's a body and in context it must be some creature that's met with a bad end. We saw them by the roadside on the way here, victims of vehicles and/or bullets. Humans like killing and wombats don't shoot back. But this body's bigger than that of a wombat – much bigger.

Baseless assumptions are bumps in the road of detecting and you try to avoid them. Or if you can't avoid them, accept them for what they're worth and work your way around them without banging your head against a brick wall. I bend and my fingers touch cloth. It's not a wombat. ANOTHER DEATH, the newspaper said.

My first assumption is that it's Mr Whimsy Baldface – Malcolm Booby. Second: that it's that creeping derelict, my putative father. And – desperately not, I find myself begging – the body of Sally. But if it's any of them, why is he or she lying here dead? And who killed him or her?

That's when I entertain the fourth assumption – no, not assumption, the very real possibility – and start shaking. Whoever belongs to the body, I made it that way. I know from experience that lack of consciousness is the killer's favourite defence. I blacked out and when I came to there was blood on my hands and this body lying on the ground. I don't remember a thing.

Before technology appropriated the name, blackberries were bushes. I drag them aside. The moon and stars are undimmed by city lights and after I lost the torch my rods and cones started adjusting to the dark. But everything's still obscure – what happened, what's in front of me. The body's on the ground with red blackberries covering its face – alizarin crimson against black leaves. All I can make out are two wide-awake eyes and the red berries.

I touch one of the eyes and it doesn't blink. ANOTHER DEATH. I run my hands down the body to the feet. It's a big corpse, hard-muscled and dressed in denim jacket and jeans, its sideways hip upthrust. People are the clothes they wear, never more so than when they're dead. And this person's very dead. I place a hand on the ground to steady myself and peer into the darkness, hoping to see the killer. My fingers close on something.

There was no shout, no scream, no indication of who it was but I know that the body must be Sally's and that I must have killed her. I try to do the visual but can't. I'm blind again but this time it's tears. You might end up killing someone you love. I blacked out – why, I don't know. What happened after I blacked out I don't know, either. And even if I didn't kill her, I'm still the prime cause of her death. I allowed myself to be followed to Hobart where she was shot at by the people who followed me, then I brought her here and now she's dead. I expected to find Pandora so why couldn't Pandora have found us first? Either that, or I'm Pandora. My vision's warped like that of a criminal adjusting to life outside after a long sentence. It was Pandora. If it wasn't, I'm mad and it was me.

I know now why I brought Sally here. It wasn't just to keep her safe, although that was one of the reasons. It was because I wanted her nearby, so she could keep an eye on me. Caligari was right – I'm a killer. Sally! I called. But I was calling the dead. And somewhere not far away my newfound paterfamilias is probably also lying dead because I killed him, too. Only he'll be less mourned – by the world, by me. TWO MORE DEATHS, the heading will read. Deaths that occurred after I blacked out.I take a breath. Watch out for the bats, my mother warned me. But it's not the bats, it's me. With a body that I can't – don't want to – identify. Keep the cases separate, Monica Best said. But it's like my mother's warning about the bats. The scissors are by your bed, she said. The bats are my fears and my weapons are my hands. A past littered with deaths when I thought I'd killed nobody; Sally accusing me of killing one of her patients; Hélène Dalmatian with a bullet in her brain and me holding the smoking gun ...

I slip the thing I picked up into my pocket. You can ignore memories but you can't hide the facts. Not when they're right in front of you, not when your latest victim's staring you in the face.

Chapter 26

BLOOD ON THE BLACKBERRIES

'What on earth are you doing?'

It's Sally's voice yet the corpse is still there, its eyes wide open and staring. Bats rise against the night sky. Someone's waving a torch in my face.

'Where's the old man?'

I barely recognise my own voice. It's a croak, a whisper, the voice of someone afraid of himself, of what he might have become, fearful he's spiralling out of control. 'Pass me your torch.'

The mist coils in the beam as she hands it to me. I haven't done cause of death because I'm afraid of what I might find. Don't get too close, Monica Best warned. I'm conscious of Sally watching me. Look before you leap and always remember that you've got the option of not leaping at all. I probe with the torchlight as well as with my hands but keep my eyes off the face because I'm afraid of what I'll see. I force myself to look down.

It was a knife to the throat – left side – leaving blood on the blackberries. Because the blackberries aren't red at all and if I hadn't been so close I would have realised. It's the second week in February, a few days before St Valentine's Day – February 14 – late summer, and this far north the berries would no longer be red but their eponymous colour – black. Blood on the blackberries, ashes to ashes, and the blood's still red which means it's a fresh death. I glance up at Sally. In the darkness she looks a lot bigger than she is and far more dangerous than I care to remember.

'Where were you?'

'I think I had some kind of dizzy spell,' she says. 'I must be overwrought after all that's happened.'

'What about the old man?'

'I think he's wandered off.'

'Wandered off where?'

The old man emerges like a wraith. 'I'm here, son.'

It's not who I expect but it's never who you expect because you don't want to expect anyone. I go into investigator mode because that way I can forget – for the moment anyway – who and what I'm investigating. It's a run-of-the-mill autopsy, I tell myself, and the body on the bench with the blood-drain around it is no-one I know. There's the wound to the side of the neck, the death wound, and, swinging the torch away from those staring eyes, there are the marks. The shirt's top three buttons are undone and the shirt's pulled open. I've got to notice that because it's my job to notice. But at the same time I sense that even in death – no, *especially* in death – there should be privacy. Because a corpse is like a child, innocent and vulnerable, and bodies should keep their secrets. I feel like a violator. At first I mistake the marks for primitive drawings, those stick figures kids make using stones in the ground, with circles for heads and lines for torsos and limbs, because kids reduce what they see to basics. But these marks weren't made in hard ground but in soft flesh and they're not figures but words. Number of letters – I force myself to count them – eleven. Dimensions: roughly an inch high – four centimetres in the new money – and scratched to the depth of the width of a small coin. Blood that's only just now blackening. Implement employed –

'Would you mind coming here for a moment, Sally?'

'What is it?'

I don't look up as she moves in beside me. I indicate the marks with the torch. 'What do the words say?'

She gives them a cursory glance; she seems hardly able to make herself look. 'Tyrannosaur or something. But is this really the time to be playing detective? Shouldn't we report it?' She straightens. 'Whatever crazy adventure you're on can't have anything to do with this. The death clearly wasn't due to natural causes. We should notify the police.'

I hold out the torch and she takes it, gripping it as she might a scalpel as she squats. She criss-crosses the corpse's chest with the beam of the torch, finally bringing it back to the marks.

'No, it's not TYRANNOSAUR. It's more like TRAN NESOL –

whatever that means – followed by the numeral 10. The implement used wasn't sharp, which rules out something like a scalpel.'

'How can you tell?'

'The edges of the incisions are rough. See there, there and there? They're rips rather than cuts. It was something like an old-fashioned tin-opener or a blunt knife. It might even have been a fork. There was no bleeding, which means the wounds were inflicted after death.'

'Why were the marks made?'

'In my work, I've seen the marks of madmen. But this isn't the work of a madman. It's as if the killer's trying to tell us something.'

Chapter 27

CUT AND RUN

She sits back. 'It reminds me of the so-called magic tricks that *shalyuns* – Brazilian witchdoctors – perform in order to instil fear in people. I think the words are intended to invoke the kind of questions we're asking. Prehistoric man made marks in caves. Was it art or did they want to convey information?' Sally shivers and draws back even further – I'd say it was the cold except that it's not cold. 'But these marks are brutal.' She glances at me. 'They remind me of the bullet you put in that man's skull, the one I operated on.'

'What do you mean – brutal?'

'I'm a pragmatist. But it's easy to guess what was at work here. It's as if the killer was fighting forces beyond reason.'

'And the cause of death?'

She brings the torchlight up to the corpse's neck. 'The carotid artery was severed. Death would have been instantaneous.'

I've checked the arms for defensive wounds – there are none; and under the fingernails for cloth, blood, skin – ditto. And while checking the arms I also came across the same non-watch that Hélène Dalmatian was wearing when she died.

'Was the same implement used on the chest as on the neck?'

She shakes her head. 'The words were an add-on extra and the weapon used was blunt while the incision to the neck was clean.'

'In your opinion were the words on the chest carved just after death or much later?'

'I can't tell.'

'How long has she been dead?'

'Not my field – I'm a surgeon not a zetetic. Death could have occurred anywhere from a few minutes to hours ago. It's a cool night.'

I know the answer but I still ask. 'Was she killed here?'

'Hard to say.' She frowns. 'But what's it got to do with me? This is your field. You knew her, didn't you?' 'Yeah, I knew her.'

'Is she an old friend from Nimbin or someone who followed us here? Was she on the bus or was she lying in wait for us?' It's a surgeon's probing, a surgeon who needs an accurate diagnosis before proceeding further, before applying the scalpel. 'She was an insurance agent who I met a long time ago and whose acquaintance I remade only recently. She was sacked because of something I did – or didn't do. Her name is Monica Best.'

At times like these, you've got two choices. You can cut and run or you can stay and listen to the music – in this case, Schubert's *Death and the Maiden*. Which means I've got no choice at all because music there will be. This might be Nimbin but there are still laws and there are still cops and they'll come running like blood from a severed artery when they learn about the corpse because that's how they're built.

A tourist on an early-morning jog will stumble upon the body and call them on his ever-handy mobile. And the first thing the cops will want to say is, Don't touch anything. Except they won't say that because there's something even more important than not touching anything and that's the identity of the caller. Who are you? they'll ask, adding: We only need your name for the records. Except that's not why they need the name at all. They need the name because the caller's the first cab off the rank, the suspect-in-chief, the person of most interest in their investigation. Until someone of even more interest comes along.

After that, they'll follow procedure, which is:

Inspect the corpse;

Interrogate the natives. During which they'll get around to interviewing Booby and – willingly or unwillingly – he'll say he dropped us where the body was found – a criminal, a derelict and an elegant dame totally out of place in that company. The cops will work back from there. Say what you like about cops, they follow procedure. Under questioning, Booby will tell them that the suspects just arrived in Nimbin; then the cops will.

Talk to the driver of the bus and the passengers.

And in so doing find that the trio boarded the bus in Casino after travelling by train from Sydney. The tickets will be by far the best lead to our identity. Country Rail, State Rail, Rack and Pinion or simply Rack Off – whatever they call themselves now – will say who bought them and under what names. Trips have to be booked and the names logged into a computer. We gave fake names but that's the best lead of all. We want to fingerprint your van, the cops will tell Booby. They'll find our prints, no trouble at all. After so many years on the streets, the old man's will be in files everywhere while Sally's will match those of a person who disappeared from a witness protection program. And mine will be all over everything – a suddenly not-so-anonymous detective.

All of which means I can't call the cops. Because if I do, they'll do two things pretty well simultaneously – they'll trace the call and at the same time hurry to the scene of the crime before anyone has a chance to interfere with the evidence. But more important still, to stop the caller doing a runner. They'll think I killed her and all they'll need after that is a motive. That will be harder but they'll still find one. The corpse's fingerprints will match those of a security officer at a refuge, prints that the cops will already have because all security personnel are fingerprinted. A cross-check will produce a court case involving the same security officer during which the following questions were asked. You say there was a private detective involved in this case. What was his name? Can you describe him? And the description will bear an uncanny resemblance to the person who – in company with two others – was dropped near the body of the woman who lost the court case because of the detective …

Making ourselves scarce is a lottery ticket but we've got to buy it.'Where are we going?' Sally asks. 'We've got to call the police.'

I retrieve the torch. 'Only if you want the people hunting for you to find you. Rank amateurs can monitor police radios and the Mafia are far from amateurs. Besides which, we're at a murder scene which means we've got to get out of here – fast.'

Monica Best was a chief starter to be Pandora. Why was she in Nimbin and why is she dead? More important, who killed her?

Chapter 28

ISLAND OF MADNESS

There's no great flash of inspiration – nothing but a sense of strangeness, a memory of hippies finding a kid with a grazed knee and murmuring trite uncertainties like: *It was meant to be.* That and the bats. I was five, for Christ's sake, no more than a kid. And in those days – those glorious, inglorious seventies – kids were Nazis: born to be borne, something to be seen and not heard, an evil to be put up with or put down.

The Mafia's after Sally; the people who killed Hélène Dalmatian and were waiting for me at Rory's are after me; Pandora's here somewhere; and now there'll be cops. I don't need to be paranoid to know I'm being followed. But I can't be distracted from the main game – and that is, proving Pandora exists. I need to think myself into the case. Method detecting, Rube used to call it.

We're heading for the hills – for no reason other than that the hills are elsewhere. Before us, Nimbin Rocks – grim, dark and foreboding – are black holes in a violet sky. I've kept the old man away from the grog and he's suffering because of it. With his hair cut and in clean clothes he looks halfway respectable. But he's still the same person who ran off when his wife and daughter were dying – a drunk, a blackmailer, a coward. I don't want him anywhere near me but there's no such thing as want. He knows where we lived, where it happened, what happened and the identity of my nemesis. He's a metal detector, a geiger counter, a sniffer dog – the key to finding Pandora. Which is also why Sally's here. I might be keeping her out of the hands of the Mafia but she's also keeping an eye on me. And since the discovery of the body, something's irrevocably changed. It's like she's at last worked something out. I expected her to become even more distant. Instead, on the occasions when we accidentally brush against one another, she no longer draws away. Then again, it's probably just my imagination.

The going's steep and every few minutes the old man demands a drink. Sally produces a Rum Crunch chocolate bar from her pack while my mind toggles between the problems of not getting tangled in the lantana and who killed Monica Best. Correction: Monica Best and Hélène Dalmatian. The dolls in my pocket – the doll that Monica Best found outside the refuge and the one from my father's place of refuge in Melbourne – have been joined by the one I just found next to the latest body.

Shadow is substance and substance shadow while behind every tree I imagine the cops, the mystery killer, the Mafia and/or Pandora. How can any of those women be Pandora if she existed forty years ago? But when shadow is substance anything's possible. You see what you want to see, the necromancer said. I hurry the old man along with more roughness than necessary. Rabbits and wombats have dug holes in our path like the hole I seem to have dug for myself. The old man's angry because I've dragged him through a patch of nettles.

'I need a drink,' he grumbles.

I turn away. Why are we doing this? I asked Rube whenever she took me off into the bush. Because one day you might need to survive in the wild, she replied. You've read the book, now put what you've learnt into practice. Survive.

It's summer but the night was cold and the old man missed his liquor. In the bright light of morning, I find Sally's fashioned a broom out of twigs and is sweeping stones, bones and bat droppings out of the cave while I scavenge for food. A kookaburra laughs and somewhere a magpie warbles. The remains of our breakfast lie among the stones. The old man has refused food – *I'm not eating any of that crap,* he muttered. All he wants is something to drink. I look down into the valley at the scattered farmlets. From the perspective of the cave, there are no trees, just green cottonwool and, from the perspective of years, memories as soft as the bush. In my mind, my childhood was danger free. 'You keep saying we're escaping from the Mafia but where are they?' Sally asks. 'And that's not all, is it?

That body has a lot to do with why we're here.' Her eyes fix on mine. 'All those years ago you solved my case but now you can't even solve your own.' It's not an accusation – it's a statement of fact. 'Who was she?'

'She was a case that went wrong. I solved the case but left her to pick up the pieces. The matter went to court and she was caught in the cross-fire. She lost her job because I wasn't there to help.'

'But who was she?'

'How would I know? A private eye never knows anyone. Just another dame with a past.'

'Well one thing's for certain, she doesn't have a future.' Sally pushes her fists deep in her pockets. 'Was there anything between you? Did you love her? People kill for love, you know.'

From the mouth of the cave the world goes on forever – the pale sky contains even paler clouds and below us are the deep blues, greens and yellows of an ocean of time. Without booze the old man seems to be death warmed up, his face wearing an expression of malevolence as he emerges back into a world he's been trying to escape. For the first time, I almost recognise him. Nothing physical – it's his air of contempt, like he's no longer a piece of flotsam scraped off a Melbourne street but a man who's worked out the meaning of life and everyone else is stupid.

'Look at us,' he sneers. 'A bunch of bloody reffos in a cave in the middle of la-la land.' He waves his skinny arms around – the cave ceiling's just high enough not to bruise his knuckles. 'Who's she? And you're not my son – what makes you think you might be?'

Suddenly I know. It's not the face or even the voice that tells me it's him. It's the attitude of a man who thinks he's right even when he knows otherwise. Who screamed and shouted and made my mother's life hell. Who cleared out, leaving others to clean up the mess. If the cops ever interviewed him about what happened that night, it would have been cursory. Because it was Nimbin, they'd already decided it was suicide, possibly drug-induced. I ignore the old man's ravings.'You brought me with you because you compromised my safety,' Sally says. 'I understand that. But why him?'

'My childhood's here somewhere and as soon as the old man's dried out he'll lead me to it. And when I get to that place of tepees, windmills and Easter Island statues, I'll have the answer.'

'The answer to what?'

'Pandora's identity and where I can find her.'

'But why do you need to find this Pandora?'

'To prove I'm not mad.'

'And after you find her what then? Do you go back to being what you were? Do I go back into the witness protection program? And if I do, will I be safe? Will I ever practise surgery again? Do you destroy everyone you meet?'

'Humans can go weeks without food but not without water. I'll go find some.'

But before I leave, I ask her for the whitener I asked her to buy and pomade my hair with it.

Chapter 29

INTO THE VALLEY OF DEATH

I told Sally I was going to look for water. It wasn't a lie but before that I've got to go into town and before that again I've got to check up on the body. Criminals return to the scene of the crime except I can't accept it was *my* crime. I left Sally with instructions to:

Keep an eye on the old man like a murderer watches an intended victim because he'll try to escape; and

Gather berries, fungi, roots, et cetera, that might be edible.

I venture into the bush. There's no movement apart from occasional grunts followed by the thump-thump-thump of marsupials, the rustle of lizards and the flapping of wings. If the cops don't know yet, I've got time – not much but some. I touch the dolls in my pocket. The old man might be the key. But first I've got to find the lock.

It looked easy. The cave gave onto an accommodating landscape in which I could make out the Palais Royale. All I had to do was head for the spire. I check the position of the sun and alter course. No fires, I told Sally, either inside the cave or out. The food can be eaten raw but not before I get back.

The corpse has gone.

I don't need to check my bearings. The building's to my right and this is the right blackberry bush but there's no corpse. It introduces a new factor into the equation only I'm not sure what it is. The police didn't take the body because they haven't been here. There's no plastic tape indicating a crime scene; no patchwork of overlapping tyre tracks; no boot prints; no body tracing; no-one on guard duty.

In the Palais Royale I come across a billy and a saucepan.

There's a lot of traffic because of the coming St Valentine's Day festival and I get a ride within minutes. I don't buy food because it would only tell Sally where I've been. The paper shop's halfway along Main Street.

'You're lucky there are any left,' the bloke behind the counter says. 'These tourists are like bloody locusts.'

'How much?'

'They come to gawp at the hippies but all they get is the censored version — the didgeridoos, the hugs, the drugs, the markets and the maypoles.'

'Would two bucks cover it?'

'There's talk of secret rites and sacrifices.'

Tourists jostle me as I leaf through the newspaper. There was no corpse, Monica Best didn't die and the cops aren't after us. Someone nudges against me but it's just another hugger.

'Did you find it, man?'

'Find what?' I say.

'Futility, man. That's what everyone's after, isn't it?' The hippy cackles. 'Or in your case, the card reader. You were looking for her, weren't you?' He frowns. 'Anyway, she was looking for you.'

It's the joker who gave me directions. Someone must pay him to keep an eye on people. What he's told me might be nothing but nothing's a lot more than I've got. And nothing says that I can't pay a return visit to her while I'm here. The sign's still in the window and she's still in the room beyond the sign. But when I look around the dolls have gone.

'Where are they?'

The dame's got her back to me and she doesn't look around. 'Where are what?'

'The dolls.'

'What dolls?'

I change tack. 'Why did you want to see me?'

She's silent for a moment. Then, 'Non-believers think we seers are all flush and bluster. What they don't know is that we can be proactive.

When someone makes an appointment to see us we find out something about them before they arrive – in that regard, the internet has made our lives a whole lot easier. But in your case I found nothing and I ask myself why.'

'That's because there's nothing to discover.'

When I emerge into the street, Booby's hail-fellow-well-meeting someone across the road. This is Nimbin and in Nimbin people are too friendly. I don't read the writing on the side of the four-wheel-drive vehicle as I climb in. Three men are inside, all of them wearing white, all of them big, all of them not to get in a vehicle with. I recognise the one in the back but he doesn't remember me. Disguise is a lot more than a change of hair colour. I've rounded my shoulders and developed a squint.

'You a local?' he asks.

'Yeah.'

'Then you might be able to help us. We're looking for someone who would be trying to pass himself off as a tourist but who's really an escapee from a lunatic asylum. He's big like you but a lot younger and with certain characteristics you don't possess. He'd be wearing bright clothes and a hat.' He fishes in a pocket and pulls out a card. 'Call this number if you happen to see him.'

Disguise is the way you talk, and my voice is a croak. 'I take it you're the law.'

'Something like that,' the man in the white coat replies.

I croak to them to let me out and stagger slowly away. Old people don't run and neither do the innocent. The writing on the card matches the writing on the side of the four-wheel drive: SIDONIA CLINIC.

It's past midday by the time I return. Whoever killed Monica Best is still around – plus the Mafia and Pandora and now also the goons from the clinic. I've picked up the pot and pan from the Palais Royale, filled the pot at a creek and done my best to hide my tracks – crossing and recrossing the creek, doubling back, walking sideways, hopping, skipping and jumping. It creates an appetite but Sally's resourceful – she will have found something.

The old man is crouching in the rear of the cave and in the mouth of the cave Sally's carving up what she's foraged. 'Where have you been?' she asks.

'Water's like a good woman,' I reply, 'hard to find.' It gets me the first smile I've seen from her in a long time. 'What did you get?'

I chuck the fungi to one side. 'Fungus kills you or at least puts you in Fantasyland – a lot of mushrooms are hallucinogenic. There are good ones and there are bad ones. For example, this is the deadly Amanita. See those white gills? Very few safe mushrooms possess white gills. Also there's a collar around the stalk – no edible mushroom has a collar around its stalk. Then there's the volva or skirt ...'

She breaks in, 'Along with a great many other subjects, I studied alternative medicine. As a doctor I'm aware humans need starch, protein and fat. The blackberry, Rubus Fruticosus, is wonderful because we can eat all parts of it. This is Bungwal fern – Blench numidicum: that's good. Some pink finger orchids – the Caladenia canea – are also good. The wild parsnip – Trachymeneincisa – is full of starch. Wattle pods – nothing wrong with them, either. Then there are the violet-coloured plants: flax lillies; geebung, high in vitamin C; lillypilly – Acmena Smithii, fruiting right now; the purple banksia' – she glances at the old man huddled in the rear of the cave – 'we can ferment that to make alcohol; more violet flora – the fig of the creek sandpaper. And there's nothing wrong with the mushrooms.'

Chapter 30

THEY CALL IT PARRICIDE

The old man staggers out of the cave, attracted by the smell of cooking. His clothes are rumpled, his mouth's puckered and his face is covered with stubble. He grabs a lump of moss out of the pan and shoves it in his mouth. There's got to be something in that pickled brain of his.

'Come on,' I say, 'it can't be that hard to remember. Preferably where we lived but if you can't manage that, something else that might prove useful.'

'Useful for what?'

He goes to pick something out of his rotten teeth, glances across at Sally and thinks better of it. Then, incredibly, coherent sounds emerge. Something's evoked memories. It must be sobriety. He waves at some point in the distance.

'Over there was a commune – Wellsprung or Mainspring or something. It's where Heather lived.' His arm makes an arc. 'Over there was Janice's.' Another arc. 'And Rosie lived there.' He's boasting about the lovers he had when he was married to my mother. 'Past that hill was little Kaska's hut. And –'

'But where did we live?'

'Calm down,' Sally says.

'Over there,' he says. 'We lived over there.'

I look in the direction he's pointing and see some trees move in the opposite way to the wind.

She packs the uncooked flora and we set off. The Australian bush is like life – you don't know you're lost until you're in it and by then it's too late. I took a bearing and there was the landmark of Nimbin Rocks but once we're among the trees both rocks and sun disappear. There's just the bush, us three – and anyone and everyone that's after us.

We're halfway down the hill when the old man starts to develop the DTs. I could nurse him out of it but I'm not in the mood. We need to replenish our water but that means travelling tangentially to any pursuers and the gap closes that much faster. After a couple of hours I accept we're not going to find any water – not this side of the mountain, anyway – and we're wasting valuable time looking for it. I motion to Sally to stop.

'We don't know if they've got dogs but in case they do we've got to take to the trees. We only need to be off the ground for a few minutes to lose them.'

'What about him?'

It's late in the afternoon and the old man's breath's coming in short, ragged gasps. He's trembling and has got a wild look in his eyes. 'I'll climb, you pass him up, then follow and swing across to the next tree. I'll shove him over to you, climb past, you hand him to me and so on.'

She shakes her head. 'Why am I even doing this? I haven't done anything wrong and I'm not paranoid like some people. I should just walk away.'

'So walk away.'

She doesn't.

Wattles are too brittle while gums have high branches and keep their distance from other trees. It's a good thirty minutes before we come across suitable trees for climbing, a group of camphor laurels. I stuff my whitesides in my backpack, collect the other packs and get up the first tree. Below, Sally and the old man are arguing.

'I'm not going.'

'You have to.'

'I don't have to do anything.'

I break in, 'If you don't do what you're told, you old bastard, I'll come down and kill you.'

He holds out his arms and the shakes go into remission. He's light but anyone's heavy when they're reluctant and you're hoisting them into a tree. He clings to a branch as Sally climbs after him. After the first tree

it gets easier but any dogs after us will have gained ground. I can't hear
them but hunting dogs are trained to be quiet. By the time we reach the
last tree they'd be less than a minute away. I drop to the ground, drag the
old man after me, Sally follows and I put on my whitesides.

'Now we'll split. I'll take the old man and head left while you go
right. We'll meet at that stringy-bark over there.'

The old man's the fisherman on the shoulders of Sinbad, the monkey
on my back, a burden I'm lumped with. I don't like him, don't want him
anywhere near me. He abandoned my mother and my sister and dumped
me. The thought of whip-back saplings lashing his face as we plunge
through the scrub affords me grim joy. To my right, Sally's making for
the rendezvous. The dogs won't see the trees move because they're short-
sighted, at least that's what the books say.

When I drop him the old man's head hits a rock. I want to pick him up
and drop him again but resist the temptation. Sally kneels and checks him
while I go over what we're doing yet again. There's a cop logic and I don't
have to be Pythagoras to follow it. It goes something like:

Identify corpse

On basis of motive and opportunity, list suspects

Locate and interrogate

Arrest and charge.

All of which means that when they find the corpse they'll round
up the local hopheads and track down recent arrivals – private vehicles,
hitchers, buses. A simple cross-check will show two men and a woman
arrived on the 11.30 am bus from Casino a couple of days back and were
last seen in the vicinity. It's not hard to work out the rest. But someone
lifted the body. The Mafia? Ariadne's people? The thugs that killed
Damnation? Pandora?

The old man's stopped shaking.

'I don't know how much of your brain's left after a lifetime pickling
it,' I tell him, 'but if you don't use what little memory you've got left we'll
all end up on a murder rap. What happened?'

'When?'

'When you were with – Christ, I don't even know the name of my
own mother!'

'Jasmine. It was Jasmine, sweet Jasmine.'

'All right, you've remembered her name, congratulations. Now try and remember more. What happened? And don't say when again or I'll kill you. How did she die? Where did it happen? Who was involved?'

'You're accusing me!' he shouts. 'You're saying I killed her but how would you know? You were a snivelly-nosed little brat then and now you're just mad. I'm going to call those dogs you reckon are after us. At least with the cops I'll get justice.'

They call it parricide but they can call it what they like. I grab him by the throat. This isn't a dream. The old man's throat's real, an organ by which he sucks air into his lungs to aerate his blood and stay alive. But Sally's strong surgeon's fingers prise my hands loose. Weals stand out on his scrawny neck. The sight fires something in me and I go to grab him again.

'Where is it?' I demand. 'Where's the funny farm?'

He cringes away from me, rubbing his throat with one hand while pointing shakily with the other. 'It's – over there.'

Chapter 31

MORNING GORY

I don't know where we are – I don't even know where we are in relation to Booby's place. I've taken another sighting and made a mental note of landmarks. In a vehicle it would be a snip but we've only got our legs and if anyone's onto us they'll have the roads covered. Slipping and sliding down rocky slopes between the trees, around spiky bushes, dragging the reluctant old man with us, it's two hours before we reach the place he indicated from the cave – a sloping patch of ground with a tangle of thorns at its centre, a couple of trees and an outcrop of rock. I don't recognise a thing.'Are you sure this is the place?' I ask him.

'What do you think I am – a bloody dementia?'

I take it as a yes and get out the binoculars. They're not much but for the first time in forty years I'm reminded how we used to live. It was the bark hut and tepee phase of Nimbin, when the druggies' god was Aquarius and life was mist and ashes. Forty years on there's not much left, even of that. Lantana, blackberries and morning glory have taken over, some of the clumps as high as –

There are none so blind as those who will not see, my mother remonstrated. Closely followed by: Seek and ye shall find. It was nonsense, even to my five-year-old mind, no more than playground prattle, a witch's curse, a voodoo mantra. Like: Close the windows or the bats will get you. Our hut didn't have windows. It's all starting to come back to me.

'My mother was stark-staring mad,' I murmur.

'Were there as many bats in your childhood as there are now?' Sally asks.

'I don't know. We saw what our parents told us to see, feared what our parents said we should fear, believed what our parents wanted us to believe.' I think of Imogene then I don't think of Imogene. 'That was how things used to be – our imaginings were far worse than any reality.' I swing around to the old man. 'Is this the bloody place?'

He's gone sullen again. 'How would I know.'

I make lunge at him again, my need to hurt him momentarily eclipsing my need to find Pandora. He steps back, a look of fear in his eyes. 'Yeah, this is it.'

A confession obtained under duress is no confession at all but there's nothing else. I can't hear the dogs but that doesn't mean they aren't coming. Someone killed Monica Best and removed her corpse. The cops will have stumbled across it in a shallow grave or someone will have found it for them. Cops feed on death. That means they can't be far off. They like to be in at the kill.

'You're lying.'

Sally intervenes and the old man decides he's safe again.

'Why would I lie to you, son?'

Forty years on and I'm back at the funny farm looking for my mother. Correction: I'm looking for *who killed her* because that would explain everything. Because I no longer believe she killed herself. The killer could have been – probably was – my father. The *idea* of suicide was something the old man fed to me on the trip to Sydney. The killer could have been Pandora because Pandora dates from my mother's death. Seeing someone kill my mother when I was five would go a long way towards explaining my paranoia. It would also explain Pandora.

The old man was the rough draft but I'm the correcting fluid. Another scrap of memory: our hut was built on a slope so the rain wouldn't turn the floor to mud. Amid her ramblings, my mother praised the old man for it because it was the one thing he got right – he built our pathetic little hut on a slope so the floor would stay dry. Seek and ye shall find.

I leave them by the odd-shaped bush – my father huddled in a heap with Sally tending to him – and make my way westward through the waist-high vegetation. I come across a fork in the road and take the left-hand one. Method detect, Rube said – put yourself in situ and relive what happened. There's something familiar about my surroundings. I stumble across what I'm looking for among the trees.

They're still there, only much bigger now – among them the Moreton Bay fig with roots like pythons. I'll go and hide, I'd tell my sister. All right, she'd reply trustingly. Then I'd disappear, not to return until nightfall. Sophie would still be waiting because she trusted me. Sometimes there were others but mostly there was just us. I ignore the ephemera – dirt tracks, rabbit holes and weeds – and keep an eye out for the more enduring landmarks.

I'm looking for a forest. Not a forest of trees but a forest of totems and a windmill. After forty years most of it will have gone but there must be remnants. That night, with my mother and sister turning into skyrockets, I found refuge among a towering array of totem poles. But so far I've found only trees. Then, around the other side of the hill – the blind side, the side I couldn't see through the binoculars – I find the shrouded ones. If this isn't the place, I tell myself, I'll kill him. At least I'll have that satisfaction. The cops will get me but they'll get me anyway.

I find an old fence, its posts splintered and sagging, the wire that links them broken and rusted. My jacket snags on barbed wire and I curse the living daylights out of it. My shoes squelch in boggy soil. There's nothing here. How could there be? It's too marshy. I pull away one last shroud …

… to expose one leering face after another, the totems that scared the hell out of a five-year-old kid, a cluster of Easter Island statues with black holes for eyes, made of wood like the fence posts, grey and leaning with age. Put yourself in that space and time, Rube said. I'm a kid again and my mother and little sister are burning. Put yourself in that space and time. But I don't need to imagine myself anywhere. I'm here. You see what you want to see.

But there's something wrong.

Daylight's fading by the time I get back and there's also darkness in my mind. She's lit a fire, tearing stuff from the odd-shaped bush in the clearing and putting a match to it to heat up the leftovers. Something registers in my mind. It's not the fire, the smell of cooking mushrooms or even Sally. The old man's curled on the rock like a goanna sucking the last of the day's heat from the sun.

'You look as if you've seen a ghost,' Sally says.

The wind shifts and the smell of cooking fungi wafts across to me.

Out of nowhere a figure steals into my brain – a giant figure, real and yet not real. There was a clump of vines around the remains of a windmill but when I dragged them away all I got was a memory – a memory and now that mind-numbing stench. A stench as strong as incense.

'There was a ceremony,' I hear myself say.

She busies herself with the pan. 'What kind of ceremony?'

'Something to do with –'

The wind shifts again, blowing the smoke towards the old man. He comes alert and suddenly there's a tension in him yet all that's happened is that the smoke blew in his face and I said: There was a ceremony. They call it the foetal position – knees drawn up to the chin, head bowed, hands between thighs. But suddenly there's nothing foetal about the old man. He's a coiled spring. Death and transfiguration, the necromancer said.

I'm waving the gun. 'That's it! I only thought I saw a burning windmill,' I hear myself say, 'because that's what he told me I'd seen. And I believed him because he was my father but also because I knew about windmills while I didn't know this other thing. Or didn't want to.'

Sally looks upset; she doesn't take her eyes off the pan. 'You disappear and when you return you look like death, waving guns about and spouting nonsense. Put that thing away and eat some of this.'

A vehicle's approaching, the rough road turning the sound of its approach into an alarm.'Put out the fire!' When I drag the old man to his feet his buttons pop. 'It's February the thirteenth, the day before St Valentine's, and you knew what happened then and you know what's going to happen now. It's a spectre that's haunted you ever since you ran away, why you became what you are. How did she die?'

'I don't know!' He's backing away from the truth as much as from me. 'I don't remember a thing!'

The car's getting closer. We could hide but they'd see the fire – it's only smoke but that would be enough. I let go of the old man, chuck the gun aside, throw the jacket onto the fire. Something's clicked into place. I'm no longer a kid, no longer at the mercy of events.

Chapter 32

FINDERS KEEPERS

After the car passes I tell the others to stay put, retrieve my coat and gun and go after it. The tracks show that it took the road to the right, the one I didn't take earlier. My foot warps in a rabbit hole and I throw out my hands to break my fall, losing my gat in the process. I scrabble around for it. It takes a while to find it – too much time. By the time I find it, the car's gone.

It's futile but I keep after them. Life's futile but it doesn't stop you living it. And sometimes, like now, it pays off. When I turn a corner, I find the car stopped and two cops standing beside it.

'What would your mother say if she could see you now, in Nimbin the day before Valentine's Day, issuing fire warnings?' one of the cops is saying.

'But that's not what we're doing, is it? We're relieving ourselves. And when we've finished we'll make a routine call on a bunch of whackos to remind them we exist then go back to the station and play cards.'

A stone rattles away under my feet and the younger cop spins around, gat in hand. I freeze.

'What was that?'

The older cop calmly zips up his fly.

'You've been in Nimbin too long, pal, and become paranoid just like the rest of them. Put away your gun – in fact, put away both your guns. All we're doing is making a routine call. We're still half an hour away, so let's go.'

When I get back, Sally's pulled away the rest of the bush, exposing the hut, and made three beds out of biddy bush. It's a long time before I can sleep. Light plays on the walls of the old hut – orange light interspersed with yellow and violet. Violent violet, violet violence. Lights − not playing but fighting, fighting for keeps. Finders keepers, losers weepers. The words meant nothing to my sister but when I chanted them she wept because she knew I was rejecting her.

We leave before dawn, the old man waking in unaccustomed sobriety. I clamp a fist over his face in case he tries to call out. It's the second time I've done that − the first being last night when the cops returned from their mission. By then we'd heaped dirt on the fire so again they didn't notice us. There were no dogs − just the car with the diagonal stripes along the side, the red and blue lights on top and two cops inside. All they'd have seen was the hut but it wouldn't have meant anything because they weren't looking for it − all they were doing was checking on a bunch of whackos preparing for St Valentine's Day.

They'd been no more than half an hour − long enough to call on whoever they had to call on but not long enough to do anyone any harm. They were travelling slow which meant they hadn't uncovered anything new. They'd made a routine visit and given their stock-standard warning − it's summer but you can have your fire as long as you're careful. I remove my hand from the old man's mouth. I would have liked to keep it there.

'Where are we going?'

'Back to my past.' I indicate the old man. 'Make sure he keeps up with us.'

There's been a change of clothing − I'm back in grey, Sally's wearing a viridian T-shirt and turquoise-coloured jeans to go with the landscape and the old man's in something similar. She might still dislike me but her attitude seems to have changed. Towards me. Towards the old man. Towards life.

'Come on, Grandpa,' she murmurs.

It's late afternoon. We've stopped, rested, then resumed walking. I'm working backwards from things known – the territory's familiar but only after I've seen it. Déjà vu's like that – no more than wisdom after the event, a murderer's confession. It would have been easy to abandon the old man at the airport or in the hut. Except that I still need what he's got locked in that silly head of his – in the unsafe safe. *Half an hour,* the cop said. Travelling at 20 kilometres an hour over rough terrain, half an hour would mean 10 kilometres. At our current rate of progress it will take us three hours – maybe a little longer.

'You're your bloody mother all over again,' the old man says. 'You'll end up topping yourself, too.'

'What do you mean – too?'

'She killed herself.'

'No, she didn't. It was a long time ago and I was five.' I'm talking more to myself than to them. 'It was dark, I was scared and I saw what I expected to see. I was a child with a sheet of butcher's paper and a bunch of crayons, drawing straight lines to depict a forest. I thought they were on a windmill because I knew about windmills. I was a kid and saw what I expected to see. This other thing was too dreadful to acknowledge.'

'You're talking nonsense,' the old man says.

'If I am it's because you brainwashed me.'

'Why would I do that?'

'Because you're guilty – of what exactly, I haven't worked out yet.'

Normally I get at the truth by waving a gun and asking if they care about their loved ones. But I'm past that stage with the old man. If I pull out the gat it'll be to kill him. I've found the well only to discover it won't give up its water. I make a stab at the truth and bank on him correcting me.

'You killed her because you wanted her out of the way so you could take up with your blonde.'

The old man's more in command of himself. 'But I'd already taken up with the blonde.'

I touch the dolls in my pocket. They're a child's dolls, the kind that Sophie used to play with. But why were they where they were and why did I keep them? I know the answer to that but I don't tell the old man – it's the only ammunition I've got. The sky's occupying that part of the spectrum between cobalt violet and mauve where nearby objects seem distant and far-off ones appear well within reach. I'm a child again, seeing the world with a child's eyes again. I nod to Sally.

'Let's go.'

It's late. Sometimes we stayed up late. What am I saying? We *always* stayed up late. There were beds if we wanted to sleep, food when we were hungry and ragged affairs made of rabbit skins if we got cold. We found food where it happened to be, slept when we felt like it and the rest of the time ran around naked. The adults worshipped symbols and the symbol that seemed to work for everyone was fire. We're close enough to smell it now. We stop to rest.

Memory: There was only one source of fire and that was the Mushroom Man. No-one else could keep it on pain of – I was going to say death but stop myself. It couldn't have been death. We were a happy little commune. But I remember now that after fire had served its purpose it had to be extinguished. The Mushroom Man sat in his cave like a giant toad. No-one saw his face. Like the bats in my mother's mind, there was a possibility he didn't exist.

There were other kids but many of them were spirited away. My closest childhood friend, Ace Mollema, left when he was four. My grandparents kidnapped me, he said the last time I saw him. They made a joke of it, calling it kin-napped. Others followed. And those that were left – me, a couple of boys, a handful of girls – had to cope as best we could. Fantasy helped.

More memories: The adults called the Mushroom Man a name far beyond our childish knowledge. We thought it was Promises. I'm off to Promises, Mum said, going off with her kerosene stick to return with fire. Only now do I realise that what she was saying was Prometheus – the name of the god that stole fire.

Chapter 33

LOSERS WEEPERS

The old man has reached a state of awareness – me and Sally having to half-drag, half-carry him. She seems to have twigged to something. I can see it in the glances she throws my way. Or maybe that's more of my imagination. The weeds didn't exist in my childhood – the hippies must have introduced them in their fruitcakes, scattering the seeds along with the crumbs. Blackberry seeds, lantana seeds, the seeds of that violet-flowered excrescence, morning glory. Anything that could survive.

Sophie had blonde hair and I was so jealous of it that one time I hacked it off with scissors. Afterwards my sister looked like a thistle and because of what I'd done I was universally hated. It was my first lesson in criminology – hurting people might make you *feel* good but doesn't necessarily make you *look* better. In fact when you're found out you look a whole lot worse. After that I made a point of taking care of her. Until the night she died on the windmill. No, *not* on the windmill.

In the mouth of his cave, the Mushroom Man was little more than a shadow. If you were lucky you caught a glimpse of the yellowed soles of his feet. People left offerings in exchange for fire. I'd forgotten about him until now — Calvary would call it *Positive Forgetting*. The figure was obscured by the dark sheet of glass placed between me and my childhood. Along with the events of that night.

The dark sheet of glass. Pandora's been with me so long it seems wrong to doubt her but what if the shrink was right? None of the women in my life could be Pandora because of their age, however much I need it to be otherwise. Forty years have passed since she first came into my life, a female figure in black, her face a blank slate on which I drew what might have been her features. I knew nothing about her except that she made me afraid. She always appeared when I was at my most vulnerable.

Calvary: She's a figment of your imagination, the embodiment of your fears. Like the gods of old, she possessed human form and your guilt turned her into a woman. Guilt over your treatment of your sister, guilt caused by your mother's death. But that's all she was — the embodiment of your fears. Because in reality she never existed. If she had existed, she'd have had a lot better things to do than follow you waving a knife. I won't say you're mad because that word's not in my professional lexicon. But your thinking's at best tangential.

In my mind the old man's mocking me: Tangential? Give me a break! Why don't we call a spade a shovel and accept that, just like your mother, you're stark, staring mad.

'Keep moving.'

There's no moon and I find myself half in, half out of reality, only dimly aware of Sally and the old man. I told her to buy black and that's what she's wearing — the kind of clothes ballerinas wear to depict evil — black, skin-hugging leotards, black tights, black sneakers. She's here because I put her in danger. Correction: she's here because *I'm* the danger. Or maybe there's another reason. The world's surreal — the sky's solid while the distant hills, the weed-shrouded buildings and the trees outlined against it are yawning chasms. The old man and the woman are conspiring against me. I feel the fire's heat and as we close in, it becomes a conflagration, reaching out of the blackness to engulf us. I stop.

'What's wrong?'

I shake my head in an attempt to clear it. 'We're almost there. I want you both in front of me where I can see you.'

The old man hangs back, reluctant to go on, like he, too, has also suddenly remembered. But that's not what he says.

'I'm not going any further.'

'You'll do what I say.'

Sally remains silent, like she's one step ahead of me, has already solved the case. What if I rule her out? What if Sophie's Pandora? What if my sister escaped the conflagration? And I suddenly realise that I've nursed that possibility – no, hope, because it would mean she's still alive – ever since it happened. However malignant she might have become, I'd be happy to the point of delirium to know my sister Sophie's still alive. Because I loved her but also because it would be one death I'm not responsible for. I hid while she was burning. But how could I be responsible for my sister's death if she's still alive?

Last seen she was small, blonde and three. Sally could be in her early forties. Which means that the two – no, three: Sophie, Sally and Pandora – could be one and the same woman. It doesn't explain the figure in the shadows the night my mother died but memories needn't be perfect. I'm back in the midst of my nightmare and shadows dance around the moon.

I blacked out and when I came to I found Monica Best dead. Sally knows her way around fungi and could have fed me anything. But why would she do that? Because she's my sister Sophie and hates me for what I did or didn't do. But isn't that like the shrink saying I imagined Pandora – one mad idea replacing another? Think, dammit, think! You're no longer a child and these aren't shadows.

'The old man won't go any further – he's says he's tired, thirsty, sick and afraid,' Sally says.

While she's tall, lithe, beautiful and dressed in black. 'And guilty,' I tell her. 'You forgot guilty.' When I take hold of the old man's arm it's a twig, so thin it could snap. 'You're coming with me and you'll tell me what's locked in that miserable head of yours if I have to kill you.'

I drag him after me and Sally follows and suddenly they're on us, a mass of leaping shadows, figures gesticulating, the past come to life, a world of terror. There's music, the kind that comes out of a loudspeaker, but I'm too busy focusing on the visual stimuli – the fire, the shadows and, closer to hand, Sally and the old man. The wind's blowing away from us and towards the flames – which is why I only caught a whiff of it before now. Before I understood that there was never any burning windmill. My sister didn't die. There's even a chance my mother's still alive, that I imagined her death, too.

I go weak at the knees. Nothing's as I thought it was. It was a child's world and this is the reality. The change of wind and the chanting bring it back to me. I was a kid and my mother and sister were in peril. People were dancing and there was a kaleidoscope of colour. I was aware of flames and my sister's mute appeals for help. Because she knew her big brother would always be there when it mattered. There were no Easter Island statues or burning windmill – that's what I imagined to soften the awful reality. But if there was no windmill, how did they die?

Apply free association, another magician's trick, this time that of the shrink. The Mushroom Man wasn't Prometheus but a magician. The medicine man, bone pointer, shyster, shalyun, shamus. Shamus: n. Private detective, person pretending to be what he's not – danger man.

You don't know what you've forgotten until something triggers the memory. I saw my mother and my sister die and after that I ceased to be a kid. Because mothers and sisters don't die, they're there forever. It's why I refused to accept the reality and why I hated my father. What I believed became the reality when I couldn't cope with what happened – a reality my father reinforced on the journey to Sydney. But what's happening now triggers the memory. I take out my dead-man's mobile and call the number on the card – the one the man in the white coat gave me. And after that, I call the cops.

We're at the pile of rubbish next to Booby's place. Only it's not a pile of rubbish at all but a pyre – from the Greek *pura* meaning *fire*. A funeral pyre. There's smoke and, deep within the smoke as if projected on a sheet of glass, a figure. This is the smoke and mirrors of a shamus. And within that smoke, upon that glass, the giant image of – Pandora. I've found her only to discover that she's a wraith, a phantom, a writhing image. And back from the fire in the swirling shadows another figure, a giant in a cloak, a high priest or a god, his arms raised either in benediction or as a threat. The fire's behind him and I can't make out his features. I look back to the fire to see something I hadn't noticed before, a flaming cross. And on the cross, a naked figure. Even from here I can make out the meaningless words – *TRANNE SOL 10*. But suddenly they're not meaningless at all. I see what's there instead of what I expect to see. It's not *10* but *IO* and the words aren't meaningless but Italian. The words read: *No-one but me.* Meaning: *You're mine.*

Memories overwhelm me. Of a giant in a cave. Of figures dancing around a volcano. Of a small boy refusing to accept what was before his eyes because it was too terrible to believe, accepting what he was told because it was easier. From a distance, I hear my mother's voice chanting, Cut off their legs. The smell's intense, dizzying, profound, and sparks dance like sins fleeing from a box. Figures – they seem more like black cut-outs than humans – dance around the flames, contorting like the figure on the cross, waving cups spilling some sort of liquid. The fire's out of control. So are the dancers. I called the cops. Where are they?

But I know where the cops are. Veni, vidi but not vici. They came, they saw and they cleared out. They had a duty, they did it and they're back at the station playing cards. Local madmen are a protected species – wild but harmless. They not supposed to be lighting fires in summer but what the hell. The cops aren't here because forewarned is disarmed, this is just another pagan rite and the cops have got better things to do with their time, like playing cards back at the station. Like the cards dealt by one of the naked figures dancing around the fire, the grandmotherly figure that dealt me the Death card while reassuring me: It's not death but transfiguration. A grandmotherly figure that's become a virago, its arms outflung, cup raised above its head – the blind necromancer. The figure in the cloak speaks.

'Come unto me, ye unsightly and infirm and be transformed.'

The smoke forms a screen, like the cracked loungeroom wall Aunt Rube showed me her old movies on. And on that screen is the figure of Pandora. I trace it back to a smaller figure beside the figure in the cloak. Somehow it's been projected – enlarged and terrible – onto the flames. Smoke and mirrors. The smoke wafts towards me and my knees buckle. Memories swamp me. Flames and flood, fire and water, primal elements worshipped by the commune long ago and still revered now. At last I remember. There was no windmill, except the one in my mind, not here, not when my mother and my sister died.

Only this.

Chapter 34

BOOBY TRAP

'In the beginning our souls were wreathed in fire. We are tempered steel and that's what makes us strong.'

'Strong!' chants the crowd as they dance around the flames. 'We're strong, strong, strong!'

Smoke and darkness impair my vision. As in a dream, I see the magician with his arms raised, the contorted, dancing figures around him and the fire with the sacrifice on the cross. Above it all the black figure of Pandora, outlined in the haze.

The wizard chants:

But first on earth, as vampire sent,

Thy corpse shall from the tomb be rent,

Then ghastly haunt thy native place

And suck the blood of all thy race.

These are real memories, not the distorted imaginings of a frightened kid. Memories of my mother and my sister spinning above the dancers' heads on a burning cross, converted by my childish mind into a windmill because it was something I could comprehend. But houses are no longer triangles perched on squares or the Australian bush a bunch of matchsticks. This is reality. It's not what I was looking for. I was looking for Pandora, not an image projected on a screen of smoke, a shamus with his arms raised and a chanting crowd drugged out of their brains.

'I am the darkness and the truth,' intones the Mushroom Man. 'Truth is in darkness, hearken to Pandora.'

'Hail Pandora!'

I'm a child again, hiding behind a totem pole before a burning windmill again. But that's what I imagined, it's not the truth. Because the truth is what's unfolding before me, a scene no five-year-old had any hope of coping with. Which is how they wanted it. They wanted us afraid, needed us vulnerable in order to mould us. He made you in His image. They're the words I heard all those years ago – declamation and response. And above it all – shrill and helpless – the pleas of my mother and sister while my father grabs me by the arm and drags me away.

'He's gone!' Sally says.

It's Walpurgisnacht with the figure of the Mushroom Man dancing attendance on Pandora and dancing figures dropping like flies. He changed hands and whisked and rioted like a dance of Walpurgis in his lonely brain. And the sacrifice. Don't forget the sacrifice.

'Get him!'

It's the wizard shouting and he's pointing at me. I head towards him, a giant figure towering above me and seared in my memory.

'Get him! Bring him back!'

Other voices, my own among them. Because out of the corner of my eye I see the frail old figure entering the flames. I've got a decision to make. Save the old man or go for shamus. I tear off my jacket and plunge forward, divesting myself of the rest of my clothes until I'm naked like the dancers, a kid again. Only this time I'm trying to save someone. I shove the dancers out of the way as I follow the matchstick figure.

I'm only dimly aware of the heat, of the incense, of the chanting figure of the shamus, the music, the dancers, the sacrifice. Or the giant, two-dimensional shape in the smoke – Pandora. Or the voice of the shamus and the response of dancers on whom whatever poison he's used hasn't taken effect yet.

'Who are we?'

'We are the indestructible.'

'Can the flames touch us?'

'No, for we can dance upon burning coals.'

The voices of the still-surviving dancers become at one with that of the wizard.

'We must make the ultimate sacrifice to Pandora. We must appease her wrath. Because only then will she be on our side, her anger abated, our protectress.'

'Burn!' the wizard screams.

'Burn! Burn! Burn!' the dancers scream back.

'Kill!'

'Kill! Kill! Kill!'

They're all about me – the ghostly figures that have peopled my mind for so long, the figures of my childhood, my nightmare. The Mafia, grey men with guns, men that might be cops, the blind necromancer, men in white coats and Pandora descend upon me. I identify the figure of the preying mantis, Caligari. I thrust aside one dancing dervish only for another to take its place. The dancers still on their feet carry knives and they're raised against me.I hear screams and they're my screams; I see blackened hands and they're my hands. And beyond the hands, beyond everything else, I see the old man emerging from the flames carrying the figure of the woman he's saved.

Only he hasn't saved her because she's dead and has been for days.

Chapter 35

THE FATHER THE BETTER

'Wake up!'

I'm dreaming. An angel is hovering over my head and I'm dreaming. The sky's the colour of violets and I smell the intemperate smell of burning geraniums. There was a night of bleeding angels, of people dying and the contorted figure of Pandora. It's not reality, not the facts. Aunt Rube wouldn't be happy at how my mind worked. You're a private eye, she'd say. You deal in facts. Because if you don't deal in facts you're not dealing. I try to focus but fail. I can't see.

'Your eyes are burnt,' says the voice of Sally. 'Try and keep them closed.'

'What happened?'

'I'll tell you if you lie still.' The shadows shift as I wait for the voice to continue. 'Forty years ago on a farm in Africa, more than 900 sect members died when their leader dosed them with cyanide. The Jonestown Massacre it was called. Booby was doing a copycat killing and while he was doing it, your father pushed through the dying dancers and entered the flames –'

'I want to hear it blow by blow.'

I already know most of it. When we arrived Booby was ready for us because of the geographical position finders in the dolls – like the ones in the tracker bracelets on Monica and Hélène's wrists. I was led by the nose – courtesy of the murders, the dolls, the necromancer and the smell of the fire. It was just a matter of joining the dots, the kind of picture puzzle children are given to solve. And for the purpose of this game I was a child. Sally worked out the hallucinogens that were fed to the dancers – a mixture of manmade ones and the kind found growing wild.

601

Like children, the dancers saw what they expected to see. Booby used props – prime among them the figure projected in the flames that seemed impervious to fire, Pandora – what he promised the dancers would be.

'Booby and his wife used smoke and mirrors. The smoke formed a screen on which the figure of Pandora was projected and next to her was the sacrifice.'

'A sacrifice that was already dead – Monica Best.'

'Monica served a twofold purpose. She led us to Booby but she was also a sacrifice. She was long dead but no-one knew that. She was what the celebrants expected to see. You, meanwhile, knew who she was and that she was already dead. But the old man saw something else – he saw his beloved wife and a second chance to save her. He dived into the flames and you went after him. Oblivious to the other sect members dying around them, the surviving celebrants went on chanting and dancing. The old man was bringing the corpse out of the flames when the police arrived.'

'Why did he try to save someone he thought was his wife when he neglected to save her all those years ago?'

'As I said, it was his second chance. In his mind, forty years hadn't passed and the dead Monica had become the live Jasmine. He saw what he most desperately wanted so see.'

'Which means that he was off his brain on something just like everyone else.'

'I know you're saying I drugged you but, believe me, I didn't. The power of suggestion was enough. The leaves in our campfire might have helped but only by way of arousing memories. The mushrooms were harmless so I think it was the leaves. You were cast back in time to when the sect sacrificed your mother and little sister.'

'So why did my father abandon her?'

'All those years ago, your father was faced with that most monstrous of choices, who to save. He chose you. He didn't abandon his wife and daughter – he rescued his son.'

'He came out of the flames.' I look around blindly. 'Is he here somewhere? Where are we?'

'We're back in the hut, safe for the moment because no-one knows we're here. After I stopped you killing Booby I tended to your father. He was badly burnt but, incredibly, still alive – in shock but still alive. He managed to say something.'

'What did he say?'

'He said, Tell Rainbow –'

'Tell Rainbow what?'

'He said, Tell my son I need a bloody drink. Those were his last words – Tell my son I need a drink. Then he died.'

I need to laugh but I also need to cry so I do neither. Private eyes don't cry, not in public anyway. That's why they call us private eyes. But right now laughter's not coming all that easy either. I never knew my father – not until he died.'How come the cops didn't arrest us?' I ask her.

'I told them the truth – that I was a doctor – so they left us alone. They were more interested in Booby and Marsha anyway and saving as many sect members as they could, the blind necromancer and your shrink from the clinic among them. Your father was taken away in an ambulance. I managed to spirit you away and we're safe for the moment but eventually the police will work out who we are and where we've gone and come after us. So as soon as you're up to it – or before if possible – we have to get out of here.'

She gives me something from her first-aid box and I get the impression of a short, disjointed journey, during which I ask, 'What about you?'

'I've decided to stop running. I'm going to tell the Witness Protection people I'm taking myself out of their program. They'll make it seem like I died along with all the others. It shouldn't be hard – people see what they expect to see. But that's one question too many because you can no longer cope with the answers.'

'Will I be able to see again?'

'Let's see, shall we? I'm sorry, that wasn't meant as a joke.'

I struggle to sit up but can't. 'I failed to do what I set out to do, didn't I? I didn't find Pandora. ... But it was you all the time, wasn't it?'

It's the first time in a long while I've heard her laugh and it's birdsong, a full-throated chuckle – all that and more. 'That'd be an easy solve, wouldn't it? Sorry to disappoint you, Rainbow, but no, I'm not Pandora.'

'Then who is she?'

She laughs again. 'I think you know who she is and that you've known all along – you just buried it in your subconscious so you could function more or less normally.'

Her voice becomes teasing. 'I can't tell you any more because you're in shock. I've given you something to make you sleep so your mind wouldn't be able to handle the information anyway.' Her voice has the quality of a late-summer landscape, the perfect landscape for a murder. 'We have a twelve-hour journey ahead of us but you need no longer worry that you're being followed. The police have arrested Booby and along with him the Mafia thugs as well as Ariadne's goons.'

'How am I travelling?'

My last thought before I fade is that she misunderstood me when I desperately needed to be understood. Because I already know how I'm travelling and it's not well. But I've had a good non-life. I've had a child and there's an outside chance she doesn't hate me all that much. What more could a private detective hope for?

I don't remember much about that journey. There was the sound of a car then the rattling of a train but like the forty-five years of my life the journey seemed to pass in a flash. As they say in the classics, I haven't died, I've been reborn. I'm dependent again, waiting for someone to change my nappy. There was nothing before this moment and I don't know what comes after it.

I just want to sleep.

One day Sister Mildred peels the bandages off my eyes and I can see – blurred images like I'm in the midst of a rainbow in which all the colours have merged into one, turning the rainbow brown. Nothing's distinct and one case dissolves into another. We don't see what's right before our eyes; we see what we want to see and what I see is Sally seated beside me.

'Did you say that all those years ago my old man saved me?'

She nods. 'It was his epiphany. Up to then he accepted the sect, went along with what they told him. It was hard not to. Booby and his wife were control freaks just like Ariadne.'

She pauses. 'Then they sacrificed his wife and daughter. It was too late to save them but not too late to save you. He grabbed you and took off. The cops never discovered anything – Booby and Marsha either disposed of the two bodies or made them look like suicides and they were fairly certain the old man wouldn't say anything. But Booby and the woman kept their eye on you – via Pandora. At first Marsha was Pandora – as long as she was young and lithe. And when Marsha grew too old they replaced her with girls from the funny farm – Monica Best, with Hélène Dalmatian as backup. But Monica blotted her copybook by rescuing you so her days were numbered. She didn't know that the doll they told her to give you was – I'm sorry, Booby-trapped. Emitting a signal that told them where you were.'

'And Caligari – where did he fit in?

'For Ariadne, the sect was a way of laundering people in the same way other crooks launder money. The sect was a handy little sideline. It was at the funny farm that she found Caligari – a bright-enough lad but about as qualified to be a psychiatrist as my little finger.'

'So she'll go down along with the rest?'

Sally shakes her head. 'People like Ariadne never go down. They get others to do their dirty work for them and if anything goes wrong they just walk away from the mess they've created and start again. A sort of metamorphosis.'

Chapter 36

DOUBLE FUGUE

There are visitors, among them my daughter Sophie – sorry, *Imogene* – relieved to find that I'm still alive, although she says that my head – both inside and out – could be improved upon. 'You'll need surgery, Daddy – *plastic* surgery, not a lobotomy. It can only be an improvement.'

'Thanks.'

'It's your fault – you taught me to tell the truth.'

'So tell me the truth about how your transfiguration into a cop's going.'

'The short answer is that it's not. Like your sect, police cadets have rituals – it's a control thing similar to the sect's, only the cadets call them initiation ceremonies rather than rites. But their self-defence skills weren't up to mine and as a result I hurt some of them. I was suspended pending an inquiry and after the inquiry I was kicked out. They decided I wasn't suitable material – I was a hairshirt when what they wanted was nice blue serge.'

'What will you do now?'

'I think you know. In fact, like the identity of Pandora, I think you've known all along.'

When I tell Sister Mildred about Monica a look of anguish crosses her face, to be replaced by acceptance, in the way of any nurse learning of the death of a terminally ill patient.

'I saw that you worked out she was my daughter – I found you studying those photographs. Yes, I was a member of the sect but I managed to escape. I tried to get Monica to come with me but she insisted on staying. You see they'd already brainwashed her. She was a gorgeous little girl and there was a lot of good in her but she was a time bomb – to me, to you, to them.'

I'm staying at Mildred's until judged fit to return to the real world. It suits us both – she's lost a daughter and I've lost a father. Sally comes around a lot and she's no longer a shrinking violet, if she ever was.

'You're not looking too bright,' she says on her next visit.

'That's what my daughter says.' My sight's nowhere near what it was but I can still make out the beautiful woman perched on the edge of the couch holding my hand. 'Imogene says no-one will ever look at me again without wincing. But in my line of business that might prove useful.'

'Can you handle the truth?'

The traffic rackets by overhead. I'm not ready to look in mirrors but, yeah, I can handle the truth. In fact, after all these years of living in ignorance I desperately need the truth. So I tell her, Yeah, I can handle the truth.

To which Sally Kane replies: 'Well, the truth is that you look quite nice to me ... And I didn't tell you everything the old man told me before he died. He said that he and his wife – your mother – joined the sect because they were looking for Utopia. At first it was okay – Booby might have been Prometheus but he was also an idealist. But he had to keep control. And as dictators have always found, real control depends on fear. People were starting to leave the sect and in order to keep them, Booby and his wife upped the bread and circuses.'It was Nero's Rome all over again. They had a strict policy towards escapees. They monitored them. They didn't worry about people like your father – he'd drunk himself into a state of harmlessness. But you were a detective so Marsha visited you from time to time in the guise of Pandora. And when she grew too old, they used younger sect members – among them Hélène and Monica. They kept tabs on you, knowing that with a little tweaking they could draw you back whenever they needed to. Which they did when you grew too inquisitive. That was when Ariadne gave "Dr" Caligari two choices – to either lobotomise you or trick you into returning to the funny farm.'

Suddenly I want to exist again; to be a proper father again. Plus something more.'Go on,' I say.

'Malcolm Booby was the front man, the shamus. He wasn't as young as he looked nor as henpecked as he made himself out to be. As a magician looking younger was a stroll in the Garden of Eden compared with his day job as some kind of jumped-up tour guide. As was appearing ten feet tall when he wanted to look ten feet tall and scaring the hell out of little kids in order to get them to do his bidding. But that's enough for now.'

I want her to keep talking because there's something therapeutic about her voice. As is her reassuring me that Pandora wasn't a figment of my imagination, that I'm not mad, and not a killer. You're too close, Monica Best warned. It might have been a warning to herself as well as to me. Because she got too close and in the end became a risk, which was why she had to die. 'But why did Monica save me?' I ask.

'Brainwashing's an inexact science and Monica's better side cut in. She put on her persona with her mask but without her mask she was still Monica and I believe that she loved you.' An interesting expression crosses Sally's face – even with my imperfect vision I can see that. 'Out of character – that is, as herself – she couldn't bring herself to hurt you. Consequently, she had to die. When Booby and Marsha succeeded in luring you to Nimbin, Hélène was killed and Monica was recalled. Everything was a set up – Booby "accidentally" meeting us; Booby showing us around while Marsha killed Monica; the phone that was supposed not to work but which Marsha answered; the "lollies" that made us black out while they deposited Monica's body in the bush.'

I've worked out most of it but I like listening to her voice; it's like sunrise on a beautiful day; a day to live for; but now it's my turn. 'Monica was Sister Mildred's daughter. That was the photo I couldn't work out – the one that showed Mildred holding a baby at the funny farm. Mildred escaped – she was wounded in the leg as she went – but her rebellious teenaged daughter refused to accompany her. Years later, when Mildred and Monica met up again, Mildred accepted Monica for what she was – a kid who'd been brainwashed but who was still, in part at least, there for her. Monica had lucid moments, one being when she killed the thug at the refuge and saved me then brought me to Mildred's.'

I think about that. 'No wonder I was paranoid. The gunman who was after you was Mafia. But the thugs that tried to kill me at the Three Sisters and the one at Rory's were from Booby's cult. Just as Monica and Hélène were trained to stalk people, the thugs were trained to kill. What I thought was a horticultural experiment was a training ground for killers. I saw what I expected to see. Speaking of which ...'

I swing my legs over the side of the couch, my bare feet touching the cold floor with the shock of sudden awareness. 'Let's take a cab ride.'

Sally puts in a call for a cab with a bump in it, takes my arm and helps me into the wheelchair. She's a doctor. She knows how it rolls.

The place looks different but that's only because the scales have fallen from my eyes. I no longer imagine I'm being followed because I no longer am. We're stopped by a new guard.

'I'm looking for answers,' I tell him from the wheelchair.

He blocks the way. 'We're all looking for answers, buddy, but you won't find any here – at least, not on my watch. You're wasting your time and everyone else's. This is private property. So why not leave before you and your companion animal get hurt.'

It's the companion animal bit that does it. 'I'm no companion animal,' Sally says warmly as she pushes the wheelchair over the goon's feet. 'So look out because that means I bite.'

We pass through the entrance and down the hall that I'd been led down before and end up outside a door with a sign on it saying: INTERVIEW ROOM. DO NOT ENTER. We enter.

She holds me upright while I check under the desk and, after that, behind the air-conditioning. It's an easy check because it was never meant to be made. The air-conditioning vents are speakers; there's a stop/start switch on the windowsill; and when I press the little red button marked PARANOID FANTASY 1, a shadow appears on the wall; PARANOID FANTASY 2 produces a series of voices muttering imprecations like Kill everyone and I hate the world; PF 3 does things to the lights. While PF 4 results in noises that sound pretty much like people trying to kill one another. Next door.

In the main building I press another button. To hear a voice like my daughter's saying: How's he coming along? To which Calvados replies: It's a bit like doing a trepan, the surgical procedure where a hole's cut in the patient's skull to relieve pressure on the brain. Your father clams up just when it seems as though we're getting somewhere. We use drugs but he seems resistant to them. It's an act of will, as if he's being tortured and would rather die than divulge his secret. Then the voice that sounds like my daughter's but isn't – yeah, you hear what you expect to hear – asks: Can you cure him? To which the shrink replies: It depends on the secret.

A shrink by any name is a shamus. I nod to Sally.

'Those marks of violence on Ariadne's neck that she said I caused weren't real; they were painted on with something like gentian violet. But they served their purpose, making me doubt myself.' I think about that then I don't think about it. 'Let's go, companion animal.'

I'm not imagining the smile in her voice as she replies, 'Any more of that and you'll be the one wearing the marks of violence. Where are we going, shamus?'

It hurts but I still shrug. 'We'll think of somewhere.'

I LOVE YOUSE ALL –
WELL ALMOST ALL

They appeared out of nowhere at the launch of the first Rainbow – two young men brandishing business cards and saying, 'We read your book, we loved it and we want to publish it'. They were Rod Morrison and Jon MacDonald who – together with David Henley – constitute Xoum, the brilliant new publishing group that, in a few years, has beautifully produced all seven volumes in what we tentatively refer to as 'our *first* Rainbow series' – in the hope they will continue to publish us.

Why us? Because my late-life flowering as an author wouldn't have been possible without the total dedication and unswerving support of Judith, my wife and helpmeet of six years. In a very real way these books are hers as much as they are mine.

I also owe a debt of gratitude to countless others. First my children who – whether they realise it or not – suffered through having a writer for a father. Then there are those who went out of their way to help. In this category are thriller writer Alan Mills, who inspired me greatly and, with his wife Yukiko, remains a close friend; one of my all-time heroes, legendary Australian novelist Barry Oakley, whom I was fortunate enough to have as mentor; author Leone Britt, who had faith in me even when I didn't; and actor, raconteur and entrepreneur Mike Cody, who not only was ever ready with advice and information but dropped everything when needed.

The other rainbows in my life (my abject apologies to those inadvertently overlooked), in alphabetical order (which serendipitously puts my mother and father first), are: Kathleen and Stewart Boag; John, Jane and Julia Boag; that wonderful wood artist and great supporter (who,

I hasten to add, is nothing like his fictional namesake), the real Malcolm Booby; Annie Carter; George and Carol Conomos; Michael and Lorise Doumani; Dick and Fay Hughes; Matt and Jessica Lamb; Lini Lee; Julia and Simeon Legian; Keith and Penelope McConnell; John and Marnie Mason; and Paddy Robinson and the other members of the Sofala-Wattle Flat book group who have provided me with such great input and friendship.

By way of balance are the fraudsters, liars and swindlers of this world who can't be named but know who they are – the thugs who provide rags like the *Terrorgraph* with their daily cannon fodder; and the crooks I've been close to – people who would sell their own mother down the creek for a shilling. They're the ones to whom I'm most indebted because they provide the basis for that essential noir – the dark clouds without which the creation of rainbows wouldn't be possible.